THE OXFORD BOOK OF

Latin American
Short Stories

THE OXFORD BOOK OF

Latin American

Short Stories

———————————— ‖ ————————————

EDITED BY

ROBERTO GONZÁLEZ ECHEVARRÍA

OXFORD UNIVERSITY PRESS

NEW YORK   OXFORD

Oxford University Press

Oxford   New York
Athens   Auckland   Bangkok   Bogotá
Buenos Aires   Calcutta   Cape Town   Chennai   Dar es Salaam
Delhi   Florence   Hong Kong   Istanbul   Karachi
Kuala Lumpur   Madrid   Melbourne
Mexico City   Mumbai   Nairobi   Paris   São Paolo   Singapore
Taipei   Tokyo   Toronto   Warsaw

and associated companies in

Berlin   Ibadan

Copyright © 1997 by Roberto González Echevarría

First published by Oxford University Press, Inc., 1997

First issued as an Oxford University Press paperback, 1999

Oxford is a registered trademark of Oxford University Press

Library of Congress Cataloging-in-Publication Data
The Oxford book of Latin American short stories / edited by Roberto
  González Echevarría.
     p.   cm.
   Includes bibliographical references (p.   ) and index.

   ISBN-13 978-0-19-513085-0 (Pbk.)

1. Short stories, Latin American—Translations into English.
   I. González Echevarría, Roberto.
   PQ7087.E509   1997
   863'.010898—dc21   97-5395

Because this page cannot legibly accommodate all of the acknowledgments, pages
477–80 constitute an extension of the copyright page.

Printed in the United States of America

Para José A. Cabranes, amigo leal, compadre

Contents

Preface

When Oxford asked me to prepare this anthology, I knew at once that I would be unable to refuse. I have been a devoted reader of Latin American short stories since grade school, but there was another reason. Beginning language teachers on their way to becoming professors of literature read many short stories with their students. The genre is made for the classroom because of the brevity of the texts and the excitement that they can generate. For years I taught mostly short stories, as did many of my colleagues in foreign-language departments. I would venture that we learned to teach literature by teaching short stories. I accepted the invitation, and here is the product.

A question that will immediately arise in the reader's mind concerns the title and scope of the book. What is meant by Latin America? To think that the name of a region, nation, or ethnic group can accurately reflect its history or demography is a kind of naïveté often feigned for political purposes. Debates about the term Latin America have not been spared. In my introduction and headnotes I refer to Latin America when I include Brazil in what I say, and Spanish America when alluding only to the countries where that language is spoken. A few instances may arise where the words, as they are prone to, will refuse to reflect differences accurately, but I have done my best to be precise. As can be imagined, what to call Latin America has been a vehemently debated issue, with some proposing the awkward but perhaps most accurate Iberoamérica for the entire continent, and others Hispanoamérica, Indoamérica, and so forth. Common usage (and sense) compels me to use Latin America, with all the caveats implicitly assumed, and not forgetting that it was the French, in their imperialist zeal during the nineteenth century, who coined the term. They opposed Latin to Anglo America to claim for political gain a historical and linguistic kinship with regions recently freed from Spanish domination. The name has stuck, although clearly many of the cultures in the region had no significant connection with the Roman Empire. Some cultures, in which Spanish or Portuguese are not spoken, still have none.

I am also aware that though cognate, Brazilian and Spanish American literary traditions are distinct; I try earnestly to do justice to the differences while acknowledging that my greater familiarity with Spanish will likely condemn me to more than the usual share of misjudgments. Brazil's is, with that of the United States, the richest national literature in the New World, Brazil having practically overtaken its former metropolis. In fact, during the nineteenth century instead of breaking away from Portugal, Brazil absorbed its mother country when the Portuguese monarchy moved to its American colony, fleeing the Napoleonic invasion. But Brazilian and Spanish American literatures have an obvious and profound kinship, and at times they enjoy a close relationship with each other. It seems to me that the closeness has increased in recent years, with writers like Haroldo de Campos and Octavio Paz functioning as literary bridges between the two traditions, and the Spanish American novelists having a tremendous impact on Brazilian ones.

An anthology is not finished without the usual lament about the difficulty of selection and the regret for all those deserving authors not included. It is true that the wealth of the Latin American short story is such that several excellent anthologies could be assembled with the authors excluded from this one. I have made my choices strictly on merit, but I cannot honestly claim that this has been the only reason for inclusion. An anthology of the Latin American short story selected on the basis of excellence alone would be quite different from this one. It would have to include several stories by Borges, Machado de Assis, and Quiroga, and certainly more than one by Cortázar and García Márquez. The number of excluded authors would have swollen considerably. So, while the criterion for selection has been quality, diversity has also been an important aim.

I decided from the start to be canonical rather than innovative, with a few deviations—but canonical from a Latin American point of view, not from that of an English-language readership. In this I believe the anthology will contribute to a better understanding and appreciation of Latin American literature. There was no room to open the canon to the very latest writers, and perhaps an anthology in a language other than Spanish or Portuguese is not the place to carry out that polemical but necessary task. The current crop of Latin American short story writers seems good and abundant, and in a future anthology like this one some of them will no doubt be featured.

This anthology's boldest innovation is the inclusion of texts from the colonial period. In this I follow a trend in the field of Latin American literary studies that in turn reflects the choice of many of the region's most distinguished authors. Fiction writers like Alejo Carpentier, Carlos Fuentes, and Gabriel García Márquez plunder the colonial record for stories, characters, and situations. Octavio Paz has written a massive literary biography of Sor Juana Inés de la Cruz, the seventeenth-century Mexican poet-nun. Severo Sarduy and Haroldo de Campos have found in the colonial baroque a worthy antecedent. I am confident that the quality of the colonial texts will convince the reader of the validity of these writers' predilections.

Although I could also rehearse the usual complaint about the agonizing process of making the final selection, I would be dishonest if I did not at the same time confess to the pleasures enjoyed while reading the stories included as well as those I finally had to exclude. There are worse tasks than reading Latin American short stories and selecting the best. I hope that the reader will experience comparable pleasures, a reason for reading literature that today is often forgotten.

During the composition of this book I was ably aided by two assistants to whom I would like to express my sincere gratitude and whose work I hereby credit. Nieves Martínez de Olcoz was invaluable during the early stages, helping in the selection of the stories and tracking down some of the more elusive texts. Christine Dolan helped in the final months finding texts, reading headnotes, making useful suggestions, and generally keeping track of the entire project until its completion. My greatest debt is to my cherished colleagues at Yale whom I have pestered all too often for opinions and information. I am particularly thankful to Josefina Ludmer, Rolena Adorno, and K. David Jackson. David's generous and expert advice has greatly strengthened coverage of Brazilian literature in this book. I am grateful to Enrique Pupo-Walker, with whom I first studied the Spanish American short story many years ago, for advice on every aspect of the book's conception. Other friends like Elizabeth Burgos, Gustavo Guerrero, and Miguel Barnet made important suggestions. The final judgment in all cases was mine as are any errors.

It has truly been a pleasure to work with Linda Halvorson Morse and to enjoy her friendship in times that were not always good. She is an ideal editor as well as a lively and witty interlocutor. I am grateful for her encouragement, patience, and good humor. I would also like to thank Ellen Chodosh, who first approached me about the project. Thanks are due to copyeditor James Tully and to Ellen Satrom for the care they took over the text and to editorial assistants Karen Murphy and Mary Jacobi for performing quite a few important tasks. I would also like to thank the staff at Sterling Memorial Library, particularly Barbara Gajewski and César Rodríguez. Denise Hibay, at the New York Public Library, helped me find some of the more elusive extant translations. Finally, I wish to acknowledge that I am beholden to the translators for making the book a literary reality in English. This is as much their book as the authors' or mine. Gregory Rabassa, Margaret Sayers Peden, Helen Lane, and Sarah Arvio are the veterans in the group. I would also like to recognize the new ones: Kathleen Ross, Rolena Adorno, Sandra Ferdman, Christine Dolan, Gabriel and Michelle Stepto, and Susan Herman.

Roberto González Echevarría
Hamden, Connecticut
July 1996

THE OXFORD BOOK OF

Latin American Short Stories

Introduction

In Latin America the short story is a major genre enjoying popularity at all levels and genuine recognition in the most demanding literary circles. Several leading Latin American authors have been exclusively short story writers—for instance, Horacio Quiroga, Jorge Luis Borges, and Juan José Arreola. And some of the novelists held in the highest regard are considered to be just as great because of their short stories; Machado de Assis, Gabriel García Márquez, and Juan Rulfo come immediately to mind. Other successful novelists, like Julio Cortázar and Reinaldo Arenas, are believed to be at their best in the short story. National anthologies of short stories abound, and several prestigious short story prizes are awarded to writers from the region. The wealth of the short story tradition in Latin America, which shares in the fabulous richness of Latin American literature and art in general, belies those who would naively equate economic underdevelopment and political instability with artistic poverty. Some of the writers mentioned are among the very best in the modern world, having influenced the literatures of the most developed areas of the globe.

Several other misconceptions abroad concerning Latin American literature should be dispelled at the outset. One, caused by the emergence of a glittering array of fiction writers in the 1960s (a phenomenon known as "the Boom of the Latin American novel"), is that Latin American literature is a recent development with no antecedents. The fact is that, given the nature of the Iberian empires from which it emerged, Latin America has enjoyed literary activity attuned to that of the West ever since the sixteenth century, particularly in the Spanish area. Another misconception, a corollary of the first, is that Latin American literature is rural in both nature and themes as a result of its history and geographic setting. But, in contrast to colonial life in North America, the Spanish Empire in particular was organized around opulent cities, the seats of elaborate viceregal courts that competed with and at times surpassed metropolitan centers. In several regions, central Mexico, for instance, the Spaniards had to contend with powerful and advanced native cultures that had large and complex cities of their own, not with nomadic tribes. Viceregal cities were a symbiosis of native and European cities. Latin American literature has been

3

since the beginning an urban activity, even when its themes have been rural because writers have taken a political interest in the jungle, the plain, or the backlands.

Finally, some have seen Latin American literature as somewhat provincial in orientation and crude in themes and techniques, reflecting a presumed proximity to nature. But quite the opposite is true. Latin American literature is predominantly cosmopolitan and sophisticated. In colonial times intellectual life was dominated by neo-scholasticism, which placed heavy emphasis on classical and patristic sources, rhetoric, and logic. Erudition, received knowledge, and elegance of argumentation prevailed over the observation of reality, mental habits that left a dire legacy in politics and cultural life in general, one might add. There was a university, Saint Thomas Aquinas, in Hispaniola as early as the sixteenth century, and in Tlatelolco, Mexico, a college to teach Latin to the sons of the native aristocracy. The Spanish Empire was ruled by the letter of the law, as was the Portuguese, but with lesser severity. The custom endured after independence. Since the nineteenth century, when Latin American literature became a deliberate and premeditated social and textual activity, Paris has been the artistic and intellectual supracapital of Latin America, a place where writers from the various countries still meet to exchange ideas. Latin American literature has been since then cosmopolitan to a fault. Latin American writers like Borges, Alejo Carpentier, and João Guimarães Rosa were individuals with immense learning and possessing several languages. The affectation of being a naïf, a natural, which seems to be prevalent among North American writers, is not common among Latin American ones, who are seldom embarrassed by their erudition. Nor has political commitment ever stood in the way of learning or refined artistic craft. José Martí, the nineteenth-century Cuban revolutionary and poet, knew at least three languages and wrote exquisite verse.

One important dimension of this long Latin American literary tradition is the quality and quantity of short stories it has produced. This can be explained in part by the convergence of narrative cycles from powerful and diverse cultural sources: the various native cultures (Aztec, Mayan, Incan, Guaraní); the several African cultures (with the Yoruba prevailing); and the Iberian culture, which includes the Portuguese, the Galician, and the Catalan, among others, as well as the entire European heritage reaching back, through the Middle Ages, to classical and biblical times and to the Indo-European sources of the Western narrative stock. But there are also more contingent reasons for the abundance of the short story in Latin America. For instance, in a region fragmented into many countries sharing a language and a literature, the short story, which travels easily, is a genre in which Latin American writers can come to know one another more rapidly.

Whatever else may explain the wealth of Latin American short stories, they share with those from all over the world not only a history but basic common features. Of all the modern prose genres, the short story is both the most and the least literary: the most because the artistic short story is notoriously exacting in matters of form and originality; the least because the short story is the only modern prose genre that has a parallel oral tradition surviving even in everyday conversation and unconcerned with formal details or innovation. Storytelling consists quite overtly of transmitting received versions of a given tale told and retold many times before. One hears many short stories in the course of daily life. Gossip is a form of short story, as are anecdotes told around a dinner table, which can have the concord and colorfulness of their literary counterparts. The same can be said of jokes, which depend so much more on the performance of the teller than on novelty. Lies, too, tend to be carefully constructed short stories, as are confessions to authorities, lawyers, or therapists. Rural storytellers in today's Venezuela combine tradition with modern technology, selling cassettes of their performances at truck stops and gas stations.

Contrary to expectations, the genre has acquired new life in the social sciences. Case histories in psychoanalysis, anthropology, and sociology are often like short stories, a fact that modern ethnography now acknowledges. Two of the most influential short story collections in the past hundred years have been Sir James G. Frazer's *The Golden Bough* (1890) and Sigmund Freud's *The Interpretation of Dreams* (1900). Karl Jung's work mapped out the relationship between mythic stories and the subconscious, and Claude Lévi-Strauss compared the deep structures of tales with those of language itself. The short story seems to be immune to time, to literary fashion, to progress, and to the diversity of cultures. Everyone, everywhere, has always told stories, although for purposes that differ according to the historical moment. The Taíno, Mayan, and Incan stories included in this anthology probably had a doctrinal, perhaps liturgical, function in their original cultural settings.

While it is difficult to define the genre, there is a feel and texture to the short story—a kind of phenomenology—determined by its limited length, by its brief duration whether heard or read. But length cannot be measured easily—although, a short story can usually be read or heard at one sitting, so that the whole of it is present in the mind of the reader as it concludes. This is doubtless why the artistic short story makes so much of its unity of action, symbolism, and tone. In this the short story resembles lyric poetry and music. A musical phrase has effect on the listener only if a previous one is still ringing in his ear. The reader of a well-wrought short story is expected to remember early incidents or other details and to establish connections in his or her mind. The aesthetic pleasure provided by a good short story, which is likely to be sudden and intense, depends on its ability to provoke such associations. But the difference between the short story and music or the lyric poem is great. A good story can probably survive a bad performance or poor execution by a clumsy writer. Its core seems to be a concurrence of incidents independent of performance and the accoutrements of literary fashion. This is why short stories can enjoy a certain anonymity, like popular ballads. Seeing this, Vladimir Propp proposed a "morphology" of the Russian folktale, as though stories were as common a property as language itself. Another reason for the richness of the Latin American short story tradition may very well be its combination of highly literary forms with very traditional ones.

The first short stories in European languages to emanate from what would become Latin America were doubtless the tales sailors told of their adventures in the taverns of ports such as Cádiz, Seville, or Lisbon. Well-worn and honed by many retellings during the tedious sea journeys, some of these yarns found their way into the writings of Peter Martyr d'Anghiera (1459–1526), the first historian of the New World, as well as the first collector of Americana, both artifacts and lore. In his *De orbe novo decades* the indefatigable d'Anghiera retells with obvious delight an anecdote about Jerónimo de Aguilar's mother, who went insane when told (erroneously) that her son had been devoured by cannibals. He also regales his reader with the heroic deeds of a one-armed monkey—so maimed during his capture—who fights off a boar determined to kill him while both are being shipped to Spain. D'Anghiera also collected many of the stories that make up Taíno cosmogony and remarks on their suggestive resemblance to classical myths. With this observation he opened up an issue that vexes philosophers and anthropologists even today: Is mythology a general phenomenon with analogous stories told in independent regions of the world? Is there a universal mind expressed through these tales? At the turn of the fourteen to the fifteen hundreds, components of what would become Latin American literature (written in Latin by the good humanist, incidentally) were already active in d'Anghiera's influential writings. His very practice as collector of tales from diverse origins, who then recasts them in a European rhetorical mold within which they adjust uneasily to one another and to the repository itself, anticipates both the predicament and some of the solutions devised by contemporary Latin American writers.

The New World was only "new" from the point of view of the Europeans, of course. Native peoples had been telling stories for centuries before Columbus's ships rose above the horizon that fateful morning of 12 October 1492. Their stories, like those in the Old Testament or classical mythology, dealt with the origins of the world and of humanity, and they involved tales of cosmological upheavals, incest, violence, betrayals, monarchic struggles, and mass migrations. These stories were a way of conceptualizing the world and of coping with the harsh realities facing men and women everywhere: fate, death, transcendence, the organization of social life. They spoke about the uncertainties of love, filial or erotic, the succession of generations, fear of natural phenomena, questions of knowledge and power. Friars, appalled by the treatment of the misnamed "Indians," gathered these stories and gave them written form partly to demonstrate that these people belonged to the human race and were also children of the Christian God. The novelty of the stories was often startling, but no more so than European lore, particularly Christianity, was for the natives.

European and American stories eventually commingled as the natives, with varying degrees of sincerity and often responding to threats and to unspeakable brutality, accepted the new doctrines. This process was renewed when Africans began to be imported as slaves to many parts of the New World, particularly the Caribbean and Brazil. Various forms of story collecting derived from the practice started by the friars are still current. It is thanks to the friars in early times, and later to the anthropologists, that we have some of the stories in this anthology, given that no writing existed in the New World before the arrival of the Europeans. The dilemmas raised by this process of collection—moral, political, literary—have often been incorporated into the fabric of stories, particularly but not exclusively in modern times. The Taíno, Maya, and Incan tales included here, therefore, are not pre-Hispanic in a chronological sense, but post-Hispanic, part of the process of rewriting and constant rediscovery provoked by colonization. They appear at the beginning of this book to respect the sequential construct that any history has to build in order to be intelligible. But the reader should be aware of the inevitable distortions that rewriting always perpetrates on original texts, no matter how much the reteller wishes or pretends to withdraw from the picture.

The stories collected by the likes of d'Anghiera, Fray Ramón Pané, or Fray Bernardino de Sahagún were not the only native tales to reach the European presses. Soon, literate descendants of the conquered Indians began to write from their peculiarly divided perspective, as inhabitants of two mental worlds who try to explain one of those worlds to the other. Writing about Garcilaso de la Vega, el Inca, Arnold Toynbee usefully identified this new class of hybrid writers, present throughout modern history, as belonging to what the Russians called the "intelligentsia"—natives who explained (made intelligible) their culture to the conqueror, incorporating in the process the conqueror's fundamental ideological and technical repertoire. In colonial Latin America these writers in fact used the very foundation of European doctrine to condemn the Europeans. Guaman Poma de Ayala—writing, like Garcilaso de la Vega, from a Christian perspective—castigates the Spaniards for not abiding by the tenets of their own religion. Neither writer questions Christianity—at the time the explicit core of Western ideology—which is the overarching set of beliefs to which they adhere. In their ambiguity and anguished hybridity these writers anticipate the quandary of modern Latin American authors: To differentiate themselves from the West, they must think using the ideological tools that the West provides.

The cosmogonies of native cultures were not the only stories with a cosmic reach in colonial Latin America. The very accounts of discovery and conquest had such universal scope. The Discovery (of the New World) was, according to Fray Bartolomé de las Casas, the greatest historical event since the birth of Christ. Since then the feeling of living through a historical watershed, of being present at a significant beginning, has permeated stories coming from Latin America. Consciousness of how momentous the Discovery was in terms of universal history constitutes nothing less than the onset of a modern sense of temporality. People believed they had fallen into a historical chasm, that they were being swept along by a large, inexorable, and irreversible temporal motion that unraveled the safety net of tradition, as represented by the reassuring reiterations of culture, including the retelling of stories. Montezuma, the defeated Aztec monarch, could only explain the arrival of Cortés and his men as the fulfillment of prophecy within the Aztec system of beliefs. It was a way of swerving away from the abyss that confronted him. The historical urgency present in many of the chronicles of the Discovery and Conquest parallels that of Saint Paul's writings; it is a consciousness of the occurrence of a break in the progression of collective life that announces a new and portentous beginning.

The actual announcement was made possible by the development of movable type—the New World was really discovered by the printing press, some will argue. Debate continues about the process of Spanish and Portuguese colonization because a stupendous original record of it is still available. We have comparatively little on the deeds and misdeeds of Alexander the Great or King Darius, and nothing on the Aztec invasions as they pushed south to the central Mexican highlands. But the Spaniards, in particular, developed in the sixteenth century a huge state bureaucracy that recorded in histories and legal papers the achievements and failings of thousands of people from all stations of life. The archives at Simancas, and particularly the Archivo de Indias in Seville, are bulging with such documents. In both the histories and the legal documents—depositions, petitions, confessions, briefs—we find myriad stories about both the colonizers and the colonized. Although not short stories in the sense the term would acquire in the nineteenth century, when the practice became a genre, these are entertaining, significant, and well-constructed tales that stand on their own. Enrique Pupo-Walker has shown how in the larger histories these tales appear as illustrations, as entertaining, imaginative digressions, as transitions, as examples, and as other rhetorical ornaments. Some tales, like Pedro Serrano's story included here, taken from Garcilaso de la Vega's *The Royal Commentaries of the Incas,* may have a political or even philosophical subtext: Europeans, when reduced to barbarity, act in the same manner as the lowest natives.

What links all of these colonial stories together is the theme and plot of escape, both physical and mental, from the strictures, and sometimes literally the prisons, of the Old World. This is why so many involve some sort of deviancy or even delinquency, as in the stories by Catalina de Erauso and Gaspar de Villarroel. It is a historical fact that many criminals came to the New World to evade the long arm of the law. Columbus himself engaged common prisoners in his first voyage, promising them freedom in exchange for their risky service. Freedom and the New World became subconsciously synonymous in the sixteenth and seventeenth centuries. Miguel de Cervantes pined for an assignment in the New World, which was denied him. The historical watershed mentioned earlier could be, at a more modest level, a change of identity, in some instances for converted Jews fleeing the Inquisition. For Catalina de Erauso, the "Lieutenant Nun," freedom meant a change of gender.

In Juan Rodríguez Freyle's *El Carnero* (1636), the first literary collection of stories from the New World, the conceit that holds the work together is that its contents were drawn from the wastepaper basket of the Bogotá court of appeals. Hence, the stories were all presumed to be the rubbish of litigation involving the good residents of that city. Illicit or immoral behavior is their common denominator. As heroic action was no longer possible because the Conquest had long ended, these adventures were erotic, often acts against the vows of matrimony. Marriage stands as the fundamental law that maintains the social order and ensures peaceful succession. Rodríguez Freyle mocks the pervasive attempts of the law to control and contain desire and turns this colonial *Decameron* into a delightful, even slightly pornographic book. Naturally, many such misadventures found their way into ecclesiastical writings, the other large and comprehensive form of archive that recorded the private, even intimate, lives of the colonists. Long and for the most part tedious histories of orders, bishoprics, and parishes occasionally contain juicy stories not devoid of artistic merit. In the seventeenth and eighteenth centuries the ecclesiastical and legal record is not as colorful as that of the sixteenth century, but it is thorough and covers a life that, although not adventurous, is the foundation of today's Latin America.

The world of the viceroyalties was baroque, not only in its artistic expression but in the very fabric of social and political life—its legal and religious writings were forms of baroque scholasticism. This was a life of pomp and ritual, in which the religious and political authorities made ostentatious displays of their power and wealth. The baroque favored and flavored the oddity of the New World, incorporating it into the received forms of European architecture, painting, and literature. Religious oratory, as in the Villarroel story, was practiced by the likes of Juan de Espinosa Medrano ("El Lunarejo"), who was also a devoted follower and apologist of Don Luis de Góngora, the leading Spanish baroque poet of the age, revered and imitated in colonial America. Others, like the Mexican nun Sor Juana Inés de la Cruz, wrote theater in the manner of Calderón de la Barca, and poetry in which the Spanish Golden Age culminated. Sor Juana's "Reply to Sor Filotea," a defense of her right as a woman to exercise her intellect and practice the art of writing, is also a synoptic autobiography—a good story caught in the web of its neo-scholastic rhetoric and lexicon. Like the lives of other unconventional and, as we saw in many cases, criminal Creoles, Sor Juana's life is one that ventures to the edges of custom and the law, where the unusual and the forbidden meet. Her baroque oddity was to be a woman and an intellectual, in the same way that Catalina de Erauso's was that of being a lieutenant nun.

In Brazil the artistic and intellectual activity was not comparable to that of the Spanish viceroyalties—although it was not insignificant, particularly by the seventeenth century with the works of the Jesuit Antônio Vieira (1608–97) and the lawyer Gregorio de Matos (1633–96). The Portuguese colonists were not confronted with advanced indigenous cultures like the Aztec, Maya, and Inca, so they had no need to compete by creating elaborate societies like the Spanish viceroyalties. Aztec temples were turned into baroque cathedrals. Further, by remaining close to the coast, the Portuguese did not engage in large-scale, epic campaigns and mass migrations like the Spanish. From the start, perhaps given the character of the Portuguese, Brazil was more open to European influence and less confrontational in its contact with native populations. Unlike Spain, Portugal, where the Arabs had been defeated much earlier, was not absorbed by questions of doctrinal and racial purity. Hence, it did not apply itself to the conversion of the Indians with the same zeal. Appropriately enough, then, the most compelling stories of the colonial encounter are those written by Jean de Léry in his *Histoire d'un voyage faict en la terre du Bresil autrement dite Amerique* (1578), still read with profit and delight by writers and anthropologists.

Latin American literature as a self-conscious activity emerged as a result of the independence process during the first decades of the nineteenth century. As the former viceroyalties and other political subdivisions (such as captaincy generals and the jurisdictions of courts of appeal) became nations, their elites sought to found with them individual literatures. A new nation had to have an expression of its own essence in art. Copied from Napoleonic models, like the bright uniforms of their armies, these new states drew up constitutions, organized legislatures, composed national anthems, and devised flags and an entire heraldry of legitimation and power. Their history was monumentalized, heroes enshrined, statues erected. The originality of each nation, its uniqueness, had to be expressed and preserved. National myths became the foundations of national literatures in vast poems devoted to American nature, like Andrés Bello's odes.

Literary activity moved from the monastic cell, the pulpit, and the viceregal court to cenacles, cafés, political clubs, newly founded newspapers, and gazettes. The founders of nations and literatures were often the same. Latin American literature was developed in the midst of intense political activity, a trait that it has not lost and that colors many of the short stories included in this anthology. (Politics thus became both the honor and the blight of modern Latin American literature.) Intellectuals and writers from various Latin American countries met in the 1830s in Paris, where they discovered their commonalities as well as their differences. They were exiles, diplomats, young men sent to Europe to be educated. For geographical and political reasons it would have been impossible for them to gather at any one Latin American city, so Paris, their common destiny, became the cradle of modern Latin American literature. France, of course, was the European hub of artistic and intellectual activity, and the place where the short story as a genre was consolidated in the works of writers like Guy de Maupassant, Flaubert, and many others. The models for Latin American gazettes were inevitably their French counterparts. So, too, with the stories. Latin American writers learned from the feuilletons they read, imitated, and often translated.

If the romantic spirit celebrated the particular, the individual, the local, and the different, as opposed to the abstract norms and rules dictated by neoclassicism, then a contradiction existed in the activities of Latin American artists and intellectuals in Paris and elsewhere. Was there a single Latin American literature or were there many? If a particular consciousness born of a specific natural and social habitat created art, then there had to be a Mexican, an Argentine, a Chilean literature, not a Latin American one. This is an unresolved problem at a theoretical but not at the practical level. The Spanish Empire had been programmatically uniform in language, law, and religion, so the new intellectuals and artists, and their successors to the present, found that they had much in common. In addition, modern communications made it possible for them to exchange books, pamphlets, ideas, and to meet in Europe or Latin America itself. They came to know and seek one another, and to publish anthologies that included works by writers from several countries (the first was *América poética*, compiled by the Argentine Juan María Gutiérrez, which appeared in Chile in 1846). The leading Latin American writers know one another's work and feel that they belong to a continental tradition, while acknowledging that they also work within national literatures that provide them with institutions such as publishing houses, jobs, and the possibilities of travel. With the usual exceptions, often created by political persecution, the best writers rise to the top and converse with one another across national borders.

The principal innovation in nineteenth-century romantic Latin American literature was the effort to look as directly as possible at the continent's reality, both natural and social, instead of through the grid of neo-scholastic philosophy. This change, which had of course taken place during the Enlightenment in Europe, was delayed in the former Spanish colonies because of the thoroughness of Catholic indoctrination, which was allied to state institutions. In Brazil it happened somewhat earlier and resulted in the foundation of state agencies devoted to the purpose of learning more about the country's vast natural resources.

This development led to *costumbrismo,* or the depiction of local natural and social phenomena. Journals such as the *Aguinaldo habanero* in Cuba published the work of naturalists like Felipe Poey along with that of poets and writers of fiction. These and others that appeared throughout the continent are precious publications, with beautiful illustrations of the flora and fauna and representations of social categories, such as peasants, gauchos, and slaves. Some of the pieces in this tradition are somewhat static and overly concerned with physical detail, but a new language was being forged to express Latin American reality. In Colombia the *cuadro de costumbres,* or local color sketch, became a leading literary manner by midcentury, particularly with a group of writers connected with the magazine *El Mosaico* (1858–72). The most important Colombian *costumbristas* were José Caicedo Rojas (1816–97), Juan de Dios Restrepo (1827–94), and José María Vergara y Vergara (1831–72). Many of these picturesque descriptions of local characters were halfway to becoming short stories, as their authors endowed with movement the bizarre figures they depicted.

A work as powerful and ambitious as Domingo Faustino Sarmiento's *Vida de Facundo Quiroga* (1845) is, among many other things, a kind of catalog or glossary of terms to represent rural Argentine reality. Quaint regionalisms became one of the most interesting aspects of the new literature, focusing on the particular, the contingent, and the local. Nineteenth-century stories enriched the language in this fashion, and as these tales traveled from one country to another, they became the basis of a Latin American literary discourse. Local types were incorporated, most notably the gaucho in Argentina, the black in Brazil and the Caribbean, and the Indian in Mexico and the Andean countries. Their language was imitated, and their poetic and narrative traditions were adapted and adopted for literary use. However, there was no small measure of reification in this process, as well as distortion and deflection of social and political ills, which made this type of literature very polemical, as it continued to be into the twentieth century.

All of the nineteenth-century literary schools advocated a more direct contact with and a deeper probe into social and natural reality. By the second half of the nineteenth century and toward its end, realist and naturalist tendencies invaded Latin America. These trends purported to wield more scientific approaches to the task, derived from the natural and social sciences. These changes are evident particularly in vast narrative projects like the Cuban novel *Cecilia Valdés* (1881) by Cirilo Villaverde, and in a good deal of Brazilian fiction. In the short story the most enduring influence was that of naturalism, which together with a pessimistic and ultimately Nietzschean conception of life furnished the discourse of modern short story writers like Horacio Quiroga. The natural so conceived offered a merciless kind of order governing individual and collective life, making of every plot a headlong race toward destruction. The proximity of teeming jungles, immense rivers, and the striking struggle for life present in those scenarios provided ample opportunity to insert the human in the same combat with forces that turned out to be as fatal as those in Greek tragedies. Many inferior short stories emerged from this, but in Quiroga, already in the twentieth century, it streamlined plots and gave the narrative a powerful tempo with no room for sentimentality.

One important aspect of nineteenth-century Latin American literature consisted of stories and vignettes describing each society; thus was born the already mentioned *cuadro de costumbres,* the most distinctive of Latin American literary creations in the nineteenth century. Writers offered graphic descriptions of particular aspects of the country that were strange, peculiar, and original to the eye of the educated observer. These writers served as intellectual spectators protesting that the essence (theirs included) of the nation was captured in these quaint pictures of country life. The methodology (or its rhetoric) was derived from European travelers who, like Alexander von Humboldt, described the New World in terms of the emerging social sciences. Out of these vignettes, which appeared in the many journals that suddenly sprang up in the nineteenth century in Lima, Mexico City, Havana, Rio de Janeiro, Buenos Aires, and Santiago, the modern Latin American short story was born. The space constraints of the journals in which they appeared began to draw the boundaries of the genre and to put a premium on a certain coherence of composition in plot and tone.

Esteban Echeverría's "The Slaughter House" is the best example—indeed, the inaugural one—of this hybrid genre we could perhaps call "a tableau of manners." Echeverría was the archetypical Latin American writer of the time: He spent his season in Paris, was imbued in French culture of the post-

Napoleonic era, and was among the founders of the Asociación de Mayo, a group of intellectuals who, in the wake of Argentine independence, engaged in the activities and produced the texts constituting the origins of Argentine literature. A socialist, poet, and political activist, he offers in his powerful story (not published during his lifetime) a horrifying vignette that reveals the violent origin of the Argentine nation. Paradoxically, the beauty—indeed, the appeal—of the story lies precisely in the barbarity the author wishes to condemn, a predicament that would beset Latin American writers from then on.

Indeed, it is the central, constitutive contradiction of the most compelling and influential literary work of the Latin American nineteenth century, Sarmiento's *Facundo* (1845), which articulates with enduring vigor the duality of "civilization versus barbarism" that characterized Latin America in Sarmiento's view. The formulation is still current. The fragment about the "tiger" included here ("The Tiger of the Plains"), which opens that memorable book, manifests the compelling nature of the barbarous and the romantic core of Latin American literature. Facundo Quiroga is a strongman *(caudillo)* who commands one of the regions into which the Argentine Republic threatens to fragment itself. He represents the barbarism opposed by Sarmiento's civilizing impulse. Facundo versus Sarmiento; the young, educated man in Echeverría's story against the thugs at the slaughterhouse; the cities against the jungle or plains; the European coastal areas against the uncultivated interior, or provinces; the rabble, often made up of people of non-European origin, against the white elites. In this dichotomy a writer as profound and contradictory as Sarmiento discovered the uneasy nucleus of Latin American culture. As president of Argentina he was to carry out a vast and controversial program of "Europeanization" that belies his own fascination with Facundo Quiroga and his habitat, the pampa. In his political mission Sarmiento also set a trend: that of the writer turned politician. Among those included in this anthology are two other presidents, Rómulo Gallegos (Venezuela) and Juan Bosch (Dominican Republic); a presidential candidate, Vargas Llosa (Peru); and several diplomats (Asturias, Guimarães Rosa, Carpentier, Fuentes).

Because Juana Manuela Gorriti lived within the maelstrom of the military and political process of independence as well as the consolidation of more than one Latin American nation, her works have begun to attract the attention they deserve. Hers is a compelling world of intrigue that reads like a novel of adventures, although historically accurate. Like the works of her better-known contemporary and fellow Argentinean José Mármol, Gorriti's writings reflect turmoils that begot nations. But the work chosen for this anthology has other literary virtues, the most visible being perhaps how she creates suspense about what lies on the other side of the wall covered by the massive armoire in her story. But in the neat separation of well-designed interior spaces and the plot centered on the attempt to see what happens beyond the obstacles dividing them (particularly the ancient, unwieldy piece of furniture), Gorriti's story has an allegorical aura much like Echeverría's. It is as though these rooms and their mystery stood for the colonial past, fraught with the dark perversions of religious and aristocratic power, a phantasmagoria that will vanish once discovered by the curious, modern eye. The story displays in miniature the mechanics of an entire historical transition.

One of the most compelling tasks confronting Latin American intellectuals after independence was the invention of a past. How could the years of colonial rule be made into a fable of origins? No one was better placed to create a past than Ricardo Palma, virtual founder and longtime director of Peru's national library (a position Jorge Luis Borges would later hold in Argentina). Palma's ploy was to focus on the quaint aspects of the colonial era, in the same way that the *costumbristas* who wrote the sketches of local color highlighted the contemporary quaintness of certain sectors of Latin American reality. It was a way to cleanse from the colonial era the many undesirable elements of its implacably stratified authoritarian society. It was also a way of focusing on and even rejoicing in the historically arrested aspects of Latin America, resistant or oblivious to modernization. Palma's *Tradiciones peruanas* frames in its entertaining plots the religiosity and credulity of the common people, a quasi-medieval belief in miracles that is the seed of a more recent tendency in Latin American fiction called "magical realism."

Other writers, particularly in the Caribbean and Brazil, saw that the question of slavery and the racial conflicts in Latin America were the central issue literature had to address. Vast narratives like *Cecilia Valdés,* by the Cuban Villaverde, used the techniques of the realist European novel to paint a vast panorama of racial strife and integration. Villaverde and other Cuban *costumbristas* wrote short stories and vignettes depicting life in the sugar mills and the cities, teeming worlds of crime, abuse, and revolt. In Brazil there were marked differences. Although institutions of higher learning did not develop until the nineteenth century, when they did, Brazil had become the seat of the Portuguese empire, so their growth was more organic and stable.

In addition, because the population had remained mostly in coastal areas, Brazil was much more receptive and active in the commerce of ideas with the rest of the world. Thus Brazilian literature blossomed in the nineteenth century, with the publication of many *folhetins,* in which translations of the best European writers appeared. In 1855 Manuel Antonio de Almeida (1831–61) published *Memórias de um sargento de milícias* (1855), a novel that was first serialized. In the second half of the nineteenth century, Brazilian fiction was unequaled in the rest of Latin America in terms of production and quality.

José M. de Alencar was one of the most important Brazilian writers of this era. In his *Iracema* (1865), *O gaucho* (1870), and *O sertanejo* (1875) he describes marginal figures of Brazilian society as well as the country's abounding natural world. Aluísio Azevedo's *O mulato* (1881) and *O cortiço* (1890) were even more explicit in their depiction of the evils of rural life, with a style that K. David Jackson has compared to that of Dickens and Zola. All this prepared the way for the emergence, at the end of the nineteenth century, of Machado de Assis, the best Latin American fiction writer of the century and the first truly masterful short story writer to appear in the region. In *Memórias póstumas de Brás Cubas* (1881), *Dom Casmurro* (1899), *Quincas Borba* (1891), and the many short stories he published in newspapers, Machado boasts such mastery and sophistication in the art of storytelling and such a profound knowledge of the racial complexities of Brazilian society (he was a mulatto himself) that he must be regarded as one of Latin America's first world-class writers. Machado's techniques and grasp of the social world are more attuned to those of contemporary literature than any of the nineteenth-century writers mentioned before. Not only does he usher in the twentieth century, but in many ways he anticipates and even exhausts it.

In Spanish America the modern arrived with Modernismo, a late-nineteenth-century poetic movement derived mostly from French models. Nicaraguan Rubén Darío was its chief figure and the first Latin American author to enjoy star status throughout the Spanish-speaking world. He was the best poet in the Spanish language since the poets of the Golden Age in the sixteenth and seventeenth centuries. No one since Góngora had so clearly revolutionized the language of poetry as Darío did beginning in the 1890s. The modern was essentially that which was not Spanish but was instead linked to the world of international commerce of goods and ideas made possible by new modes of communication. The *modernistas* created a discourse that cut itself off from tradition, and they did so by writing in an exquisite, elegant, and euphonious style that described not nature but a world of luxury created by the products of human industry. Theirs is an indoor, decadent milieu cluttered with exotica from the farthest reaches of the world, like the statue in Darío's "The Death of the Empress of China," and redolent of a languorous kind of forbidden eroticism, as in Arévalo Martínez's "The Man Who Resembled a Horse."

For the short story, Modernismo meant a sharp turn to the most intense concerns with form—the contemporary Spanish American short story began with the movement and its aftermath in the works not only of Darío but also of Leopoldo Lugones, Ricardo Güiraldes, and above all Horacio Quiroga. Quiroga even wrote, tongue in cheek to be sure, yet as a reflection of his mastery, a much-quoted "Decalogue of the Good Short Story Writer" (1917). Like those of Machado de Assis in Brazil, the works of these writers are already part of twentieth-century literature. The proliferation of journals of all kinds at the height of Modernismo increased enormously the quantity and quality of short stories. Since then the output remains unabated.

The climate of perversion, the ghoulishness, the vague aura of disease—both mental and physical—that permeate the short fiction of writers like Quiroga, Lugones, Levinson, and others reveal the decisive influence of Edgar Allan Poe at this moment in the evolution of the Spanish American short story. It is one that endures through Borges and Julio Cortázar, who translated Poe into Spanish much later. But at this point Poe was read mostly in French translation, as if to emphasize the artificiality of the entire Modernist enterprise.

Two competing tendencies would emerge from the *modernista* short story in the first decades of the twentieth century. One, preoccupied with formal experimentation, would lead to the avant-garde. Another, allied to political movements and as a continuation of nineteenth-century realism, would be part of regionalist fiction. The meeting of the two would yield, in Spanish America, a tendency that has been known as "magical realism," but also as the expression of Latin American "marvelous reality." In all this, in the broadest of terms, one could still see the dichotomy between civilization and barbarism, the urban and the rural, the coastal and the jungle—in short, the uneasy coexistence of the modern and the premodern in Latin America. The leading Spanish American writers in the regionalist vein and their popular novels were Ricardo Güiraldes, *Don Segundo Sombra* (1926); Rómulo Gallegos, *Doña Bárbara* (1929); and Eustasio Rivera, *La vorágine* (1924). These vast sagas, often allegorical, depicted social conditions in the hinterlands and included many stories from those regions.

In Brazil a parallel tendency emerged also in the 1930s in what is known as the "novel of the Northeast," depicting for the most part the evils of the sugar industry in that region. The chief practitioners of this trend, which was partly inspired by the work of rural sociologist Gilberto Freyre, were Graciliano Ramos (1892–1953), José Lins do Rêgo (1901–57), and Jorge Amado (b. 1912). In both the Spanish American regionalist novel and the Brazilian novel of the Northeast, we are dealing with a very politicized form of literature.

The leading short story writer in contemporary Latin America, and one of the best in the world, was Jorge Luis Borges. His influence on all writers of fiction since the publication of *Ficciones* in 1944, and even before, is immeasurable. It could be argued that this was the most influential collection of short stories published anywhere during the twentieth century. Borges worked against the grain by declaring himself not to be fond of the novel, which he found amorphous and tedious. In a famous prologue to Adolfo Bioy Casares's *La invención de Morel* (1940), Borges complained that there were too many pages in Proust as boring as life itself, and he decried the vogue of the psychological novel, alluding to the great Russian novelists and their disciples.

Borges proclaimed that the short story was a better genre and that the best ones were the detective stories. For Borges, the story worked as a minor tragedy because of the inexorable concatenation of events, the tight web of details that determined the outcome with their interconnectedness, as in "The Garden of Forking Paths." He also maintained the absolute artificiality of fiction and denounced the false claims of realism. Borges wrote all this in great measure as a reaction against the massive regionalist novels, which were supposed to express the essence of each region by means of detailed descriptions of social ills in a rural context. To him, these were crude creations with opportunistic political programs often concocted from the comfort and safety of studies in large urban capitals. There is no small measure of truth in all this, incidentally.

To them Borges opposed his avowedly fictitious, bookish, and tightly woven tales, written in a terse Spanish devoid of rhetoric—a major accomplishment in a romance language. Some of the early stories, collected in *A Universal History of Infamy* (1935), shared with *modernista* fiction a rarefied atmosphere, often Oriental. The pieces in *Ficciones* also take place in foreign settings or involve foreign characters. All of Borges's fiction is traversed by an elegant yet profound irony, as if the universe were, as he put it, the "creation of a subaltern god." This does not mean, however, that Borges's writing does not share some fundamental characteristics with Latin American fiction. Perhaps the most important is his unabashed preoccupation with vast themes involving the very creation of the universe and the origins of mankind, as opposed to the bourgeois hardships of a mediocre hero, which tends to be the case in most Western fiction to the present (to wit, John Updike). This is a romantic tendency, very much present in a story such as "The Circular Ruins," that is also prevalent in the works of Borges's contemporaries, like Alejo Carpentier. It is perhaps a throwback to the colonial stories about the Discovery and Conquest in which the chasm created by the emergence of a "new" world unsettles the narrative of universal history.

Borges's philosophical fiction generated a subgenre within the short story, namely, the essay-story, or story-essay. In this type of short fiction a vexing philosophical question is probed openly, not as an allegorical construct. In other words, solving an enigma constitutes the plot of the story. It is an ironic misalliance of the philosophical treatise with the detective story. The best-known among these is Borges's "Tlön, Uqbar, Orbis Tertius," which is the account of the completely artificial construction of a region. Few have been able to discern behind it a parody of the regionalist novel, but it is obvious that Borges is making a wry comment about the artificiality and utter fictionality of the regions depicted in those widely circulating works.

Of course, the issue is not strictly Latin American but a more fundamental question concerning both the possibility of knowledge about an area and the very process by which real regions may have been created in the beginning. Adding to the humor is the fact that in the story the region, provided with a language and a literary tradition, is the product of a hoax perpetrated by a society of individuals scattered throughout the world. "Tlön, Uqbar, Orbis Tertius" had a tremendous impact on Latin American fiction, being one of the main sources in the creation of Macondo, the fictional region in Gabriel García Márquez's *One Hundred Years of Solitude*. In Borges's "The Garden of Forking Paths"—collected here—all of these elements converge, including Borges's ironic view of the unwieldy infinity of the novel and its futile effort to represent the world. The story is a minitragedy, contained in what appears at first glance as a very mannered spy thriller.

There is more pathos in Borges than he was probably willing to concede. In "The Circular Ruins" there is a heroic yet futile attempt to play the role of God, replaced by a feeling of dejection when the narrator realizes that he himself may just be a part of someone else's dream. Yet the story itself is the creation of Borges, a "subaltern god" unable to produce anything beyond this minor, mediated fiction: He is destined, in this fallen modern world, not to be able to write a monumental work akin to Dante's *Divine Comedy*. In this, too, Borges still falls within the largely romantic cast of modern Latin American literature.

Borges would never have allowed himself to be associated with what has come to be known as "magical realism" because of its regionalist, somewhat provincial air—although he did write stories in the strictest Argentine tradition (about gauchos, for instance). Yet his experimental fiction, his attention to craft, and his penchant for the fantastic had a strong effect on those who did write in a magico-realist vein, like Alejo Carpentier. Magical realism results from the meeting of the two tendencies mentioned before. One is the formal experiments of the avant-garde, partly inspired by new conceptions of temporality and perception derived from the sciences. The other is the realism popularized in the nineteenth century and taken up as a program by politically motivated artistic trends such as socialist realism.

On the whole, magical realism was an effort to express counterintuitively the world as if the presuppositions of Western, bourgeois society could be erased and a fresh look made possible. To Latin American writers such a new look could be attained if reality could be observed through the eyes of those Latin Americans whose cultural presuppositions were different because of their ethnic or class origin—those believers in miracles like the characters in Palma's *Tradiciones peruanas*. Magical realism answered the desire not just to know the other within—the Cuban black, the Colombian Indian—but actually to become him in the act of creation. Seen from such a perspective, the "defamiliarization" of objects and customs that the avant-garde artist labored for could be achieved. Magic would explain the difference; realism would provide the contrasting background of ordinary experience that made it discernible. In the case of Carpentier, the origin of this practice is surrealism (a movement with which he was associated in Paris in the late 1920s) and the Afro-Cuban movement. Others, in their theoretical or programmatic formulations, derived their conception of magical realism from Franz Roh and German expressionism.

Carpentier's "Journey Back to the Source," included in this volume, is as good an example as any of magical realism. The story is a violent technical tour de force: It is told backward because the black sorcerer at the beginning, by moving his magic wand, has made time flow in reverse. Framed by the actions of the black sorcerer, the plot moves from the protagonist's death to his return to the womb. Language, which as Saint Augustine memorably discovered was the very measure of human time as it races toward death, is not reversible. If "Journey Back to the Source" were read into a tape recorder and played backward, only unintelligible sounds would be heard. To tell the story backward highlights the conventionality of language, which cannot truly reflect that which it purports to express. The result is often very humorous, as the reader will discover. All of this serves to defamiliarize both the objects described and one's perception of the passage of time. Carpentier adds to this compelling mix a cabalistic scheme involving the numbers of the chapters and a rich and detailed historical backdrop that makes of "Journey Back to the Source" a veritable masterpiece independent of its "magical realism."

In Brazil the synthesis of the avant-garde and regionalism achieved by Carpentier occurred in the monumental work of João Guimarães Rosa, one of the very best Latin American writers of all time; unfortunately, he is not betterknown abroad because of the difficulties in translating his major novel, *The Devil to Pay in the Backlands* (1956). The avant-garde reached Brazil in the 1920s and had an impact that was greater than in the rest of Latin America, culminating in a movement called Modernismo, not to be confused with the earlier Spanish American Modernismo of the late nineteenth century. Brazilian artists and writers celebrated what seemed to be a movement made for their country, always projected to the new and the daring. (It has been said, sardonically, that Brazil is and will always be the country of the future.) A whole "Week of Modern Art" was celebrated in São Paulo in 1922, and a notorious movement, the *Antropófagos,* emerged touting cannibalism as the ultimate form of rebellion and homage to the native cultures. Fortunately, all was in jest, a metaphor in the spirit of Carnival, the country's most famous explosion of joy and abandonment of societal norms, and no one was actually eaten.

The confluence of the Carnival and the avant-garde underlines the *modernista* program to discover a truly Brazilian form of expression. The avant-garde produced major works in fiction, such as Mário de Andrade's *Mucanaíma* (1928), a novel whose hero, a spoiled, foul-mouthed, indolent creature, is supposed to be a representation of the country, and is a composite of myths from the various ethnic strains that make up Brazilian society.

Meanwhile, as we saw, the Brazilian novel of the Northeast portrayed the toils of the poor in desperately rural settings following a realist formula. They were in opposition to the cosmopolitanism of the *modernistas*. Guimarães Rosa was the synthesis. He produced a profound portrait of the *sertão*, the barren Brazilian plain, with techniques that are Joycean in the play of language, and Goethean in theme and plot (*The Devil to Pay in the Backlands* is yet another version of the Faustian pact). In his stories, Guimarães Rosa's style is much less complicated, but his tales still deal with major themes and display astonishing originality in the plots. Anyone tempted to believe that plots and situations have already been exhausted by literature should read in Guimarães Rosa, for instance, about the blind Don Juan–type who depends on his guide for descriptions of the women he intends to seduce. "The Third Bank of the River," understated in tone, is a profound story, one of the masterpieces of the genre.

The Boom of the Latin American novel with which this introduction began was really also a Boom of the Latin American short story. In fact, if one were to place the point at which Latin American fiction began to attain wide international recognition as the Formentor Prize that Borges shared with Samuel Beckett in 1962, then it was the short story that really sparked that Boom. Although Cortázar's *Hopscotch,* García Márquez's *One Hundred Years of Solitude,* and other famous novels were celebrated, everyone seemed to agree that Borges was the major fiction writer from Latin America. Moreover, stories by Borges himself, Cortázar, García Márquez, Donoso, Vargas Llosa, Fuentes, and many others began to appear in magazines with mass circulation, while others were turned into films. Michelangelo Antonioni's film *Blowup* was based on Cortázar's "Las babas del diablo" (translated as "Blow Up"), and Jean Luc Goddard's *Weekend* on the same writer's "Southern Thruway." Borges's *Ficciones* became, twenty years after its original publication, a classic, read and studied throughout the world. In revolutionary Cuba the annual prize for the short story revealed new talent, like the Cuban Antonio Benítez Rojo, while disciples of Borges, García Márquez, Cortázar, and Carpentier appeared everywhere.

These Boom stories did not differ from the acclaimed novels in theme, tone, or texture, and they gained in concision and polish what they may have lacked in epic breadth. The Latin American short story became a standard of measure throughout the world in the 1960s, recognizable to some because of its often fantastic elements, all too quickly associated with magical realism. Neither the abundance nor the quality of Latin American short stories has diminished, although no figure of Borges's stature appears on the horizon. But the major contemporary writers—particularly Fuentes, Vargas Llosa, and García Márquez—continue to produce fiction of the highest quality, as do younger writers like Cristina Peri Rossi, Luis Rafael Sánchez, Rosario Ferré, Augusto Monterroso, Nélida Piñón, Alvaro Mutis, and many others. A major blow to the renewal of the Latin American short story was the early death of Cuban Reinaldo Arenas, perhaps the most original of the younger group; nevertheless, he left a considerable oeuvre. Less fortunate was his compatriot Calvert Casey, who committed suicide just as he was beginning to produce some of the best short fiction in the continent.

Guatemalan Augusto Monterroso is the practitioner of a new subgenre of his own, the "mini-story," perhaps the answer to the modern world's pre-occupation with speed and instantaneous gratification. Monterroso's one-liner "The Dinousaur"—"When he awoke, the dinosaur was still there"—was highly praised by another master of the short story, Italo Calvino (who was, incidentally, born in Cuba).* "The Dinosaur" is a meeting of the short story with the lyric, conveying a concise and evocative power. But it is possessed of a very Latin American cosmic quality that reaches back to the Discovery and Conquest and reminds one of Carpentier or Guimarães Rosa, as well as a comic element with which the likes of Cortázar would have been pleased. Finally, it is a fantastic imaginative flash of which all the writers in this anthology would have been proud.

*Augusto Monterroso, *Complete Works and Other Stories,* translated by Edith Grossman, with an introduction by Will H. Corral (Austin: University of Texas Press, 1995).

Part I

The Colonial Period

Colonial Latin American history can be divided into three broad periods. The first spans the Discovery and settlements in the Caribbean. The second begins around 1520 with the conquest of Mexico, which relegated the Antilles to a secondary role. (Havana, however, became the center where the fleets coming and going to Spain met.) There followed the conquest of Peru in the 1530s and the consolidation of the Spanish Empire. By the second half of the sixteenth century, the empire had taken the shape it would have until independence, although territories were added as expansion continued at a slower pace, and new political units were created. Two viceroyalties, one in Mexico and the other in Peru, with splendid capitals and many cities and dependencies stretching from California to Tierra del Fuego, plus the faraway Philippines, made up this vast domain ruled by the Spanish Crown from the distant Castilian plateau.

First the conquistadores conquered America, then the Crown had to conquer them using an army of lawyers. A vast, minutely organized legal system was devised, aided by the newly developed printing press and enforced by a huge bureaucracy. When a compilation of the "Laws of the Indies" was made in 1681, the rate of production was shown to have averaged one law per day following the discovery of the New World, if one excludes Sundays. Most stories of colonial times are entangled in the web of legal writing. Fray Ramón Pané's *Relación* was one such document, which slipped out of the legal archive to find and lose its way into another vast repository of tales: the histories of the New World that soon appeared, beginning with Peter Martyr d'Anghiera's *De orbe novo decades*.

These histories, by the likes of Bartolomé de las Casas, Gonzalo Fernández de Oviedo, Francisco López de Gómara, and Bernal Díaz del Castillo, were massive, detailed, and cast in medieval and Renaissance rhetorical molds. They provided fascinating accounts of broad historical movements, large campaigns, widespread malevolence, and humble achievements or misdeeds. The historiography of the New World was polemical from the very beginning, particularly in the work of las Casas; many brief stories appear as examples of abuses. Modern Latin American writers, beginning with Manuel de Jesús Galván and

Ricardo Palma in the nineteenth century, discovered in the chronicles a marvelous repository of tales and character types. In recent times, Alejo Carpentier, Gabriel García Márquez, Abel Posse, and Carlos Fuentes, among others, have used them to create their fictions, both brief and long. The chronicles constitute an origin, and their currency in fiction signals the writers' belief that the wounds of the Conquest have not healed, that the historical process they narrate is yet to close, that we still live in the temporal chasm cloven in history by the Discovery.

The imposition of the reigning neo-scholastic philosophy, the zeal to convert the natives, and the aggressive attitude the Spanish took against Protestantism gave the colonial world a quasi-medieval cast. Juan Rodríguez Freyle's *El Carnero,* a collection of bawdy stories, was written, like many medieval works, as a warning against the lures of the flesh. But the examples are so vivid and the irony so clear that no one but the most naive would believe protestations to that effect. The story about sorceress and go-between Juana García is a legitimate heir of *Celestina*'s (1499), and the book's overall composition has much in common with *El Conde Lucanor* (1335). At the same time, and as a clear example of the mixture of narrative traditions, it contains echoes of an African myth: that of the flying black who can soar home after death in a literal flight from oppression. The stories in the histories and legal record have been elevated to literary status by the backward glance of modern writers in search of a tradition. But there was much literature being produced in colonial America.

Literary life in the viceroyalties and elsewhere was abundant, particularly in Mexico City and Lima. Hundreds of Renaissance-style poets participated in frequent competitions, writing sonnets, eclogues, and epics in the manner of Ariosto and his followers. In Lima, in the late sixteenth and early seventeenth centuries, an Academia Antártica flourished in the style of the literary academies of Renaissance Europe. Italian was spoken by some of its members to emulate the masters of the Renaissance. In Mexico's viceregal court, Sor Juana Inés de la Cruz blossomed as the last great poet of the Spanish Golden Age, attaining widespread fame through the empire (including the mother country).

The Taíno, Mayan, and Incan stories included here and the others drawn from histories and legal record are not short stories in the modern sense. The first are fragments of theogonic cycles, the latter parts of larger narratives in which they serve a variety of functions. Nevertheless, they are compelling stories, as modern Latin American writers have shown.

Fray Ramón Pané

Spain
(late fifteenth century)

———————\\———————

A shadowy figure lost in a textual maze of Borgesian intricacy, Fray Ramón Pané came to the New World with Columbus on the admiral's second voyage (1494). He lived for almost a year among the natives of Hispaniola to learn about their beliefs and to write a report for the authorities. The report, *Relación acerca de las antigüedades de las Indias*, was lost, but not before it had been copied verbatim in Diego Columbus's biography of his father. The manuscript of this book, however, was also lost; fortunately, it had earlier been translated into Italian. Professor José J. Arrom's recent superb edition of Pané's *Relación* is his translation of the text back to its "original" Spanish. But even that original text is somewhat imprecise. Being a Catalan, Pané's Spanish was not perfect. Hence, Arrom's version is an improvement on the original as well as a careful rendition of the entangled names of Taíno gods. Pané was an attentive listener and was for the most part devoid of the prejudices of other Europeans, so his account has an air of authenticity, even with the textual uncertainties. His *Relación* is a quilt of brief narratives whose theogonic order he cannot quite make out. The following story, "How the Men Were Parted from the Women," is among the most original, although there are echoes of classical myths; one cannot tell whether they are the product of Pané's mind, or proof of the commonality of all mythical narratives, which certain branches of anthropology have proposed.

How the Men Were Parted from the Women

It happened that one, whose name was Guahayona, told another, whose name was Yahubaba, to gather a weed called *digo,* which was used for cleansing the body during a bath. He went out before dawn, but the Sun overtook him, and he turned into a bird that sings in the morning like the nightingale, and whose name was *yahubabayael.* Seeing that the one he had sent to gather *digo* had not returned, Guahayona determined to leave the cave known as Cacibajagua.

And he said to the women: "Leave your spouses, and let us go to other lands and bear with us much *güeyo.* Leave your children and let us bear with us only the weed, and later we shall return for them."

Guahayona parted with all the women, and went in search of other

25

lands, and came to Matininó, where he left the women, and went on to a further region, known as Guanín, having left the small children beside a stream. When hunger began to vex them, they wept and called for their mothers, who had parted; and the fathers could do nothing to calm the children, who cried hungrily for their mothers, saying "mama," when what they really wanted was a suck of milk. Weeping and fussing for the breast, saying *"toa, toa,"* very slowly and with much desire, they turned into tiny animals, much like frogs, and which were known as *tona,* after the sound they made when they wept for milk; and thus were the men left without women.

When Guahayona parted, the one who carried off the women, he carried off also the women of his *cacique,* whose name was Anacacuya, fooling him as he had fooled the others. Anacacuya, also the spouse of his sister, went to sea with him; and the above-named Guahayona, seated in the canoe, said to his sister's spouse, "Look at that lovely *cobo* in the water," *cobo* being the sea conch. And when Anacacuya gazed into the water, Guahayona, the brother of his wife, seized him by the feet and pitched him into the sea; and thus he took all the women to himself, and left them in Matininó, where still today there are only women. And he went to another island, called Guanín, so named for what he took from it when he parted.

When Guahayona was on the land to which he went, he saw that he had left a woman in the sea, and from her he took much pleasure, and then at once sought places where he could wash, being as he was covered with the sores we call the French sickness. Then she put him in a *guanara,* which means a place apart, and there he was healed of his sores. Then she asked him leave to go on her way, and he gave it her. This woman was known as Guabonito. And Guahayona changed his name, and was called thereafter Albeborael Guahayona. And the woman named Guabonito gave to Albeborael Guahayona many *guanines,* and many *cibas* to wear lashed to his arms, for in those lands *cibas* are stones that look much like marble, and they wear them lashed to their arms and neck, and they pierce holes in the ears of small children, and put *guanines* in their ears, made of a metal much like florins. (They say the source of those *guanines* was Guabonito, Albeborael Guahayona, and the father of Albeborael.) Guahayona stayed on the land with his father, whose name was Hiauna. His son on his father's side*
was called Híaguaili Guanín, which means son of Hiauna, and thereafter he was called Guanín, as he is today. And because they have no alphabet and no writing, they cannot tell these stories well, nor can I write them well. And I think I therefore put first what should go last and last first. But

---

*His son by his sister, daughter of his father.

all I write is as they have told it, so I write it; so I put it down as I have heard it in the land.

One day the men went to wash, and while they were in the water, it rained much, and they much desired women; and often when it rained they went seeking some sign of the women, but found no trace. But that day, washing, they saw falling from the trees, dropping down among the branches, a certain shape of person that was not man or woman, and whose sex was not of man or of woman, but when they went to gather them, they slipped away like eels. Since they could not be caught, the *cacique* ordered that two or three men should be sent to count them, and that for each should be found a man who had *caracaracol*. They counted four, and then they summoned four *caracaracoleros,* who had rough hands and could therefore grip them tightly. *Caracaracol* is a sickness like mange, which makes the body very rough. After seizing them, they held a council about how to turn them into women, since they had neither the sex of man or of woman.

They sought a bird called *inriri,* known in ancient times as *inriri cahu-babayael,* which pecks trees, and which in our language is called a wood-pecker. And they took the women, who had the sex neither of man nor of woman, bound their feet and their hands, brought the above-named bird, and tied it to their bodies. And believing they were made of wood, it began its usual chore, pecking and jabbing at the spot where the sex of a woman usually is. And thus there came to be women, say the Indians, or so say the oldest among them.

TRANSLATED BY SARAH ARVIO

Popol Vuh

Guatemala
(mid-sixteenth century)

———— \\\\ ————

The *Popol Vuh* contains the creation myths of the Quiche Maya, one of the groups that commanded the Guatemalan Highlands when the Spanish arrived. Though these stories still bear strong resemblance to Mayan myths of centuries before (the so-called Classic Maya), they are more recent retellings—retellings in a literal sense, since a new translation by Dennis Tedlock seems to prove that the work originated as an oral performance lasting several days. As Mary E. Miller demonstrates in her beautiful and authoritative *The Blood of Kings: Dynasty and Ritual in Maya Art* (with Linda Schele), Western views of the Maya have often been influenced by preconceptions based on parallels and contrasts with other cultures. The idea of a sacred book may very well be the central construct at work in the *Popol Vuh:* "No native Maya hieroglyphic books recounting extensive mythic narrative survive; one, however, was transcribed into European script in the middle of the sixteenth century by a young Quiche noble in Guatemala" (Miller, 31). Since then the *Popol Vuh* has evolved through translations and editions, shaped by Western anthropological and literary criteria. This is precisely its value for Latin American fiction. Ever since the nineteenth century these re-cycled Mayan stories have been part of the invention of a Latin American literature, most famously in the works of Guatemalan novelist and short story writer Miguel Angel Asturias. The *Popol Vuh,* in the tradition of all theogonies, particularly those committed to the book, deals with the origins of the world and the culture in which the story arises. After several failed attempts, the gods succeed in creating man by making him out of maize, the principal staple of the Mayan diet. The Mayan mythic core and its Westernized reconstructions constitute a beautiful collection of stories, such as the one reproduced here.

A Maiden's Story

A girl heard of this tree and came to see for herself. She was the daughter of Gathered Blood, one of the Lords of the Underworld. Her name was Xquic, little blood, woman's blood. She came and stood near the tree and gazed up into its branches. "Such strange fruit," she murmured. "It's impossible that I should die for picking one." Then the skull that nestled in the graveyard of the branches spoke: "What do you want? Skulls are the fruit of this tree. Is that what you want, a skull?"

"Yes, give me one," the girl answered.

"All right," said the skull, "reach up here." The girl reached her hand upward, ready to catch the fruit. The skull let a few drops of spittle fall directly into her palm. She looked quickly into the palm of her hand, but the spittle had disappeared into her flesh. "In my saliva and spittle," the voice again came from the tree, "I have given you my descendants. My head has a different look now without flesh, for the beauty of all men lies in their flesh. When death takes a handsome prince, men are frightened by his bones. But descendants are saliva and spit. Saliva and spit are the sons of kings, and when they die they keep their substance. The king or soothsayer or lawyer leaves his image to his son or daughter, and this I have left to you. Now go to the surface of the world and keep your life. Believe in my words, and they will be true."

All that these two did together was under the direction of Huracan, Chipi-Caculha, and Raxa-Caculha. The girl returned home, sons in her belly conceived of spittle. And thus Hunahpu and Xbalanque were conceived. One day, her father noticed her roundness. He went to the Lords. "My daughter is pregnant, Sirs," he told them. "She's a useless little whore."

"At least question her," advised the Lords. "Search her mouth for truth. If she doesn't confess, punish her. Send her far into the hills to be sacrificed." Gathered Blood returned home to question his daughter. "I want a direct answer," he told her. "Who is the father of the children that you carry?"

"I have no child, Father," the girl answered. "I haven't yet known the face of a man."

"A real whore!" the father exploded. "Not another word! Lord Messenger!" he called to the owls. "Take her. Come back with a bowl containing her deceitful heart." The four owls took the bowl and a sacrificial knife of flint. They lifted the girl in their arms, and set out.

Along the way the girl spoke to the owls. "Oh, messengers!" she said. "I can't believe you will kill me! I'm innocent. What I carry in my stomach is no disgrace, it's a miracle! I became pregnant standing by the magic tree. I can't believe that you would sacrifice me!"

"But what can we bring in place of your heart?" asked the owls. "You heard your father's command! Do your duty, he said, bring her heart to me. We can't take back an empty bowl. We don't want to kill you, but what can we do?"

"My heart does not belong to them!" the girl answered. "Don't let them force you to take it. You don't belong here yourselves. Why should you be forced to kill men? The time will come when I will defeat the Lords of Death. The time will come when the real criminals will be at your mercy. Come with me. On earth you will have all that belongs to you. You will be loved there." Just then they were passing a tree from which a red sap flowed. Seeing this the girl stopped. "Here," she said, "fill the bowl with the red sap from this tree. That will satisfy the Lords."

"We shall do it," the owls said, "and we shall go with you to the Upperworld." The red sap gushed out of the tree. The owls filled the bowl. The sap looked exactly like blood. It glistened red as it flowed into the bowl, clotting in the shape of a heart. The tree itself glowed radiantly as the owls and the girl stood there gathering the sap. From that day on the tree was called the Blood Tree. While the girl traveled on toward the upper regions, the owls returned with the sap for the Lords of Death.

The Lords were assembled, waiting, when the owls returned. "Have you finished?" they asked.

"It is finished," the owls replied. "Here is the girl's heart."

"Let's have a look," said Hun-Came, and the bowl broke as he grabbed it in his eager fingers, and the red blood leaked in a stream. "Stir up the fire," he said, "put it on the coals." As soon as it was on the fire, and the wet smoke began to rise, all the Lords of the Underworld drew close and began to sniff. To them the fragrance of the heart was very, very sweet. As the Lords of Death sat deep in thought, the owls rose as one body and flew from the abyss, earthbound to serve their new mistress in the upper regions.

TRANSLATED BY RALPH NELSON

Felipe Guaman Poma de Ayala

Peru
(seventeenth century)

———— \\ ————

Felipe Guaman Poma de Ayala's *El primer nueva corónica i buen gobierno*, discovered in the Royal Library of Copenhagen in 1908, was composed around 1615. In recent years this convoluted text has become part of the canon of Latin American history and literature. Guaman Poma's prolix work, which contains many drawings by the author, is a letter to the Spanish king arguing for a restoration of Peru to its native inhabitants. It also contains a bitter and detailed indictment of the Spaniards for not having followed the principles of their own Christian religion. Written in a laborious Spanish, laced with Quechua words and syntax, the *Primer nueva corónica* paints a horrendous picture of Peru under Spanish rule, literally so in the drawings. Venal officials, abusive colonists, lustful would-be grandees, and irresponsible priests all populate this vast canvas. Guaman Poma provides a minute description and narrative of the Incas, their customs, and their beliefs, as did Garcilaso de la Vega, el Inca, but in greater detail and more from within the Incan way of life. Guaman Poma is also a much angrier and engaged witness, whose plans for restoration include having his own son named king of Peru. But Guaman Poma was not overly optimistic about his chances of convincing the Spanish king. As one of his best exegetes (and translator here), Rolena Adorno, has written: "Through pictures and prose, Guaman Poma declares that there is no point of productive contact between European and Andean cultures; each remains hopelessly separate from the other, an understanding between the two is impossible." The cosmogonic story included here is not pre-Hispanic in the strict chronological sense, given that the author wrote it during the seventeenth century, but it is as authentic a rendition as there probably is of myths that antedate the European invasion of the Andean world. In this ethnographic self-analysis Guaman Poma anticipates the stance of several modern Peruvian writers.

Tocay Capac, The First Inca

The first account of the first Inca king, who came from the aforementioned legitimate descendants of Adam and Eve and the progeny of Noah, and of the first people, of *Uari Uira Cocha Runa* and *Uari Runa* and *Purun Runa* and *Auca Runa:* From here came forth *Capac Ynga, Tocay*

Capac, Pinau Capac, the original Incas. And this house and lineage came to an end. And about their own coat of arms that they painted. And they called them the most authentic ones.

About how *Intip Churin* was declared to be the son of the sun by the first chronicler: First he said that his father was the sun and his mother the moon and his brother the morning star. And his idol was *Uana Cauri.* And it is said that the place where they came forth was called *Tanbo Toco* and, by another name, *Pacari Tanbo.* They adored and made sacrifices to all of these. But the first Inca, *Tocay Capac,* had neither idol nor ceremonies; he was innocent of that until *Mango Capac Ynga's* mother and wife began to rule. And their clan was of the lineage of the *Amarus* serpents. And all the rest they say and paint about the aforementioned Incas is nonsense.

These said Incas came to an end and *Mango Capac Ynga* began to rule. And this said Inca had neither a place with a ceremonial center nor lands nor fields nor forts nor clan nor relatives nor anything that symbolized the first ancestors from the times of *Uari Uira Cocha Runa* and *Uari Runa* and *Purun Runa* and *Auca Runa.*

So he could not determine whether he was descended from the progeny of the first Indians of the *Uari Uira Cocha Runa* who descended from Adam and Noah in the time of the Flood, or whether he was of the lineage of grandees of *Capac Apo,* powerful lords. As a result, he said that he was the son of the sun.

The aforementioned first Inca *Mango Capac* did not have a known father; because of that they told him he was the son of the sun, *Yntip Churin, Quillap Uanan,* son of the sun, son of the moon. But in truth his mother was *Mama Uaco.* They say that this said woman was a great deceiver, idolater, sorceress, one who spoke with the demons of hell and performed ceremonies and witchcraft. And thus she made stones and boulders and logs and hilltops and lagoons speak, because the demons responded to her. And thus this said woman was the inventor of the aforementioned *uacas,* idols and witchcraft and enchantments. And with all that she deceived the said Indians at first. Then, the whole kingdom was deceived by Cuzco and consistently taken in and dominated by Cuzco, because the Indians saw it as a miraculous thing that a woman could speak with stones and rocks and hilly summits. And thus this said woman, *Mama Uaco,* was obeyed and served. And for this reason they called her *"Coya,"* queen of Cuzco. They say that she slept with the men she wanted from the entire realm. In this deception she went about for many years, according to what the previously mentioned very old Indians say.

And this said *mama* was first called *Mama.* When she became a matron she was called *Mama Uaco.* After she married her son and became a lady and queen she was called *Mama Uaco Coya.* And she learned from the devil that she was pregnant with a son. And the devil instructed her to give birth to the said child and not to show him to anyone but to give him to a nurse called *Pillco Ziza*. And the devil ordered her to take the infant to a cave called *Tanbo Toco* and not to bring him out until two years later. And they should care for him and proclaim that from the *Pacari Tanbo* there would come forth a *Capac Apo Ynga*, a powerful Inca lord, king, called *Mango Capac Ynga*, the son of the sun and his wife the moon and the brother of the morning star. And his god was to be *Uana Cauri*. And this king was to rule the land. And he was to be, like them, a *Capac Apo Ynga*, a powerful Inca lord. And this is the way the *Guaca Bilcas*, the supernaturals who are the demons in Cuzco, declared and commanded it.

And the said *Ynga* had no land nor sacred ceremonial center and there had not appeared—nor would there appear—any known father or lineage. They say that his mother was of low birth and a sorceress, the first one who began to serve and confer with demons. But how can it be that the sun and the moon, in the highest part of the heavens, can make a child? It's a lie. And being king of the kingdom did not come to him by the authority of God or by justice. And they say that he is an *Amaru* serpent and a devil, that the right to be lord and king does not belong to him, as they write.

In the first place, he had neither the lands nor the ancient home required to be lord. Second, he was the son of the devil, the enemy of God and man, the evil serpent *Amaru*. Third, saying that he is the son of the sun and the moon is a lie. Fourth, because of being born without a father and of a lowly mother who was the first sorceress, the greatest and chief servant of the demons, he had neither lineage nor honor nor can he be represented as a man for all the generations of the world. It cannot be, even though he be a wild beast, being the son of the devil who is an *Amaru* serpent.

TRANSLATED BY ROLENA ADORNO

Fray Bartolomé de las Casas

Spain
(1484–1566)

———\\———

A towering figure of colonial Latin America, Fray Bartolomé de las Casas is known as the defender of the Indians. He began, in fact, as one of the Spanish settlers who went to the New World in search of fortune. But the young Bartolomé was so repelled by the atrocities committed against the natives that he became a Dominican friar and devoted his life to their defense. It was a long life of struggle that bore some immediate fruit: Laws were passed curtailing the *encomienda* system by which Indians were given to Spaniards. Fray Bartolomé's protracted polemic was cast in the most scholastic, historical, and legal discourse of the time. He used Christian doctrine to damn abusive practices, cannily protesting that the Spanish Crown allowed the crimes only because it was unaware of what was happening across the ocean. His prolix *History of the Indies,* which was not published until 1875, is an angry appeal and indictment, as was his widely circulated *Brief History of the Destruction of the Indies.* Fray Bartolomé's accusations often took on a biblical air and included many stories as evidence. Several scholars had noted the literary quality of those narratives, but it was Cuban author and critic Antonio Benítez Rojo (an accomplished short story writer himself, who is featured in this anthology) who saw the power of the particular excerpt included here. "Plague of Ants," from the *History,* uncannily anticipates themes and techniques of contemporary Latin American fiction, particularly those associated with magical realism. Las Casas, needless to say, had no aesthetic intentions; in fact, he wrote more like a lawyer or preacher than as a historian.

Plague of Ants

A round this time, in the year 1518 or 1519, something else happened on this island. By the will or consent of God, to relieve them of the anguished and tortured lives they endured toiling in all sorts of labor, but mostly in the mines, and to punish those who oppressed them by making them suffer their absence, there came a terrible plague in which nearly all the few Indians left perished, with only a small number surviving. The epidemic was smallpox, brought over by someone from Castile, and which attacked the poor Indians. The pox, which burns like fire, grew out of the earth's heat. The Indians, whose custom it was to wash themselves in the

34

rivers at every opportunity, took to washing themselves even more in their anguish. As a result the smallpox was locked inside their bodies, and, as in a devastating pestilence, all died in a short time. Added to these causes were the thinness and meager substance of their bodies from lack of food, their nakedness, their sleeping on the ground, the excessive labor, and the little or no care for their health and preservation they received from those whom they served. Finally, seeing that the Indians were dying, the Spaniards began to understand the need they had and would continue to have of them, which moved them to make some effort to cure them, but this was of little help to most, for it ought to have begun many years earlier. I do not believe that 1,000 souls were left alive or escaped this misery, from the infinite number of people who had lived on this island and whom we saw with our own eyes, as is explained in book I. No Christian can doubt that, although God by his secret judgments might have permitted afflicting these peoples in this way and with such inhumanity, and, in short, putting an end to them, that on the day of final judgment, and on the day of universal judgment, those who were ministers of such harshness and caused the loss of so many souls, will be severely punished by divine justice. If they did not repent while still alive they will pay for their greed and cruelty, for taking lives before their time, before their conversion, and so for the loss of so many souls (because all others on this island and on the neighboring ones believe, and I do not doubt it because I saw much of it myself, that they died without faith and without sacraments in their simple paganism). No Christian doubts this.

And because they realized that the Indians were dying, they began to slacken off and leave the mines, for they had no one left to send there to die or even to kill, and so they looked instead for other profits and new ways to acquire wealth, one of which was to plant cassia trees, which grew so quickly and in such numbers that it seemed as if this soil had not been created for any other tree, nor these trees for any other soil but this one, so ordered by Divine Providence and nature. In a very few days, many great estates were established of these cassia trees, from which the entire populated world could have been supplied. Their stalks were very big and thick, full of pulp, very honey-sweet. Ask the doctors and pharmacists if their virtue is lesser or greater than that of Alexandria.

The citizens of this island, that is to say, the Spaniards, because there is nothing left to say about the Indians, were not just a little proud, promising themselves many riches by putting all their hopes in the cassia tree. It would be good to believe that they might have attributed to God a part of this prospect, but they were already beginning to enjoy the fruits of their labors and to fulfill their expectations when God sent over this whole island and over the island of Saint John, principally, a plague. One might have feared, if it continued to grow, that the plague would totally depopulate them.

This plague was an infinite number of ants that were on this island and on the other and that could not be stopped in any way nor by any human means because of the sheer number of them. The ants bred on this island had an advantage over the ones on Saint John in the amount of damage done to the trees they destroyed, and the ants of the other island had an advantage over these in their fierceness, as they bit and caused greater pain than wasps that bite and hurt men. They could not defend themselves from these ants at night in their beds, nor could they survive if the beds were not placed on four small troughs filled with water. The ants on this island began to eat the trees from the root up, and as though fire had fallen from the sky and burned them, they stood all scorched and dried out. They also attacked the orange and pomegranate trees, of which there were many groves, very pretty and full on this island, and they left none without burning them out completely. To see it was a great pity. Many groves were destroyed in the city of Santo Domingo, and among them a very important one belonging to the Dominicans' monastery (of pomegranate trees and sweet, dry, and bitter orange trees), and in a place called La Vega another one, quite notable, belonging to the Franciscans. These trees stood behind the cassia trees, and, as they were sweeter, they destroyed them even more quickly and burned them out. I believe that they devastated over one hundred million trees that were planted for profit. It was, certainly, a great shame to see so many properties, so rich, annihilated by such a relentless plague. The grove of Saint Francis in La Vega, already mentioned, was full of orange trees that gave sweet, dry, and bitter fruit. There I saw very beautiful pomegranate trees and cassia trees, and great stalks of cassia, nearly four hands in length. And just a short time later I saw all of it charred out. I saw the same thing in many other cassia tree estates that were in that area. The spreads of cassia trees on that land, and those that could have been planted, would without doubt have been enough, alone, to provide for all of Europe and Asia, even if they had been eaten as one eats bread, because of the great fertility of that land and its size. It extends for 80 leagues from sea to sea, full of rivers and happiness, and as flat as the palm of one's hand. We have talked about this at great length in our *Apologética historia*.

Some looked for remedies to extirpate this plague of ants. They dug around the trees as deeply as they could and killed the ants by drowning them in water. Other times they burnt them with fire. They found, inside the earth, three and four and more hands deep, their seedbeds and eggs, as white as snow, and they would burn one and two measures* of them every day, and by dawn, they would find an even greater quantity of live ants. The priests from Saint Francis of La Vega placed a mercury chloride stone,

---

Celemín—old Castilian measure for land and grain *(Simon & Schuster International Dictionary)*; dry measure consisting of 4,625 liters *(Pequeño Larousse)*.

which must have weighed three or four pounds, on a roof railing. All the ants of the house rushed there, and after eating from the stone they all fell dead. As if they had sent messengers to those who were within one and a half leagues, inviting them to the banquet of mercury chloride, not one ant, I believe, failed to come. One could see the roads filled with those coming to the monastery. They finally climbed up on the roof and ate from the mercury chloride and then fell dead, so that the roof was as black as if they had sprayed it with charcoal dust. This lasted as long as the stone of mercury chloride did. The stone was like two great fists and like a ball; I saw it as large as I said it was when they first put it there, and a few days later I saw it again, only now the size of a hen's egg or a little bigger.

Once the priests saw that the mercury chloride was of no use, except to soil their home, they decided to take it away. They marveled at two things, which were worthy of admiration. First, at the natural instinct and the strength with which it endows sensitive and insensitive creatures, as is apparent in the case of these ants, who from such a distance could feel the mercury chloride, if one may put it this way, and how the same instinct guided them and brought them to it. Second, how a little animal so tiny and small (like these ants, which were very tiny) could have such strength as to be able to bite the mercury chloride, and, finally, to diminish it and finish it off, the mercury chloride in stone form, before it is ground, being as hard as a stone of alum, if not more so, and almost like a small rock.

As the citizens of Santo Domingo saw the affliction of this plague grow, doing such damage to them, and as they could not end it by any human means, they agreed to ask for help from the Highest Tribunal. They made great processions begging Our Father to free them from such a plague so harmful to their worldly goods. In order to receive divine blessing more quickly, they thought of taking a saint as a lawyer, whichever one by chance Our Lord should declare best suited. Thus, with the procession over one day, the bishop, and clergy, and the whole city cast lots over which of the litany's saints Divine Providence would see fit to give them as a lawyer. Fortune fell on Saint Saturnin, and receiving him with happiness and joy as their patron, they celebrated him with a feast of great solemnity, as they have each year since then, by vow, as I believe. I do not know if they even fast on the eve. From that day on one saw by plain sight that the plague was diminishing, and if it did not end altogether, it was because of their sins. I now believe that it no longer exists, because they have again restored some of the cassia trees, and orange and pomegranate trees. I say restore referring not to what the ants burned out, but to the new trees that were planted. Some believed and said that the ants originated with the importation and cultivation of banana trees. Petrarch recounts in his *Trionfi* that in the realm of Pisa a certain city was depopulated by a plague of ants that came over it like this one. Nicolaus Leonicus, book II, chapter 71 of *Varia Historia,* refers to two very great cities, one named Miunte and the other Atarnense, which were depopulated by a multitude of mosquitos that at a certain time came upon them. Thus it is that, when God wishes to punish lands or the men who live in them for their sins, he does not lack the means to afflict them, and can even do so with the tiniest little creatures. So it was with the plagues of Egypt.

TRANSLATED BY SANDRA FERDMAN

Garcilaso de la Vega, el Inca

Viceroyalty of Peru
(1539–1616)

———— \\ ————

Considered the first Latin American writer because of his anxieties about the complications of his genealogy, Garcilaso de la Vega, el Inca, was born from the unsanctified union of a Spanish nobleman and an Inca woman, also of aristocratic lineage. Because of this double and conflicting origin, Garcilaso's most important work, *The Royal Commentaries of the Incas,* from which the present story is taken, is an elegant and probing history of both pre- and post-Hispanic Peru. The first part, dedicated to Incan history and lore, is based on stories Garcilaso heard from relatives on his mother's side. The second part recounts the civil wars among the conquistadores, in which his father was implicated. Garcilaso's primary intellectual preoccupation was the philosophy of history, more specifically the place of the New World in history. He argues that the Incas were the equals of classical Romans, civilized but lacking Christianity. Garcilaso moved to Spain in his early twenties and remained there the rest of his life. He became an accomplished humanist, and published, in addition to *The Royal Commentaries,* a history of Florida and a translation of Leon Hebreo's Neoplatonic book, *The Dialogues of Love.* Enrique Pupo-Walker has argued persuasively that the brief stories that Garcilaso includes in his books give his work an imaginative quality. "The Story of Pedro Serrano," the selection presented here, has a philosophical and even political edge. The shipwrecked Spaniard, a precursor of Robinson Crusoe, is put in the position of a savage, devoid of nearly all the accoutrements of culture.

The Story of Pedro Serrano

Before going further, it would be as well to tell here the story of Pedro Serrano mentioned above, so that it is not too far from its place, and in order that this chapter may not be too short. Pedro Serrano swam to the hitherto unnamed desert island, which, as he said, would be about two leagues in circumference. The chart shows this to be so: it gives three small islets with a great many banks round about, and the same appearance is given to the one called Serranilla, which is five islets with more shoals than Serrana: there are many banks in all these parts, and ships avoid them so as not to fall into danger.

It was Pedro Serrano's fate to be wrecked among them and to reach the island swimming. He was in a state of despair, for he found no water nor fuel nor even grass he could graze on, nor anything else to maintain life till some ship might pass to rescue him before he perished from hunger and thirst; this seemed to him a harder fate than death by drowning, which is quicker. So he spent the first night bewailing his misfortune, and was as cast down as one would suppose a man to be in such a plight. As soon as dawn came, he again walked round the island, and found some shellfish from the sea, crabs, shrimps, and other creatures. He caught what he could and ate them raw, having no flame to roast or boil them with. Thus he kept himself going until he saw turtles come forth. Seeing them some distance from the sea, he seized one and turned it over, and did the same to as many as he could, for they are clumsy in righting themselves when on their backs. Drawing a knife he used to wear in his belt, and which saved his life, he beheaded one and drank its blood instead of water. He did the same with the rest, and laid out their flesh in the sun to make dried meat and cleaned out the shells to catch rainwater, for the whole region is, of course, very rainy. Thus he sustained himself during the first days by killing all the turtles he could. Some were as big as and bigger than the biggest shields, and others like smaller shields and targes. They were in fact of all sizes. The largest of them he could not contrive to turn over on their backs, because they were stronger than he, and though he climbed on them to subdue them by tiring them, it was no use because they could make their way to the sea with him astraddle. So experience taught him which turtles he could attack and which to abandon. In their shells he collected a great deal of water, for some could hold two arrobas, and others less. Finding himself adequately supplied with food and drink, Pedro Serrano thought that if he could make fire so as to be able to roast his food and produce smoke in case a ship should pass, he could lack nothing. With this idea, being a man with long experience of the sea (and they certainly have a great advantage over other men in any sort of task), he looked for a pair of pebbles that he could use as flint, hoping to use his knife to strike fire from them. But not finding any such stones on the island, which was covered with bare sand, he swam into the sea and dived, carefully searching the sea bottom in all directions, and persisting in his labors until he found pebbles and collected what he could, picking out the best and breaking them on one another so as to make edges to strike the knife on. He then tried out his idea, and seeing that he could strike fire, made shreds of a piece of his shirt, torn very small like carded cotton. This served as tinder, and by dint of industry and skill, after great perseverance, he made himself a fire. Having got it, he counted himself fortunate and sustained it by collecting the jetsam thrown up by the sea. He spent hours collecting weeds called sea-pods, timber from ships lost at sea, shells, fish bones, and other

THE STORY OF PEDRO SERRANO \ 41

material to feed his fire. So that the showers should not extinguish it, he made a hut with the biggest shells from the turtles he had killed, and tended the fire with great diligence lest it should slip from his hands. Within two months or less, he was as naked as when he was born, for the great rain, the heat, and the humidity of the region rotted the few clothes he had. The sun wearied him with its great heat, for he had no clothes to protect himself nor any shade. When he was very extenuated, he entered the water and submerged himself. He lived three years amidst these hardships and cares, and though he saw several ships pass in that time, and made smoke (the usual signal for people lost at sea), they did not see him, or else feared the shoals and did not dare to approach, but passed well out to sea, all of which left Pedro Serrano so discouraged that he had resigned himself to dying and ending his misery. Owing to the harshness of the climate hair grew all over his body till it was like an animal's pelt, and not just any animal's, but a wild boar's. His hair and beard fell below his waist.

After three years, one afternoon when he was not expecting anything, he saw a man on the island. This man had been wrecked on the shoals the night before and had saved himself on a ship's plank. As soon as dawn appeared, he saw the smoke of Pedro Serrano's fire, and guessing what it was, made for it, aided by the plank and his good swimming. When they saw one another, it would be hard to say which was the more surprised. Serrano thought it was the Devil come in human form to tempt him to some desperate act. His guest thought Serrano was the Devil in his true form, he was so coated with hair, beard, and hide. Each fled from the other, and Pedro Serrano went off crying: "Jesus! Jesus! Oh Lord, deliver me from the demon!"

Hearing this, the other was reassured, and turned toward him saying: "Flee me not, brother, for I am a Christian too," and to prove it, as he still ran away, shouted the Credo. Pedro Serrano heard it, turned back, and they advanced with the greatest tenderness and many tears and groans, seeing that they were both in the same plight with no hope of escape. Each briefly told the other the story of his past life. Pedro Serrano, realizing his guest's need, gave him some of his food and drink, which comforted him a little, and they again discussed their plight. They arranged their life as best they could, dividing the hours of the day and night between the duties of collecting shellfish to eat and sea-pods and wood and fish bones and anything else thrown up by the sea to sustain the fire, and especially the perpetual vigil they had to keep on it, hour by hour, lest it go out. They lived in this way for some days, but it was not long before they quarrelled, and so violently that they lived apart and nearly came to blows (which shows how great is the misery of human passions). The cause of the strife was that one accused the other of not doing the necessary duties properly. This accusation and the words they exchanged were enough to destroy their harmony and divide them. But they themselves soon realized their folly, asked one another's forgiveness, made friends, and lived together again. Thus they continued for four years. During this time they saw some ships pass and made their smoke signals, but in vain, and this so depressed them that they all but died.

At the end of this long time, a ship chanced to pass so near that their smoke was sighted and a boat put out to pick them up. Pedro Serrano and his companion, who had grown a similar pelt, seeing the boat approach, fell to saying the Credo and calling on the name of our Redeemer aloud, so that the sailors should not think they were demons and flee from them. This availed them, for otherwise the mariners would doubtless have fled: they no longer looked like human beings. So they were carried to the ship, where they astounded all who saw them and heard about their labors. The companion died at sea returning to Spain. Pedro Serrano reached here and went on to Germany, where the emperor then was. He kept his pelt as it was, as a proof of his wreck and all he had gone through. In every village he passed through on the way he earned much money whenever he chose to exhibit himself. Some of the lords and principal knights who liked to see his figure contributed toward the cost of the journey, and his imperial majesty, having seen and heard him, gave him a reward of 4,000 pesos in income, or 4,800 ducats, in Peru. On the way to enjoy this, he died at Panama, and never saw it. All this story, as I have repeated it, is told by a gentleman called Sánchez de Figueroa, from whom I heard it. He knew Pedro Serrano and warrants that he had heard it from him, and that after seeing the emperor, Pedro Serrano cut his hair and beard to just above the waist; and to enable him to sleep at night, he plaited it, for otherwise it spread out over the bed and disturbed his rest.

TRANSLATED BY HAROLD V. LIVERMORE

Gaspar de Villarroel

Viceroyalty of Peru
(1587–1665)

———— // ————

An Augustinian friar, Gaspar de Villarroel was celebrated in Lima and other cities of the Viceroyalty of Peru for his sermons. Baroque oratory was an important subgenre in the seventeenth century in Spain and her colonies. Villarroel lived for a time in Lisbon, where he published the first volume of his notable work *Semana Santa o Comentarios y discursos sobre los evangelios de Cuaresma,* the second volume of which appeared in Madrid in 1633 and the third in Seville in 1634. Philip II named him to the bishopric of Santiago, Chile, in 1637. He distinguished himself for his erudition and concern for the people, particularly in the aftermath of the 1647 earthquake. His *Gobierno eclesiástico y pacífico* (1656–57), the source of this story, is one of the best seventeenth-century chronicles, not only for its wealth of information but also for Villarroel's lively style. Like the legal documents drawn up to police the vast Spanish Empire, church histories were the most prevalent forms of writing in colonial America, providing a rich record of social activity as well as a prolix display of wit, scholarship, and intelligence. Some ecclesiastical prose, adhering to neo-scholastic discourse, assumed the form of polemics. The best-known is the "Reply" by Mexican nun Sor Juana Inés de la Cruz in which she defends her right to cultivate her intellect. Villarroel's history is a vast tapestry of human action, portrayed with a slight ironic tone. In "The Adventurer Who Pretended That He Was a Bishop," the selection chosen here, we see how a resourceful rogue bilks the system of support the church maintained for her servants. Villarroel was a master of the significant physical detail, such as the description of the hands of his main character.

The Adventurer Who Pretended That He Was a Bishop

A fairly well-educated priest, who was also quite clever, had come over from Spain to attend to certain business and licenses concerning his superiors. He did not belong to any of the orders that have taken residence in the Indies, and I shall refrain from mentioning the one to which he actually belonged because I do not make it a habit of mentioning those where it might be construed that I intend to tarnish their reputation. He had made a stop a few leagues from Cuzco at a *doctrina,* which is what we call, here, in these parts, parishes in which the congregation is made up entirely of Indians. He had been very warmly received.

From there he wrote to the magistrate of Cuzco, to the prelates of the religious orders, and to several private gentlemen, informing them that His Majesty had granted him the favor of naming him to the bishopric of Venezuela, known as Caracas here in the Indies; also, that in the time remaining before he took possession of his parish he wished to travel to Potosí to bring to a close some of the matters that had pulled him out of his monastery cell. That city is known for being very hospitable to foreigners and extremely deferential to bishops, so it rejoiced with the visit, which unleashed a holy war among the prelates over who would host such a distinguished guest. The prior of the Augustinians came out the winner. He was Master Fray Lucas de Mendoza, a man of great virtue and learning, who died as Provincial and Chair of Holy Scriptures at the University of Lisbon, where he was deeply mourned by all the ecclesiastics. (I do not mean to exaggerate vainly his enormous talents, but I mention them to show how subtle the swindler had to be.)

And so the "bishop" entered Cuzco with solemn accompaniment. A room was richly appointed for him in the convent. (I was put up in the same room when I succeeded the Prior, a fact I bring up here so that it be known that the imbroglio was still so fresh when I learned of it that I could almost give testimony as an eyewitness.) Gentlemen made precious gifts to the prelate, as did all the orders. They entrusted him with the sermon on the feast of my holy father Saint Augustine. The pulpit was lavishly decorated. The preacher entered it with great pomp, not the least part of which was that he was allowed to speak from a chair with a cushion. He then proceeded to remove perfumed and amber-colored gloves from his hands, performing this ceremony so deliberately that he was able to conclude as he did a protracted argumentation to the effect that the grave responsibilities that assuming the bishopric entailed, the immense rewards that came with such a distinguished position, so occupied his mind that he would be unable to preach to the level of expectations. He wound up this harangue just as he left his hands bare, whereupon he made the sign of the cross and declared the theme of his oration. Having finished the sermon, he was congratulated with all the pomp and circumstance due a bishop.

The applause brought him a good sum of money, with which he left Cuzco as well provided as if he had been visiting his own bishopric. He reached Potosí, having picked up all he could along the way; and this town, which astonishes with its great magnanimity, made such donations to him that he needed a mule train for the money alone. He made several money runs, and reached the proximity of Arequipa loaded with silver. Because Peru is like an alley and Arequipa sticks outside the main road, and also because of its historical wealth, the city is called "the Indies money bag."

He found out there through a confidante of his that the Council of the Indies had issued a warrant for his arrest, asking the Viceroy to detain him and ship him back to Spain. Given the fleets' itineraries this shows that the hoax had lasted a full three years. He shrewdly scattered his servants by sending them with letters to various parts, and finding himself rid of such witnesses, got lost with a few poor little Indians, making himself and his money so scarce that to this day nothing has been heard of him.

If this clergyman, in the same way that he passed himself off as the bishop of such a faraway church, had decided to take over one of the many vacant churches in the kingdom of Peru, and he would have managed to take possession of it without the proper bulls, couldn't one fear many other misfortunes? Of course one could. For which reason it is also clear that the law's regulations are prudent and holy.

TRANSLATED BY ROBERTO GONZÁLEZ ECHEVARRÍA

Catalina de Erauso ("The Lieutenant Nun")

Spain
(1584–1650)

———— \\\\ ————

"The Lieutenant Nun" ("Monja Alférez"), whose story is one of the more captivating tales to emerge from colonial Latin America, summarizes her life thus to Bishop don Agustín de Carvajal:

> The truth is this: that I am a woman, that I was born in such and such a place, the daughter of this man and this woman, that at a certain age I was placed in a certain convent with a certain aunt, that I was raised there and took the veil and became a novice, and that when I was about to profess my final vows, I left the convent for such and such a reason, went to such and such a place, undressed myself and dressed myself up again, cut my hair, traveled here and there, embarked, disembarked, hustled, killed, maimed, wreaked havoc, and roamed about, until coming to a stop in this very instance, at the feet of Your Eminence.

The *relación,* a deposition or petition, in which Catalina de Erauso fills in the blanks, reads like a strange combination of picaresque and Byzantine romance, with the sustained suspense of the imminence of her real gender being discovered. She barely escapes being exposed several times, and at other times, such as in this fragment, she skirts disaster by inciting the desire of women or the matchmaking wiles of fathers and mothers. Catalina, a fierce soldier and fearless adventurer, managed to preserve her virginity intact through it all, which garners her the favor of first the bishop, later the king of Spain, and finally the pope himself. She is a fugitive from power who is ultimately rewarded for her military deeds as a man and her dogged chastity as a woman. According to her writings—which are legal documents—Catalina lived out each gender role without a modern sense of ambiguity.

Amorous and Military Adventures

I set out along the coast, suffering a good deal, especially from thirst, for there was no fresh water to be had for miles around. Along the way, I fell in with two other soldiers, deserters both, and we continued on our way together, determined to die rather than let ourselves be arrested. We had our horses, our swords, our firearms, and the guidance of God on high. We ascended into the mountains, climbing for more than thirty leagues, and in all of them and the three hundred more we traveled, we didn't meet up with a single mouthful of bread, and only rarely some water or a clump of rough herbs, or some small animals, and now and then a gnarled root to keep us alive, and now and then an Indian who fled before us. We were forced to kill one of the horses and dry its meat, but we found that it was little more than skin and bones—and as we pressed onward, step by step, mile after mile, the others met the same fate, until we were left with only our feet to carry us and barely enough strength to stand.

The land grew cold—so cold we were half-frozen. One day from a distance we saw two men leaning against a rock and this gave us heart. We pushed on towards them, calling out as we came, asking what they were doing there, but they never answered. When we came to the spot, we saw they were dead—frozen through, their mouths hanging open as if they were laughing, and this filled us with terror.

We pressed on and three nights later, as we rested against a rock, one of the others gave out and died. The two of us went on and the next day, at about four in the afternoon, my companion dropped to the ground sobbing, unable to go another step, and he died. I found eight pesos in his pocket and pressed on blindly, clutching my rifle and the last scrap of dried meat, expecting any moment to share my companions' fate. You can imagine my wretched state, dead tired, barefoot, my feet in shreds. I propped myself against a tree and wept—for what I think was the first time in my life—I recited the rosary, commending myself to the Most Holy Virgin and to her husband, glorious Saint Joseph. I rested a little, got back on my feet, and began to walk again, and judging by the climate I must have walked clear out of the kingdom of Chile and into Tucumán.

I kept on going and the next morning, as I lay stretched out on the ground, overcome by fatigue and hunger, I caught sight of two men approaching on horseback. And I didn't know whether to rejoice or tremble—were they cannibals or Christians? I couldn't tell—and without even the strength to take aim, I loaded my rifle.

They rode up and asked me what I was doing in that godforsaken place, and I could see they were Christians, and the heavens seemed to open before me. I told them I was lost, that I didn't know where I was, that I was wracked with fatigue, dead with hunger, too weak to even stand. It pained them to see me like that and, dismounting, they gave me what food they had, loaded me up on one of the horses, and carried me to what they said was their mistress's ranch, some three leagues away, and we arrived there around five in the afternoon.

The lady was a half-breed, the daughter of a Spaniard and an Indian woman, a widow and a good woman. When she saw how broken and friendless I was, she took pity on me, gave me a decent bed to sleep in, a good meal, and told me to rest—after which, I felt much better. The next morning, she fed me well, and seeing as I was so entirely destitute she gave me a decent cloth suit, and went on treating me handsomely, making me small gifts of this and that. The lady was well-off, with a good deal of livestock and cattle, and it seems that, since Spaniards were scarce in those parts, she began to fancy me as a husband for her daughter.

After I'd been there for eight days, the good woman said she wanted me to stay on and manage the place. I let her know how grateful I was, seeing how I was penniless, and told her I would serve her to the best of my abilities. And a couple of days later, she let me know it would be fine by her if I married her daughter—a girl as black and ugly as the devil himself, quite the opposite of my taste, which has always run to pretty faces. Still, I pretended to be overcome with happiness—so much good fortune, and for one so undeserving!—and I threw myself at her feet, telling her I was hers to dispose of as she pleased, as one she had snatched from the jaws of ruin, and I went on serving her as well as I knew how.

The woman tricked me out like a dandy and gave me full run of the house and the lands. After two months, we went into Tucumán for the wedding, and there I remained for another two months, delaying the thing on one pretext or another until, finally, I couldn't take it anymore and I stole a mule and cleared out—and that was the last they ever saw of me.

It was during this time in Tucumán that I had another adventure of the same sort. In the two months while I was putting off the Indian woman, I struck up a casual friendship with the bishop's secretary, who made quite a fuss over me and more than once invited me to his house, where we played cards and where I met a certain churchman, don Antonio de Cervantes, the bishop's vicar-general. This gentleman also took a fancy to me, and gave me gifts and wined me and dined me at his house until, finally, he came to the point, and told me that he had a niece living with him who was just about my age, a girl of many charms, not to mention a fine dowry, and that he had a mind to see the two of us married—and so did she.

I pretended to be quite humbled by his flattering intentions. I met the girl, and she seemed good enough. She sent me a suit of good velvet, twelve shirts, six pairs of Rouen breeches, a collar of fine Dutch linen, a dozen handkerchiefs, and two hundred pesos in a silver dish—all of this a gift, sent simply as a compliment, and having nothing to do with the dowry itself.

Well, I received it all gratefully and composed the best thank-you I knew how, saying I was on fire for the moment when I would kiss her hand and throw myself at her feet. I hid as much of the stuff as I could from the Indian woman, and as for the rest I led her to believe it was a gift from don Antonio, something on the occasion of my marriage to her daughter, whom that gentleman had heard of and thought the world of—especially considering I was so crazy about her myself.

This is how things stood when I saddled up and vanished. And I have never heard exactly what became of the black girl or the little vicaress.

TRANSLATED BY MICHELE STEPTO AND GABRIEL STEPTO

Juan Rodríguez Freyle

Nueva Granada
(1566–1640)

A Creole son of a conquistador, Juan Rodríguez Freyle wrote what purports to be a history of the Kingdom of Nueva Granada (today's Colombia), which came to be known by its short title, *El Carnero* (1636–38). The book covers from the Conquest to Rodríguez Freyle's time. But the historical part is a mere pretext, a flimsy frame, for what turns out to be the meat of the book: a series of scandalous stories about the adventures and misadventures of philandering husbands and unfaithful wives in the city of Bogotá. The historical disguise of *El Carnero,* not to mention its enigmatic title, led many scholars astray, until Susan Herman discovered the true meaning of both. *Carnero* does not mean sheep here, but wastebasket, from the Latin *carnarium,* a place where scraps were discarded in a butcher shop. Hence the book's self-deprecating title refers to it as the wastebasket of the Bogotá court of appeals—the place where the least worthy cases wound up. This mock archive of lost causes and cases contained spicy stories that make up a kind of Spanish colonial *Decameron.* The best-known among these is the story included here, "A Deal with Juana García," a minor masterpiece of colonial Latin American literature. The story contains elements that go back to the Spanish *Celestina,* the story of a go-between, as well as elements from African lore, such as that of the flying African who can return home after death by soaring through the sky. But it is also a delightfully ironic description of the corruptions of the colonial regime, particularly of its religious and lay administrators, who are presumably in charge of public morality and the orderly observance of the law.

A Deal with Juana García

While the first president of this land is arriving, I want to pluck two flowers from the garden of Santa Fe de Bogotá, the New Kingdom of Granada, the first being the events concerning His Excellency, Bishop Juan de los Barrios, and the Real Audencia, so the reader will understand that there is nothing new in confrontations between these two tribunals.

This segment from Rodríguez Freyle's chronicle of the Conquest and Discovery of the New Kingdom of Granada contains numerous references to the colonial insti-

50

I recounted, following the arrest of Juan de Montaño, the names of the *oidores* who had sat in judgment on the *licenciado* Alonso de Grajeda. Well, then, it happened that a cleric, in habit, had come from Peru to this city, about whom nothing more was known at the time. After him followed a requisitory from the Audencia of Lima that he be taken and remanded to that city. This Real Audiencia ordered the requisitory to be carried out. The cleric, who knew of it, betook himself to the church, where His Excellency the Bishop was to be found. As requested, a senior *oidor* went to the church to carry out the mandate of the Real Audencia. His Excellency held out against it to the degree he was able; the *oidor* took the cleric prisoner. The prelate acted and brought proceedings against the entire Audencia, according to the articles of law, and, finally, issued a *cessatio divinis* against the Audencia and left this city to return to Castile.

The conquistadors and captains were aroused; the entire city suffered great emotion upon the departure of their prelate, leaving it deprived of spiritual consolation. In the end, there was sufficient stir that those gentlemen came into line, and, all being in agreement, sent after His Excellency the Bishop. The captain-conquistadors went to fetch him. As His Excellency returned, night fell upon the Hill of Alfonso Díaz, which today is called the Hill of Juan de Melo. The first among the lords of the Real Audencia to see him was the Treasurer, señor García de Valverde, whom the Bishop received warmly, and absolved, giving him a penance, which was that from said Hill he come to this city on foot, that distance being some five leagues. Which penance he fulfilled, accompanied by other señores who had no blame. His Excellency then set out for this city, where he was warmly received. The *oidores* came out to meet him along the way, and where he came across them he absolved them, giving them the same penance as the Treasurer. With which that commotion was ended, all remaining very good friends.

The second flower was also born of this plaza, which was that broadside placed on the walls of the Cabildo on said plaza, years earlier, having to do with the deaths of the two *oidores* Góngora and Galarza, and the loss of the *Capitana,* her General and men, during a stopover in Bermuda. Which happened in this way.

On one of the ships coming and going from Castile following the imprisonment of Montaño, there traveled a resident of this city to make good

tutions of seventeenth-century Colombia, among them the Real Audencia, or Royal Court, and its *oidores,* or judges. The Cabildo is the city hall. A *licenciado* is someone who has completed the advanced degree of the licenciature. *Comadre* has several meanings: a midwife, the word denoting the relationship between the mother of a child and the child's godmother, and here, a term of familiarity. *Translator's note.*

use of his money. He was a married man, having a young and beautiful wife; and in the absence of her husband this wife did not wish to waste her beauty, but to take pleasure from it. As she was negligent, she soon found that her beauty had borne fruit, but believed that with time she might rid herself of it. Before the natural course of things, however, there came to her door news of the arrival of a flotilla in Cartagena, at which the poor señora grew greatly alarmed and made every effort to rid herself of her problem, though without effect. She then endeavored to work out an arrangement with *madre* Juana García, her *comadre,* she being an emancipated black woman who had arrived in this land with Governor don Alonso Luis de Lugo. Juana García had two daughters, who went about the city decked out in silks and gold, and even drew into their train some men of the city. This black woman was somewhat given to fanciful flights, as was ascertained. The enceinte lady consulted this *comadre* and told her her needs, and what she wished to have done, and asked for a remedy to her problem. The *comadre* said to her:

"Who has told you that your husband is arriving with these ships?"

Replying to her, the lady said that her husband himself had said it, that he would return at the first opportunity, without fail. The *comadre* responded:

"If it is thus, wait, do nothing, for I want to hear this news of the ships, and learn if your husband is coming with them. Tomorrow I will come to you again and arrange what we must arrange; and so saying, go with God."

The following day, the *comadre* returned, having busied herself throughout the night, and she came well informed of the truth. She said to the enceinte lady:

"Señora *comadre*: I have worked diligently to learn about your husband. It is true that the ships are in Cartagena, but I have found no word of your husband, nor is there anyone who says that he is arriving with them."

The enceinte lady was much disturbed, and pleaded with the *comadre* to give her the remedy that would rid her of her problem, to which she responded:

"Do nothing until we learn the truth, whether or not he is coming. What you can do is . . . Do you see that green basin there?"

The lady said, "Yes."

"Well, *comadre,* fill it with water and place it in your chamber, and make preparations for us to dine, for I shall come this evening and bring my daughters, and we shall make merry, and also undertake some remedy for what you say you wish to do."

With this, she took her leave and went to her home. She advised her daughters, and when night fell, along with them, she went to the home of the enceinte lady, who had not forgotten the task of filling the basin. She also sent for other young neighbor women, who came to revel with her that night. They gathered together, and as the young women were singing and dancing, the enceinte *comadre* said to her *comadre*:

"My belly gives me great pain. Will you look at it for me?"

The *comadre* responded:

"Yes, I will do that. Take one of those candles and we will go to your bed chamber."

The lady took up the candle and they went into the chamber. After they were inside, she closed the door and said:

"*Comadre*, there is the basin with the water."

And she replied:

"Well, take that candle and observe what is in the water."

She did as directed, and looking, said to her:

"*Comadre*, here I see a land I do not know, and here is a man, my husband, seated on a chair, and a woman is nearby at a table, and a tailor with scissors in his hand, who wants to cut her a gown of fine scarlet cloth."

The *comadre* said to her:

"Then wait, for I, too, wish to see."

She neared the basin and saw everything she had been told. The *comadre* asked: "What land is that?"

And she answered:

"Hispaniola, the Isla Española of Santo Domingo."

With this, the tailor availed himself of his scissors and cut a sleeve, and threw it over his shoulder. The *comadre* said to the enceinte lady:

"Do you want me to take that sleeve from the tailor?"

And the woman replied:

"Well, how will you do that?"

She replied:

"As you shall see, I shall take it from him."

The lady said:

"Well, then, take it, *comadre*, by your life."

And scarcely had the woman spoken when the *comadre* said to her:

"Well, here you have it," and handed her the sleeve.

They were a while watching the tailor cut the gown, which he did in a thrice, and when he was done everything faded, and there was nothing but the basin and the water. The *comadre* said to the lady:

"You have seen that your husband takes his leisure. You may be rid of this belly and even grow another."

The enceinte lady was very content. She threw the sleeve of scarlet cloth into a trunk beside her bed. And with this, the two went out to the hall, where the young women were making merry. They set the table and they supped richly, after which they went to their own homes.

Let us add: It is well known that the Devil was the one who tangled these threads, and that he is exceeding wise in the ways of the sons of man; but he cannot work within them, because this is reserved for God. He prevails through conjecture, and by attending to the path man is taking, the direction in which he is heading. I do not wonder at what he showed in the water to these women, because to this I reply that he who had the boldness to take our Lord Jesus Christ and lead Him to a high mountain, and from there show Him all the kingdoms of the world, and the glory thereof, of which God had no need, because he knows all before Him, offered a demonstration that was beyond doubt fantastic; and so also what he showed to the women in the basin of water. What does cause wonder is the dispatch with which he delivered the sleeve, for scarcely had the one said, "Well, take it, then, *comadre*," than the other replied, "Well, here you have it," and handed it to her. I also say that the Devil knew well the steps in which these women were following, and was forewarned in everything. And with this we come to the lady's husband, who was the one who uncovered all these fanciful flights.

Having arrived in the city of Seville, at the place and the time when relatives and friends of his had arrived, and who came from the Isla Española of Santo Domingo, the husband was told of the riches of that island and counseled to make good use of his money and come with them to that island. The man did so; he went to Santo Domingo and it turned out well. He returned to Castile and again made use of his money, and made a second journey to Isla Española. It was during this second voyage that the gown of fine scarlet cloth was cut. He sold his merchandise and returned to Spain and again invested his money in goods. And with this investment, he came to this New Kingdom at a time when the child was already some years old, and being brought up in the house as an orphan. Husband and wife welcomed each other gladly. For some days they were very content and in harmony, until the wife began to ask for some gew-gaw, and then another, and in the asking inserted little pinpricks of jealousy, so that the husband began to be annoyed, and suffered miserable dinners and worse suppers because his wife badgered him about the women he had had in Isla Española. At this the husband grew suspicious that some friend of his, one among those who had been with him on that island, had said something to his wife. Then, against his own nature, he began to give gifts to his wife, to see whether he might draw from her the name of the one who had done the harm. Finally, one evening while the two were at supper, very content, the wife asked her husband for a petticoat of green woolen, with a fine border. The husband did not respond well to her request, offering numerous excuses, to which the wife replied:

"By my faith, you were prepared to give gifts to the lady in Santo Domingo, the one to whom you gave the gown of fine scarlet cloth, and offered no excuses to her."

With this, the husband was defeated and confirmed in his suspicion. And in order to learn more, he gave his wife many gifts. He gave her the petticoat she had asked for, and other gew-gaws, with which she was very content. Then, one evening when they were happily together, the husband said to his wife:

"Sister, by your life, will you not say who it was told you I had dressed a lady in Isla Española in fine scarlet?"

His wife replied:

"So you wish to deny it? Tell me the truth, and I will tell you who told me."

The husband had found what he was seeking, and told her:

"Wife, it is true, because a man away from his home and in foreign lands must have some entertainment. I did give that gown to a lady."

She said:

"Tell me, then, when it was being cut, what was lacking?"

He replied to her:

"Nothing was lacking."

The woman spoke again, saying:

"What a one you are for denials! Was not a sleeve lacking?"

The husband searched his memory and said:

"It is true that the tailor forgot to cut it, and it was necessary to obtain more cloth."

Then the woman said to him:

"If I show you the sleeve that was lacking, will you know it?"

The husband said to her:

"Why, do you have it?"

She replied:

"Yes, come with me, and I will show it to you."

Together they went to her chamber, and from the tray in the trunk she took out the sleeve, saying to him:

"Is this the sleeve that was lacking?"

The husband said:

"This is it, wife; and I swear by God that we shall know who it was who brought the sleeve from Isla Española to the city of Santa Fe."

And with this he took the sleeve and went with it to His Excellency the Bishop, who was a judge for the Inquisition, and informed him of the matter. His Holiness was diligent in his duty. He called the woman before him; he took her statement. She fully confessed what she had seen in the basin of water. He then had the black woman Juana García seized, and her daughters. She confessed everything, as well as how it was she who had put up the broadsheet regarding the death of the two *oidores*. He heard the testimony of many other women, as recorded in the proceedings. The cause being substantiated, His Excellency pronounced sentence upon all those culpable. The word spread that many had fallen into the net, and that the guilt touched many illustrious people. In the end, the Governor don Gonzalo Jiménez de Quesada, Captain Zorro, Captain Céspedes, Juan Tafur, Juan Ruiz de Orejuela, and other important persons went to his Excellency, pleading with him not to execute the sentence in the given case, and to take into consideration that the land was new and that his judgment would be a stain upon it.

They so pressed His Holiness that he set aside the sentence. It fell only upon Juana García, whose punishment was to be placed on a platform before [the church of] Santo Domingo, during the hours of High Mass, with a noose around her neck and a lighted candle in her hand, at which she said, weeping, "Each of us women did it, but I alone pay!" She, and her daughters, were banished from this land. In her confession, she said that when she had gone to Bermuda, where the *Capitana* had gone down, she had flown from the hill that lies behind Nuestra Señora de las Nieves, there where one of the crosses is, and later, after much time had passed, they called it Juana García, or the Hill of Juana García.

TRANSLATED BY MARGARET SAYERS PEDEN

Part II

New Nations

\\\\

One of the clearest clues that nineteenth-century Latin American writers knew that they belonged to a tradition larger than those of their respective countries is that they wrote about one another and included one another's works in general anthologies. These intellectuals and artists founded journals, and some became scholars of colonial Latin American writing in an effort to endow the new literature with a common past, with a fable of origins. The pioneer in these activities was the Argentine Juan María Gutiérrez, whose anthology *América poética* appeared in Valparaíso, Chile, in 1846. Before him the Venezuelan Andrés Bello and the Argentine Domingo Faustino Sarmiento had played vital roles in the emergence of Chilean literature and the constitution of an educational system in that country.

Gutiérrez also published in 1848 a critical edition of Pedro de Oña's Renaissance epic *Arauco domado* (1570), which deals with the conquest of Chile, as if attempting to put an epic poem at the bottom of Latin American literature, in the same way that nineteenth-century literary history placed the *Poema de Mío Cid,* the *Chanson de Roland, Beowulf,* and *The Nibelungenlied* at the root of Spanish, French, English, and German literatures, respectively. The Chilean Diego Barros Arana followed suit with an edition of Fernando Alvarez de Toledo's *Purén indómito* (1862), a similar poem on the same topic, and even founded a collection in Paris titled *Bibliotheca americana: Collection d'ouvrages inédits ou rares sur l'Amérique,* to publish other works of the same nature.

Meanwhile, the Colombian José María Torres Caicedo published in 1862–63 (also in Paris) his three volumes of *Ensayos biográficos y de crítica literaria sobre los principales publicistas, historiadores, poetas y literatos de América Latina.* By 1893 the Argentine Martín García Merou had issued his gossipy *Confidencias literarias,* which recounted his travels throughout Europe and Latin America and his meetings with authors from many countries from the New World. It is a lively testimony of a literature in the making at the most personal level. A significant number of these scholar-critics were also writers, among them the earliest short story writers in Latin America, such as the Chilean José Victoriano Lastarria (1817–88).

Although there were exceptions, the production of short stories in the modern sense did not really begin in Latin America until the second half of the nineteenth century, and the *cuadro de costumbres* often had plots that turned them into short stories for all intents and purposes. Nineteenth-century Latin American literature preferred large fictional constructs linked to the foundation of national myths, as Doris Sommer has shown. But there were also stories in historical accounts, such as those by Juana Manuela Gorriti, not to mention Ricardo Palma's *Tradiciones peruanas,* which created a genre of their own. Many of the influential European short story writers were published in translation; their work appeared in journals throughout Latin America. The most influential turned out to be the North American Edgar Allan Poe, who was read in French, probably in Baudelaire's translation. By the end of the century an increase in short story production was stimulated by this influence.

But it was the *cuadro de costumbres* that prevailed in the nineteenth century, influencing the voluminous novels being published and giving the measure of the new literature's zeal to portray the realities of the new nations. This movement was stimulated by the dissemination of works by European scientific travelers who became the new discoverers of America. These travelers were often accompanied by artists who painted human types as well as specimens from the local flora and fauna. Literary *costumbrismo* was parallel to various schools of painting that pursued the same ends. These paintings ran from the scientific plate to pictures by artists who had decided to abandon the abstract models learned in the academies, focusing instead on the reality around them. Painting, with its inherent static quality, influenced the *cuadro de costumbres,* as Enrique Pupo-Walker has shown. In Cuba a Spanish artist, Landaluze, was the first to paint blacks. He portrayed memorable scenes of typical country life. The trend extended to the emerging popular culture. Urban types, particularly blacks and mulattoes, were depicted in magnificent cigarette wrappers. The typical scenes in these depictions are storylike because they are more often than not dramatic situations of social life at all levels.

In Brazil short story production seems to have been greater than in the Spanish American nations, perhaps because having been the seat of the Portuguese Crown for a protracted period, no need existed for nation-founding fictions. João Manuel Pereira da Silva (1817–97) published many short stories of a historiographic bent in *O Jornal dos Debates* in the 1830s. As in Spanish America, variations of regionalism prevailed in the second half of the century, until the appearance of Machado de Assis, who surpassed its limitations.

Esteban Echeverría

Argentina
(1805–1851)

———— \\\\ ————

Although Esteban Echeverría's renown rests on his intellectual and political activities, he was an important writer, and "The Slaughter House," the selection chosen for this volume, is a landmark in the history of Latin American short fiction. Echeverría was one of the young Argentines who founded in 1838 the Asociación de Mayo. This organization hoped to develop a national literature reflecting Argentina's realities. Having spent four formative years in Paris (1825–30), Echeverría was imbued in the romantic spirit, and he became one of the movement's promoters. Back in Argentina he devoted himself to the overthrow of the Rosas dictatorship. In 1841 he went into exile in nearby Uruguay, where he stayed until his death. Echeverría's "The Captive," a narrative poem about a white woman abducted by Indians, is among the better-known tales from nineteenth-century Latin America. "The Slaughter House," written about 1838, was published thirty years later, so its immediate political aim was not realized, but it became one of the most important stories in Latin American literary history. Its opening, which proposes the colonial chronicles as a narrative model, is a programmatic and prophetic statement on the relationship between Latin American history and fiction. "The Slaughter House" is mostly significant, however, because it displays the clash between "civilization and barbarism" that Sarmiento saw at the core of Latin American culture. Read in this light the story is a political allegory. Its more specific design was to accuse Rosas of cuddling the thugs who slay the civilized young man. A deeper conflict perhaps is between the liberal ideology of "The Slaughter House" and its painstaking representation of the ritual murder, an atavistic story of sacrifice that appears to be the source of its quasi-religious power.

The Slaughter House

Although the following narrative is historical, I shall not begin it with Noah's ark and the genealogy of his forebears as was wont once to be done by the ancient Spanish historians of America who should be our models. Numerous reasons I might adduce for not pursuing their example, but I shall pass them over in order to avoid prolixity, stating merely that the events here narrated occurred in the 1830's of our Christian era. Moreover, it was during Lent, a time when meat is scarce in Buenos Aires because the Church, adopting Epictetus' precept—*sustine abstine* (suffer, abstain)—orders vigil and abstinence to the stomachs of the faithful because carnivorousness is sinful and, as the proverb says, leads to carnality. And since the Church has, *ab initio* and through God's direct dispensation, spiritual sway over consciences and stomachs, which in no way belong to the individual, nothing is more just and reasonable than for it to forbid that which is both harmful and sinful.

The purveyors of meat, on the other hand, who are staunch Federalists and therefore devout Catholics, knowing that the people of Buenos Aires possess singular docility when it comes to submitting themselves to all manner of restrictions, used to bring to the Slaughter House during Lent only enough steers for feeding the children and the sick whom the Papal Bull excused, and had no intention of stuffing the heretics—of which there is no dearth—who are always ready to violate the meat commandments of the Church and demoralize society by their bad examples.

At this time, then, rain was pouring down incessantly. The roads were inundated; in the marshes water stood deep enough for swimming, and the streets leading to the city were flooded with watery mire. A tremendous stream rushed forth from the Barracas rivulet and majestically spread out its turbid waters to the very foot of the Alto slopes. The Plata, overflowing, enraged, pushed back the water that was seeking its bed and made it rush, swollen, over fields, embankments, houses, and spread like a huge lake over the lowlands. Encircled from north to east by a girdle of water and mud, and from the south by a whitish sea on whose surface small craft bobbed perilously and on which were reflected chimneys and treetops, the city from its towers and slopes cast anxious glances to the horizon as if imploring mercy from the Lord. It seemed to be the threat of a new deluge. Pious men and women wept as they busied themselves with their novenaries and continuous prayers. In church preachers thundered and made the pulpit creak under the blows of their fists. This is the day of judgment, they proclaimed, the end of the world is approaching! God's wrath runs over, pouring forth an inundation. Alas you poor sinners! Alas you impious Unitarians who mock the Church and the Saints and hearken not with veneration to the word of those anointed by the Lord! Alas you who do not beg mercy at the foot of the altars! The fearful hour of futile gnashing of teeth and frantic supplications has come! Your impiety, your heresies, your blasphemies, your horrid crimes, have brought to our land the Lord's plagues. Justice and the God of the Federalists will damn you.

The wretched women left the church breathless, overwhelmed, blaming the Unitarians, as was natural, for this calamity.

However, the torrential rainfall continued and the waters rose, adding credence to the predictions of the preachers. The bells tolled plaintively by order of the most Catholic Restorer, who was rather uneasy. The libertines, the unbelievers, that is to say, the Unitarians were frightened at seeing so many contrite faces and hearing such clamor of imprecations. There was much talk about a procession which the entire population was to attend barefoot and bareheaded, accompanying the Host, which was to be carried under a pallium by the Bishop to the Balcarce slope, where thousands of voices exorcising the demon of inundation were to implore divine mercy.

Fortunately, or rather unfortunately, for it might have been something worth seeing, the ceremony did not take place, because the Plata receded and the overflow gradually subsided without the benefit of conjuration or prayer.

Now what concerns my story above all is that, because of the inundation, the Convalescencia Slaughter House did not see a single head of cattle for fifteen days and that, in one or two days, all the cattle from nearby farmers and watercarriers were used up in supplying the city with meat. The unfortunate little children and sick people had to eat eggs and chickens, and foreigners and heretics bellowed for beefsteak and roast. Abstinence from meat was general in the town which never was more worthy of the blessing of the Church, and thus it was that millions and millions of plenary indulgences were showered upon it. Chickens went up to six pesos and eggs to four reales and fish became exceedingly expensive. During Lent there were no promiscuities or excesses of gluttony, and countless souls went straight to heaven and things happened as if in a dream.

In the Slaughter House not even one rat remained alive from the many thousands which used to find shelter there. All of them either perished from starvation or were drowned in their holes by the incessant rain. Innumerable Negro women who go around after offal, like vultures after carrion, spread over the city like so many harpies ready to devour whatever they found eatable. Gulls and dogs, their inseparable rivals in the Slaughter House, emigrated to the open fields in search of animal food. Sickly old men wasted away from the lack of nutritive broth; but the most remarkable event was the rather sudden death of a few heretic foreigners who committed the folly of glutting on sausages from Extremadura, on ham and dry codfish, and who departed to the other world to pay for the sin of such abominations.

Some physicians were of the opinion that if the shortage of meat continued, half the town would fall in fainting fits, since their stomachs were accustomed to the stimulating meat juice; and the discrepancy was quite noticeable between this melancholy prognosis of science and the anathemas broadcast from the pulpit by the reverend fathers against all kinds of animal nutrition and promiscuity during days set aside by the Church for fasting and penitence. Therefore a sort of intestinal war between stomachs and consciences began, stirred by an inexorable appetite and the not less inexorable vociferations of the ministers of the Church, who, as is their duty, tolerated no sin whatsoever which might tend to slacken Catholic principles. In addition to all this, there existed a state of intestinal flatulence in the population, brought on by fish and beans and other somewhat indigestible fare.

This war manifested itself in sighs and strident shrieks during the sermons as well as in noises and sudden explosions issuing from the houses and the streets of the city and wherever people congregated. The Restorer's government, as paternal as it is foreseeing, became somewhat alarmed, believing these tumults to be revolutionary in origin and attributing them to the savage Unitarians, whose impiety, according to Federalist preachers, had brought upon the nation the deluge of divine wrath. The Government, therefore, took provident steps, scattered its henchmen around town, and, finally, appeasing consciences and stomachs, decreed wisely and piously that without further delay and floods notwithstanding, cattle be brought to the Slaughter Houses.

Accordingly, on the sixteenth day of the meat crisis, the eve of Saint Dolores' day, a herd of fifty fat steers swam across the Burgos pass on their way to the Alto Slaughter House. Of course this was not much considering that the town consumed daily from 250 to 300 and that at least one-third of the population enjoyed the Church dispensation of eating meat. Strange that there should be privileged stomachs and stomachs subjected to an inviolable law, and that the Church should hold the key to all stomachs!

But it is not so strange if one believes that through meat the devil enters the body, and that the Church has the power to conjure it. The thing is to reduce man to a machine whose prime mover is not his own free will but that of the Church and the government. Perhaps the day will come when it will be prohibited to breathe, to take walks and even to chat with a friend without previous permission from competent authorities. Thus it was, more or less, in the happy days of our pious grandparents, unfortunately since ended by the May Revolution.

Be that as it may, when the news about the action of the government spread, the Alto Slaughter House filled with butchers, offal collectors, and inquisitive folk who received with much applause and outcry the fifty steers.

"It's surely wonderful!" they exclaimed. "Long live the Federalists! Long live the Restorer!" The reader must be informed that in those days the Federalists were everywhere, even amid the offal of the Slaughter House, and that no festival took place without the Restorer—just as there can be no sermon without Saint Augustine. The rumor is that on hearing all the hubbub the few remaining rats dying in their holes of starvation revived and began to scamper about, carefree, confident, because of the unusual joy and activity, that abundance had once more returned to the place.

The first steer butchered was sent as a gift to the Restorer, who was exceedingly fond of roasts. A committee of butchers presented it to him in the name of the Federalists of the Slaughter House and expressed to him, *viva voce,* their gratitude for the government decree and their profound hatred for the savage Unitarians, enemies of God and men. The Restorer replied to their harangue by elaborating on the same theme, and the ceremony ended with vivas and vociferations from both spectators and protagonists. It is to be assumed that the Restorer had special dispensation from His Most Reverend Father, excusing him from fasting, for otherwise, being such a punctilious observer of laws, such a devout Catholic, and such a staunch defender of religion, he would not have set such a bad example by accepting such a gift on a holy day.

The slaughtering went on, and in a quarter of an hour forty-nine steers lay in the court, some of them skinned, others still to be skinned. The Slaughter House offered a lively, picturesque spectacle even though it did contain all that is horribly ugly, filthy, and deformed in the small proletarian class peculiar to the Plata River area. That the reader may grasp the setting at one glance, it might not be amiss to describe it briefly.

The Convalescencia, or Alto Slaughter House, is located in the southern part of Buenos Aires, on a huge lot, rectangular in shape, at the intersection of two streets, one of which ends there while the other continues eastward. The lot slants to the south and is bisected by a ditch made by the rains, its shoulders pitted with ratholes, its bed collecting all the blood from the Slaughter House. At the junction of the right angle, facing the west, stands what is commonly called the *casilla,* a low building containing three small rooms with a porch in the front facing the street and hitching posts for tying the horses. In the rear are several pens of ñandubay picket fence with heavy doors for guarding the steers.

In winter these pens become veritable mires in which the animals remain bogged down, immobile, up to the shoulder blades. In the casilla the pen taxes and fines for violation of the rules are collected, and in it sits the judge of the Slaughter House, an important figure, the chieftain of the butchers, who exercises the highest power, delegated to him by the Restorer, in that small republic. It is not difficult to imagine the kind of man required for the discharge of such an office.

The casilla is so dilapidated and so tiny a building that no one would notice it were it not that its name is inseparably linked with that of the terrible judge and that its white front is pasted over with posters: "Long live the Federalists! Long live the Restorer and the Heroine Doña Encarnación Escurra! Death to the savage Unitarians!" Telling posters, indeed, symbolizing the political and religious faith of the Slaughter House folk!

But some readers may not know that the above mentioned Heroine is the deceased wife of the Restorer, the beloved patroness of the butchers, who even after her death is venerated by them as if she were still alive, because of her Christian virtues and her Federalist heroism during the revolution against Balcarce. The story is that during an anniversary of that memorable deed of the *mazorca*, the terrorist society of Rosas' henchmen, the butchers feted the Heroine with a magnificent banquet in the casilla. She attended, with her daughter and other Federalist ladies, and there, in the presence of a great crowd, she offered the butchers, in a solemn toast, her Federalist patronage, and for that reason they enthusiastically proclaimed her patroness of the Slaughter House, stamping her name upon the walls of the casilla, where it will remain until blotted out by the hand of time.

From a distance the view of the Slaughter House was now grotesque, full of animation. Forty-nine steers were stretched out upon their skins and about two hundred people walked about the muddy, blood-drenched floor. Hovering around each steer stood a group of people of different skin colors. Most prominent among them was the butcher, a knife in his hand, his arms bare, his chest exposed, long hair dishevelled, shirt and sash and face besmeared with blood. At his back, following his every movement, romped a gang of children, Negro and mulatto women, offal collectors whose ugliness matched that of the harpies, and huge mastiffs which sniffed, snarled, and snapped at one another as they darted after booty. Forty or more carts covered with awnings of blackened hides were lined up along the court, and some horsemen with their capes thrown over their shoulders and their lassos hanging from their saddles rode back and forth through the crowds or lay on their horses' necks, casting indolent glances upon this or that lively group. In mid-air a flock of bluewhite gulls, attracted by the smell of blood, fluttered about, drowning with strident cries all the other noises and voices of the Slaughter House, and casting clear-cut shadows over that confused field of horrible butchery. All this could be observed at the very beginning of the slaughter.

But as the activities progressed, the picture kept changing. While some groups dissolved as if some stray bullet had fallen nearby or an enraged dog had charged them, new groups constantly formed: here where a steer was being cut open, there where a butcher was already hanging the quarters on the hook in the carts, or yonder where a steer was being skinned or the fat taken off. From the mob eyeing and waiting for the offal there issued ever and anon a filthy hand ready to slice off meat or fat. Shouts and explosions of anger came from the butchers, from the incessantly milling crowds, and from the gamboling street urchins.

"Watch the old woman hiding the fat under her breasts," someone shouted.

"That's nothing—see that fellow there plastering it all over his behind," replied the old Negro woman.

"Hey there black witch, get out of there before I cut you open," shouted a butcher.

"What am I doing to you, Ño Juan? Don't be so mean! Can't I have a bit of the guts?"

"Out with the witch! Out with the witch!" the children squalled in unison. "She's taking away liver and kidneys!" And with that, huge chunks of coagulated blood and balls of mud rained upon her head.

Nearby two Negro women were dragging along the entrails of an animal. A mulatto woman carrying a heap of entrails slipped in a pool of blood and fell lengthwise under her coveted booty. Farther on, huddled together in a long line, four hundred Negro women unwound heaps of intestines in their laps, picking off one by one those bits of fat which the butcher's avaricious knife had overlooked. Other women emptied stomachs and bladders and after drying them used them for depositing the offal.

Several boys gamboling about, some on foot, other on horseback, banged one another with inflated bladders or threw chunks of meat at one another, their noise frightening the cloud of gulls which celebrated the slaughtering in flapping hordes. Despite the Restorer's orders and the holiness of the day, filthy words were heard all around, shouts full of all the bestial cynicism which characterizes the populace attending our slaughter houses—but I will not entertain the reader with all this dirt.

Suddenly a mass of bloody lungs would fall on somebody's head. He forthwith would throw it on someone else's head until some hideous mongrel picked it up as a pack of other mongrels rushed in, raising a terrific growl for little or no reason at all, and snapping at one another. Sometimes an old woman would run, enraged, after some ragamuffin who had smeared her face with blood. Summoned by his shouts his comrades would come to his rescue, harassing her as dogs do a bull, and showering chunks of meat and balls of dung upon her, accompanied by volleys of laughter and shrieks, until the Judge would command order to be restored.

In another spot two young boys practicing the handling of their knives, slashed at one another with terrifying thrusts, while farther on, four lads, much more mature than the former, were fighting over some offal which they had filched from a butcher. Not far from them some mongrels, lean from forced abstinence, struggled for a piece of kidney all covered with mud. All a representation in miniature of the savage ways in which individual and social conflicts are thrashed out in our country.

Only one longhorn, of small, broad forehead and fiery stare, remained in the corrals. No consensus of opinion about its genitals had been possible: some believed it to be a bull, others a steer. Now its hour approached.

Two lasso men on horseback entered the corral while the mob milled about its vicinity on foot or on horseback, or dangled from the forked stakes of the enclosure. A grotesque group formed at the corral's gate: a group of goaders and lasso men on foot, with bare arms and provided with slipknots, their heads covered with red kerchiefs, and wearing vests and red sashes. Behind them several horsemen and spectators watched with eager eyes.

With a slipknot already round its horns, the angrily foaming animal bellowed fiercely; and there was no demon strong or cunning enough to make it move from the sticky mud in which it was glued. It was impossible to lasso it. The lads shouted themselves hoarse from the forked stakes of the corral and the men tried in vain to frighten it with blankets and kerchiefs. The din of hissing, handclapping, and shrill and raucous voices which issued from that weird orchestra was fearful.

The witty remarks, the obscene exclamations traveled from mouth to mouth, and either excited by the spectacle or piqued by a thrust from some garrulous tongue, everyone gratuitously showed off his cleverness and caustic humor.

"So—they want to give us cat for rabbit!"

"I'm telling you, it's a steer—that's no bull!"

"Can't you see it's an old bull?"

"The hell it is—show me its balls and I'll believe you!"

"Can't you see them hanging from between its legs? Each one bigger than the head of your roan horse. I guess you left your eyes by the roadside!"

"It's your old woman who was blind to have given birth to a chump like you! Can't you see that the mess between its legs is just mud?"

"Bull or steer, it's as foxy as a Unitarian!"

On hearing this magic word "Unitarian," the mob exclaimed in unison: "Death to the savage Unitarians!"

"Leave all sons of bitches to One-Eye!"

"You bet, One-Eye has guts enough to take care of all the Unitarians put together!"

"Yes—Yes—leave the bull to Matasiete, the beheader of Unitarians. Long live Matasiete!"

"The bull for Matasiete!"

"There it goes!" shouted someone raucously, interrupting the interlude of the cowardly mob. "There goes the bull!"

"Get ready! Watch out, you fellows near the gate! There it goes, mad as hell!"

And so it was. Maddened by the shouts and especially by two sharp goads which pricked its tail, the beast, divining the weakness of the slipknot, charged on the gate, snorting, casting reddish, phosphorescent glances right and left. The lasso man strained his line taut, till his horse squatted. Suddenly the knot broke loose from the steer's horns and slashed across the air with a sharp hum. In its wake there came instantly rolling down from the stockade the head of a child, cut clean from the trunk as if by an ax. The trunk remained immobile, perched in the fork of a pole, long streams of blood spurting from every artery.

"The rope broke and there goes the bull!" one of the men shouted. Some of the spectators, overwhelmed and puzzled, were quiet. It all happened like lightning.

The crowd by the gate trickled away. Some, clustered around the head and palpitating trunk of the beheaded child, registered horror in their astonished faces; others, mostly horsemen, who had not witnessed the mishap, slipped away in different directions in the tracks of the bull. All of them shouted at the top of their voice: "There goes the bull! Stop it! Watch out! Lasso it, Sietepelos! It's coming after you, Botija! He's mad, don't get too close! Stop it, Morado, stop it! Get going with that nag of yours! Only the devil will stop that bull!"

The hubbub and din was infernal. A few Negro women who were seated along the ditch huddled together on hearing the tumult and crouched amid the intestines which they were unraveling with a patience worthy of Penelope. This saved them, because the beast, with a terrifying bellow, leaped sideways over them and rushed on, followed by the horsemen. It is said that one of the women voided her self on the spot, that another prayed ten Hail Mary's in a few seconds, and that two others promised San Benito never to return to the damned corrals and to quit offal-collecting forever and anon. However, it is not known whether they kept their promises.

In the meantime the bull rushed toward the city by a long, narrow street which, beginning at the acutest point of the rectangle previously described, was surrounded by a ditch and a cactus fence. It was one of the so-called "deserted" streets because it had but two houses and its center was a deep marsh extending from ditch to ditch. A certain Englishman, on his way home from a salting establishment which he owned nearby, was crossing this marsh at the moment on a somewhat nervous horse. Of course he was so absorbed in his thoughts that he did not hear the onrush of horsemen or the shouts until the bull was crossing the marsh. His horse took fright, leaped to one side, and dashed away, leaving the poor devil sunk in half a yard of mire. This accident did not curb the racing of the bull's pursuers; on the contrary, bursting into sarcastic laughter—"The gringo's sunk. Get up, gringo!"—they shouted and crossed the marsh, their horses' hoofs trampling over his wretched body. The gringo dragged himself out as best he could, but more like a demon roasting in the fires of hell than a blond-haired white man.

Farther on, at the shout of "the bull! the bull!" four Negro women who were leaving with their booty of offal dived into a ditch full of water, the only refuge left them.

The beast, in the meantime, having run several miles in one direction and another, frightening all living beings, got in through the back gate of a farm and there met his doom. Although weary, it still showed its spirit and wrathful strength, but a deep ditch and a thick cactus fence surrounded it and there was no escape. The scattered pursuers got together and decided to take it back convoyed between tamed animals, so that it could expiate its crimes on the very spot where it had committed them.

An hour after its flight, the bull was back in the Slaughter House where the dwindling crowd spoke only of its misdeeds. The episode of the gringo who got stuck in the mud moved them to laughter and sarcastic remarks.

Of the child beheaded by the lasso there remained but a pool of blood: his body had been taken away.

The men threw a slipknot over the horns of the beast which leaped and reared, uttering hoarse bellows. They threw one, two, three lassos—to no avail. The fourth, however, caught it by a leg. Its vigor and fury redoubled. Its tongue, hanging out convulsively, drooled froth, its nostrils fumed, its eyes emitted fiery glances.

"Knock that animal down!" an imperious voice commanded. Matasiete dismounted at once from his horse, hocked the bull with one sure thrust, and, moving on nimbly with a huge dagger in his hand, stuck it down to the hilt in the bull's neck and drew it out, showing it smoking and red to the spectators. A torrent gushed from the wound as the bull bellowed hoarsely. Then it quivered and fell, amid cheers from the crowd, which proclaimed Matasiete the hero of the day and assigned him the most suc- culent steak as his prize. Proudly Matasiete stretched out his arm and the bloodstained knife a second time, and then with his comrades bent down to skin the dead bull.

The only question still undecided was whether the animal was a steer or a bull. Although it had been provisionally classified as bull because of its indomitable fierceness, they were all so fatigued with the long drawn out performance that they had overlooked clearing up this point. But sud- denly a butcher shouted: "Here are the balls!" and sticking his hands into the animal's genitals he showed the spectators two huge testicles.

There was much laughter and talk and all the aforementioned unfor- tunate incidents of the day were readily explained. It was strictly forbidden to bring bulls to the Slaughter House and this was an exceptional occur- rence. According to the rules and regulations this bull should have been thrown to the dogs, but with the scarcity of meat and so many hungry people in town the Judge did not deem it advisable.

In a short while the bull was skinned, quartered, and hung in the cart. Matasiete took a choice steak, placed it under the pelisse of his saddle and began getting ready to go home. The slaughtering had been completed by noon, and the small crowd which had remained to the end was leaving, some on foot, others on horseback, others pulling along the carts loaded with meat.

Suddenly the raucous voice of a butcher was heard announcing: "Here comes a Unitarian!" On hearing that word, the mob stood still as if thunderstruck.

"Can't you see his U-shaped side whiskers? Can't you see he carries no insignia on his coat and no mourning sash on his hat?"

"The Unitarian cur!"

"The son of a bitch!"

"He has the same kind of saddle as the gringo!"

"To the gibbet with him!"

"Give him the scissors!"

"Give him a good beating!"

"He has a pistol case attached to his saddle just to show off!"

"All these cocky Unitarians are as showy as the devil himself!"

"I bet you wouldn't dare touch him, Matasiete."

"He wouldn't, you say?"

"I bet you he would!"

Matasiete was a man of few words and quick action. When it came to violence, dexterity, skill in the handling of an ox, a knife, or a horse he did not talk much, but he acted. They had piqued him; spurring his horse, he trotted away, bridle loose, to meet the Unitarian.

The Unitarian was a young man, about twenty-five years old, elegant, debonair of carriage, who, as the above-mentioned exclamations were spouting from these impudent mouths, was trotting towards Barracas, quite fearless of any danger ahead of him. Noticing, however, the significant glances of that gang of Slaughter House curs, his right hand reached automatically for the pistol-case of his English saddle. Then a side push from Matasiete's horse threw him from his saddle, stretching him out. Supine and motionless he remained on the ground.

"Long live Matasiete!" shouted the mob, swarming upon the victim.

Confounded, the young man cast furious glances on those ferocious men and hoping to find in his pistol compensation and vindication, moved towards his horse, which stood quietly nearby. Matasiete rushed to stop him. He grabbed him by his tie, pulled him down again on the ground, and whipping out his dagger from his belt, put it against his throat.

Loud guffaws and stentorian vivas cheered him.

What nobility of soul! What bravery, that of the Federalists! Always ganging together and falling like vultures upon the helpless victim!

"Cut open his throat, Matasiete! Didn't he try to shoot you? Rip him open, like you did the bull!"

"What scoundrels these Unitarians! Thrash him good and hard!"

"He has a good neck for the 'violin'—you know, the gibbet!"

"Better use the Slippery-One on him!"

"Let's try it," said Matasiete, and, smiling, began to pass the sharp edge of his dagger around the throat of the fallen man as he pressed in his chest with his left knee and held him by the hair with his left hand.

"Don't behead him, don't!" shouted in the distance the Slaughter House Judge as he approached on horseback.

"Bring him into the casilla. Get the gibbet and the scissors ready. Death to the savage Unitarians! Long live the Restorer of the laws!"

"Long live Matasiete!"

The spectators repeated in unison "Long live Matasiete! Death to the Unitarians!" They tied his elbows together as blows rained upon his nose, and they shoved him around. Amid shouts and insults they finally dragged the unfortunate young man to the bench of tortures just as if they had been the executioners of the Lord themselves.

The main room of the casilla had in its center a big, hefty table, which was devoid of liquor glasses and playing cards only in times of executions and tortures administered by the Federalist executioners of the Slaughter House. In a corner stood a smaller table with writing materials and a notebook and some chairs, one of which, an armchair, was reserved for the Judge. A man who looked like a soldier was seated in one of them, playing on his guitar the "Resbalosa," an immensely popular song among the Federalists, when the mob rushing tumultuously into the corridor of the casilla brutally showed in the young Unitarian.

"The Slippery-One for him!" shouted one of the fellows.

"Commend your soul to the devil!"

"He's furious as a wild bull!"

"The whip will tame him!"

"Give him a good pummeling!"

"First the cowhide and scissors."

"Otherwise to the bonfire with him!"

"The gibbet would be even better for him!"

"Shut up and sit down," shouted the Judge as he sank into his armchair. All of them obeyed, while the young man standing in front of the Judge exclaimed with a voice pregnant with indignation:

"Infamous executioners, what do you want to do with me?"

"Quiet!" ordered the Judge, smiling. "There's no reason for getting angry. You'll see."

The young man was beside himself. His entire body shook with rage: his mottled face, his voice, his tremulous lips, evinced the throbbing of his heart and the agitation of his nerves. His fiery eyes bulged in their sockets, his long black hair bristled. His bare neck and the front of his shirt showed his bulging arteries and his anxious breathing.

"Are you trembling?" asked the Judge.

"Trembling with anger because I cannot choke you."

"Have you that much strength and courage?"

"I have will and pluck enough for that, scoundrel."

"Get out the scissors I use to cut my horse's mane and clip his hair in the Federalist style."

Two men got hold of him. One took his arms and another his head and in a minute clipped off his side whiskers. The spectators laughed merrily.

"Get him a glass of water to cool him off," ordered the Judge.

"I'll have you drink gall, you wretch!"

A Negro appeared with a glass of water in his hand. The young man kicked his arm and the glass smashed to bits on the ceiling, the fragments sprinkling the astonished faces of the spectators.

"This fellow is incorrigible!"

"Don't worry, we'll tame him yet!"

"Quiet!" said the Judge. "Now you are shaven in the Federalist style—all you need is a mustache, don't forget to grow one!"

"Now, let's see: why don't you wear any insignia?"

"Because I don't care to."

"Don't you know that the Restorer orders it?"

"Insignia become you, slaves, but not free men!"

"Free men will have to wear them, by force."

"Indeed, by force and brutal violence. These are your arms, infamous wretches! Wolves, tigers, and panthers are also strong like you and like them you should walk on all fours."

"Are you not afraid of being torn to pieces by the tiger?"

"I prefer that to having you pluck out my entrails, as the ravens do, one by one."

"Why don't you wear a mourning sash on your hat in memory of the Heroine?"

"Because I wear it in my heart in memory of my country which you, infamous wretches, have murdered."

"Don't you know that the Restorer has ordered mourning in memory of the Heroine?"

"You, slaves, were the ones to order it so as to flatter your master and pay infamous homage to him."

"Insolent fellow! You are beside yourself. I'll have your tongue cut off if you utter one more word. Take the pants off this arrogant fool, and beat him on his naked ass. Tie him down on the table first!"

Hardly had the Judge uttered his commands when four bruisers bespattered with blood lifted the young man and stretched him out upon the table.

"Rather behead me than undress me, infamous rabble!"

They muzzled him with a handkerchief and began to pull off his clothes. The young man wriggled, kicked, and gnashed his teeth. His muscles assumed now the flexibility of rushes, now the hardness of iron, and he squirmed like a snake in his enemy's grasp. Drops of sweat, large as pearls, streamed down his cheeks, his pupils flamed, his mouth foamed, and the veins on his neck and forehead jutted out black from his pale skin as if congested with blood.

"Tie him up," ordered the Judge.

"He's roaring with anger," said one of the cutthroats.

In a short while they had tied his feet to the legs of the table and turned his body upside down. In trying to tie his hands, the men had to unfasten them from behind his back. Feeling free, the young man, with a brusque movement which seemed to drain him of all his strength and vitality, raised himself up, first upon his arms, then upon his knees, and collapsed immediately, murmuring: "Rather behead me than undress me, infamous rabble!"

His strength was exhausted, and having tied him down crosswise, they began undressing him. Then a torrent of blood spouted, bubbling from the young man's mouth and nose, and flowed freely down the table. The cutthroats remained immobile and the spectators, astonished.

"The savage Unitarian has burst with rage," said one of them.

"He had a river of blood in his veins," put in another.

"Poor devil, we wanted only to amuse ourselves with him, but he took things too seriously," exclaimed the Judge, scowling tiger-like.

"We must draw up a report. Untie him and let's go!"

They carried out the orders, locked the doors, and in a short while the rabble went out after the horse of the downcast, taciturn Judge.

The Federalists had brought to an end one of their innumerable feats of valor.

Those were the days when the butchers of the Slaughter House were apostles who propagated by dint of whip and poignard Rosas' Federation, and it is not difficult to imagine what sort of Federation issued from their heads and knives. They were wont to dub as savage Unitarians (in accordance with the jargon invented by the Restorer, patron of the brotherhood) any man who was neither a cutthroat nor a crook; any man who was kindhearted and decent; any patriot or noble friend of enlightenment and freedom; and from the foregoing episode it can be clearly seen that the headquarters of the Federation were located in the Slaughter House.

TRANSLATED BY ANGEL FLORES

Domingo Faustino Sarmiento

Argentina
(1811–1888)

––––––– \\

Domingo Faustino Sarmiento is one of the most prominent figures in nineteenth-century Latin American literature, politics, social thought, and education. President of Argentina from 1868 to 1874, Sarmiento was a prolific writer and polemicist, but his fame rests on *Facundo: Civilización y barbarie: Vida de Juan Facundo Quiroga* (1845), which might legitimately be considered the most influential book in Latin American history: it set the basis for the civilization versus barbarism debate. *Facundo* is so powerful a statement that it has had a shaping effect even on texts attacking it, and there have been many. Imbued in the racialist thinking of his time, Sarmiento believed that the future of Argentina lay in its becoming more Western and more like the United States, a country that fascinated him (as president he encouraged immigration from Europe). But he was such a complex thinker and a supple writer that Sarmiento has come to be known for his portrait of Facundo Quiroga, a provincial strongman whom he saw as the kernel of the political barbarism that led to the Rosas dictatorship. To understand Quiroga, Sarmiento collected much material on rural Argentina and painted a compelling picture of the pampa and its gauchos. The civilization that he promoted could not be as attractive as their barbarism, despite his protestations. Sarmiento's compelling biography of Quiroga is at the same time a socioeconomic treatise, a study of folklore, and a philosophical meditation on the sources of evil and violence. His analysis of the clash between the coastal capital and the interior provinces of Argentina is applicable to much of the rest of Latin America. *Facundo* is, in addition, a loving description of the motherland by an exile (Sarmiento wrote it in Chile during the Rosas reign) and, perhaps foremost, an oblique yet impassioned autobiography. The story presented here, "The Tiger of the Plains," opens the biography of Juan Facundo Quiroga.

The Tiger of the Plains

Between the cities of San Luis and San Juan there lies a vast desert, which because of its complete lack of water is given the name *travesía.**

* *Travesía*: The distance or passage between two places. In nineteenth-century Argentina, the term came to mean certain provincial areas totally lacking in water or vegetation.

In general, these solitudes have a sad and abandoned aspect, and no traveler coming from the east passes the last reservoir or cistern of the countryside without supplying his *chifles*[†] with a sufficient quantity of water. In this *travesía*, there once took place the following strange scene. The knife fights so common among our gauchos had forced one of them to abandon the city of San Luis precipitously and to reach the *travesía* on foot, with his saddle over his shoulder, in order to escape the pursuit of the law. Two companions were to catch up with him as soon as they could rob horses for all three.

At that time, hunger and thirst were not the only dangers awaiting him in that desert, where a "stoked"[‡] tiger[§] had been roaming for a year following the track of voyagers, and by then more than eight were those who had become victims to his predilection for human flesh. It sometimes happens, in those areas where man and beast dispute the dominance of nature, that the former falls beneath the bloody claw of the latter; then the tiger begins to prefer the taste of human flesh, and is called "stoked" when it becomes accustomed to this new sort of hunt, the manhunt. The country judge of the area adjacent to the scene of this devastation summons a posse of able men to the chase, and under his authority and direction they pursue the "stoked" tiger, who rarely escapes the sentence that declares the animal outside the law.

When our fugitive had walked some six leagues, he thought he heard the tiger roar in the distance, and his muscle fibers shuddered. The tiger's roar is a grunt like that of a hog, but sharp, prolonged, strident, and even when there is no reason to fear, it causes an involuntary shaking of the nerves, as if the flesh all by itself were trembling at the announcement of death.

Some minutes later, he heard the roar to be more distinct and more immediate; the tiger was onto his track now, and all he could see, only at a great distance, was a small carob tree. He needed to hurry his pace, even to run, because the roars were following each other with increasing frequency, and each was more distinct, more vibrant than the last.

Finally, throwing his saddle down by the side of the road, the gaucho headed for the tree he had perceived, and despite its weak trunk, luckily quite a tall one, he was able to climb up to the top and sway continuously, half hidden among the branches. From there, he could observe the scene

---

[†]*Chifles*: The horns of cattle, fitted with a wooden base at the wide end and a plugged hole at the point, used as a water canteen.

[‡]The Argentine expression Sarmiento uses is *cebado*, variously meaning fed or fattened, as livestock or a fire; primed, as a gun; excited, as a passion or rage.

[§]The South American *tigre*, of course, is not a tiger at all, but a jaguar, erroneously named by the Spanish conquerors.

unfolding on the road: the tiger marched at a hurried pace, sniffing the ground and roaring more frequently as it sensed the proximity of its prey. The beast passed the point where the gaucho had left the road and lost the track; it became infuriated and whirled around until it saw the saddle, which it tore to pieces with a slap of the paw, scattering all the gear through the air. Irritated all the more by this disappointment, the animal returned to search for the track, finally finding the direction in which it went, and, lifting its gaze, perceived its prey using his weight to keep the little carob tree balancing, as does the fragile reed when birds perch on its tip.

From that moment, the tiger roared no more: it bounded over, and in the blink of an eye, its enormous paws were bearing upon the slender trunk two yards above the ground, sending it a convulsive tremor that worked its way into the nerves of the badly secured gaucho. The beast tried to make a leap, but in vain; it took a turn around the tree, measuring its height with eyes reddened by the thirst for blood, and finally, roaring with rage, lay down on the ground, ceaselessly switching its tail, eyes fixed on its prey, mouth partly open and parched. This horrible scene had now lasted two deadly hours; the strained pose of the gaucho and the terrifying fascination exerted over him by the bloody, immobile gaze of the tiger, from which, owing to an invincible force of attraction, he could not avert his eyes, had begun to weaken his strength, and he could feel the moment coming when his exhausted body would fall into the tiger's wide mouth. Suddenly, the far-off sound of galloping horses gave him hope for salvation.

In fact, his friends had seen the tiger's tracks, and they had raced forward with little hope of saving the gaucho. But the scattered saddle gear showed them the place, and to fly there, unroll their lassos, throw them over the tiger, heels dug in and blind with fury, was but the work of a moment. The beast, stretched between two ropes, could not escape the repeated knife blows with which, in vengeance for his prolonged agony, the one who would have been its victim ran it through.

"That's when I found out what being afraid means," General Juan Facundo Quiroga used to say, telling a group of officers this story.

TRANSLATED BY KATHLEEN ROSS

Juana Manuela Gorriti

Argentina
(1818–1892)

————\\————

Juana Manuela Gorriti's life was as dramatic and fascinating as most novels, and she knew it and exploited it. Juana Manuela was the daughter of Argentine general José Ignacio Gorriti. Not only was he a participant in the May Revolution that led to the independence of his country, but he routed the Spanish at Jujuy. Juana Manuela, who began writing at an early age, witnessed the political and military processes that led to the foundation of several new republics. She was herself involved when she married General I. Belzú, who was named president of Bolivia and was assassinated while in office. Her considerable literary output is an absorbing account of all these events from the perspective of a privileged observer. Juana Manuela spent the last years of her life in Lima, where she founded and directed a grade school. She wrote short stories and novellas, as well as memoirs and historical works, among which the best-known are *Güemes: recuerdos de la infancia* and *El General Vidal*. Juana Manuela wrote vignettes redolent with local color, in the style of the *costumbristas* of the period. But her world is one of intrigue, in the manner of Hugo and Dumas, though in an ironic tone. The present story, "He Who Listens May Hear," contains two narratives separated, like the massive armoire in the two rooms, by time. The old black man who eventually reveals the secret passage and the voluminous piece of furniture function as mediators between these two epochs, concealing and unveiling at the same time the secret. The narrator's predicament is to be able to reconstruct, and in a way invent, the story of what has happened on the other side of the wall. Objects like the armoire and the bed acquire through Gorriti's writing, a meaningful substantiality that verges on the symbolic. The ending suddenly casts the story in a broader historical and political frame.

He Who Listens May Hear—To His Regret: Confidence of a Confidence

I. Confidence of a confidence

"When we have erred," a certain friend said to me one day, "and restitution is impossible, we have but one option, and that is expiation through explicit and frank confession. Do you, my dearest friend, wish to be my confessor?"

"Why, yes," I answered readily.

"A confessor bound by all attending conditions?"

"Yes, except for one."

"Which is that?"

"Secrecy."

"Bah, women! Women! You cannot refrain from talking even when your life depends on it. Women, who in your idolatrous chatter profess to form a cult. Women who . . . Women! Whom we must accept as you are!

"Ah, well, I plead guilty," he began, already resigned to my restriction in regard to not keeping his confidence. "I plead guilty to a serious, a very grave, offense, and repent to the degree that an inveterate busybody may repent for having satisfied his devouring passion.

"Not long ago I was involved in a plot and denounced by government agents. I found it necessary to go into hiding. I took refuge with a friend. Naturally, in the most hidden corner of his home, which was a room located at the back of the garden. The door was invisible, overgrown by heavy vines.

"The walls of the room were covered with crimson damask, and gave a sense of antiquity. The room had served as a bed chamber to the grandfather of the house whose enormous gilded bed, left empty at his death, I now occupied. But, ah, in such a different manner! The aged gentleman—I believed—slept the sleep of the blessed amid the thick bed hangings of green velvet, now stirred by the unrelenting insomnia that throbbed through the veins of a conspirator, and, something more: a busybody. You will judge.

"From my first night in that room, I heard—without being able to determine exactly from where—a voice, the soft and beautiful voice of a woman intermingled with the voices of men. When she appeared to be alone, she read prose and poetry aloud, as Rachel must have recited, and like Malibrán she sang the most sublime pieces from the contemporary repertoire, among them, a Schubert serenade whose solemn notes wove a heavenly melody.

"I spent several days investigating, listening at the gilded molding that was the mounting for the tapestries, tapping on the walls, and searching everywhere for the source from which that voice was issuing.

"I concluded, finally, that when I approached a large armoire standing in one corner of the room, I heard the voice more clearly and at closer range, and looked no further. That piece of furniture was so heavy that I knew it was pointless for me to try to move it by myself. That did not, however, in the least lessen my determination to learn what lay behind it.

"So that night when the old black man charged with looking after me in my seclusion brought me my supper, I placed a doubloon in his hand and asked him to help me move the armoire.

"At my words, the servant's eyes opened wide, and he paled.

"'Oh, no, señor,' he said in a strained voice. 'Not for all the gold in the world. The Mistress is still living, and if she ever came to know that her husband was unfaithful to her in this very place, she could easily guess that I was the one—dear Jesus!—that I was the one who cut through the door so the Master, may he rest in peace!— could slip into the monastery. Blessed Mary! Oh, no, señor. Besides, the armoire is bolted to the wall, and can't be moved.'

"It was extremely difficult, but I calmed the man's fears, and after I had promised him absolute secrecy, he told me that the neighboring house had once been part of a convent, and that his master had had the temerity to fall in love with a bride of God, and how, not satisfied with the enormity of that crime, he had, with the help of his mason-and-carpenter slave, profaned the house of God by opening a door through the wall that corresponded to the interior of the armoire.

"'And that is why, señor,' the servant concluded, 'that ever since the Master died, that armoire has been my nightmare. Always afraid that the Devil will tug at my shirttails, always in fear and trembling that repairs to the house will uncover the door and the name of the one who cut it open will be revealed, because there is no doubt that the Mistress would roast me alive.'

"'Have no fear, Juan,' I said to calm him. 'Who is going to tell her? I will be quiet as the tomb, and when I leave here, the secret will go with me forever.'

"'Oh, señor,' the black replied, yielding despite himself to the wish to reminisce. 'Those were the days! The Master's love lasted as long as the little nun lived, which was not very long. His poor little turtle dove (for that is what the Master called her, that being what beaus called their beloved back then), his little caged dove, loved too passionately, and as that love could no longer breathe in the poisonous atmosphere of the cloister, it bore her soul off to a better place.

"'At first my master was inconsolable, but then he did what they all do: he forgot his dove and visited the convents of others he loved no less; in those loves, though, he had no need for his slave.'

"'Juan,' I said, interrupting his confidences. 'Remember that what I want now is for you to help me, and then you may leave.'

"So the former Mercurio to the seducer of nuns, with the skill of someone who knew exactly what he was doing, opened the armoire doors. Removing the backboard, he revealed a small opening blocked by a postern on the other side of my wall.

"He showed me the latch that opened it, and fled in terror.

"When I found myself alone and lord of that mysterious door, my heart began to beat violently, whether from delight or fear, I can't say. I now held in my hand the tip of the veil I so longed to draw back.

"But how could I? What right had I to intrude in the intimate life of a person confidently sleeping two steps away?

"With my hand on the latch and my ear cocked, I vacillated a long moment between curiosity and discretion.

"Suddenly from the neighboring room I heard the swish of a skirt and the familiar voice murmuring close to my ear.

" 'Two months with no news of him! The ingrate left without telling me goodbye. Where could he be? In his cold indifference he did not find it necessary to tell me where my love might seek him. But I shall learn. The science whose power men without faith deny—he among them—that science shall tell me. Yes, I love him!' she added emphatically.

"A door closed, and everything was quiet.

"How could I withstand the overwhelming curiosity that swept over me when I heard that expression of unique love revealed in these mysterious words? I could do nothing now to contain myself. My whole being surrendered to the desire to touch with my own hands the secrets of that strange existence.

"Standing with my forehead against the postern, I waited fifteen minutes. The same silence. Nothing was moving on the other side. Then, ridding myself of any thought that might deter me, I resolutely pressed the latch the servant had pointed out to me.

"The shrill screech of the latch forgotten for half a century frightened me, but at that moment the small postern, narrow as a carriage door, swung open. Stepping forward, I found myself in my neighbor's rooms.

II. The bed chamber of an eccentric woman

"The faint light from a small spirit lamp sitting on a night table beside a small bed hung with white draperies cast a pale glow in the dark and deserted room. At the foot of the bed, on a marble-topped bureau, was a small library whose authors included Andral, Huffeland, Raspail, and others that, along with various skulls and anatomical drawings, would have led one to believe that this was the room of a man of science had a simple glance around not argued the contrary. Here, in a knitting basket, a half-finished garland; there, a veil draped around a column of the dressing table; over there, a filmy ribbon-trimmed skirt tossed carelessly across a hassock, lovingly arranged flowers in vases of every size, the subtle perfume of English oils, bluish smoke rising from a clay incense burner, all revealed the gender of their owner.

"Above the head of the bed, beneath a painting representing the infant Jesus, was the portrait of a handsome youth, and these images of the two ages at which love is lavished upon man seemed to preside over that simple and modest artistic abode.

"The walls of the room were completely lined with dark panels of carved wood. The mysterious postern was disguised by a small, rectangular section of panel bordered by a wreath of roses in bas relief. So, then, I was at last in the former cell of the nun, the sanctuary of her love now the temple of one no less impassioned. There was in this coincidence motive to unleash my fancy to fly in pursuit of past scenes, before the staring eyes of the voluptuous caryatids and chubby-cheeked cherubim on that age-mellowed carving. But I had no time to waste. Since I was a trespasser, I decided that I may as well not settle for half measures and determined to open a hole so that I could spy upon the room of my eccentric neighbor at any time.

"I went through her knitting basket, which, I might say in passing, was in a terrible jumble. Nervous fingers had tangled the silk skeins as threads were broken off, rather than cut; nearly a dozen needles, loose amongst the lace and ribbons, pricked my fingers as I felt for the scissors that I finally found and used to gouge a hole in the center of one of the carved roses on the panel.

"Just in time. I had barely closed the postern and, after stepping through the armoire, returned to my own room, when my host arrived for his customary evening visit.

"I confess that never had the company of the most detestable bore been as unbearable as my friend's was that evening. His conversation, usually so interesting and animated—for he was a talented man with vast knowledge—seemed dull and monotonous. My restlessness increased as I heard a door open in the adjoining room. I knew it was she, the mysterious occupant. Had she fulfilled her design? What was the science she had spoken of, and what had its arcane secrets revealed to her?

"The silence that followed seemed a bad omen, and I, transfixed in the chair opposite my friend, was not free to investigate. I was consumed with anxiety, and replied to my friend with an abstraction that finally he perceived.

"'Are you ill?'

"'No, not at all,' I hastened to reply.

"'You seem preoccupied. At any rate, go to bed. Until tomorrow.'

"'Until tomorrow!' I answered. My enthusiasm surprised him, and he left smiling.

"The moment I was alone, I ran and closed myself inside the armoire to peer through the opening I had made with the scissors.

"Nothing was changed, except now the room was not empty. In the center, seated in an armchair, a man was looking about him with an expression of amazement. I could read nothing more from his eyes, nor from the set of his large mouth with its thin, pale lips. His brow, broad and high, would have been of great interest to a phrenologist.

"Just then a small door covered by a red tapestry opened, and outlined against the darkness behind her stood the figure of a woman. She was tall and slender. She was wearing a long white peignoir whose flowing folds were loosely held by a blue cord. Her black hair fell in long curls to her shoulders, and from her quick step and cheerful attitude one might have thought her to be the happiest creature on earth. At close inspection, however, one realized that tears lay behind that smile, and that *le nuage au coeur laissait son front serein.*

"As she entered, she focused upon the man sitting there a soft, insistent look that caused him to shudder. The young man's eyes, as if mesmerized by her gaze, locked on hers for a long moment, but gradually a strange languor caused his lids to close until his cheek was shadowed by his eyelashes.

"Then the woman, walking toward him with a slow, measured tread, passed her right hand three times before his closed eyes, tracing the length of his face then swerving toward his shoulder, only to repeat the gesture. Then, holding her left hand parallel to and at the height of her heart, she said in a soft but imperious tone, .

"'Samuel!'

"'What do you wish of me?' he replied in a choked voice.

"Again, several times, she made the motion with her left hand across her chest, as he repeated, 'What do you wish of me? I am ready to obey you.'

"'Good,' she said, placing her thumb and index finger of the right hand upon the man's forehead. 'Look deep into my heart and search for an image.'

"The youth's head dropped toward his chest, and he seemed to sink into a deep slumber. Then a violent spasm shook his body and his lips murmured a name. She smiled sadly, gazing tenderly toward the portrait. Then, taking the sleeping man's hand, she said, 'Samuel! Turn your all-seeing gaze toward the boundless horizon in that direction (her hand pointed north) and seek the one whose name you have just spoken.'

"The sleeping man's head again dropped to his chest; his breathing gradually grew more agitated, more labored, and perspiration bathed his temples.

"The woman, still standing, arms crossed, observed with a tenacious and imperious gaze the emotions that played across those closed eyes.

"The hour, the place, the surroundings, all contributed to the truly fantastic character of the scene. Seeing how that fragile creature, through some mysterious influence, dominated the powerful man, watching her there in her sheer, flowing robes, her hand held above the head of the man subjected to the power of her gaze, one would have thought her a magus celebrating the rituals of some unknown cult.

"A second convulsion interrupted the sleeping man's impassivity.

"'I see him there!' he exclaimed.

"'Where?'

"'Silvery moonbeams are playing over the waves of a great river wending its placid course between a forest and a city fantastic as a febrile reverie.

"'Below the city, secured by heavy anchors, a ship gently rocked by calm waves casts pools of glittering light as far as the foliage on the far shore. Upon the broad deck of the ship adorned with banners and fragrant garlands, a hundred beautiful women dressed in white and crowned with flowers languidly surrender themselves to the arms of their partners in the ardent emotion of the dance. Oh, their eyes are so beautiful! You would think they had stolen their splendor from the dazzling sun of the tropics.'

"'But he? Where is he?'

"'Oh,' the sleeping man replied in a tone of supplication. 'Let me watch the magical canvas of this dance upon the waters beneath a fiery sky. They are so beautiful! So beautiful! I see one who is standing apart from the enchanted vortex. She is strolling toward the bow of the ship with her gallant, and now she is leaning over the railing to point out the trembling image of stars reflected in the watery depths. Oh!'

"'Samuel!' said the woman, interrupting him, as yet again a spasm contracted his impassive features. 'Samuel, what are you seeing?'

"'I see him. He is the one with the beauty.'

"'And why are you trembling?'

"'Oh,' the answer was muted. 'Don't ask, you don't want to know.'

"'I must. I want you to tell me. Say it.'

"He lowered his head in painful resignation, but as he began to speak, his words emerged in a strange tongue, perhaps so that they would wound less deeply the heart of the woman whom he obeyed with such visible sadness.

"As he spoke, a cloud obscured the woman's brow. Her eyes blazed like lightning in a storm, and her lips murmured confused and inarticulate words. Suddenly she grew calm.

"'Samuel,' she said. 'Read the heart of that man.'

"The youth concentrated deeply; one might have said that his spirit descended into an abyss.

"Then, like molten lead, these words fell from his lips.

"'He loves the woman.'

"A new spasm choked off his words, as if he had been wounded by the same blow that had been dealt the woman's heart.

"She, however, stood motionless and silent; not a single muscle moved in her face, and were it not for her extreme pallor, nothing would have revealed the pain in that heart of exceptional fortitude.

"She paced the length of the room several times; she approached the portrait, stared at it a long while with an unreadable expression, and then, as if to pluck out a beloved memory, she touched her hand to her brow, tossed back the long curls, covered the portrait with a black cloth, and walking to a door opposite the one through which she had entered, turned toward the sleeping man, holding out her hand, palm upward, and beckoned to him. He rose and moved in the direction that hand indicated.

"When he had crossed the threshold and the door had closed behind him, I heard the woman's voice:

"'Samuel, wake up!'

"Then I saw her come sit at the foot of her bed and hide her face in her hands.

"I no longer had anything to see or learn there. The lamp had died out, I could not see the woman, yet I stood glued to the postern that separated her from me. Silence reigned about us, yet in my brain roared a tumultuous crashing like waves in a stormy sea. It was my heart beating. It was a desperate, uncontainable rage that reverberated deep in my soul. It was . . . , it was jealousy! I was in love with that woman who loved another with a burning, impossible love. I wanted her for myself, while another possessed her heart."

"He who listens may hear—to his regret," I proclaimed, with the sententious tone of a confessor.

"As daylight crept into her room, she was revealed in the same position. Neither she nor I had shifted position."

Suddenly, interrupting himself, my penitent asked, "Did you hear that?"

"Hear what?"

"That train whistle. The Southern Express is due today, and it should be carrying interesting news from Arequipa."

Without a thought for my pleas, my cries, my protests, even the formal threat of refusing him absolution, my irreverent friend seized his hat and was outside in a flash. He boarded the train for Islay province, and from there he traveled to Arequipa and furtively slipped into the plaza, fought in the trenches on March 7 and, miraculously freeing himself from "liberating" shackles, crossed into Chile, where it is well known that in order not to get out of practice he played an active part in the revolution that soon broke out in that country. When the revolution failed, he went to Europe, accompanied Garibaldi in his expedition to Sicily, then followed him and fell at his side in Aspromonte—not dead but a prisoner.

He escaped, and now is wandering somewhere like a needle in God's haystack.

Incorrigible conspirator! May Heaven watch over him so that one day he can complete his confession and we can learn, my beautiful Cristina, the end of his tale of culpable and severely punished espionage.

TRANSLATED BY MARGARET SAYERS PEDEN

Ricardo Palma

Peru
(1833–1919)

One of the most important cultural figures of nineteenth-century Latin America, and certainly the leading Peruvian writer of the period, Ricardo Palma is credited with having "created" a genre with his *tradiciones*. These were brief, light, mildly satirical stories about colonial Peru. Peru had such a rich colonial past (Lima was one of the most populous and sumptuous viceregal capitals) that the quarry was nearly inexhaustible. But once he found his formula, Palma fell into recognizable patterns of plot, character, and incident. Because of his care for style and structure, Palma was influential in the development of the artistic short story in Latin America. The *tradiciones* were published as collections in 1872, 1874, 1875, 1877, 1879, and 1891, after having appeared in newspapers. Romantic in their evocation of the past, the *tradiciones* present the colonial period as devoid of the dreadful conflicts that truly characterized it. Through Palma's miniaturist art, Peru under Spanish rule seemed like a world of legend and romance. Palma found a receptive public in a postindependence Peruvian bourgeoisie that longed for an imagined past of privilege and pageant. One of the first Latin American writers recognized abroad, Palma was instrumental in the development of Latin American literature as a continentwide phenomenon. Like many Latin American writers to follow, Palma was multifaceted: a senator, journalist, playwright, and author of historical texts, the best known being *Anales de la inquisición de Lima* (1863). In 1860 he was exiled to Chile, where he spent three years and honed his skills as a writer. During the War of the Pacific with Chile, Peru's national library was ravaged. Named director of the library in 1883, Palma devoted many years to replenishing it. Because their effect is cumulative, two *tradiciones* are reproduced here. They both appeal to an element seldom mentioned when referring to what came to be known as magical realism: popular piety. The written tradition behind these texts is that of the popular collections of saints' lives.

Fray Gómez's Scorpion

In diebus illis—that is to say, when I was a boy—I often heard old women say, in praising the beauty or value of a piece of jewelry: "It's as valuable as Fray Gómez's scorpion."

I've got a little girl who is a treasure, everything that is winning and delightful, with a pair of eyes that are more roguish and mischievous than a couple of notaries:

> A girl that is like
> The morning star
> At the break of day.

In my paternal besottedness I have nicknamed this flower of mine "Fray Gómez's little scorpion." And now I am going to explain the old wives' saying and the tribute to my Angélica by relating this tradition.

I

Once upon a time there was a lay brother who lived at the same time as Don Juan de la Pipirindica, the silver-tongued, and San Francisco Solano. This lay brother lived in Lima, in the convent of the Franciscans, where he performed the duties of refectioner in the nursing home or hospital of the devout friars. The people called him Fray Gómez, Fray Gómez he is called in the conventual records, and tradition knows him as Fray Gómez. I believe that in the petition for his beatification and canonization that was sent to Rome this is the only name he is given.

Fray Gómez performed miracles right and left in my land, without even knowing that he was working them, and as though against his will. He was a born miracle-worker, like the man who talked in prose without suspecting it.

One day the lay brother happened to be crossing a bridge when a runaway horse threw its rider on the flagstones. The poor fellow lay there, stiff as a board, his head as full of holes as a sieve, and blood gushing from his mouth and nose.

"He's fractured his skull. He's dying. Go quick and bring a priest from San Lázaro to administer the last rites." The noise and confusion were indescribable.

Fray Gómez walked calmly over to the fallen man, touched his mouth with the cord of his girdle, pronounced three blessings over him, and without further doctoring or medication the dying man got to his feet as though nothing had happened.

"A miracle! A miracle! Long live Fray Gómez," shouted the multitude that had witnessed the scene. And in their enthusiasm they wanted to carry the lay brother in a triumphal procession. But the latter, to avoid this demonstration, started off at a run for his convent and shut himself up in his cell.

The Franciscan chronicle gives a different version of what happened at this point. It says that Fray Gómez, to escape from his admirers, rose in the air and flew from the bridge to the belfry of his convent. I neither deny nor affirm this. Perhaps he did, perhaps he didn't. In questions of miracles I do not intend to waste ink either defending them or refuting them.

That must have been Fray Gómez's day for working miracles, because as he came out of his cell on his way to the hospital, he found San Francisco Solano stretched out on a bench with a terrible sick headache. The lay brother felt his pulse and said to him:

"Father, you are very weak and you ought to have something to eat."

"Brother," answered the saint, "I'm not the least bit hungry."

"Make an effort, Reverend Father, and take something, even if it's just a bite."

And the refectioner kept at him so long that the sick man, to stop his nagging, hit upon the idea of asking him for something that it would have been impossible even for the Viceroy to get, because it was out of season then.

"Well, brother, the only thing I'd like to eat would be a couple of smelts."

Fray Gómez put his right hand into the left sleeve of his habit and pulled out a pair of smelts that were as fresh as though they had just come out of the water.

"There you are, father, and let's hope they make you feel better. I'll cook them for you right away."

And the fact of the matter is that the blessed smelts cured San Francisco like a charm.

These two little miracles I have mentioned just in passing do not seem to me chaff. And I am leaving in my inkwell many others this lay brother performed, because I do not propose to relate his life and miracles. Nevertheless, to satisfy the demands of the curious, I shall jot down that over the door of the first cell of the small cloister that is still used as a hospital, there is an oil painting depicting the two miracles I have described, which bears the following inscription:

"The Venerable Fray Gómez. Born in Extremadura in 1560. Took the habit in Chuquisaca in 1580. Came to Lima in 1587. Was a nurse for forty years, displaying all virtues, and was endowed with celestial gifts and favors. His life was a continuous miracle. He died on May 2, 1631, and was held to be a saint. The following year his body was laid in the chapel of Aranzazú, and on October 13, 1810, was placed beneath the high altar in the same vault where the remains of the priors of the convent are interred. Doctor Don Bartolomé María de las Heras was a witness to this transfer. This venerable painting was restored on November 30, 1882, by M. Zamudio."

• • •

II

Fray Gómez was in his cell one morning, given over to meditation, when a couple of timid knocks sounded on his door, and a plaintive-toned voice said:

"*Deo gratias*. . . . Praised be the Lord."

"Forever, amen. Come in, brother," answered Fray Gómez.

And the door of the humble cell opened to admit a ragged individual, a *vera efigies* of a man crushed by poverty, but whose face revealed the proverbial forthrightness and honesty of the Old Castilian.

The entire furnishings of the cell comprised four rawhide chairs, a table that had seen better days, a cot without mattress, sheets, or blankets and with a stone for a pillow.

"Sit down, brother, and tell me frankly what brings you here," said Fray Gómez.

"Well, father, I want to tell you that I am an honest and decent man. . . ."

"That is plain, and I hope you will continue that way, for it will give you peace of heart in this life, and bliss in the next."

"You see, I am a peddler, and I have a big family, and my business does not prosper because I am short of capital, not because of laziness or lack of effort on my part."

"I am glad, brother, for God helps a man who works as he should."

"But the fact of the matter is, father, that so far God hasn't heard me, and He is slow in coming to my help. . . ."

"Don't lose heart, brother, don't lose heart."

"But the fact of the matter is that I have knocked at many doors asking for a loan of five hundred duros and I have found them all locked and bolted. And last night, turning things over in my mind, I said to myself: 'Come, Jerónimo, cheer up and go ask Fray Gómez for the money, for if he wants to, a mendicant friar and poor as he is, he'll find a way to give you a hand.' And so here I am because I have come, and I beg and request you, father, to lend me that trifling sum for six months, and you can be sure that it will never be said of me:

> The world is full of folks
> Who reverence certain saints,
> But whose gratitude ends
> When they've answered their plaints."

"What made you think, son, that you would find such a sum in this poor cell?"

"Well, father, the fact is that I wouldn't know how to answer that; but I have faith that you will not let me leave empty-handed."

"Your faith will save you, brother. Wait a minute."

And running his eyes over the bare, whitewashed walls of the cell, he saw a scorpion that was crawling calmly along the window-frame. Fray Gómez tore a page out of an old book, walked over to the window, carefully picked up the insect, wrapped it in the paper, and, turning to his visitor, said:

"Take this jewel, good man, and pawn it; but don't forget that you are to return it to me in six months."

The peddler could hardly find words to express his gratitude; he took his leave of Fray Gómez and like a flash was on his way to a pawnbroker's shop.

The jewel was magnificent, worthy of a Moorish queen, to say the least. It was a brooch in the shape of a scorpion. A magnificent emerald set in gold formed the body, and the head was a sparkling diamond, with rubies for eyes.

The pawnbroker, who understood his business, greedily examined the jewel, and offered the peddler two thousand duros on it; but the Spaniard insisted that he would accept only five hundred duros for six months, at a Jewish rate of interest, of course. The papers or tickets were made out and signed, and the moneylender comforted himself with the hope that after a time the owner of the jewel would come back for more money, and that with the compound interest that would pile up, he would be unable to redeem it, and he would become the owner of a jewel so valuable in itself and because of its artistic merit.

With this little capital the peddler's affairs went so well that, when the time was up, he was able to redeem the jewel, and wrapping it in the same paper in which he had received it, he returned it to Fray Gómez.

The latter took the scorpion, set it upon the windowsill, blessed it, and said:

"Little creature of God, go your way!"

And the scorpion began to crawl happily about the walls of the cell.

Where and How the Devil Lost His Poncho

"So there you are, my dear fellow. I lost my head, and went about riding a wild mule with the stirrups dangling over a girl that came from the country where the devil lost his poncho."

This was the way my friend Don Adeodato de la Mentirola concluded the account of one of the adventures of his youth. Don Adeodato is an old fellow who took up arms in the royalist cause with Colonel Sanjuanena and who even today prefers the paternal rule of Fernando VII to all the republican forms of government, theoretical and practical, there ever have been or ever will be. Aside from this weakness or peculiarity, my friend Don Adeodato is a jewel of great price. There is no one who is better informed on the subject of Bolívar's philanderings with the ladies of Lima, or who can quote, with chapter and verse, from the history of all the old scandals that have taken place in this City of the Kings. He relates the things with a frankness and familiarity that is amazing; and as I have an insatiable curiosity about the life and doings, not of the living, but of those who have turned to dust and are pushing up the daisies, I stick to him like a button to a shirt, and I wind him up, and Don Adeodato unlimbers his tongue.

"Now how and where was it that the devil lost his poncho?" I asked him.

"What! You who write verses, and pretend to be a historian or story-teller, and have things printed in the public newspapers, and have been a congressman, don't know what in my days even the two-year-olds knew? That's what literary fame has become since 'the birth of a nation.' Dry leaves and chaff! Tinsel, nothing but tinsel!"

"I'm sorry, Don Adeodato. But I confess my ignorance and beg you to enlighten me; to teach those who do not know is a precept of the Christian doctrine."

Apparently my humility flattered this last leaf upon the tree from the times of Pezuela and La Serna, for after lighting a cigarette and settling himself comfortably in an armchair, he began with the story that follows. Of course, as you all know, neither Christ nor His disciples dreamed of crossing the Andes (although there are learned historians who affirm that the apostle Thomas preached the gospel in America), nor was there such a thing as the telegraph in those days, or steamboats or printing presses. But just overlook these and other anachronisms, and here is the story, *ad pedem littere*.

I

Well, sir, when Jesus Christ Our Lord was traveling about the world, riding a gentle little donkey, restoring sight to the blind and the use and abuse of their limbs to the paralyzed, He came to a region where there was nothing but sand as far as the eye could see. Here and there a slender, rustling palm raised itself aloft, and under its shade the Divine Teacher used to stop with His favorite disciples who, seemingly absent-mindedly, would fill their knapsacks with dates.

That stretch of sand seemed eternal, sort of like God, without beginning or end. Night was falling, and the travelers were heavy-hearted at the idea of having to spend the night with only the starry sky for a canopy, when with the last ray of the setting sun the silhouette of a belfry appeared upon the horizon.

The Lord, raising His hand to His eyes like a visor to see better, said:

"There's a town there. Peter, you know about navigation and geography, could you tell me what that city is?"

St. Peter licked his chops at the compliment and answered:

"Master, that city is Ica."

"Get along, then, get along."

And all the apostles fetched their donkeys a kick with their heels, and off the cortege trotted toward the town.

When they were just outside the city, they all got off to slick themselves up a bit. They perfumed their whiskers with balm of Judea, tightened the straps of their sandals, brushed off their tunics and cloaks, and then continued on their way, not without a word of advice from the gentle Jesus to His favorite apostle:

"Remember, Peter, you're not to go losing your temper and cutting off people's ears. Your hotheadedness is always getting us into trouble."

The apostle blushed to the whites of his eyes, and nobody would have said, to see him so kindly and contrite, that he had ever been so handy with a knife.

The people of Ica rolled out the red carpet, so to speak, for the distinguished visitors; and although they were anxious to be on their journey, the inhabitants found so many ways to detain them and they were the object of such attentions and celebrations that a week had gone by before you could say scat.

Wine of the finest brands, Elías, Boza y Falconi, flowed like water. During those eight days Ica was like a foretaste of paradise. The doctors sat idle, the druggists sold no medicines; there wasn't even a toothache or the mildest case of measles.

The notaries' pens got all rusty because not once did they have a complaint to draw up. Not a cross word was heard between man and wife, and even those rattlesnakes known as mothers-in-law and sisters-in-law—and this really was a miracle!—lost their venom.

How apparent it was that the Supreme Good was dwelling in Ica! The city breathed peace, joy, happiness.

The kindness, charm, and beauty of the ladies of Ica inspired St. John to write a sonnet with an *envoi* which was published on the same day in *El Comercio, Nacional,* and *Patria.* The Icans, between drink and drink, made the apostle poet promise to write the Apocalypse,

A Pindaric poem, a work immortal,
If lacking in sense, with genius glowing,

a poet friend of mine says.

So with one thing and another the eighth day had come to an end when Our Lord received a telegram urging Him to return to Jerusalem at once to keep the Samaritan woman from pulling out Mary Magdalen's hair; and fearing that the people, in their affection, might put obstacles in His way, He sent for the patriarch of the apostles, closed the door, and said to him:

"Peter, you handle this any way you think best, but we have to leave here tomorrow without a soul knowing it. There are circumstances under which one has no choice but to take French leave."

St. Peter drew up his plans, informed the others, and the next morning the guests had disappeared from the house where they had slept.

The city council had prepared a surprise serenade for that morning, but they were left all dressed up and no place to go. The travelers had already crossed Huacachina Lake and had disappeared beyond the horizon.

Ever since then the waters of Huacachina have the property of curing all ailments except the bite of wild monkeys.

When they had put several miles between themselves and the city, the Lord turned back for a last look and said:

"You say this place is called Ica, Peter?"

"Yes, sir, Ica."

"My, what a fine place!"

And raising His right hand, He blessed it in the name of the Father, the Son, and the Holy Ghost.

II

As the correspondents of the newspapers had written to Lima describing at length, in detail, and with flowery phrases the celebrations and banquets with which the visitors had been honored, the devil received the news by the first European mail-boat.

They say that *Cachano* bit his lips with envy, the rascally old snout-nose, and exclaimed:

"What the devil! I'm just as good as He. The very idea! . . . Nobody is going to get ahead of me!"

And calling up straightway twelve of his courtiers he disguised them to look like the apostles. For that is true, *Cucufo* knows more about the art of make-up and fixing over faces than an actor and a coquette put together.

But as the journalists had forgotten to describe the attire of Christ and His disciples, the *Maldito* decided that he could get around the difficulty by looking at the pictures in some travel book. And so, without further ado, he and his comrades dressed themselves up in high boots and threw over their shoulders a four-cornered cape, the poncho.

The people of Ica, when they saw the group coming, thought the Lord was coming back with His elect and rushed out to meet him, prepared to throw the house out of the window this time, so that the Man-God should have no cause for complaint and would decide to establish Himself for good in their city.

Until then the Icans had been happy, very happy, superlatively happy. They never mixed in politics, paid their taxes without a word, and did not give a hoot whether Prester John or the Moor Muza was in power. There was no gossip or tale-bearing from one neighborhood to another or from house to house. All they thought about was cultivating their vineyards and doing as much good as they could to one another. It was a land so flowing with happiness and well-being that it made the other regions jealous.

But *Carrampempe,* whose teeth begin to chatter with rage when he sees anybody happy, made up his mind the minute he arrived to stick his tail in the pie and ruin the whole thing.

El Cornudo reached Ica just as a marriage was about to take place between a young man like the flower of the flock and a girl like a ewe. They were a couple that seemed made for each other, they were so well suited in disposition and character, and they gave promise of living out their lives in peace and in the grace of God.

"I couldn't have come more opportunely if they had sent for me," said the devil to himself. "By St. Tecla, the patroness of out-of-tune pianos!"

But unfortunately for him, the couple had been to confession and had taken communion that morning, so the snares and temptations of *El Patudo* could not prevail against them.

With the first toasts drunk to the happy couple, the wine went to everyone's head, producing not that fine, genial, harmless exhilaration of the spirit that reigned at the banquets Our Lord honored with His presence, but a gross, sensual, indecent frenzy.

One young fellow, a Don Juan in his salad days, began to make insinuating remarks to the bride; and a middle-aged woman, with service stripes, began making eyes at the groom. That old girl was pure gasoline, and with one spark of willingness from the young man a blaze would have started that the Garibaldi fire-engine and all the fire companies would have been unable to put out. And things did not stop here.

The lawyers and notaries got together to drum up trade; the doctors and druggists went into cahoots to raise the price of *aqua fontis;* the mothers-in-law decided to scratch out their sons-in-law's eyes; the wives began to whine and beg for jewelry and velvet dresses; the upright citizens began to talk about larks and hot times; and, to put the whole thing in a nutshell, even the town council began to shout that they would have to tax people ten cents for each sneeze.

That was anarchy with all its horrors. It was as plain as the nose on your face that *El Rabudo* was at the bottom of the business.

And the hours went by, and drinking was no longer by the glass but by the bottle, and people who used to get mildly mellow that night went on such a bender as had never been seen before.

The poor bride, who, as I have said, was in a state of grace, was in complete distress, and was doing her best to get people to separate two groups of rowdies who, armed with cudgels, were tanning each other's hide.

"The devil has got into them; that's what it is," the poor girl kept saying to herself, and her guess was not far off. Going over to *Uñas Largas,* she took him by the poncho, saying:

"But, Lord, don't you see that they're going to kill one another?"

"And what's that to me?" answered *El Tiñoso* coolly. "I'm not from this parish. . . . More power to them. Let them. So much the better for the priest and for me. I'll act as sexton."

The girl, who of course could not take in the full implication of these gross remarks, answered him:

"Jesus! What a hard heart Your Excellency has! By the sign of this cross, you must be the devil!"

El Maligno had no sooner seen the girl's fingers forming the cross than he tried to rush off like a dog with a firecracker tied to its tail; but as she had hold of his poncho, *El Tunante* had to slip his head through the opening, leaving the four-cornered cape in the bride's hands.

El Patón and his acolytes evaporated, but it is said that since then, every once in a while, His Satanic Majesty comes back to the city of Ica looking for his poncho. When this happens, the elbow-benders go on a proper spree and . . .

TRANSLATED BY HARRIET DE ONÍS

Joaquim Maria Machado de Assis

Brazil
(1839–1908)

———— //

Joaquim Maria Machado de Assis, or simply Machado, is the premier nineteenth-century Latin American writer and one of the best of all time anywhere. Had he been born French or English, there is little doubt that his works would be prominently featured in the Western canon. In the Americas he is certainly on the level of Melville, Hawthorne, and Poe. No one in Spanish comes close to his polish and originality. A mulatto from a poor background who was orphaned early, Machado made a living in a printing shop, later as a journalist, and finally as a writer. In Brazil he attained fame and respect, was elected as the first president of the Brazilian Academy of Letters, and was reelected in perpetuity until his death. He published nine novels, of which the best known are *Epitaph for a Small Winner* (1880), *The Heritage of Quincas Borba* (1891), *Dom Casmurro* (1899), and *Esau and Jacob* (1904), and more than two hundred short stories, some of which were collected in English as *The Psychiatrist and Other Stories* (1963). A master of subtle psychological intrigues and of dramas involving the great questions vexing humankind, Machado was devoted to Shakespeare, who, he said, wrote in ''the language of the soul.'' He was also deeply influenced by biblical stories. Machado painted Brazilian society with elegant, satirical flair. He anticipates and equals Borges's penchant for ironic detachment and authorial self-effacement, but his skepticism was less corrosive and more compassionate. ''Midnight Mass'' is one of Machado's most celebrated pieces. It is so indirect and understated that the drama is merely insinuated by the protagonists' gestures and clothing and by the decor. Brief as it is, ''Midnight Mass'' has the breadth of a whole novel. The sociohistorical background is all there, but it is not intrusive. The ending leaves one with the melancholy of squandered possibilities and the quiet despair of wasted lives.

Midnight Mass

I have never quite understood a conversation that I had with a lady many years ago, when I was seventeen and she was thirty. It was Christmas Eve. I had arranged to go to Mass with a neighbor and was to rouse him at midnight for this purpose.

The two-story house in which I was staying belonged to the notary

Menezes, whose first wife had been a cousin of mine. His second wife, Conceição, and her mother had received me hospitably upon my arrival a few months earlier. I had come to Rio from Mangaratiba to study for the college entrance examinations. I lived quietly with my books. Few contacts. Occasional walks. The family was small: the notary, his wife, his mother-in-law, and two female slaves. An old-fashioned household. By ten at night everyone was in his bedroom; by half-past ten the house was asleep.

I had never gone to a theater and, more than once, on hearing Menezes say that he was going, I asked him to take me along. On these occasions his mother-in-law frowned and the slaves tittered. Menezes did not reply; he dressed, went out, and returned the next morning. Later I learned that the theater was a euphemism. Menezes was having an affair with a married woman who was separated from her husband; he stayed out once a week. Conceição had grieved at the beginning, but after a time she had grown used to the situation. Custom led to resignation, and finally she came almost to accept the affair as proper.

Gentle Conceição! They called her the saint and she merited the title, so uncomplainingly did she suffer her husband's neglect. In truth, she possessed a temperament of great equanimity, with extremes neither of tears nor of laughter. Everything about her was passive and attenuated. Her very face was median, neither pretty nor ugly. She was what is called a kind person. She spoke ill of no one, she pardoned everything. She didn't know how to hate; quite possibly she didn't know how to love.

On that Christmas Eve (it was 1861 or 1862) the notary was at the theater. I should have been back in Mangaratiba, but I had decided to remain till Christmas to see a midnight Mass in the big city. The family retired at the usual hour. I sat in the front parlor, dressed and ready. From there I could leave through the entrance hall without waking anyone. There were three keys to the door: the notary had one, I had one, and one remained in the house.

"But Mr. Nogueira, what will you do all this while?" asked Conceição's mother.

"I'll read, Madame Ignacia."

I had a copy of an old translation of *The Three Musketeers,* published originally, I think, in serial form in *The Journal of Commerce.* I sat down at the table in the center of the room and, by the light of the kerosene lamp, while the house slept, mounted once more D'Artagnan's bony nag and set out upon adventure. In a short time I was completely absorbed. The minutes flew as they rarely do when one is waiting. I heard the clock strike eleven, but almost without noticing. After a time, however, a sound from the interior of the house roused me from my book. It was the sound of footsteps, in the hall that connected the parlor with the dining room. I raised my head. Soon I saw the form of Conceição appear at the door.

"Haven't you gone?" she asked.

"No, I haven't. I don't think it's midnight yet."

"What patience!"

Conceição, wearing her bedroom slippers, came into the room. She was dressed in a white negligee, loosely bound at the waist. Her slenderness helped to suggest a romantic apparition quite in keeping with the spirit of my novel. I shut the book. She sat on the chair facing mine, near the sofa. To my question whether perchance I had awakened her by stirring about, she quickly replied:

"No, I woke up naturally."

I looked at her and doubted her statement. Her eyes were not those of a person who had just slept. However, I quickly put out of my mind the thought that she could be guilty of lying. The possibility that I might have kept her awake and that she might have lied in order not to make me unhappy did not occur to me at the time. I have already said that she was a good person, a kind person.

"I guess it won't be much longer now," I said.

"How patient you are to stay awake and wait while your friend sleeps! And to wait alone! Aren't you afraid of ghosts? I thought you'd be startled when you saw me."

"When I heard footsteps I was surprised. But then I soon saw it was you."

"What are you reading? Don't tell me, I think I know: it's *The Three Musketeers*."

"Yes, that's right. It's very interesting."

"Do you like novels?"

"Yes."

"Have you ever read *The Little Sweetheart*?"

"By Mr. Macedo? I have it in Mangaratiba."

"I'm very fond of novels, but I don't have much time for them. Which ones have you read?"

I began to name some. Conceição listened, with her head resting on the back of her chair, looking at me past half-shut eyelids. From time to time she wet her lips with her tongue. When I stopped speaking she said nothing. Thus we remained for several seconds. Then she raised her head; she clasped her hands and rested her chin on them, with her elbows on the arms of her chair, all without taking from me her large, perceptive eyes.

"Maybe she's bored with me," I thought. And then, aloud: "Madame Conceição, I think it's getting late and I . . ."

"No, it's still early. I just looked at the clock; it's half-past eleven.

There's time yet. When you lose a night's sleep, can you stay awake the next day?"

"I did once."

"I can't. If I lose a night, the next day I just have to take a nap, if only for half an hour. But of course I'm getting on in years."

"Oh, no, nothing of the sort, Madame Conceição!"

I spoke so fervently that I made her smile. Usually her gestures were slow, her attitude calm. Now, however, she rose suddenly, moved to the other side of the room, and, in her chaste disarray, walked about between the window and the door of her husband's study. Although thin, she always walked with a certain rocking gait as if she carried her weight with difficulty. I had never before felt this impression so strongly. She paused several times, examining a curtain or correcting the position of some object on the sideboard. Finally she stopped directly in front of me, with the table between us. The circle of her ideas was narrow indeed: she returned to her surprise at seeing me awake and dressed. I repeated what she already knew, that I had never heard a midnight Mass in the city and that I didn't want to miss the chance.

"It's the same as in the country. All Masses are alike."

"I guess so. But in the city there must be more elegance and more people. Holy Week here in Rio is much better than in the country. I don't know about St. John's Day or St. Anthony's . . ."

Little by little she had leaned forward; she had rested her elbows on the marble top of the table and had placed her face between the palms of her hands. Her unbuttoned sleeves fell naturally, and I saw her forearms, very white and not so thin as one might have supposed. I had seen her arms before, although not frequently, but on this occasion sight of them impressed me greatly. The veins were so blue that, despite the dimness of the light, I could trace every one of them. Even more than the book, Conceiçã's presence had served to keep me awake. I went on talking about holy days in the country and in the city, and about whatever else came to my lips. I jumped from subject to subject, sometimes returning to an earlier one; and I laughed in order to make her laugh, so that I could see her white, shining, even teeth. Her eyes were not really black but were very dark; her nose, thin and slightly curved, gave her face an air of interrogation. Whenever I raised my voice a little, she hushed me.

"Softly! Mama may wake up."

And she did not move from that position, which filled me with delight, so close were our faces. Really there was no need to speak loudly in order to be heard. We both whispered, I more than she because I had more to say. At times she became serious, very serious, with her brow a bit wrinkled. After a while she tired and changed both position and place. She came around the table and sat on the sofa. I turned my head and could see the tips of her slippers, but only for as long as it took her to sit down: her negligee was long and quickly covered them. I remember that they were black. Conceição said very softly:

"Mama's room is quite a distance away, but she sleeps so lightly. If she wakes up now, poor thing, it will take her a long time to fall asleep again."

"I'm like that, too."

"What?" she asked, leaning forward to hear better.

I moved to the chair immediately next to the sofa and repeated what I had said. She laughed at the coincidence, for she, too, was a light sleeper, we were all light sleepers.

"I'm just like mama: when I wake up I can't fall asleep again. I roll all over the bed, I get up, I light the candle, I walk around, I lie down again, and nothing happens."

"Like tonight."

"No, no," she hastened.

I didn't understand her denial; perhaps she didn't understand it either. She took the ends of her belt and tapped them on her knees, or rather on her right knee, for she had crossed her legs. Then she began to talk about dreams. She said she had had only one nightmare in her whole life, and that one during her childhood. She wanted to know whether I ever had nightmares. Thus the conversation re-engaged itself and moved along slowly, continuously, and I forgot about the hour and about Mass. Whenever I finished a bit of narrative or an explanation she asked a question or brought up some new point, and I started talking again. Now and then she had to caution me.

"Softly, softly . . ."

Sometimes there were pauses. Twice I thought she was asleep. But her eyes, shut for a moment, quickly opened: they showed neither sleepiness nor fatigue, as though she had shut them merely so that she could see better. On one of these occasions I think she noticed that I was absorbed in her, and I remember that she shut her eyes again—whether hurriedly or slowly I do not remember. Some of my recollections of that evening seem abortive or confused. I get mixed up, I contradict myself. One thing I remember vividly is that at a certain moment she, who till then had been such engaging company (but nothing more), suddenly became beautiful, so very beautiful. She stood up, with her arms crossed. I, out of respect for her, stirred myself to rise; she did not want me to, she put one of her hands on my shoulder and I remained seated. I thought she was going to say something but she trembled as if she had a chill, turned her back, and sat in the chair where she had found me reading. She glanced at the mirror above the sofa and began to talk about two engravings that were hanging on the wall.

"These pictures are getting old. I've asked Chiquinho to buy new ones."

Chiquinho was her husband's nickname. The pictures bespoke the man's principal interest. One was of Cleopatra; I no longer remember the subject of the other, but there were women in it. Both were banal. In those days I did not know they were ugly.

"They're pretty," I said.

"Yes, but they're stained. And besides, to tell the truth, I'd prefer pictures of saints. These are better for bachelors' quarters or a barber shop."

"A barber shop! I didn't think you'd ever been to . . ."

"But I can imagine what the customers there talk about while they're waiting—girls and flirtations, and naturally the proprietor wants to please them with pictures they'll like. But I think pictures like that don't belong in the home. That's what I think, but I have a lot of queer ideas. Anyway, I don't like them. I have an Our Lady of the Immaculate Conception, my patron saint; it's very lovely. But it's a statue, it can't be hung on the wall, and I wouldn't want it here anyway. I keep it in my little oratory."

The oratory brought to mind the Mass. I thought it might be time to go and was about to say so. I think I even opened my mouth but shut it before I could speak, so that I could go on listening to what she was saying, so sweetly, so graciously, so gently that it drugged my soul. She spoke of her religious devotions as a child and as a young girl. Then she told about dances and walks and trips to the island of Paquetá, all mixed together, almost without interruption. When she tired of the past she spoke of the present, of household matters, of family cares, which, before her marriage, everyone said would be terrible, but really they were nothing. She didn't mention it, but I knew she had been twenty-seven when she married.

She no longer moved about, as at first, and hardly changed position. Her eyes seemed smaller, and she began to look idly about at the walls.

"We must change this wallpaper," she said, as if talking to herself.

I agreed, just to say something, to shake off my magnetic trace or whatever one may call the condition that thickened my tongue and benumbed my senses. I wished and I did not wish to end the conversation. I tried to take my eyes from her, and did so out of respect; but, afraid she would think I was tired of looking at her, when in truth I was not, I turned again towards her. The conversation was dying away. In the street, absolute stillness.

We stopped talking and for some time (I cannot say how long) sat there in silence. The only sound was the gnawing of a rat in the study; it stirred me from my somnolescence. I wanted to talk about it but didn't know how to begin. Conceição seemed to be abstracted. Suddenly I heard a beating on the window and a voice shouting:

"Midnight Mass! Midnight Mass!"

"There's your friend," she said, rising. "It's funny. You were to wake him, and here he comes to wake you. Hurry, it must be late. Goodbye."

"Is it time already?"

"Of course."

"Midnight Mass!" came the voice from outside, with more beating on the window:

"Hurry, hurry, don't make him wait. It was my fault. Goodbye until tomorrow."

And with her rocking gait Conceição walked softly down the hall. I went out into the street and, with my friend, proceeded to the church. During Mass, Conceição kept appearing between me and the priest; charge this to my seventeen years. Next morning at breakfast I spoke of the midnight Mass and of the people I had seen in church, without, however, exciting Conceição's interest. During the day I found her, as always, natural, benign, with nothing to suggest the conversation of the prior evening.

A few days later I went to Mangaratiba. When I returned to Rio in March, I learned that the notary had died of apoplexy. Conceição was living in the Engenho Novo district, but I neither visited nor met her. I learned later that she had married her husband's apprenticed clerk.

TRANSLATED BY WILLIAM L. GROSSMAN AND HELEN CALDWELL

Part III

The Contemporary Period

The history of the contemporary Latin American short story can be organized around the publication of pivotal collections, books that are peaks of Latin American literature in the same way as novels such as Gabriel García Márquez's *One Hundred Years of Solitude* (1967) or poems like Pablo Neruda's *Canto general* (1950). The first such collection has to be Rubén Darío's *Azul* (1888), even if it is traditional to think of that book as a turning point in the history of Latin American poetry. But the revolution in literary language brought about by Darío, a Nicaraguan, affected all genres, and he did include in *Azul* brief prose pieces like "The Death of the Empress of China" (featured in the second edition of 1890). The succession of collections is easier to plot after that.

Horacio Quiroga's *Cuentos de amor, de locura y de muerte* (1917) inaugurates, for many, the modern Latin American short story. In Latin America, Quiroga was the most accomplished disciple of Edgar Allan Poe, and the presence of Poe divides for many critics the history of the Latin American short story into two periods—before Poe and after. Only that, if Brazil is included, as it is here, then Machado de Assis's *Contos fluminenses* (1870) has to take precedence, even over *Azul*. Important collections between those dates and Jorge Luis Borges's *Ficciones* (1944) number many, but none had a more profound and lasting effect. A case could be made for Miguel Angel Asturias's *Leyendas de Guatemala* (1930), which continued the tradition initiated by Ramón Pané, Peter Martyr d'Anghiera, and others in the colonial period, of collecting native American tales and recasting them in a European language. Asturias's book was influential throughout Latin America and beyond, partly because of its endorsement in the prologue by the French poet Paul Valéry. But the Latin American short story was never the same after *Ficciones,* and neither was the international short story after that collection began to be disseminated world-wide in the 1960s. Borges's appeal was not only the craft of his stories but their philosophical cast, which seemed to compose a philosophical position—a kind of programmatic skepticism. João Guimarães Rosa's *Sagarana* (1946) had a comparable effect on the Brazilian short story, though not in the international arena. In the 1950s there were four influential short story collections: Juan Carlos Onetti's *Un sueño realizado y otros relatos* (1951), Juan José Arreola's

Confabulario total (1952), Juan Rulfo's *The Burning Plain* (1953), and Alejo Carpentier's *War of Time* (1958). Rulfo and Onetti were doubtlessly influenced by the work of another great American writer, William Faulkner, who left a definitive imprint on Latin American fiction.

All these collections had a tremendous impact on the writers who emerged in the 1960s. Since then the decisive short story collections have been Julio Cortázar's *The Secret Weapons* (1964) and *All Fires the Fire* (1966). Cortázar was the premier short story writer among those who came to be known during the Boom, but Gabriel García Márquez was a very close second, with *No One Writes to the Colonel* (1957), a novella, and *Los funerales de la Mamá Grande* (1962)—all collected in English under the title *No One Writes to the Colonel and Other Stories* (1968). Cortázar's appeal was due in part to his trendy reflection of the international counterculture movement of the 1960s.

Each nation has its own history of the short story that can also be mapped by the publication of decisive short story collections. From Cuba, to use the example I know best, there are collections by Alfonso Hernández Catá, Enrique Labrador Ruiz, Lydia Cabrera, Onelio Jorge Cardoso, Lino Novás Calvo, Guillermo Cabrera Infante, and Antonio Benítez Rojo. Novás Calvo, who wrote stark, dramatic stories in the manner of Hemingway, was more influential within the local tradition than was Carpentier, who was better known internationally. Lydia Cabrera, on the blurry divide between anthropology and literature, rewrote Afro-Cuban stories. Jorge Cardoso followed the practice of the rural storyteller and published some first-rate fantastic tales drawn from folk sources. Labrador Ruiz wrote well-crafted, often comical avant-garde stories. Hernández Catá composed urban, decadent tales that still had traces of Modernismo in their elaborate style. He was so prominent in the early decades of the twentieth century that a short story prize was given his name after his untimely death in 1940. Cabrera Infante wrote the first stories with revolutionary themes after 1959, and Benítez Rojo, a historical novelist in the manner of Carpentier, crafted some magnificent tales about the crumbling Cuban bourgeoisie in the aftermath of Fidel Castro's takeover. A detailed history of each national literature would reveal the depth, indeed the abundance, of the Latin American short story tradition.

Because of the wider circulation of books, today local short story writers are more likely to see themselves in terms of an international rather than a national literary market. This is stimulated, as always, by various forms of exile that forced many writers to live abroad all or part of their careers: Augusto Roa Bastos in France; Nélida Piñón in Barcelona; Benítez Rojo in the United States; Cristina Peri Rossi in Spain; and so forth. Thus, we are perhaps witnessing the final dissolution of the national traditions of short story writing.

Rubén Darío

Nicaragua
(1867–1916)

———— \\ ————

Rubén Darío is not only the most important poet in Spanish since Góngora but he also revolutionized all of Latin American literary discourse. Feted throughout the Spanish-speaking world, Darío was the first Latin American international literary celebrity. His initial success was *Azul* (1888), a combination of poems and poetic prose that became immensely influential almost at once. A second edition in 1890 incorporated the story included here. Darío's innovation consisted mainly of an effort to achieve perfection, the unabashed cultivation of the artful and the exclusion of the sentimentalism of postromantic poetry. Artistic excellence was an ideal to which everything should be sacrificed, and Darío pursued that ideal both in literature and in life. It was a typically decadent manner, and some of the artfulness of the verse was derived from the French Parnassians. But the effect on Spanish-language literature was such that a movement, Modernismo, emerged around Darío. It was the first literary movement to have arisen in Latin America. *Modernista* art cultivated the foreign, rejecting what appeared to be the obsolete, nonmodern ways of the Spanish. The alien, be it French or Oriental, was akin to art in that it was unnatural, not part of the received, familiar (in all senses) culture of the Spanish motherland. "The Death of the Empress of China," reprinted here, could not be more typical of Modernismo, not only in style and content but even in the atmosphere in which the characters live, surrounded by the exotic, particularly chinoiserie. The story is a brilliant case study of idolatry, with the porcelain figure as the fetish wherein all desires converge.

The Death of the Empress of China

In the little house, the rugs of whose parlor were faded blue, lived a pink-skinned girl as rare and fine as a jewel. It was her jewel box.

Who was the owner of that luscious happy bird with black eyes and red mouth? For whom did she sing her sublime song when, in the sun's glory, little Miss Springtime showed her pretty laughing face and opened the meadow flowers and shook out the nests? Suzette was the name of the little bird that had been stuck in a cage primped in plush and lace and silk

105

by a dreamy Artist Hunter who had trapped her one May morning with sun in the air and many blowzy roses.

Recaredo—paternal whim!—Was it his fault his name was Recaredo?— had married one and a half years before. "Do you love me?" "I love you." "And you?" "With all my heart."

Gorgeous was the golden day after the visit to the priest. They had gone to the new meadow to luxuriate in the pleasures of love. Beside the stream- let, the fragrant bellflowers and wild violets murmured in their leafy sheafs as the two lovers passed, arms laced around each other's waists, their lips' red bloom blowing kisses. Then home to the big city and the nest redolent of youth and happy heat.

Did I tell you Recaredo was a sculptor? If I haven't, I say so now.

He was a sculptor. He kept his studio in the little house, a clutter of works in marble, plaster, bronze, and clay. Sometimes those passing heard, through the grates and blinds, a voice singing and a hammer ringing. Suzette and Recaredo, the mouth that made the song, the clink of the chisel.

And infinite nuptial bliss. On tiptoe, to his place of work, showering his neck in her hair, smothering him with little kisses. Stealing ever so quietly to where she dozed on her divan, her little black-stocking-shod feet propped crisscross, on her lap an open book; planting a kiss on her lips that drank up her breath and started open her indescribably brilliant eyes. And at all this, the blackbird chortled, a blackbird in a cage that turned downcast and declined to sing when Suzette played Chopin. The black- bird's chortle! It was no slight thing.

"Do you care for me?" "Don't you know I do?" "Do you love me?" "I adore you!" And by then the little beast would be cackling away, beak in the air. If they let him out of his cage, he would flap around the blue parlor and perch on the head of the plaster Apollo or on the spear of some old Teuton in dark bronze. *Friiiit! . . . rit!* Was his babble ever rude and fresh sometimes! But how prettily he perched on Suzette's hand, and she cooed and caught his beak between her teeth till he begged for mercy. And then she would say to him in a severe voice trembling with tenderness: "Mr. Blackbird, you're a rogue!"

The two lovers groomed each other's hair. "Sing," he said, and she sang languidly. Though they were just two youngsters in love, they thought they were splendid, regal, handsome. She was Elsa to him; to her he was Lohengrin. Love, oh young ones full of blood and dreams, sets a pane of blue crystal glass before the eyes and lavishes infinite bliss.

How they loved! He envisaged her among the stars of God; his love ranged over the full spectrum of the passions, now muted, now wild, now nearly mystical. The artist, it might even be said, was a theosophist who saw in his beloved something supreme and superhuman, like Rider Haggard's Ayesha. He sipped her like a flower, he smiled as to a star, and he felt eminently powerful when he clasped against his chest her lovely little head, which resembled, when she was hushed and pensive, the proud profile of a Byzantine empress on the head of a coin.

Recaredo loved his art. He had a passion for form; from the marble sprang graceful naked goddesses with smooth white eyes lacking pupils; his studio was peopled with a nation of silent statues, metal beasts, dread gargoyles, griffins with long leafy tails, Gothic confections of possible occult inspiration. And his greatest love, Japanese and Chinese exotica. In this, Recaredo was an original. I don't know what he would have given to speak the tongues of Japan and China. He had perused the best albums; he had read fine exotica; he worshipped Loti and Judith Gautier. He had scrimped to buy authentic works from Yokohama, Nagasaki, Kyoto, Nanking, and Peking: knives, pipes, weird and hideous masks like faces in drugged dreams; mandarin minidwarfs with bloated bellies and indented eyes; frog-mouthed freaks with big, gaping, toothy grins; tiny, gruff Tartar soldiers.

"Oh how I hate your horrid workshop," Suzette said to him, "your wizard's hutch, your strange strongbox that keeps you from my kisses." Grinning, he would come forth from his place of work, his temple of rare curios, and hurry to the blue parlor to coddle his living jewel, and to hear the happy blackbird chant and chortle.

When he came in that morning, he saw his sweet Suzette lying drowsily beside a three-legged stool bearing a bowl of roses. Was she Sleeping Beauty? Her delicate body showed shapely under a white robe, her ruddy hair coiled on one shoulder, all of her emanating a soft feminine smell: she was like the lovely maiden in one of those pretty tales that begins: "Once upon a time there lived a king . . ."

He woke her: "Suzette, my beauty!" His face was joyful; his black eyes shone beneath the red fez he wore when he worked; in his hand he carried a letter.

"A letter from Robert, Suzette. That rat's in China! 'Hong Kong, 18 January . . . ' "

Suzette had sat up a bit woozily and taken the sheet of paper. Who would have thought that globetrotter would get so far! "Hong Kong, 18 January . . ." What a fine boy that Robert was, always good for a laugh, mad to travel! He meant to reach the ends of the earth. Best of friends, all but family. He had left for San Francisco, California, two years before. Crazy as they come!

He began to read:

Hong Kong, 18 January 1888

My dear Recaredo:

I came and I saw. (I have not yet conquered.)
In San Francisco I had word of your marriage and was glad. One
leap and I landed in China. I'm the agent for a California im-
porting firm that deals in silk, enamels, ivory, and other chinoi-
series. A gift shall follow; given your love for the things of this
golden country, to you it shall be as gold. My compliments to
Suzette, cherish this memento from

Robert

That was all. Both broke into peals of laughter. The blackbird, for his part,
had a paroxysm of musical screaks that rocked the cage.

The package had arrived: a medium-size box covered with stamps,
numbers, and black hieroglyphics avouching the extreme fragility of its
contents. Open came the box, and forth came the mystery. It was a fine
porcelain bust, the superb bust of a woman, waxen, smiling, and winsome.
On its mount was an inscription in Chinese, English, and French: *the Empress of China*. The hands of what Far Eastern artist had molded those
mysterious and alluring shapes? A tight knot of hair, a look of enigma, the
exotic, lowered eyes of a sublime princess, the smile of a sphinx, her neck
craned above a pair of dovelike shoulders draped in a wave of silk embroidered with dragons, an enchantment of perfect pale white porcelain
innocence. The Empress of China! Suzette passed her pink fingers over
the eyes of that marvelous monarch, over the slope of her eyes slanting
beneath the pure and noble curve of her brows. She was happy. And
Recaredo felt proud to possess such a porcelain. He would build a cabinet,
a sacred niche in which she would live and reign alone, triumphant and
imperially canopied like the Venus de Milo.

And so he did. At one end of his studio he created a tiny cupboard out
of folding screens decorated with cranes and rice fields. Yellow was the
most noticeable color. The full range of yellows: flame-gold, eastern ochre,
autumn leaf, and that ever so pale yellow that fades, dying, into white.
And among them her exotic Imperial Highness sat laughing, on a black-
and-gold pedestal. Around her Recaredo had placed all his Chinese and
Japanese knickknacks. Over her he had placed a big Nipponese parasol
painted with camellias and fat bleeding roses. And when, setting aside his
pipe and chisels, the dreamy-eyed artist stood before the Empress, hands
folded over his breast, bowing and scraping, it was almost funny. He visited
her once, twice, twenty times daily. She was his passion. Every day he

placed fresh flowers for her in a Yokohama enamel bowl. At moments, he felt truly touched and transported by the lovely and motionless majesty of the Oriental bust. He studied her every detail, the curl of her ear, the curve of her lip, her polished nose, the slope of her eyefold. His idol, the far-famed Empress! Suzette called to him:

"Recaredo!"

"Coming!"

And he continued to gaze at his work of art. Until Suzette came to drag him away, with tugs and kisses.

One day the flowers vanished from the enamel bowl as though by magic.

"Who swiped the flowers!" shouted the artist from his studio.

"I did," said a voice that trembled.

And Suzette drew aside a curtain, blushing and flashing her dark eyes.

Somewhere in the depths of his mind, señor Recaredo, sculptor, asked himself: What's wrong with my darling? She barely eats. Those fine books deflowered with her ivory paperknife lie shut on their little black shelf, longing for her smooth pink hands and her warm, sweet-smelling lap. Recaredo found her sad. What's gotten into my girl? She sits down at the table but she doesn't eat. She's glum, so very glum. Sometimes he observed her out of the corner of an eye, and her dark pupils looked moist as though they wished to cry. And when she replied, she spoke like a child who has been refused a sweet. "Nothing." She said that "nothing" with a whimper, and tears slipped between the syllables.

Oh, señor Recaredo! What's wrong with your darling is you're a hateful man. Haven't you noticed that ever since that beauty queen the Empress of China came into your home, the blue room has gone glum and the blackbird has ceased to sing and laugh his pearly laugh? Suzette revived Chopin and his morbid melancholy melody rose slowly and sonorously from the black piano. She's jealous, señor Recaredo. She's drowning and burning with jealousy, which strangles the soul like a snake. Jealousy! Perhaps he did understand, for one evening he said these words to the love of his life through the steam of a cup of coffee:

"You're too unjust. Don't I love you with all my soul? Can't you read in my eyes what I feel in my heart?"

Suzette broke into tears. So he loved her! No, he no longer loved her; the splendid shining hours had fled, and their smacks and smooches had scattered like a flight of birds. He no longer loved her. He had left her, his religion, his sweet, his dream, his queen, for another woman.

Another woman! Recaredo started. She was mistaken. Did she mean blond Eulogia, for whom he had once composed madrigals?

She shook her head. "No." Or plump rich Gabriela with long black hair and skin as white as alabaster, whose bust he had sculpted? Or Luisa, the dancer with smoldering eyes and willowy waist and the breasts of a wet nurse? Or the widow Andrea, who stuck out the pink catlike tip of her tongue between shiny ivory teeth when she laughed?

No, it was none of these. Recaredo was puzzled. "Tell me, my darling, tell me the truth. Who is she? You know how I love you, my Elsa, my Juliet, my love, my life. . . ."

Those breathless words trembled with such true love that Suzette, the tears now dry in her puffy eyes, got to her feet, tossing her pretty aristocratic head.

"Do you love me?"

"You know I do."

"Then allow me to take revenge upon my rival. Choose between me and her. If you love me, will you let me banish her forever, so I may be sure you love me and me alone?"

"So be it," said Recaredo. And he went on sipping his coffee black as ink as he watched his jealous stubborn little bird leave the room.

He had taken only three sips when he heard a great crash and clatter in his studio.

In he went. What did he see? The bust had disappeared from its black-and-gold mount, and on the floor, among a scatter of tiny fallen mandarins and fans, lay shards of porcelain that crunched beneath Suzette's little feet. Flushed, her hair mussed, giggling silvery giggles to her startled husband, and awaiting kisses: "I have wreaked my revenge. The Empress of China is dead!"

And when their lips so passionately met and made up in the blue room brimming with joy, the blackbird in his cage died laughing.

TRANSLATED BY SARAH ARVIO

Leopoldo Lugones

Argentina
(1874–1938)

———— \\\\ ————

A prolific poet, essayist, and polemicist, Leopoldo Lugones led a frenzied life that took him from being a young socialist poet to a fascist defender of military rule and national values. A follower of Darío and the *modernista* movement in the last decade of the nineteenth century, Lugones's was widely influential with his first important collection of poems, *Las montañas de oro* (1897), as well as with his even better-known *Los crepúsculos del jardín* (1905) and *Lunario sentimental* (1909). His lectures on the Argentine gaucho epic *Martín Fierro*, published as *El payador* in 1916, were just as influential. Lugones's poetry shed the poetic glitter and prosodic gymnastics of Modernismo to acquire a simpler tone, imitated from rural verse. *Romancero* (1924) and *Poemas solariegos* (1928) display this new predilection for what are presumed to be Argentine national attributes. These books announced his turn to conservatism, which is openly articulated in *La patria fuerte* (1930), a call for military rule. It was perhaps these violent contradictions that led to his unexplained suicide in 1938. As the title of the short story collection in which "Yzur" appeared, *Las fuerzas extrañas* (1906), suggests Lugones was haunted by the fantastic in ways that are reminiscent of Poe. He is also curious about how those "strange forces or powers" that he perceives can be controlled or unleashed by modern scientific knowledge. But "Yzur" also reveals his fascination with violence, dominance, and the power of language, and it can be seen as anticipating his later fascist period. In Lugones, the quest for the beautiful that he inherited from *modernistas* like Darío unveils an ugly, fetishistic side.

Yzur

I bought the ape at auction from a circus that had gone bankrupt.

The first time it occurred to me to try the experiment described in these pages was an afternoon when I happened to read, somewhere or other, that the natives of Java ascribe the absence of articulate speech among the apes to deliberate abstention, not to incapacity. "They keep silent," the article stated, "so as not to be set to work."

This idea, which at first struck me as superficial, in the end engaged my mind until it evolved into this anthropological theory: apes were men who for one reason or another had stopped speaking, with the result that the vocal organs and the centers of the brain that control speech had atrophied; the connection between the two was weakened nearly to the breaking-point; the language of the species was arrested at the stage of the inarticulate cry; and the primitive human being sank to the animal level.

Clearly if this could be proved it would readily account for all the anomalies which make the ape such a singular creature. But there could be only one proof possible: to get an ape to talk.

Meanwhile I had travelled the world over with my ape, and our experiences, our ups and downs, had bound him closer and closer to me. In Europe he attracted attention everywhere, and had I chosen to I could have made him as famous as Consul*—but this sort of buffoonery was unsuited to a sober man of business.

In the grip of my obsession I exhausted the entire literature on the subject of speech among the apes, with no appreciable result. All that I knew, with absolute certainty, was that *there is no scientific explanation for the fact that apes do not speak.* And this took five years of study and thought.

Yzur (where he got this name I could never find out, for his former owner did not know either) was certainly a remarkable animal. His training in the circus, even though it was restricted almost exclusively to mimicry, had greatly developed his faculties; and this prompted me to try out on him a theory that seemed, on the face of it, nonsensical. Moreover I knew that of all the apes the chimpanzee (which Yzur was) is equipped with the best brain, and is also one of the most docile: my chances of success were thus increased. Every time I saw him, rolling along like a drunken sailor, with his hands behind his back to keep his balance, I felt more strongly convinced that he was a retarded human being.

Actually there is no way of accounting for the fact that an ape does not articulate at all. His native speech, that is, the system of cries he uses to communicate with his fellows, is varied enough; his larynx, although very different from a human being's, is not so different as the parrot's, yet the parrot speaks; and, not to mention that a comparison of the ape's brain with the parrot's must banish all doubt, we need only recall that, although the idiot's brain is also rudimentary, there are cretins able to pronounce a few words. As for Broca's convolution, it depends, of course, on the total development of the brain; moreover, it has yet to be proved, beyond dispute, that this is the area that controls speech. Anatomy may have established it as the most probable site, but there are still incontrovertible arguments against it.

Fortunately, among so many bad traits, the ape has a taste for learning, as his aptitude for mimicry proves, an excellent memory, a capacity for

*The Roman emperor Caligula (A.D. 12–41), who showed his contempt for the Republic by naming his horse, Incitatus, as Consul.

reflection that can turn him into a profound dissembler, and an attention span comparatively better developed than a human child's. Hence he is a most promising subject for pedagogy.

My ape was young, moreover, and we know that it is in youth that the ape's intelligence reaches its peak. The only difficulty lay in choosing what teaching method to use. I was well aware of the fruitless endeavors of my predecessors, and when I considered all the effort expended, with no result, by so many, some of them of the highest competence, my purpose faltered more than once. But all my thinking on the subject led me to this conclusion: *the first step is to develop the organs which produce sound.*

Actually this is the method one uses with deaf mutes before getting them to articulate; and the moment I began to consider this, analogies between the deaf mute and the ape crowded into my mind. First of all, there is that extraordinary aptitude for mimicry, compensating for the lack of articulated speech, and proving that failure to speak does not argue failure to think, even though the second faculty may be impaired by the paralysis of the first. Then there are other traits, more particular because more specific: diligence in work, fidelity, fortitude—increased, certainly, by two factors which (and surely this is revealing) are allied: an aptitude for feats of balance, and resistance to dizziness.

I decided, then, to begin with a series of exercises for the lips and tongue, treating my ape as I would a deaf mute. After that his ear would enable me to establish direct communication, I should not have to resort to the sense of touch. The reader will see that in this I was planning ahead too optimistically.

Happily, of all the great apes the chimpanzee has the most mobile lips; and in this particular case Yzur, having been subject to sore throat, knew how to open his mouth wide for examination. The first inspection partly confirmed my suspicions: his tongue lay on the floor of his mouth like an inert mass, moving only in order to swallow. The exercises shortly began to produce results: at the end of two months he could stick out his tongue at me. This was the first association he made between the movement of his tongue and an idea, an association, moreover, quite in accordance with his nature.

The lips gave more trouble: they even had to be stretched with pincers. But he fully realized—perhaps from the expression of my face—the importance of that singular task, and performed it with zeal. While I demonstrated the lip movements he was supposed to imitate, he would sit there with one arm twisted behind him, scratching his rump, his face screwed up in mingled concentration and doubt, or rubbing his hairy cheeks, for all the world like a man using rhythmic gestures as an aid to setting his thoughts in order. In the end he learned how to move his lips.

But speech is a difficult art: for proof there is the child's extended period of stammering, paralleling the development of his intellect, until speech becomes a habit with him. Indeed, it has been shown that the center of voice production is linked with the speech center of the brain; as early as 1785 Heinicke, inventor of the oral method of teaching deaf mutes, had guessed that this was a logical consequence. The profound lucidity of his phrase "the dynamic concatenation of ideas" would do honor to more than one present-day psychologist.

With regard to speech, Yzur was in the same situation as the child, who already understands many words before he begins to talk; but his greater experience of life made him far quicker to associate ideas and to reach conclusions. Conclusions not based on mere impressions; to judge by their varied character they must have been the fruit of intellectual curiosity and a spirit of inquiry. All this indicated a capacity for abstract reasoning and a superior intelligence which would be highly favorable to my purpose.

If my theory appears too bold, you have only to reflect that there are many animals to whose mind the syllogism, the basis of all logic, is not foreign. For the syllogism is primarily a comparison between two sensations. Otherwise, why is it that animals who know man avoid him, while those who have never known him do not?

And so I began Yzur's phonetic education. The point was to teach him the mechanics first of all, leading him on gradually to rational speech. Since the ape possessed a voice—he had this advantage over the deaf mute, besides having a rudimentary control of the organs of articulation—the question was how to train him to modulate that voice, how to produce those sounds which speech teachers call static if they are vowels, dynamic if they are consonants.

Considering the greediness of the ape tribe, and following a method which Heinicke had employed with deaf mutes, I decided to associate each vowel with something tasty to eat: *a* with *potato*, *e* with *cream*, *i* with *wine*, *o* with *cocoa*, *u* with *sugar*, in such a way that the vowel would be contained in the name of the tidbit either alone and repeated as in *cocoa*, or combining the basic sounds in both accented and unaccented syllables, as in *potato*. All went smoothly while we were on the vowels, the sounds, that is, which are formed with the mouth open. Yzur learned them in two weeks. The *u* was the hardest for him.

But I had the devil of a time with the consonants. I was soon forced to admit he would never be able to pronounce those consonants which involve the teeth and the gums. His long eye teeth were an absolute impediment. He would always be limited to the five vowels, plus *b*, *k*, *m*, *g*, *f* and *c*, the consonants which require the action of the tongue and the palate only. Even for this much, his hearing alone was not sufficient. I had to resort to the sense of touch, as one does with deaf mutes, placing his hand first on my chest and then on his, so that he could feel the sound vibrations.

Three years passed, and I had still not succeeded in getting him to form a single word. He tended to name things after the letter that predominated in them. That was all.

In the circus he had learned to bark, like the dogs he worked side by side with; and when he saw me in despair over my vain attempts to wrest a word from him, he would bark loudly, as though trying to offer me all he had to give. He could pronounce isolated vowels and consonants, but he could not combine them. The best he could produce was a dizzying series of repeated *p*'s and *m*'s.

For all the slowness of his progress, a great change had come over him. His face was less mobile, his expression more serious, his attitudes were those of a creature deep in thought. He had acquired, for instance, the habit of gazing at the stars. . . . And at the same time his sensibilities had developed: I noticed that he was easily moved to tears.

The lessons continued with unremitting determination, but with no greater success. The whole business had become a painful obsession with me; and as time went on I felt inclined to resort to force. The failure was embittering my disposition, filling me with unconscious resentment against Yzur. As his intellect developed he withdrew into a stubborn silence which I was beginning to believe I should never draw him out of, when I suddenly discovered that he wasn't speaking because he chose not to!

One evening the horrified cook came to tell me he had overheard the ape "speaking real words." According to his story, Yzur had been squatting beside a fig-tree in the garden; but the cook's terror prevented him from recalling what was the real point, the actual words. He thought he could remember two: *bed* and *pipe*. I came near to kicking him for his stupidity.

Needless to say the profoundest agitation preyed upon me the whole night through; and what I had not done in the three years, the mistake that ruined everything was the result of the exasperation that followed on that sleepless night, and of my overweening curiosity as well. Instead of allowing the ape to arrive at his natural pace to the point of revealing his command of speech, I summoned him the next day and tried to compel him to it. All I could get out of him was the *p*'s and *m*'s I'd already had my fill of, the hypocritical winks, and—may God forgive me—a hint of mockery in the incessant grimaces. I lost my temper: without thinking twice, I beat him. The only result was tears and absolute silence, unbroken even by moans.

Three days later he fell ill, with a kind of deep depression complicated by symptoms of meningitis. Leeches, cold showers, purgatives, counter-irritants, tincture of alcohol, bromides—every remedy for the terrible illness was applied to him. Driven by remorse and fear, I struggled with desperate energy. Remorse for the cruelty which had made him its victim, fear for the secret he might perhaps be carrying with him to the grave.

After a long time he began to improve, but he was still too feeble to stir from his bed. The closeness of death had ennobled and humanized him. His eyes, filled with gratitude, never left me, following me about the room like two revolving globes, even when I was behind him; his hand sought mine in the companionship of convalescence. In my great solitude he was rapidly assuming the importance of a person.

Yet the demon of investigation, which is only one other form of the spirit of perversity, kept urging me on to renew my experiment. The ape had actually talked. It was impossible simply to let it go at that.

I began very slowly, asking for the letters he knew how to pronounce. Nothing! I left him alone for hours at a time, spying on him through a chink in the wall. Nothing! I spoke to him in brief sentences, trying to appeal to his loyalty or his greediness. Nothing! When my words moved him, his eyes would fill with tears. When I uttered a familiar phrase, such as the "I am your master" with which every lesson began, or the "You are my ape" with which I completed the statement, to impress upon his mind the conviction of a total truth, he would close his eyelids by way of assent; but he would not utter a sound, not even move his lips.

He had reverted to sign language as the only way of communicating with me; and this circumstance, together with the analogies between him and deaf mutes, led me to redouble my precautions, for everyone knows that mutes are extremely subject to mental illness. I had moments of wishing he would really lose his mind, to see if delirium would at last break his silence.

His convalescence had come to a halt. The same emaciation, the same depression. It was clear he was ill and suffering, in body and mind. The abnormal effort demanded of his brain had shattered his organic unity, and sooner or later he would become a hopeless case. But for all his submissiveness, which increased still more as the illness took its course, his silence, that despairing silence my fury had driven him to, would not yield. Out of a dim past of tradition that had petrified and become instinct, the species was forcing its millennial mutism on the animal, whose ancestral will was strengthened by his own inner being. The primitive men of the jungle, driven into silence, to intellectual suicide that is, were guarding their secret; ancient mysteries of the forest, formidable with the immense weight of ages, dictated that unconscious decision that Yzur was now making.

In the race we call evolution, man had overtaken the anthropoid and crushed him with savage brutality, dethroning the great families who ruled their primitive Eden, thinning their ranks, capturing their females so that organized slavery might begin in the very womb. Until, beaten and helpless, they expressed their human dignity by breaking the higher but fatal bond—speech—that linked them to the enemy, and as their last salvation took refuge in the dark night of the animal kingdom.

And what horrors, what monstrous excesses of cruelty the conquerors must have inflicted upon this half-beast in the course of his evolution to make him—once he had tasted the joys of the intellect, the forbidden fruit of the Bible—resign himself to stultifying his mind in degrading equality with inferior beings; to that retrogression which fixed his intelligence for ever, leaving him a robot, an acrobat, a clown; to that fear of life which would bend his servile back as a sign of his animal condition, and imprint upon him that melancholy bewilderment which is his basic trait.

This is what had aroused my evil temper, buried deep in some atavist limbo, on the very brink of success. Across the millions of years the magic of the word still kept its power to stir the simian soul; but against that temptation which was about to pierce the dark shadows of animal instinct, ancestral memories that filled his race with some instinctive horror were heaping age upon age as a barrier.

Yzur did not lose consciousness as death approached. It was a gentle death, with closed eyes, faint breathing, feeble pulse, and perfect tranquillity, interrupted only at intervals, when he would turn his sad old mulatto face toward me with a heart-rending expression of eternity. And the last afternoon, the afternoon he died, the extraordinary thing occurred that decided me to write this account.

Overcome by the heat, drowsy with the quiet of the twilight coming on, I had dozed off by his bedside. Suddenly I felt something gripping my wrist. I woke up with a start. The ape, his eyes wide open, was dying, unmistakably, and his look was so human that I was seized with horror; yet something expressive in his hands and in his eyes impelled me to bend over him. And then with his last breath, the last breath which at once crowned and blasted all my hopes, he murmured (how can I describe the tone of a voice which has not spoken for ten thousand centuries?) these words, whose humanity reconciled our two species:

"Water, master. Master, my master. . . ."

TRANSLATED BY GREGORY WOODRUFF

Horacio Quiroga

Uruguay
(1878–1937)

———— \\ ————

Most historians agree that the modern Latin American short story began with
Horacio Quiroga, still considered a master worthy of imitation. Quiroga managed
to combine Latin American settings and themes, like the jungle and violence,
with flawless execution, devoid of sentimentality or local color. Quiroga's own
life was haunted by violent death. His father was killed in a hunting accident and
his stepfather committed suicide. Quiroga's wife also committed suicide, as did
Quiroga, who was ill with cancer at the time. His fascination with morbid states
of mind and the deleterious effects of nature on the individual are topics of the
period, and it is not difficult to see in some of his stories the influence of Edgar
Allan Poe. After attending university at Montevideo and a ritual season in Paris,
in 1906 he settled in the tropical jungle region of Misiones, in northern Argentina,
which became the source of many of Quiroga's works. *Cuentos de amor, de
locura y de muerte,* or *Stories about Love, Madness and Death,* appeared in
1917. This influential short story collection combined his experiences in Misiones
with a somber, even gruesome sense of life. Quiroga's world is one ruled by
tragedy. "The Decapitated Chicken," which anticipates some of William Faulkner's obsessions and themes, is perhaps Quiroga's most representative story.
However he has so many excellent ones that it would be difficult to claim that it
is his best. His *Cuentos de la selva,* published in 1918 and in English as *South
American Jungle Tales* in 1922, confirmed him as the leader of a new type of
writing, one free of the often superficial glitter of the *modernistas*. Quiroga practiced the short story as his main genre and theorized about it, somewhat tongue
in cheek, in his famous "Decalogue of the Perfect Story Teller." In Quiroga's
writings it was as if literature had been kicked outside to face the turbulent natural
and human landscape of the New World. Most major prose writers of the Southern Cone, such as Güiraldes, Borges, and Cortázar, recognized their debt to
Quiroga, a tragic figure in his own right.

The Decapitated Chicken

All day long the four idiot sons of the couple Mazzini-Ferraz sat on a
bench in the patio. Their tongues protruded from between their lips;
their eyes were dull; their mouths hung open as they turned their heads.

The patio had an earthen floor and was closed to the west by a brick wall. The bench was five feet from the wall, parallel to it, and there they sat, motionless, their gaze fastened on the bricks. As the sun went down, disappearing behind the wall, the idiots rejoiced. The blinding light was always what first gained their attention; little by little by little their eyes lighted up; finally, they would laugh uproariously, each infected by the same uneasy hilarity, staring at the sun with bestial joy, as if it were something to eat.

Other times, lined up on the bench, they hummed for hours on end, imitating the sound of the trolley. Loud noises, too, shook them from their inertia, and at those times they ran around the patio, biting their tongues and mewing. But almost always they were sunk in the somber lethargy of idiocy, passing the entire day seated on their bench, their legs hanging motionless, dampening their pants with slobber.

The oldest was twelve and the youngest eight. Their dirty and slovenly appearance was testimony to the total lack of maternal care.

These four idiots, nevertheless, had once been the joy of their parents' lives. When they had been married three months, Mazzini and Berta had oriented the self-centered love of man and wife, wife and husband, toward a more vital future: a son. What greater happiness for two people in love than that blessed consecration of an affection liberated from the vile egotism of purposeless love and—what is worse for love itself—love without any possible hope of renewal?

So thought Mazzini and Berta, and, when after fourteen months of matrimony their son arrived, they felt their happiness complete. The child prospered, beautiful and radiant, for a year and a half. But one night in his twentieth month he was racked by terrible convulsions, and the following morning he no longer recognized his parents. The doctor examined him with the kind of professional attention that obviously seeks to find the cause of the illness in the infirmities of the parents.

After a few days the child's paralyzed limbs recovered their movement, but the soul, the intelligence, even instinct, were gone forever. He lay on his mother's lap, an idiot, driveling, limp, to all purposes dead.

"Son, my dearest son!" the mother sobbed over the frightful ruin of her first-born.

The father, desolate, accompanied the doctor outside.

"I can say it to you; I think it is a hopeless case. He might improve, be educated to the degree his idiocy permits, but nothing more."

"Yes! Yes . . . !" Mazzini assented. "But tell me: do you think it is heredity, that . . . ?"

"As far as the paternal heredity is concerned, I told you what I thought when I saw your son. As for the mother's, there's a lung there that doesn't sound too good. I don't see anything else, but her breathing is slightly ragged. Have her thoroughly examined."

With his soul tormented by remorse, Mazzini redoubled his love for his son, the idiot child who was paying for the excesses of his grandfather. At the same time he had to console, to ceaselessly sustain Berta, who was wounded to the depths of her being by the failure of her young motherhood.

As is only natural, the couple put all their love into the hopes for another son. A son was born, and his health and the clarity of his laughter rekindled their extinguished hopes. But at eighteen months the convulsions of the first-born were repeated, and on the following morning the second son awoke an idiot.

This time the parents fell into complete despair. So it was their blood, their love, that was cursed. Especially their love! He, twenty-eight; she, twenty-two; and all their passionate tenderness had not succeeded in creating one atom of normal life. They no longer asked for beauty and intelligence as for the first-born—only a son, a son like any other!

From the second disaster burst forth new flames of aching love, a mad desire to redeem once and for all the sanctity of their tenderness. Twins were born; and step by step the history of the two older brothers was repeated.

Even so, beyond the immense bitterness, Mazzini and Berta maintained great compassion for their four sons. They must wrest from the limbo of deepest animality, not their souls, lost now, but instinct itself. The boys could not swallow, move about, or even sit up. They learned, finally, to walk, but they bumped into things because they took no notice of obstacles. When they were washed, they mewed and gurgled until their faces were flushed. They were animated only by food or when they saw brilliant colors or heard thunder. Then they laughed, radiant with bestial frenzy, pushing out their tongues and spewing rivers of slaver. On the other hand, they possessed a certain imitative faculty, but nothing more.

The terrifying line of descent seemed to have been ended with the twins. But with the passage of three years Mazzini and Berta once again ardently desired another child, trusting that the long interim would have appeased their destiny.

Their hopes were not satisfied. And because of this burning desire and exasperation from its lack of fulfillment, the husband and wife grew bitter. Until this time each had taken his own share of responsibility for the misery their children caused, but hopelessness for the redemption of the four animals born to them finally created that imperious necessity to blame others that is the specific patrimony of inferior hearts.

It began with a change of pronouns: your sons. And since they intended to trap, as well as insult each other, the atmosphere became charged.

"It seems to me," Mazzini, who had just come in and was washing his hands, said to Berta, "that you could keep the boys cleaner."

As if she hadn't heard him, Berta continued reading.

"It's the first time," she replied after a pause, "I've seen you concerned about the condition of your sons."

Mazzini turned his head toward her with a forced smile.

"Our sons, I think."

"All right, our sons. Is that the way you like it?" She raised her eyes.

This time Mazzini expressed himself clearly.

"Surely you're not going to say *I'm* to blame, are you?"

"Oh, no!" Berta smiled to herself, very pale. "But neither am I, I imagine! That's all I needed . . . ," she murmured.

"What? What's all you needed?"

"Well, if anyone's to blame, it isn't me, just remember that! That's what I meant."

Her husband looked at her for a moment with a brutal desire to wound her.

"Let's drop it!" he said finally, drying his hands.

"As you wish, but if you mean . . ."

"Berta!"

"As you wish!"

This was the first clash, and others followed. But, in the inevitable reconciliations, their souls were united in redoubled rapture and eagerness for another child.

So a daughter was born. Mazzini and Berta lived for two years with anguish as their constant companion, always expecting another disaster. It did not occur, however, and the parents focused all their contentment on their daughter, who took advantage of their indulgence to become spoiled and very badly behaved.

Although even in the later years Berta had continued to care for the four boys, after Bertita's birth she virtually ignored the other children. The very thought of them horrified her, like the memory of something atrocious she had been forced to perform. The same thing happened to Mazzini, though to a lesser degree.

Nevertheless, their souls had not found peace. Their daughter's least indisposition now unleashed—because of the terror of losing her—the bitterness created by their unsound progeny. Bile had accumulated for so long that the distended viscera spilled venom at the slightest touch. From the moment of the first poisonous quarrel Mazzini and Berta had lost respect for one another, and if there is anything to which man feels himself drawn with cruel fulfillment it is, once begun, the complete humiliation of another person. Formerly they had been restrained by their mutual failure; now that success had come, each, attributing it to himself, felt more strongly the infamy of the four misbegotten sons the other had forced him to create.

With such emotions there was no longer any possibility of affection for the four boys. The servant dressed them, fed them, put them to bed, with gross brutality. She almost never bathed them. They spent most of the day facing the wall, deprived of anything resembling a caress.

So Bertita celebrated her fourth birthday, and that night, as a result of the sweets her parents were incapable of denying her, the child had a slight chill and fever. And the fear of seeing her die or become an idiot opened once again the ever-present wound.

For three hours they did not speak to each other, and, as usual, Mazzini's swift pacing served as a motive.

"My God! Can't you walk more slowly? How many times . . . ?"

"All right, I just forget. I'll stop. I don't do it on purpose."

She smiled, disdainful.

"No, no, of course I don't think that of you!"

"And I would never have believed that of you . . . you consumptive!"

"What! What did you say?"

"Nothing!"

"Oh, yes, I heard you say something! Look, I don't know what you said, but I swear I'd prefer anything to having a father like yours!"

Mazzini turned pale.

"At last!" he muttered between clenched teeth. "At last, viper, you've said what you've been wanting to!"

"Yes, a viper, yes! But I had healthy parents, you hear? Healthy! My father didn't die in delirium! I could have had sons like anybody else's! Those are your sons, those four!"

Mazzini exploded in his turn.

"Consumptive viper! That's what I called you, what I want to tell you! Ask him, ask the doctor who's to blame for your sons' meningitis: my father or your rotten lung? Yes, viper!"

They continued with increasing violence, until a moan from Bertita instantly sealed their lips. By one o'clock in the morning the child's light indigestion had disappeared, and, as it inevitably happens with all young married couples who have loved intensely, even for a while, they effected a reconciliation, all the more effusive for the infamy of the offenses.

A splendid day dawned, and as Berta arose she spit up blood. Her emotion and the terrible night were, without any doubt, primarily responsible. Mazzini held her in his embrace for a long while, and she cried hopelessly, but neither of them dared say a word.

At ten, they decided that after lunch they would go out. They were pressed for time so they ordered the servant to kill a hen.

The brilliant day had drawn the idiots from their bench. So while the servant was cutting off the head of the chicken in the kitchen, bleeding it parsimoniously (Berta had learned from her mother this effective method of conserving the freshness of meat), she thought she sensed something like breathing behind her. She turned and saw the four idiots, standing shoulder to shoulder, watching the operation with stupefaction. Red. . . . Red. . . .

"Señora! The boys are here in the kitchen."

Berta came in immediately; she never wanted them to set foot in the kitchen. Not even during these hours of full pardon, forgetfulness, and regained happiness could she avoid this horrible sight! Because, naturally, the more intense her raptures of love for her husband and daughter, the greater her loathing for the monsters.

"Get them out of here, María! Throw them out! Throw them out, I tell you!"

The four poor little beasts, shaken and brutally shoved, went back to their bench.

After lunch, everyone went out; the servant to Buenos Aires and the couple and child for a walk among the country houses. They returned as the sun was sinking, but Berta wanted to talk for a while with her neighbors across the way. Her daughter quickly ran into the house.

In the meantime, the idiots had not moved from their bench the whole day. The sun had crossed the wall now, beginning to sink behind it, while they continued to stare at the bricks, more sluggish than ever.

Suddenly, something came between their line of vision and the wall. Their sister, tired of five hours with her parents, wanted to look around a bit on her own. She paused at the base of the wall and looked thoughtfully at its summit. She wanted to climb it; this could not be doubted. Finally she decided on a chair with the seat missing, but still she couldn't reach the top. Then she picked up a kerosene tin and, with a fine sense of relative space, placed it upright on the chair—with which she triumphed.

The four idiots, their gaze indifferent, watched how their sister succeeded patiently in gaining her equilibrium and how, on tiptoe, she rested her neck against the top of the wall between her straining hands. They watched her search everywhere for a toe hold to climb up higher.

The idiots' gaze became animated; the same insistent light fixed in all their pupils. Their eyes were fixed on their sister, as the growing sensation of bestial gluttony changed every line of their faces. Slowly they advanced toward the wall. The little girl, having succeeded in finding a toe hold and about to straddle the wall and surely fall off the other side, felt herself seized by one leg. Below her, the eight eyes staring into hers frightened her.

"Let loose! Let me go!" she cried, shaking her leg, but she was captive.

"Mama! Oh, Mama! Mama, Papa!" she cried imperiously. She tried still to cling to the top of the wall, but she felt herself pulled, and she fell.

"Mama, oh, Ma——" She could cry no more. One of the boys

squeezed her neck, parting her curls as if they were feathers, and the other three dragged her by one leg toward the kitchen where that morning the chicken had been bled, holding her tightly, drawing the life out of her second by second.

Mazzini, in the house across the way, thought he heard his daughter's voice.

"I think she's calling you," he said to Berta.

They listened, uneasy, but heard nothing more. Even so, a moment later they said good-by, and, while Berta went to put up her hat, Mazzini went into the patio.

"Bertita!"

No one answered.

"Bertita!" He raised his already altered voice.

The silence was so funereal to his eternally terrified heart that a chill of horrible presentiment ran up his spine.

"My daughter, my daughter!" He ran frantically toward the back of the house. But as he passed by the kitchen he saw a sea of blood on the floor. He violently pushed open the half-closed door and uttered a cry of horror.

Berta, who had already started running when she heard Mazzini's anguished call, cried out, too. But as she rushed toward the kitchen, Mazzini, livid as death, stood in her way, holding her back.

"Don't go in! Don't go in!"

But Berta had seen the blood-covered floor. She could only utter a hoarse cry, throw her arms above her head and, leaning against her husband, sink slowly to the floor.

TRANSLATED BY MARGARET SAYERS PEDEN

João do Rio (Paulo Barreto)

Brazil
(1881–1921)

A bohemian interested in decadent types, Paulo Barreto (who published under the name João do Rio) chronicled the adventures of the Carioca (people from Rio) upper class. He himself was engaged in many of the activities portrayed in his stories. According to K. David Jackson's elegant formulation, Barreto's life and art "imitated each other in polished phrases." He delights in presenting cases of sexual deviancy and the various other pastimes of bored pseudo-aristocrats looking for thrills to animate their lives. Barreto's stories are titillating, vaguely pornographic, an experience in themselves of what they depict. But they contain, too, rather explicit social criticism. They have been collected in *Dentro da noite* (1910), *A mulher e os espelhos* (1918), and *Rosário da ilusão* (1912). Barreto's production was substantial despite his very short life. "The Baby in Pink Buckram" is his best-known tale. It is a story within a story, with a built-in coterie of readers who comment upon it. Barreto takes advantage of Rio de Janeiro's famous Carnival to have his main character, Heitor de Andrade, sink in an atmosphere of systematic amorality. There is bitter social commentary in de Andrade's pursuit of pleasure among the lower classes, the lumpen, of Rio. He goes slumming in search of a sexual jolt. The woman he encounters, disguised as a baby in pink, is a mockery of the romantic notion of human innocence perverted by society. De Andrade's depraved desire is a form of truly repulsive pedophilia. The grotesqueness of the woman's real face gives the story a baroque exemplariness: she becomes an image of death while in the guise of a newborn. In this the story reflects and partakes of the profound meaning of Carnival as a collective ritual of renewal.

The Baby in Pink Buckram

"A h! A tale of masks! Is there anyone who hasn't been through one during his lifetime? Carnival is only interesting because it gives us that feeling of something anticipated and unforeseen. Everybody has a Carnival story, delightful or macabre, chilling or full of heavy lust. Carnival without adventure isn't Carnival. I had an adventure just this year. . . ." And Heitor de Andrade stretched lazily on the couch, enjoying our curiosity.

125

In the study were Baron Belfort; Anatólio de Azambuja, who'd earned the ill will of so many women; and Maria de Flor, the extravagant bohemian; and they were all burning to find out about Heitor's adventure. An expectant silence fell. Heitor, lighting up a genuine Gianaclis, seemed absorbed.

"Was it a pleasant adventure?" Maria asked.

"That depends on one's temperament."

"Scroungy?"

"Grisly to say the least."

"During the day?"

"No. Between midnight and dawn."

"So come on there, tell us about it!" Anatólio begged. "Look how Maria's suffering."

Heitor took a long drag on his cigarette. "During Carnival everybody comes out all ready to go the limit, ready for raptures of the flesh and all kinds of wild things. Desire, close to being morbid, is kind of instilled, infiltrated into the atmosphere. Everything is giving off lust, everything's all full of anxiety and ecstasy, and during those four paranoid days, with the jumps, the yells, the unlimited familiarity, everything's possible. Nobody's satisfied with just one woman. . . ."

"Or just one man," Anatólio put in.

"Smiles are given easily, eyes entreat, throats catch the tingle of nettles in the air. It's possible that a lot of people manage to be indifferent. I get that feeling. And when I go out into the low life of the city I go along the way Phoenician sailors went during the Spring Procession or Alexandrians on Aphrodite's night."

"Right on!" Maria de Flor whispered.

"Of course, this year I got together with a group of four or five actresses and four or five buddies. I didn't have the courage to be all alone like a limp rag in the swells of sensuality and pleasure all through the city. The group was my life jacket. On the first day, Saturday, we went by car to all the balls. We went along without any distinction, drinking champagne at athletic clubs that advertised balls and on to the basest dance halls. It was rather amusing and by the time we got to the fifth club we were all worked up. That was when I thought about a visit to the public dance on the Recreio. 'Good God!' the first music-hall star with us said. 'It's awful! All those common people, sailors in civvies, sluts from the depths of the Rua de São Jorge, an awful stink, fights all the time . . .' So what? Shall we all go?

"That was it. We all went, with the women in costume. There was nothing to be afraid of and we were able to fulfill our greatest desire: to go degenerate, to do a thorough job of debasing ourselves. We went, naturally, and it was a disaster of thick-lipped, toothless black women lounging in their stinking velveteens on the platform with the military band, all the johns from their dismal alleys, and the strange figures of diabolical larvae, incubi in bottles of alcohol, that lost women from certain streets have, young, but with their features kind of squashed in, all of them pale, as pale as blotting paper or onion skin. It was nothing new. Except that since the group had stopped in front of the dancers, rubbing against me, chubby and appealing, I felt a baby in pink buckram. I looked at her legs in knee socks. Nice. I checked her arms, the slope of her shoulders, the curve of her breasts. Quite nice. As for her face, it was a bold little face, with two perverse eyes and a fleshy mouth that was kind of offering itself. The only thing artificial about her was the nose, such a well-shaped nose, just right, and you had to take a close look to see that it was false. I was sure of it. I stuck out my hand and pinched her. The baby sank down even lower and said with a sigh, 'Oh, that hurts!' You're all waiting to see how I was immediately ready to get away from the group. But there were five or six elegant ladies with me, capable of debauchery but not ready to forgive excesses in others and it was out of bounds for me to run off like that, abandoning them, chasing after someone from the dances at the Recreio. We went back to our cars and went off to dine at the most chic and boring club in the city."

"What about the baby?"

"The baby was left behind. But on Sunday, right there on the Avenida, riding next to the driver in that wild turmoil, I felt a pinch on my leg and a hoarse voice saying, 'That's to pay you back for yesterday.' I looked. It was the pink baby, smiling at me with her artificial nose, that so perfect nose. I just had time to ask her, 'Where are you off to today?' 'Everywhere,' she answered, getting lost in a raucous group."

"She was chasing you!" Maria de Flor commented.

"Maybe it was a man," friendly old Anatólio snorted suspiciously.

"Don't interrupt Heitor!" the baron said, holding up his hand.

Heitor lighted another gold-tipped Gianaclis, smiled, and went on. "I didn't see her again that night and I didn't see her on Monday either. On Tuesday I broke away from the group and fell into the high seas of depravity, alone, wearing light clothing over my skin and with all my evil instincts riding high. The whole city was like that too. It's the time when, behind their masks, girls confess their passions to boys, it's the moment when the most secret unions become transparent, it's when virginity becomes dubious and all of us find it useless, chastity a bore, and common sense wearisome. At that moment everything's possible, the wildest bits of absurdity, the greatest crimes. At that moment there's laughter that galvanizes the senses and kisses are turned loose naturally.

"I was thrilled, with an almost morbid urge toward swinishness. I wanted nothing to do with showy whores all perfumed and too well-known, nothing to do with familiar contacts, but I wanted an anonymous debauchery, the ritual debauchery of arriving, grabbing, finishing, going on my way. It was ignoble. Fortunately a lot of people suffer from the same malady at Carnival."

"You can say that again! . . ." Maria de Flor sighed.

"But I was out of luck, with a case of *guigne,* with the bad luck our departed Indians used to call *caiporismo.* It was a matter of getting close and the projected prey's running away. I ran into São Pedro, got involved in the dances, rubbing up against people who weren't so clean. I repeated it here, there. Nothing doing!"

"That's when you get the most nervous!"

"Exactly. I was nervous all the way to the end of the dancing. I watched everybody leaving and I went off all the more desperate. It was three o'clock in the morning. The movement on the streets had let up. Other dances had finished now. The squares, all lighted up before with spotlights and smoking trails from Roman candles had fallen into the shadows— shadows that were the accomplices of the pre-dawn city. And showing the revelry, the excitement of the city, only here and there was an exhausted car carrying masked people kissing or someone in costume swinging a ratchet along the street fluffy with confetti. Oh, what a debilitating sight, those unreal figures in the half-shadows of the silent hours, scraping along the pavement, giving off the last sound of a ratchet here and there! It's like something you can't touch, vague, enormous, coming out of the shadows piece by piece. . . . And the hooded costumes, the crumpled ballerinas, the undecided collection of last-minute maskers dragging themselves along in exhaustion! I decided to walk through the Largo do Rocio and was passing by the Interior Ministry when I saw there, standing, the baby in pink buckram.

"There she was! I felt my heart beating. I stopped. 'Good friends always find each other,' I said. The baby smiled without saying a word. 'Are you waiting for someone?' She nodded her head no. I put my arm around her. 'Will you come with me?' 'Where?' she asked in her harsh, hoarse voice.

"'Wherever you want!' I took her hands. They were damp but well cared for. I tried to give her a kiss. She drew back. My lips only touched the tip of her nose. I was out of my mind.

"Almost . . .

"It wasn't necessary anymore in Carnival, especially when she said in her panting and lecherous voice, 'Not here!' I put my arm around her waist and we walked along without saying a word. She was leaning against me, but she was the one leading the way and her moist eyes seemed to be gathering in all the bestial desire that mine were speaking. There's no talking in those phrases of love. We didn't exchange a single word. She could feel the disordered rhythm of my heart and my desperate blood. What a woman! What vibrations! We'd gone back to the park. At the entrance on the Rua Leopoldina she stopped, hesitated. Then she tugged me along, crossed the square. We went into the dark street without lights. At the end was the Fine Arts building, desolate and mournful. I hugged her closer. She snuggled up more. The way her eyes shined! We crossed the Rua Luís de Camões and were right under the thick shadows of the Conservatory of Music. The silence was enormous and the atmosphere had a vaguely reddish tint as darkness was pushed back a bit by the glow of the distant streetlights. My pink and chubby little baby looked like something sin had forgotten in the austerity of the night. 'So, shall we go?' I asked. 'Where?' 'To your place.' 'Oh, no, you can't at my place. . . . ' 'Anywhere then.' 'Go in, go out, get undressed. I'm not that kind!' 'What do you want, child? We can't stay here on the street. A policeman might come by at any moment.' 'What's that got to do with it?' 'It's not impossible for them to pick us up here and make a nice end of it all as Ash Wednesday dawns. Then, when four o'clock comes you've got to take off your mask.' 'What mask?' 'The nose.' 'Oh, yes!' And without saying another word she pulled me toward her. I hugged her. I kissed her arms, I kissed her neck, I kissed her chin. Her mouth was offered to me greedily. All around us the world was kind of opaque and indecisive. I sucked on her lip.

"But my nose felt the contact with her artificial nose, a nose that smelled of resin, a nose that made things bad. 'Take off your nose!' She whispered, 'No! No! It's so hard to put on!' I tried not to touch that nose, so cold over that fire-hot flesh.

"The piece of cardboard bulged, however, seemed to grow, and I felt a curious upset, a state of strange inhibition. 'Hell! You're not going home with that! After all, it doesn't disguise anything.' 'Yes, it does disguise something!' 'No!' I looked for the cord in her hair. There wasn't any. But, hugging me, kissing me, the baby in pink buckram was like a possessed woman in a hurry. Once more her lips came close to my mouth. I gave in. The nose rubbed up against mine, the nose wasn't hers, a mask nose. Then, unable to resist, I raised my hand, brought it closer while I hugged her tighter with the left one, and in a flash I grabbed the piece of cardboard, tore it off. Caught by my lips, with two eyes where rage and fright seemed to be joined, I found a strange head, a head without a nose, with two bloody holes stuffed with cotton, a head that was a hallucination—a skull with flesh. . . .

"I let go of her as if vomiting myself up. I was shaking all over with horror and nausea. The baby in pink buckram fell to the ground, her skull turned up toward me with a weeping that revealed her lips in a singular way under the hole that was her nose, her white teeth. 'I'm sorry! I'm sorry! Don't beat me! It's not my fault! It's only at Carnival that I can have fun, so I take advantage of it, understand? I take advantage. It was you who wanted . . .'

"I shook her furiously, stood her up with a wrench that must have put her bones out of joint. An urge to spit, to bring up phlegm clutched my throat and I got an urgent desire to punch that nose, break those teeth, kill that atrocious reverse side of lust. . . . But a whistle sounded. The policeman was on the corner looking at us, taking in that scene in the half-light. What was I to do? Take that skull to the police station? Tell everybody I'd kissed her? I gave up. I went off, picked up my pace, and when I got to the square I unconsciously took off on the run for home, with my jaws chattering, burning with fever.

"When I stopped at the door of the house to take out my key, I noticed that my right hand was clutching an oily, bloody mess. It was the nose of the baby in pink buckram. . . ."

Heitor de Andrade stopped. The cigarette between his fingers was out. Maria de Flor was showing the tightness of horror on her face and sweet Anatólio looked ill. The narrator himself had to daub drops of sweat off his face. There was an agonizing silence. Finally, Baron Belfort stood up, rang the bell for the servant to bring some drinks, and summed it up with:

"An adventure, my friends, a nice adventure. Who doesn't have his or her adventure at Carnival time? This one was thrilling at least."

And he went over to sit down at the piano.

TRANSLATED BY GREGORY RABASSA

Rafael Arévalo Martínez

Guatemala
(1884–1975)

———— \\ ————

Director of the national library for more than twenty years and his country's representative before the Pan American Union in 1946–47 in Washington, Rafael Arévalo Martínez was the political and literary counterpart of his better-known countryman, Nobel Prize winner Miguel Angel Asturias. Arévalo was an unabashed admirer of the United States, where, he said, "every superiority found its home." The selection included here, "The Man Who Resembled a Horse," according to John A. Crow's now dated judgment in *The Epic of Latin America* (1946), is "the most famous short story to come out of Latin America in this century." (A measure of the story's fame is this translation by the great American poet William Carlos Williams, done with his father.) The tale was first published in 1915 and was so successful that Arévalo embarked on other experiments in the same vein, which he called "psychozoological stories," involving a dog, a lioness, and so forth (probably remembering Kipling). He wrote many other stories, several novels, and also poetry, but Arévalo will forever be remembered for this story, which began as a satirical portrait of Colombian poet Porfirio Barba Jacob. The story's appeal lies in its luxuriant, indirect account of homoerotic desire. Señor de Aretal's resemblance to a horse includes his elegant yet brutal sexuality and his absolute disregard for morals. In this the story is very fin de siècle, much in tune with Nietzsche and Freud. Sexuality is transmuted into colors, gestures, physical beauty, and strength, untrammeled by the morals of the weak. Its language is like one would imagine that of the subconscious unleashed to be, except for the pull of desire toward the beautiful. All this is tempered by the ironic tone of the narrator, whose satirical stance nevertheless enters into the play of desire and rejection above which it wishes to place itself.

The Man Who Resembled a Horse

At the time we were presented he was at one end of the apartment, his head on one side, as horses are accustomed to stand, with an air of being unconscious of all going on around him. He had long, stiff, and dried-out limbs, strangely put together, like those of one of the characters in an English illustration of *Gulliver's Travels*. But my impression that the man in some mysterious way resembled a horse was not obtained then,

131

except in a subconscious manner, which might never have risen to the full life of consciousness had not my abnormal contact with the hero of this story been prolonged.

In this very first scene of our introduction Señor de Aretal began by way of welcome to exhibit the translucent strings of opals, amethysts, emeralds, and carbuncles which constituted his intimate treasure. In a first moment of dazzlement I spread myself out; I opened myself completely like a great white sheet, in order to make greater my surface of contact with the generous giver. The antennae of my soul went out, felt him and returned, tremulous, moved, delighted to give me the good news: "This is the man you awaited; this is the man in search of whom you peered into all unknown souls, for your intuition had affirmed to you long since that some day you would be enriched by the advent of a unique being. The avidity with which you have seized, stared into, and cast aside so many souls which made themselves desired and deceived your hope shall today be amply satisfied: Stoop and drink of this water."

And when he arose to go, I followed him, tied and a captive, like the lamb which the shepherdess bound with garlands of roses. Once in the living room of my new friend, having no more than crossed the threshold which gave him passage to a propitious and habitual environment, his entire person burst into flame. He became dazzling, picturesque like the horse of an emperor in a military parade. The skirts of his coat had a vague resemblance to the inner tunic of a steed of the Middle Ages harnessed for a journey. They fell below his meager buttocks, caressing his fine and distinguished thighs, and his theatrical performance began.

After a ritual of preparation carefully observed—knight initiate of a most ancient cult—and when our souls had already become concave, he brought forth his folio of verses with the unctuous deportment of a priest who draws near the altar. He was so grave that he imposed respect. A laugh would have been put to the knife in the instant of its birth.

He drew forth his first string of topazes, or, better said, his first series of strings of topazes, translucent and brilliant. His hands were raised with such cadence that the rhythm extended three worlds removed. By the power of the rhythm our room was moved entirely to the second floor, like a captive balloon, until it broke free from its earthly ties and carried us on a silent aerial journey. They were the translucid and radiant soul of minerals; they were the symmetrical and flinty soul of minerals.

And then the officiant of mineral things brought forth his second necklace. Oh, emeralds, divine emeralds! And he showed the third. Oh, diamonds, clear diamonds! And he brought the fourth and the fifth, which were again topazes like drops of light, with accumulations from the sun, with parts opaquely radiant. And then the seventh: his carbuncles! His carbuncles were—almost warm; they nearly moved me as might pomegranate pips or the blood of heroes; but I touched them and I felt them hard. By every means the soul of mineral things invaded me; that inorganic aristocracy seduced me strangely, without my fully comprehending. So much was this true that I could not translate the words of my inner master who was confused and made a vain effort to become hard and symmetrical and limited and brilliant; I remained dumb. And then, in an unforeseen explosion of offended dignity, believing himself deceived, the officiant took from me his necklace of carbuncles with a movement so full of violence but so just that it left me more perplexed than hurt. If it had been he of the roses he would not have acted in this way.

And then, as upon the breaking of a charm by that act of violence, the enchantment of the rhythm was shattered; and the little white boat in which we had been flying through the blue of the sky found itself solidly planted on the first floor of the house.

Later, our mutual friend, Señor de Aretal and I lunched together on the lower floor of the hotel.

In those moments I looked into the well of the soul of the master of the topazes. I saw many things reflected. As I looked in I had instinctively spread my peacock's tail; but I had spread it without an inner sense of the thing; simply urged by so much beauty perceived and desiring to show my best aspect in order to place myself in tone with it.

Oh, the things I saw in that well! The well was for me the very well of mystery itself. To look into a human soul, wide open as a well, which is an eye of the earth, is the same thing as to get a glimpse of God. We never can see the bottom. But we saturate ourselves in the moisture of the water, the great vehicle of love; and we are bedazzled with reflected light.

This well reflected the multiple external aspect of things in the very manner of Señor de Aretal. Certain figures showed more clearly than others on the surface of the water: there were reflected the classics—that treasure of tenderness and wisdom, the classics: but above all there was reflected the image of an absent friend with such purity of line and such exact coloring that the fact that this parallel should give me knowledge of the soul of *el Señor de la Rosa,* the absent friend so admired and loved, was not one of the least interesting attractions which the soul of Señor de Aretal possessed for me. Above all else there was reflected God, God, from whom I was never less distant. The great soul which for a time is brought into focus. I understood as I looked into the well of Señor de Aretal that he was a divine messenger. He brought a message to humanity—the human message, which has the greatest value of all. But he was an unconscious messenger. He lavished good, but he had it not in his possession.

Soon I interested my noble host to an unusual degree. I leant over the clear water of his spirit with such avidity that he was enabled to get a clear likeness of me. I had drawn sufficiently near and besides I was in addition a clear thing which did not intercept the light. Possibly I obscured him as much as he did me. It is a quality of things brought under hallucination to be in their turn hallucinators. This mutual attraction drew us together and brought us into intimate relationship. I frequented the divine temple of that beautiful soul. At its contact I began to take fire. Señor de Aretal was a lighted lamp and I was stuff ready to burn. Our souls communicated with each other. I held my hands extended and the soul of each one of my ten fingers was an antenna through which I received the knowledge of the soul of Señor de Aretal. Thus I became aware of many things unknown before. Through aerial routes—what else are the fingers, or velvety leaves, for what else but aerial routes are the leaves—I received something from that man which I had lacked till that time. I had been an adventurous shrub which prolongs its filaments until it finds the necessary humus in new earth. And how I fed! I fed with the joy of tremulous leaves of chlorophyll that spread themselves to the sun; with the joy with which a root encounters a decomposing corpse; with the joy with which convalescents take their vacillating steps in the light-flooded mornings of spring; with the joy with which a child clings to the nutritious breast and afterward, being full, smiles in his dreams at the vision of a snowy udder. Bah! All things which complete themselves have had that joy. God, some day, will be nothing more than a food for us: something needed for our life. Thus smile children and the young when they feel themselves gratified by nutrition.

Beyond that I took fire. Nutrition is combustion. Who knows what divine child shook over my spirit a sprinkling of gunpowder, of naphtha, of something easily inflammable; and Señor de Aretal, who had known how to draw near me, had set fire to it. I had the pleasure of burning; that is to say, of fulfilling my destiny. I understood that I was a thing easily inflammable. Oh, father fire, blessed be thou! My destiny is to burn. Fire is also a message. What other souls will take fire from me? To whom would I communicate my flame? Bah! Who can foretell the nature of a spark?

I burnt, and Señor de Aretal saw me burn. In marvelous harmony our two atoms of hydrogen and oxygen had approached so closely that, stretching themselves, throwing out particles, they almost succeeded in uniting into a living thing. At times they fluttered about like two butterflies which seek each other and make marvelous loops over the river and in the air. At other times they rose by virtue of their own rhythm and harmonious consonance, as rise the two wings of a distich. One was impregnating the other. Until . . .

Have you heard of those icebergs which, drawn into warm water by a submarine current, disintegrate at their base until, marvelous equilibrium being lost, they revolve upon themselves in an apocalyptic turning, rapid, unforeseen, presenting to the face of the sun what had before been hidden beneath the sea? Inverted they appear unconscious of the ships which, when their upper part went under, they caused to sink into the abyss. Unconscious of the loss of nests which had been built in their part heretofore turned to the light, in the relative stability of those two fragile things: eggs and ice.

Thus, suddenly, there began to take shape in the transparent angel of Señor de Aretal a dark, little, almost insubstantial cloud. It was the projected shadow of the horse that was drawing near.

Who could express my grief when there appeared in the angel of Señor de Aretal that thing—obscure, vague, and formless. My noble friend had gone down to the bar of the hotel in which he lived. Who was passing? Bah! A dark thing possessed of a horrible flattened nose and thin lips. Do you understand? If the line of the nose had been straight then also something would have been straightened in his soul. If his lips had been full, his sincerity would have been increased also. But no. Señor de Aretal had called him. There he was. . . . And my soul which at that instant had power to discern clearly, understood that that dwarf whom I had until then thought to be a man, since I one day saw his cheeks color with shame, was no more than a pygmy. With such nostrils one could not be sincere.

Invited by the master of the topazes, we seated ourselves at a table. They served us cognac and refreshments to take or leave. Here the harmony was broken. The alcohol broke it. I did not take any. He drank. But the alcohol was near me on the white marble table. It came between us and intercepted our souls. Furthermore, the soul of Señor de Aretal was no longer blue like mine. It was red and flat like that of the companion who separated us. Then I understood that what I had most loved in Señor de Aretal was my own blue.

Soon the flattened soul of Señor de Aretal began to speak of low things. All his thoughts had the crooked nose. All his thoughts drank alcohol and materialized grossly. He told us of a legion of Jamaican negresses, lewd and semi-naked, pursuing him with the offer of their odious merchandise for a nickel. His speech pained me, and soon his will pained me. He asked me insistently to drink alcohol. I yielded. But hardly had my sacrifice been consummated than I felt clearly that something was breaking between us— that our inner masters were withdrawing and that a divine equilibrium of crystals was tumbling down in silence. I told him so: "Señor de Aretal, you have broken our divine relationship in this very instant. Tomorrow you will see me arrive at your apartment, a man only, and I will meet only a man in you. In this very instant you have dyed me in red."

The following day in effect, I do not know what we did, Señor de Aretal and I. I believe we were walking along the street bent upon some sort of business. He was again ablaze. I was walking, thinking to myself that mystery had never opened so wide a slit for me to look through as in my relations with my strange fellow voyager. I had never felt so thoroughly the possibilities of man; I had never so well understood the intimate God as in my relations with Señor de Aretal.

We arrived at his room. His forms of thought were awaiting us. And all the while I felt myself far from Señor de Aretal. I felt far for many days, on many successive visits. I went to him, obeying inexorable laws. Because precisely that contact was required to consume a part in me, so dry until then, as if prepared the better to burn. All my pain of dryness hitherto now rejoiced in burning; all the pain of my emptiness hitherto now rejoiced in fullness. I sallied out of the night of my soul into a blazing dawn. It is well. Let us be brave. The dryer we are the better we shall burn. And so I went to that man and our inner masters rejoiced. Ah! But the enchantment of the first days. Now where?

When I had become resigned to find a man in Señor de Aretal, there returned anew the enchantment of his marvelous presence. I loved my friend. But it was impossible for me to throw aside the melancholy of the departed god. Translucid, diamantine lost wings! How might I recover them and return where we were?

One day Señor de Aretal found the medium propitious. We his hearers were several; verses were being recited in the room enchanted by his habitual creations. Suddenly, in the presence of some more beautiful than the rest, as upon a horn blast, our noble host arose pawing and prancing. And then and there I had my first vision: *Señor de Aretal stretched his neck like a horse.*

I attracted his attention: "Worthy host, I beg you to take this and this attitude." Yes: it was true: *he stretched his neck like a horse.*

Later, the second vision; the same day. We went out to walk. Of a sudden I perceived, I perceived it: *Señor de Aretal fell like a horse.* Suddenly his left foot gave way, then his haunches nearly touched the ground, like a horse that stumbles. He recovered himself quickly; but he had already given me the impression. Have you seen a horse fall?

Afterward another vision. Señor de Aretal looked at things like a horse. When he was drunk with his own words, as his own generous blood makes a high-bred steed drunk, tremulous as a leaf—trembling like a steed mounted and curbed, trembling like all living forms of nervous and fine fiber—he would bend down his head, he would turn his head sidewise, and thus he looked about, while his arms knitted something in the air, like the forepaws of a horse. What a magnificent thing a horse is! He almost stands upon two feet! And then I felt that the spirit was riding him.

And later a hundred visions more. Señor de Aretal approached women like a horse. In sumptuous parlors he could not remain quiet. He would draw alongside some lovely woman, newly introduced, with elastic and easy movements, bow his head and hold it on the side; he would take a turn around her and take a turn around the room.

Thus he looked sidelong. I was able to observe that his eyes were blood-shot. One day he broke one of the small vessels which color them with a delicate network: the little vessel broke and a tiny red stain colored his sclera. I called it to his attention.

"Bah," said he to me, "that is an old matter. I have suffered with it for three days. But have no time to see a doctor."

He walked to a glass and looked into it fixedly. When I returned on the following day, I found that one more virtue ennobled him. I asked him: "What beautifies you in this hour?" And he replied: "A hue." And he told me that he had put on a red necktie that it might harmonize with his red eye. Then I understood what had attracted my attention when saluting him. For the crystal spirit of Señor de Aretal was wont to take on the hue of surrounding things. And this is what his verses were: a marvelous collection of crystals tinged by the things about them: emeralds, rubies, opals. . . .

But this was at times sad because at times surrounding things were dark or discolored: the greens of the manure pile, the pale greens of sickly plants. I came to deplore finding him with others and when this happened I would leave Señor de Aretal under any pretext if his companion were not a person of clear colors.

For unfailingly Señor de Aretal reflected the spirit of his companion. One day I found him, he the noble steed, dwarfed and honeyed. And as in a mirror, I saw in the room a person dwarfed and honeyed. Sure enough, there she was. He presented her. A woman flattened, fat and low. Her spirit likewise was a low thing. Something trailing and humble; but inoffensive and desirous of pleasing. That person was the spirit of flattery. And Señor de Aretal also at that moment possessed a small soul, servile and obsequious. What convex mirror has brought about this horrible transformation? I asked myself, terrified. And at once all the air of the room appeared to me as a transparent convex glass which distorted the objects. How flattened the chairs were! Everything offered itself to be sat upon. Aretal was one hack horse the more.

On another occasion, at the table of a noisy group which laughed and drank, Aretal was one human the more, one more of the heap. I drew alongside him and saw him listed and the price fixed. He cracked jokes and brandished them like weapons of defense. He was a circus horse. All in that group were on exhibition. Another time he was a *jayán*. He entangled himself in abusive words with a brute of a man. He was like a market woman. He would have disgusted me; but I loved him so much that it made me sad. He was a kicking horse.

Finally there appeared on the physical plane a question which I had long been shaping: Which is the true spirit of Señor de Aretal? And I answered it quickly. Señor de Aretal with his fine mentality had no soul: He was amoral. He was amoral as a horse and allowed himself to be mounted by any spirit whatever. At times his riders were fearful or miserly and then Señor de Aretal would fling them from him with a proud buck. That moral vacuum of his being would fill, as do all vacuums, with ease. It ended to fill itself.

I proposed the question to the very exalted mind of my friend and he took it up at once. He made me a confession:—Yes: it is true. I show you who loves me the better part of me. I show you my inner god. But, it is painful to say it, between two human beings around me I tend to take on the color of the lower. Flee from me when I am in bad company.

Upon the base of this discovery I entered still more deeply into his spirit. He confessed to me one day, in grief, that no woman had ever loved him. All his being bled as he said this. I explained to him that no woman could love him, because he was not a man; the union would have been monstrous. Señor de Aretal did not know modesty and was indelicate in his relations with ladies, like an animal. And he:

—But I heap them with money.

—That also would be given them by valuable property rented.

And he:

—But I caress them with passion.

—Their little wooly dogs also lick their hands.

And he:

—But I am faithful and generous to them; I am humble to them; I am self-denying to them.

—Well; man is more than that. But, do you love them?

—Yes, I love them.

—But do you love them as a man? No, friend, no. You break in those delicate and divine beings a thousand slender cords which constitute a life entire. That last prostitute, who denied you her love and has disdained your money, defended her one inviolate part: her inner master; that which is not sold. You have no shame. Now listen to my prophecy: A woman will redeem you. You, obsequious and humble to lowliness with the ladies; you proud to carry a lovely woman on your back, with the pride of the favorite nag which delights in its burden; when this beautiful woman shall love you, you will be redeemed; you will acquire chastity by conquest.

And at another time propitious for confidences:

—I have never had a friend. And his entire being bled as he said this. I explained to him that no man could give him his friendship because he was not a man, and the friendship would have been monstrous. Señor de Aretal did not comprehend friendship and was indelicate in his relations with men, like an animal. . . . He knew only comradeship. He galloped, joyful and open-hearted, upon the plain with his companions; he liked to go in droves with them; primitive and primordial he galloped, drunk with the air, the verdure and the sun; but later he would withdraw with indifference from his companion of a year. The horse, his brother dead beside him, sees him rot beneath the dome of the heavens without a tear rising to his eyes. . . . And Señor de Aretal, when I had finished expressing my last concept, radiant:

—This is the glory of nature. Matter, immortal, does not die. Why weep for a horse when a rose remains? Why weep for a rose when a bird is there? Why lament for a friend when a meadow remains? I feel the radiant light of the sun which possesses us all, which redeems us all. To weep is to sin against the sun. Men, cowards, miserable and low, sin against nature, which is God.

And I, reverent, on my knees before that beautiful animal soul which filled me with the unction of God!

—Yes, it is true; but man is a part of nature; he is nature evolved. I respect evolution! There is force and there is matter; I respect them both! They are all one.

—I am beyond the moral.

—You are on this side of morality; you are below the moral. But the horse and the angel touch one another, and for this reason you at times appear to me as divine. St. Francis d'Assisi, like you, loved all beings and all things; but that being true, he loved them in another manner; he loved them beyond the circle, not this side of it as you do.

And then he:

—I am generous with my friends. I shower them with gold.

—It would also be given them by a valuable property leased, or by an oil well, or a working mine.

And he:

—But I pay them a thousand little attentions. I have been nurse to the sick friend and a boon companion in an orgy to the hale friend.

And I:

—Man is more than that; man is solidarity. You love your friends but do you love them with human love? No; you offended in us a thousand tangible things. I, who am the first man who has loved you, have sown the germ of your redemption. That egoist friend who separated himself, in leaving you, from a benefactor, did not feel himself united to you by any human bond. You have no solidarity with men.

— . . . . . .

—You have no modesty with women nor solidarity with men nor respect for the law. You lie, and find in your exalted mentality an excuse for your lie, although you are by nature truthful, like a horse. You flatter and deceive and find in your exalted mentality an excuse for your flattery and your deceit, although you are by nature noble, like a horse. I have never so loved horses as I love them in you. I understand the nobility of the horse; it is nearly human. You have always borne a human load upon your back; a woman, a friend. . . . What would become of that woman and that friend in the difficult passes without you, the noble, the strong, who bore them upon himself with a generosity which will be your redemption! He who bears a burden covers the road most swiftly. But you have borne them like a horse. Faithful to your nature, begin to bear them like a man.

I took leave of the master of the topazes and a few days later there occurred the last act of our relationship. Of a sudden Señor de Aretal sensed that my hand was unsteady, that it was held out to him in a cowardly and ungenerous manner and his nobility of the brute revolted. With a swift kick he threw me far from him. I felt his hoofs on my forehead. Then a rapid gallop, rhythmic and martial, scattering to the winds the sands of the desert. I turned my eyes toward the place where the sphynx had stood in her eternal repose of mystery and I no longer saw her. The sphynx was Señor de Aretal who had revealed to me his secret which was the same as that of the centaur!

It was Señor de Aretal, drawing away at a rapid gallop, with a human face and the body of a beast.

TRANSLATED BY WILLIAM GEORGE WILLIAMS AND WILLIAM CARLOS WILLIAMS

Ricardo Güiraldes

Argentina
(1886–1927)

———— \\ ————

Ricardo Güiraldes was one of the most influential Argentine writers and intellectuals of the early years of the twentieth century. Born to a well-to-do family, the young Güiraldes spent his first years in Paris, where he learned French before Spanish. He was to die in the French capital when he was only forty-one. His interests were multifarious and his production substantial for such a short life. Güiraldes was a literary associate and friend of Jorge Luis Borges, with whom he founded in the 1920s the avant-garde magazines *Martín Fierro* and *Proa*. In 1915 Güiraldes published his *Cuentos de muerte y de sangre,* from which "The Braider" is taken. It met with great success. Güiraldes also published several collections of verse in a metaphysical vein. But his claim to international fame rests on his 1926 novel *Don Segundo Sombra,* a classic of Latin American letters that paints an idealized picture of the life of gauchos in the Argentine pampa. It is an effort to discover the depths of the nation's psyche in the figure of old Don Segundo, a sage whose wisdom emerged from his contact with the land. It is, needless to say, a very urban view of the countryside by one of its owners and a kind of paean to the cattle industry. Yet Güiraldes fixed forever in the Latin American imagination another literary myth, comparable to Doña Bárbara, in the novel of the same name by the Venezuelan Rómulo Gallegos: the old gaucho. "The Braider," very much in line with *Don Segundo Sombra,* is the portrait of a natural artist, a man endowed with a unique talent who gives his all to his work like a cultivated poet. This romantic view of the gaucho is clearly a projection of Güiraldes's notion of his own practice as an artist. Art is its own reward and demands a special, all-consuming devotion. The story's intricate lexicon, derived from the gaucho's world, is elaborately woven like the strands of leather in the main character's hands.

The Braider

Núñez braided like Bach made music; Goya, paintings; Dante, poetry. His natural talent led him on an unbending path, and he lived fully consumed by his art.

Núñez suffered the eternal tragedy of all great men. In compliance with divine law, he engendered and painfully gave birth to his craft. To his disciples he left a thousand different ways of following his example, concealing a secret that even his most accomplished prophets have yet to understand.

In the beginning Núñez made imperfect buttons out of leather for old Nicasio, wetting the straps until they became malleable. In time he learned many things, some of the most onerous lessons one could hope to ascertain. Núñez watched Nicasio silently, without asking questions, absorbing with voracious facility his various styles, as the complex braid coiled around itself in ways that could not be taught.

Once Núñez had acquired a breadth of techniques, he had the urge to turn his dreams into reality. For this, he locked himself up in idle moments. In the secrecy of his room, while the others napped, Núñez began the difficult tasks of making braids and buttons, skills he easily perfected.

It was a typical Núñez bridle, intricate and delicately woven. To traditional decorative motifs, Núñez would add his own personal touches, finding inspiration in trees and various animals.

He proceeded slowly owing to various factors: the time needed to prepare the leather straps—fine as horse hair; the lack of free time; and the gibes of his friends that he tried to avoid like the plague for they would only destroy his art.

What could Núñez be doing confined in his room for so many hours on end? The laborers' curiosity reached the boss, who wanted to know more. He entered Núñez's room by surprise, finding Núñez so absorbed in an array of leather straps that he left without being heard.

When the siesta was over, the patron ordered Núñez to be summoned, ironically charging him to make some reins fashioned after the inimitable four-button model of a dead braider. The following day the reins were finished. The dead braider's handiwork looked shoddy in comparison. It marked Núñez's arrival. His reputation spread like wildfire.

The requests piled up and Núñez had to quit his job to finish them all. From that moment on, the rest of his days were filled with work, and he had neither time to look regretfully back nor to enjoy the change.

Months later, to comply with the demands of his clients, Núñez moved to the town where he had a house that served all of his work-related needs.

Núñez was perfecting his craft, yet against his will a dark cloud seemed to overshadow his glory.

There was never anyone more admired. They said Núñez was capable of braiding himself a poncho as fine, flexible, and supple as the most prized vicuña. He finished buttons and sewed invisible seams with a perfection that hinted at witchcraft. They appointed him the whip-maker.

His pumice stone was a part of his fist; his knife, an extension of his agile fingers. Between the blade and his thumb streamed the leather strips that curled up upon being separated from the strap.

The awl handles, of assorted shapes and sizes, fit into the hollow of his hand as if it were a habitual niche. He wetted the straps, causing them to glide between his lips. After that, he ran them across the back of the knife until they were pliant and unbreakable.

It is also known that Núñez had a rather rare pinto. Every year the mare gave birth to one dark colt and one light foal. Núñez would decapitate them when they were three months old and hang the skins up to dry, later combining black with white, in expert and unrepeatable variations.

Over the course of forty years he used his ample talent to comply with and satisfy his customers. He made money, a lot of money, and the local tycoons lavished him with attention, but there was always a skeptical look in Núñez's eyes.

Already old, his vision began to fail him at times, and he could not spend more than four hours each day working. Whenever he tried to work beyond the point of fatigue, his braids turned out uneven. That was when Núñez abandoned his craft. The poor, nearly decrepit man was finally able to freely take charge of his life.

He had absolutely no desire to touch another leather strap, and he avoided all conversations that dealt with his trade until, suddenly, he seemed to revert to childhood. That malady overcame him one day when, while rearranging a closet, he came across the bridle that he had begun making in his youth. At that exact moment, the old man lost his mind. He embraced the moldy straps and, forgetting his promise to never braid again, resumed the task he had abandoned fifty years earlier, without pause and to the detriment of his spent eyes and body, whose stooped posture caused him tremendous pain. More and more bent with each passing day on his fatal attention to work, don Crisanto Núñez died.

When they found him stiff and curled up, it was impossible to take from his grasp the bridle that he clutched tightly against his chest with bony claws. They had to place it on his deathbed along with him.

Friends, family, and admirers went to the wake and everyone commented on the desperation with which he hung on to the unfinished work. Someone, asserting that it was his best work, proposed to cut off the old man's fingers so as not to bury him with such a marvelous piece. They all stared at him angrily: "Cut off Núñez's fingers, Núñez's divine fingers?"

The strange and inexplicable image still lingers of the gesture with which the old man cuddled his first and last work. Was it an attempt not to leave behind something he considered inferior? Was it out of love? Or was it simply the artist's desire to be buried with his most intimate creation?

TRANSLATED BY CHRISTINE A. DOLAN

Afonso Henriques
de Lima Barreto

Brazil
(1881–1922)

A mulatto, Afonso Henriques de Lima Barreto was a civil servant most of his life. He is one of the most important Brazilian novelists, often compared to Machado de Assis. Lima Barreto was a more direct social critic than was Machado, and his style did not achieve the purity and perfection of the author of *Dom Casmurro*. Eminent Brazilian critic Antonio Candido writes that Lima Barreto was "an irreverent bohemian and one of the greatest Brazilian novelists." And leading North American authority on Brazilian literature, K. David Jackson, says that Lima Barreto "makes of his writings an instrument of social criticism and revolt." In *O triste fim de Policarpo Quaresma* (1915), Lima Barreto draws a satiric picture of Brazilian society. In his earlier, somewhat autobiographical *Recordações do escrivão Isaías Caminha* (1909), there is a touch of resentment perhaps sparked by his race and class. But Lima Barreto received acclaim in the last years of his life, and after his death he was enshrined in the Brazilian literary canon. His short stories were collected in *Histórias e sonhos* (1920). "The Man Who Knew Javanese" is the tale of a hoax, the self-creation of one impelled by dire economic need. The narrator, Castelo, is caught in the web of his own lies, which acquire with time a virtual truth that takes over his life, determining its course. It is a bitter and extremely comical satire of the Brazilian (and by extension Latin American) diplomatic elite, often allied to venal academics and writers in need of jobs. Castelo's initial ineligibility by virtue of his looks—he is dark, obviously a mulatto like Lima Barreto—is a clear expression of the author's personal bitterness. The fact that he is eventually assigned to Havana is a mockery of the diplomats' geographic knowledge: Castelo's appointment is made on the strength of the similarity in the sound of Javanese and Havana, land, one assumes, of the "Havanese."

The Man Who Knew Javanese

In a sweet shop once I was relating to my friend Castro the liberties I'd taken with convictions and respectable matters in order to be able to go on living.

There was even one particular time in Manaus when I was obliged to hide my status as a lawyer in order to gain greater respect from the clients who sought my advice as a sorcerer and soothsayer. That was what I was telling him about.

My friend listened in silence, rapt, enjoying the living Gil Blas that I was until, during a pause in the conversation as we emptied our glasses, he observed casually: "You've led quite an amusing life, Castelo!"

"It's the only way to live. . . . That business of a regular job, leaving home at a fixed time, returning at another is boring, don't you think? I don't see how I was able to stand it off there at the consulate!"

"It's wearisome, but that's not what amazes me. What amazes me is how you've had so many adventures in this imbecilic and bureaucratic Brazil of ours."

"Come, now! Precisely right here, my dear Castro, is where you can write some of the most beautiful pages of life. Can you imagine, I was a teacher of Javanese once!"

"When? Here, after you got back from the consulate?"

"No, before that. And, as a matter of fact, I was named consul because of it."

"Tell me what happened. Do you want some more beer?"

"I do."

We ordered another bottle, filled our glasses, and I continued:

"I'd arrived in Rio a short while before and was dead broke. I was sneaking out of one boarding house after another, not knowing where or how I could earn some money, when I read the following want ad in the *Jornal do comércio*:

"'Wanted: Teacher of the Javanese language. Letters, etc.'

"Well, I said to myself, here's a job that won't have too many applicants. If I can pick up four or five words I'll put in an appearance. I left the café and walked the streets, thinking all the time about myself as a teacher of Javanese, earning money, riding trolleys, and not being 'boned' by creditors. Without thinking I headed toward the National Library. I didn't know what book to ask for, but I went in, checked my hat, got my pass, and went upstairs. On the way it occurred to me to ask for the *Grande Encyclopédie*, letter *J*, with an aim to looking up the article on Java and the Javanese language. No sooner said than done. After a few minutes I learned that Java was a large island in the Sonda archipelago, a Dutch colony, and that Javanese, an agglutinative language of the Malay-Polynesian group, possessed a literature worthy of note and was written in characters derived from the old Hindu alphabet.

"The *Encyclopédie* gave me the names of studies on that Malayan language and I made up my mind to consult one of them. I copied down the alphabet, its representative pronunciation, and I left. I went along the street strolling and chewing letters.

"Hieroglyphics were dancing in my head. From time to time I'd consult my notes. I'd go into parks and write those scrawls in the sand in order to fix them in my memory and get my hand used to writing them.

"At night, when I could get into the house without being seen so as to avoid the clerk's indiscreet queries, in my room I went on digesting my Malayan ABCs and with such doggedness that I felt I'd know them perfectly by the next day.

"I convinced myself that it was the easiest language in the world, and I went out, but not early enough to avoid running into the clerk in charge of boarders' accounts.

"'Mr. Castelo, when are you going to pay your bill?'

"I answered him then with the most charming optimism:

"'Shortly. . . . Just wait a bit. . . . Be patient. . . . I'm about to get a position as a teacher of Javanese, and . . .'

"At that point the man interrupted me:

"'What the devil is that, Mr. Castelo?'

"I liked the diversion and I went after the man's patriotism:

"'It's a language spoken out there in the neighborhood of Timor. Do you know where that is?'

"'Oh, the poor innocent soul! The man forgot all about my bill and said to me with that strong accent the Portuguese have:

"'I can't really say I know myself, but I've heard tell that it's a place we own out there near Macao. And you can speak it, Mr. Castelo?'

"Perked up by the happy out that Javanese had given me, I went back to find the advertisement. There it was. I eagerly resolved to apply for the position of teacher of the overseas language. I drew up my answer, passed by the *Jornal,* and dropped the letter off. I immediately went back to the library and continued my studies of Javanese. I didn't make any great progress that day; I don't know whether because I thought the Javanese alphabet was the only thing a teacher of the Malayan language had to know or because I got more interested in the bibliography and literary history of the language I was going to teach.

"At the end of two days I received a letter telling me to come and speak to Dr. Manuel Feliciano Soares Albernaz, Baron of Jacuecanga, on the rua Conde de Bonfim; I can't remember what number too well. You must keep in mind that in the meantime I was continuing the study of my Malayan, that is, the Javanese language in question. In addition to the alphabet I got to know the names of some authors, also to ask and answer 'How are you?' and two or three grammatical rules. All of that knowledge was buttressed by twenty vocabulary words.

"You can't imagine the trouble I ran into trying to put the four hundred

reis fare together. It was easier—you can be sure of that—to learn Javanese.
. . . I went on foot. I got there all covered with sweat and the ancient
mango trees along the drive leading to the nobleman's house greeted me,
sheltered me, and comforted me with maternal affection. That was the
only moment in my whole life in which I had a warm feeling for nature. . . .

"It was a huge deserted-looking house. It was run-down, but, I don't
know why, the thought occurred to me that its poor shape was due more
to negligence and weariness with life than to actual poverty. It must have
been years since it had been painted. The walls were peeling and the eaves,
with those glazed tiles of times gone by, had pieces missing here and there,
like a set of decaying or neglected teeth.

"I took a quick look at the garden and saw the vengeful growth with
which the sedge and burrs had driven out the caladiums and begonias. The
crotons were still there, however, surviving with their dull foliage. I
knocked. It took a long time for the door to be opened. Finally an ancient
African black arrived, with a cottony beard and hair that gave his face a
look of old age, gentleness, and suffering.

"There was a gallery of portraits in the parlor. Haughty bearded gentlemen in high collars were lined up in huge gilded frames, and the gentle
rows of ladies in tight coiffures, with large fans, seemed to be trying to
ascend into the air, billowed by their hoopskirts. But of all those old items
on which the dust had laid down even more antiquity and respect, the
thing I liked best was a beautiful porcelain vase from China or India, as
they say. The purity of that chinaware, its fragility, the innocence of its
design, and its dull moonlight glow told me that the object there could
have been made by the hands of a dreamy child for the enchantment of
the weary eyes of disillusioned old men. . . .

"I waited a while for the master of the house. He took some time in
coming. Tottering a bit, handkerchief in hand, venerably taking some fine
snuff left from days gone by, he filled me with respect as I watched him
come in. I felt like leaving. Even if he weren't the pupil, it would still be
a crime to deceive that old man whose age brought something august,
sacred to the surface of my thought. I hesitated but I stayed.

"'I'm the teacher of Javanese that you said you needed,' I began.

"'Sit down,' the old man replied. 'Are you from here, from Rio?'

"'No, I'm from Canavieiras.'

"'What?' he said. 'Speak a little louder, I'm deaf.'

"'I'm from Canavieiras, in Bahia,' I repeated.

"'Where did you study?'

"'In São Salvador.'

"'Where did you learn Javanese?' he asked with that insistence peculiar
to old people.

"I hadn't counted on that question, but I immediately fabricated a lie. I told him that my father was Javanese. A seaman on a merchant ship, he'd ended up in Bahia. He'd settled down near Canavieiras as a fisherman, got married, prospered, and it was from him that I'd learned Javanese."

"And did he believe you? What about your physical appearance?" my friend, who'd been listening in silence until then, asked.

"I'm not all that different from a Javanese," I argued. "This straight hair of mine, thick and hard, and my tanned skin could easily give me the look of a Malayan mixed breed. . . . You know quite well that we've got everything in us: Indian, Malayan, Tahitian, Malgache, Guanche, even Goth. A whole array of races and types that's the envy of the entire world."

"So continue, then," my friend said.

"The old man," I went on, "listened to me attentively, looking me over carefully, and he seemed to accept me as the son of a Malayan and asked me softly: 'So, are you ready to teach me Javanese?'

"The answer came out in spite of myself: 'Of course.'

"'You must be surprised,' the Baron of Jacuecanga put in, 'that at this age I still want to learn something, but . . .'

"'I have no reason to be amazed. There have been examples and very worthy examples . . .'

"'What I want, my dear Mr. . . . ?'

"'Castelo,' I hastened to add.

"'What I want, my dear Mr. Castelo, is to fulfill a family pledge. I don't know if you're aware that I'm the grandson of Counselor Albernaz, the one who accompanied Pedro I when he abdicated. Returning from London, he brought back a book in a strange language and which he thought highly of. It had been a Hindu or a Siamese who'd given it to him in London as thanks for some service my grandfather had done for him. When he was dying my grandfather summoned my father and told him, "Son, I have this book written in Javanese here. The person who gave it to me said that it forestalls misfortune and brings good luck to the one who owns it. I'm not sure of any of that. In any case, hold on to it, and if you want the prophecy of the Oriental wise man who left it to me to be fulfilled, have your son understand it so that our line will always be fortunate." My father,' the old baron went on, 'didn't put too much faith in the story but he kept the book. On the threshold of death he gave it to me and told me what he'd promised his father. At first I didn't pay much attention to the story of the book. I put it away and went about with my life. I even came to forget about it, but recently I've experienced so many displeasures, so much misfortune has fallen upon my old age that I remembered the family talisman. I've got to read it, understand it if I don't want my last years to be the announcement of disaster for my posterity, and in order to understand it, of course, I've got to understand Javanese. There you have it all.'

"He fell silent and I noticed that the old man's eyes had become dewy. He discreetly wiped them and asked me if I wished to see the book. I said I did. He called the servant, gave him some instructions, and explained to me that he'd lost all his sons and nephews and all he had left was a married daughter whose offspring, however, was limited to one son, physically weak and in fragile and uneven health.

"The book arrived. It was a big old tome, an ancient quarto bound in leather and printed in large letters on thick, yellowing paper. The title page was missing and so it was impossible to read the date of publication. It still had some pages of preface written in English where I read that it involved the stories of Prince Kulanga, a Javanese writer of great merit.

"I immediately informed the old baron of that and, not perceiving that I'd come by the information by means of the English, he showed a great respect for my knowledge of Malayan. I was still thumbing through the bulky old book in the manner of someone who had a masterful knowledge of that gibberish when we finally came to an agreement on the conditions of price and time, with my promising him that he would be able to read that old book before a year was up.

"A short while later I gave him my first lesson, but the old man wasn't as diligent as I. He couldn't get to learn to distinguish and write even four letters. Ultimately it took us a month for half the alphabet and my lord Baron of Jacuecanga didn't master much of the material. He would learn and unlearn.

"His daughter and son-in-law (I don't think that even then they knew anything about the book's story) came to see how the old man's studies were going. It didn't bother them. They found it amusing and thought it was a good thing to keep him occupied.

"But what will surprise you, my dear Castro, is the admiration that the son-in-law ended up having for the teacher of Javanese. What a unique thing! He never tired of repeating, 'It's amazing! He's so young! If I could have had that knowledge, oh, where I could have been today!'

"The husband of Dona Maria da Glória (that was the name of the baron's daughter) was a chief magistrate, a man with connections and power, but he wasn't ashamed to display for everyone his amazement over my Javanese. Furthermore, the baron was extremely content. At the end of two months he gave up his apprenticeship and asked me to translate a passage from the enchanted book for him every day. 'All I have to do is understand it,' he told me. There was nothing wrong with someone else's translating it and his listening. In that way he could avoid the fatigue of studying and still fulfill his duty.

"You know quite well that even today I don't know any Javanese, but I composed some rather silly stories and palmed them off on the old man as coming from the chronicle. The way he listened to that nonsense! . . .

"He was ecstatic, as if he were listening to the words of an angel. And I got bigger in his eyes!

"He brought me to live in his house, smothered me with presents, raised my stipend. In short, I was leading a bountiful life.

"Greatly contributing to that was the fact that an inheritance from a forgotten relative who lived in Portugal had come his way. The good old man attributed it to my Javanese, and I was almost ready to believe him too.

"I was losing any remorse, but, just the same, I was still afraid that someone who knew the Malayan patois would put in an appearance. And my fears were great when the baron sent me off with a letter to the Viscount of Caruru asking that he get me into the diplomatic service. I made all kinds of objections: my ugliness, my lack of elegance, my Tagalog looks. 'Come, now!' he retorted. 'Get along with you, boy. You know Javanese!' I went. The viscount sent me to the Foreign Ministry with several recommendations. It was a success.

"The director called in the section heads: 'Just look, a man who knows Javanese—a miracle!'

"The section heads took me to the officials and the clerks and there was one of the latter who looked at me more with hatred than with envy or admiration. And they all said, 'So, you know Javanese? Is it hard? There's nobody here who knows it!'

"The clerk who'd looked at me with hatred then put in, 'That's true, but I know Kanaka. Are you familiar with it?' I told him I wasn't and was brought before the minister.

"That high authority got up, put his hands on his hips, adjusted his pince-nez on his nose, and asked, 'So, you know Javanese?' I answered that I did and to his question as to where I'd learned it I told him the tale of that Javanese father. 'Well,' the minister told me, 'you're not for the diplomatic service. Your physical appearance isn't right for it. . . . The best thing would be a consulate in Asia or Oceania. At the moment there's no vacancy, but I'm going to make some changes and you can go in. Starting today, however, you'll be attached to my ministry and I hope that within the year you'll leave for Bâle, where you'll represent Brazil at the Congress on Linguistics. Study, read Hovelacque, Max Müller, and the rest!'

"Just imagine, I, who up till then knew nothing of Javanese, was hired and would represent Brazil at a conference of scholars.

"The old baron passed away, turned the book over to his son-in-law so he could turn it over to his grandson when he reached the proper age, and left me a legacy in his will.

"I assiduously went to work studying the Malay-Polynesian languages, but there was no way!

"Eating well, dressing well, sleeping well, I didn't have the necessary energy to get those strange things into my noggin. I bought books, sub-scribed to journals: *Revue Anthropologique et Linguistique, Proceedings of the English-Oceanic Association, Archivo Glottologico Italiano,* the whole devilish lot, but nothing doing! And my fame was growing. On the street people who knew would point me out and tell others, 'There goes the fellow who knows Javanese.' In bookstores grammarians would consult with me over the placement of pronouns in such-and-such a jargon from the Sonda Islands. I would receive letters from scholars in the interior, newspapers would mention my knowledge, and I turned down a group of students eager to understand Javanese. At the invitation of the editor I wrote a four-column article for the *Journal do Comércio* on ancient and modern Javanese literature. . . ."

"How, if you didn't know anything?" the attentive Castro asked me.

"Quite simple. First, I described the island of Java with the help of dictionaries and some geography books and then I quoted anything I could."

"And they never suspected?" my friend persisted.

"Never. That is, I was almost lost once. The police had arrested a fellow, a sailor, a bronzed type who only spoke some strange language. They called in several interpreters and nobody could understand him. I was called in too, with all the respect that my wisdom deserved, of course. I took my time in going, but finally I went. The man had already been released, thanks to the intervention of the Dutch consul, whom he was able to make understand with a half dozen words in Dutch. And that sailor had been Javanese—Wow!

"The time for the congress finally arrived and off I went to Europe. What a delight! I attended the opening and the preparatory sessions. I was registered in the Tupi-Guarani section and I took off for Paris. First, how-ever, I had my picture and some biographical and bibliographical notes published in the *Bâle Messenger.* When I got back the president begged my forgiveness for having assigned me to that section. He hadn't been familiar with my work and had judged that as a South American Brazilian the Tupi-Guarani section seemed to be the indicated one. I accepted his explanations and I still haven't been able so far to write my works on Javanese in order to send them to him as I'd promised.

"When the congress was over I had excerpts from the article in the *Bâle Messenger* published in Berlin, Turin, and Paris, where the readers of my works gave a banquet in my honor presided over by Senator Gorot. That whole hoax, including the banquet given me, cost me close to ten thousand francs, almost the entire inheritance from the credulous and good Baron of Jacuecanga.

"I hadn't wasted my time or my money. I got to be a national glory, and when I landed at the Pharoux docks I received an ovation from every

social class, and a few days later the President of the Republic invited me
to have lunch with him.

"Inside of six months I was sent to Havana as consul. I spent six months
there and I shall return in order to perfect my studies of the languages of
Malaya, Melanesia, and Polynesia."

"It's fantastic," Castro observed, holding his glass of beer.

"Look. If I hadn't been content, do you know what I was going to
be?"

"What?"

"An eminent bacteriologist. Shall we go?"

"Let's go."

TRANSLATED BY GREGORY RABASSA

Rómulo Gallegos

Venezuela
(1884–1969)

———— \\\\ ————

Rómulo Gallegos was the first Latin American novelist to gain international acclaim when he published an undisputed classic, *Doña Bárbara* in 1929. The
protagonist of the novel's title is one of the most enduring literary mythic figures
in Latin America, revered and reviled, but never forgotten. Gallegos was a liberal
who opposed Venezuelan dictator Juan Vicente Gómez (in power from 1909 to
1935) and suffered exile as a result. In 1948, during a brief period of democratic
rule, Gallegos was elected president of Venezuela. But he was deposed within
a year by the military, which installed Marcos Pérez Jiménez, who ruled with an
iron hand until 1958. Gallegos spent the years of Jiménez's rule abroad in Cuba,
Mexico, and the United States. The success of *Doña Bárbara* was such that
Gallegos was warmly received everywhere, but it also obscured some of his other
worthy novels, like *Canaima* (1935). *Doña Bárbara* embodied the central duality
of Latin American thought and culture: the conflict between barbarism and civilization, between the city and the countryside, between Europe and a savage
"other." But such is the allure of the barbarous, as represented in the perversely
attractive protagonist, that, against Gallegos's liberal ideology, it becomes much
more compelling than the plans for progress and rule propounded by the narrator. Gallegos was a folklorist who was interested in the customs and particularly
the stories told by country folk, especially those of the plains, the endless *llano*.
He was also a powerful stylist with a rhetorical loftiness that was the equal of the
jungle settings described in novels such as *Canaima*. Though often criticized by
Latin American novelists in the 1960s for his outmoded realism and his liberal
politics, Gallegos is their most powerful precursor and an unavoidable influence.

Peace on High

In a wild mountainous region, at the edge of a steep precipice garlanded
with tough creepers and bushes, a ruinous cabin huddles, above whose
thatched roof no chimney-smoke has risen for a long time. A boy sits in
the doorway.

He is a miserable, sad creature: a huge head held up by a scrawny neck
bristled with a thin brush of filthy hairs, on a wasted body: the stomach
bloated, arms skeletal, legs full of runny scabs, with enormous knees and

153

feet deformed by malarial edema. His face is striking with its pasty skin stuck to its bones, a peeling mouth exposing its teeth. The whites of his eyes are horribly yellow deep in their staring sockets. There is a shadow of dumb, furious pain in the muddy pupils of his eyes.

He remains motionless and silent, looking over the sea of small hills that fill the immense distance of low land that stretches out before his eyes to reach a barrier of blue mountains, far off, sketched against the scudding golden cloud-background of the horizon. A bitter, stubborn grief scratches without stopping into his small heart, already scarred by a hate for everything that lives and moves around him. This feeling permanently keeps a knot in his throat, like a crying fit about to break out, but tears never come into his eyes. A wave of rage often surges in his breast and then he closes his fists and his teeth rattle in a disturbing way until, when he has torn whatever he can get his hands on, the furious feeling dies down and leaves him in a logy state. At other times, he spends whole days brooding, without talking, sitting in the doorway or lying on the hard ground, looking straight ahead, intensely, at something fascinating and terrible that seems to be in front of his eyes. During such moments of depression, the feelings of his body sapped by sickness become confused in his mind and end up by making him forget who he is. First a tickling sensation begins at the soles of his feet and slowly floods up through his entire body, and it is a horde of things that eat him up as if he were already dead. Then a horrible sensation of puffing up inside, as if his bowels suddenly started to grow big fast the way he hears the hills grow inside the precipice in the silence of dark nights, when his stomach stifles him and does not let him sleep. Finally, the emptiness inside his head: the chatter of millions of crickets approaching, a crazy whirl of stars around his eyes. And last of all, a sudden, definite silence that seems as if it will never come to an end. . . . And in the middle of all this, the obsessive vision of a man, the coalman, hugging his mother, as he himself lies in a corner of the hovel, shaking with the cold that precedes a fever. . . .

This scene witnessed by Felipe shortly after his father's death had been printed on his memory in such a way that, without knowing why—since he has never tried to figure out what it meant—he could never look at his mother without seeing her as he had seen her that night, held close in the arms of the coalman who had placed his big black hands on her shoulders.

That is how the unswerving intense dislike for his mother had started in his small injured heart. Her efforts to prod him out of his silence from which he shut her out were useless and besides, since she never tried to do it with affection but by throwing harsh words at him or battering his broken skin with hard blows, the secret revulsion of the boy began to turn into a fierce hatred that twisted in his heart with such violence that he turned it on her blindly, fists squeezed tight, showing her his teeth grinding with a terrible sound.

In the beginning, when this happened the mother smothered his anger with a storm of blows that, no matter how hard, could never draw a single tear from him. He howled like a cornered animal and rolled about on the ground, after which he would stay there still as a corpse for hours. But then his mother adopted a different tactic that angered him even more. She stopped beating him and simply pinned back his arms until, worn out by the violence of his anger which flowed through his body like a poisonous drug, he would drop to the ground and go into his morbid condition of half-sleep. Then the woman would leave him, speaking in a low frightened way:

"Holy Mother of God!"

About this time the woman's absences from the farm began to last longer and longer. She spent whole days in the woods where she went each morning to look for a bundle of sticks or for ears of corn to steal from the cornfields and sell in the town nearby. Often she came back at nightfall with the miserable product of her sales converted into rough sheets of cassava bread and occasionally a chunk of salted fish on which Felipe would fall with voracious hunger, the excessive hunger that was never satisfied and filled his lonely days and sleepless nights with tormenting images of fantastic, delicious scenes of gluttony.

One day Felipe found a friend. From morning he had been listening to the barking of a dog as it wandered through the woods, sniffing at the footpaths as if it were looking for its lost owner. That afternoon it came toward the hut and, seeing him sitting in the doorway, stopped in front of him, wagging its tail, and then lay down at his feet panting, without interrupting its friendly stare into the horrible little face of the sick boy. Felipe, in turn, looked at it a long time, like a friend he had been expecting and had received without being surprised. He did not try to pet it or speak a single word to it. It seemed natural to him that the dog had come and settled near him. He did not think about it, just knew that he was the master the dog had been looking for all day across the farms, along the footpaths. It had found him and he was certain that the dog would never leave him. After a while an unusual thought brushed the stillness of his mind: inexplicable, nameless ideas that pass through your mind without being quite seen, the way you feel the shadow of a hand that is about to caress or harm you. He thought—without realizing that he was doing it— that the dog had come from the unknown, from the place that soared overhead, and he had not been able to see it but it had been seen by the rooster who then let out its terrible cry, stretching its neck and following its ominous flight with a frightened eye. And he thought that it had come in search of him to save him from something that was about to happen to him.

Breaking his silence, he finally said:

"I heard you barking in that cornfield this morning. I knew you were looking for me."

The dog began to bark a friendly playful bark. But it stopped suddenly and began to growl suspiciously. Felipe, who had also heard the sound of footsteps in the thicket, told him:

"It's mama. Be quiet."

Plácida was annoyed at finding the dog there and tried to scare it away, but the dog took cover between Felipe's legs, growling and looking at her with threatening eyes. She was afraid of it and stopped trying to drive it away, but you could see that she was uneasy.

She deposited the bundle of provisions for their skimpy evening meal in the hut, placing it where Felipe could not reach it, took one sheet of cassava from it, and went to eat it near the edge of the precipice.

Excited by hunger, the boy approached her greedily. She did not let him reach her, stopping him a few steps away by throwing him a piece of cassava that fell near the bushes that hung like garlands from the edge of the precipice. Felipe picked it up and sat on the ground to eat it. The dog at his side wagged its tail. The boy offered it a piece of what he was eating but, after sniffing it, the animal turned away from it and stretched out on the ground contemptuously, its head toward the woman.

Meanwhile, she could not take her eyes off her son's face, made uglier by the grotesque way it moved up and down as he chewed. He seemed more horrible than ever, and as she looked at him her heart filled more and more with a terrible grudge. That repulsive creature who was like a filthy rag already dangling in the clutch of death, yet would never stop living, was the reason for her misery. Because of him she could not find housework when she went to the town to offer her services. No one would have such a revolting creature in his house. And because of him Crisanto, the coalman, who loaded her ears with words of love, had not wanted her to move in with him. That same day he had said to her:

"Honey, if it wasn't fer that boy, you wouldna be havin' all this trouble, 'cause I gotta house and food and if you decide to come live with me, you won't have no need to go all over the place stealin' corn or pickin' up halfburned sticks down the ravines. But that kid, I wouldn't want 'im if you covered 'im with gold. Ha, the little basta'd's a bad egg. Ya just gotta look at 'is eyes. There's badness all over him. . . . For my money, that little bast'd's the Devil's own son! Holy Mother of God! He ain't even a kid: he's like a grown man. Kids don't think about things like that one thinks. Looks to me like a man hidin' in a kid's body fer you to get careless and he c'n jump out at you. If, fer instance, I meet 'im at night on that mountain road, I c'n tell ya I wouldn't stop. . . . Ah! Sure! That's the Devil's own son. If I was you. . . ."

Their conversation had reached this point when, some distance back along the precipice where they were talking, the dog he was now used to finding there lying beside Felipe appeared. The animal, which looked as if it had lost sight of its master and was desperately searching for him, had come near them and, after sniffling around their feet, had started to bark furiously, just as Plácida was answering Crisanto:

"And if they find me out?"

"They're not gonna find ya out! The easiest thing is fer a kid that can't stay on 'is two legs to fall down that rock . . . !"

Now, gazing at the cadaverous face of her hated son, whom she blamed for her miserable life, Plácida was savoring Crisanto's insinuation:

"Who's gonna find out?"

She looked around her suspiciously. Everything seemed solitary and empty. The immense low land full of green small hills that stretched silently toward the distant horizon. Below, far off, could be seen a few farmhouses scattered among the fields and patches of wild vegetation, but they were so far away that it was impossible to make out people near them. You could just manage to see the frail smoke lifting slowly from the chimneys into the air, above the roofs.

This exploration of the lonely landscape pulled the knot in her throat painfully tighter. Over the precipice floated a heavy atmosphere that almost made you choke. Black masses of clouds rolled through the sky, filling the hollow of the low land with violet shadows. On the horizon, along the barrier of the last hilltops, you could see the bluish stain of the rain coming closer. A low rumble of distant thunder groaned in the atmosphere charged with omens.

Plácida felt herself dragged irresistibly towards the whirlpool of an evil thought.

"Don't it look like the Devil 'imself's crouchin' inside that kid? Look at the way he's starin' at me! Holy Mother of God! His eyes are rollin' and 'is teeth are rattlin'! God save us from 'im! What c'n he get out of livin' like that, a rotten sack of diseases . . . ! Those worms he's got in 'is stomach are eatin' 'im alive! And the chills he gets when the fever starts to get 'im. To live like that all the time I'd rather die. . . ."

The dog stared at him, growling.

"And who could that dog be . . . ? Holy Mother of God! Look how there's things in this life ya can't explain."

Felipe had finished devouring the piece of cassava and, turning to his mother, told her roughly:

"Gimme more! I'm hungry! I want it all 'cause I'm hungry!"

The woman gave him a frightened look. The horrible whites of his eyes had flashed in an evil way. She felt that a mysterious force lurked powerfully behind the boy's words. At the same time, the imperative demand of the boy coincided with a thought that had just crossed her mind.

Trembling anxiously, she threw the piece of cassava she had left in her hand, in such a way that it fell on the bushes dangling at the edge of the precipice over the emptiness below.

Felipe stood up and fixed her with a penetrating look of fury that upset her. He had understood her intention: if he went to reach for the piece of cassava, the bushes would give under his weight and he would crash down into the ravine. There was an instant that lasted an eternity. Plácida felt that madness was whirling all around her. Felipe, with sudden resolve, took a step toward the bushes.

At the same time the dog pounced quickly on the piece of cassava caught in the bushes, letting out a strange howl. The vegetation gave under its weight and the animal's body rolled down the side of the precipice.

A dreadful night. Rain is pouring down furiously on the workfields. Crash after crash of lightning rattles endlessly like moving furniture in the solitude of the low land. You can hear the water hissing down the gullies like furious serpents. . . . For a long while you could hear the painful barking of the dog that was probably tangled in the brambles down the side of the ravine, but he stopped barking some time ago. . . .

In the hut, whose roof leaks streams of water falling from the clouds, Plácida and Felipe lie far apart, silent. By the light of the lightning flashes that brighten the place, Plácida sees the horrible whites of Felipe's eyes shining wickedly. She dare not sleep. She is afraid of the boy who carries something crouched inside, something that frightens her and at the same time holds her fascinated.

From time to time he says, with an implacable insistence that is almost driving her out of her mind:

"Mama, why do you want me to die . . . ?"

TRANSLATED BY HARDIE ST. MARTIN

Mário de Andrade

Brazil
(1893–1945)

With Oswald de Andrade (no relation), Mário de Andrade was one of the pro-moters of the Brazilian avant-garde. Although Oswald was the first in bringing about the movement's consolidation, Mário, a better organizer, made possible many of its activities. Emir Rodríguez Monegal called him the Saint Paul of Mod-ernismo,* as the movement came to be called. Mário was a prolific writer who published several volumes of poetry, three books of short stories, a novel, essays on art and literature, and a voluminous and important correspondence with other writers. His first collection of poetry, *There Is a Drop of Blood in Every Poem* (1917), was conventionally Parnassian, but his second, *Hallucinated City* (1922), was already imbued in the modernist spirit. He read from it during the Week of Modern Art celebrated in São Paulo the year of its publication. From 1934 to 1937 Mário directed the Culture Department of the city of São Paulo. He was profoundly interested in anthropology and folklore. His only novel, *Macunaíma* (1928), endeavors to portray a hero representative of Brazil. Based on myths from the various cultures that make up the country, including modern ones brought over by Italian immigrants, it is written in a rambling, dialectal language reminiscent of James Joyce. It is outrageously obscene and humorous in a Ra-belaisian vein, full of the antibourgeois, defiant spirit of the avant-garde. "The Christmas Turkey" is a brilliant, skillful short story that is both a satire of the Brazilian middle class and a deep psychological, even anthropological, probe into the function of sacrifice in human society. There is dark humor in the asso-ciation of the turkey with the protagonist's dead father and with Christ, the ar-chetypical sacrificial victim, on whose feast day the bird is consumed. The last line seems to indicate that only after this family ritual will the protagonist be free to love.

The Christmas Turkey

Our first family Christmas after the death of my father five months earlier had decisive consequences for family happiness. We hadn't

---

*This Modernismo is not to be confused with the literary movement of the same name in Spanish America, which took place in the late nineteenth century.

always been happy in a family way, in that very abstract meaning of happiness: honorable people, no crimes, a home without internal strife or serious economic difficulties. But owing mainly to the gray nature of my father, a creature devoid of any lyricism, exemplary in his incapacity, well bedded down in mediocrity, we'd never been able to take full advantage of life, of the pleasures of material happiness, a good wine, a vacation at a resort, getting a refrigerator, things like that. My father had been one of those people who sought the good in a mistaken way, an almost full-blooded dramatic killjoy.

My father died, and we were all very sad, etc. As we were getting close to Christmas I still couldn't get that obstructive memory of the dead man out of my mind. He still seemed to have systematized the obligation of a mournful memory at every meal, in the most insignificant act of the family. Once, when I suggested to Mama the idea of going to see a movie, the result was tears. Where had I ever heard of such a thing as going to the movies during a period of deep mourning! Grief was already being cultivated for appearances and I, who'd only liked my father according to the rules, more out of filial instinct than any spontaneous love, saw myself getting to the point of hating the good dead man.

The reason for my having been born most certainly, yes, spontaneously, was the idea of performing one of my so-called crazy things. That had been, furthermore and from a very early age, my splendid victory over the family environment. From an early age, from the time of high school, when I managed to get failing grades every year; from the hidden kiss with a cousin at the age of ten, caught by Tia Velha, a detestable old aunt; and most of all since the time of the lessons I gave or received, I don't know which, with a servant girl of relatives: it got me imprisonment at home and within the vast array of relatives the conciliatory reputation of a "nut." "He's crazy, poor thing!" they would say. My parents would speak with a certain condescending sadness; the rest of my relatives found an example for their children and probably had that pleasure of those who've convinced themselves of a certain superiority. There were no loonies among their children. Well, that was my salvation, that reputation. I did everything that life laid before me, and my being demanded that it be done with integrity. And they let me do it all because I was crazy, poor thing. The result of that was an existence without complexes, and I can't make one single complaint about it.

Christmas dinner had always been a custom in the family. A cheap dinner, as you've probably guessed: a dinner after the likes of my father, chestnuts, figs, raisins, after midnight mass. Stuffed with walnuts and almonds (the way we three children fought over the nutcrackers . . .), stuffed with chestnuts and monotony, we would embrace and go to bed. It was remembering it all that caused me to break out with one of my "crazy things."

"Well, I want to eat some turkey this Christmas."

It was one of those shocks that are impossible to imagine. Immediately my saintly single aunt who lived with us gave notice that we couldn't invite anyone because of the mourning.

"But, who said anything about inviting anyone? That mania . . . When did we ever eat turkey in our lifetime? Turkey in this house is a party dish, all those devilish relatives come . . ."

"Don't talk like that, my son. . . ."

"Well, I am talking like that, all right?"

And I unloaded my icy indifference concerning our infinite relatives who say they're the descendants of pioneers; what do I care? It was precisely the moment to develop my crazy, poor-thing theory; I couldn't let the opportunity slip by. I soaked myself in great tenderness for Mama and Aunty, my two mothers, three with my sister, the three mothers who always made my life a divine thing. It had always been like that: someone's birthday would come along and only then would they cook a turkey in that house. Turkey was a party dish: a whole stinking bunch of relatives, already prepared by tradition, would invade the house because of the turkey, the pastries, and the sweets. My three mothers, three days before, no longer were aware of anything else in life except working, working in the preparation of sweetmeats and delicacies, exquisitely made. The relatives would devour everything and still carry off little packages for the ones who had been unable to come. My three mothers could barely get through, they were so exhausted. Only at its funeral the next day were Mama and Aunty then able to taste a slice of turkey leg, vague, dark, lost in the midst of the white rice. And Mama was the one who served, keeping everything for the old man and the children. No one really knew what turkey was like in our house; turkey meant party leftovers.

No, there'd be no guests; it was a turkey for us, five people. And it would be served with two kinds of manioc stuffing, the fatty kind with the giblets and the dry kind all golden with lots of butter. I only wanted to fill my gullet with the fatty stuffing, to which we had to add black plums, walnuts, and a glass of sherry, as I'd learned at Rose's house; we went around together a lot. Naturally I omitted telling where I'd learned the recipe, but they all suspected. And they sat there afterward with that look of smoke, as if incense was being wafted around as if it were a temptation of the Devil to enjoy such a tasty recipe. And ice-cold beer, I guaranteed that, almost shouting. It's true that with my "tastes," quite refined now away from home, I'd first thought of a good wine, a hundred percent

French, but a tender feeling for Mama overcame the nut. Mama adored beer.

When I finished outlining my plans, I took good note of how very happy they were with a wild desire to follow along with the madness, but they all let themselves imagine that I alone was the only person who was wanting all that and it was an easy way to push them past me to . . . the guilt of their huge desires. They smiled, looking at one another, timid as distraught doves until my sister brought out the general feeling:

"He really is crazy!"

The turkey was bought, the turkey was cooked, etc. And after a poorly sung midnight mass we had our most delightful Christmas. It was funny: since I remembered that I was finally going to make Mama eat turkey, I couldn't do anything else those days except think about her, feel tenderness toward her, love my adorable little old lady. And my brother and sister were also caught up in the same fervent rhythm of love, all dominated by the new happiness that the turkey was giving the family. So that still covering up I very calmly watched Mama cutting the whole breast of the turkey. A moment later she paused, with strips from one side of the bird's breast, unable to resist those laws of frugality that had always held her prisoner in a meaningless near-poverty.

"No, ma'am, the whole piece! I could eat it all myself!"

It was a lie. Family love was burning so brightly in me that I was incapable of eating even a little bit in order for the other four to eat too much. And the others' tempo was the same. That turkey, eaten all by ourselves, was making each one rediscover what daily routine had completely smothered: love, the love of a mother, the love of children. God forgive me, but I'm thinking about Jesus. . . . In that modest middle-class house a miracle worthy of a Christmas of God was taking place. The turkey's breast had been reduced completely to wide slices.

"I'll serve!"

"He really is crazy!" Because why should I serve since Mama always served in that house? In the midst of laughter the big full plates were passed to me and I began a heroic distribution while I told my brother to pour the beer. I immediately noticed an admirable piece of "bark," skin full of fat, and I put it on the plate. Then some broad strips of white meat. Mama's voice, turning stern, cut through the anxious space in which everyone was aspiring for a particular part of the turkey:

"Don't forget your brother and sister, Juca!"

When would she realize, poor thing, that it was her plate, Mother's, that of my poor mistreated friend, who knew about Rose, about my crimes, to whom I only remembered telling things that made her suffer! The plate was sublime.

"Mama, this plate is for you! No! Don't pass it on, no!"

That was when she couldn't take any more of such commotion and began to cry. My aunt, too, perceiving that the next sublime plate would be hers, joined in the refrain of tears. And my sister, who could never see tears without opening her faucet, enlarged the area of weeping also. Then I began to say a lot of wild things so I wouldn't cry, too, I was nineteen. . . . What kind of a family is this that looks at a turkey and cries? Things like that. They all made an effort to smile, but happiness had become impossible now. It was because the weeping, by association, had brought up the undesirable image of my dead father. My father, with his gray look, had come to ruin our Christmas once and for all. I was angry.

Well, we started eating in silence, mournfully, and the turkey was perfect. The soft meat, with such a delicate texture, was floating gently amidst the tastes of the stuffings and the ham, wounded from time to time, disturbed and redesired by the intervention of a black plum or the petulant annoyance of a walnut. But Papa, sitting there, gigantic, incomplete, a censure, a wound, an incapacity. And the turkey was so tasty with Mama's finally learning that turkey was a morsel worthy of the newborn Christ Child.

A dull battle began between the turkey and Papa's image. I thought that by praising the turkey I could help it in the fight and, naturally, I was on the turkey's side. But the dead have slippery and very hypocritical ways of winning: no sooner had I praised the turkey than Papa's image was victorious, insupportably obstructive.

"The only thing missing is your father. . . ."

I wasn't eating. I couldn't enjoy that perfect turkey because I was so interested in that battle between the two dead creatures. I got to hate Papa. And I don't know what stroke of genius suddenly turned me political and hypocritical. At that moment, which today seems to me decisive to our family, I apparently took the side of my father. I pretended, sadly:

"That's right. . . . But Papa, who loved us so much, who died from working so hard for us, Papa, up there in heaven, must be happy . . . (I hesitated, but I decided not to mention the turkey anymore) happy to see all of us gathered here together as a family."

And they all began, very calmly, to talk about Papa. His image grew smaller and smaller and became a bright little star in the sky. Now they were all eating the turkey sensually, because Papa had been very good, had always sacrificed himself for us, had been a saint who "you, my children, will never be able to repay what you owe your father," a saint. Papa had become a saint, a pleasant thing to contemplate, a steadfast little star in the sky. He wasn't harming anyone anymore; he was only the object of sweet contemplation. The only dead one there was the turkey, dominating, completely victorious.

My mother, my aunt, all of us were overflowing with happiness. I was going to write "gustatory happiness," but it wasn't just that. It was happiness with a capital *H*, a love for all, a forgetting of relationships that were a distraction of the great family love. And it was, I know it was, that first turkey ever eaten in the bosom of the family, the beginning of a new love, reestablished, more complete, richer, and more inventive, more satisfied and aware of itself. A family happiness was born of that moment for us that—I'm not being an exclusionist—although there may be one as great, a more intense one than ours is impossible for me to imagine.

Mama ate so much turkey that I thought for a moment that it might do her harm. But then I thought: Oh, let her alone; even if it kills her, for once in her life at least she'll really have eaten turkey!

Such a lack of selfishness had been given to me by our infinite love. . . . Afterwards there were light grapes and some cookies that in my country carry the name of *bem-casados,* the happily married. But not even that dangerous name was associated with the memory of my father, whom the turkey had already converted into a dignitary, something secure, a cult for contemplation.

We got up from the table. It was almost two o'clock, and all of us were merry, staggering from two bottles of beer. We all went off to sleep, to sleep or toss in bed, it didn't really matter which, because happy insomnia is good. The devilish part is that Rose, Catholic before she was Rose, had promised to wait for me with a bottle of champagne. In order to get out I lied, said that I was going to a male friend's party. I kissed Mama, winked at her as a way of letting her know where I was going and making her suffer a little. I kissed the two other women without winking. And now for Rose!

TRANSLATED BY GREGORY RABASSA

Felisberto Hernández

Uruguay
(1902–1964)

———— \\\\ ————

Felisberto Hernández is a writer's writer, more admired by his colleagues than known by the public at large—except for "The Daisy Dolls," one of the most astonishingly original short stories written anywhere in the twentieth century and the one selected for this volume. Felisberto, as he is generally known because his first name is so much more distinctive than his last, is also a covert classic because of his colorful, if pathetic, life.

Born into poverty, he was a self-taught pianist who earned a living for years playing in movie theaters during the silent-film era. Critics, perhaps not without reason, have attempted to see a connection between his fiction and the somewhat mindless yet creative effort to match melody to plot. Film and movie house, with their Platonic-cave quality, do seem to play a role in the intricate levels of representation at work in "The Daisy Dolls." The protagonist's frenzied—though to his mind perfectly logical—arrangements, his *son et lumière* pornographic shows so carefully constructed, his sadomasochist tendencies, reveal one of the most bizarre constructions of a subconscious mind on the loose. Felisberto seems to revamp, reshape, parody, and scorn both the bourgeois family structure in which the protagonist placidly lives and the common manifestations of erotic desire. The human itself appears to be in peril in the manipulations of the body, and in the reconstruction of both physical shape and psychic phenomena. Nothing short of Kafka's "The Metamorphosis" is an apt parallel to Felisberto's creation, and only the accident of his birth in remote Montevideo has kept this literary masterpiece from finding a wider audience (his countryman and antecedent Lautréamont was fortunate to write in French his no more eccentric *Chants de Maldoror*).

The Daisy Dolls

I

Next to a garden was a factory, and the noise of the machines seeped through the plants and trees. And deep in the garden was a dark weathered house. The owner of the "black house" was a tall man. At dusk his slow steps came up the street into the garden, where—in spite of the noise of the machines—they could be heard chewing on the gravel. One autumn evening, as he opened the front door, squinting in the strong light of the hall, he saw his wife standing halfway up the grand staircase, which widened out into the middle of the courtyard, and it seemed to him she was wearing a stately marble gown, gathered up in the same hand that held on to the balustrade. She realized he was tired and would head straight up to the bedroom and she waited for him with a smile. They kissed and she said:

"Today the boys finished setting up the scenes. . . ."

"I know, but don't tell me anything."

She saw him up to the bedroom door, ran an affectionate finger down his nose and left him to himself. He was going to try to get some sleep before dinner: the dark room would divide the day's worries from the pleasures he expected of the night. He listened fondly, as he had since childhood, to the muffled sound of the machines, and fell asleep. In a dream he saw a spot of lamplight on a table. Around the table stood several men. One of them wore tails and was saying: "We have to turn the blood around so it will go out the veins and back through the arteries, instead of out the arteries and back through the veins." They all clapped and cheered, and the man in tails jumped on a horse in the courtyard and galloped off, through the applause, on clattering hooves that drew sparks from the flagstones. Remembering the dream when he woke up, the man in the black house recognized it as an echo of something he had heard that same day— that the traffic, all over the country, was changing from left- to right-hand driving—and smiled to himself. Then he put on his tail coat, once more remembering the man in the dream, and went down into the dining room. Approaching his wife, he sank his open hands in her hair and said:

"I always forget to bring a lens to have a good look at the plants in the green of your eyes. I know how you get your complexion, though: by rubbing olives on your skin."

She ran her forefinger down his nose again, then poked his cheek, until her finger bent like a spider leg, and answered:

"And I always forget to bring scissors to trim your eyebrows!"

As she sat down at the table he left the room, and she asked:

"Did you forget something?"

"Could be . . ."

He came right back and she decided he had not had time to use the phone.

"Won't you tell me where you went?"

"No."

"Then I won't tell you what the men did today."

He had already started to answer:

"No, my dear olive, don't tell me anything until after dinner."

THE DAISY DOLLS \ 167

And he poured himself a glass of the wine he imported from France.

But his wife's words had dropped like pebbles into the pond where his obsessions grew, and he could not get his mind off what he expected to see later that night. He collected dolls that were a bit taller than real women. He had had three glass cases built in a large room. In the biggest one were all the dolls waiting to be chosen to compose scenes in the other cases. The arrangements were in the hands of a number of people: first of all, the caption writers (who had to express the meaning of each scene in a few words). Other artists handled settings, costumes, music, and so on. Tonight was the second show. He would watch while a pianist, seated with his back to him, across the room, played programmed works. Suddenly the owner of the black house remembered he must not think of all this during dinner. So he took a pair of opera glasses out of his pocket and tried to focus them on his wife's face.

"I'd love to know if the shadows under your eyes are also plants."

She realized he had been to his desk to fetch the opera glasses, and decided to humor him. He saw a glass dome, which turned out to be a bottle. So he put down the opera glasses and poured himself some more wine from France. She watched it gurgle into his glass, splashing black tears that ran down the crystal walls to meet the wine on its way up. At that moment, Alex—a White Russian with a pointed beard—came in, bowing at her, and served her a plate of ham and beans. She used to say she had never heard of a servant with a beard, and he would answer that it was the one condition Alex had set for accepting the job. Now she shifted her eyes from the glass of wine to the man's wrist, where a tuft of hair grew out of his sleeve, crawling all the way down his hand to his fingers. As he waited on the master of the house, Alex said:

"Walter" (the pianist) "is here."

After dinner, Alex removed the wineglasses on a tray. They rang against each other, as if happy to meet again. The master, half-asleep—in a sort of quiet glow—was pleasantly roused by the sound and called out after him:

"Tell Walter to go to the piano. He mustn't talk to me as I come in. Is the piano far from the glass cases?"

"Yes, sir, on the other side of the room."

"Good. Tell Walter to sit with his back to me, to start on the first piece in the program and keep repeating it without stopping until I flash the light at him."

His wife was smiling. He went up to kiss her and for a moment rested his flushed face on her cheek. Then he headed for the little parlor off the big show room. There he started to smoke and sip his coffee, collecting himself: he had to feel completely isolated before going in to see the dolls. He listened for the hum of the machines and the sounds of the piano. At first they reached him in what seemed like watery murmurs, as if he were wearing a driver's helmet. Then he woke up and realized some of the sounds were trying to tell him something, as if he were being singled out from among a number of persons snoring in the room. But when he tried to concentrate on the sounds, they scattered like frightened mice. He sat there puzzled for a moment, then decided to ignore them. But suddenly he realized he was not in his chair any more: he had gotten up without noticing it. He remembered having just opened the door, and now he felt his steps taking him toward the first glass case. He switched on the light in the case and through the green curtain he saw a doll sprawled on a bed. He opened the curtain and mounted the podium, which was actually a small rolling platform on rubber casters, with a railing. From there, seated in an armchair at a little table, he had a better view of the scene. The doll was dressed as a bride and her wide open eyes stared at the ceiling. It was impossible to tell whether she was dead or dreaming. Her arms were spread in an attitude of what could be either despair or blissful abandon. Before opening the drawer of the little table to read the caption, he wanted to see what his imagination could come up with. Perhaps she was a bride waiting for the groom, who would never arrive, having jilted her just before the wedding. Or perhaps she was a widow remembering her wedding day, or just a girl dressed up to feel like a bride. He opened the drawer and read: "A moment before marrying the man she doesn't love, she locks herself up, wearing the dress she was to have worn to her wedding with the man she loved, who is gone forever, and poisons herself. She dies with her eyes open and no one has come in yet to shut them." Then the owner of the black house thought, "She really was a lovely bride." And after a moment he savored the feeling of being alive when she was not. Then he opened the glass door and entered the scene to have a closer look. At the same time, through the noise of the machines and the music, he thought he heard a door slam. He left the case and, caught in the door to the little parlor, he saw a piece of his wife's dress. As he tiptoed over to the door, he wondered whether she had been spying on him—or maybe it was one of her jokes. He snatched the door open and her body fell on him. But when he caught it in his arms it seemed very light . . . and he recognized Daisy, the doll who resembled her. Meantime his wife, who was crouching behind an armchair, straightened up and said:

"I wanted to give you a surprise, too. I just managed to get her into my dress."

She went on talking, but he did not listen. Although he was pale, he thanked her for the surprise: he did not want to discourage her, because he enjoyed the jokes she made up with Daisy. But this time he had felt uneasy. So he handed Daisy back to her, saying he did not want too long an intermission. Then he returned to the show room, closing the door behind him, and walked toward Walter. But he stopped halfway and opened another door, which gave onto his study, where he shut himself in, took a notebook from a drawer, and proceeded to make a note of the joke his wife had just played on him with Daisy, and the date. First he read the previous entry, which said: "July 21. Today, Mary"—his wife's name was Daisy Mary, but she liked to be called Mary, so when he'd had a doll made to look like her they had dusted off the name Daisy for the doll—"was in the balcony, looking out over the garden. I wanted to put my hands over her eyes and surprise her. But before I reached her I saw it was Daisy. Mary had seen me go to the balcony—she was right behind me, laughing her head off." Although he was the only one to read the notebook, he signed each entry with his name, Horace, in large letters and heavy ink. The entry before last said: "July 18. Today I opened the wardrobe to get my suit and found Daisy hanging there. She was wearing my tail coat, which looked comically large on her."

Having entered the latest surprise, he was back in the show room, heading for the second glass case. He flashed a light at Walter for him to go on to the next piece in the program and started to roll up the podium. In the pause Walter made before taking up the new piece, he felt the machines pounding harder, and as the podium moved the casters seemed to rumble like distant thunder.

The second case showed a doll seated at the head of a table. Her head was tilted back and she had a hand on each side of her plate, on a long row of silverware. Her posture and the way her hands rested on the silverware made her look as if she were at a keyboard. Horace looked at Walter, saw him bowed over the piano with his tails dangling over the edge of the bench, and thought of him as a bird of ill omen. Then he stared at the doll and had the sudden feeling—it had happened to him before—that she was moving. The movements did not always begin right away, nor did he expect them when the doll was dead or lying down, but this time they started too soon, possibly because of her uncomfortable position. She was straining too hard to look up at the ceiling, nodding slightly, with almost imperceptible little jerks that showed the effort she was making, and the minute he shifted his gaze from her face to her hands, her head drooped noticeably. He in turn quickly raised his eyes to her face again—but she had already recovered her stillness. He then began to imagine her story. Her dress and surrounding objects suggested luxury, but the furniture was coarse and the walls were of stone. On the far wall there was a small window, and behind her a low, half-open door, like a false smile. She might be in a dungeon in a castle. The piano was imitating a storm and every now and then lightning flashed in the window. Then he remembered that a minute ago the rolling casters had reminded him of distant thunder and the coincidence unsettled him. Also, while collecting himself in the little parlor, he had heard those sounds that had been trying to tell him something. But he returned to the doll's story: maybe she was praying, asking God to liberate her. Finally, he opened the drawer and read: "Second scene. This woman is expecting a child soon. She is now living in a lighthouse by the sea. She has withdrawn from the world, which has blamed her for loving a sailor. She keeps thinking, 'I want my child to be alone with himself and listen only to the sea.'" He thought, "This doll has found her true story." Then he got up, opened the glass door, and slowly went over her things. He felt he was defiling something as solemn as death. He decided to concentrate on the doll and tried to find an angle from which their eyes could meet. After a moment he bent over the unhappy girl, and as he kissed her on the forehead it gave him the same cool, pleasant sensation as Mary's face. He had hardly taken his lips off her forehead when he saw her move. He was paralyzed. She started to slip to one side, losing her balance, until she fell off the edge of the chair, dragging a spoon and a fork with her. The piano was still making sea noises, and the windows were still flashing and the machines rumbling. He did not want to pick her up and he blundered out of the case and the room, through the little parlor, into the courtyard. There he saw Alex and said:

"Tell Walter that's enough for today. And have the boys come in tomorrow to rearrange the doll in the second case."

At that moment Mary appeared:

"What's the matter?"

"Nothing: a doll fell—the one in the lighthouse. . . ."

"How did it happen? Is she hurt?"

"I must have bumped into the table when I went in to look at her things. . . ."

"Now let's not get upset, Horace!"

"On the contrary, I'm very happy with the scenes. But where's Daisy? I loved the way she looked in your dress!"

"You'd better go to bed, dear," answered Mary.

But instead they sat on a sofa, where he put his arms around her and asked her to rest her cheek on his for a moment, in silence. As their heads touched, his instantly lit up with memories of the two fallen dolls, Daisy and the girl in the lighthouse. He knew what this meant: the death of Mary. And, afraid his thoughts might pass into her head, he started to kiss her ears.

When he was alone again in the darkness of the bedroom, his mind throbbing with the noise of the machines, he thought of the warning signs he had been receiving. He was like a tangled wire that kept intercepting calls and portents meant for others. But this time all the signals had been aimed at him. Under the hum of the machines and the sound of the piano he had detected those other hidden noises scattering like mice. Then there had been Daisy falling into his arms when he opened the door to the little parlor, as if to say: "Hold me, for Mary is dying." And it was Mary herself who had prepared the warning, as innocently as if she were showing him a disease she did not yet know she had. Just before, there had been the dead doll in the first case. Then, when he was on his way to the second case, the unprogrammed rumble of the podium, like distant thunder, announcing the sea and the woman in the lighthouse. Finally, the woman slipping out from under him, falling off her chair, condemned to be childless, like Mary. And, meantime, Walter, like a bird of ill omen, with his flapping coattails, pecking away at the edge of his black box.

II

Mary was not ill and there was no reason to think she was going to die. But for some time now he had been afraid of losing her and dreading what he imagined would be his unhappiness without her. So one day he had decided to have a doll made to resemble her. At first the result had been disappointing: he had felt only dislike for Daisy, as for a poor substitute. She was made of kidskin that attempted to imitate Mary's coloring and had been perfumed with Mary's favorite scents, yet whenever Mary asked him to kiss her he expected to taste leather and had the feeling he was about to kiss a shoe. But in time he had begun to notice a strange relationship developing between Daisy and Mary. One morning he saw Mary singing while she dressed Daisy: she was like a girl playing with a doll. Another time, when he got home in the evening, he found Mary and Daisy seated at a table with a book in front of them. He had the feeling Mary was teaching a sister to read, and said:

"It must be such a relief to confide in someone who can keep a secret!"

"What do you mean?" said Mary, springing up and storming out of the room.

But Daisy, left behind, held firmly in place, tipped over the book, like a friend maintaining a tactful silence.

That same night, after dinner, to prevent him from joining her on their customary sofa, Mary sat the doll next to her. He examined Daisy's face and disliked it once more. It was cold and haughty, as if to punish him for his hateful thoughts about her skin.

A bit later, he went into the show room. At first he strolled back and forth among the glass cases. Then, after a while, he opened the big piano top, removed the bench, replaced it with a chair—so he could lean back—and started to walk his fingers over the cool expanse of black and white keys. He had trouble combining the sounds, like a drunk trying to unscramble his words. But meantime he was remembering many of the things he had learned about the dolls. Slowly he had been getting to know them, almost without trying. Until recently, Horace had kept the store that had been making his fortune. Alone, after closing time every day, he liked to wander through the shadowy rooms, reviewing the dolls in the show windows. He went over their dresses, with an occasional sidelong glance at their faces. He observed the lighted windows from various angles, like a stage manager watching his actors from the wings. Gradually he started finding expressions in the dolls' faces similar to those of his salesgirls. Some inspired the same distrust in him, others the certainty that they were against him. There was one with a turned-up nose that seemed to say, "See if I care." Another, which he found appealing, had an inscrutable face: just as she looked good in either a summer or a winter dress, she could also be thinking almost anything, accepting or rejecting him, depending on her mood. One way or another, the dolls had their secrets. Although the window dresser knew how to display each of them to her best advantage, at the last moment she always added a touch of her own. It was then that he started to think the dolls were full of portents. Day and night they basked in covetous looks and those looks nested and hatched in the air. Sometimes they settled on the dolls' faces like clouds over a landscape, shadowing and blurring their expressions, and at other times they reflected back on some poor girl innocently happening by, who was tainted by their original covetousness. Then the dolls were like creatures in a trance, on unknown missions, or lending themselves to evil designs. On the night of his quarrel with Mary, Horace had reached the conclusion that Daisy was one of those changeable dolls who could transmit warnings or receive signals from other dolls. Since she lived in the house, Mary had been showing increasing signs of jealousy. If he complimented one of his salesgirls, he felt Mary's suspicion and reproach in Daisy's brooding look. That was when Mary had started nagging him until she got him to give up the store. But soon her fits of jealousy, after an evening in mixed company, had reached the point where he had also had to give up visiting friends with her.

On the morning after the quarrel he had made up with both of them. His dark thoughts bloomed at night and faded in the daytime. As usual, the three of them had gone for a walk in the garden. He and Mary carried Daisy between them—in a long skirt, to disguise her missing steps—as if gently supporting a sick friend. (Which had not prevented the neighbors from concocting a story about how they had let a sister of Mary's die so as to inherit her money, and then, to atone for the sin, had taken in a doll who resembled her, as a constant reminder of their crime.)

After a period of happiness, during which Mary prepared surprises for him with Daisy and he hastened to enter them in his notebook, had come the night of the second show, with its announcement of Mary's death.

Horace had then hit on the idea of buying his wife a number of dresses made of durable material—he intended these memories of her to last a long time—and asking her to try them on Daisy.

Mary was delighted, and he also pretended to be, when, at her urging—but in response to his subtle hints—they had some of their closest friends to dinner one night. It was stormy out, but they sat down to eat in a good mood. He kept thinking of all the memories the evening was going to leave him with and tried to provoke some unusual situations. First he twirled his knife and fork—like a cowboy with a pair of six-shooters—and aimed them at a girl next to him. She went along with the joke and raised her arms, and he tickled her shaved armpits with the knife. It was too much for Mary, who burst out:

"Horace, you're being a brat!"

He apologized all around and soon everyone was having fun again. But when he was serving his wine from France, over dessert, Mary saw a black stain—the wine he was pouring outside the glass—growing on the table-cloth, and, trying to rise, clutching at her throat, she fainted. They carried her into the bedroom, and, when she recovered, she said she had not been feeling well for days. He sent at once for the doctor, who said it was nothing serious but she had to watch her nerves. She got up and saw off her guests as if nothing had happened. But, as soon as they were alone, she said:

"I can't stand this life any more. You were messing with that girl right under my nose."

"But, my dear . . ."

"And I don't just mean the wine you spilled gaping at her. What were you up to in the yard afterward when she said, 'Horace, stop it'?"

"But, darling, all she said was 'a boring topic.' "

They made up in bed and she fell asleep with her cheek next to his. But, after a while, he turned away to think about her illness. And the next morning, when he touched her arm, it was cold. He lay still, gazing at the ceiling for several grueling minutes before he managed to shout: "Alex!" At that moment the door opened and Mary stuck her head in—and he realized it was Daisy he had touched and that Mary had put her there, next to him, while he slept.

After much reflection, he decided to call his friend, Frank, the doll manufacturer, and ask him to find a way to give Daisy some human warmth.

Frank said:

"I'm afraid it's not so easy, dear boy. The warmth would last about as long as a hot-water bottle."

"All right, I don't care. Do what you want, just don't tell me. I'd also like her to be softer, nicer to touch, not so stiff. . . ."

"I don't know about that, either. Think of the dent you'd make every time you sank a finger in her."

"Well, all the same, she could be more pliant. And, as for the dent—that might not be such a bad idea."

The day Frank took Daisy away, Horace and Mary were sad.

"God knows what they'll do to her," Mary kept saying.

"Now then, darling, let's not lose touch with reality. After all, she was only a doll."

"Was! You sound as if she were dead. Anyway, you're a fine one to talk about losing touch with reality!"

"I was just trying to comfort you. . . ."

"And you think dismissing her like that is the way to do it? She was more mine than yours. I dressed her and told her things I've never told anyone, do you realize? And how she brought us together—have you ever thought of that?"

He was heading for his study, but she went on, raising her voice:

"Weren't you getting what you wanted with our surprises? Wasn't that enough, without asking for 'human warmth'?"

By then he had reached the study and slammed the door behind him. The way she pronounced "human warmth" not only made him feel ridiculous but soured all the pleasures he was looking forward to when Daisy returned. He decided to go for a walk.

When he got back, Mary was out, and when she returned they spent a while hiding the fact that they were unexpectedly glad to see each other.

That night he did not visit his dolls. The next morning he was busy. After lunch he and Mary strolled in the garden. They agreed that Daisy's absence was temporary and should not be made too much of. He even thought it was easier and more natural to have his arm around Mary instead of Daisy. They both felt light and gay and enjoyed being together. But later, at dinnertime, when he went up to the bedroom for her, he was surprised to find her there alone. He had forgotten for a moment that Daisy was gone, and now her absence made him strangely uneasy. Mary might well be a woman without a doll again, but his idea of her was no longer complete without Daisy, and the fact that neither she nor the house seemed to miss Daisy was like a kind of madness. Also, the way Mary drifted back and forth in the room, apparently not thinking of Daisy, and the blankness of her expression, reminded him of a madwoman forgetting to dress and wandering naked. They went down to dinner, and there, sipping his wine from France, he stared at her in silence, until finally it seemed he caught her with Daisy on her mind. Then he began to go over what the two women meant to each other. Whenever he thought of Mary, he remembered her fussing over Daisy, worrying about how to get her to sit straight without sagging, and planning to surprise him with her. If Mary did not play the piano—as Frank's girlfriend did—it was because she expressed herself in her own original manner through Daisy. To strip her of Daisy would be like stripping an artist of his art. Daisy was not only part of her being but her most charming self, so that he wondered how he ever could have loved her before she had Daisy. Perhaps in those days she had found other means or ways to express that side of her personality. Alone in the bedroom, a while back, without Daisy, she had seemed insignificant. Yet— Horace took another sip of his wine from France—there was something disquieting about her insignificance, as if Daisy had still been there, but only as an obstacle she had put up for him to trip over on his way to her.

After dinner he kissed Mary's cool cheek and went in to look at his glass cases. One of them showed a Carnival scene. Two masked dolls, a blonde and a brunette, in Spanish costumes, leaned over a marble balustrade. To the left was a staircase with masks, hoods, paper streamers and other objects scattered on the steps with artful neglect. The scene was dimly lit—and suddenly, watching the brunette, Horace thought he recognized Daisy. He wondered whether she had been ready sooner than expected and Mary had sent for her as a surprise. Without looking again, he opened the glass door. On his way up the staircase he stepped on a mask, which he picked up and threw over the balustrade. The gesture gave the objects around him physical reality and he felt let down. He moved to the podium, irritated because the noise of the machines and the sound of the piano did not blend. But after a few seconds he turned to the dolls again and decided they were probably two women who loved the same man. He opened the drawer and read the caption: "The blonde has a boyfriend. He discovered, some time ago, that he preferred her friend, the brunette, and declared his love to her. She was also secretly in love with him but tried to talk him out of it. He persisted, and, earlier on this Carnival night, he has told the blonde about her rival. Now the two girls have just met for the first time since they both learned the truth. They haven't spoken yet as they stand there in a long silence, wearing their disguises." At last he had guessed the meaning of one of the scenes: the two girls in love with the same man. But then he wondered whether the coincidence was not a portent or sign of something that was already going on in his own life and whether he might not really be in love with Daisy. His mind flitted around the question, touching down on other questions: What was it about Daisy that could have made him fall in love with her? Did the dolls perhaps give him something more than a purely artistic pleasure? Was Daisy really just a consolation in case his wife died? And for how long would she lend herself to a misunderstanding that was always in Mary's favor? The time had come to reconsider their roles and personalities. He did not want to take these worries up to the bedroom where Mary would be waiting for him, so he called Alex, had him dismiss Walter, then sent him for a bottle of wine from France and sat for a while, alone with the noise of the machines. Then he walked up and down the room, smoking. Each time he came to the glass case he drank some wine and set out again, thinking: "If there are spirits that inhabit empty houses, why wouldn't they also inhabit the bodies of dolls?" He thought of haunted castles full of spooked objects and furnishings joined in a heavy sleep, under thick cobwebs, where only ghosts and spirits roam, in concert with whistling bats and sighing marshes . . . At that moment he was struck by the noise of the machines and he dropped his glass. His hair stood on end as it dawned on him that disembodied souls caught the stray sounds of the world, which spoke through them, and that the soul inhabiting Daisy's body was in touch with the machines. To shake off these thoughts he concentrated on the chills going up and down his spine. But, when he had settled in his armchair, his thoughts ran on: no wonder such strange things had happened on a recent moonlit night. They were out in the garden, all three of them, and suddenly he started chasing his wife. She ran, laughing, to hide behind Daisy—which, as he well re-alized, was not the same as hiding behind a tree—and when he tried to kiss her over Daisy's shoulder he felt a sharp pinprick. Almost at once he heard the machines pounding, no doubt to warn him against kissing Mary through Daisy. Mary had no idea how she could have left a pin in the doll's dress. And how—he asked himself—could he have been so foolish as to think Daisy was there to grace and adorn Mary, when in fact they were meant to grace and adorn each other? Now, coming back to the noise of the machines, he confirmed what he had been suspecting all along: that it had a life of its own, like the sound of the piano, although they belonged to different families. The noise of the machines was of a noble family, which was perhaps why Daisy had chosen it to express her true love. On that thought he phoned Frank to ask after Daisy. Frank said she was nearly ready, that the girls in the workshop had found a way to . . . But at this point Horace cut him off, saying he was not interested in tech-nical details. And, hanging up, he felt secretly pleased at the thought of girls working on Daisy, putting something of themselves into her.

The next day, at lunchtime, Mary was waiting for him with an arm around Daisy's waist. After kissing his wife, he took the doll in his arms, and for a moment her soft warm body gave him the happiness he had been hoping for, although when he pressed his lips to hers, she seemed feverish. But he soon grew accustomed to this new sensation and found it com-forting.

That same night, over dinner, he wondered: "Why must the transmi-gration of souls take place only between people and animals? Aren't there cases of people on their deathbed who have handed their souls over to some beloved object? And why assume it's a mistake when a spirit hides in a doll who looks like a beautiful woman? Couldn't it be that, looking for a new body to inhabit, it guided the hands that made the doll? When someone pursues an idea, doesn't he come up with unexpected discoveries, as if someone else were helping him?" Then he thought of Daisy and wondered whose spirit could be living in her body.

Mary had been in a vile mood since early evening. She had scolded Daisy while dressing her, because she would not hold still but kept tipping forward—and now that she was full of water, she was a lot heavier than before. Horace thought of the relationship between his wife and the doll and of the strange shades of enmity he had noticed between women who were such close friends that they could not get along without one another. He remembered observing that the same thing often happened between mother and daughter. . . . A minute later, he raised his eyes from his plate and said:

"Tell me something, Mary. What was your mother like?"

"May I ask the reason for your question? Do you want to trace my defects to her?"

"Of course not, darling. I wouldn't think of it!"

He had spoken in a soothing voice, and she said:

"Well, I'll tell you. She was my complete opposite. Calm as a clear day. She could spend hours just sitting in a chair, staring into space."

"Perfect," he said to himself. Although, after pouring himself a glass of wine, he thought: "On the other hand, I can't very well have an affair with the spirit of my mother-in-law in Daisy's body."

"And what were her ideas on love?"

"Do you find mine inadequate?"

"Mary, please!"

"She had none, lucky for her. Which was why she was able to marry my father to please my grandparents. He was wealthy. And she made him a fine wife."

Horace, relieved, thought: "Well, that's that. One thing less to worry about."

Although it was spring, the night turned cold. Mary refilled Daisy, dressed her in a silk nightie and took her to bed with them, like a hot-water bottle. As he dropped off to sleep, Horace felt himself sinking into a warm pond where all their legs tangled, like the roots of trees planted so close together he was too lazy to find out which ones belonged to him.

III

Horace and Mary were planning a birthday party for Daisy. She was going to be two years old. Horace wanted to present her on a tricycle. He told Mary he had seen one at the Transportation Day fair and he was sure they would let him have it. He did not tell her the reason for using this particular device was that he had seen a bride elope with her lover on a tricycle in a film years ago. The rehearsals were a success. At first he had trouble getting the tricycle going, but as soon as the big front wheel turned it grew wings.

The party opened with a buffet dinner. Soon the sounds from human throats and necks of bottles mixed in an increasingly loud murmur. When it was time to present Daisy, Horace rang a school bell in the courtyard and the guests went out holding their glasses. They saw him come tearing down a long carpeted hallway, struggling with the front wheel. At first the tricycle was almost invisible beneath him. Of Daisy, mounted behind him, only her flowing white dress showed. He seemed to be riding the air, on a cloud. Daisy was propped over the axle that joined the small back wheels, with her arms thrust forward and her hands in his trouser pockets. The tricycle came to a stop in the center of the courtyard, and, acknowledging the cheers and applause, he reached over with one hand and stroked her hair. Then he began pedaling hard again, and as the tricycle sailed back up the carpeted hallway, gathering speed, everyone watched in breathless silence, as if it were about to take flight. The performance was such a success that Horace tried to repeat it, and the laughter and applause were starting up again when suddenly, just as he reached the yard, he lost a back wheel. There were cries of alarm, but when he showed he was not hurt there was more laughter and applause. He had fallen on his back, on top of Daisy, and was kicking his legs in the air like an insect. The guests laughed until they cried. Frank gasped and spluttered:

"Boy, you looked like one of those wind-up toys that go on walking upside down!"

Then they all went back into the dining room. The men who arranged the scenes in the glass cases surrounded Horace, asking to borrow Daisy and the tricycle to make up a story with them. He turned them down, but he was so pleased with himself that he invited everybody into the show room for a glass of wine from France.

"If you wouldn't mind telling us what you feel watching the scenes," said one of the boys, "I think we could all learn something."

He had started to rock back and forth on his heels, staring at his guests' shoes. Finally he made up his mind and said:

"It's very difficult to put into words, but I'll try . . . if you promise meantime to ask no more questions and to be satisfied with anything I care to say."

"Promised!" said one who was a bit hard of hearing, cupping a hand to his ear.

Still, Horace took his time, clasping and unclasping his hands. To quiet the hands, he crossed his arms and began:

"When I look at a scene . . ." Here he stopped, then took up the speech again, with a digression: "(It's very important to see the dolls through a glass, because that gives them the quality of memories. Before, when I could stand mirrors—now they're bad for me, but it would take too long to explain why—I liked to see the rooms that appeared in them.) So . . . when I look at a scene, it's like catching a woman in the act of remembering an important moment in her life, a bit—if you'll forgive the expression—as if I were opening a crack in her skull. When I get hold of the memory, it's like stealing one of her undergarments: I can use it to imagine the most intimate things and I might even say it feels like a defilement. In a way, it's as if the memory were in a dead person and I were picking a corpse, hoping the memory will stir in it. . . ." He let his voice trail off, not daring to describe the weird stirrings he had seen.

The boys were also silent. One of them thought of emptying his glass of wine at a swallow and the others imitated him. Then another said:

"Tell us something more about yourself—your personal tastes, habits, whatever."

"Ah, as for that," said Horace, "I don't think it would be of any help to you in making up your scenes. For instance, I like to walk on a wooden floor sprinkled with sugar. It's that neat little sound . . ."

Just then Mary came in to ask them all out into the garden. It was a dark night and the guests were requested to form couples and carry torches. Mary took Horace's arm and together they showed the way. At the door that led into the garden, each guest picked a small torch from a table and lit it at a flaming bowl on another table. The torchlight attracted the neighbors, who gathered at the low hedge, their faces like shiny fruit with watchful eyes among the bushes, glinting with distrust. Suddenly Mary crossed a flowerbed, flicked a switch, and Daisy appeared, lit up in the high branches of a tall tree. It was one of Mary's surprises and was greeted with cheers and exclamations. Daisy was holding a white fan spread on her breast. A light behind the fan gave her face a theatrical glow. Horace kissed Mary and thanked her for the surprise. Then, as the guests scattered, he saw Daisy staring out toward the street he took on his way home every day. Mary was leading him along the hedge when they heard one of the neighbors shout at others still some distance away, "Hurry! The dead woman's appeared in a tree!" They staggered back to the house, where everyone was toasting the surprise. Mary had the twins—her maids, who were sisters—get Daisy down from the tree and change her water for bed.

About an hour had gone by since their return from the garden when Mary started looking around for Horace and found him back in the show room with the boys. She was pale, and everyone realized something serious had happened. She had the boys excuse Horace and led him up to the bedroom. There he found Daisy with a knife stuck under one breast. The wound was leaking hot water down her dress, which was soaked, and dripping on the floor. She was in her usual chair, with big open eyes. But when Mary touched her arm she felt it going cold.

Collapsing into Horace's arms, Mary burst out crying:

"Who could have dared to come up here and do such a thing?"

After a while she calmed down and sat in a chair to think what was to be done. Then she said:

"I'm going to call the police."

"You're out of your mind," he said. "We can't offend all our guests just because one of them misbehaved. And what will you tell the police? That someone stuck a knife in a doll and that she's leaking? Let's keep this to ourselves. One has to accept setbacks with dignity. We'll send her in for repairs and forget about it."

"Not if I can help it," said Mary. "I'm going to call a private detective. Don't let anyone touch her—the fingerprints must be on the knife."

Horace tried to reason with her, reminding her the guests were waiting downstairs. They agreed to lock the doll in, as she was. But, the moment Mary had left the room, he took out his handkerchief, soaked it in bleach, and wiped off the handle of the knife.

IV

Horace had managed to convince Mary to say nothing about the wounded doll. The day Frank came for her, he brought his mistress, Louise. She and Mary went into the dining room, where their voices soon mixed like twittering birds in connecting cages: they were used to talking and listening at the same time.

Meantime, Horace and Frank shut themselves in the study. They spoke one at a time, in undertones, as if taking turns at drinking from a jug. Horace said, "I was the one who stuck the knife in her so I'd have an excuse to send her in to you . . . without going into explanations." And they stood there in silence, with their heads bowed.

Mary was curious to know what they were discussing. Deserting Louise for a minute, she went to put her ear to the study door. She thought she recognized her husband's voice, but it sounded hoarse and blurred. (At that moment, still mumbling into his chin, Horace was saying, "It may be crazy, but I've heard of sculptors falling in love with their statues.") In a while, Mary went back to listen again, but she could only make out the word "possible," pronounced first by her husband, then by Frank. (In fact, Horace had just said: "It must be possible," and Frank had answered, "If it's possible, I'll do it.")

One afternoon, a few days later, Mary realized Horace was acting strangely. He would linger over her, with fond eyes, then abruptly draw back, looking worried. As he crossed the courtyard at one point, she called after him, went out to meet him and, putting her arms around his neck, said:

"Horace, you can't fool me. I know what's on your mind."

"What?" he said, staring wildly.

"It's Daisy."

He turned pale:

"Whatever gave you that idea?"

He was surprised that she did not laugh at his odd tone.

"Oh, come on, darling. . . . After all, she's like a daughter to us by now," Mary insisted.

He let his eyes dwell on her face, and with them his thoughts, going over each of her features as if reviewing every corner of a place he had visited daily through many long happy years. Then, breaking away, he went and sat in the little parlor to think about what had just happened. His first reaction, when he suspected his wife had found him out, had been to assume she would forgive him. But then, observing her smile, he had realized it was madness to suppose she could imagine, let alone forgive, such a sin. Her face had been like a peaceful landscape, with a bit of golden evening glow on one cheek, the other shaded by the small mound of her nose. He had thought of all the good left in the innocence of the world and the habit of love, and the tenderness with which he always came back to her face after his adventures with the dolls. But in time, when she discovered not only the abysmal nature of his more than fatherly affection for Daisy but also the care with which he had gone about organizing his betrayal, her face and all its features would be devastated. She would never be able to understand the sudden evil in the world and in the habit of love, or feel anything but horror at the sight of him.

So he had stood there, gazing at a spot of sun on his coat sleeve. As he withdrew his arm, the spot had shifted, like a taint, to her dress. Then, heading for the little parlor, he had felt his twisted insides lump and sag, like dead weights. Now he sat on a small bench, thinking he was unworthy of being received into the lap of a family armchair, and he felt as uncomfortable as if he had sat on a child. He hardly recognized the stranger in himself, disillusioned at being made of such base metal. But, to his surprise, a bit later, in bed with the covers pulled up over his ears, he went straight to sleep.

Mary was on the phone to Frank, saying:

"Listen, Frank, you'd better hurry with Daisy. Horace is worrying himself sick."

Frank said:

"I have to tell you, Mary, it's a bad wound, right in the middle of the circulatory system. We can't rush it. But I'll do my best, I promise."

In a while, Horace woke up under his pile of blankets. He found himself blinking down a kind of slope, toward the foot of the bed, and saw a picture of his parents on the far wall. They had died in an epidemic when he was a child. He felt they had cheated him: he was like a chest they had left full of dirty rags instead of riches, fleeing like thieves in the dark before he could grow up and expose the fraud. But then he was ashamed of these monstrous thoughts.

At dinner, he tried to be on his best behavior.

Mary said:

"I called Frank about hurrying Daisy."

If only she had known the madness and betrayal she was contributing to by hastening his pleasure! he thought, blindly casting right and left, like a horse trying to butt its way out.

"Looking for something?" asked Mary.

"No, here it is," he said, reaching for the mustard.

She decided that if he had not seen it standing there in front of him, he must not be well.

Afterward he got up and slowly bent over her, until his lips grazed her cheek. The kiss seemed to have dropped by parachute, onto a plain not yet touched by grief.

That night, in the first glass case, there was a doll seated on a lawn, surrounded by huge sponges, which she seemed to think were flowers. He did not feel like guessing her fate, so he opened the drawer with the captions and read: "This woman is sick in the head. No one has been able to find out why she loves sponges." "That's what I pay them for, to find out," he said to himself, and then, bitterly: "The sponges must be to wipe away her guilt."

In the morning he woke up rolled into a ball and remembered the person he had become. It seemed to him even his name had changed, and if he signed a check it would bounce. His body was sad, as it had been once before, when a doctor told him he had thin blood and a small heart. But that other time he had gotten over the sadness. Now he stretched his legs and thought: "Formerly, when I was young, I had far stronger defenses against guilt: I cared much less about hurting others. Am I getting weak with age? No, it's more like a late flowering of love and shame." He got up, feeling better. But he knew the dark clouds of guilt were just over the horizon, and that they would be back with night.

V

The next days, Mary took Horace for long walks. She wanted to get his mind off Daisy. Yet she was convinced it was not Daisy he missed but the real daughter she could never have.

The afternoon Daisy was returned, Horace did not show any particular affection for her, and again Mary feared she was not the reason for his sadness. But, just before dinner, she noticed him lingering over Daisy with restrained emotion, and felt relieved.

After that, for several nights, as he kissed his wife before going to see his dolls, he watched her face intently, with searching eyes, as if to make sure there was nothing strange hidden anywhere. He had not yet been alone with Daisy.

Then came a memorable afternoon when, in spite of the mild weather, Mary replenished Daisy's hot water, packed Horace comfortably into bed with her for his nap, and went out.

That evening he kept scanning every inch of her face, watching for the enemy she would soon become. She noticed his fidgety gestures, his stilted walk. He was waiting for the sign that he had been found out.

Finally, one morning, it happened.

Once, some time ago, when Mary had been complaining of Alex's beard, Horace had said: "At least he's not like one of those twin maids of yours that you can't tell apart."

She had answered: "Why, do you have anything special to say to either of them? Has there been some mix-up that has . . . inconvenienced you?"

"Yes, I was calling you once—and who do you think turned up? The one who has the honor to bear your name."

After which the twins had been ordered to stay out of sight when he was home. But, seeing one vanish through a door once at his approach, he had plunged after her, thinking she was an intruder, and run into his wife. Since then Mary had them come in only a few hours in the morning and never took her eyes off them.

The day he was found out, Mary had caught the twins raising Daisy's nightie when it was not time to dress her or change her water. As soon as they had left the bedroom, she went in. In a little while the twins saw the lady of the house rush across the courtyard into the kitchen. On her way back she was carrying a carving knife. They were terrified and tried to follow her, but she slammed the door on them. When they peeped through the keyhole her back blocked their view, so they moved to another door. She had Daisy flat on a table, as if to operate on her, and was in a frenzy, stabbing her all over. She looked completely disheveled: a jet of water had caught her in the face. Two thin spurts rose in an arc from one of Daisy's shoulders, mixing in the air, like the water from the fountain in the garden, and her belly gushed through a rip in her nightgown. One of the twins had knelt on a cushion, with a hand over one eye, the other eye stuck, unblinking, to the keyhole. When the draft that blew through the hole made her eye run, her sister took her place. Mary also had tears in her eyes when she finally dropped the knife on Daisy and slumped into an armchair, sobbing, with her face buried in her hands. The twins lost interest in the scene and returned to the kitchen. But soon the lady called them back up to help her pack. She had decided to handle the situation with the wounded dignity of a fallen queen. Determined to punish Horace and, meantime, to adopt the appropriate attitude in case he showed up, she instructed the twins to say she could not receive him. She began making arrangements for a long trip and gave the twins some of her dresses. They followed her out into the garden, and when she drove off in the family car they finally realized what was happening and started to howl over the lady's misfortune. But, back in the house with their new dresses, they were gleeful. They drew open the curtains that covered the mirrors—to spare Horace the unpleasantness of seeing himself in them—and held the dresses up to their bodies for effect. One of them saw Daisy's mangled shape in a mirror and said: "What a beast!" She meant Horace, who had just appeared in a door and was wondering how to ask them to explain the dresses and the bare mirrors. But, suddenly catching sight of Daisy sprawled on the table in her torn nightie, he directed his steps toward her. The twins were trying to sneak out of the room, but he stopped them:

"Where's my wife?"

The one who had said "What a beast!" stared him full in the face and answered:

"She left on a long trip. And she gave us these dresses."

He dismissed them and the thought came to him: "The worst is over." He glanced at Daisy again: the carving knife still lay across her belly. He was not too unhappy and for a moment even imagined having her repaired. But he pictured her all stitched up and remembered a rag horse he had owned as a child, with a hole ripped in it. His mother had wanted to patch it up, but it had lost its appeal and he had preferred to throw it away.

As for Mary, he was convinced she would come back. He kept telling himself: "I have to take things calmly." He welcomed the return of the bold and callous self he had been in his prime. Looking back over the morning's events, he could easily see himself betraying Daisy as well. A few days ago Frank had shown him another doll: a gorgeous blonde with a shady past. Frank had been spreading word of a manufacturer in a northern country who made these new dolls. He had imported the designs and—after some experimenting—found them workable. Soon a little shy man had come by, with big pouchy eyes gleaming under heavy lids, to inquire about the dolls. Frank had brought out pictures of the available models, saying: "Their generic name is Daisy, but then each owner gives them whatever pet name he wants. These are the models we have designs for." After seeing only three of them the little shy man had picked one almost at random and put in an order for her, cash in hand. Frank had quoted a stiff sum, and the buyer had batted his heavy lids once or twice, but then he had signed the order, with a pen shaped like a submarine. Horace had seen the finished blonde and asked Frank to hold her for him, and Frank, who had others on the way, had agreed. At first Horace had considered setting her up in an apartment, but now he had a better idea: he would bring her home and leave her in the glass case where he kept the dolls waiting to be assigned their roles. As soon as everyone was asleep he would carry her up to the bedroom, and before anyone was up in the morning he would put her back in the glass case. He was counting on Mary not returning in the middle of the night. From the moment Frank had set the doll apart for him, he had felt himself riding a lucky streak he had not known since adolescence. Just happening to have been out until it was all over with Daisy meant a higher power was on his side. With this assurance, in addition to his new youthful vigor, he felt in command of events. Having decided to exchange one doll for another, he could not stop to shed tears over Daisy's mutilated body. Mary was certain to be back, now that he no longer cared about her, and she could dispose of the corpse.

Suddenly Horace started to edge along the wall like a thief. Sidling up to a wardrobe, he drew the curtain across the mirror. He repeated the gesture at the other wardrobe. He had had the curtains hung years ago. Mary was always careful to shield him from the mirrors: she dressed behind closed doors and made sure the curtains were in place before leaving the room. Now he was annoyed to think the twins had not only been wearing Mary's clothes but had left the mirrors uncovered. It was not that he disliked seeing things in mirrors, but his sallow face reminded him of some wax dolls he had seen in a museum one afternoon. A shopkeeper had been murdered that day, as had many of the people whose bodies the dolls represented, and the bloodstains on the wax were as unpleasant to him as if, after being stabbed to death, he had been able to see the wounds that had killed him. The only mirror in the bedroom without a curtain was the one over the dresser: a low mirror before which he bent just far enough for a quick glimpse at the knot of his tie as he went by absently each day. Because he combed and shaved by touch, from the mirror's point of view he had always been a man with no head. So now, after covering the other mirrors, he went by it as blithely as usual. But when it reflected his hand against his dark suit he had the same queasy sensation as when he caught sight of his face. He realized then that his hands were also the color of wax. At the same time, he remembered some loose arms he had seen in Frank's office that morning. They were pleasantly colored and as shapely as those of the blonde doll, and, like a child asking a carpenter for scraps, he had told Frank:

"I could use some arms and legs, if you have any left over."

"Whatever for, dear boy?"

"I'd like the men to make up some scenes with loose arms and legs.

For instance, an arm hanging from a mirror, a leg sticking out from under a bed, and so on."

Frank, wiping his face, had watched him askance.

At lunch that day, Horace drank his wine and ate as calmly as if Mary were out spending the day with relatives. He kept congratulating himself over his good luck. He got up feeling elated, sat at the piano for a while, letting his fingers wander over the keys, and finally went up for his nap. On his way past the dresser he thought: "One of these days I'll get over my dread of mirrors and face them." He had always enjoyed being surprised and confused by the people and objects reflected in mirrors. With another glance at Daisy, who would simply have to wait until Mary got back, he lay down. As he stretched out under the covers, he touched a strange object with the tip of his foot, and he jumped out of bed. For a moment he just stood there, then he pulled back the covers. It was a note from Mary that said: "Horace, here's what's left of your mistress. I've stabbed her, too. But I can admit it—not like a certain hypocrite I know who only wanted a pretext to send her in and have those sinful things done to her. You've sickened my life and I'll thank you not to look for me. Mary."

He went back to bed but could not sleep and got up again. He avoided looking at Mary's things on the dresser as he avoided her face when they were angry at each other. He went out to a movie. There he shook hands with an old enemy, without realizing it. He kept thinking of Mary.

When he got back to the black house, there was still a bit of sunlight shining in the bedroom. As he went by one of the covered mirrors, he saw his face in it, through the wispy curtain, lit by a glint of sun, bright as an apparition. With a shiver, he closed the shutters and lay down. If the luck he used to have was coming back, at his age it would not last long, nor would it come alone but accompanied by the sorts of strange events that had been taking place since Daisy's arrival. She still lay there, a few feet away. At least, he thought, her body would not rot. And then he wondered about the spirit that had once inhabited that body like a stranger and whether it might not have provoked Mary's destructive fury so that Daisy's corpse, placed between him and Mary, would keep him away from her. The ghostly shapes of the room disturbed his sleep: they seemed to be in touch with the noise of the machines. He got up, went down to dinner and began to drink his wine. He had not known until then how much he missed Mary—and there was no after-dinner kiss before he headed for the little parlor. Alone there with his coffee, he decided he ought to avoid the bedroom and dinner table while Mary was gone. When he went out for a walk a bit later he remembered seeing a student hotel in a neighborhood nearby, and found his way there. It had a potted palm in the doorway and parallel mirrors all the way up the stairs, and he walked on. The sight of so many mirrors in a single day was a dangerous sign. He remembered what he had told Frank that morning, before encountering the ones in the bedroom: that he wanted to see an arm hanging from a mirror. But he also remembered the blonde doll and decided, once again, to overcome his dread. He made his way back to the hotel, brushed past the potted palm, and tried to climb the stairs without looking at himself in the mirrors. It was a long time since he had seen so many at once, wherever he turned, right and left, with their confusion of images. He even thought there might be someone hidden among the reflections. The lady who ran the place met him upstairs and showed him the vacant rooms: they all had huge mirrors. He chose the best and promised to return in an hour. In his dark house he packed a small suitcase, and on his way back to the hotel he remembered that it had once been a brothel—which explained the mirrors. There were three in the room he had chosen, the largest one next to the bed, and since the room that appeared there was prettier than the real one, he kept his eyes on the one in the mirror, which must have been tired of showing the same mock-Chinese scenery over the years, because the gaudy red wallpaper looked faded, as if sunk in the bottom of a misty lake with its yellowish bridges and cherry trees. He got into bed and put out the light, but he went on seeing the room in the glow that came in from the street. He had the feeling he had been taken into the bosom of a poor family, where all the household objects were friends and had aged together. But the windows were still young and looked out: they were twins, like Mary's maids, and dressed alike, in clinging lace curtains and velvet drapes gathered at the sides. It was all a bit as if he were living in someone else's body, borrowing well-being from it. The loud silence made his ears hum, and he realized he was missing the noise of the machines and wondered whether it might not be a good idea to move out of the black house and never hear its sounds again. If only Mary had been lying next to him now, he would have been perfectly happy. As soon as she came back he would invite her to spend a night with him in the hotel. But then he dozed off thinking of the blonde doll he had seen that morning. He dreamed of a white arm floating in a dark haze. The sound of steps in a neighboring room woke him up. He got out of bed, barefoot, and started across the rug. He saw a white spot following him and recognized his face, reflected in the mirror over the fireplace. He wished someone would invent a mirror that showed objects but not people, although he immediately realized the absurdity of the idea, not to mention the fact that a man without an image in the mirror would not be of this world. He lay down again, just as someone turned on a light in a room across the street. The light fell on the mirror by the bed, and he thought of his childhood and of other mirrors he remembered, and went to sleep.

VI

Several days had gone by. Horace now slept in the hotel and the same pattern of events repeated itself every night: windows went on across the street and the light fell on his mirrors, or else he woke up and found the windows asleep.

One night he heard screams and saw flames in his mirror. At first he watched them as if they were flickers on a movie screen, but then he realized that if they showed in the mirror they must be somewhere in reality, and, springing up and swinging around, all at once, he saw them dancing out a window across the street, like devils in a puppet show. He scrambled out of bed, threw on his robe and put his face to one of his windows. As it caught flashes in its glass, his window seemed frightened at what was happening to the one across the street. There was a crowd be-low—he was on the second floor—and the firetruck was coming. Just then, he saw Mary leaning out another window of the hotel. She had already noticed him and was staring as if she did not quite recognize him. He waved, shut his window and went up the hall to rap on what he figured was her door. She burst right out saying:

"You're wasting your time following me."

And she slammed the door in his face.

He stayed there quietly until he heard her sobbing inside, then he answered:

"I wasn't following you. But since we've met, why don't we go home?"

"You go on if you want," she said.

He thought he had sensed a note of longing in her voice, in spite of everything, and the next day he moved back happily into the black house. There he basked in the luxury of his surroundings, wandering like a sleep-walker among his riches. The familiar objects all seemed full of peaceful memories, the high ceilings braced against death, if it struck from above.

But when he went into the show room after dinner that evening, the piano reminded him of a big coffin, the silence of a wake. It was a resonant silence, as if it were mourning the death of a musician. He raised the top of the piano, and, suddenly, terrified, let it fall with a bang. For a moment he stood there with his arms in the air, as if someone were pointing a gun at him, but then he rushed out into the courtyard shouting:

"Who put Daisy in the piano?"

As his shouts echoed, he went on seeing her hair tangled in the strings, her face flattened by the weight of the lid. One of the twins answered his call but could not get a word out. Finally Alex appeared:

"The lady was in this afternoon. She came to get some clothes."

"These surprises of hers are killing me," Horace shouted, beside himself. But suddenly he calmed down: "Take Daisy to your room and have Frank come for her first thing in the morning. Wait!" he shouted again. "Something else." And—after he had made sure the twins were out of earshot—lowering his voice to a whisper: "Tell Frank he can bring the other doll when he comes for her."

That night he moved to another hotel. He was given a room with a single mirror. The yellow wallpaper had red flowers and green leaves woven in a pattern that suggested a trellis. The bedspread was also yellow and irritated him with its glare: it would be like sleeping outdoors.

The next morning he went home and had some large mirrors brought into the show room to multiply the scenes in the glass cases. The day passed with no word from Frank. That evening, as Alex came into the show room with the wine, he dropped the bottle. . . .

"Anything wrong?" Horace said.

He was wearing a mask and yellow gloves.

"I thought you were a bandit," said Alex as Horace's laugh blew billows in the black silk mask.

"It's hot behind this thing, and it won't let me drink my wine. But before I remove it I want you to take down the mirrors and stand them on the floor, leaning on chairs—like this," said Horace, taking one down and showing him.

"They'd be safer if you leaned the glass on the wall," Alex objected.

"No, because I still want them to reflect things."

"You could lean their backs on the wall then."

"No, because then they'd reflect upward and I have no interest in seeing my face."

When Alex had done as he was told, Horace removed his mask and began to sip his wine, pacing up and down a carpeted aisle in the center of the room. The way the mirrors tipped forward slightly, toward him, leaning on the chairs that separated them from him, made him think of them as bowing servants watching him from under their raised eyelids. They also reflected the floor through the legs of the chairs, making it seem crooked. After a couple of drinks he was bothered by this effect and decided to go to bed.

The following morning—he had slept at home that night—the chauffeur came, on Mary's behalf, to ask for money. He gave him the money without asking where she was, but assumed it meant she would not be back any time soon. So when the blonde arrived, he had her taken straight up to the bedroom. At dinnertime he had the twins dress her in an evening gown and bring her to the table. He ate with her sitting across from him. Afterward, in front of one of the twins, he asked Alex:

"Well, what do you think of this one?"

"A beauty, sir—very much like a spy I met during the war."

"A lovely thought, Alex."

The next day he told the twins:

"From now on you're to call her Miss Eulalie."

At dinnertime he asked the twins (who no longer hid from him):

"Can you tell me who's in the dining room?"

"Miss Eulalie," both twins said at once.

But, between themselves, making fun of Alex, they kept saying:

"It's time to give the spy her hot water."

VII

Mary was waiting in the student hotel, hoping he would return there. She went out only long enough for her room to be made. She carried her head high around the neighborhood, but walked in a haze, oblivious to her surroundings, thinking, "I am a woman who has lost her man to a doll. But if he could see me now he would be drawn to me." Back in her room, she would open a book of poems bound in blue oilcloth and start to read aloud, in a rapt voice, waiting for Horace again. When he failed to show up, she would try to see into the poems, and if their meaning escaped her she abandoned herself to the thought that she was a martyr and that suffering would add to her charm. One afternoon she was able to understand a poem: it was as if someone had left a door open by chance, suddenly revealing what was inside. Then, for a moment, it seemed to her the wallpaper, the folding screen, even the washbowl with its nickel-plated taps also understood the poems, impelled by something in their nature to reach out toward the lofty rhythms and noble images. Often, in the middle of the night, she switched on her lamp and chose a poem as if she could choose a dream. Out walking again the next day in the neighborhood, she imagined her steps were poetry. And one morning she decided, "I would like Horace to know I'm walking alone among trees with a book in my hand."

Accordingly, she packed again, sent for her chauffeur and had him drive her out to a place belonging to a cousin of her mother's: it was in the outskirts and had trees. The cousin was an old maid who lived in an ancient house. When her huge bulk came heaving through the dim rooms, making the floor creak, a parrot squawked: "Hello, milksops!" Mary told Prairie of her troubles without shedding a tear. The fat cousin was horrified, then indignant, and finally tearful. But Mary calmly dispatched the chauffeur with instructions to get money from Horace. In case Horace asked after her, he was to say, as if on his own, that she was walking among trees with a book in her hand. If he wanted to know where she was, he should tell him. Finally, he was to report back at the same time the next day. Then she went and sat under a tree with her book, and the poems started to float out and spread through the countryside as if taking on the shapes of trees and drifting clouds.

At lunch Prairie was silent, but afterward she asked:

"What are you going to do with the monster?"

"Wait for him and forgive him."

"Not at all like you, my dear. This man has turned your head and has you on a string like one of his dolls."

Mary shut her eyes in beatific peace. But later that afternoon the cleaning woman came in with the previous day's evening paper and Mary's eyes strayed over a headline that said: "Frank's Daisy Dolls." She could not help reading the item: "Springwear, our smartest department store, will be presenting a new collection on its top floor. We understand some of the models sporting the latest fashions will be Daisy Dolls. And that Frank, the manufacturer of the famous line of dolls, has just become a partner in Springwear Enterprises. One more example of the alarming rate at which this new version of Original Sin—to which we have already referred in our columns—is spreading among us. Here is an example of a propaganda leaflet found at one of our main clubs: 'Are you homely? Don't worry. Shy? Forget it. No more quarrels. No budget-breaking expenses. No more gossip. There's a Daisy Doll for you, offering her silent love.' "

Mary had awakened in fits and starts:

"The nerve! To think he could use the name of our . . . !"

Still grasping for words, her eyes wide with outrage, she took aim and pointed at the offending spot in the paper:

"Prairie, look at this!"

The fat cousin blinked and rummaged in her sewing basket, searching for her glasses.

"Have you ever heard anything like it?" Mary said, reading her the item. "I'm not only going to get a divorce but kick up the biggest row this country has ever seen."

"Good for you, at last you've come down out of your cloud!" shouted Prairie, extricating her hands, which were raw from scrubbing pans. And, at the first chance she had, while Mary strode frantically up and down, tripping over innocent plants and flowerpots, she hid the book of poems from her.

The next day the chauffeur drove up wondering how to evade Mary's questions about Horace, but she only asked him for the money and then sent him back to the black house to fetch the twin called Mary. Mary—the twin—arrived in the afternoon and told her all about the spy they had to call Miss Eulalie. At first Mary—Horace's wife—was aghast. In a faint voice, she asked:

"Does she look like me?"

"No, Madam—she's blonde and she dresses differently."

Mary—Horace's wife—jumped up, but then dropped back into her armchair, crying at the top of her lungs. The fat cousin appeared and the twin repeated the story. Prairie's huge breasts heaved as she broke into pitiful moans, and the parrot joined the racket screeching:

"Hello, milksops!"

VIII

Walter was back from a vacation and Horace was having his nightly showings again. The first night, he had taken Eulalie into the show room with him, sat her next to him on the podium and kept his arms around her while he watched the other dolls. The boys had made up scenes with more important characters than usual. There were five in the second glass case, representing the board of a society for the protection of unwed mothers. One of them had just been elected president of the board; another, her beaten rival, was moping over her defeat. He liked the beaten rival best and left Eulalie for a moment to go and plant a kiss on her cool forehead. When he got back to the podium he listened for the buzz of the machines through the gaps in the music and recalled what Alex had told him about Eulalie's resemblance to a war spy. Nevertheless, he feasted his eyes greedily on the varied spectacle of the dolls that night. But the next day he woke up exhausted and toward evening he had dark thoughts of death. He dreaded not knowing when he would die, or what part of his body would go first. Every day it was harder for him to be alone. The dolls were no company but seemed to say, "Don't count on us—we're just dolls." Sometimes he whistled a tune, but only to hang from the thread of sound as if it were a thin rope that snapped the moment his attention wandered. Other times, he talked to himself aloud, stupidly commenting on what he was doing, "Now I'm in my study. I've come to get my inkpot." Or he described his actions as if he were watching someone else: "Look at him, poor idiot—there he is, opening a drawer, unstopping the inkpot. Let's see how long he has left." When his fear caught up with him, he went out.

Then, one day, he received a box from Frank. He had it pried open: it was full of arms and legs. He remembered asking Frank for discards and hoped the box did not include any loose heads, which would have unsettled him. He had it carried in to the glass cases where he kept the dolls waiting to be assigned their roles, and called the boys on the phone to explain how he wanted the arms and legs incorporated into the scenes. But the first trial angered him: it was a disaster. The moment he drew the curtain, he saw a doll dressed in mourning, seated at the foot of what looked like the steps of a church. She was staring straight ahead, with an incredible number of legs—at least ten or twelve—sticking out from under her skirt.

On each step above her lay an arm with the palm of the hand turned up. "The clumsy fools," he said to himself. "They didn't have to use all the arms and legs at once." Without trying to figure out the meaning of the scene, he opened the drawer with the captions and read, "This is a poor widow who has nothing to eat. She spends her day begging and has laid out hands like traps to catch alms." "What a dumb idea," he went on mumbling to himself. "And what an undecipherable mess they've made of it." He went to bed in a bad mood. On the point of falling asleep, he saw the widow walking with all her legs, like a spider.

After this setback Horace felt very disappointed in the boys, the dolls, and even Eulalie. But a few days later Frank took him out for a drive. Suddenly, on the highway, Frank said:

"See that small two-story house by the river? That's where that little shy man—you remember, the one who bought your blonde's sister—lives with your—uh—sister-in-law." He slapped Horace on the leg and they both laughed. "He only comes at night. Afraid his mother will find out."

The next morning, toward noon, Horace returned to the spot alone. A dirt road led down to the shy man's house by the river. At the entrance to the road stood a closed gate, and next to it a gatehouse probably belonging to the forest ranger. He clapped, and an unshaven man in a torn hat came out chewing on a mouthful of something:

"Yeah—what is it?"

"I've been told the owner of that house over there has a doll. . . ."

The man, now leaning back on a tree, cut him short:

"The owner's out."

Horace drew several bills from his wallet, and the man, eyeing the money, began to chew more slowly. Horace stood there thoughtfully rippling the bills as if they were a hand of cards. The man swallowed his mouthful and watched. After giving him time to imagine what he could do with the money, Horace said:

"I might just want to have a quick look at that doll. . . ."

"The boss'll be back at seven."

"Is the house open?"

"No, but here's the key," said the man, reaching for the loot and pocketing it. "Remember, if anyone finds out, I ain't seen you. . . . Give the key two turns. . . . The doll's upstairs. . . . And, mind you, don't leave nothing out of place."

Horace strode with brisk steps down the road, once again full of youthful excitement. The small front door was as dirty as a slovenly old hag, and the key seemed to squirm in the lock. He went into a dingy room with fishing poles leaning against a wall. He picked his way through the litter and up a recently varnished staircase. The bedroom was comfortable—but there was no doll in sight. He looked everywhere, even under the bed, until he found her in a wardrobe. At first it was like running into one of Mary's surprises. The doll was in a black evening gown dotted with tiny rhinestones like drops of glass. If she had been in one of his showcases he would have thought of her as a widow sprinkled with tears. Suddenly he heard a blast, like a gunshot. He ran to look over the edge of the staircase and saw a fishing pole lying on the floor below, in a small cloud of dust. Then he decided to wrap the doll in a blanket and carry her down to the river. She was light and cold, and while he looked for a hidden spot under the trees, he caught a scent that did not seem to come from the forest and traced it to her. He found a soft patch of grass, spread out the blanket, holding her by the legs, slung over his shoulder, and laid her down as gently as if she had fainted in his arms. In spite of the seclusion, he was uneasy. A frog jumped and landed nearby. As it sat there for a long moment, panting, he wondered which way it was going to leap next and finally threw a stone at it. But, to his disappointment, he still could not devote his full attention to this new Daisy Doll. He dared not look her in the face for fear of her lifeless scorn. Instead, he heard a strange murmur mixed with the sound of water. It came from the river, where he saw a boy in a boat, rowing toward him with horrible grimaces. He had a big head, gripped the oars with tiny hands, and seemed to move only his mouth, which was like a piece of gut hideously twisted in its strange murmur. Horace grabbed the doll and ran back to the shy man's house.

On his way home, after this adventure with a Daisy belonging to someone else, he thought of moving to some other country and never looking at another doll. He hurried into the black house and up to the bedroom, grimly determined to get rid of Eulalie—and found Mary sprawled face down on the bed, crying. He went up and stroked her hair, but realized Eulalie was on the bed with them. So he called in one of the twins and ordered her to remove the doll and to have Frank come for her. He stretched out next to Mary and they both lay there in silence waiting for night to fall. And then, taking her hand and searching painfully for words, as if struggling with a foreign language, he confessed how disappointed he was in the dolls and how miserable his life had been without her.

IX

Mary thought Horace's disappointment in the dolls was final, and for a while they both acted as if happier times were back. The first few days, the memories of Daisy were bearable. But then they began to fall into unexpected silences—and each knew who the other was thinking of. One morning, strolling in the garden, Mary stopped by the tree where she had put Daisy to surprise Horace. There, remembering the story made up by the neighbors and the fact that she had actually killed Daisy, she burst into tears. When Horace came out to ask her what was wrong, she met him with a bleak silence, refusing to explain. He realized she had lost much of her appeal, standing there with folded arms, without Daisy. Then, one evening, he was seated in the little parlor, blaming himself for Daisy's death, brooding over his guilt, when suddenly he noticed a black cat in the room. He got up, annoyed, intending to rebuke Alex for letting it in, when Mary appeared saying she had brought it. She was in such a gay mood, hugging him as she told him about it, that he did not want to upset her by throwing it out, but he hated it for the way it had taken advantage of his guilty feelings to sneak up on him. And soon it became a source of further discord as she trained it to sleep on the bed. He would wait for her to fall asleep, then start an earthquake under the covers until he dislodged it. One night she woke up in the middle of the earthquake:

"Was that you kicking the cat, Horace?"

"I don't know."

She kept coming to the defense of the cat, scolding him when he was mean to it. One night, after dinner, he went into the show room to play the piano. For some days now he had called off the scenes in the glass cases and, against his habit, left the dolls in the dark, alone with only the drone of the machines. He lit a footlamp by the piano, and there, on the lid, indistinguishable from the piano except for its eyes, was the cat. Startled, he brushed it off roughly and chased it into the little parlor. There, jumping and clawing to get out, it ripped a curtain off the door to the courtyard. Mary was watching from the dining room. She saw the curtain come down and rushed in with strong words. The last he heard was:

"You made me stab Daisy and now I suppose you want me to kill the cat."

He put on his hat and went out for a walk. He was thinking that, if she had forgiven him—at one point, when they were making up, she had even said, "I love you because you're a bit mad"—Mary had no right now to blame him for Daisy's death. In any case, seeing her lose her attraction without Daisy was punishment enough. The cat, instead of adding to her appeal, cheapened her. She had been crying when he left and he had thought, "Well, it's her cat—so it's her guilt." At the same time, he had the uneasy feeling that her guilt was nothing compared to his, and that, while it was true that she no longer inspired him, it was also true that he was falling back into his old habit of letting her wash his sins away. And so it would always be, even on his deathbed. He imagined her at his side still, on his predictably cowardly last days or minutes, sharing his unholy dread. Perhaps, worse still—he hadn't made up his mind on that point— he would not know she was there.

At the corner he stopped to gather his wits so he could cross without being run over. For a long time he wandered in the dark streets, lost in thought. Suddenly he found himself in Acacia Park. He sat on a bench, still thinking about his life, resting his eyes on a spot under the trees. Then he followed the long shadows of the trees down to a lake, where he stopped to wonder vaguely about his soul, which was like a gloomy silence over the dark water: a silence with a memory of its own, in which he recognized the noise of the machines, as if it were another form of silence. Perhaps the noise had been a steamboat sailing by, and the silence was the memories of dolls left in the wreck as it sank in the night. Suddenly coming back to reality, he saw a young couple get up out of the shadows. As they approached, he remembered kissing Mary for the first time in a fig tree, nearly falling out of the tree, after picking the first figs. The couple walked by a few feet away, crossed a narrow street and went into a small house. He noticed a row of similar houses, some with "for rent" signs. When he got home, he made up again with Mary. But, later that night, alone for a moment in the show room, he thought of renting one of the small houses on the park with a Daisy Doll.

The next day at breakfast something about the cat caught his attention: it had green bows in its ears. Mary explained that all newborn kittens had the tips of their ears pierced by the druggist with one of those machines used for punching holes in file paper. He found this amusing and decided it was a good sign. From a street phone he called Frank to ask him how he could distinguish the Daisy Dolls from the others in the Springwear collection. Frank said that at the moment there was only one, near the cash register, wearing a single long earring. The fact that there was only one left seemed providential to Horace: she was meant for him. And he began to relish the idea of returning to his vice as to a voluptuous fate. He could have taken a trolley, but he did not want to break his mood, so he walked, thinking about how he was going to tell his doll apart in the throng of other dolls. Now he was also part of a throng, pleasantly lost—it was the day before Carnival—in the holiday crowd. The store was farther away than he had anticipated. He began to feel tired—and anxious to meet the doll. A child aimed a horn at him and let out an awful blast in his face. He started to have horrible misgivings and wondered whether he should not put things off until afternoon. But when he reached the store and saw costumed dolls in the show windows he decided to go in. The Daisy Doll was wearing a wine-colored Renaissance costume. A tiny mask added to her proud bearing and he felt like humbling her. But a salesgirl he knew came up with a crooked smile and he withdrew.

In a matter of days he had installed the doll in one of the small houses by the park. Twice a week, at nine in the evening, Frank sent a girl from his shop over with a cleaning woman. At ten o'clock the girl filled the doll with hot water and left. Horace had kept the doll's mask on. He was delighted with her and called her Hermione. One night when they were sitting in front of a picture he saw her eyes reflected in the glass: they shone through the black mask and looked thoughtful. From then on he always sat in the same place, cheek to cheek with her, and whenever he thought the eyes in the glass—it was a picture of a waterfall—took on an expression of humbled pride he kissed her passionately. Some nights he crossed the park with her—he seemed to be walking a ghost—and they sat on a bench near a fountain. But suddenly he would realize her water was getting cold and hurry her back into the house.

Not long after that there was a big fashion show in the Springwear store. A huge glass case filled the whole of the top floor: it was in the center of the room, leaving just enough space on all four sides for the spectators to move around it. Because people came not only for the fashions but also to pick out the Daisy Dolls, the show was a tremendous success. The showcase was divided into two sections by a mirror that extended to the ceiling. In the section facing the entrance, the scene—arranged and interpreted by Horace's boys—represented an old folk tale, "The Woman of the Lake." A young woman lived in the depths of a forest, near a lake. Every morning she left her tent and went down to the lake to comb her hair. She had a mirror which some said she held up behind her, facing the water, in order to see the back of her head. One morning, after a late party, some high-society ladies decided to pay the lonely woman a visit. They were to arrive at dawn, ask her why she lived alone, and offer their help. When they came up on her, the woman of the lake was combing. She saw their elegant gowns through her hair, and curtsied humbly before them. But at their first question she straightened up and set out along the edge of the lake. The ladies, thinking she was going to answer the question or show them some secret, followed her. But the lonely woman only went round and round the lake, trailed by the ladies, without saying or showing them anything. So the ladies left in disgust, and from then on she was known as "the madwoman of the lake." Which is why, in that part of the country, a person lost in silent thought is said to be "going round the lake."

In the showcase, the woman of the lake appeared seated at a dressing table on the edge of the water. She wore a frilly white robe embroidered with yellow leaves. On the dresser stood a number of vials of perfume and other objects. It was the moment in the story when the ladies arrived in their evening gowns. All sorts of faces enthralled by the scene went by outside the glass, looking the dolls up and down, and not only for their fashions. There were glinting eyes that jumped suspiciously from a skirt to a neckline, from one doll to the next, distrusting even the virtuous ones like the woman of the lake. Other wary eyes seemed to tiptoe over the dresses as if afraid of slipping and landing on bare flesh. A young girl bowed her head in Cinderella-like awe at the worldly splendors that she imagined went with the beautiful gowns. A man knit his brows and averted his eyes from his wife, hiding his urge to own a Daisy Doll. The dolls, in general, did not seem to care whether they were being dressed or undressed. They were like mad dreamers oblivious to everything but their poses.

The other section of the showcase was subdivided into two parts—a beach and a forest. The dolls on the beach wore bathing suits. Horace had stopped to observe two in a "conversational" pose: one with concentric circles drawn on her belly, like a shooting target (the circles were red), the other with fish painted on her shoulderblades. Carrying his small head stiffly, like another doll head, among the spectators, Horace moved on to the forest. The dolls in that scene were natives and half-naked. Instead of hair, some grew plants with small leaves from their heads, like vines that trailed down their backs; they had flowers or stripes on their dark skins, like cannibals. Others were painted all over with very bright human eyes. He took an immediate liking to a negress, who looked normal except for a cute little black face with red button lips painted on each breast. He went on circling the showcase until he located Frank and asked him:

"Which of the dolls in the forest are Daisies?"

"Why, dear boy, in that section they're all Daisies."

"I want the negress sent to the house by the park."

"I'm sold out right now. It'll take at least a week."

In fact, no less than twenty days went by before Horace and the negress could meet in the house by the park. She was in bed, with the covers drawn up to her chin.

He found her less interesting than expected, and when he pulled back the covers she let out a fiendish cackle in his face. It was Mary, who proceeded to vent her spite on him with bitter words. She explained how she had learned of his latest escapade: it turned out his cleaning woman also worked for her cousin Prairie. Noticing his strange calm—he seemed distraught—she stopped short. But then, trying to hide her amazement, she asked:

"So now what do you have to say for yourself?"

He went on staring blankly, like a man sunk into a stupor after an exhaustion of years. Then he started to turn himself around with a funny little shuffle. Mary said, "Wait for me," and got up to wash off the black paint in the bathroom. She was frightened and had started to cry and sneeze at the same time. When she got back he had vanished. But she found him at home, locked in a guest room, refusing to talk to anyone.

X

Mary kept asking Horace to forgive her for her latest surprise. But he remained as silent and unyielding as a wooden statue that neither represented a saint nor was able to grant anything. Most of the time he was shuttered in the guest room, almost motionless (they knew he was alive only because he kept emptying bottles of wine from France). Sometimes he went out for a while in the evening. When he returned he had a bite to eat and then lay flat on the bed again, with open eyes. Often Mary went in to look at him, late at night, and found him rigid as a doll, always with the same glassy stare. One night she was stunned to see the cat curled up next to him. She decided to call the doctor, who began giving him injections. He was terrified of the injections but seemed to take more of an interest in life. So, with the help of the boys who worked on the glass cases, she convinced him to let them set up a new show for him.

That night they had dinner in the dining room. He asked for the mustard and drank a considerable amount of wine from France. He took his coffee in the little parlor, then went straight into the show room. The first scene had no caption: among plants and soft lights, in a large rippling pool, he made out a number of loose arms and legs. He saw the sole of a foot stick out through some branches, like a face, followed by the entire leg, which reminded him of a beast in search of prey. As it glanced off the glass wall, it hesitated before veering in the opposite direction. Then came another leg, followed by a hand with its arm, slowly winding and unwinding around each other like bored animals in a cage. He stood there for a while, dreamily watching their different combinations, until there was a meeting of toes and fingers. Suddenly the leg began to straighten out in the commonplace gesture of standing on its foot. He was dismayed and flashed his light at Walter, as he moved the podium to the next scene. There he saw a doll on a bed, wearing a queen's crown. Curled up next to her was Mary's cat. This distressed him and he was angry at the boys for letting it in. At the foot of the bed were three nuns kneeling on prayer stools. The caption read, "The queen died giving alms. She had no time to confess, but her whole country is praying for her." When he looked again, the cat was gone. But he had the uneasy feeling it would turn up again somewhere. He decided to enter the scene—gingerly, watching for the unpleasant surprise the cat was about to spring on him. Bending to peer into the queen's face, he rested a hand on the foot of the bed. Almost at once, a hand belonging to one of the nuns settled on his. He must not have heard Mary's voice pleading with him, because the minute he felt her hand he straightened up, stiff as death, stretching his neck and gasping like a captive bird trying to flap its wings and caw. Mary took hold of his arm, but he pulled away in terror and began turning himself around with a little shuffle, as he had done the day she had painted her face black and laughed in his face. She was rattled and frightened again and let out a scream. He tripped on a nun, knocking her over. Then, on his way out of the case, he missed the small door and walked into the glass wall. There he stood pounding on the glass with his hands, which were like birds beating against a closed window. Mary did not dare take hold of his arm again. She ran to call Alex, who was nowhere to be found. Finally he appeared, and, thinking she was a nun, asked politely what he could do for her. Crying, she said that Horace was mad. They went into the show room but could not find him. They were still looking for him when they heard his steps in the gravel of the garden. They saw him cut straight through the flowerbeds. And when they caught up with him, he was going toward the noise of the machines.

TRANSLATED BY LUIS HARSS

Enrique Amorim

Uruguay
(1900–1960)

———— \\ ————

Enrique Amorim lived most of his life and pursued his literary career in Argentina. He was barely twenty when he published his first book, *20 años*, a collection of poetry. Beginning in 1923 Amorim wrote stories, essays, poems, plays, screenplays, and novels dealing with rural life, gauchos, farmlands, and the city. His three most recognized novels are *La carreta* (1929), *El paisano Aguilar* (1934), and *El caballo y su sombra* (1941). Amorim's short stories were published as a collection in *Después del temporal* (1953, 1958). Though his longer works verge on a kind of rural realism that was quickly outdated, Amorim was no crude practitioner of local color or of the regionalist variety of Spanish American fiction. "The Photograph" shows that he was a subtle, sensitive writer, with the ability to temper and elevate a potentially melodramatic situation. He deals here with a broad sociohistorical phenomenom: European immigration to South America. But instead of focusing on the coarse and tawdry details of immigrant labor, he captures a touching individual quandary: how a Frenchwoman, who wants to reassure her mother back home of the respectability of her position in the New World, goes about getting herself photographed in such a way as to convey that message. To center on the issue of the photograph's composition and production frames the story's own, picturelike, deceptive simplicity. It is only indirectly, by the evasive behavior of the schoolteacher, for instance, that the reader discerns the sad reality of the woman's trade.

The Photograph

The town photographer turned out to be very accommodating. He showed her various painted backdrops. Grayish, cracked, and faded scenery. One featured trees of primeval verdure, a Nature of ages past. Another, with several truncated columns that—according to him—went with a horseshoe-shaped wrought iron table resting on three hunting crops.

The photographer wanted to make her fit in. Madame Dupont was a very pleasant person despite the aggressive tint of her hair, the thick layers of face powder, and a jewel that threatened the unprotected eyes of the entire neighborhood. With a different perfume, perhaps with no scent at

201

all, she might have gained a respectable position in that small-town atmosphere. But the woman simply did not know how to abandon a very foreign intimacy.

"Unless the señora would prefer a snapshot taken in the plaza. But I don't believe you capable of such bad taste," the photographer said. And laughed to underscore his observation. "I think it is more suitable to take one that looks as if you were in a lovely garden, taking tea. . . . Have I interpreted your wishes correctly?"

And he pulled a dusty railing and the iron table over before the painted columns. The photographer arranged two chairs at a cozy distance, and then stepped back, looking for the best angle. He disappeared for a few seconds beneath the black cloth, then returned to the conversation as one returns after making a sensational discovery.

"Magnificent. Mag-ni-fi-cent!" The cloth sailed into a corner. "I have just seen exactly what you have in mind."

The woman stared at the scenery rather dubiously. The poor creature knew nothing about such matters. She had been photographed only twice in her life. Once when she set sail from Marseilles, for her passport. And a picture taken in America with a sailor, in an amusement park. Naturally, she hadn't sent that picture to her mother. What would she say when she saw her with a sailor, considering how her mother despised the sea and anyone connected with it?

Again she explained to the photographer what she planned.

"I want a portrait to send to my mother. It must give the impression that it was taken in a real house. My own house."

The photographer already knew her explanation by heart. She wanted a portrait eloquent enough to speak for her. He knew the inscription she would write at the bottom: "To my dearest beloved mother, in the patio of my home with my best friend."

It was easy to fake the house. The backdrops would do admirably. What was lacking was the companion, the friend.

"That is up to you, señora. I can't help you there. Have her come with you and I guarantee you a perfect picture of the two of you."

Madame Dupont returned three or four times. The photographer was helpful, encouraging.

"Only yesterday I took two ladies sitting before this same canvas. Fantastic. It's been tested now. And it's perfect for two people. Look at this proof. It looks like the garden of an elegant home."

The client smiled as she looked at the proof. The photographer was right. A truly handsome portrait. Two ladies, in their small garden, taking tea.

She was light-hearted as she returned to her shabby home on the outskirts of town.

Some hundred meters from her own dark corner lived the school-teacher, the only neighbor who ever responded to her timid greeting.

"Buenas tardes."

"Buenas. . . ."

The pitiful woman with the peroxided hair felt her legs tremble. Her words of greeting evaporated on her lips. And she hugged the wall, without looking up.

Maybe some day she would work up the courage to pause and speak to her neighbor. There on her marble balcony, the schoolmarm looked withered. Melancholy, and defeated. The balcony itself looked very much like the one on the backdrop. Perhaps she would ask her the favor. Why not try? She would never refuse such an innocuous request.

Finally, one afternoon, she stopped. An afternoon when there were no people about, only stray dogs. A cart carrying hay was just passing by, one of those you make a wish on. And it is granted. . . .

She stopped impulsively. Of course, she was not expected. She explained the situation as best she could. Yes, it was just to have a picture taken to send to her mother. A picture of her with someone else, someone like the señorita, respectable. . . . She smiled, sure that her expression would help. The photograph would be taken of the two of them, and then she would add the inscription. Her mother, a woman getting along in years now, would see that her daughter lived in a decent house and had lady friends, good friends, nearby. The setting had been ready for days now. Would she be so kind as to do her this favor? Madame Dupont's own relationships were few and far between, and not suitable for something like this. Not appropriate. Besides, they wouldn't understand. Might she expect her at the photographer's? Yes, she would wait until after school hours. Tomorrow. After all the children had gone home.

"Merci, merci. . . ."

Madame Dupont could not remember whether she had been the only one to speak. Whether the teacher had said yes or no. But she remembered a phrase she had not heard for a long time: "With pleasure."

And she gave thanks with her mother's words. And before going to bed she kissed her mother's picture, then put it back where she kept it in a pile of sheets, shrouded.

Finally, someone from the other side of the world had deigned to hold out a hand to help her make the leap. She was thinking, as she walked to the photographer's studio, that maybe this was the beginning of a new stage in her life. The teacher had answered normally, as if it were no effort at all to agree. That detail soothed her.

They kept arranging the chairs, moving the table, flicking the feather duster over the dusty pâpier maché balcony.

The photographer, weary of rearranging the scene, went to the open doorway to watch the people passing by in the street. After the children had poured out of the school, he came back inside to inform his client. The teacher would be on her way now.

"She'll be here any moment," the woman assured the photographer. "She's probably touching up her makeup."

Fifteen minutes later, the students had all hung up their white smocks and were back outside, dirty, noisy, eating bananas and tossing the peels on the sidewalks with sadistic intent, waiting for someone to slip. Days they felt contrary without knowing why.

"She should be here by now," the photographer said. "I'm sorry to tell you, but soon there won't be enough light to get a good plate."

Still the woman waited, enjoying her peaceful little corner, happy in her expectations. She had never sat so long in such a pleasant and cozy place. She was filled with an honorable, simple, unfamiliar happiness.

With the first shadows, Madame Dupont left the studio. She walked away hiding her despondency. She said she would be back the following day. The teacher, she was sure, had forgotten the appointment.

When she turned the corner into her street, she saw the teacher flee her balcony. The bang of the shutter resounded like a slap in the face. She felt it blazing on her cheek.

Such an episode is not easy to forget. Even less if you live such a monotonous, such an unvaryingly monotonous life. Although Madame Dupont was accustomed to going out once a week, she has reduced the number of her outings. Months go by that she never steps outside the horrible walls of her house.

She has never again seen the schoolteacher withering on her marble balcony, waiting for love, for happiness.

The photographer stored away the backdrop, the cloth dominated by the tree with the fanciful foliage. A fine dust—the soul of the town, the mark of its peaceful hours—has settled over the railing.

The children still toss banana peels on the sidewalks out of pure perversity. Especially when a norther is blowing. When you hear the shouting of irritated mothers, angry fathers.

Sometimes, it is not an exaggeration to say it, you have to shrug your shoulders and go on living.

TRANSLATED BY MARGARET SAYERS PEDEN

Luisa Mercedes Levinson

Argentina
(1914–1988)

———— \\ ————

A compelling novelist, short story writer, playwright, and journalist, Luisa Mercedes Levinson has unfortunately been eclipsed by the popularity of her daughter, novelist Luisa Valenzuela. Levinson epitomized the upper-class Argentine woman: of foreign descent, brought up speaking English and French, and exquisitely educated, she played the piano and the harp and sang very well, lived some time in Europe, and was involved in literary activities. Her father was Australian and her mother the daughter of a Spanish diplomat. Because of illness Levinson was educated mostly at home by her British governess, and at nineteen she married Dr. Pablo Valenzuela. She was associated with the magazine *Sur* and its leading figure, Jorge Luis Borges, and wrote sentimental counseling in a newspaper column she called "Sharing Secrets with Lisa Lenson," her pseudonym then. She also published short stories in *Sur* and in the literary supplement of *La Nación*. The quality of her work was far from common or stereotypical, however. Levinson received some recognition in her lifetime, although she did not publish her novel *La casa de los Felipe* until 1951, when she was already thirty-seven years old. Her second novel, *Concierto en mi,* won the Buenos Aires Municipal Prize in 1956. Her play *El tiempo de Federica* (1962) was awarded first prize of the Teatro Municipal General San Martín. By 1959 Levinson's work had been translated into English, French, Italian, and German. "The Clearing," a powerful tale of eros and violence, could not have been written by a man, according to distinguished Venezuelan author Elizabeth Burgos. The story was first collected in *El estigma del tiempo* (1977).

The Clearing

In a clearing on Mendihondo's land onto which the brush had begun to clamber stood a two-room shack with porches on both sides and a zinc roof savaged by sunlight. The clearing was less than a league wide; the Misiones jungle ringed the place like a noose and threatened it with death by choking. Only the occasional monkey or rhea visited that dry island, or, still more rare, some Indian message-runner like myself, driven by poverty across the jungle and the red *páramo.**

páramo" a plain

205

Years ago the shack had been whitewashed, and cows grazed in the yard. Now a pitiful well with a she-mule lashed to the crossbar was the only source of water. In a Paraguayan hammock slung from the porch beams, a dark woman with short, plump limbs lay stretched, cooling herself with a reed fan. Despite the dark hue of her skin, she looked foreign; the thick shadow under her eyes suggested kohl. She wore a pale dress that showed her shapely curves. The hammock swayed under the weight of her small, thick figure. Around her hovered a murk, like a halo or aura. Though it may have been merely the wafting swarm of flies and mosquitos.

One night don Alcibíades had brought her back from Oberá, and there she had stayed. He called her by no name: he said only *hey you! look here you!* Her name was hard to pronounce. She had fancied that this bearded man with deadpan eyes, quick gestures, and a silver-plated buckle would whisk her away to cities, to fairgrounds where great wheels whirled through the sky over the distant blare of trumpets, where at dusk the flasks of rum passed from lip to lip, gently swollen by the secret vows of many men.

There they had stayed without a guitar or a dog. And then he hired Ciro, the ranchhand. Ciro led the animals to the trough; he spayed, he butchered, he cooked, he brewed maté,* and he washed clothes. He also toted the hammock from post to post, in search of shade, with or without the woman in it. He rarely spoke; he passed the nights alone in the dark, leaning against the last post. Since he took no maté, nothing shone but the hectic gleam of his eyes, now and again. The stars burned bright in the night sky; they were out beyond, along the rim of the celestial dome.

In darkness now, don Alcibíades tossed his cigarette butt and approached the hammock. There he stood for some time. Then he took up the woman and carried her into the shack.

Ciro brewed maté in the early dawn. By then the woman was back in the hammock, as though she had never stirred, fanning, fanning, her eyes blackened with kohl. The look on her face resembled the look on the faces of so many women from the villages and cities: a mask of sadness or boredom, and behind the mask, nothing.

Squatting, Ciro passed her the maté, the pot just beyond, on the red ground; on his knees now, he handed her a cigarette rolled in corn husks, a morsel of fruit, a partridge from the laguna fifteen leagues off. His boss watched from within, fingering his silver buckle and stretching his dry lips. The boy was a good worker, a hard worker, and he was learning respect.

One morning before dawn, eating her breakfast of coconut, the woman saw a snake: she took up the gun that lay beside her in the hammock and fired a shot into its head. As she so often had. Don Alcibíades stepped through the door of the shack.

maté a kind of tea

"Good shot, hon. You get a prize for good shootin'. I'm taking the bullocks to the fair, and I'll buy you a blouse."

"Can I come along, boss?"

"No," said don Alicibíades. Then he turned to the woman. "You got one shot left. That'll do you." And he stalked off.

The mask of her face never fazed.

Ciro mounted the mare and took a turn around the field, as usual. He flushed three stray cows from the jungle, dewormed a calf, picked the ticks off another, and patched the twig fence. When he returned to the shack, he started in on the chores: he lit the fire for the roast in the wind and dust; squatting, as always, he watched the woman out of the corner of his eye. She stretched and unbuttoned her blouse, as though the buttons bothered her breasts. Lying stretched there in the hammock, fanning, her face never fazed; only her body stirred; it writhed in the netting like many shimmering freakish deep-sea fishes struggling and flailing in some unnatural place. With distant, savage beauty. On his knees, Ciro neared her slowly and silently and began to stroke the hand that dangled over the edge of the hammock. She lifted her hand to her breast, bringing his with hers. He leapt into the netting, as rash and reckless as a breaking storm. And their hot sweat mixed with deep salts and the secret of the world was at last divulged. The woman's lips parted. A pale voluptuous peace rose over the red earth. There were no birds. At a cry from the woman, Ciro started. A shot rang out, and he fell stiff from the hammock and struck the hard earth.

"Not expecting me home so soon, eh?" And then: "Don't bitch and moan! I didn't drop him on you, did I?"

Alicibíades approached, tucking the gun in his belt. Then he plucked up the edges of the hammock and wove them together, end to end, with his rope. The woman lay still, silently, sightlessly gazing at the rope that closed first over her face, then the length of her body. He worked neatly and deftly. He finished up with her feet, in a big double knot.

She still didn't know what had happened. The rope squeezed her face and her breasts. Something sticky had spattered both thighs and one of her arms. A smell arose from the hard ground, a mix of dust and love, of things distant and deep, perhaps oceans. With one quick twist, the hammock turned over; and there she was, staring at Ciro, dead: his blown-out brow, his timid nose and the helpless wound of his lips, his sweet obliging lips, the freshly kissed lips of a boy.

The woman lay awash in that departed peace. Though she felt no fear, she understood that almost nothing could be worse. Some time had passed since she had touched bottom; what was happiness but a blur, a fleeting memory, a moment with no future. She had drunk, just then, the depths of happiness for the first time, and in spite of everything she lay awash in happiness, a sea of happiness which mattered more than the fact, which havocked time, which held her in a moment that had already passed. At doña Jacinta's she had known the desires of many men, but never had she tasted the bliss that beckons back faraway days: childhood and a boat and the wisp of a song. She felt as though her breasts and her womb were the nub of the universe. She opened her eyes. Ciro lay motionless below her on the ground. She twisted in the net, and a dull, stony hatred began to rise through her, as though from the very bowels of the red earth. A clay hatred, that took her and overtook her. By rubbing her sides, she managed to turn on her side. Her hatred did not arise from torment or weakness; it did not result from the fact of her lying there mortified, roped, trapped. It was a hard hatred against the man with the power, against her boss Alcibíades, standing beside the post; there, in that place that had held her hope, her patience, her poverty and her love: for Ciro.

Her mask revealed nothing, as ever. And yet now she was reliving the moment in which the man with the beard had turned up at around dusk on doña Jacinta's terrace, the man whose boots squeaked as though with every step he were stamping out the light of the world, to eye the line-up of girls: la Zoila, so thin she looked fit to break; la Wilda, with her green eyes, puffy lips and frizzed hair; and the rest: how he had chosen her, how he had made her lie down and tuck her arms behind the nape of her neck, and how, for the first time, a wave of revulsion had risen in her throat. He vowed to show her the cities; he offered her cigarettes rolled in corn husks; and she forgot her disgust and went away with him, leaving her sack of clothes to the girls, for he would buy her new dresses and a blue silk slip. And then they came here to the clearing where, as on the terrace, as in the village, the days were ever the same, and more so the same, dusk to dawn and night to day, from one round of heat to the next.

The hatred choked her, rising in waves from her womb. It resembled that sudden access of nausea she had felt when Alcibíades first kissed her. Something that had been stagnant within, a stagnant pond, now rushed, flushed through her body and mind, carrying the mirrored shards of what she had just seen, stunned and stupefied. And as it washed through her, it cleared her and clarified her, and readied her revenge. She heard the man moving back and forth in the room, she heard him counting his coins, she heard him snapping open the suitcase, she heard him packing his clothes and the rug for the bed. Which meant that he was going away, that he was leaving her to waste and die beneath the sun that was even now turning the corner of the porch and shining its rays on the green sticky swarm of mosquitos rising upward toward her from the head of the dead man. The caracaras and the crows skulked in the distance, waiting.

Her dry tongue stuck to her palate; her stomach clenched and was scratched from within by a hundred tiny fingernails; but she never thought of hunger or even thirst. Her hatred was fiercer than any need. A dull smell rose from the ground. A sweet smell that resembled their recent sweat, mixing. And the palm fronds he brought from afar. And the mule's trough.

Alcibíades, suitcase in hand, halted nearby, stretching his lips into a sort of smirk. His deed seemed to bulk large, larger than he. He admired himself; he admired his force. He had killed a man, a boy. He had cleanly excised what he did not like. And now he had to run. But nor did he like that. He didn't know what to do. It was hot; it was time for his siesta.

The woman looked like a puma, short limbs, round stomach and breasts, some big red splotches on her skin under the sun-dappled net. She began to twist. The sun struck her right shoulder and hip, then it rayed the length of her side. She positioned herself face up, with her back to the dead man, the sun on her heavy breast that lay against the rope, one purple nipple poking through a square in the mesh. A tangle of black hair hid her face; through barely a gap, only her eyes shone. A drone, a husky moan, or a coo, if wild animals could coo, swayed with the hammock, and from her depths an ancient wisdom rose into the narrow brow on which her heavy hair pressed; if she knew how to call that man, he would come, he would rush to her side and untie the knot and unwind the rope and free the rims of the hammock, and that would mean life and power and the reign of women, and then revenge.

Alcibíades stood by the post, uncertain. He set the suitcase on the ground and took a step toward her. Then he halted again.

"You're roasting in the sun, hon," he said in a strange, groggy voice.

She twisted and whimpered. In a thick voice, as though it pained him to speak, he said: "Now nobody'll bother us, not even the sun."

He came closer, he halted, then stepped closer again. She watched him growing larger. Now, at any moment, he would pounce. In his impatience, he might even slit the rope, the net, with his *facón*.

There was a jerk, a rhythmic alteration, in the swaying of the woman that the man did not notice. In waves, in flashes, her hatred mastered her; her every quirk and fluke, her lust, her laziness, all she had ever been until now. She was a swell of hot, clenching hatred. Her hate was hotter and more urgent than his desire. Now nothing mattered but revenge, not even life. Her hatred was forceful, furious, fiercely noble. It swelled inside her; she could not contain it. . . . A shot rang out.

"Bitch," muttered the man, between his teeth; he fell back and smacked the ground, still spitting curses. He held one hand to his chest.

The gun lay in the hammock, empty, useless. She too lay like that. The last shot, the last sound that would ever break the drone, the torpor, the thirst. For her it was the world's last sound. Alcibíades writhed and cursed where he lay; he was a dark blotch against the sunlight, agony and oath. And then at last nothing, a death beneath the post, just beyond the old, misshapen suitcase. A dribble of blood on his none-too-white shirt, below his beard.

The woman yielded to the sunlight, which lavishly took her. Her hatred, slaked, left her the way a man leaves a woman, and she sank into a heavy, sluggish peace so unlike the peace that had followed love. Though this peace at least would last.

All the sunlight that was allotted to that patch of red dirt merged mercilessly on the moist, naked body that lay beneath the net slowly drying. And the lavish audience of flies traveling back and forth from her body to those of the dead men, iridescent as they passed from sun to shadow, flexing their wings and tiny feet, knew nothing of the difference between a blown-out head, a chest from which blood still seemed to run, and her thirst. She fed her hatred with that thirst; something was slaked, sated. For a while she lay still, dozing. Then she began to gnaw the net, desperately. One square tore, then another. Her skin smarted, her lips, her eyes. Her insides were burning though night was already falling, slowly, as heavy as a hundred men, and the jungle had begun to recoil in the distance; it recoiled first slowly and then with furious speed, yanking its lasso around the clearing and choking it. The lakes shimmered and dazzled; the rivers fluxed and fled. Night, sun, and night again. She gnawed on cold, fear, loneliness. Her cries spawned more cries; they took shape in the air; they hovered and dazed and drowned out the night. And then silence, and the knot hanging above her feet loomed larger and larger in the air, unattainable and almighty.

The jungle rushes, faster, faster. Shadows, caws, sticky wings swat at her face, peck at her thighs and hips, splatter her with darkness and death: "La Wilda and la Zoila are asleep under the mosquito net! The men have begun to arrive. Doña Jacinta will be angry. The garters twist on my thighs, and the men squeeze the girls' breasts which flow with bitter yellow milk that fools their thirst. The wet nurse! No, burn the afterbirth with palm fronds and snakes. Beneath, below the hard ground, the black beard and the silver money burn; now they're a river of black sludge.

The wheel rolls through the cities. Ciro! Ciro! Untie me from this wheel! Below, on the terrace climbing with jasmine vines, the soldiers in their handsome blue suits, the blare of trumpets. And angels wing through the air and sing. They've brought silk blouses for the girls. Let us all pray to the Virgin for this miracle: a lace slip and a man who will never depart. The jungle conceals me in its leafy luxuriance. . . . Little Virgin, knot of air, do not blind me in your light. . . ."

When I, the poor message-runner, arrived, the hammock was swaying over death like a bridge of rope, like a murmuring dream.

TRANSLATED BY SARAH ARVIO

Jorge Luis Borges

Argentina
(1899–1986)

The best-known writer from Latin America, and no doubt the most influential
worldwide, Jorge Luis Borges, a bookish man, was, paradoxically, blind for most
of his adult life. He made self-effacement his trademark and his most self-
assertive ploy, both in life and in fiction. Borges had a thorough education in
Buenos Aires (mostly in his father's library) and in Switzerland. During his childhood he traveled through Europe with his family. As a result, Borges learned
several languages, being especially fond of English and German writers, whom
he read in the original. His first collection of stories was *A Universal History of
Infamy* (1935), where he began to experiment with apocryphal attributions and
bogus bibliographies. The stories are deceptively simple, with adventuresome
and variously villainous protagonists. But Borges's most significant book was the
collection of stories he calculatedly entitled *Ficciones* (1944), which had enormous impact on the following generations of Latin American writers and which
became a classic of world literature. He had a particularly strong influence on
Latin American novelists like Gabriel García Márquez, though Borges claimed to
abhor the novel as a genre for being too diffuse and prolix. Borges's stories are
often like metaphysical riddles but without sacrificing plot and suspense or becoming allegories. They question not only reality but also all pieties about writing,
never indulging in sentimentalism. Borges was particularly adept at the detective
story, but his most original creation is the essaylike tale that pretends to solve
an enigma. This is the case of "The Garden of Forking Paths," which blends all
of the aforementioned traits with violence, another predilection of Borges's,
although the calm surface of the stories and his terse prose manage to con-
ceal it.

The Garden of Forking Paths

To Victoria Ocampo

In his *A History of the World War* (page 212), Captain Liddell Hart reports
that a planned offensive by thirteen British divisions, supported by fourteen hundred artillery pieces, against the German line at Serre-Montauban,
scheduled for July 24, 1916, had to be postponed until the morning of the

29th. He comments that torrential rain caused this delay—which lacked any special significance. The following deposition, dictated by, read over, and then signed by Dr. Yu Tsun, former teacher of English at the Tsingtao *Hochschule,* casts unsuspected light upon this event. The first two pages are missing.

* * * * * * * * * *

. . . and I hung up the phone. Immediately I recollected the voice that had spoken in German. It was that of Captain Richard Madden. Madden, in Viktor Runeberg's office, meant the end of all our work and—though this seemed a secondary matter, *or should have seemed so to me*—of our lives also. His being there meant that Runeberg had been arrested or murdered.* Before the sun set on this same day, I ran the same risk. Madden was implacable. Rather, to be more accurate, he was obliged to be implacable. An Irishman in the service of England, a man suspected of equivocal feelings if not of actual treachery, how could he fail to welcome and seize upon this extraordinary piece of luck: the discovery, capture and perhaps the deaths of two agents of Imperial Germany?

I went up to my bedroom. Absurd though the gesture was, I closed and locked the door. I threw myself down on my narrow iron bed, and waited on my back. The never changing rooftops filled the window, and the hazy six o'clock sun hung in the sky. It seemed incredible that this day, a day without warnings or omens, might be that of my implacable death. In spite of my dead father, in spite of having been a child in one of the symmetrical gardens of Hai Feng, was I to die now?

Then I reflected that all things happen, happen to one, precisely *now.* Century follows century, and things happen only in the present. There are countless men in the air, on land and at sea, and all that really happens happens to me. . . . The almost unbearable memory of Madden's long horseface put an end to these wandering thoughts.

In the midst of my hatred and terror (now that it no longer matters to me to speak of terror, now that I have outwitted Richard Madden, now that my neck hankers for the hangman's noose), I knew that the fast-moving and doubtless happy soldier did not suspect that I possessed the Secret—the name of the exact site of the new British artillery park on the Ancre. A bird streaked across the misty sky and, absently, I turned it into an airplane and then that airplane into many in the skies of France, shat-

*A malicious and outlandish statement. In point of fact, Captain Richard Madden had been attacked by the Prussian spy Hans Rabener alias Viktor Runeberg, who drew an automatic pistol when Madden appeared with orders for the spy's arrest. Madden, in self defense, had inflicted wounds of which the spy later died.—*Note by the original manuscript editor.*

tering the artillery park under a rain of bombs. If only my mouth, before it should be silenced by a bullet, could shout this name in such a way that it could be heard in Germany. . . . My voice, my human voice, was weak. How could it reach the ear of the Chief? The ear of that sick and hateful man who knew nothing of Runeberg or of me except that we were in Staffordshire. A man who, sitting in his arid Berlin office, leafed infinitely through newspapers, looking in vain for news from us. I said aloud, "I must flee."

I sat up on the bed, in senseless and perfect silence, as if Madden was already peering at me. Something—perhaps merely a desire to prove my total penury to myself—made me empty out my pockets. I found just what I knew I was going to find. The American watch, the nickel-plated chain and the square coin, the key ring with the useless but compromising keys to Runeberg's office, the notebook, a letter which I decided to destroy at once (and which I did not destroy), a five-shilling piece, two single shillings and some pennies, a red and blue pencil, a handkerchief—and a revolver with a single bullet. Absurdly I held it and weighed it in my hand, to give myself courage. Vaguely I thought that a pistol shot can be heard for a great distance.

In ten minutes I had developed my plan. The telephone directory gave me the name of the one person capable of passing on the information. He lived in a suburb of Fenton, less than half an hour away by train.

I am a timorous man. I can say it now, now that I have brought my incredibly risky plan to an end. It was not easy to bring about, and I know that its execution was terrible. I did not do it for Germany—no! Such a barbarous country is of no importance to me, particularly since it had degraded me by making me become a spy. Furthermore, I knew an Englishman—a modest man—who, for me, is as great as Goethe. I did not speak with him for more than an hour, but during that time, he *was* Goethe.

I carried out my plan because I felt the Chief had some fear of those of my race, of those uncountable forebears whose culmination lies in me. I wished to prove to him that a yellow man could save his armies. Besides, I had to escape the Captain. His hands and voice could, at any moment, knock and beckon at my door.

Silently, I dressed, took leave of myself in the mirror, went down the stairs, sneaked a look at the quiet street, and went out. The station was not far from my house, but I thought it more prudent to take a cab. I told myself that I thus ran less chance of being recognized. The truth is that, in the deserted street, I felt infinitely visible and vulnerable. I recall that I told the driver to stop short of the main entrance. I got out with a painful and deliberate slowness.

I was going to the village of Ashgrove, but took a ticket for a station further on. The train would leave in a few minutes, at eight-fifty. I hurried, for the next would not go until half-past nine. There was almost no one on the platform. I walked through the carriages. I remember some farmers, a woman dressed in mourning, a youth deep in Tacitus' *Annals* and a wounded, happy soldier.

At last the train pulled out. A man I recognized ran furiously, but vainly, the length of the platform. It was Captain Richard Madden. Shattered, trembling, I huddled in the distant corner of the seat, as far as possible from the fearful window.

From utter terror I passed into a state of almost abject happiness. I told myself that the duel had already started and that I had won the first encounter by besting my adversary in his first attack—even if it was only for forty minutes—by an accident of fate. I argued that so small a victory prefigured a total victory. I argued that it was not so trivial, that were it not for the precious accident of the train schedule, I would be in prison or dead. I argued, with no less sophism, that my timorous happiness was proof that I was man enough to bring this adventure to a successful conclusion. From my weakness I drew strength that never left me.

I foresee that man will resign himself each day to new abominations, that soon only soldiers and bandits will be left. To them I offer this advice: *Whosoever would undertake some atrocious enterprise should act as if it were already accomplished, should impose upon himself a future as irrevocable as the past.*

Thus I proceeded, while with the eyes of a man already dead, I contemplated the fluctuations of the day which would probably be my last, and watched the diffuse coming of night.

The train crept along gently, amid ash trees. It slowed down and stopped, almost in the middle of a field. No one called the name of a station. "Ashgrove?" I asked some children on the platform. "Ashgrove," they replied. I got out.

A lamp lit the platform, but the children's faces remained in a shadow. One of them asked me: "Are you going to Dr. Stephen Albert's house?" Without waiting for my answer, another said: "The house is a good distance away but you won't get lost if you take the road to the left and bear to the left at every crossroad." I threw them a coin (my last), went down some stone steps and started along a deserted road. At a slight incline, the road ran downhill. It was a plain dirt way, and overhead the branches of trees intermingled, while a round moon hung low in the sky as if to keep me company.

For a moment I thought that Richard Madden might in some way have divined my desperate intent. At once I realized that this would be impossible. The advice about turning always to the left reminded me that such was the common formula for finding the central courtyard of certain labyrinths. I know something about labyrinths. Not for nothing am I the great-grandson of Ts'ui Pên. He was Governor of Yunnan and gave up temporal power to write a novel with more characters than there are in the *Hung Lou Mêng,* and to create a maze in which all men would lose themselves. He spent thirteen years on these oddly assorted tasks before he was assassinated by a stranger. His novel had no sense to it and nobody ever found his labyrinth.

Under the trees of England I meditated on this lost and perhaps mythical labyrinth. I imagined it untouched and perfect on the secret summit of some mountain; I imagined it drowned under rice paddies or beneath the sea; I imagined it infinite, made not only of eight-sided pavilions and of twisting paths but also of rivers, provinces and kingdoms. . . . I thought of a maze of mazes, of a sinuous, ever growing maze which would take in both past and future and would somehow involve the stars.

Lost in these imaginary illusions I forgot my destiny—that of the hunted. For an undetermined period of time I felt myself cut off from the world, an abstract spectator. The hazy and murmuring countryside, the moon, the decline of the evening, stirred within me. Going down the gently sloping road I could not feel fatigue. The evening was at once intimate and infinite.

The road kept descending and branching off, through meadows misty in the twilight. A high-pitched and almost syllabic music kept coming and going, moving with the breeze, blurred by the leaves and by distance.

I thought that a man might be an enemy of other men, of the differing moments of other men, but never an enemy of a country: not of fireflies, words, gardens, streams, or the West wind.

Meditating thus I arrived at a high, rusty iron gate. Through the railings I could see an avenue bordered with poplar trees and also a kind of summer house or pavilion. Two things dawned on me at once, the first trivial and the second almost incredible: the music came from the pavilion and that music was Chinese. That was why I had accepted it fully, without paying it any attention. I do not remember whether there was a bell, a push-button, or whether I attracted attention by clapping my hands. The stuttering sparks of the music kept on.

But from the end of the avenue, from the main house, a lantern approached; a lantern which alternately, from moment to moment, was criss-crossed or put out by the trunks of the trees; a paper lantern shaped like a drum and colored like the moon. A tall man carried it. I could not see his face for the light blinded me.

He opened the gate and spoke slowly in my language.

"I see that the worthy Hsi P'eng has troubled himself to see to relieving my solitude. No doubt you want to see the garden?"

Recognizing the name of one of our consuls, I replied, somewhat taken aback.

"The garden?"

"The garden of forking paths."

Something stirred in my memory and I said, with incomprehensible assurance:

"The garden of my ancestor, Ts'ui Pên."

"Your ancestor? Your illustrious ancestor? Come in."

The damp path zigzagged like those of my childhood. When we reached the house, we went into a library filled with books from both East and West. I recognized some large volumes bound in yellow silk—manuscripts of the Lost Encyclopedia which was edited by the Third Emperor of the Luminous Dynasty. They had never been printed. A phonograph record was spinning near a bronze phoenix. I remember also a rose-glazed jar and yet another, older by many centuries, of that blue color which our potters copied from the Persians. . . .

Stephen Albert was watching me with a smile on his face. He was, as I have said, remarkably tall. His face was deeply lined and he had gray eyes and a gray beard. There was about him something of the priest, and something of the sailor. Later, he told me he had been a missionary in Tientsin before he "had aspired to become a Sinologist."

We sat down, I upon a large, low divan, he with his back to the window and to a large circular clock. I calculated that my pursuer, Richard Madden, could not arrive in less than an hour. My irrevocable decision could wait.

"A strange destiny," said Stephen Albert, "that of Ts'ui Pên—Governor of his native province, learned in astronomy, in astrology and tireless in the interpretation of the canonical books, a chess player, a famous poet and a calligrapher. Yet he abandoned all to make a book and a labyrinth. He gave up all the pleasures of oppression, justice, of a well-stocked bed, of banquets, and even of erudition, and shut himself up in the Pavilion of the Limpid Sun for thirteen years. At his death, his heirs found only a mess of manuscripts. The family, as you doubtless know, wished to consign them to the fire, but the executor of the estate—a Taoist or a Buddhist monk—insisted on their publication."

"Those of the blood of Ts'ui Pên," I replied, "still curse the memory of that monk. Such a publication was madness. The book is a shapeless mass of contradictory rough drafts. I examined it once upon a time: the hero dies in the third chapter, while in the fourth he is alive. As for that other enterprise of Ts'ui Pên . . . his Labyrinth. . . ."

"Here is the Labyrinth," Albert said, pointing to a tall, laquered writing cabinet.

"An ivory labyrinth?" I exclaimed. "A tiny labyrinth indeed . . . !"

"A symbolic labyrinth," he corrected me. "An invisible labyrinth of time. I, a barbarous Englishman, have been given the key to this transparent mystery. After more than a hundred years most of the details are irrecoverable, lost beyond all recall, but it isn't hard to image what must have happened. At one time, Ts'ui Pên must have said; 'I am going into seclusion to write a book,' and at another, 'I am retiring to construct a maze.' Everyone assumed these were separate activities. No one realized that the book and the labyrinth were one and the same. The Pavilion of the Limpid Sun was set in the middle of an intricate garden. This may have suggested the idea of a physical maze.

"Ts'ui Pên died. In all the vast lands which once belonged to your family, no one could find the labyrinth. The novel's confusion suggested that *it* was the labyrinth. Two circumstances showed me the direct solution to the problem. First, the curious legend that Ts'ui Pên had proposed to create an infinite maze, second, a fragment of a letter which I discovered."

Albert rose. For a few moments he turned his back to me. He opened the top drawer in the high black and gilded writing cabinet. He returned holding in his hand a piece of paper which had once been crimson but which had faded with the passage of time: it was rose colored, tenuous, quadrangular. Ts'ui Pên's calligraphy was justly famous. Eagerly, but without understanding, I read the words which a man of my own blood had written with a small brush: "I leave to various future times, but not to all, my garden of forking paths."

I handed back the sheet of paper in silence. Albert went on:

"Before I discovered this letter, I kept asking myself how a book could be infinite. I could not imagine any other than a cyclic volume, circular. A volume whose last page would be the same as the first and so have the possibility of continuing indefinitely. I recalled, too, the night in the middle of *The Thousand and One Nights* when Queen Scheherezade, through a magical mistake on the part of her copyist, started to tell the story of *The Thousand and One Nights*, with the risk of again arriving at the night upon which she will relate it, and thus on to infinity. I also imagined a Platonic hereditary work, passed on from father to son, to which each individual would add a new chapter or correct, with pious care, the work of his elders.

"These conjectures gave me amusement, but none seemed to have the remotest application to the contradictory chapters of Ts'ui Pên. At this point, I was sent from Oxford the manuscript you have just seen.

"Naturally, my attention was caught by the sentence, 'I leave to various future times, but not to all, my garden of forking paths.' I had no sooner read this, than I understood. *The Garden of Forking Paths* was the chaotic novel itself. The phrase 'to various future times, but not to all' suggested the image of bifurcating in time, not in space. Rereading the whole work confirmed this theory. In all fiction, when a man is faced with alternatives he chooses one at the expense of the others. In the almost unfathomable Ts'ui Pên, he chooses—simultaneously—all of them. He thus *creates* various futures, various times which start others that will in their turn branch out and bifurcate in other times. This is the cause of the contradictions in the novel.

"Fang, let us say, has a secret. A stranger knocks at his door. Fang makes up his mind to kill him. Naturally there are various possible outcomes. Fang can kill the intruder, the intruder can kill Fang, both can be saved, both can die and so on and so on. In Ts'ui Pên's work, all the possible solutions occur, each one being the point of departure for other bifurcations. Sometimes the pathways of this labyrinth converge. For example, you come to this house; but in other possible pasts you are my enemy; in others my friend.

"If you will put up with my atrocious pronunciation, I would like to read you a few pages of your ancestor's work."

His countenance, in the bright circle of lamplight, was certainly that of an ancient, but it shone with something unyielding, even immortal.

With slow precision, he read two versions of the same epic chapter. In the first, an army marches into battle over a desolate mountain pass. The bleak and somber aspect of the rocky landscape made the soldiers feel that life itself was of little value, and so they won the battle easily. In the second, the same army passes through a palace where a banquet is in progress. The splendor of the feast remained a memory throughout the glorious battle, and so victory followed.

With proper veneration I listened to these old tales, although perhaps with less admiration for them in themselves than for the fact that they had been thought out by one of my own blood, and that a man of a distant empire had given them back to me, in the last stage of a desperate adventure, on a Western island. I remember the final words, repeated at the end of each version like a secret command: "Thus the heroes fought, with tranquil heart and bloody sword. They were resigned to killing and to dying."

At that moment I felt within me and around me something invisible and intangible pullulating. It was not the pullulation of two divergent, parallel, and finally converging armies, but an agitation more inaccessible, more intimate, prefigured by them in some way. Stephen Albert continued:

"I do not think that your illustrious ancestor toyed idly with variations. I do not find it believable that he would waste thirteen years laboring over a never ending experiment in rhetoric. In your country the novel is an inferior genre; in Ts'ui Pên's period, it was a despised one. Ts'ui Pên was a fine novelist but he was also a man of letters who, doubtless, considered himself more than a mere novelist. The testimony of his contemporaries attests to this, and certainly the known facts of his life confirm his leanings toward the metaphysical and the mystical. Philosophical conjectures take up the greater part of his novel. I know that of all problems, none disquieted him more, and none concerned him more than the profound one of time. Now then, this is the *only* problem that does not figure in the pages of *The Garden*. He does not even use the word which means *time*. How can these voluntary omissions be explained?"

I proposed various solutions, all of them inadequate. We discussed them. Finally Stephen Albert said: "In a guessing game to which the answer is chess, which word is the only one prohibited?" I thought for a moment and then replied:

"The word is *chess*."

"Precisely," said Albert. "*The Garden of Forking Paths* is an enormous guessing game, or parable, in which the subject is time. The rules of the game forbid the use of the word itself. To eliminate a word completely, to refer to it by means of inept phrases and obvious paraphrases, is perhaps the best way of drawing attention to it. This, then, is the tortuous method of approach preferred by the oblique Ts'ui Pên in every meandering of his interminable novel. I have gone over hundreds of manuscripts, I have corrected errors introduced by careless copyists, I have worked out the plan from this chaos, I have restored, or believe I have restored, the original. I have translated the whole work. I can state categorically that not once has the word *time* been used in the whole book.

"The explanation is obvious. *The Garden of Forking Paths* is a picture, incomplete yet not false, of the universe such as Ts'ui Pên conceived it to be. Differing from Newton and Schopenhauer, your ancestor did not think of time as absolute and uniform. He believed in an infinite series of times, in a dizzily growing, ever spreading network of diverging, converging and parallel times. This web of time—the strands of which approach one another, bifurcate, intersect or ignore each other through the centuries— embraces *every* possibility. We do not exist in most of them. In some you exist and not I, while in others I do, and you do not, and in yet others both of us exist. In this one, in which chance has favored me, you have come to my gate. In another, you, crossing the garden, have found me dead. In yet another, I say these very same words, but am an error, a phantom."

"In all of them," I enunciated, with a tremor in my voice, "I deeply appreciate and am grateful to you for the restoration of Ts'ui Pên's garden."

"Not in *all*," he murmured with a smile. "Time is forever dividing itself toward innumerable futures and in one of them I am your enemy."

Once again I sensed the pullulation of which I have already spoken. It seemed to me that the dew-damp garden surrounding the house was infinitely saturated with invisible people. All were Albert and myself, secretive, busy and multiform in other dimensions of time. I lifted my eyes and the short nightmare disappeared. In the black and yellow garden there was only a single man, but this man was as strong as a statue and this man was walking up the path and he was Captain Richard Madden.

"The future exists now," I replied. "But I am your friend. Can I take another look at the letter?"

Albert rose from his seat. He stood up tall as he opened the top drawer of the high writing cabinet. For a moment his back was again turned to me. I had the revolver ready. I fired with the utmost care: Albert fell without a murmur, at once. I swear that his death was instantaneous, as if he had been struck by lightning.

What remains is unreal and unimportant. Madden broke in and arrested me. I have been condemned to hang. Abominably, I have yet triumphed! The secret name of the city to be attacked got through to Berlin. Yesterday it was bombed. I read the news in the same English newspapers which were trying to solve the riddle of the murder of the learned Sinologist Stephen Albert by the unknown Yu Tsun. The Chief, however, had already solved this mystery. He knew that my problem was to shout, with my feeble voice, above the tumult of war, the name of the city called Albert, and that I had no other course open to me than to kill someone of that name. He does not know, for no one can, of my infinite penitence and sickness of the heart.

TRANSLATED BY HELEN TEMPLE AND RUTHVEN TODD

Alejo Carpentier

Cuba
(1904–1980)

———— ⫫ ————

One of the most influential writers in Latin America during the twentieth century, Alejo Carpentier was a man of encyclopedic culture. In addition to history and literature, he was especially learned in music, architecture, and painting. This knowledge is present in his textured, baroque prose, which sometimes reflects the archaic discourse of the historical document. Carpentier began as an avant-garde artist in the Cuba of the 1920s, spreading the gospel of the new art through lectures, articles, and librettos for ballets and operas. He was also implicated in revolutionary politics and wound up an exile in Paris in 1928. Being of French descent, which endowed his Spanish with raspy Gallic *r*s Carpentier was thus at home in the French capital, where he became involved with the surrealists. His achievements as a writer began with *The Kingdom of This World* (1949), a novel about the Haitian Revolution that is purported to have begun the "magical realist" mode in Latin American fiction. Cast in a rigorous historical mold, the novel highlights the repetitions, reiterations, and sudden concurrences of events in time. Indeed, the question of time, viewed with the technical eye of the musicologist he was, informs Carpentier's fiction from then on. Novels such as *The Lost Steps* (1953), *Explosion in a Cathedral* (1962), *The Harp and the Shadow* (1979), and *Concierto barroco* (1974) all display this combination of excruciating attention to historical detail with the convoluted shapes that human action displays through the ages. A most daring and influential work was Carpentier's *War of Time* (1958), a collection of short stories in which he carries out many of his experiments in briefer narrative pieces. "Journey Back to the Source," included here, contains a memorable tour de force: It is told backward, as though language were reversible.

Journey Back to the Source

I

"What d'you want, pop?"
Again and again came the question, from high up on the scaffolding. But the old man made no reply. He moved from one place to another, prying into corners and uttering a lengthy monologue of incom-

prehensible remarks. The tiles had already been taken down, and now covered the dead flower beds with their mosaic of baked clay. Overhead, blocks of masonry were being loosened with picks and sent rolling down wooden gutters in an avalanche of lime and plaster. And through the crenellations that were one by one indenting the walls, were appearing—denuded of their privacy—oval or square ceilings, cornices, garlands, dentils, astragals, and paper hanging from the walls like old skins being sloughed by a snake.

Witnessing the demolition, a Ceres with a broken nose and discolored peplum, her headdress of corn veined with black, stood in the back yard above her fountain of crumbling grotesques. Visited by shafts of sunlight piercing the shadows, the gray fish in the basin yawned in the warm weed-covered water, watching with round eyes the black silhouettes of the workmen against the brilliance of the sky as they diminished the centuries-old height of the house. The old man had sat down at the foot of the statue, resting his chin on his stick. He watched buckets filled with precious fragments ascending and descending. Muted sounds from the street could be heard, while overhead, against a basic rhythm of steel on stone, the pulleys screeched unpleasantly in chorus, like harsh-voiced birds.

The clock struck five. The cornices and entablatures were depopulated. Nothing was left behind but stepladders, ready for tomorrow's onslaught. The air grew cooler, now that it was disburdened of sweat, oaths, creaking ropes, axles crying out for the oil can, and the slapping of hands on greasy torsos. Dusk had settled earlier on the dismantled house. The shadows had enfolded it just at that moment when the now-fallen upper balustrade used to enrich the façade by capturing the sun's last beams. Ceres tightened her lips. For the first time the rooms would sleep unshuttered, gazing onto a landscape of rubble.

Contradicting their natural propensities, several capitals lay in the grass, their acanthus leaves asserting their vegetable status. A creeper stretched adventurous tendrils toward an Ionic scroll, attracted by its air of kinship. When night fell, the house was closer to the ground. Upstairs, the frame of a door still stood erect, slabs of darkness suspended from its dislocated hinges.

II

Then the old Negro, who had not stirred, began making strange movements with his stick, whirling it around above a graveyard of paving stones.

The white and black marble squares flew to the floors and covered them. Stones leaped up and unerringly filled the gaps in the walls. The nail-studded walnut doors fitted themselves into their frames, while the screws rapidly twisted back into the holes in the hinges. In the dead flower beds, the fragments of tile were lifted by the thrust of growing flowers and joined together, raising a sonorous whirlwind of clay, to fall like rain on the framework of the roof. The house grew, once more assuming its normal proportions, modestly clothed. Ceres became less gray. There were more fish in the fountain. And the gurgling water summoned forgotten begonias back to life.

The old man inserted a key into the lock of the front door and began to open the windows. His heels made a hollow sound. When he lighted the lamps, a yellow tremor ran over the oil paint of the family portraits, and people dressed in black talked softly in all the corridors, to the rhythm of spoons stirring cups of chocolate.

Don Marcial, Marqués de Capellanías, lay on his deathbed, his breast blazing with decorations, while four tapers with long beards of melted wax kept guard over him.

III

The candles lengthened slowly, gradually guttering less and less. When they had reached full size, the nun extinguished them and took away the light. The wicks whitened, throwing off red sparks. The house emptied itself of visitors and their carriages drove away in the darkness. Don Marcial fingered an invisible keyboard and opened his eyes.

The confused heaps of rafters gradually went back into place. Medicine bottles, tassels from brocades, the scapulary beside the bed, daguerreotypes, and iron palm leaves from the grille emerged from the mists. When the doctor shook his head with an expression of professional gloom, the invalid felt better. He slept for several hours and awoke under the black beetle-browed gaze of Father Anastasio. What had begun as a candid, detailed confession of his many sins grew gradually more reticent, painful, and full of evasions. After all, what right had the Carmelite to interfere in his life?

Suddenly Don Marcial found himself thrown into the middle of the room. Relieved of the pressure on his temples, he stood up with surprising agility. The naked woman who had been stretching herself on the brocade coverlet began to look for her petticoats and bodices, and soon afterward disappeared in a rustle of silk and a waft of perfume. In the closed carriage downstairs an envelope full of gold coins was lying on the brass-studded seat.

Don Marcial was not feeling well. When he straightened his cravat before the pier glass he saw that his face was congested. He went downstairs to his study where lawyers—attorneys and their clerks—were waiting for him to arrange for the sale of the house by auction. All his efforts had been in vain. His property would go to the highest bidder, to the rhythm of a hammer striking the table. He bowed, and they left him alone. He thought

how mysterious were written words: those black threads weaving and unweaving, and covering large sheets of paper with a filigree of estimates;
weaving and unweaving contracts, oaths, agreements, evidence, declara-
tions, names, titles, dates, lands, trees, and stones; a tangled skein of threads,
drawn from the inkpot to ensnare the legs of any man who took a path
disapproved of by the Law; a noose around his neck to stifle free speech
at its first dreaded sound. He had been betrayed by his signature; it had
handed him over to the nets and labyrinths of documents. Thus constricted,
the man of flesh and blood had become a man of paper.

It was dawn. The dining-room clock had just struck six in the evening.

IV

The months of mourning passed under the shadow of ever-increasing remorse. At first the idea of bringing a woman to his room had seemed quite
reasonable. But little by little the desire excited by a new body gave way
to increasing scruples, which ended as self-torment. One night, Don Marcial beat himself with a strap till the blood came, only to experience even
intenser desire, though it was of short duration.

It was at this time that the Marquesa returned one afternoon from a
drive along the banks of the Almendares. The manes of the horses harnessed
to her carriage were damp with solely their own sweat. Yet they spent the
rest of the day kicking the wooden walls of their stable as if maddened by
the stillness of the low-hanging clouds.

At dusk, a jar full of water broke in the Marquesa's bathroom. Then
the May rains came and overflowed the lake. And the old Negress who
unhappily was a maroon and kept pigeons under her bed wandered
through the patio, muttering to herself: "Never trust rivers, my girl; never
trust anything green and flowing!" Not a day passed without water making
its presence felt. But in the end that presence amounted to no more than
a cup spilled over a Paris dress after the anniversary ball given by the Governor of the Colony.

Many relatives reappeared. Many friends came back again. The chandeliers in the great drawing room glittered with brilliant lights. The cracks
in the façade were closing up, one by one. The piano became a clavichord.
The palm trees lost some of their rings. The creepers let go of the upper
cornice. The dark circles around Ceres' eyes disappeared, and the capitals
of the columns looked as if they had been freshly carved. Marcial was more
ardent now, and often passed whole afternoons embracing the Marquesa.
Crow's-feet, frowns, and double chins vanished, and flesh grew firm again.
One day the smell of fresh paint filled the house.

V

Their embarrassment was real. Each night the leaves of the screens opened a little farther, and skirts fell to the floor in obscurer corners of the room, revealing yet more barriers of lace. At last the Marquesa blew out the lamps. Only Marcial's voice was heard in the darkness.

They left for the sugar plantation in a long procession of carriages—sorrel hindquarters, silver bits, and varnished leather gleamed in the sunshine. But among the pasque flowers empurpling the arcades leading up to the house, they realized that they scarcely knew each other. Marcial gave permission for a performance of native dancers and drummers, by way of entertainment during those days impregnated with the smells of eau de cologne, of baths spiced with benzoin, of unloosened hair and sheets taken from closets and unfolded to let a bunch of vetiver drop onto the tiled floor. The steam of cane juice and the sound of the angelus mingled on the breeze. The vultures flew low, heralding a sparse shower, whose first large echoing drops were absorbed by tiles so dry that they gave off a diapason like copper.

After a dawn prolonged by an inexpert embrace, they returned together to the city with their misunderstandings settled and the wound healed. The Marquesa changed her traveling dress for a wedding gown and the married pair went to church according to custom, to regain their freedom. Relations and friends received their presents back again, and they all set off for home with jingling brass and a display of splendid trappings. Marcial went on visiting María de las Mercedes for a while, until the day when the rings were taken to the goldsmiths to have their inscriptions removed. For Marcial, a new life was beginning. In the house with the high grilles, an Italian Venus was set up in place of Ceres, and the grotesques in the fountain were thrown into almost imperceptibly sharper relief because the lamps were still glowing when dawn colored the sky.

VI

One night, after drinking heavily and being sickened by the stale tobacco smoke left behind by his friends, Marcial had the strange sensation that all the clocks in the house were striking five, then half past four, then four, then half past three . . . It was as if he had become dimly aware of other possibilities. Just as, when exhausted by sleeplessness, one may believe that one could walk on the ceiling, with the floor for a ceiling and the furniture firmly fixed between the beams. It was only a fleeting impression, and did not leave the smallest trace on his mind, for he was not much given to meditation at the time.

And a splendid evening party was given in the music room on the day he achieved minority. He was delighted to know that his signature was no longer legally valid, and that worm-eaten registers and documents would now vanish from his world. He had reached the point at which courts of justice were no longer to be feared, because his bodily existence was ignored by the law. After getting tipsy on noble wines, the young people took down from the wall a guitar inlaid with mother-of-pearl, a psaltery, and a serpent. Someone wound up the clock that played the *ranz-des-vaches* and the "Ballad of the Scottish Lakes." Someone else blew on a hunting horn that had been lying curled in copper sleep on the crimson felt lining of the showcase, beside a transverse flute brought from Aranjuez. Marcial, who was boldly making love to Señora de Campoflorido, joined in the cacophony, and tried to pick out the tune of "Trípili-Trápala" on the piano, to a discordant accompaniment in the bass.

Then they all trooped upstairs to the attic, remembering that the liveries and clothes of the Capellanías family had been stored away under its peeling beams. On shelves frosted with camphor lay court dresses, an ambassador's sword, several padded military jackets, the vestment of a dignitary of the Church, and some long cassocks with damask buttons and damp stains among their folds. The dark shadows of the attic were variegated with the colors of amaranthine ribbons, yellow crinolines, faded tunics, and velvet flowers. A picaresque *chispero*'s costume and hair net trimmed with tassels, once made for a carnival masquerade, was greeted with applause. Señora de Campoflorido swathed her powdered shoulders in a shawl the color of a Creole's skin, once worn by a certain ancestress on an evening of important family decisions in hopes of reviving the sleeping ardor of some rich trustee of a convent of Clares.

As soon as they were dressed up, the young people went back to the music room. Marcial, who was wearing an alderman's hat, struck the floor three times with a stick and announced that they would begin with a waltz, a dance mothers thought terribly improper for young ladies because they had to allow themselves to be taken round the waist, with a man's hand resting on the busks of the stays they had all had made according to the latest model in the *Jardin des Modes*. The doorways were blocked by maidservants, stableboys, and waiters, who had come from remote outbuildings and stifling basements to enjoy the boisterious fun. Afterward they played blindman's buff and hide-and-seek. Hidden behind a Chinese screen with Señora de Campoflorido, Marcial planted a kiss on her neck, and received in return a scented handkerchief whose Brussels lace still retained the sweet warmth of her low-necked bodice.

And when the girls left in the fading light of dusk, to return to castles and towers silhouetted in dark gray against the sea, the young men went to the dance hall, where alluring *mulatas* in heavy bracelets were strutting about without ever losing their high-heeled shoes, even in the frenzy of the guaracha. And as it was carnival time, the members of the Arara Chapter Three Eyes Band were raising thunder on their drums behind the wall in a patio planted with pomegranate trees. Climbing onto tables and stools, Marcial and his friends applauded the gracefulness of a Negress with graying hair, who had recovered her beauty and almost become desirable as she danced, looking over her shoulder with an expression of proud disdain.

VII

The visits of Don Abundio, the family notary and executor, were more frequent now. He used to sit gravely down beside Marcial's bed, and let his acana-wood cane drop to the floor so as to wake him up in good time. Opening his eyes, Marcial saw an alpaca frock coat covered with dandruff, its sleeves shiny from collecting securities and rents. All that was left in the end was an adequate pension, calculated to put a stop to all wild extravagance. It was at this time that Marcial wanted to enter the Royal Seminary of San Carlos.

After doing only moderately well in his examinations, he attended courses of lectures, but understood less and less of his master's explanations. The world of his ideas was gradually growing emptier. What had once been a general assembly of peplums, doublets, ruffs, and periwigs, of controversialists and debaters, now looked as lifeless as a museum of wax figures. Marcial contented himself with a scholastic analysis of the systems, and accepted everything he found in a book as the truth. The words "Lion," "Ostrich," "Whale," "Jaguar" were printed under the copperplate engravings in his natural history book. Just as "Aristotle," "St. Thomas," "Bacon," and "Descartes" headed pages black with boring, close-printed accounts of different interpretations of the universe. Bit by bit, Marcial stopped trying to learn these things, and felt relieved of a heavy burden. His mind grew gay and lively, understanding things in a purely instinctive way. Why think about the prism, when the clear winter light brought out all the details in the fortresses guarding the port? An apple falling from a tree tempted one to bite it—that was all. A foot in a bathtub was merely a foot in a bathtub. The day he left the seminary he forgot all about his books. A gnomon was back in the category of goblins; a spectrum a synonym for a phantom; and an octandrian an animal armed with spines.

More than once he had hurried off with a troubled heart to visit the women who whispered behind blue doors under the town walls. The memory of one of them, who wore embroidered slippers and a sprig of sweet basil behind her ear, pursued him on hot evenings like the toothache. But one day his confessor's anger and threats reduced him to terrified tears. He threw himself for the last time between those infernal sheets, and then forever renounced his detours through unfrequented streets and that last-minute faintheartedness which sent him home in a rage, turning his back on a certain crack in the pavement—the signal, when he was walking with head bent, that he must turn and enter the perfumed threshold.

Now he was undergoing a spiritual crisis, peopled by religious images, paschal lambs, china doves, Virgins in heavenly blue cloaks, gold paper stars, the three Magi, angels with wings like swans, the Ass, the Ox, and a terrible St. Denis, who appeared to him in his dreams with a great space between his shoulders, walking hesitantly as if looking for something he had lost. When he blundered into the bed, Marcial would start awake and reach for his rosary of silver beads. The lampwicks, in their bowls of oil, cast a sad light on the holy images as their colors returned to them.

VIII

The furniture was growing taller. It was becoming more difficult for him to rest his arms on the dining table. The fronts of the cupboards with their carved cornices were getting broader. The Moors on the staircase stretched their torsos upward, bringing their torches closer to the banisters on the landing. Armchairs were deeper, and rocking chairs tended to fall over backward. It was no longer necessary to bend one's knees when lying at the bottom of the bath with its marble rings.

One morning when he was reading a licentious book, Marcial suddenly felt a desire to play with the lead soldiers lying asleep in their wooden boxes. He put the book back in its hiding place under the washbasin, and opened a drawer sealed with cobwebs. His schoolroom table was too small to hold such a large army. So Marcial sat on the floor and set out his grenadiers in rows of eight. Next came the officers on horseback, surrounding the color sergeant; and behind, the artillery with their cannon, gun sponges, and linstocks. Bringing up the rear were fifes and tabors escorted by drummers. The mortars were fitted with a spring, so that one could shoot glass marbles to a distance of more than a yard.

Bang! . . . Bang! . . . Bang!

Down fell horses, down fell standard-bearers, down fell drummers. Eligio the Negro had to call him three times before he could be persuaded to go to wash his hands and descend to the dining room.

After that day, Marcial made a habit of sitting on the tiled floor. When he realized the advantages of this position, he was surprised that he had not thought of it before. Grown-up people had a passion for velvet cushions, which made them sweat too much. Some of them smelled like a notary— like Don Abundio—because they had not discovered how cool it was to lie at full length on a marble floor at all seasons of the year. Only from the floor could all the angles and perspectives of a room be grasped properly.

There were beautiful grains in the wood, mysterious insect paths and shadowy corners that could not be seen from a man's height. When it rained, Marcial hid himself under the clavichord. Every clap of thunder made the sound box vibrate, and set all the notes to singing. Shafts of lightning fell from the sky, creating a vault of cascading arpeggios—the organ, the wind in the pines, and the crickets' mandolin.

IX

That morning they locked him in his room. He heard whispering all over the house, and the luncheon they brought him was too delicious for a weekday. There were six pastries from the confectioner's in the Alameda—whereas even on Sundays after Mass he was only allowed two. He amused himself by looking at the engravings in a travel book, until an increasing buzz of sound coming under the door made him look out between the blinds. Some men dressed all in black were arriving, bearing a brass-handled coffin. He was on the verge of tears, but at this moment Melchor the groom appeared in his room, his boots echoing on the floor and his teeth flashing in a smile. They began to play chess. Melchor was a knight. He was the king. Using the tiles on the floor as a chessboard, he moved from one square to the next, while Melchor had to jump one forward and two sideways, or vice versa. The game went on until after dusk, when the fire brigade went by.

When he got up, he went to kiss his father's hand as he lay ill in bed. The Marqués was feeling better, and talked to his son in his usual serious and edifying manner. His "Yes, Father's" and "No, Father's" were fitted between the beads of a rosary of questions, like the responses of an acolyte during Mass. Marcial respected the Marqués, but for reasons that no one could possibly have guessed. He respected him because he was tall, because when he went out to a ball his breast glittered with decorations; because he envied him the saber and gold braid he wore as an officer in the militia; because at Christmas time, on a bet, he had eaten a whole turkey stuffed with almonds and raisins; because he had once seized one of the *mulatas* who were sweeping out the rotunda and had carried her in his arms to his room—no doubt intending to whip her. Hidden behind a curtain, Marcial watched her come out soon afterward, in tears and with her dress unfastened, and he was pleased that she had been punished, as she was the one who always emptied the jam pots before putting them back in the cupboard.

His father was a terrible and magnanimous being, and it was his duty to love him more than anyone except God. To Marcial he was more godlike even than God because his gifts were tangible, everyday ones. But he preferred the God in heaven because he was less of a nuisance.

X

When the furniture had grown a little taller still, and Marcial knew better than anyone what was under the beds, cupboards, and cabinets, he had a great secret, which he kept to himself: life had no charms except when Melchor the groom was with him. Not God, nor his father, nor the golden bishop in the Corpus Christi procession was as important as Melchor.

Melchor had come from a very long distance away. He was descended from conquered princes. In his kingdom there were elephants, hippopotamuses, tigers, and giraffes, and men did not sit working, like Don Abundio, in dark rooms full of papers. They lived by outdoing the animals in cunning. One of them had pulled the great crocodile out of the blue lake after first skewering him on a pike concealed inside the closely packed bodies of twelve roast geese. Melchor knew songs that were easy to learn because the words had no meaning and were constantly repeated. He stole sweetmeats from the kitchens; at night he used to escape through the stable door, and once he threw stones at the police before disappearing into the darkness of the Calle de la Amargura.

On wet days he used to put his boots to dry beside the kitchen stove. Marcial wished he had feet big enough to fill boots like those. His right-hand boot was called Calambín; the left one Calambán. This man who could tame unbroken horses by simply seizing their lips between two fingers, this fine gentleman in velvet and spurs who wore such tall hats, also understood about the coolness of marble floors in summer, and used to hide fruits or a cake, snatched from trays destined for the drawing room, behind the furniture. Marcial and Melchor shared a secret store of sweets and almonds, which they saluted with "Urí, urí, urá" and shouts of conspiratorial laughter. They had both explored the house from top to bottom, and were the only ones who knew that beneath the stables there was a small cellar full of Dutch bottles, or that in an unused loft over the maids' rooms was a broken glass case containing twelve dusty butterflies that were losing their wings.

XI

When Marcial got into the habit of breaking things, he forgot Melchor and made friends with the dogs. There were several in the house. The large one with stripes like a tiger; the basset trailing its teats on the ground; the greyhound that had grown too old to play; the poodle that was chased by the others at certain times and had to be shut up by the maids.

Marcial liked Canelo best because he carried off shoes from the bedrooms and dug up the rose trees in the patio. Always black with coal dust or covered with red earth, he devoured the dinners of all the other dogs, whined without cause, and hid stolen bones under the fountain. And now and again he would suck dry a new-laid egg and send the hen flying with a sharp blow from his muzzle. Everyone kicked Canelo. But when they took him away, Marcial made himself ill with grief. And the dog returned in triumph, wagging his tail, from somewhere beyond the poorhouse where he had been abandoned, and regained his place in the house, which the other dogs, for all their skill in hunting, or vigilance when keeping guard, could never fill.

Canelo and Marcial used to urinate side by side. Sometimes they chose the Persian carpet in the drawing room, spreading dark, cloud-like shapes over its pile. This usually cost them a thrashing. But thrashings were less painful than grown-up people realized. On the other hand, they gave a splendid excuse for setting up a concerted howling and arousing the pity of the neighbors. When the cross-eyed woman from the top flat called his father a "brute," Marcial looked at Canelo with smiling eyes. They shed a few more tears so as to be given a biscuit, and afterward all was forgotten. They both used to eat earth, roll on the ground, drink out of the goldfish basin, and take refuge in the scented shade under the sweet-basil bushes. During the hottest hours of the day quite a crowd filled the moist flower beds. There would be the gray goose with her pouch hanging between her bandy legs; the old rooster with his naked rump; the little lizard who kept saying *"Urí, urá"* and shooting a pink ribbon out of his throat; the melancholy snake, born in a town where there were no females; and the mouse that blocked its hole with a turtle's egg. One day someone pointed out the dog to Marcial.

"Bow-wow," Marcial said.

He was talking his own language. He had attained the ultimate liberty. He was beginning to want to reach with his hands things that were out of reach.

XII

Hunger, thirst, heat, pain, cold. Hardly had Marcial reduced his field of perception to these essential realities when he renounced the light that accompanied them. He did not know his own name. The unpleasantness of the christening over, he had no desire for smells, sounds, or even sights. His hands caressed delectable forms. He was a purely sensory and tactile being. The universe penetrated him through his pores. Then he shut his eyes—they saw nothing but nebulous giants—and entered a warm, damp body full of shadows: a dying body. Clothed in this body's substance, he slipped toward life.

But now time passed more quickly, rarefying the final hours. The minutes sounded like cards slipping from beneath a dealer's thumb.

Birds returned to their eggs in a whirlwind of feathers. Fish congealed into roe, leaving a snowfall of scales at the bottom of their pond. The palm trees folded their fronds and disappeared into the earth like shut fans. Stems were reabsorbing their leaves, and the earth reclaimed everything that was its own. Thunder rumbled through the arcades. Hairs began growing from antelope-skin gloves. Woolen blankets were unraveling and turning into the fleece of sheep in distant pastures. Cupboards, cabinets, beds, crucifixes, tables, and blinds disappeared into the darkness in search of their ancient roots beneath the forest trees. Everything that had been fastened with nails was disintegrating. A brigantine, anchored no one knew where, sped back to Italy carrying the marble from the floors and fountain. Suits of armor, ironwork, keys, copper cooking pots, the horses' bits from the stables, were melting and forming a swelling river of metal running into the earth through roofless channels. Everything was undergoing metamorphosis and being restored to its original state. Clay returned to clay, leaving a desert where the house had once stood.

XIII

When the workmen came back at dawn to go on with the demolition of the house, they found their task completed. Someone had carried off the statue of Ceres and sold it to an antique dealer the previous evening. After complaining to their trade union, the men went and sat on the seats in the municipal park. Then one of them remembered some vague story about a Marquesa de Capellanías who had been drowned one evening in May among the arum lilies in the Almendares. But no one paid any attention to his story because the sun was traveling from east to west, and the hours growing on the right-hand side of the clock must be spun out by idleness— for they are the ones that inevitably lead to death.

TRANSLATED BY HARRIET DE ONÍS

María Luisa Bombal

Chile
(1910–1980)

———— // ————

At twelve, María Luisa Bombal went to study in Paris and stayed until 1931. In 1933 she settled in Argentina, where she was associated with the group of writers who published the magazine *Sur,* the most important of whom, Jorge Luis Borges, expressed admiration for her work. Bombal married Count Raphael de Saint-Phalle in 1941 and moved to New York, where she lived until his death in 1970, whereupon she returned to Chile. Her production as a writer was meager, but of the highest quality. She wrote an unaffected prose devoid of rhetoric, but precise and hauntingly poetic in the expression of moods. Bombal's major work was her novella *Shrouded Woman,* in which the narrator-protagonist, who has just died, reviews her life as relatives and friends come to view her body. The major theme of Bombal's work is the dissatisfaction of middle- to upper-class married women, which she manages to raise to a universal discontent with life itself. In another superb short novel, *House of Mist,* a married woman obsessively evokes a brief affair she had one night as she roamed the city in a state of agitation and yearning. When she retraces her steps many years later in search of the man's house, memory and reality fail to mesh, and she is left in doubt about whether her adventure was real or imagined. Bombal is masterful in her portrayal of desire, which is manifested as a general craving for fulfillment, yet is always tinged with erotic longings. She was ahead of her time in the openness with which sexuality is expressed in her fiction. "The Tree" is a characteristic story, but unique in the way that music is blended into both the plot and the feelings of the narrator.

The Tree

> *To Nina Anguita:*
> *great artist, magical friend,*
> *who gave life and breath to my imaginary tree,*
> *I dedicate this story which, unknowingly,*
> *I wrote for her long before we ever met*

The pianist sits down, coughs from force of habit, and concentrates for a moment. The clusters of lights illuminating the hall gradually dim

233

until they glow like dying embers, whereupon a musical phrase rises in the silence, swells: clear, sharp, and judiciously capricious.

Mozart, maybe, Brígida thinks to herself. As usual, she has forgotten to ask for the program. Mozart—or perhaps Scarlatti . . . She knew so little about music! And it was not because she lacked an ear or the inclination. On the contrary, as a child it had been she who demanded piano lessons; no one needed to impose them on her, as was the case with her sisters. Today, however, her sisters could sight-read perfectly, while she . . . she had abandoned her studies after the first year. The reason for the inconstancy was as simple as it was shameful: she had never been able, never, to learn the key of F. "I don't understand—my memory serves me only to the key of C." And her father's indignation! "Would that I could lay down this burden: a miserable widower with children to educate! My poor Carmen! How she would have suffered with such a daughter! The creature is retarded!"

Brígida was the youngest of six girls—all endowed with different temperaments. She received little attention from her father, for dealing with the other five daughters reduced him to such a perplexed and worn-out state that he preferred to ease his burden by insisting on her feeblemindedness. "I won't struggle any longer—it is useless. Leave her alone. If she chooses not to study, so be it. If she would rather spend her time in the kitchen listening to ghost stories, that is fine with me. If she favors playing with dolls at the age of sixteen, let her play." And so Brígida had kept to her dolls, remaining almost totally ignorant as far as formal education was concerned.

How pleasant it is to be ignorant! Not to know exactly who Mozart was—to ignore his origins, his influences, the particularities of his technique! To simply let oneself be led by the hand, as now . . .

For in truth Mozart leads her—transporting her onto a bridge suspended above crystal water running over a bed of pink sand. She is dressed in white, tilting on one shoulder an open parasol of Chantilly lace, elaborate and fine as a spider's web.

"You look younger every day, Brígida. Yesterday I ran into your husband—I mean, your ex-husband. His hair is now completely white."

But she makes no reply, unwilling to tarry while crossing the bridge Mozart has fabricated toward the garden of her youth.

Tall blossoming spouts in which the water sings. Her eighteen years; her chestnut braids that, unbound, cascaded to her waist; her golden complexion; her dark eyes so wide and questioning. A small mouth with full lips; a sweet smile; and the lightest, most gracious body in the world. Of what was she thinking, seated by the fountain's edge? Of nothing. "She is as silly as she is pretty," they used to say. But she did not mind being silly, nor acting the dunce at parties. One by one, her sisters received proposals of marriage. No one asked her.

Mozart! Now he conducts her to a blue marble staircase on which she descends between two rows of ice lilies. And now he opens a wrought-iron gate of spikes with golden tips so that she may throw herself on Luis, her father's intimate friend. From childhood, she would run to Luis when everyone else abandoned her. He would pick her up and she would encircle his neck between giggles that were like tiny bird cries and kisses she flung like disorderly raindrops on his eyes, his forehead, and his hair—which even then was graying (had he never been young?). "You are a necklace," Luis would say. "You are like a necklace of sparrows."

For which she had married him. Because at the side of that solemn and taciturn man she felt less culpable for being what she was: foolish, playful, and indolent. Yes—now, after so many years, she realizes that she had not married Luis for love; yet she cannot put her finger on why, why she left him so suddenly one day . . .

But at this moment Mozart takes her nervously by the hand, drawing her into a rhythm second by second more urgent—compelling her to retrace her steps across the garden and onto the bridge at a pace that is almost like fleeing. And after stripping her of the parasol and the transparent crinoline, he closes the door on her past with a note at once firm and sweet—leaving her in the concert hall, dressed in black, applauding mechanically as the artificial lights rekindle their flame.

Again shadows, and the prelude of silence.

And now Beethoven begins to stir the lukewarm tide of his notes beneath a vernal moon. How far the sea has retreated! Brígida walks seaward down the beach toward the distant, bright, smooth water; but all at once the sea rises, flowing placidly to meet and envelop her—the gentle waves pushing at her back until they press her cheek against the body of a man. And then the waves recede, leaving her stranded on Luis's chest.

"You have no heart, you have no heart," she used to say to him. His heartbeat was so faint that she could not hear it except in rare and unexpected moments. "You are never with me when you are by my side," she would protest in their bedroom when, before going to sleep, he would ritually open the evening paper. "Why did you marry me?"

"Because you have the eyes of a startled fawn," he would reply, giving her a kiss. And she, abruptly cheerful, would proudly accept the weight of his gray head on her shoulder. Oh, that silvery, radiant hair!

"Luis, you have never told me exactly what color your hair was when you were a boy. Or how your mother felt when you began going gray at the age of fifteen. What did she say? Did she laugh? Cry? And you—were you proud or ashamed? And at school—what did your classmates say? Tell me, Luis, tell me . . ."

"Tomorrow. I am sleepy, Brígida. Very tired. Turn off the light."

Unconsciously, he would turn away from her in sleep; just as she unconsciously sought her husband's shoulder all night long, searching for his breath, groping blindly for protection as an enclosed and thirsty plant bends its tendrils toward warmth and moisture.

In the mornings, when the maid would open the Venetian blinds, Luis was no longer next to her. He had departed quietly without so much as a salutation, for fear the necklace of sparrows would fasten obstinately around his neck. "Five minutes, five minutes, no more. Your office will not disappear if you are five minutes late, Luis."

Her awakenings. Ah, how sad her awakenings! But—it was curious—no sooner had she entered her boudoir than the sadness vanished as if by an enchantment.

Waves crash, clashing far away, murmuring like a sea of leaves. Beethoven? No.

It is the tree outside her dressing-room window. She had only to enter the room to experience an almost overpowering sense of well-being. How hot the bedroom always was of a morning! And what harsh light! By contrast, in the boudoir, even her eyes felt rested, refreshed. The faded cretonne curtains; the tree casting shadows that undulated on the walls like cold, moving water; the mirrors refracting foliage, creating the illusion of a green and infinite forest. How enjoyable that room was! It seemed a world submerged in an aquarium. And how that huge rubber tree chattered! All the birds in the neighborhood took refuge in it. It was the only tree on that narrow, falling street that sloped from one side of the city directly to the river.

"I am busy. I can't be with you . . . Lots of work to do, I won't be home for lunch . . . Hello—yes, I am at the club. An engagement. Eat and go to bed . . . No. I don't know. Better not wait for me, Brígida."

"If only I had friends!" she would sigh. But she bored everyone. "If I tried to be a little less foolish! Yet how does one recover so much lost ground at a single stroke? To be intelligent, you must start very young—isn't that true?"

Her sisters' husbands took them everywhere, but Luis—why had she denied it to herself?—had been ashamed of her, of her ignorance, her shyness, even of her eighteen years. Had he not urged her to pretend that she was at least twenty-one, as though her youth were an embarrassing secret they alone shared?

And at night—he always came to bed so weary! Never paying full attention to what she said. He smiled, yes—a mechanical smile. His caresses were plentiful, but bestowed absentmindedly. Why *had* he married her?

To continue their acquaintance, perhaps simply to put the crowning touch on his old friendship with her father.

Maybe life for men was based on a series of established and continuous customs. Rupturing this chain would probably produce disorder, chaos. And after, men would stumble through the streets of the city, roosting on park benches, growing shabbier and more unshaven with each passing day. Luis's life, therefore, was patterned on keeping occupied every minute of the day. Why had she failed to see this sooner? Her father had been right: she *was* retarded.

"I would like to see snow sometime, Luis."

"This summer I will take you to Europe, and since it will be winter there, you shall have your snow."

"I am quite aware that winter in Europe coincides with our summer. I am not *that* stupid!"

At times, to rouse him to the rapture of true love, she would throw herself on him and cover him with kisses: weeping, calling: "Luis, Luis, Luis . . ."

"What? What is the matter? What do you want?"

"Nothing."

"Why do you cry out my name like that, then?"

"No reason. To say your name. I like to say your name."

And he would smile benevolently, pleased with the new game.

Summer came—her first summer as a married woman. Several new business ventures forced Luis to postpone the promised European trip.

"Brígida, the heat will be terrible in Buenos Aires shortly. Why don't you spend the summer on your father's ranch?"

"Alone?"

"I would visit you every week, from Saturday to Monday."

She sat down on the bed, primed to insult him. But she could not find the hurting words. She knew nothing, nothing—not even how to offend.

"What is wrong with you? What are you thinking of, Brígida?"

He was leaning over her, worried, for the first time in their marriage unconcerned about violating his customary punctuality at the office.

"I am sleepy," Brígida had replied childishly, hiding her face in the pillow.

For once, he rang her up at lunchtime from his club. But she had refused to come to the phone, wielding angrily a weapon she had discovered without thinking: silence.

That same evening she dined across from him with lowered eyes and nerves strung tight.

"Are you still angry, Brígida?"

But she did not answer.

"You know perfectly well that I love you. But I can't be with you all the time. I am a very busy man. When you reach my age, you become a slave to a thousand obligations."

. . .

"Shall we go out tonight?"

. . .

"No? Very well, I will be patient. Tell me, did Roberto call from Montevideo?"

. . .

"What a lovely dress! Is it new?"

. . .

"Is it new, Brígida? Answer me. Say something."

But she refused to break her silence.

And then the unexpected, the astonishing, the absurd. Luis rises from his chair and slaps his napkin on the table, slamming the door as he stomps from the house.

She, too, had gotten to her feet, stunned, trembling with indignation at such injustice. "And I . . . and I . . ." she stammered, "I, who for almost an entire year . . . when for the first time I take the liberty of lodging a complaint . . . Ah, I am leaving—I am leaving this very night! I shall never set foot in this house again . . ." And she jerked open the armoires in her dressing room, strewing clothes furiously in all directions.

It was then that she heard a banging against the windowpane.

She ran to the window and opened it, not knowing how or whence her courage came. It was the rubber tree, set in motion by the storm, knocking its branches on the glass—as though calling her to witness how it twisted and contorted like a fierce black flame under the burning sky of that summer night.

Heavy rain soon began to lash its cold leaves. How lovely! All night long she could hear the rain thrashing, splashing through the leaves of the rubber tree like a thousand tiny rivers sliding down imaginary canals. All night long she heard the ancient trunk creak and moan, the storm raging outside while she curled into a ball between the sheets of the wide bed, very close to Luis.

Handfuls of pearls raining on a silver roof. Chopin. *Etudes* by Frédéric Chopin.

How many mornings had she awakened as soon as she sensed that her husband, now likewise maintaining an obstinate silence, had slipped from bed.

Her dressing room: the window thrown wide, the odor of river and grass floating in that hospitable chamber, and the mirrors wearing a veil of fog.

Chopin intermingles in her turbulent memory with rain hissing through the leaves of the rubber tree like some hidden waterfall—so palpable that even the roses on the curtains seem moist.

What to do in summer when it rains so often? Spend the day in her room feigning sadness, a convalescence? One afternoon Luis had entered timidly. Had sat down stiffly. There was a long silence.

"Then it is true, Brígida? You no longer love me?"

A sudden joy seized her. She might have shouted: "No, no. I love you, Luis, I love you," if he had given her time, if he had not almost immediately added, with his habitual calm: "In any case, I do not think it would be convenient for us to separate, Brígida. Such a move requires much thought."

Her impulse sank as fast as it had surfaced. What was the use of exciting herself! Luis loved her tenderly, with moderation; if he ever came to hate her, it would be a just and prudent hatred. And that was life. She walked to the window and placed her forehead against the cold glass. There was the rubber tree, serenely accepting the pelting rain. The room was fixed in shadow, quiet and ordered. Everything seemed to be held in an eternal and very noble equilibrium. That was life. And there was a certain grandeur in accepting it thus: mediocre, like something definite and irremediable. While underneath it all there seemed to rise a melody of grave and slow words that transfixed her: "Always. Never" . . .

And in this way the hours, days, and years pass. Always! Never! Life! Life!

Collecting herself, she realized that her husband had stolen from the room.

"Always! Never!" . . . And the rain, secret and steady, still whispered in Chopin.

Summer stripped the leaves from its burning calendar. Luminous and blinding pages fell like golden swords; pages also of malignant dampness like breeze from a swamp; pages of furious and brief storms, of hot wind—the wind that carries the "carnation of the air" and hangs it on the huge rubber tree.

Some children used to play hide-and-seek among the enormous, twisted roots that pushed up the paving stones on the sidewalk, and the tree overflowed with laughter and whispering. On those days she would look from the window and clap her hands; but the children dispersed in fear, without noticing the childlike smile of a girl who wanted to join the game.

Alone, she would lean on her elbows at the window for a long time, watching the foliage swaying—a breeze blew along that street which sloped directly to the river—and it was like staring deep into moving water or the dancing flames in a fireplace. One could kill time in this fashion, no need for thought, made foolish by peace of mind.

She lit the first lamp just as the room began to fill with twilight smoke, and the first lamp flickered in the mirrors, multiplying like fireflies eager to hasten the night.

And night after night she dozed beside her husband, suffering at intervals. But when her pain tightened so that it pierced like a knife thrust, when she was besieged by the desire to wake Luis—to hit him or caress him—she tiptoed to her dressing room and opened the window. Immediately the room came alive with discreet sounds and discreet presences, with mysterious footsteps, the fluttering of wings, the sudden rustling of vegetation, the soft chirping of a cricket perched on the bark of the rubber tree under the stars of a hot summer night.

Little by little her fever went down as her bare feet grew cold on the reed mat. She did not know why it was so easy to suffer in that room.

Chopin's melancholy stringing of one *Etude* after another, stringing of one melancholy after another, imperturbably.

And autumn came. The dry leaves hovered an instant before settling on the grass of the narrow garden, on the sidewalk of that sloping street. The leaves came loose and fell . . . The top of the rubber tree remained green but underneath it turned red—darkened like the worn-out lining of a sumptuous evening cape. And now the room seemed to be submerged in a goblet of dull gold.

Lying on the divan, she waited patiently for the dinner hour, and the improbable arrival of Luis. She had resumed speaking to him, had become his again without enthusiasm or anger. She no longer loved him. But she no longer suffered. On the contrary, an unexpected feeling of fulfillment and placidity had taken hold of her. Nothing, no one could now hurt her. It may be that true happiness lies in the conviction that one has irremediably lost happiness. It is only then that we can begin to live without hope or fear, able finally to enjoy all the small pleasures, which are the most lasting.

A thunderous noise, followed by a flash of light from which she recoils, shaking.

The intermission? No. The rubber tree.

Having started work early in the morning without her knowledge, they had felled it with a single stroke of the ax. "The roots were breaking up the sidewalk, and, naturally, the neighborhood committee . . ."

Dazed, she has shielded her eyes with her hands. When she recovers her sight, she stands and looks around. What does she see?

The concert hall suddenly ablaze with light, the audience filing out?

No. She is imprisoned in the web of her past, trapped in the dressing room—which has been invaded by a terrifying white light. It was as if they had ripped off the roof; a crude light entering from every direction, seeping through her very pores, burning her with its coldness. And she saw everything bathed in that cold light: Luis, his wrinkled face, his hands crisscrossed with ropy discolored veins, and the gaudy cretonnes.

Frightened, she runs to the window. The window now opens directly on a narrow street, so narrow that her room almost brushes against a shiny skyscraper. On the ground floor, shop windows and more shop windows, full of bottles. At the corner, a row of automobiles lined up in front of a service station painted red. Some boys in their shirtsleeves are kicking a ball in the middle of the street.

And all that ugliness lay embedded in her mirrors, along with nickelplated balconies, shabby clotheslines, and canary cages.

They had stolen her intimacy, her secret; she found herself naked in the middle of the street, naked before an old husband who turned his back on her in bed, who had given her no children. She does not understand why, until then, she had not wanted children, how she had resigned herself to the idea of life without children. Nor does she comprehend how for a whole year she had tolerated Luis's laughter, that overcheerful laughter, that false laughter of a man who has trained himself in joviality because it is necessary to laugh on certain occasions.

Lies! Her resignation and serenity were lies; she wanted love, yes, love, and trips and madness, and love, love . . .

"But, Brígida—why are you leaving? Why did you stay so long?" Luis had asked.

Now she would have known how to answer him.

"The tree, Luis, the tree! They have cut down the rubber tree."

TRANSLATED BY RICHARD AND LUCIA CUNNINGHAM

Miguel Angel Asturias

Guatemala
(1899–1974)

To many, Miguel Angel Asturias was the quintessential modern Latin American writer: he was visibly Indian, the author of novels of protest against the United Fruit Company, and a practitioner of what came to be known as "magical realism." In 1967, Asturias was the first Latin American novelist to be awarded the Nobel Prize, and some in Latin America believed it was because he fit the prevailing stereotype. But Asturias was a great writer independent of any preconceptions or misconceptions. He was of Mayan and Spanish ancestry, and in his youth the brutal dictatorship of Estrada Cabrera in Guatemala forced his family to move from the capital to the countryside. While there he came into intimate contact with indigenous cultures in ways that would not have been available in the capital, Guatemala City. But it was not until he studied anthropology in Paris that Asturias truly learned about Mayan culture. It was at the Sorbonne that he translated into Spanish the *Popol Vuh,* or sacred book of the Mayas, from a French translation, and published in 1930 *Legends of Guatemala* to no small acclaim and with a prologue by the French poet Paul Valéry. While in Paris, Asturias also associated with the surrealists and quite a few Latin American artists and writers, such as the Cuban Alejo Carpentier. Surrealism and ethnography, in addition to a profound political commitment, are the most significant characteristics of Asturias's work. His best-known book, *El señor presidente* (1946), is the story of Estrada Cabrera's dictatorship, told in a poetic, often grotesque tone that betrays Asturias's surrealist past. These are the qualities that led some to associate him with magical realism. *Men of Maize* (1949) retells the history of Guatemala, as well as that of Asturias's own life, in the mold of Mayan myths. Asturias's literary experiments had a decisive influence on Latin American novelists of the 1960s. Even when they denied him, they learned from him how to write engaged novels that were not realistic or propagandistic. In the powerful "The Legend of 'El Cadejo,' " he, like Ricardo Palma earlier, takes recourse to popular piety and to stories about bizarre events and miracles often recounted in saints' lives.

The Legend of "El Cadejo"

And El Cadejo, *who steals girls with long braids and knots the manes of horses, makes his appearance in the valley.*

In the course of time, Mother Elvira of St. Francis, abbess of the monastery of St. Catherine, would be the novice who cut out the hosts in the convent of the Conception, a girl noted for her beauty and manner of speaking, so ingenuous that on her lips the word was a flower of gentleness and love.

From a large window without glass, the novice used to watch the flights of leaves dried by the summer's heat, the trees putting on their flowers and ripe fruit dropping in the orchards next to the convent, through the part that was in ruins, where the foliage, hiding the wounded walls and the open roofs, transformed the cells and the cloisters into paradises filled with the scent of *búcaro* clay and wild roses; bowers of feasting, as the chroniclers recorded, where nuns were replaced by pigeons with pink feet and their canticles by the warble of the cimarron mockingbird.

Outside her window, in the collapsed rooms, the warm shade, where butterflies worked the dust of their wings into silk, joined the silence of the courtyard, interrupted by the coming and going of the lizards, and the soft aroma of the leaves that multiplied the tender feeling of the trees whose roots were coiled into the very ancient walls.

And inside, in the sweet company of God, trimming the peel from the fruit of angels to disclose the meat and seed that is the Body of Christ, long as the orange's medulla—*vere tu es Deus absconditus!*—Elvira of St. Francis reunited her spirit and her flesh to the house of her childhood, with its heavy locks and its light roses, its doors that split sobs into the loose seams of the wind, its walls reflected in the troughs of the fountains like clouds of breath on clean glass.

The voices of the city broke the peace of her window: last-minute blues of the passenger that hears the movement of the port at sailing time; a man's laughter as he brings his galloping horse to a stop, a cart wheeling by, or a child crying.

Horse, cart, man, child passed before her eyes, evoked in country settings, under skies whose tranquil appearance put under a spell the wise eyes of the fountain troughs sitting around the water with the long-suffering air of old women servants.

And the images were accompanied by odors. The sky smelled like a sky, the child like a child, the fields like fields, the cart like hay, the horse like an old rosebush, the man like a saint, the troughs like shadows, the shadows like Sunday rest and the Lord's day of rest like fresh washing. . . .

Dark was coming on. The shadows erased their thought, luminous mixture of dust particles swimming in a shaft of sunlight. The bells drew their lips towards the cup of evening without a sound. Who talks of kisses? The wind shook up the heliotropes. Heliotropes or hippocampi? And the hummingbirds quenched their desire for God in streams of flowers. Who talks of kisses?

The tap of heels hurrying brought her to herself. Their sound frilled along the corridor like drumsticks.

Could she be hearing right? Could it be the man with the long eyelashes who came by late on Fridays for the hosts to take them nine towns away from there, to the Valley of the Virgin, where a pleasant hermitage rested on a hill's top?

They called him the poppy-man. The wind moved in his feet. When the sound of his goat's footsteps stopped, there he would be, like a ghost: hat in hand, tiny boots, a goldish color, wrapped in his blue greatcoat; and he waited for the wafer boxes in the doorway.

Yes, it was he; but this time he rushed in looking very frightened, as if to prevent some catastrophe.

"Miss, oh miss!" he came in shouting, "they're going to cut off your hair! They're going to cut it off!"

When she saw him coming in, livid and elastic, the novice sprang to her feet intending to reach the door. But, wearing shoes she had charitably inherited from a paralytic nun who had worn them in life, when she heard his shout, she felt as if the nun who had spent her life motionless had stepped on her feet, and she couldn't move a step. . . .

. . . A sob, like a star, trembled in her throat. Birds scissored the twilight among the grey, crippled ruins. Two giant eucalyptus trees were saying prayers of penance.

Bound to the feet of a corpse, unable to move, she wept disconsolately, swallowing her tears silently as sick people whose organs begin to dry up and turn cold, bit by bit. She felt as if she were dead, covered with dirt; she felt that in her grave—her orphan's dress being filled with clay—rosebushes of white words bloomed and, little by little, her dismay changed into a quiet sort of happiness. Walking rosebushes, the nuns were cutting off one another's roses to dress the altars of the Virgin and the roses became the month of May, a spider web of fragrances that trapped Our Lady like a fly of light.

But the sensation of her body's flowering after death was a shortlived happiness.

Like a kite that suddenly runs out of string among the clouds, the weight of her braid pulled her headlong, with all her clothes, into hell. The mystery was in her braid. Sum of anguished instants. She lost consciousness for as long as a couple of her sighs lasted and felt herself back on earth only when she had almost reached the boiling pit where devils bubble. A fan of possible realities opened around her: the night sweetened with puff paste, pine trees that smell like altars, the pollen of life in the hair of the air, formless, colorless cat that scratches the waters of the fountain troughs and unsettles old papers.

The window and she herself became filled with heaven. . . .

"Miss, when I receive Holy Communion, God tastes like your hands!" the one in the greatcoat whispered, laying the grille of his lashes over the coals of his eyes.

The novice pulled her hands away from the hosts when she heard the blasphemy. No, it wasn't a dream! Then she touched her arms, her shoulders, her neck, her face, her braid. She held her breath one moment, long as a century, when she felt her braid. No, it wasn't a dream! Under the warm handful of hair she came alive, aware of her womanly charms, accompanied in her diabolic nuptials by the poppy-man and a candle burning at the end of the room, oblong as a coffin. The light supported the impossible reality of the lover, who stretched out his arms like a Christ who had turned into a bat in a viaticum, and this was her own flesh! She closed her eyes to escape, wrapped in her blindness, from that vision from hell, from the man who caressed her down to where she was a woman, simply by being a man—the most abominable of concupiscences!—but as soon as she lowered her round pale eyelids the paralytic nun seemed to step from her shoes, soaked in tears, and she quickly opened them. She tore through the darkness, opened her eyes, left their deep interior with their pupils restless as mice in a trap, wild, insensible, the color drained out of her cheeks, caught between the stertor of a strange agony she carried in her feet and her braid's stream of live coals twisted like an invisible flame on her back.

And that's the last she knew about it. Like someone under a spell that can't be broken, with a sob on her tongue which seemed to be filled with poison, like her heart, she broke away from the presence of the corpse and the man, half mad, spilling the wafers about, in search of her scissors and, finding them, she cut off the braid and, free of the spell, she fled in search of the sure refuge of the Mother Superior, no longer feeling the nun's feet on hers. . . .

But when the braid fell it was no longer a braid: it moved, undulated over the tiny mattress of hosts scattered on the floor.

The poppy-man turned to look for light. Tears quivered on his eyelashes like the last little flames on the black of the match that is about to go out. He slid along the side of the wall with bated breath, without disturbing the shadows, without making a sound, desperate to reach the flame he believed would be his salvation. But his measured step soon dissolved into a flight of fear. The headless reptile was moving past the sacred leaf-pile of hosts and filing towards him. It dragged itself right under his feet like the black blood of a dead animal and suddenly, as he was about to take hold of the light, leaped with the speed of water that runs free and light to coil itself like a whip around the candle which it caused to weep until it consumed itself for the soul of him who was being extinguished, along with it, forever. And so the poppy-man, for whom cactus plants still weep white tears, reached eternity.

The devil had passed like a breath through the braid, which fell lifeless on the floor when the candle's flame went out.

And at midnight, changed into a long animal—twice as long as a ram by full moon, big as a weeping willow by new moon—with goat's hoofs, rabbit's ears and a bat's face, the poppy-man dragged down to hell the black braid of the novice who, in the course of time, would be Mother Elvira of St. Francis—that's how "El Cadejo" was born—while, on her knees in her cell, smiling like an angel, she dreamed of the lily and the mystic lamb.

TRANSLATED BY HARDIE ST. MARTIN

Juan Bosch

Dominican Republic
(b. 1909)

The son of a Catalan father and a Puerto Rican mother, Juan Bosch is a well-known Dominican writer of the twentieth century (his fame is outstripped only by that of outstanding scholar and essayist Pedro Henríquez Ureña). A novelist, historian, and essayist, Bosch is most accomplished as a short story writer. In 1929, Bosch began publishing his stories in literary journals and newspapers. His first collection, *Camino real,* appeared in 1933. In 1943, his story "Luis Pie" won in Cuba the Alfonso Hernández Catá Prize. In 1936 Bosch published the first of his two novels, *La Mañosa.* His second, *El oro y la paz,* appeared in 1964. Bosch devoted himself to the overthrow of Dominican dictator Rafael Trujillo and was exiled for a long period, mostly in Cuba. He returned to the Dominican Republic in 1961, after Trujillo's assassination, and was elected president in 1963. He was overthrown by a military coup only seven months later. Social and political themes dominate Bosch's later essayistic and historical writings: *Crisis de la democracia de América en la República Dominicana* (1964), *Pentagonismo, sustituto del imperialismo* (1968), *Composición social dominicana* (1968), *De Cristóbal Colón a Fidel Castro* (1970), and *El próximo paso: dictadura con respaldo popular* (1970). "Encarnación Mendoza's Christmas Eve," reprinted here, is built upon a series of ironies, not the least of which is that Encarnación's own son, unwittingly, brings about his death. But there is a broader irony in that the Christmas Eve celebration—the most important in the Caribbean and in Latin America in general—is the background of the incidents. Moved to celebrate Christ's birth, Encarnación (his name is significant) is himself the victim of a sacrifice. This is a story that combines Bosch's well-known social and political concerns, as well as his realism, with a sense of cosmic injustice in which the elements (the rain, the sunlight) play important roles.

Encarnación Mendoza's Christmas Eve

With his keen eye of a fugitive, Encarnación Mendoza had been able to discern the outline of a tree from twenty paces, which is why he thought that night would soon be lifting. He was accurate in his calculations; where he began to go wrong was in drawing a conclusion based on the observation. For, as daylight approached, finding a hiding place took

247

on the utmost urgency, and he pondered whether to immerse himself in the hills to his right or in the sugarcane field that lay to the left. To his misfortune, he chose the cane field. An hour and a half later, the December 24 sun was lighting up the fields and gently warming Encarnación Mendoza, who was stretched out head-up on a bed of cane leaves.

At seven in the morning things seemed to be going as the runaway had predicted; no one had come along the nearby paths. Besides, the breeze was fresh and it might well rain, as it did almost every year on Christmas Eve. And even if it didn't, the men weren't likely to leave the company store, where they'd gotten an early start downing rum and talking in loud voices, as custom dictated, in an attempt to be cheerful. On the other hand, had he turned toward the hills, he couldn't have felt as secure. He knew the place well; the families that lived up in the hollows produced firewood, yuca root, and some corn. If any of the men who lived in the shacks around there came down that day to sell supplies in the sugar mill's store, and if any of them happened to see him, he was a goner. For miles around there was no one who'd dare keep the encounter quiet. Anyone who'd cover for Encarnación Mendoza would never be pardoned; despite the fact that the matter was never talked about, all the neighbors in the district knew that whoever saw him was to report the incident immediately to the nearest guard-house.

Encarnación Mendoza was just starting to calm down, because he was sure he'd chosen the best spot for hiding during the daylight hours, when fate began to work against him.

For at that very moment, Mundito's mother was thinking along the same lines as the fugitive: no one would come down the footpaths in the morning, and if Mundito quickened his steps he'd make the trip to the store before the usual Christmas Eve drunks began to travel the roads. Mundito's mother had a few cents she'd saved from the little she charged for washing clothes and for peddling hens at the highway crossing almost a half day's walk to the west. With these pennies she could send Mundito to the store to buy flour, a piece of codfish, and some lard. Meager as it might be, she wanted to celebrate Christmas Eve with her six little ones, even if it meant eating cod fritters.

The hamlet where they lived—there on the hillside, in the road that divided the cane fields from uncultivated land—counted some fourteen or fifteen poor dwellings, most of whose roofs were thatched with palm bark. As he was leaving his home to go on the mission to the store, Mundito stopped for a moment in the middle of the dry clay where carts loaded with cane would pass by during the sugar-making season. It was a long haul to the store. The sky was clear, radiant with light scattered over the horizon of cane shoots; the breeze was pleasant and the silence sadly sweet. Why should he go alone only to get bored walking along the never-changing footpaths? Mundito paused for ten seconds to contemplate going into the neighboring shack, where six weeks earlier a black bitch had given birth to six pups. The animal's owners had given away five, but one was left "to nurse the mother," and Mundito had displaced onto it all the affection accumulated in his own little tenderness-starved soul. His nine years burdened with precocious wisdom, the lad was aware that if he took the puppy he'd have to carry it almost the whole while, because it wouldn't be able to cover such a long distance on its own. Mundito felt that this insight almost authorized him to enlist the pup. Suddenly, with no further thought, he ran toward the hut yelling, "Miss Ophelia, loan me Azabache, 'cause I'm gonna take him anyways!"

Whether they heard him or not, he'd already asked permission, and that was enough. He whirled in like the wind, took the little animal in his arms, and dashed out running at full speed, until lost in the distance. And that's how destiny started to play into Encarnación Mendoza's plans.

For it happened that a bit before nine, when young Mundito was passing in front of the section where the runaway lay hiding, tired, or simply motivated by a curiosity in the here and now, by that kind of indifference that is a privilege of small animals, Azabache ventured into the cane field. Encarnación Mendoza heard the boy's voice commanding the pup to stop. For a second he feared the lad might be the scout for some search party. The morning was clear. With his sharp eye of a fugitive, he could see as far as the confusion of stalks and leaves would allow. The boy was not there within range of his sight. Encarnación Mendoza was nobody's fool. He quickly calculated that if they found him lurking about, he was lost; the best thing would be to pretend he was sleeping, turning his back to the side where he'd heard noises. To be even safer, he used his hat to cover his face.

The black puppy ran back and forth, playing with the cane leaves, trying to jump in awkward motions, and when he saw the stretched-out fugitive, he burst into tiny funny barks. Calling him loudly and crawling to move forward, Mundito kept coming closer when suddenly he became paralyzed: he'd seen the man. But for him, this was not simply a man but something terrible and imposing; it was a corpse. There was no other way to explain its presence there, much less in that position. He froze with terror. His first thought was to flee, and to do so in silence so the corpse wouldn't notice. But it seemed criminal to leave Azabache abandoned, exposed to the danger of the dead man's getting upset with his barking and breaking him into pieces, squeezing him with his hands. Unable to leave without his little animal and unable to stay there, the boy thought he'd faint. Absent of any willpower, he raised a hand and fixed his gaze on the deceased, trembling while the pup sat back on his haunches launching his diminutive barks. Mundito was sure the corpse would rise up at any moment. In his state of fright, he tried to approach the dead man. He swooped down over the little puppy, which he grabbed by the neck with nervous impetuousness, and then, head bent into the cane stalks, cutting his face and hands, impelled by sheer terror and gasping for air, he broke into a run for the store. As he arrived there, on the verge of fainting from exertion and fear, he shouted, pointing to the distant site of his adventure, "There's a dead man in Adela District!"

To which a great big rough voice yelled back, "What's that boy sayin'?"

And as this was the voice of Sergeant Rey, station chief for the sugar mill, it commanded supreme interest in those present, as did the pieces of information he solicited from the boy.

One couldn't count on La Romana's judge to perform an inquest on the corpse on Christmas Eve day, since he was probably wandering around the capital enjoying his end-of-the-year holiday. But the sergeant was quick on his feet; fifteen minutes after listening to Mundito, Sergeant Rey, with two troops and ten or twelve curiosity seekers, headed for the location where the presumed corpse was lying. This turn of events had not entered into Encarnación Mendoza's plans.

Encarnación Mendoza's goal was to spend Christmas Eve with his wife and children. Hiding by day and walking by night, he had covered mile after mile from the mountain range's first buttresses, in Seybo Province, by keeping away from all encounters and avoiding all shacks, corrals, tree clearings or land burns. Everyone in the entire region knew he'd killed Corporal Pomares, and no one was unaware he was a condemned man wherever they found him. He mustn't let himself be seen by a soul, except for Nina and the children. And he'd see them for only an hour or two, on Christmas Eve. He'd been fleeing for six months now, for it was on St. John's Day when the events that cost Corporal Pomares his life took place.

He absolutely had to see his wife and children. It was an animal impulse pushing him on, a blind force he couldn't resist. When all was said and done, free of all sentiment, Encarnación Mendoza understood that the desire to embrace his wife and to spin a yarn for the children was mixed with a tinge of jealousy. And besides, he needed to see the cozy hut, the lamp light illuminating the room where they'd gather when he'd return from work and the children would surround him so he could make them laugh with his witty remarks. His body urged him on to the dusty road that would turn into a mud hole in the rainy season. He had to go or he'd die of a dreadful sorrow.

Encarnación Mendoza was used to doing whatever he pleased; he never yearned after anything bad, and he respected himself. The whole St. John's Day affair, when Corporal Pomares insulted him by slapping him in the face, had happened because of his self-respect. To strike him, he who in order to not offend, didn't drink, and who was driven by nothing but concern for his family. No matter what, and even if the devil himself opposed him, Encarnación Mendoza would spend Christmas Eve in his own hut. To even imagine Nina and the boys feeling sad, with not a dime to celebrate the holiday, maybe weeping for him, was breaking his heart and made him curse with pain.

But his plan had become somewhat complicated. It was a matter of considering whether the boy would talk or if he'd keep quiet. He'd left running, something Encarnación could gather by the speed of his footsteps, and perhaps the lad thought that this was just a case of a sleeping field hand. Perhaps it would have been prudent to distance himself from there and go into another patch of cane. Nevertheless, it was worth thinking about twice because, if he should be so unlucky as to have someone pass along the footpath either coming or going, and that person should see him crossing the road, and recognize him, he was a lost man. He shouldn't be precipitous; there, for the present, he was safe. At nine at night he could leave, walk cautiously toward the edge of the hills, and he'd be in the house at eleven, maybe eleven-fifteen. He knew what he was going to do. He'd call through the window in a low voice and he'd tell Nina to open it, that it was he, her husband. It already seemed like he was watching Nina with her black hair falling across her cheeks, her dark shining eyes, her full mouth, her prominent chin. This moment of homecoming was his life's reason for being; he couldn't chance being caught before that. To change sections in full daylight was too risky. The best thing would be to rest, to sleep. . . .

He awoke to the sound of tramping footsteps and the voice of the little boy saying, "He's there, Sergeant."

"But in which patch? In that one or the one over there?"

"In that one there," the boy assured him.

"In that one there" could mean that the boy was pointing out the one Encarnación was occupying, the one next to it, or the one in front of him. For, to judge from the voices, the boy and the sergeant were in the pathway, perhaps at the intersection between several patches of cane. It depended on which direction the boy was indicating when he said "that one there." The situation was really serious, because what there could be no doubt about was that people were already close to finding the fugitive. The moment, then, was not for doubting, but for acting. Quick to decide, Encarnación Mendoza began to crawl with extreme caution, being careful that any sound he made could be confused with that of the wind-whipped leaves in the cane field. He had to get out of there at once, without losing a second. He heard the sergeant's rough voice, "Go in over there, Nemesio, 'cause I'm goin' over here! You, Solito, stay here!"

There were sounds of mumbling and grumbling. As he moved farther away, crouching and using feline steps, Encarnación could gather that there were several men in the group searching for him. There was no doubt things were getting ugly.

Ugly for him and ugly for the boy, whoever he was. Because when Sergeant Rey and Private Nemesio Arroyo searched the patch of cane they'd gone into, destroying the most tender stalks and cutting their arms and hands, and when they didn't see a single corpse, they got to thinking the story about the dead man in Adela District was all a joke.

"Ya sure it was here, boy?" asked the sergeant.

"Yes, it was here," affirmed Mundito, quite frightened now.

"Those are boys' doin's, Sergeant; there's no one there," put in Private Arroyo.

The sergeant fixed his glare on the boy, a spine-chilling one that filled him with dread.

"Look, I be comin' along here with Azabache," Mundito started to explain, "and he be runnin' like so," which he said while putting the puppy down on the ground, "and he mustered himself up and went on in there."

But Private Solito Ruiz interrupted Mundito's performance by asking, "What was the dead man like?"

"I ain't seen his face," said the boy, trembling with fear. "I only seen his clothes. He had a hat over his face. He be like this, on his side. . . ."

"What color was his pants?" inquired the sergeant.

"Blue, and his shirt kinda yellow, and he had a black hat over his face. . . ."

But poor Mundito could hardly speak; he was in a state of terror, wanting to cry. According to his childish notion of things, the dead man had gone from the spot only to avenge his denunciation and to make a liar out of him. Surely at night, he'd appear in his house and chase after him his whole life long.

In any event, whether Mundito knew it or not, they wouldn't come upon the corpse, at least not in this patch. Encarnación Mendoza had crossed with surprising speed to another one, and then to yet another; and he was already crossing the path to go into a third one when the boy, already dismissed by the sergeant, passed by running with the puppy under his arm. His fear stopped him cold as he saw the deceased's torso and leg entering the cane field. It couldn't be anyone else, given that the clothes were the ones he'd seen that morning.

"He here, Sergeant, he here!" he yelled, pointing toward the spot were he'd lost sight of the fugitive. "He gone in there!"

And, since he was very scared, he kept on running until he reached home, breathless and filled with self-pity for the mess he'd gotten himself into. The sergeant, along with the soldiers and curiosity seekers who accompanied him, had come back after hearing the little lad's voice.

"Boy's stuff," soothed Nemesio Arroyo.

But the sergeant, experienced in his job, was suspicious. "Look, there's something to this. Let's surroun' this patch once 'n for all!" he shouted.

And so the hunt began without the hunters knowing what prey they were chasing.

It was a bit past midmorning. Divided into groups, each soldier was followed by three or four field hands, looking here and there, running along the paths, all of them a little drunk and everyone excited. Slowly, the small, dark blue clouds that rested level with the horizon began to grow and climb upward into the sky. Encarnación Mendoza knew he was more or less surrounded. It was just that unlike his pursuers, who didn't know for whom they were looking, he figured the objective of the cane-field search was to apprehend him, and that they were coming to collect for what happened on St. John's Day.

While not being dead sure about where the soldiers were, the fugitive stuck to his instinct and will to escape, and he kept running from one patch to another, avoiding any encounter with the soldiers. He was now distant enough from them that if he'd remained calm he'd have been able to wait until dark with no danger of being found. But he didn't feel safe and he kept on passing from patch to patch. He was seen from afar while crossing a lane, and a voice proclaimed at the top of its lungs, "There he goes, Sergeant, there he goes; and he looks like Encarnación Mendoza!"

Encarnación Mendoza! All at once everyone stopped, paralyzed in their tracks. Encarnación Mendoza!

"Come on!" The sergeant shouted his orders. He broke into a run, revolver in hand, in the direction to which the field hand who'd seen the fugitive pointed.

It was now close to noon, and though the increasingly large clouds were turning the atmosphere suffocatingly hot, the man hunters hardly noticed; they kept running and running, yelling back and forth, zigzagging, shooting above the sugarcane. Encarnación let himself be seen on a distant path, for just a moment, running away with the speed of a fleeing shadow, and he didn't give Private Solito Ruiz time to aim his gun at him.

"One o' you go to the mill compound and tell 'em from me to send two troops," the sergeant ordered, shouting.

Nervous, stirred up, breathing as one, and looking in all directions at once, the pursuers ran from one side to the other, yelling back and forth among themselves, recommending prudence when anyone threatened to go in among the canes.

Noon came and went. Not two, but three soldiers arrived with some nine or ten more field hands; they dispersed into groups and the hunt stretched out over various sections of cane. In the distance a soldier and four or five field hands would suddenly be seen, which hindered movement, for it was risky to shoot if friendly people were at the other end.

Men, and even a woman, kept coming out of the compound, and no one was left in the store except the clerk, who asked every mother's son that passed by if "they'd nabbed him yet."

Encarnación Mendoza was no easy man. But around three o'clock, on the road that divided the cane field from the hills, that is, more than two hours from the mill compound, a sure shot broke his spinal column at the moment he was crossing to plunge into the undergrowth. He was wallowing on the ground, spouting blood, when he received fourteen more shots, for the soldiers kept shooting him as they approached. And it was precisely then that the first drops of rain, which had been creeping in since midmorning, started to fall.

Encarnación Mendoza was dead. He retained the lines on his face, though his teeth were destroyed by a blast from a Mauser. It was Christmas Eve day and he had come down from the mountains to spend Christmas Eve, dead or alive, at home, not in the sugar mill. It was beginning to rain, though not yet strongly. And the sergeant was mulling something over. If he removed the corpse to the highway to the west, he could take him this very day to Macorís and deliver the captain this Christmas present; if he took it to the compound, he'd have to catch a company train there in order to go to La Romana, and since the train's departure could be quite delayed, he'd arrive in the city late at night, maybe too late to transfer to Macorís. On the highway things were different; vehicles frequently passed by, he could stop a car, make the people get out and put the corpse in it, or load it up on top of a truck's cargo.

"Look for a horse right now 'cause we're gonna take this bum out to the highway!" he said, addressing the nearest person.

Not a horse, but a burro, turned up, and at that after four o'clock, when the heavy downpour sounded without let-up on the plots of newly sown cane. The sergeant didn't want to waste any time. Several field hands, all getting into each other's way, placed the corpse across the donkey and tied him as best they could. Followed by two soldiers and three onlookers he'd chosen to drive the burro, the sergeant issued the command to march in the rain.

The road turned out not to be easy. Three times, before arriving at the first village, the dead man slipped off and wound up hanging under the donkey's belly. The latter snorted and made an effort to trot in the mud that was starting to form. Covered at first only by their regulation hats, the soldiers made use of palm bark strips and large leaves yanked off trees, or, when the rain was most intense, they took refuge in the cane fields for a spell. The dismal retinue kept on going without stopping, most of the time in silence, though a soldier's voice would once in a while comment: "Look at that bastard." Or he'd simply allude to Corporal Pomares, whose blood had finally been avenged.

It became completely dark, undoubtedly earlier than usual due to the rain; and with darkness, the road got more difficult, which is why the pace of the march slowed down. It must have been around seven, and it was now hardly raining, when one of the hands said, "I can see a little light over there."

"Yes, from the village," explained the sergeant, and immediately he wove a plan that made him feel enormously satisfied.

Well, for the sergeant, the death of Encarnación Mendoza was not enough. The sergeant wanted something more. So, when fifteen minutes later he found himself in front of the first shack in the place, he commanded in his rough voice, "Untie this dead man and throw him there inside. We can't keep on gettin' wet."

He said this when the rain was quite light, for it looked like it was about to let up, and as he was speaking he observed the men struggling with the task of freeing the corpse from the ropes. Once the body was loose, he knocked on the hut's door just in time for the woman who opened it to receive, at her feet, thrown down like a dog, the body of Encarnación Mendoza. The dead man was drenched in water, blood and mud, and his teeth were shattered by a bullet, which gave his previously serene and kindly face the illusion of a horrible grimace.

The woman looked at that inert mass; her eyes all at once took on the expressionless fix of madness; and bringing a hand to her mouth, she began to slowly draw back, until she stopped three steps away; then, dejected, she rushed onto the corpse while screaming, "Oh my chil'ren! They's left orfins . . . they's killed Encarnación!"

Frightened, stumbling over each other, the children came out from the room, flinging themselves at their mother's skirt.

Then, in a blend of tears and horror, a young child's voice could be heard: "Mamma, mommy! . . . That's him! . . . That's the dead man I seen today . . . out there in the cane field."

TRANSLATED BY SUSAN HERMAN

João Guimarães Rosa

Brazil

(1908–1967)

———— \\\\ ————

A medical doctor by training and a career diplomat to improve his lot, João Guimarães Rosa wrote fiction that was a brilliant combination of the regionalist novel of northeastern Brazil with the avant-garde poetics of groups centered in São Paulo. He worked in Brazil's diplomatic corps in many places and for many years, including a mission in Nazi Germany, where he was detained for helping Jews escape the country. His interest in folklore started early. As a young doctor in the remote Brazilian plain, Guimarães Rosa would ask his destitute patients to compensate him by telling him stories. Many of these he wove into his complicated and ambitious novel *Grande sertão, veredas* (1956) (published in 1963 in English as *The Devil to Pay in the Backlands*) set in the Brazilian plains known as the *sertão* (literally, the title means "Broad Plain, Pathways"). Some critics, like the late Emir Rodríguez Monegal, rank it as the best Latin American novel ever written. The text consists of a protracted, digressive, and haunting monologue by Riobaldo, the protagonist, who returns over and again to the most significant incidents of his life, elaborating in the process a discourse full of puns, allusions, and other linguistic devices reminiscent of James Joyce. Guimarães Rosa was also a leading short story writer, perhaps the best in the Portuguese language since Machado de Assis. He published several collections in his lifetime: *Sagarana* (1946), *Corpo de baile* (1954), and *Primeras estórias* (1962). Some of these have been collected in *The Third Bank of the River and Other Stories* (1968). Other stories were collected posthumously in *Estas estórias* (1969). "The Third Bank of the River," perhaps Rosa's finest story and the selection here, begins with a deliberate effort to highlight the conventional, even colorless character of the father, who literally embarks on a strange adventure without end that takes on allegorical connotations. Is the river time or death or both?

The Third Bank of the River

M y father was a dutiful, orderly, straightforward man. And according to several reliable people of whom I inquired, he had had these qualities since adolescence or even childhood. By my own recollection, he was neither jollier nor more melancholy than the other men we knew. Maybe a little quieter. It was mother, not father, who ruled the house. She scolded us daily—my sister, my brother, and me. But it happened one day that father ordered a boat.

He was very serious about it. It was to be made specially for him, of mimosa wood. It was to be sturdy enough to last twenty or thirty years and just large enough for one person. Mother carried on plenty about it. Was her husband going to become a fisherman all of a sudden? Or a hunter? Father said nothing. Our house was less than a mile from the river, which around there was deep, quiet, and so wide you couldn't see across it.

I can never forget the day the rowboat was delivered. Father showed no joy or other emotion. He just put on his hat as he always did and said goodbye to us. He took along no food or bundle of any sort. We expected mother to rant and rave, but she didn't. She looked very pale and bit her lip, but all she said was:

"If you go away, stay away. Don't ever come back!"

Father made no reply. He looked gently at me and motioned me to walk along with him. I feared mother's wrath, yet I eagerly obeyed. We headed toward the river together. I felt bold and exhilarated, so much so that I said:

"Father, will you take me with you in your boat?"

He just looked at me, gave me his blessing, and, by a gesture, told me to go back. I made as if to do so but, when his back was turned, I ducked behind some bushes to watch him. Father got into the boat and rowed away. Its shadow slid across the water like a crocodile, long and quiet.

Father did not come back. Nor did he go anywhere, really. He just rowed and floated across and around, out there in the river. Everyone was appalled. What had never happened, what could not possibly happen, was happening. Our relatives, neighbors, and friends came over to discuss the phenomenon.

Mother was ashamed. She said little and conducted herself with great composure. As a consequence, almost everyone thought (though no one said it) that father had gone insane. A few, however, suggested that father might be fulfilling a promise he had made to God or to a saint, or that he might have some horrible disease, maybe leprosy, and that he left for the sake of the family, at the same time wishing to remain fairly near them.

Travelers along the river and people living near the bank on one side or the other reported that father never put foot on land, by day or night. He just moved about on the river, solitary, aimless, like a derelict. Mother and our relatives agreed that the food which he had doubtless hidden in the boat would soon give out and that then he would either leave the river and travel off somewhere (which would be at least a little more respectable) or he would repent and come home.

How far from the truth they were! Father had a secret source of provisions: me. Every day I stole food and brought it to him. The first night after he left, we all lit fires on the shore and prayed and called to him. I was deeply distressed and felt a need to do something more. The following day I went down to the river with a loaf of corn bread, a bunch of bananas, and some bricks of raw brown sugar. I waited impatiently a long, long hour. Then I saw the boat, far off, alone, gliding almost imperceptibly on the smoothness of the river. Father was sitting in the bottom of the boat. He saw me but he did not row toward me or make any gesture. I showed him the food and then I placed it in a hollow rock on the river bank; it was safe there from animals, rain, and dew. I did this day after day, on and on and on. Later I learned, to my surprise, that mother knew what I was doing and left food around where I could easily steal it. She had a lot of feelings she didn't show.

Mother sent for her brother to come and help on the farm and in business matters. She had the schoolteacher come and tutor us children at home because of the time we had lost. One day, at her request, the priest put on his vestments, went down to the shore, and tried to exorcise the devils that had got into my father. He shouted that father had a duty to cease his unholy obstinacy. Another day she arranged to have two soldiers come and try to frighten him. All to no avail. My father went by in the distance, sometimes so far away he could barely be seen. He never replied to anyone and no one ever got close to him. When some newspapermen came in a launch to take his picture, father headed his boat to the other side of the river and into the marshes, which he knew like the palm of his hand but in which other people quickly got lost. There in his private maze, which extended for miles, with heavy foliage overhead and rushes on all sides, he was safe.

We had to get accustomed to the idea of father's being out on the river. We had to but we couldn't, we never could. I think I was the only one who understood to some degree what our father wanted and what he did not want. The thing I could not understand at all was how he stood the hardship. Day and night, in sun and rain, in heat and in the terrible midyear cold spells, with his old hat on his head and very little other clothing, week after week, month after month, year after year, unheedful of the waste and emptiness in which his life was slipping by. He never set foot on earth or grass, on isle or mainland shore. No doubt he sometimes tied up the boat at a secret place, perhaps at the tip of some island, to get a little sleep. He never lit a fire or even struck a match and he had no flashlight. He took only a small part of the food that I left in the hollow rock—not enough, it seemed to me, for survival. What could his state of health have been? How about the continual drain on his energy, pulling and pushing the oars to control the boat? And how did he survive the annual floods, when the river rose and swept along with it all sorts of dangerous objects—branches of trees, dead bodies of animals—that might suddenly crash against his little boat?

He never talked to a living soul. And we never talked about him. We just thought. No, we could never put our father out of mind. If for a short time we seemed to, it was just a lull from which we would be sharply awakened by the realization of his frightening situation.

My sister got married, but mother didn't want a wedding party. It would have been a sad affair, for we thought of him every time we ate some especially tasty food. Just as we thought of him in our cozy beds on a cold, stormy night—out there, alone and unprotected, trying to bail out the boat with only his hands and a gourd. Now and then someone would say that I was getting to look more and more like my father. But I knew that by then his hair and beard must have been shaggy and his nails long. I pictured him thin and sickly, black with hair and sunburn, and almost naked despite the articles of clothing I occasionally left for him.

He didn't seem to care about us at all. But I felt affection and respect for him, and, whenever they praised me because I had done something good, I said:

"My father taught me to act that way."

It wasn't exactly accurate but it was a truthful sort of lie. As I said, father didn't seem to care about us. But then why did he stay around there? Why didn't he go up the river or down the river, beyond the possibility of seeing us or being seen by us? He alone knew the answer.

My sister had a baby boy. She insisted on showing father his grandson. One beautiful day we all went down to the river bank, my sister in her white wedding dress, and she lifted the baby high. Her husband held a parasol above them. We shouted to father and waited. He did not appear. My sister cried; we all cried in each other's arms.

My sister and her husband moved far away. My brother went to live in a city. Times changed, with their usual imperceptible rapidity. Mother finally moved too; she was old and went to live with her daughter. I remained behind, a leftover. I could never think of marrying. I just stayed there with the impedimenta of my life. Father, wandering alone and forlorn on the river, needed me. I knew he needed me, although he never even told me why he was doing it. When I put the question to people bluntly and insistently, all they told me was that they heard that father had explained it to the man who made the boat. But now this man was dead and nobody knew or remembered anything. There was just some foolish talk, when the rains were especially severe and persistent, that my father was wise like Noah and had the boat built in anticipation of a new flood; I dimly remember people saying this. In any case, I would not condemn my father for what he was doing. My hair was beginning to turn gray.

I have only sad things to say. What bad had I done, what was my great guilt? My father always away and his absence always with me. And the river, always the river, perpetually renewing itself. The river, always. I was beginning to suffer from old age, in which life is just a sort of lingering. I had attacks of illness and of anxiety. I had a nagging rheumatism. And he? Why, why was he doing it? He must have been suffering terribly. He was so old. One day, in his failing strength, he might let the boat capsize; or he might let the current carry it downstream, on and on, until it plunged over the waterfall to the boiling turmoil below. It pressed upon my heart. He was out there and I was forever robbed of my peace. I am guilty of I know not what, and my pain is an open wound inside me. Perhaps I would know—if things were different. I began to guess what was wrong.

Out with it! Had I gone crazy? No, in our house that word was never spoken, never through all the years. No one called anybody crazy, for nobody is crazy. Or maybe everybody. All I did was go there and wave a handkerchief. So he would be more likely to see me. I was in complete command of myself. I waited. Finally he appeared in the distance, there, then over there, a vague shape sitting in the back of the boat. I called to him several times. And I said what I was so eager to say, to state formally and under oath. I said it as loud as I could:

"Father, you have been out there long enough. You are old. . . . Come back, you don't have to do it anymore. . . . Come back and I'll go instead. Right now, if you want. Any time. I'll get into the boat. I'll take your place."

And when I had said this my heart beat more firmly.

He heard me. He stood up. He maneuvered with his oars and headed the boat toward me. He had accepted my offer. And suddenly I trembled, down deep. For he had raised his arm and waved—the first time in so many, so many years. And I couldn't . . . In terror, my hair on end, I ran, I fled madly. For he seemed to come from another world. And I'm begging forgiveness, begging, begging.

I experienced the dreadful sense of cold that comes from deadly fear, and I became ill. Nobody ever saw or heard about him again. Am I a man, after such a failure? I am what never should have been. I am what must be silent. I know it is too late. I must stay in the deserts and unmarked plains of my life, and I fear I shall shorten it. But when death comes I want them to take me and put me in a little boat in this perpetual water between the long shores; and I, down the river, lost in the river, inside the river . . . the river . . .

TRANSLATED BY WILLIAM L. GROSSMAN

Juan Carlos Onetti

Uruguay
(1909–1994)

———\\———

Although his first novel, *The Pit,* dates from 1939, and he had published a minor masterpiece, *A Brief Life,* in 1959, Juan Carlos Onetti was largely ignored until the 1960s. He was then discovered as a forerunner of the novelists who brought about the Boom of the Latin American novel (Cortázar, Fuentes, Vargas Llosa, García Márquez) and recognized as a great writer in his own right. His output was quite remarkable for someone who spent so much time in exile (twice in Buenos Aires for lengthy durations, later in Spain). In 1980 Onetti received the Miguel de Cervantes Prize, the most prestigious in the Spanish language. His best-known novel in English is *The Shipyard* (1961, translated 1978). Onetti was an early Latin American disciple of Faulkner (there were many others later): He uses several unreliable narrators who tell the same story differently and creates in the city of Santa María a self-contained fictional world, and there is a Faulknerian sense of doom in his novels and stories. But his work is darker, more concerned with perversion than that of the American master. Onetti's is a more aberrant, Dostoyevsky-like world—of madness, sadism, and masochism. His sense of dejection, his pessimism, and the degradation of his characters also recall Céline. All of these traits were already present in *A Brief Life,* which his best critic, Josefina Ludmer, considers the foundational fiction of Onetti's oeuvre. Onetti's chief virtue is how he probes into the perverse motives and the contradictory structures of fictions, both personal and literary. In ''The Image of Misfortune,'' the protagonist's self-indictment is an oblique way of showing his guilt for the death of his brother.

The Image of Misfortune

I

At dusk, despite the high wind, I was in shirtsleeves, leaning on the rail of the hotel porch, alone. The light made the shadow of my head reach as far as the edge of the sandy trail through the bushes that links the highway and the beach with the cluster of houses.

The girl appeared, pedaling along the road, only to be immediately lost from sight behind the A-frame cabin, vacant but still adorned with the sign

261

in black letters above the mailbox. It was impossible for me not to look at the sign at least once a day; though lashed by rain, siestas, and the sea wind, it showed a proud face and a lasting glow, and stated: "My Rest."

A moment later the girl appeared again along the sandy margin surrounded by thickets. She held her body erect on the seat, moving her legs at a slow, easy pace, her legs wrapped with calm arrogance in thick gray wool socks, tickled by the pine needles. Her knees were amazingly round and mature considering the age of the rest of her body.

She braked the bicycle right beside the shadow of my head, and her right foot, seeking balance, released the pedal and came to rest in the short dead grass, all brown now, on the shadow of my body. All at once she pulled the hair from her forehead and looked at me. She was wearing a dark sweater and a pink skirt. She looked at me calmly and attentively as if her brown hand, pulling the hair away from her eyes, were sufficient to hide her examination of me.

I calculated there were sixty feet between us and less than thirty years. Leaning on my forearms I held her gaze, changing the position of the pipe in my mouth, looking steadily toward her and her heavy bicycle, the colors of her thin body set against a backdrop of a landscape of trees and sheep sinking into the calm of the evening.

Suddenly sad and irritated, I looked at the smile the girl offered my exhaustion, her hair stiff and messy, her thin curved nose moving as she breathed, the childish angle at which her eyes had been stuck onto her face (which had nothing to do by now with her age, which had been formed once and for all and would remain that way until death), the excessive space left for the sclerotic membrane lining the eye. I looked at the glow of sweat and fatigue gathered together by the last or perhaps first light of sunset, covering and highlighting the coming darkness.

The girl laid her bicycle gently down on the bushes and looked at me again, her hands touching her hips, the thumbs sunk below the waist of her skirt. I don't know if she was wearing a belt; that summer all the girls were using wide belts. Then she looked around. Now she was facing sideways, her hands joined behind her back, without breasts as yet, still breathing with an odd shortness of breath, her face turned toward the spot in the afternoon where the sun would set.

Suddenly she sat down on the grass, took off her sandals, and shook them; one at a time she held her bare feet in her hands, rubbing the short toes and moving them in the air. Over her broad shoulders I watched her shake her dirty reddish feet. I saw her stretch out her legs, take out a comb and a mirror from the large monogrammed pocket on the lap of her skirt. She carelessly combed her hair, almost without looking at me.

She put her sandals back on and got up, then stood for a moment banging on the pedals with swift kicks. Repeating a sharp quick movement, she turned toward me, standing alone by the porch railing, still as ever, looking at her. The smell of honeysuckle was starting; the light from the hotel bar made pale splotches of light on the grass, the areas of sand, and the round driveway that circled the terrace.

It was as if we had seen each other before, as if we knew each other, as if we had fond memories. She looked at me with a defiant expression while her face slipped off into the meager light; she looked at me with the defiance of her whole scornful body, of the shiny metal of the bicycle, of the landscape with the A-frame cabin and the privet hedges and the young eucalyptus with milky trunks. For a moment that's all there was; everything that surrounded her became a part of her and her absurd pose. She climbed back on her bicycle and pedaled off beyond the hydrangeas, behind the empty benches painted blue, ever more quickly through the lines of cars in front of the hotel.

II

I emptied my pipe and watched the sun dying through the trees. I already knew what she was, perhaps too well. But I didn't want to name her. I thought of what was awaiting me in the hotel room around dinnertime. I tried measuring my past and my guilt with the rod I had just discovered: the profile of the thin girl looking toward the horizon, her brief, impossible age, the pink feet a hand had hit and squeezed.

By the door of my room, I found an envelope from the management with the biweekly bill. When I picked it up, I caught myself bending over to smell the honeysuckles' perfume barely floating in the room, feeling expectant and sad, without any new reason I could point to. I lit a match so as to reread the framed *Avis aux passagers* on the door, then lit my pipe again. For several minutes I stood there, washing my hands, playing with the soap; I looked at myself in the mirror above the washstand in almost total darkness, until I could pick out my thin, badly shaven, white face, perhaps the only white face among the guests in the hotel. It was my face; all the changes of the last few months had no real importance. I realized that the custom of playing with the soap had begun when Julian died, perhaps the very night of the wake.

I went back to the bedroom and opened the suitcase, after pushing it out from under the bed with my foot. It was a stupid ritual, but a ritual; however, perhaps it would be better for everyone if I stuck faithfully to this form of madness until using it up or getting used up myself. Without looking, I sorted things out, separated clothes and two little books, and found the folded newspaper at last. I knew the story by heart; it was the fairest, the most profoundly mistaken, and the most respectful of any of the ones published. I pulled the armchair up to the light and began not reading, just looking at, the big black headline across the top of the page, now starting to fade: FUGITIVE TREASURER KILLS SELF. Underneath was the picture, the gray spots forming the face of a man looking at the world with an expression of astonishment, his mouth almost smiling under a mustache that slanted down at the edges. I remembered the sterility of having thought about the girl, a few minutes earlier, as if she might be the beginning of some melody that would resound elsewhere. This place, my place, was a private world, narrow, irreplaceable. No friendship, presence, or dialogue could find a place there, apart from that ghost with the listless mustache. Sometimes he allowed me to choose between Julian and the Fugitive Treasurer.

Anyone would admit the possibility of having influence on, or of doing something for, one's younger brother. But Julian was—or had been until a few days more than a month before—a little more than five years older than I was. Nonetheless, I should write nonetheless. I may have been born, and continued to live, to spoil his condition as an only child; I may have forced him, by means of my fantasies, my aloofness, and my scant sense of responsibility, to turn into the man he became: first into the poor devil proud of his promotion, then into a thief. Also, of course, into the other, into the relatively young dead man we all looked at but whom only I could recognize as my brother.

What has he left me? A row of crime novels, some childhood memories, clothes I cannot use because they are too tight and too short. And the photo in the newspaper beneath the long headline. I looked down on his acceptance of life. I knew he was a bachelor for lack of spirit. How many times would I pass, almost always by chance, in front of the barbershop where he went for a shave every day. His humility irritated me and it was hard for me to believe in it. I was aware of the fact that a woman visited him punctually every Friday. He was very affable, incapable of bothering anyone, and from the time he was thirty, his clothes gave off the smell of an old man. A smell that cannot be defined, that comes from God knows where. When he doubted something, his mouth formed the same grimace as our mother's. Had circumstances been different he would never have been my friend; I would never have chosen him or accepted him as that. Words are pretty, or try to be, when they point toward an explanation. From the first, all these words are useless, at odds with one another. He was my brother.

Arturo whistled in the garden, jumped over the railing, and came straight into the room, dressed in a bathrobe, shaking sand from his hair as he crossed toward the bathroom. I saw him rinse in the shower and hid the newspaper between my leg and the back of the chair. But I heard him shout: "The ghost, same as always."

I did not answer and once again lit my pipe. Arturo came out of the bathroom whistling and closed the door on the night. Sprawled on the bed, he put on his underwear and then continued dressing.

"And my belly keeps growing," he said. "I barely had any lunch, swam out to the breakwater. Result: my belly keeps growing. I would have bet anything that of all the men I know, this wouldn't have happened to you. Yet it happens, and happens hard. About a month ago, right?"

"Yes. Twenty-eight days."

"You've even counted," Arturo continued. "You know me well. I say it without any disrespect. Twenty-eight days since that wretch shot himself, and you—you, no less—go on playing with feelings of remorse. Like some hysterical spinster. Because not even all spinsters would behave like this. It's unbelievable."

He sat on the edge of the bed drying his feet and putting on his socks.

"Yes," I said. "If he shot himself, he was apparently none too happy. Not so happy, at least, as you are at this moment."

"It's maddening," Arturo went on. "As if you had killed him. And don't ask me again. . . ." He stopped for a moment to look at himself in the mirror, "Don't ask me again whether in one of the seventeen dimensions you are guilty of the fact that your brother shot himself."

He lit a cigarette and lay down on the bed. I stood up, put a pillow over the rapidly yellowing newspaper, and began walking around in the heat of the room.

"As I told you, I'm leaving tonight," Arturo said. "What do you intend to do?"

"I don't know," I answered softly, with some feeling of indifference. "For the moment I'll stay here. The summer will last for a while yet."

I heard Arturo sigh and listened as his sigh turned into a whistle of impatience. He got up, throwing his cigarette in the toilet.

"It so happens that my moral duty is to kick you a few times and take you with me. You know that everything is different there. When you get very drunk, on toward dawn, completely distracted, then it will be all over."

I shrugged my shoulders, just my left shoulder, and recognized a gesture that Julian and I had inherited, not chosen.

"I'm telling you again," Arturo said, poking a handkerchief in his lapel pocket. "I'm telling you, insisting over and over, with a bit of anger and with the respect I mentioned earlier. Did you tell your unfortunate brother to shoot himself to escape from the trap? Did you tell him to buy Chilean pesos and change them into liras and then turn the liras into francs and the francs into Swedish crowns and the crowns into dollars and the dollars into pounds and the pounds into yellow silk slips? No, don't shake your head. Cain in the depths of the cave. I want a yes or a no. Although I don't really need an answer. Did you advise him (which is all that matters) to steal? Never. You're incapable of that. I told you so, many times. And you'll never know whether that's a compliment or a reproach. You didn't tell him to steal. And so?"

I sat down on the armchair again.

"We already talked about all that so many times. Are you leaving tonight?"

"Sure, on the bus at nine something. I have five days off and have no intention of spending them getting healthier and healthier only to waste it all right afterward on the office."

Arturo chose a tie and began knotting it.

"It's just that it doesn't make sense," he said once more in front of the mirror. "I admit that I too have shut myself in with a ghost one time or another. The experiment always turned out badly. But with your own brother, the way you're doing now . . . A ghost with a wiry mustache. Never. The ghost isn't your brother, that much we know. But now it's the ghost of nothingness, that's all. This time it came from misfortune. It was the treasurer of a cooperative who wore the mustache of a Russian general."

"Won't you be serious for this one last time?" I said in a low voice. I wasn't asking him for anything: I just wanted to keep my promise, and even today I don't know to whom, or even what promise.

"The last time," said Arturo.

"I see the reason well enough. I didn't tell him, didn't make the least suggestion, that he should use the Cooperative's money for the currency exchange business. But one night, just to encourage him or so his life would be a little less boring, I explained to him that there were things that could be done in this world to make money and spend it, something other than picking up a check at the end of the month . . ."

"I know," Arturo said, sitting down on the bed with a yawn. "I swam too hard; I'm not up for such things anymore. But it was the last day. I know the whole story. Now explain to me—and I would like to remind you that the summer is coming to an end—what good can you hope to do by staying shut in up here? Explain to me why it's your fault if the other guy did something stupid."

"Something is my fault," I mumbled with my eyes half-closed, my head resting on the armchair; my words were sluggish and choppy. "It's my fault that I was enthusiastic, that I lied maybe. It's my fault that I spoke for the first time to Julian of something we cannot define, something we call the world. It's my fault that I made him feel, though I can't say believe, that if he took risks that thing I called the world would be his."

"And so what," Arturo said, looking at his hair in the mirror at the far end of the room. "Brother. All of that is just complicated idiocy. Well, life is also just complicated idiocy. One of these days this phase of yours will pass; when that happens come visit me. Now get dressed and let's go have a drink before dinner. I have to leave early. But, before I forget, I want to leave you with one last argument. Maybe it will be good for something."

He touched my shoulder and looked me in the eye.

"Listen," he said. "In the middle of all this happy complicated idiocy, did your brother Julian use the money properly, did he use it in exact accordance with the silly things you had told him?"

"Him?" I asked with surprise, getting up. "Please. When he came to see me, it was already too late. At first, I'm almost certain, he made good buys. But he got frightened right away and did unbelievable things. I know few of the details. It was something like a combination of bonds and foreign currency, of casinos with racehorses."

"You see?" Arturo said, nodding his head. "A certificate of irresponsibility. I give you five minutes to get dressed and meditate on that. I'll wait for you in the bar."

III

We had a drink while Arturo tried to find a woman's picture in his wallet.

"It's not here," he said finally. "I lost it. The picture, not the woman. I wanted to show it to you because there was something unique about her that few people saw. And before you went crazy you understood such things."

And, I thought, there were memories of childhood that would surge up and become clear in the next days, weeks, or months. There was also the deceitful, perhaps deliberate, deformation of memory. In the best possible case, it was a choice I had not made. I would see the two of us, in a moment of recollection or in nightmares, dressed in ridiculous clothes, playing in a damp garden, or hitting one another in a bedroom. He was older but weaker. He was tolerant and kind, had accepted the burden of my faults, lied sweetly about the marks my blows had made on his face, about a broken cup, about coming home late. It was strange that it all had not yet begun during the month of fall vacation at the beach; perhaps, without meaning to, I was holding back the torrent with the newspaper articles and the evocation of the last two nights. During one of them Julian was alive, on the next he was dead. The second night was of no importance, and all the interpretations of it had been mistaken.

It was his wake; they had just hung his jaw back on his head; the bandage around his head grew old and yellow before dawn. I was very busy offering drinks and comparing the similarity of the regrets. As he was five years older than I, Julian had turned forty some time before. He had never asked life for anything of importance, or perhaps only for this: that he be left in peace. As in childhood, he came and went, asking permission. His residence on earth, unsurprising but long, stretched out by me, had not been any use to him, not even to become known. All the whispering and listless people, drinking coffee or whiskey, agreed to judge and feel sorry for the suicide as a sort of mistake. Because with a good lawyer, after a couple of years in jail . . . And besides, everyone found the ending out of proportion and grotesque in relation to the crime as they understood it. I thanked them and nodded; afterward I wandered around the hall and the kitchen, carrying drinks or empty glasses. Without any information to help me, I was trying to imagine what the cheap tart who visited Julian every Friday or every Monday (days when there were few clients) must be thinking. I pondered the invisible, never revealed truth of their relationship. I asked myself what her judgment would be, attributing an impossible degree of intelligence to her. She who each day endured the fact of being a prostitute, what could she think about Julian, who accepted the idea that he was a thief for a few weeks but who could not, as she could, endure the idea that the fools who inhabit and form the world might learn of his slip? But she did not come at any point during the night, or at least I did not recognize a face, an insolence, a perfume, a meekness that could be identified as hers.

Without stirring from the bar stool, Arturo had bought the bus ticket and seat reservation—9:45.

"There's time to spare. I can't find the picture. Today there's no use talking anymore. Bartender, another round."

I already said that the night of the wake was of no importance. The one before was much briefer and more difficult. Julian could have waited for me in the hallway of the apartment. But he was already thinking about the police and chose to wander around in the rain until light appeared in my window. He was soaked—he was born to use an umbrella and this time he had forgotten it—and he sneezed various times, begging pardon, joking, before sitting down next to the electric heater, before using my house. All of Montevideo knew the story of the Cooperative, and at least half of the newspaper readers desired, absentmindedly, that nothing more be discovered about the treasurer.

But Julian had not waited an hour and a half in the rain to see me, to say goodbye with words announcing the suicide. We had a few drinks. He accepted the alcohol without display, without resistance: "Now in any case . . ." he mumbled, laughing almost, shrugging one shoulder.

Nonetheless, he had come to say goodbye to me in his own way. Memory was unavoidable: thoughts of our parents, of the now demolished house and garden of our childhood.

He moistened his long mustache and said worriedly, "It's strange. I always thought you knew and I didn't. Since I was a child. And I don't think it's a problem of character or intelligence. It's something else. There are people who instinctively find their way in the world. You do and I don't. I always lacked the necessary faith." He stroked his unshaven jawbones. "But neither is it a case of my having had to adjust to deformities or vices. There was no handicap, or at least I never knew of one."

He stopped and emptied his glass. When he raised his head—the head I have been looking at on the front page of a newspaper every day for the last month—he showed me his healthy, tobacco-stained teeth.

"But," he continued as he stood up, "your strategy was very good. You should teach it to someone else. The failure is not yours."

"Sometimes it works out and other times it doesn't," I said. "You can't go out in this rain. You can stay on here forever, as long as you want."

He leaned on the back of the armchair and was making fun of me without looking at me.

"In this rain. Forever. As long as you want." He came up to me and grasped my arm. "Forgive me. There will be trouble. There is always trouble."

He had already gone. He was bidding me farewell with his presence, cowering as always, with his generous, well-trimmed mustache, with a reference to everything dead and dissolved which the blood tie could (can) revive for a couple of minutes at a time.

Arturo was speaking of swindles at the races. He looked at his watch and asked the bartender for a last drink. "But with a little more gin, please," he said.

Then, not listening to him, I caught myself linking my dead brother with the girl on the bicycle. I didn't want to remember his childhood or his passive goodness, nothing in fact except his impoverished smile, his body's meek posture during our final conversation (if I could give that name to what I allowed to happen between us when he came to my apartment, soaked to the skin, to say goodbye to me in his own way).

I knew nothing about the girl on the bicycle. But then, all of a sudden, while Arturo was speaking of Ever Perdomo or the poor promotion of tourism, I felt my throat penetrated by a whiff of the old, unfair, almost always mistaken feeling of pity. What was clear was that I loved her and wanted to protect her. I could not guess from what or against what. Angry, I sought to save her from herself and from all danger. I had seen her unsure of herself and defiant; I had seen her face turn into a haughty image of misfortune. Such an image might last but is usually crushed in a premature way, out of all proportion. My brother had paid for his excess of simplicity. In the case of the girl—whom I might never see again—the debts were different. But, by very different paths, both of them coincided in their anxious approach to death, to the definitive experience. Julian, by inertia; she, the girl on the bicycle, by trying to do everything in a great hurry.

"But," Arturo said, "even if they show you that all the races are fixed, you go on betting just the same. Hey, now it looks to me like it's going to rain."

"For sure," I answered, and we went into the dining room. I saw her right away.

She was near a window, breathing in the stormy air of the night, with a lock of dark, wind-ruffled hair hanging down over her eyes and forehead, and areas of light freckles—now, beneath the unbearable fluorescent light of the dining room—on her cheeks and nose, while her childish, watery eyes absentmindedly looked at the shadow of the sky or at the mouths of her table companions, with strong, thin bare arms reaching out from under what could be considered a yellow evening gown, a hand over each shoulder.

An old man was sitting next to her and was talking to a woman sitting across the table, a young woman whose fleshy white back faced us, a wild rose in her hair above one ear. And when she moved, the little white circle of the flower would cover the girl's absent profile, then would uncover it again. When the woman laughed, tossing her head toward the shiny skin on her back, the girl's face would be left alone against the night.

While talking with Arturo, I looked at the table, trying to guess the origin of her secret, the sensation that she was something extraordinary. I wanted to remain quiet forever beside the girl and take charge of her life. I saw her smoke as she drank her coffee, her eyes now fixed on the old man's slow mouth. Suddenly she looked at me as she had earlier on the path, with the same calm, defiant eyes, accustomed to contemplating or imagining disdain. With an inexplicable feeling of desperation, I felt the girl's eyes on me, pulling mine in the direction of the long noble young head, then escaping from the tangible secret only to plunge into the stormy night, to conquer the intensity of the sky and scatter it, impose it on the young face that observed me, still and expressionless. The face which let flow the sweetness and adolescent modesty of scarlet freckled cheeks in the direction of my serious and exhausted grown man's face, for no purpose, unconsciously.

Arturo smiled, smoking.

"Et tu, Brute?" he asked.

"What?"

"The girl on the bicycle, the girl in the window. If I didn't have to leave at this very moment . . ."

"I don't understand."

"That one, the one in the yellow dress. Hadn't you seen her before?"

"Once. This afternoon, from the porch. Before you came back from the beach."

"Love at first sight," Arturo agreed. "Intact youth, scarred experience.

It is a pretty story. But, I must confess, there is someone who tells it better. Wait."

The waiter came up to clear the plates and the fruit bowl. "Coffee?" he asked. He was small, with a dark monkey face.

"OK," Arturo smiled, "what passes for coffee. They also say 'miss' to the girl in yellow by the window. My friend is very curious; he wants to know something about the girl's nocturnal excursions."

I unbuttoned my jacket and sought out the girl's eyes. But her face had turned to one side, and the old man's black sleeve cut diagonally across the yellow dress. Right then the hairdo of the woman with the flower leaned forward, covering the freckled face. All that was left of the girl was a bit of her dark brown hair, metallic-looking at the top of her head where the light was reflected. I remembered the magic of her lips and her glance; *magic* is a word I cannot explain, which I use now because I have no other choice, not the slightest possibility of substituting another one.

"Nothing bad," Arturo continued with the matter. "The gentleman, my friend, is interested in cycling. Tell me, what happens at night when daddy and mommy, if that's who they are, are asleep?"

The waiter rocked back and forth smiling, the empty fruit bowl raised to shoulder height.

"That's right," he said finally. "Everybody knows. At midnight the young lady rides off on her bicycle; sometimes she goes to the woods, other times to the dunes." He had managed to look serious, repeating without malice: "What else can I tell you? I don't know anything else, no matter what anyone says. I never watched. That she returns with her hair mussed up and without makeup. That one night I was on duty and I ran into her and she put ten pesos in my hand. The English fellows who are staying at the Atlantic talk a lot. But I won't say anything because I didn't see it."

Arturo laughed, patting the waiter's leg.

"There you have it," he said, as if he had scored a victory.

"Excuse me," I asked the waiter. "How old do you think she is?"

"The young lady?"

"Sometimes, this afternoon, she seems like a child to me; now she seems older."

"This much I know for certain, sir," the waiter said. "According to the register she is fifteen. Her birthday was a few days ago. So, two cups of coffee?" He leaned over before leaving.

I tried to smile at Arturo's merry look; at the corner of the tablecloth, my hand trembled as it held the pipe.

"In any case," Arturo said, "whether it works out or not, it is a more interesting program than living shut up with a ghost with a mustache."

When she got up from the table, the girl turned to look at me again, from a higher angle now, one hand still wrapped in the napkin—for a moment, while the air from the window tossed the stiff hair on her forehead—and I stopped believing what the waiter had said and what Arturo accepted as the truth.

In the hallway, carrying his suitcase, his overcoat over his arm, Arturo patted me on the shoulder.

"One more week and we'll see one another again. I'll go to the Jauja and meet you at a table savoring the flower of knowledge. Well, happy cycling."

He went out into the garden and then toward the group of cars parked across from the terrace. When Arturo had crossed the lighted area, I lit my pipe, leaned on the railing, and smelled the air. The storm seemed far-off. I went back to the bedroom and lay there, sprawled on the bed, listening to the music that wafted in endlessly from the hotel dining room, where perhaps they had already started dancing. I held the warmth of my pipe in my hand and went slipping into a heavy dream of a grimy, airless world where I had been condemned to go forward, with enormous effort and no desire to do so, my mouth open, toward an entrance where the intense light of the morning was shining indifferently, always out of reach.

I woke up in a sweat and went to sit down again in the armchair. Neither Julian nor the memories of childhood had appeared in the nightmare. I left the dream forgotten on the bed, inhaled the air that was blowing in the window from the storm, pulled the paper out from under my body and looked at the headline, smelled the heavy, hot smell of a woman. Almost without moving, I saw Julian's faded picture. I dropped the paper, turned out the bedroom light, and jumped over the railing onto the soft earth of the garden. The wind was making thick zigzags and wrapped around my waist. I decided to cross the lawn as far as the patch of sand where the girl had been sitting that afternoon. Her gray socks riddled by the pine needles, then their bare feet in her hands, the skinny buttocks flattened on the ground. The woods were off to my left, the dunes to the right; everything was black and the wind struck my face. I heard steps and immediately saw the luminous smile of the waiter, the monkey face next to my shoulder.

"Bad luck," the waiter said. "She's gone."

I felt like striking him but quickly calmed my hands, scratching at the pockets of my raincoat. I stood panting, facing the noise of the sea, still, my eyes half-closed. "What you can do is wait for her when she comes back. If you give her a good scare . . ."

I slowly unbuttoned the raincoat without turning around; I took a bill out of my pants pocket and gave it to the waiter. I waited until the sound of his footsteps disappeared in the direction of the hotel. Then I bent my head down—my feet held firm on the spongy ground and the grass where she had sat—sunken in that memory (the girl's body and movements in the seemingly so distant afternoon), protected from myself and my past by an indestructible aura of belief and hope without object, breathing the hot air where everything was forgotten.

IV

I saw her all of a sudden, under the excessive autumn moon. She was walking by herself along the shore, dodging the rocks and the bright puddles that were growing ever larger, pushing her bicycle, no longer wearing the comical yellow dress, with tight pants and a sailor's jacket on instead. I had never seen her wear those clothes, and her body and footsteps had not had time to become familiar to me. But I recognized her immediately and crossed the beach almost in a straight line toward her.

"Night," I said.

A while later she turned to look me in the eye; she stopped and turned her bicycle toward the water. She looked at me attentively for a time, and there was already something solitary and helpless about her when I greeted her again. This time she answered me. On the deserted beach her voice shrieked like a bird. It was an unpleasant and alien voice, utterly separate from her, from the beautiful face, so sad and thin; it was as if she had just learned a language, some dialogue in a foreign language. I reached out to hold the bicycle. Now I was looking at the moon and she was protected by the shadow.

"Where were you going," I said, then added: "Baby."

"Nowhere in particular," her strange voice uttered laboriously.

I thought of the waiter, of the English boys at the Atlantic; I thought of everything I had lost forever, through no fault of my own, without anyone consulting me.

"They say . . ." I said. The weather had changed: it was no longer cold or windy. Helping the girl hold up the bicycle in the sand beside the pounding sea, I had a sensation of solitude that no one had ever allowed me to feel before: solitude, peace, and trust.

"If you don't have anything better to do, they say that very nearby there is a boat that's been turned into a bar and restaurant."

The hard voice repeated with mysterious joy, "They say that very nearby there is a boat that's been turned into a bar and restaurant."

I heard her struggle with her shortness of breath; after a rest she added, "No, I don't have anything to do. Is that an invitation? And like this, with these clothes on?"

"Yes. Like that."

When she turned away I saw her smile; she was not making fun of me; she seemed happy and unaccustomed to happiness.

"You were at the next table with your friend. Your friend left this evening. But one of my tires burst as soon as I left the hotel."

She irritated me with her recollection of Arturo; I took the handlebar from her, and we began walking along the shore toward the boat.

Two or three times I spoke some idle phrase, but she didn't answer. The heat and air of a storm were increasing again. I felt the girl growing sad at my side; I spied her firm steps, the resolute erectness of her body, the boyish buttocks hugged by the ordinary trousers.

The boat was there, pointed toward land, all its lights off.

"There is no boat, no party," I said. "I beg your pardon for having made you walk all this way for nothing."

She had stopped to look at the tilted freighter under the moon. She stayed like that for a while, her hands behind her back as if she were alone, as if she had forgotten about me and the bicycle. The moon was going down toward the watery horizon or was coming up from there. All of a sudden the girl turned and came toward me; I did not let the bicycle fall. She took my face in her rough hands and moved it until it was facing the moon.

"What?" she said hoarsely. "You spoke. Once more."

I could hardly see her but I remembered her. I remembered many other things for which she could serve effortlessly as a symbol. I had begun to love her, and sadness was beginning to leave her and fall on me.

"Nothing," I said. "There's no boat, no party."

"No party," she repeated. I glimpsed a smile in the darkness, white and brief as the foam of the little waves that lapped a few yards down the beach. She suddenly kissed me; she knew how to kiss and I felt her warm face damp with tears. But I did not release the bicycle.

"There's no party," she said again, now with lowered head, smelling my chest. The voice was more confused, almost guttural. "I had to see your face." Once again she raised it toward the moon. "I had to know that I was not mistaken. Does that make sense?"

"Yes," I lied; then she took the bicycle from my hands, climbed on, and made a large circle on the wet sand.

When she came around next to me, she rested a hand on the back of my neck, and we returned toward the hotel. We avoided the rocks and made a detour toward the woods. It was not her doing, or mine. She stopped next to the first pine trees and let the bicycle drop.

"Your face. Once more. I don't want you to get angry with me," she begged.

I obediently looked toward the moon, toward the first clouds that were appearing in the sky.

"Something," she said in her strange voice. "I want you to say something. Anything."

She put her hand on my chest and stood on tiptoe to bring her girlish eyes nearer my mouth.

"I love you. And it's no good. It's just another kind of misfortune," I said after a while, speaking with almost the same slowness as she did.

Then the girl mumbled "poor thing" as if she were my mother, with her strange voice, now tender and protective, and we began to go crazy with kisses. We helped one another undress her to the extent necessary, and I suddenly had two things I did not deserve: her face shaped by weeping and happiness beneath the moon and the disconcerting certainty that she had never been penetrated before.

We sat down near the hotel on the dampness of the rocks. The moon was covered up. She began throwing pebbles; sometimes they fell in the water with a loud sound, other times they barely went beyond her feet. She did not seem to notice.

My story was grave and definitive. I told it with a serious masculine voice, resolving furiously to tell the truth, unconcerned whether she believed it or not.

All the facts had just lost their meaning; from now on they could only have the meaning she desired to give them. I spoke, of course, of my dead brother. However, since that night, the girl had turned into the central theme of my story, even going back in time to become a principal obsession in the previous days. From time to time I heard her move and tell me yes with her strange malformed voice. It was also necessary to refer to the years that separated us, to feel excessively sad about it, to feign a disconsolate belief in the power of the word *impossible,* to display a certain degree of discouragement in the face of the inevitable struggles. I did not want to ask her any questions; her affirmatives, not always uttered during the right pauses, did not demand confessions. There was no doubt that the girl had freed me from Julian and from many other failures and complications that Julian's death represented or had brought to the surface; there was no doubt that I, since a half hour earlier, needed her and would continue to need her.

I accompanied her almost to the hotel door, and we parted without telling each other our names. As she drew away I thought I noticed that the two bicycle tires were full of air. Perhaps she had lied to me about that, but nothing mattered any more. I didn't even see her go into the hotel; just the same, I went into the shadow parallel to the hallway outside my room, I continued laboriously toward the dunes, wanting to think of nothing, at last, and to wait for the storm.

I walked along the dunes and then, already some distance away, returned toward the eucalyptus grove. I walked slowly through the trees, between the twisting wind and its cry, beneath thunderclaps threatening to rise up from the invisible horizon, closing my eyes against the stinging sand that was blowing in my face. Everything was dark and—as I had to repeat several times afterward—I saw no bicycle lamp, were anyone to use one on the beach, nor did I see the burning cigarette tip of anyone walking or resting on the sand, seated on the dry leaves, leaning against a trunk, with legs drawn up, tired, damp, happy. That was the way I was, and although I did not know how to pray, I wandered around giving thanks, refusing to accept the way things were, incredulous.

I finally reached the end of the trees, a hundred yards from the sea, just opposite the dunes. I felt cuts on my hands and stopped to suck on them. I walked toward the noise of the surf until I felt the damp sand of the shore underfoot. I did not see, I repeat once more, I saw no light, no movement in the shadow; I heard no voice breaking or deforming the wind.

I left the shore and began climbing up and sliding down the dunes, slipping on the cold sand that trickled into my shoes, pushing aside the bushes with my legs, almost running, angry and with a sort of joy that had pursued me for years and was now within reach, excited as if I would never be able to stop, laughing in the midst of the windy night, running up and down the little peaks, falling to my knees and relaxing my body until I could breathe without pain, my face turned toward the storm that was coming off the water. Afterward it was as if all of my discouragement and renunciation had given me chase; for hours I looked, unenthusiastically, for the path that would take me back to the hotel. Then I encountered the waiter and I repeated the act of not speaking to him, of putting ten pesos in his hand. The man smiled and I was so tired that I thought he had understood, that all of the world understood and for all time.

Half-dressed, I fell back to sleep on my bed as if on the sand, listening to the storm that had finally decided to break, knocked by the thunderclaps, sinking thirstily into the angry noise of the rain.

V

I had just finished shaving when I heard fingers knocking on the glass of the door that opened onto the porch. It was very early; I knew that the nails of those fingers were long and painted fiery colors. Still carrying my towel, I opened the door. It was unavoidable: there she was.

Her hair was dyed blond and perhaps it had been blond when she was twenty. She wore a tailor-made herringbone suit that the years and the frequent washings made cling to her body. She carried a green umbrella with an ivory handle that had perhaps never been opened. Of the three things, I had guessed at two of them—correctly, to be sure—in the course of my brother's life and of his wake.

"Betty," she said as she turned around, with the best smile she could put on.

I pretended that I had never seen her, that I did not know who she was. It was just a sort of compliment, a twisted form of tact that no longer interested me.

I thought, this was, and will never again be, the woman whose blurry image I saw behind the dirty windows of a neighborhood cafe, touching Julian's fingers during the long prologues to the Fridays or Mondays.

"Excuse me," she said, "for coming so far to bother you and at this time of day. Especially at these moments when you, the best of Julian's siblings . . . Even now, I swear to you, I cannot accept that he is dead."

The light of the morning made her look older; she must have looked different in Julian's apartment, even in the cafe. To the end, I had been Julian's only sibling, not the best or the worst. She was old and it seemed easy to soothe her. I too, despite everything I had seen and heard, despite the memory of the night before on the beach, had not fully accepted Julian's death. It was only when I raised my head and held out my arm to ask her into my room that I discovered that she was wearing a hat and that she decorated it with fresh violets surrounded by ivy leaves.

"Call me Betty," she said, choosing to sit on the armchair where I hid the newspaper, the picture, the headline, the sordid (yet not utterly sordid) article. "But it was a matter of life or death."

No trace remained of the storm, and the night might well not have happened. I looked at the sun in the window, the yellowish splotch that was heading for the rug. Nonetheless it was certain that I felt different, that I breathed the air with eagerness, that I felt like walking and smiling, that indifference—and also cruelty—seemed to me possible forms of virtue. But all of that was confused and I could only understand it a bit later.

I drew my chair up near the armchair and offered my excuses to the woman, to that outmoded form of slovenliness and unhappiness. I took out the newspaper, struck several matches, and let the burning paper dance out over the porch rail.

"Poor Julian," she said behind me.

I went back to the center of the room, lit my pipe, and sat down on the bed. I suddenly discovered that I was happy and tried to calculate how many years separated me from the last time I had felt happiness. The smoke of the pipe irritated my eyes. I lowered it to my knees and sat there happily, looking at the trash there on the armchair, the mistreated filth that lay half-conscious in the fresh morning.

"Poor Julian," I repeated. "I said it many times during the wake and afterward. Now I'm fed up, enough is enough. I was waiting for you during the wake and you didn't come. But, please understand, thanks to the anticipation I knew what you were like; I could have met you on the street and recognized you."

She observed me, disconcerted, and smiled again. "Yes, I think I understand."

She was not very old, though far from my age or Julian's. But our lives had been very different, and what was lying there on the armchair was nothing but fat, a wrinkled baby face, suffering, veiled rancor, the grease of life stuck forever to her cheeks, to the corners of her mouth, to the wrinkled dark circles under her eyes. I felt like hitting her and throwing her out. But I sat there quietly, began smoking again and speaking to her with a sweet voice.

"Betty. You gave me permission to call you Betty. You said it was a matter of life or death. Julian is dead, out of the picture. What is it then, who else?"

She sprawled back on the armchair covered in faded cretonne, on a cover with hideous huge flowers, and sat there looking at me as if at a possible client: with the inevitable quota of hatred and calculation.

"Who dies now?" I insisted. "You or me?"

She relaxed her body and was preparing a touching expression. I looked at her, admitted that she could be convincing, and not just to Julian. Behind her the autumn morning stretched without a cloud, the little offering of glory to mankind. The woman, Betty, twisted her mouth and composed a bitter smile.

"Who?" she said, speaking in the direction of the announcement on the door. "You and me."

"I don't think so; the business is just beginning."

"There are IOUs with his signature and no money to back them up, and they're coming into court now. And there is the mortgage on my house, the only thing I possess. Julian assured me that it was no more than an offer, but the house, my little house, is mortgaged. And it has to be paid off right away. If we want to save something from the disaster. Or if we want to save ourselves."

By the violets on her hat and the sweat on her face, I had foreseen that it was inevitable that sooner or later on this sunny morning I would listen to some such phrase.

"Yes," I said, "you may be right, maybe we have to join together and do something."

For many years I had not derived so much pleasure from a lie, from sham and iniquity. But I had turned young again and didn't owe any explanations even to myself.

"I don't know," I said cautiously, "how much you know about my guilt, about my part in Julian's death. In any case, I can assure you that I never advised him to mortgage your house, your little house. But I am going to tell you everything. I was with Julian about three months ago: one brother eating in a restaurant with his older brother. And it was a matter of brothers who did not see one another more than once a year. I think it was somebody's birthday—his, our dead mother's. I don't remember and it isn't important. The date, whatever it was, seemed to dishearten him. I spoke to him about speculation, about some exchange of foreign currency, but I never told him to steal money from the Cooperative."

She had let the time go by with the help of a sigh and stretched her high heels toward the rectangular patch of sun on the carpet. She waited for me to look at her and then smiled once again; now she looked as if it was somebody's birthday—Julian's or my mother's. She was tenderness and patience, wanted to help me get through without stumbling.

"Kid," she mumbled, her head leaning on one shoulder, the smile brandished against the limit of tolerance. "Three months ago?" she snorted while raising her shoulders. "Kid, Julian was stealing from the Cooperative for the last five years. Or four. I remember. You spoke to him, dear, about some deal with dollars, right? I don't know whose birthday it was that night. And I'm not being disrespectful. But Julian told me the whole story and I couldn't stop laughing hysterically. He didn't even think about the dollar deal, whether it was a good idea or not. He stole and bet on the horses. For the last five years, since before I met him."

"Five years," I repeated, chewing on my pipe. I got up and went over to the window. There was still water on the weeds and the sand. The fresh air had nothing to do with us or with anybody.

In some hotel room upstairs, the girl must have been sleeping peacefully, sprawled out, beginning to stir amid the insistent desperation of dreams and hot sheets. I imagined her and kept on loving her, loving her breathing, her smell, the references I imagined to the memory of the previous night, to me, that might fit into her morning slumber. I returned heavily to the window and looked without revulsion or pity at what destiny had located in the armchair of my hotel room. She was arranging the lapels of the tailored jacket, which was perhaps not herringbone after all; she smiled at the empty air, waited for me to return, for my voice. I felt old, with little strength left. Perhaps the obscure dog of happiness was licking my knees, my hands; perhaps it was something else altogether: that I was old and tired. But, in any case, I felt the need to let time pass, to light the pipe again, to play with the flame of the match, with its sputtering.

"As far as I'm concerned," I said, "everything's fine. It's true that Julian did not use a revolver to make you sign a mortgage application. And I never signed an IOU. If he forged the signature and was able to live that way for five years—I think you said five—then you had quite something, you both had something. I look at you, think about you, and it doesn't matter to me at all that they take away your house or bury you in jail. I never signed an IOU for Julian. Unfortunately for you, Betty—and the name does not seem particularly apt to me, I don't think it fits you—no danger or threats will work for you. We cannot be partners in anything, and that is always a sad thing. I think it's especially sad for women. I would be very grateful to you if you left right away, if you made no fuss, Betty."

I went outside and continued insulting her in a low voice, searching for defects in the wondrous autumn morning. Very far away, I heard the apathetic cursing she directed at my back. I heard, almost immediately, a door slamming. A blue Ford appeared near the cluster of houses.

I was small and all of that seemed undeserved to me, organized by the poor uncertain imagination of a child. Since adolescence I had always displayed my defects; I was always right, inclined to converse and argue without reserve or silence. Julian, on the other hand—and I began to feel sympathy and some very different form of pity for him—had deceived us all for many years. This Julian I had only become acquainted with after his death was laughing softly at me ever since he began to confess the truth, exhibiting his mustache and his smile in the coffin. Maybe he was still laughing at all of us a month after his death. But it was useless for me to invent rancor or disillusionment.

Above all, I was irritated by the memory of our last conversation, by the gratuitous nature of his lies, and could not understand why he had come to visit me, considering all the risks, to lie for one last time. For, though Betty provoked only my pity or contempt, I believed her story and felt sure of the unending filth of life.

The blue Ford sputtered its way up the hill, behind the cabin with the red roof; it left the road and crossed parallel to the porch until reaching the hotel door. I saw a policeman get out in a faded summer uniform and an extraordinarily tall, thin man in a suit with thick stripes on it and also a young blond man dressed in gray, no hat, smiling at every phrase, holding a cigarette to his mouth between two long fingers.

The hotel manager went slowly down the staircase and approached them, while the waiter from the night before came out from behind a column on the stairs in shirtsleeves, his dark brown hair shining. They all spoke with few gestures, almost without moving the position of their feet. The manager took a handkerchief from the inner pocket of his jacket, wiped his lips with it, and put it back, only to pull it out again a few seconds later with a rapid movement, squeeze it, and rub his mouth with it. I went inside to confirm that the woman had gone; when I came out on the porch again, paying attention to my own movements, to the lethargy with which I wanted to live, to assume each pose as if trying to caress everything that my hands had made, I felt happy in the morning air, felt that other days might be waiting for me somewhere.

I saw that the waiter was looking at the ground and that the four other men had raised their heads and that their faces revealed an absentminded observation of me. The young blond man tossed away his cigarette; then I began to part my lips into a smile and, nodding my head, greeted the manager, and just after, before he could answer, before he could bow, staring up at the porch, wiping his mouth with the handkerchief, I raised a hand and repeated my greeting. Then I went back to my room to finish getting dressed.

I passed quickly through the dining room, watching the guests have breakfast, and then decided to have a gin, just one, at the bar; I bought cigarettes and went down the stairs to the group that was waiting at the bottom. The manager greeted me again, and I noticed that his jaw was trembling a little. I uttered a few words and heard them talking; the young blond man came up to me and touched my arm. They were all in silence, and the blond and I looked at each other and smiled. I offered him a cigarette, and he lit it without taking his eyes off my face; then he stepped three steps back and looked at me again. Perhaps he had never seen the face of a happy man; such was my case also. He turned his back on me, walked over to the first tree in the garden, and leaned there beside some man. All of that had some meaning, and without understanding, I found I agreed and nodded my head in assent. Then the very tall man said: "Shall we go to the beach in the car?"

I walked forward and got in the front seat. The tall man and the blond sat down in the back seat. The policeman slowly got into the driver's seat and started the car. Right away we were riding quickly through the calm morning; I could smell the cigarette the young man was smoking, could feel the silence and stillness of the other man, the will at work in that silence and stillness. When we got to the beach, the car stopped by a pile of gray rocks that separated the road from the sand. We got out, crossed the rock wall, and went down toward the sea. I walked beside the blond youth.

We stopped by the shore. The four of us were silent, our ties whipped by the wind. We lit cigarettes once more.

"The weather seems uncertain," I said.

"Shall we go?" the young blond answered.

The tall man in the striped suit stretched out one arm until he touched the young man's chest and said in a thick voice: "Notice. From here to the dunes. Two blocks. No more, no less."

The other nodded in silence, shrugging his shoulders as if it were of no importance. He smiled again and looked at me.

"Let's go," I said, starting to walk toward the car. When I was about to get in, the tall man stopped me.

"No," he said. "It's over there, on the other side."

In front of us there was a shed made of bricks stained with the dampness. It had a corrugated tin roof and dark letters painted above the door. We waited while the policeman came back with a key. I turned to see the midday sun close at hand over the beach; the policeman took off the open lock, and we all went into the shadow and the unexpected cold. The rafters were a shiny black, softly painted with tar, and bits of burlap were hanging from the ceiling. When we walked in the gray twilight, I felt the shed grow bigger as every step moved us farther from the long table made of sawhorses in the middle of the room. I saw the form stretched out, wondering who teaches the dead the posture of death. There was a little puddle of water on the ground, dripping from one corner of the table. A barefoot man, his shirt open to his ruddy chest, came up, clearing his throat, and put one hand on a corner of the plank table, his short index finger covered instantly by the shiny water that had not yet dripped off. The tall man stretched out one arm and, pulling on the canvas, uncovered the face that was lying on the planks. I looked at the air, at the man's striped arm, still stretched out against the light of the door, holding the ringed edge of the canvas. I looked once more at the bareheaded blond and made a sad grimace.

"Look at this," the tall man said.

Then, little by little, I saw that the girl's face was bent backward, that it looked as if the head—purple, with spots of a reddish purple atop a more delicate bluish purple—would roll away at any moment were anyone to speak too loudly, were anyone to step hard on the floor, were time simply to pass.

From the back, invisible to me, someone was beginning to recite in a hoarse, common voice, as if speaking to me. Who else?

"The hands and feet, the skin whitened a bit and folded at the edges of the fingers and toes, also exhibit a small amount of sand and mud under the nails. There is no wound or scarring on the hands. On the arms, particularly on the forearms near the wrists, there are various superimposed ecchymoses on the transversal, the results of violent pressure on the upper limbs."

I didn't know who it was, I didn't have any desire to ask questions. I had the lone defense, I repeated to myself, of silence. Silence for us. I went closer to the table and touched the stubborn bones of the forehead. Perhaps the five men were waiting for something more, and I was prepared for anything.

The idiot, back at the end of the shed, was now listing in his vulgar voice: "The face is stained with a bluish bloodlike liquid that has flowed out of her mouth and nose. After having washed her carefully, we recognize extensive flaying and ecchymosis and the marks of teeth sunken into the flesh. Two similar marks exist below the right eye, the lower lid of which is deeply bruised. Besides marks of violence obviously made while the subject was still alive, on the face numerous contusions are visible on the skin, scoring, without redness or ecchymosis, a simple drying of the skin produced by the rubbing of the body on the sand. There is a clot of blood on either side of the larynx. The tegumenta have begun to decay, but vestiges of contusions or ecchymosis are visible in them. The interior of the trachea and of the bronchial tube contains a small amount of a cloudy (though not foamy) dark liquid mixed with sand."

It was a good answer; everything was lost. I leaned over to kiss her forehead and then, out of pity and love, the reddish liquid that was bubbling out of her lips.

But the head with its stiff hair, the squat nose, the dark mouth stretched in the shape of a sickle, the edges pointing down, limp, dripping, remained there without moving, the size of the head unchanging in the dark air smelling of bilge, as if harder each time my eyes passed over cheekbones and forehead and chin that refused to hang open. They, the tall man and the blond, spoke to me one after another, as if they were playing a game, banging away with the same question. Then the tall man let go of the canvas, sprang up, and shook me by the lapels. But he didn't believe in what he was doing—it was enough to look at his round eyes—and when I smiled at him out of fatigue, he quickly showed me his teeth and with hatred opened his hand.

"I understand, I guess, that you have a daughter. Don't worry: I will sign whatever you want without even reading it. The funny part is that you have made a mistake. But that doesn't matter. Nothing, not even this, really matters."

I paused before the violent light of the sun and asked the tall man in a proper voice, "I may be overly curious and I beg pardon—do you believe in God?"

"I will answer, of course," the giant said, "but first, if you don't mind, and not for the record of the proceedings, just, as in your case, out of simple curiosity . . . Did you know that the girl was deaf?"

We had stopped halfway between the renewed summery heat and the cool shade of the shed.

"Deaf?" I asked. "I was indeed with her last night. She never seemed deaf to me. But that's neither here nor there. I asked you a question; you promised to answer it."

The lips were too thin to call the grimace the giant made a smile. He looked at me again without disdain, with sad surprise, and crossed himself.

TRANSLATED BY DANIEL BALDERSTON

Juan Rulfo

Mexico
(1918–1986)

Juan Rulfo is one of the most important prose writers in modern Latin America, although his fame abroad is not as great as that of lesser figures. A reclusive, shy, and self-destructive man obsessed with artistic perfection and integrity, Rulfo published only two books: *Pedro Páramo* (1955), which some consider the best modern Latin American novel, and a collection of stories, *The Burning Plain* (1953), a classic nearly on the same level as Borges's *Ficciones,* though for very different reasons. Set in rural Mexico, Rulfo's fiction chronicles events in the aftermath of the Mexican Revolution (1910–17). His is a tragic world of resentments, violence, and hopelessness. *Pedro Páramo* is an intricately wrought novel that some have likened to Dante's *Inferno* in its portrayal of sin. Some of its narrators are dead and speak from their graves. Its multilayered temporal sequence reconstructs the times and deeds of a local strongman, Pedro Páramo, and the fate of Comala, the town he rules. The novel begins with one of his long-lost sons, Juan Preciado, asking about his father's whereabouts. The selection included here, "Tell Them Not to Kill Me!" is also a story about sons and fathers. Here a son, a colonel in the Mexican army, returns to take revenge on his father's murderer, who committed the crime many years before. The story begins with the captured assassin pleading with his own son to ask the colonel, invested with military authority after the revolution, for mercy. The scorched, merciless plain on which these stories take place plays a decisive role in this as in other acts of violence. Rulfo's fiction owes much to Faulkner, and the world Rulfo creates, full of sound and fury and signifying little, is very much like the postbellum South.

Tell Them Not to Kill Me!

"Tell them not to kill me, Justino! Go on and tell them that. For God's sake! Tell them. Tell them please for God's sake."

"I can't. There's a sergeant there who doesn't want to hear anything about you."

"Make him listen to you. Use your wits and tell him that scaring me has been enough. Tell him please for God's sake."

284

"But it's not just to scare you. It seems they really mean to kill you. And I don't want to go back there."

"Go on once more. Just once, to see what you can do."

"No. I don't feel like going. Because if I do they'll know I'm your son. If I keep bothering them they'll end up knowing who I am and will decide to shoot me too. Better leave things the way they are now."

"Go on, Justino. Tell them to take a little pity on me. Just tell them that."

Justino clenched his teeth and shook his head saying no.

And he kept on shaking his head for some time.

"Tell the sergeant to let you see the colonel. And tell him how old I am—How little I'm worth. What will he get out of killing me? Nothing. After all he must have a soul. Tell him to do it for the blessed salvation of his soul."

Justino got up from the pile of stones which he was sitting on and walked to the gate of the corral. Then he turned around to say, "All right, I'll go. But if they decide to shoot me too, who'll take care of my wife and kids?"

"Providence will take care of them, Justino. You go there now and see what you can do for me. That's what matters."

They'd brought him in at dawn. The morning was well along now and he was still there, tied to a post, waiting. He couldn't keep still. He'd tried to sleep for a while to calm down, but he couldn't. He wasn't hungry either. All he wanted was to live. Now that he knew they were really going to kill him, all he could feel was his great desire to stay alive, like a recently resuscitated man.

Who would've thought that old business that happened so long ago and that was buried the way he thought it was would turn up? That business when he had to kill Don Lupe. Not for nothing either, as the Alimas tried to make out, but because he had his reasons. He remembered: Don Lupe Terreros, the owner of the Puerta de Piedra—and besides that, his compadre—was the one he, Juvencio Nava, had to kill, because he'd refused to let him pasture his animals, when he was the owner of the Puerta de Piedra and his compadre too.

At first he didn't do anything because he felt compromised. But later, when the drought came, when he saw how his animals were dying off one by one, plagued by hunger, and how his compadre Lupe continued to refuse to let him use his pastures, then was when he began breaking through the fence and driving his herd of skinny animals to the pasture where they could get their fill of grass. And Don Lupe didn't like it and ordered the fence mended, so that he, Juvencio Nava, had to cut open the hole again.

286 \ JUAN RULFO

So, during the day the hole was stopped up and at night it was opened again, while the stock stayed there right next to the fence, always waiting—his stock that before had lived just smelling the grass without being able to taste it.

And he and Don Lupe argued again and again without coming to any agreement.

Until one day Don Lupe said to him, "Look here, Juvencio, if you let another animal in my pasture, I'll kill it."

And he answered him, "Look here, Don Lupe, it's not my fault that the animals look out for themselves. They're innocent. You'll have to pay for it, if you kill them."

And he killed one of my yearlings.

This happened thirty-five years ago in March, because in April I was already up in the mountains, running away from the summons. The ten cows I gave the judge didn't do me any good, or the lien on my house either, to pay for getting me out of jail. Still later they used up what was left to pay so they wouldn't keep after me, but they kept after me just the same. That's why I came to live with my son on this other piece of land of mine which is called Palo de Venado. And my son grew up and got married to my daughter-in-law Ignacia and has had eight children now. So it happened a long time ago and ought to be forgotten by now. But I guess it's not.

I figured then that with about a hundred pesos everything could be fixed up. The dead Don Lupe left just his wife and two little kids still crawling. And his widow died soon afterward too—they say from grief. They took the kids far off to some relatives. So there was nothing to fear from them.

But the rest of the people took the position that I was still summoned to be tried just to scare me so they could keep on robbing me. Every time someone came to the village they told me, "There are some strangers in town, Juvencio."

And I would take off to the mountains, hiding among the madrone thickets and passing the days with nothing to eat but herbs. Sometimes I had to go out at midnight, as though the dogs were after me. It's been that way my whole life. Not just a year or two. My whole life.

And now they've come for him when he no longer expected anyone, confident that people had forgotten all about it, believing that he'd spend at least his last days peacefully. "At least," he thought, "I'll have some peace in my old age. They'll leave me alone."

He'd clung to this hope with all his heart. That's why it was hard for him to imagine that he'd die like this, suddenly, at this time of life, after having fought so much to ward off death, after having spent his best years running from one place to another because of the alarms, now when his body had become all dried up and leathery from the bad days when he had to be in hiding from everybody.

Hadn't he even let his wife go off and leave him? The day when he learned his wife had left him, the idea of going out in search of her didn't even cross his mind. He let her go without trying to find out at all who she went with or where, so he wouldn't have to go down to the village. He let her go as he'd let everything else go, without putting up a fight. All he had left to take care of was his life, and he'd do that, if nothing else. He couldn't let them kill him. He couldn't. Much less now.

But that's why they brought him from there, from Palo de Venado. They didn't need to tie him so he'd follow them. He walked alone, tied by his fear. They realized he couldn't run with his old body, with those skinny legs of his like dry bark, cramped up with the fear of dying. Because that's where he was headed. For death. They told him so.

That's when he knew. He began to feel that stinging in his stomach that always came on suddenly when he saw death nearby, making his eyes big with fear and his mouth swell up with those mouthfuls of sour water he had to swallow unwillingly. And that thing that made his feet heavy while his head felt soft and his heart pounded with all its force against his ribs. No, he couldn't get used to the idea that they were going to kill him.

There must be some hope. Somewhere there must still be some hope left. Maybe they'd made a mistake. Perhaps they were looking for another Juvencio Nava and not him.

He walked along in silence between those men, with his arms fallen at his sides. The early morning hour was dark, starless. The wind blew slowly, whipping the dry earth back and forth, which was filled with that odor like urine that dusty roads have.

His eyes, that had become squinty with the years, were looking down at the ground, here under his feet, in spite of the darkness. There in the earth was his whole life. Sixty years of living on it, of holding it tight in his hands, of tasting it like one tastes the flavor of meat. For a long time he'd been crumbling it with his eyes, savoring each piece as if it were the last one, almost knowing it would be the last.

Then, as if wanting to say something, he looked at the men who were marching along next to him. He was going to tell them to let him loose, to let him go; "I haven't hurt anybody, boys," he was going to say to them, but he kept silent. "A little further on I'll tell them," he thought. And he just looked at them. He could even imagine they were his friends, but he didn't want to. They weren't. He didn't know who they were. He watched them moving at his side and bending down from time to time to see where the road continued.

He'd seen them for the first time at nightfall, that dusky hour when everything seems scorched. They'd crossed the furrows trodding on the tender corn. And he'd gone down on account of that—to tell them that the corn was beginning to grow there. But that didn't stop them.

He'd seen them in time. He'd always had the luck to see everything in time. He could've hidden, gone up in the mountains for a few hours until they left and then come down again. Already it was time for the rains to have come, but the rains didn't come and the corn was beginning to wither. Soon it'd be all dried up.

So it hadn't even been worthwhile, his coming down and placing himself among those men like a hole, never to get out again.

And now he continued beside them, holding back how he wanted to tell them to let him go. He didn't see their faces, he only saw their bodies, which swung toward him and then away from him. So when he started talking he didn't know if they'd heard him. He said, "I've never hurt anybody." That's what he said. But nothing changed. Not one of the bodies seemed to pay attention. The faces didn't turn to look at him. They kept right on, as if they were walking in their sleep.

Then he thought that there was nothing else he could say, that he would have to look for hope somewhere else. He let his arms fall again to his sides and went by the first houses of the village, among those four men, darkened by the black color of the night.

"Colonel, here is the man."

They'd stopped in front of the narrow doorway. He stood with his hat in his hand, respectfully, waiting to see someone come out. But only the voice came out, "Which man?"

"From Palo de Venado, colonel. The one you ordered us to bring in."

"Ask him if he ever lived in Alima," came the voice from inside again.

"Hey, you. Ever lived in Alima?" the sergeant facing him repeated the question.

"Yes. Tell the colonel that's where I'm from. And that I lived there till not long ago."

"Ask him if he knew Guadalupe Terreros."

"He says did you know Guadalupe Terreros?"

"Don Lupe? Yes. Tell him that I knew him. He's dead."

Then the voice inside changed tone: "I know he died," it said. And the voice continued talking, as if it was conversing with someone there on the other side of the reed wall.

"Guadalupe Terreros was my father. When I grew up and looked for him they told me he was dead. It's hard to grow up knowing that the thing we have to hang on to to take roots from is dead. That's what happened to us.

"Later on I learned that he was killed by being hacked first with a machete and then an ox goad stuck in his belly. They told me he lasted more than two days and that when they found him, lying in an arroyo, he was still in agony and begging that his family be taken care of.

"As time goes by you seem to forget this. You try to forget it. What you can't forget is finding out that the one who did it is still alive, feeding his rotten soul with the illusion of eternal life. I couldn't forgive that man, even though I don't know him; but the fact that I know where he is makes me want to finish him off. I can't forgive his still living. He should never have been born."

From here, from outside, all he said was clearly heard. Then he ordered, "Take him and tie him up awhile, so he'll suffer, and then shoot him!"

"Look at me, colonel!" he begged. "I'm not worth anything now. It won't be long before I die all by myself, crippled by old age. Don't kill me!"

"Take him away!" repeated the voice from inside.

"I've already paid, colonel. I've paid many times over. They took everything away from me. They punished me in many ways. I've spent about forty years hiding like a leper, always with the fear they'd kill me at any moment. I don't deserve to die like this, colonel. Let the Lord pardon me, at least. Don't kill me! Tell them not to kill me!"

There he was, as if they'd beaten him, waving his hat against the ground. Shouting.

Immediately the voice from inside said, "Tie him up and give him something to drink until he gets drunk so the shots won't hurt him."

Finally, now, he'd been quieted. There he was, slumped down at the foot of the post. His son Justino had come and his son Justino had gone and had returned and now was coming again.

He slung him on top of the burro. He cinched him up tight against the saddle so he wouldn't fall off on the road. He put his head in a sack so it wouldn't give such a bad impression. And then he made the burro giddap, and away they went in a hurry to reach Palo de Venado in time to arrange the wake for the dead man.

"Your daughter-in-law and grandchildren will miss you," he was saying to him. "They'll look at your face and won't believe it's you. They'll think the coyote has been eating on you when they see your face full of holes from all those bullets they shot at you."

TRANSLATED BY GEORGE D. SCHADE

Osman Lins

Brazil
(1924–1978)

———— // ————

Osman Lins, one of the most innovative modern Brazilian writers, lived two different, consecutive lives. Graduating with a degree in economics from the University of Recife in 1946, he found a job in banking. But then, in 1961, he received a fellowship from the Alliance Française that made it possible for him to spend some time in Paris. When Lins returned home he settled in São Paulo, a hotbed of artistic activity, and devoted himself entirely to literature. His first novel, *O visitante,* appeared in 1955, and his collection of stories, *Nove, Novena,* in 1966. It was the latter book, extremely original and experimental, that made Lins well-known. *Avalovara,* another novel, called "a modern epic in the grand scale," was first published in 1973, and an English translation appeared in 1979. During his career Lins won several awards: the Coehlo Neto Prize of the Brazilian Academy of Letters, the Municipal Prize of São Paulo, and the José Anchieta Prize. His last published novel (1976) was *A Rainha dos Cárceres da Grécia.* "Hahn's Pentagon," the selection here, is an intensely lyrical story despite the multiple levels of discourse, the graphic symbols (ideograms) used to denote them, and the temporal fragmentation. The ideograms give it a whimsical look, like that of a text a child would produce. This quality complements the central themes of the story. "Hahn's Pentagon" is like a vast allegory that displays how memories are inscribed and later recalled, a story of education with various remembered moments held apart, dangling in discrete times like the pieces of a mobile. The central figure, Hahn, is a circus elephant who seems to embody the innocence of childhood and the melancholy that remains when it vanishes. The author's penchant for structural games, for a kind of geometric orderliness, might be interpreted as a throwback to his initial love of numbers.

Hahn's Pentagon

⸲ In different towns, ⊦ I here in Goiana, ⸲ I in Vitória, ⸲ we attend Hahn's performance, and both those times ⸲ were ⊦ are ⸲ identical, everything working out with smooth regularity in the rehearsals. ⸲ I used to have, always had, a warm spot for that species of animal. Even though I was already forty-five years old I'd still get all excited when I saw them. I was fascinated by that shapeless creature etched on the walls of caves when our destiny as humans hadn't been settled, as the matrix of coins, the transport of kings, the mount of gods, itself revered and designated as the beast who carries the world on its back. In addition to that, knowing them to be a breed on the way to extinction impressed me, perhaps because I was a celibate. Miss Hahn entered to the sound of the Triumphal March from *Aida*. ¶ A crimson mat on her head, Persian rugs on her back, ¶ appeared, | comes out, ¶ ears flapping, tusks glittering under the lights; ¶ danced, | dances, ¶ with her trainer, | with the great general, a waltz, ¶ passages from the "Blue Danube"; ¶ joined, | joins ¶ put ¶ her feet together on two colored drums, raising her trunk and twirling slowly, with extreme care, on that reduced pedestal, ¶ where she drank, | drinks ¶ had ¶ a glass of beer; ¶ presented, | gives, ¶ offered, ¶ to someone sitting in the first row, ¶ a bouquet of dahlias, | three yellow roses; ¶ left, | goes away, ¶ disappeared, ¶ softly stepping on the ground; ¶ had | I have ¶ the impression that, finding an egg in her path, ¶ would remain, | will remain ¶ would remain ¶ in the air, suspended, so as not to break it. | In my nightmare I open the window: the entire space between the right angles is filled with a gray barrier, wrinkled and wavy. Is it a wall erected in secret melting away, threatening to come through the window into the room to bury me? I shout: "Hahn!" Adélia hears my cries, takes me into her arms.

‖ Busy with our old brother, the priest, who wasn't doing well at the time, I learned about the performance through Nassi Latif. I never even got to see the elephant, even though the house we live in is, in a manner of speaking, right off the same area where she spent afternoons and mornings; it was so close that my sister and I could hear her calls all day long. At first I would shout to Helônia to go see her after we did the housework. For a long time now she wouldn't go out with me, saying it was ridiculous for two old maids to be out on the street taking a walk together; she might just possibly have been right, but not that much. Were we that old? She hadn't reached seventy and I was just a little over sixty-three. There are people who get married at that age, and she was even hoping to marry Nassi. Massi Latif was going to the circus—I don't know where he got the money for it—and on the following day he appeared, crazy as ever, recounting the same things in great detail as if he hadn't told them to my sister and me countless other times. Helônia, even though she denied it, adored him; she would stay with him, listening to him, asking questions, devouring him with her eyes. Out of pity, she would say. I would go off to look in on the sick man. He indeed was old. Deaf, almost blind, he couldn't even hear the elephant's cries (God preserve him in His holy glory), and it's hard to imagine what would have become of him if he hadn't had the care of sisters like the two of us, still young and capable of anything to be of use to him. When Latif left (Helônia would say her good-byes at the gate) the argument would begin. My sister, no matter how much I opened her eyes, refused to understand that those daily visits didn't bode well: Nassi Latif was no child, but a man of some thirty-odd years, irresponsible, a vagabond, half-crazy, quite capable of compromising us poor women whose only possessions were our priest brother, our family name, our reputation, and our virginity, these last valuable by themselves and principally because of the zeal with which we'd guarded them for more than half a century.

⚲ Raising my bust and my nephew (he's six years old, five years younger than my breasts) as high as I can, here I am in the presence of Hahn, in a light brown dress, looking at her nipples, small, like her clear-lidded, teary eyes, gray butterflies gnawed at—not dead—by moths and ants. Night began in the elephant's big belly. Those of us who surrounded her, offering her lumps of salt, cakes, candy, sugar cane, and pieces of indigo, will soon leave the square, sunny now, and go home. If only the afternoon lasted longer! If I could only stay among the schoolboys longer, if they could all see me in this dress of mine. Not because it's new, but because, not being blonde and pretty like Patricia Lane, Marjorie Reynolds, or Carole Lombard, my shining lights are my breasts—large, firm—the blouse makes them stand out. It's the beginning of serious events in my dull life. I'm unaware of the fact that I'm only being swept along by the current (my nephew hasn't been thrown into those waters) and I look at Hahn. Her joy carries beyond the festive circle made up of students, old people, housewives, shopkeepers; it spreads out on the sunny square as if she weren't a clumsy and not very noisy animal but a musical band or a fireworks display. Her huge ears, like dirty old rags streaked with yellow gold, stained white and faded pink—bouquets of withered flowers, of decay dust—wave over the crowd, making me think of pennants, plumes, ribbons, and banners. Her hide has the somber color of old iron, brought out by some kind of tricks by the light, giving off greenish reflections like the sea. Only then do I see Bartolomeu's eyes, also teary, but blue, and I think that they're the source of the inexplicable marine tones that soften the elephant's back, and I feel myself bathed in blue for a second. He must be twelve or thirteen years old at the most. I'm not deceived by the perplexity or the fascination or the doubt at that first look. We're both the same height.

⊖ It's been almost two months since I've been to the town. Borne by the sudden desire to see once more—it wasn't there years ago—the open shops and grocery stores, the barber shop I used to go to in my adolescence, and the students with books under their arms on their way to the school where I'd studied, things I haven't seen for a long time because I only visit the town on Sundays (and it's also possible I'm apprehensive—tomorrow will be a holiday in Recife—about spending Sunday and Monday at home, enduring the unpleasant presence in the midst of everyone of someone we've stopped loving). I left after breakfast, giving my wife a quick kiss on the cheek, for in spite of our awareness of an intervening distance that was growing and final between us, we still maintained those little dead, so deeply painful, rites. If I'd chosen to go by train I wouldn't have seen the elephant: the route from the station to my grandmother's house doesn't pass by the square at the main church. By bus, however, I get off right across from the circus. Therefore I see Miss Hahn at one in the afternoon, sheltered by the canopy like those Oriental potentates that we see in the movies, enveloped in sunlight, on cushions, with the look of privileged people as proud of their square of shade as of their daggers and their cool emeralds. An old man is looking at her. The two of them are all alone, all alone in the shade, surrounded by the scalding silence, and Hahn has one of her feet in the air. She's executing an interminable dance with a swaying motion on which her very weight, her vastness imposes a solemn rhythm. She's a model Asian, with five nails on her front feet, four on the others. The tip of her tail reminds me of a peacock feather. The old man asked me if I didn't think it cruel to trap the elephant, isolate it from its companions, train it with baths, songs, deceitful pleasures, shouts, all for money. I smiled without answering. How could I agree since I think that untamed words, loose in limbo alone or in a band, in a savage state, are useless powers? With a wavy motion Hahn sticks out her trunk, blows on me between the fingers.

¶ In the office, more frigid and empty than my existence of a celibate, I couldn't manage to forget Miss Hahn. I've got two quite different brothers and maybe I'm the fusion, the midpoint between them. The elder, Oséas, owned a fine shoe store in which the other one, Armando, had become a partner. In that capacity he would show up two or three times a week, putter around the shelves or stand in the doorway, dreamy-eyed, always dressed in white, with his hands in his pants pockets and after a while in those of his jacket, the way George Raft would do in one of his films. Suddenly, without taking leave of Oséas, walking calmly, he would head off for home, passing through my office without turning his head, pick up some paints and brushes and shut himself up in his studio, painting saints, Scandinavian landscapes, and animals he'd never seen: hippopotamuses, herons, whales, sharks. Oséas, at the age of twenty-something, took a wife. Without any great demands, paying attention only to her teeth (for him an infallible reflection of good or bad health) and to the slimness of her legs. He thought that a fat-legged woman tends to be lazy. He liked to go fishing, ate well and a lot, drank even more, always having a good supply of wine at home, caring little about brand or origin. "It's all wine!" He detested sadness, only going to see movies with pleasant titles: *Three Cheers for the Navy, The Captain's Daughter, Delightful, Youth Will Be Served.* This was the weak point in the healthy makeup he affected, the false note in his identification: my brother was a timid soul like the rest of us, turning his face away from life. A man can't call himself brave or avid for the things of the world if he's incapable of facing up, no matter where they might occur, to images of what's frightful. He wouldn't let prostitutes (he visited them even after he was married) tell him about their troubles. "A whore is born a whore. There's not a single one who's worth anything." He was the creature least given to subtleties that I've ever known. Without having cultivated that quality, without having possessed it in the slightest, I managed to get my life involved in distinctions and minute details, not blind enough to crush what I craved nor crazy enough to get into a dream and become part of it. Since the girls in town didn't seem fabulous enough to arouse any passion in me and since I never conceived of a marriage that wasn't magnified by an exaltation, illusory that it was, of the senses and the soul, casual relationships were abhorrent to me. I had too strong a sense of the real, also, which hindered me from using my imagination to transcend the trivial and the base, rather like setting aside a nonexistent being, drawing out, like Adam, from my own insides, a woman without stain, perfect, invulnerable—and loving that imaginary character with a real love. In that way, free of the office, almost every night I would set about roaming the streets all by myself, no longer knowing (how many?) how many years it had been since I'd felt the body of a woman against mine, thinking about leaving town, knowing I never would, wishing for the impossible and sudden appearance on one of those out-of-the-way streets that seemed wrapped in their own misery of the woman who would come to my rescue, freeing from its loneliness someday this being of mine that was drenched in a silence like that of predawn courtyards.

‖ There was also a lot of it—in my sister, in our brother the priest, in me—a lot of loneliness. I can say that not all saints were as virtuous as he. Maybe for that very reason, even after having exercised his priestly duties in the town for thirty-nine years, baptizing, performing weddings, saying prayers for the dead, and organizing processions, he had almost no visitors. It was understandable, therefore even though I was apprehensive of the consequences of Nassi's daily visits and not very tolerant of his ways, that I wanted them, getting restless if by some chance he was late in appearing. It was also understandable that two weeks after the arrival of the elephant, after hearing so much talk about her antics, when her trumpet sounded I should get a strange feeling, a joy. I had the impression that she was calling to me, that I had to answer those calls, feeling guilty if I didn't respond.

↙The sacristy with its dim light. The priest at the main altar, the two acolytes, lighted candles, the gold of the images, white embroidered cloths, the red carpet. The sacred hymn sung in Latin. The old organ. The moonlight enters through the wide-open window by the square with its mango trees, reflected on the mosaic floor and lighting up the benches of dark wood. Bartolomeu beside me, erect, his hands in his pockets. Five days passed before he got up the courage to speak to me. Today he followed me resolutely, taking measured steps, a little quicker than mine. I let him catch up. I went ahead more quickly when I sensed that he was on the verge of the decision I was eagerly awaiting. We went into the church almost at the same time and I guessed—more than I heard—his choked voice asking if we could talk. Without looking at him, I was perturbed too, although reluctantly, I answered yes. The hymn, the voice of the priest, the sound of the bell, the moonlight in the sacristy. I'm standing a bit in front of Bartolomeu. I look at him from time to time. He responds with his withdrawn and delicate way of smiling. I know: and ever since this first contact I've had the premonition that something out of the ordinary is in store for me. His fragile body (it gives me an almost obsessive impression of some rare piece of clockwork), was it assembled secretly? It's like catching sight in the shadows of a stretch of terrain where vague movements indicate a structure of intentions, an attack, a flight, a conspiracy, something whose nature and aim are unknown to us. This child alarms me.

⊖ My grandmother's house, door and window, fifteen feet across. The layout, following the plan that local designers and builders have copied for decades—front parlor, hallway along the bedrooms, dining room, kitchen, bathroom, backyard—gives it the look of an old dwelling. It was built less than eight years ago and its material is cheaper than that in old houses. No stone, no tiles, no pine wood in the eaves, no cedar or metal grillwork. It isn't even tall. On the right, in a gabled chalet, lives the married daughter she visits every day and who, not given much to walks, finds her relaxation in that always thankful ritual. Doors closed, everybody sleeping the siesta. I pushed open the small gate to the chalet, crossed the veranda. My grandmother had left the kitchen door to her house open. Because of an irregularity in the terrain, the other side of the wall, the side in her yard, is lower. I took a ladder (no Oriental would dare reach the back of an elephant by that vulgar method), climbed the wall without any difficulty, and I'm in the clean, silent interior among the shelves of dishes, the chairs with cane bottoms, and the bare square table, all made of light-colored wood. My grandmother's presence touches the smell of things. Between the yard and this dining room I go along squeezing the elephant's breath between my fingers as if it were warm, damp sand. For the first time I perceive how sterile my life has become and how hostile is the milieu through which it has flowed for the greater part of my days. A monster, in sun and silence; a pachyderm, not in sheer size but in aridity and inner poverty, with the aggravating circumstance that everything in me is secret, incapable of arousing, even accidentally, the interest of others and with the attenuating circumstance of not being mute but bestowed with speech, an instrument

I handle poorly, able to control myself enough to register, if not my exile, a persevering feeling that I am breaking it. Here amidst this furniture I find out that seeing the town on Monday again is a kind of disguise. Because for a long time, during the monthly visits to my grandmother, I haven't been able to find a certain undefined taste that I'm sure existed in my childhood. I imagine—with the logic of the destitute—that I have fled from that taste or that atmosphere of Sundays in search of other days. Matters of a coward.

╷ The street we live on is one of the oldest in town. It has risen in status over the years. The original tiled sidewalk, almost buried, has retreated little by little over a long period, and street pavement and sidewalk merge. What month can it be? The end of August? The beginning of September? The sky is peopled with restless kites. Other boys send them up all day long on the street with buried sidewalks. Across from our house there lives a woman. She makes up for everything old and drab around. Adélia is her name. In the morning, after her husband, a dealer in corn and beans, leaves for work, she leans out of her green-framed window. At that time I, too, on the tips of my toes, lean out of mine. She waves, I smile, she allows herself to be adored by what she judges to be the innocence of a child. Having noticed my envy—I was getting sunburned watching the buzzing antelopes, the imposing Indians as the kites go up: rectangular, nervous, threatening, with sharp pieces of glass at the end of their tails— in the midst of oranges, hearts of lettuce, and dwarf bananas from the market she brought me this crimson Indian that quivered on top of the delivery boy's basket, and I sensed its strength with pride. I had to overcome the resistance of the grownups at home: They claim that kites bring smallpox germs loose in the upper air down to earth. They're probably right. I've seen it myself and it's always in October, after the kite season, that smallpox cases turn up in town, along with fevers and other illnesses. How could Adélia have guessed that of all the kites it's the Indian I like best, the Indian, a great colored square with one of its points turned downward, decorated with a strip of tissue paper that hangs from the tips on the side and manages at the same time, like the crown of a king, to increase both its grandeur and its stability? Leaning out the window, Adélia smiled. A brief, short-lived smile, just like all of my joys. After sending my red Indian two or three "messages" (by the hand of what miracle do the small disks of paper climb up to the head of the kites?), the curved, tense line will break, the Indian, wavering, will get tangled in the strip of tissue paper, the round "message" will fly off with it. I'll never see it again.

‖ There were arguments with Helônia. "You're getting too sweet on Latif!" She would insult me: she was of age and would do what she felt like doing with her life. We have the same family name, I answered, her mistakes would stick to me. She broke into tears, saying she was unhappy, and she shouted that I was jealous. Nassi Latif would be the last person for me to be jealous over, I declared. A nut. A vagabond. There was no understanding. Even with a bad leg he was capable of running off again, crutch and all, leaving for Acre or for Mato Grosso, for Venezuela, the way he'd done so many times. He was a born vagabond, he'd lived as a vagabond up till then, and he'd die of old age still a vagabond. She lay down on the floor moaning and kicking her feet. After that Nassi Latif didn't visit us for three days. Thinking that he'd stopped coming because of me, because of my advice, a letter I'd sent or something like that, she poisoned my food. When she saw me filling my plate she repented, confessed her crime, knelt and asked for my forgiveness. Our brother the priest knew nothing about it.

↙I know that the relationship between me and this adolescent has got to be a passing thing. I was hoping, though, to see it die as a consequence of its own absurdity—a game in which somebody accepts being King or Captain and only takes on that role, not vagabond forever. I recognize that the perversity of those to whom we've done no harm turns against us as soon as we fall in love—or try to fall in love—condemning what in itself is transitory with an even more premature end than the one determined by its nature. My nephew alerted me to the whistles. Bartolomeu might have noticed them too. He didn't say anything about them to me. He had good manners, even though he was just a boy. In the beginning, in hopes that he was still unaware of that inexplicable reaction of people, I avoided meeting him in the light of day. I would seek out the darkest places. He didn't take advantage of those circumstances one single time: hands in his pockets, he looks at me furtively (his looks have something of the watchful and frightened examination of a little rat who ventures out of his hiding place for an instant, even though they twinkled with adoration) and that charms me. After a while, however, we don't know from where—from some sealed up and darkened house or from behind a wall— the whistling would start, the Triumphal March from *Aida*. Delicately, without letting on that he could hear it, he would suggest that we go somewhere else. As I moved I could feel the volume of my thighs and I became aware that with my heavy walk, my swaying hips, my torso that lacked a waist, it was possible to discover with just a touch of the requisite malice certain similarities with Hahn. Even my breasts, of which I'd always been so proud, seemed huge to me. Our sad love affair, precarious and fragile, will dissolve in ridicule. All we'll be left with will be a humiliating memory. For that reason I look at the houses of this suddenly hateful town, facing which I became Hahn and Bartolomeu my trainer. It's the first time he's taken my hand in his. I wanted to give him a bouquet of dahlias as a sign of recognition.

Θ I contemplate the hollow roof tiles. What is this feeling coming over me? What mysterious space have I penetrated by climbing the wall and invading this silent house by a route that's not the usual one? My grandmother was sleeping, is asleep, a sheet over her legs. She's no longer of an age to occupy the whole house with her presence and there are corners and furniture that are almost abandoned, like this canvas cot I've dusted off and covered, where I've lain down and which was covered with dust. Opening the dresser drawer, taking out sheets, pillow, pillowcase, old pajamas, stretching out on my back on the bed. Banal movements—why?—by some transcendent substance. My grandmother writes me on the night of my nineteenth birthday: "I've prepared a special meal for you. Your aunt and her husband, who are planning to live near me because of my years, which, unfortunately, are many now, have come over from their place. As it was Sunday we were sure you wouldn't miss it. We ate alone at two in the afternoon, all upset because we had been dreaming of your presence at that lunch for many weeks." Where could I have been that Sunday? Gently, some door, maybe the one in the kitchen, keeps moving, bumping the door frame, the hinges creaking musically. Ancient sounds hang in the silence of extinct summers. A need to weep. The vivid impression that I'm being carried like a religious litter in a procession toward something vague and therefore no less solemn. Are all the currents of time fleeing simultaneously? Can there be dikes, detours, stagnant times, perhaps? Will certain hours return, taking on flesh through a kind of transmigration in the substance of smells and sounds, of clarities, temperatures enveloping us? The white elephant, because it was so rare, was honored for a long time with homages, sacred candles, theatrical performances, luxurious vestments, jewels, processions. It was intimidating. I also feel fear before the premonition that a dead time, enormous and white, is getting close to me, or, more than a time, huge blocks, a fleet of ghost ships, full of astrolabes, winds, compasses, the sound of bare feet, the beating of hearts, deserted tables, three shapes concentrated in a vain wait, cellars with barrels full of cool water, which I disdained in past times, seeking it in dry vats. A breaking out of sails, a swaying of masts, waves.

⊦ In the midst of kites gliding in the smallpox-infested breezes the Novelty, the Event arose. A well-known street-theater group is sharing people's attention with Hahn. (I attend a performance with Adélia and her husband. In my left hand the woman's, in the right that of the dealer in corn and beans. In order to endure the latter contact I transform myself into a sack into which the man is pouring grain and my lady friend different kinds of sugar—brown, refined, crystal—along with bees and ants. On a raised wooden platform lighted by two carbide lamps and Japanese lanterns the shepherd girls are singing, with heavy makeup, bows in their hair, tambourines ringed with artificial flowers, red or blue boleros with small gold medallions and embroidered with glass beads, very short skirts and long silk stockings fastened at the thigh. They wear rings in their ears and black beauty marks on their chins, foreheads, or next to their noses. Crêpe-paper streamers, also blue and crimson, are strung over the bandstand, joining one lantern to another. The orchestra: a fife, a banjo, and a triangle. The rumble of the audience is so great that I can barely hear the instruments and the hoarse voices of the shepherd girls.) Well, the impresario, on the days when the singer-dancers are performing, discovered this festive way of announcing the performance to the public: at four-thirty he releases a blue, red, and orange kite, built by him and which isn't like the others, not like any of them. It's enormous, regal, glowing, with more than one level, festooned with garlands, looking like a fish, a hawk, an umbrella, a jewel box, a pinwheel. It fascinates me. I decide to make a kite like that, with new shapes different from the rest and even more festive. I'm going to make one.

¶ I closed the office early. I went to Oséas's store, invited him to look at the excited crowd that every afternoon surrounded the sort of tent where the elephant, with the same grace, received tree branches, balls of honey, blocks of salt, banana leaves, bundles of hay from the people. He refused my invitation and went so far as to ask if I thought him capable of leaving the store just to look at an animal. "Even if it were Ann Sheridan!" Armando also refused to go with me:

"Too many people."

"Have you been there already?"

"No."

"Don't you like to paint animals?"

"It's not a matter of liking to, it's a necessity."

"But why not go take a look at an elephant from close up?"

"I don't have to take a look at it. I know quite well what an elephant's like."

"That's what you think. What direction do the wrinkles in the back take? Do they go along the body or are they up and down?"

"Up and down."

"Wrong. They've got the shape of a boat. They look like a canoe sketched in profile."

I left, grinding my teeth. It was absurd how, unable to find any substitute for them, I preserved things from my twenties: narrow sideburns, padded shoulders, the custom of using suspenders, and even a certain way of walking along the streets—unworried, relaxed, hands behind my back, a wandering look. I knew I wasn't the only one still hanging on to those marks common to all elegant young men who were my contemporaries; to change myself, however, was only a little less than impossible. Maybe underneath it all I was proud of the faithfulness that was transforming me into a museum piece. Despite my anger with my brothers after the ridiculous discussion about wrinkles on the back of elephants, my walk was the same as usual. I had to maintain my usual look of indifference, my usual calm. No one had any right to catch my moments of anger. Older people would greet me with respect and at the same time with condescension, as if there were something threatening and despicable about me: I was a mature man but a confirmed bachelor. I went along in the direction of the elephant like someone going to talk to his lady-love. I went along like someone running away from home, who's broken away from punishment, risen up against oppression, and is on his way to a pre-arranged meeting filled with a love that our parents don't understand and want to destroy. Happy, I drew close to Hahn. She was dancing, as always, and groups of people followed each other in endless succession. She seemed to be laughing and she was most certainly celebrating being the center of attraction in that small and happy universe. When I saw her the joy with which I'd approached disappeared. With the sight of lovers, groups of girls, I suddenly felt like a character out of some film or other, or from some book or some nightmare, tossed invisibly into a world that wasn't mine and which would never hear my voice. How could they hear me if two decades stood between us, if I was shouting to them from far away, from the year 1930? I didn't have any dinner. I crossed the town, went to remote neighborhoods, was hungry. The hunger passed and I headed for the red-light district.

It was the last time we saw each other in public. We didn't exchange a single word in that regard even though we knew it was the last time. I was the one who had the idea of meeting at the movies during the matinee of the Sabu film. We arrived when there were only a few people as yet and we sat together. Were we any different from all the others because of those precautions? The theater was full of couples, girls with boys, adolescents, sweethearts. I was getting more and more afraid to be with him. It was like someone committing adultery or being watched by the police. I can see now: I was right. First it was a distant whistle that others, timidly then deliberately, joined in with, a swarm of angry wasps insistently repeating it, mixed with belches, cackles, and imitations of an elephant trumpeting that March, which was never Triumphal for us, but, instead, despairing and which was immediately accompanied by a rhythmic stamping of feet, fifty feet, three hundred feet, which ran right through us. I tried to smile at first, then I had to control myself so as not to cry. Without saying anything, Bartolomeu gripped my hand and remained like that, even though they'd stopped, but not without a kind of whistling hoot. He's very pale. His lips, bruised and tight, look like a withered flower, a petal that's lost its bloom. When the lights go out I'll leave. Maybe he will too. We won't see the Sabu film and it's possible that we won't see each other again, separated from each other forever because of that sort of conspiracy, those whistles directed at us.

⊖I don't know what woke me up. I remain motionless, first just listening, then with my eyes open. My grandmother and her daughter are conversing in the parlor. If I pay close attention I'll be able to tell what they're talking about; the walls are thin, the house is small, the door to my room is open. I sway along with the back-and-forth of those voices, interrupted by bits of laughter. The phrases have the rhythm of the town, and the conversation is the same that went on decades ago, continued during absences, repeated itself, and went back to the beginning. They chat about certain events, about old conversations they'd had. The sun slips lower. Orange remnants penetrate the hollow tiles, light up the cobwebs hidden among the rafters. A thin breeze also passes through the tiles. The cobwebs flutter, along with the light in the room. Then what had been foretold was true. I'd penetrated the past. I'm simultaneously in this Sunday afternoon and in another remote time. I'm ubiquitous, getting to know in time the state that some men must have enjoyed in another dimension, in space. Would the same thing have happened if I'd come in through the door? I know with certainty that I'll never get to know an experience like that. I'll reach happiness at other times, but now, amidst the thousand possibilities of life, a space has opened up, a sphere, a beneficial bit of chance, a propitious configuration of factors of great duration and breadth: a harmony between the moment I'm immersed in and the most profound necessities of being. Trying to be aware of everything, I wait, on the *qui vive*, for the interruption, the end. With my spirit on the alert for some new element (the opening of a door, the crowing of a cock, a cloud over the sun) that will undo that rare conjunction forever. I can't perceive that this vigilance is dissociating me from the well-being, the privileged center of that instant, because even though I remain motionless, there is still a deadly tightening in me. And at the exact moment when, turned toward my ecstasy, I discover my expectation to be among its causes, it actually begins to die, vanishes, impossible for it to be replaced in view of the evidence that, contained in the very structure of my joy, are my discouragement, my emptiness, all the poisons that are replacing the juice of life, and they make me waste away. So, I zealously drink that ghostly resurrection of the past that's still left in the sound of voices, in the quivering of the light, in the cobwebs.

⏐ I've been working on the kite for days. Nights, rather, after finishing my lessons in Grammar, Geography, History, and Science. I've wasted sticks, cola cans, and sheet after sheet of tissue paper that Adélia gives me. I've designed and imagined impossible sketches, I've wept. My imagination goes astray, despairs. In town, many years ago, decades ago, there used to be piped water. With time and people's not knowing how to take care of what was given them, the installations went to wrack and ruin and the supply went back to being brought on donkey back. The houses are crammed with kegs of water dozing behind doors. Inside the kegs piaba fish swim, feeding on mosquito larvae. Some vestiges of the old pipes remain, lost underground and connected to hidden springs: large valves, green with verdigris, dry and eternally open over slimy concrete tanks. Without anyone's knowing why, those faucets will suddenly start giving off a trickle of water. Grownups say: "The spring woke up." That gift, that water, which doesn't cost poor people like us a penny, seems like a miracle. It can last just a short while or for a long time, whole nights, never whole days: the spring doesn't like to be watched. In the same way, as an offering, the kite was born tonight in my spirit with its framework of lines, surfaces, and other things that its subsequent construction will go about revealing, sensing, accomplishing. I'm going to put together a kite that's never existed before, with lots of colors, beautiful, complex—and capable of flying.

¶ That grimy neighborhood had been transformed, the houses torn down, new walls put up in place of the others—old, set in like milk teeth— the women from those days have died or have survived by begging or are rotting away in homes for the aged. Some have husbands, children, complain about life. What brought me there? My restlessness or the drumming, that dull, interminable rhythm that kept retreating and returning according to the direction of my steps or the wind, while hunger grew and then disappeared, as if going without food had calmed it? Elephants live in herds and are affectionate creatures. There are, however, examples of loners, rebels, intractable ones. Elephants love each other and are gentle. The loners refuse to take part in hunts and pilgrimages, drive off the females, drink by themselves, bathe by themselves, grow old by themselves. I was willing to join any herd at all, to be taken back into any relationship, to caress a woman's haunch. Down the broad street, long and poorly lighted, criss-crossed by the echoes of the drumming, I was hounded by dogs. There were a lot of other men and women besides me, children were begging, an old woman squatting next to a pile of trash was moaning a pleading song. The song was coming from another throat buried in the garbage. The dogs, however, ignored everything, everybody, people and song. They only came up to me, barked at my feet, a pack of luminous throats. Go back? There was no place to go. Going back was the same as going on, the same as not going on, as not going back. There was no voice waiting for me. A whore in gray was staring at me timidly, leaning against a doorway. There was dancing inside the house. Some of the men had their hats on. They were all spiritless, their bodies stiff, legs far apart. My hands were icy. The dogs roamed about, sniffing the night air, bristling, ears up, blue, black, green, lead-colored. I saw how thin they were. It was a woman with large breasts, jolly, hair like Robespierre's, the back of her neck shaved, who took me by the arm and led me inside. The one in gray—I could see out of the corner of my eye that she couldn't have been more than fifteen—was still looking at me and I thought, one of those thoughts that last only a second, that even there I didn't have a choice in life.

‖ Our priest brother had spent a bad night, with the two of us giving him medicine, teas, massages, and boiling water for his feet. It was our custom not to bother the neighbors. The patient was our penance and our usefulness. We were happy even though afflicted when he had urgent need of us. Toward morning he finally fell asleep. Exhausted, we also slept. I awoke with the argument, the muffled shouts, Helônia's sobs. "He's died!" I came out bare-footed. He was snoring. Then I heard the thump of the crutch in the parlor. Nassi Latif was leaving and my sister was following him, weeping, her arms in the air. When she saw me with no slippers on, she shouted that I was spying on her. I gave it right back to her: "I'm not like you." Nassi turned: "Have you both gone crazy? I'm not coming back here anymore." "So much the better. The whole neighborhood's probably talking about us. It doesn't look right for two maiden ladies living alone with their brother who never leaves his bed to be visited by a man every day. Worse yet by a man whose intentions nobody knows." Nassi Latif lifted his crutch and began to laugh that creaky laugh of his. "Who's crazy enough to gossip about you two? The pair of you fell into your last stage a hundred years ago! Next to you Miss Hahn is a child. You can go to hell, you decrepit old women!" Helônia told me the reason for her desperation after he'd left. Latif had got a job. He was going off with the circus. He was going to be a guard or keep for Hahn. Helônia's laments: "He called us old. I know that we're not children, but love is a little late in coming sometimes. I've always been proper, a talented and virtuous girl. There was even a time when I knew how to embroider. And my brother will guarantee that even today he's never seen anyone better at darning socks. I had my daydreams about the lieutenant when I was a child. His uniform was a dream. He always ignored me. Everybody, even today, is ignorant of my qualities. You know I'm not lying: Latif is the first boy in my whole life who's ever paid any attention to me." Hard as I tried I couldn't remember the lieutenant she'd daydreamed about. It must have been a long time ago.

⊖ My grandmother is in the kitchen washing the lunch dishes. I'm all wrapped up in dead air, dead sounds, inert clarity. The canvas cot creaks. The look of the town on Monday has brought me nothing. I wonder what had happened to me on the previous afternoon, even as I know that the experience won't be repeated. The feeling of uselessness caused by that search is joined now to the more acute awareness of my poverty regarding the present. I say to myself: "It's understandable for a man to look back to the past if there's a profitable purpose in that look. As for me, I'm looking for it because I haven't got the courage to follow again—or simply follow—the direction of my days." Writing. Would I find any salvation in that? I'm frightened by its indispensable and arduous apprenticeship. They're dismantling the circus. The sun is burning my head. As I observe the elephant I think about her delicate sense of smell, her keen hearing. I remember the old man who asked me a question the day before. Hunters after this animal that's capable of destroying whole villages in a matter of minutes make use of spider webs to tell which way the wind is blowing so as not to be discovered. Spider webs are instruments of cunning. They help trap elephants. Silence, perseverance, audacity, patience, webs, senses on the alert, weapons I'll have to obtain in order to encircle words, tame them with prods and baths. What crafts will I need to train them? But writing is one way—not the most efficient one—of breaking out of exile. I go along like a drunkard on the sun-drenched streets. The essential decisions a man makes never come by chance, incidentally, the same as with a work of art. We come to them slowly, with illumination and, above all, with maturing, effort, meditation, practice. During the hours of the hottest sun many people take a siesta. Only an occasional bird insists on singing. At the moment in which I suddenly conceive the space around me as made up of blinding panes of glass, there is formulated in me, and I accept it, this judgment that's so full of demands, most certainly engendered in my spirit over a long time and through a long and secret gestation: I've got to search energetically in my life for contentment and peace. A conquest, not a recollection. But I'm still like someone who gets ready mentally to take a trip without knowing that he needs to create in his soul conditions for the conquest of his habits, his fears, before he leaves. My grandmother's putting away the silverware and china that she's washed.

ᛁ My high kite, as original as the one in the shepherd play, fascinates people while another red one approaches it. All around me, looking at it condescendingly, are my relatives, whom I'd called. Not once do they offer in my praise the words that would be so pleasing for me to hear. That doesn't destroy my exaltation: I feel that I've beaten them, raising the new object up over their indifference, but it's impossible to get a lift in their spirits. The jubilation comes undone a second later. Looking at the end of the tail on the red kite, long and wavy like a wounded snake, I see the piece of glass wickedly placed there, which with a rapid and precise maneuver cuts my line. I still don't know what to do. Even though the tension of the falling kite had disappeared on the dead line I still keep my arm extended. As people whose vision has been clouded by despair must know, I can't make out its face, although I am the owner, the maker, rather, of the kite that's falling rapidly, out of control—and even then more splendid than ever in my eyes—over the masts of the circus, over the belfries, the square, the crowd, and the trees, and, moving the people out of its path, it relegates Hahn to a secondary level for a moment. I have trouble imagining it. The vision of a nightmare, fragmented and painful. My own hands, in the midst of fifty others, make a useless attempt to catch it. I think it's within reach—but it's unreachable because of some kind of evil enchantment. There are other voracious hands that get control of the prey, but to destroy it. Its ribs and colors are broken up in seconds. They fly apart in an explosion and a sob also explodes in my mouth. I choke. Then they surround me. They shout, run around me, and—I'll never know why—they throw stones at me. In my growing rage I try to grab one of those devils, hit him, fight with him. But they run off and the hooting grows louder. I look around into the distance, impotent, looking for support. A stone hits some part of my body and my rage suddenly leaves me. I need protection, any kind. I see a tree, the crown of a tree, I gather my strength together, run, and hug its trunk.

¶ There was something old-fashioned about the way I got together with the woman. She asked me what town I was from, didn't seem to accept my answer, told me she'd never met anyone just like me. Does that change too? Is a man's manner transformed when he goes to bed with a whore? She was greasy, with a shapeless body; her shoulders and her frizzled hair were drenched with an abominable perfume, maybe to get rid of the breath of the men she'd been with before me. She'd left the light on. The incessant music shook the room. I stared at her feet, broad and with ankles misshapen by a brutal life, the nails painted a bright red. I wondered if, with the girl in gray, I would have entered the community of men for a moment, escaped from my loneliness a little, and I thought, almost joyfully, that I would soon be back on the street with the dogs barking around my legs. Oséas was waiting for me. He went along with me through the dogs, who weren't even looking at me (I had the smell of their world now), took me to a bar three blocks away, bought me some wine, and started talking about women and laughing at the chance that had allowed him to catch me in the act. I listened to him vaguely, glimpsing him far off in a white cloud. That was it, then, the cloud that separated me from other people. I saw him the way charlatans say they can see the evil spirit that afflicts us beside us. Overcoming the urge to reach out my hand into the mist that enveloped Oséas, I thought about Hahn in her isolation. The desire came over me to buy her, take her far away to the companionship of her brothers and sisters, her species, in the Congo or in Burma, give her the companionship, the love I was incapable of. I took Oséas's hand: "I'm going to get married. A man has the need to cry sometimes. Just today, tonight, Oséas, I've had the need to cry. But in whose arms? I'm going to get married, it doesn't matter how, to anybody at all!" I drank the last glass down in one gulp, reached the street with decisive steps, starving, with no despair at all, a bold and happy drunk. In the silence of the night, all alone, my drive petered out: I have trouble believing I'd experienced it. I put my hands behind my back and continued on slowly.

‖ I've known dozens of cases of old age, I might even say hundreds. No one can teach me what it's like to be old. I've seen people age ten years on a trip that took only months, twenty after an operation, thirty on the death of a child. Always by leaps, however, in the night of absences. With Helônia it was different. I watched her grow old hour by hour, at five in the afternoon as she had a look about her that she hadn't had at four, hunched over a little more with each new morning, growing forgetful, wandering, talking about events of the day before as if they'd taken place years ago. A famous, bitter week. They were my brother's last days. I had to confront those hours all by myself because Helônia would ask to go get some medicine and wouldn't come back, would look at the sick man indifferently, would go to bed at the least opportune times, wander through the house at night talking to spirits, to herself, or to the images of our past. I begged God to keep her on her feet for a month or two at least. It was too much for me to take care of two invalids at the same time.

Having made a date with Bartolomeu to meet by the reservoir, I managed to get out of taking my nephew. You can see almost the whole town from there. It's a privileged place in a region with no relief. In earlier times there'd been a hospital on this very spot: the Shelter. Smallpox victims came on litters, were quarantined from healthy people. Later on smallpox became rare, and since this was the highest elevation in the town they tore down the hospital and built the reservoir. They put benches alongside it and swings for the children among the trees. At eight in the morning on Sundays the gates are opened; they're closed at six. Too long a schedule: almost nobody climbs up the steep and rough red clay slope in the afternoon. It's always on sunny mornings after Mass that families fill the area and the voices of children ring out in the clear air like the clashing of swords. In the afternoon they prefer going to the movies, walking the streets, watching the passing of the train, a kind of god or hieroglyphic of our common dreams, the symbol of the journey we're all so anxious to make. So the two of us are alone, holding hands beside the invisible waters that supply the town at our feet. The silence all around is like an absolution. We exchange few words. We walk under the trees, play on the swings, talk from one side of the reservoir to the other through the air holes, making our voices echo through the water that we couldn't see, hidden in that huge covered well where every sound was returned and, in a way, broken up into remnants. That was when he told me at a distance of a hundred feet and without our seeing each other, in a timid voice, for the first time, for the only time, that he loved me. He didn't have the courage to look me in the face right after those words. Holding hands, silent, looking at the tiled roofs among walls and garden fences, the towers, the greens and browns immersed in a peace that took us away from the land and its differences, its rigors. We're unaware of the passage of time and the formation of an approaching storm in the cloudless sky. Our hands, joined in jubilation before, tighten with fear. It's a world of low, black clouds darkening the earth as during an eclipse, a premature dusk. Neither of us has a watch. It's impossible to tell how much time there is before the gates are closed. The 5:20 train from Recife, if it's on time, could be our reference. But had we been unaware of it perhaps? If we go down on the run we'll need at least five minutes to get to the gate, cross the street, and find shelter. But what can we do if this rain, which promises to be heavy, catches us halfway there? In two minutes I'll have taken a bath, with my summer dress sticking to my body. I won't be able to go through town. Also, if they close the gates we'll be trapped. Frightened, we catch sight of the train, quite far off, its headlight on. Maybe it's late, as so often happens: are the lights of the town turned on against the growing and oppressive darkness? The trees are growing dark, too; the ground has the color of night. We look at the afternoon, we look at each other, and each time we meet the anxious face of the other it's a sight that heightens our nervousness. Does that voice so like my nephew's belong to him? "A lot of smallpox victims died here. They buried them here and not in the cemetery. Among these trees." I exclaim to myself, trying to put his pale face out of my eyes: "It's absurd, it's absurd." I don't want myself to be bewitched by his words or by his fear. In spite of my efforts there's the fear of our being trapped, spending the night here along with the ghosts of the smallpox dead. At the same time I don't dare go downhill on the run: the clouds seem to be closer and closer to the point of opening up, pouring down on us. His mouth is on my breast, sucking slowly, sheltered by the cover of the reservoir, indifferent to the rain that's falling beside us. I sense that I've calmed him, sheltering him with a cloak, with a protection whose existence even I was unaware of. I didn't reflect. Opening my blouse, I unhooked my bra, drew his head toward me with both hands. I can feel myself transmitting to him a kind of nourishment through his mouth, something of my twenty years and, looking into the future, I have the intuition that I'm diving forever into a sacred place. At this precise moment I'm a memory in formation being born in the rain.

A hazy crowd, a heavy-hearted multitude. We'd all known for a week now that the elephant would be leaving today. It had rained all afternoon and so Hahn goes along leaving her deep footprints in the ground. I can't see her because she's way up front. I can hear her frequent cries of contentment, frightening the Raven perched on the Hydra and alerting the Wolf to the Centaur's lance at the ready. The corn and beans dealer luckily didn't want to accompany her on her lamented start of a journey, my parents wouldn't have let me go out on the street all by myself after eight o'clock, so the two of us, Adélia and I, mutual chaperones, go along hand in hand, happy under the hundred and ten eyes of the Virgin, beneath whose influence we act and dream that night. Striving as hard as I can for her affection, I reveal my misfortunes: the wickedness of the others, who destroyed my kite, the chase, the stoning. As for my rage, I hid it.

"Why did you run to a tree?"

"There was nobody on my side. They were all against me. When I hugged the aglaia tree I felt a burning. A fire worm."

"On your hand?"

"I wish it had been! Here, on my face."

"Did they put something on it at home?"

"No. They thought it was funny. It hurt like hell."

Adélia kissed me where the fire worm had burned me. The tramping of the people going along, their unintelligible voices. Children, grownups. We must be a long way from town by now. Even so, we continue on, following the elephant. Even I, who hadn't gone to see her too often, find that I'm sad at her leaving. Why?

"You'll see when you grow up. People don't always find things the way they left them. I wish I'd had a son! Just like you!"

"I wouldn't want to be your son."

"No?"

"You're too pretty. I'd like to be your brother. Nephew. Or cousin. Cousin's best."

I say this and the heavy rain starts falling out of the starry sky. Hahn, coming upon a large puddle of water, sucks it in and sprays mud into the air. Adélia and I, instead of running the way the others do, stand stock still, serious, facing each other. Covered with mud, the only nonmoving people in the midst of the rout. My chest shows through my shirt, the woman's dress clings to her figure, and our inner parts, too, hidden in our bodies. I enter my friend, I enter a market, she's waiting for me, I take her hand and go forward, go forward with her into the market, through her body. Canvas stalls, prostitutes, horses with packsaddles, merchants, oxcarts covered with chintz, crocheted pieces of cloth, colored hammocks, straw mats, clay animals, fruit, vegetables, kites. Adélia leans over, picks up a red Indian and comes over to me, barefoot, naked, the kite swaying a little above her like a canopy, its restless shadow marking her white body. Adélia, her dress soaked, penetrates me and discovers in my eyes, hunched over, weeping, spying, an early ripening man. She smiles with understanding and strokes my wet head.

¶ Either a pole has fallen or the generator has broken down. There are no lights in the town. Small groups keep on coming out of the streets leading to the square. With the circus dismantled, everything had left by train or in the two old trucks. All that remained was Hahn, happy in the moonlight. People leaning out of windows, standing on benches in the square, on the steps of the church, on cornices, on ropes, on rooftops. Hands behind my back, I was in the crowd, my eyes on the trunk raised up to the full moon. We wanted to pay our respects to the elephant for the last time. Bicycle lights coiled around in the dusty air, roping in the crowd. In the shadows I caught sight of Armando's face, his lost look, his ethereal eyes, his right hand in his jacket pocket. He hadn't come to look at Hahn. He wanted to see the square in the moonlight. He liked the moonlight. With the moon he doesn't see the garbage, the dirty walls, the faces of the drunkards. With a little effort he can discover a fiord. Or one of the animals he keeps on inventing in his oil paintings. There was something of an ancient ritual in the crowd as it marched along slowly. Someone was singing the march from *Aida,* already familiar to us. Other voices joined in with that initial voice after a while. Where had I read about the case of the elephant who for a dozen years—yes, a dozen—had traveled all alone across the Bay of Bengal from island to island, covering hundreds of miles? What was it looking for? And how long have I been going about this town, a gulf of consternation, in pursuit of what might not exist? Two young girls in front of me were holding up tree branches. Hungering to give them my arm, I ambled along in their company, singing like the others. How many women besides them might be going along? Might there not be among all of them someone, real and fictitious at the same time, who could dissolve the invisible cloud that was separating me from life? No one? In a hoarse voice I shouted: "Goodbye, Hahn!" I didn't know for certain what profound good, what essential hope I was getting rid of. The girls with the branches turned around, smiling. Ashamed, I ducked into an alley. Once more, aimlessly, howling inside myself, I went out onto the sleeping streets.

‖ Standing on the veranda facing the frail corpse I didn't know—my left hand holding the candle, the right leaning on the wall—which direction to take, what to do. My body from the hips down was bathed in moonlight; with the tips of my toes I was caressing the earth. How had it been possible? Alongside the priest, who was dying, I heard it all: children blowing on horns, the animal's trumpeting, the small circus band playing the music that had been heard so many times, the clamor, then the marching off, singing. I asked Helônia to go to the neighbors, to call somebody. She paid no attention to me: she remained in the chair, facing the closed window. It was I who went knocking on neighbors' doors, trying to get some people to accompany me in the prayers. Nobody seemed to be home, they'd all gone to see the elephant. I think I got all confused after that. I put the candle in our brother's hands all by myself, calling to Helônia in vain. After death had come I shouted for her, hunting for her in the darkness of the house with the funeral candle. The people's singing, quite far off now, was following Hahn's trail; Nassi Latif too, aimless once again, carried along by his madness, his sickness of being unable to stay in one place. A madman. And Helônia, where was she hiding with her great passion? I returned to the bedroom to be with the dead man. Then there was a moan, a creaking, was it some foreboding? I'll never know. I know that I went out and found my sister hanging over her empty slippers by a silk cord, brushing the floor with her ankles. Like those land birds that rise up but can't get to fly. Poor, poor Helônia, so full of hopes, with so much life still to be lived.

↙ "I'm writing you by candlelight, with tears in my eyes. My father's been transferred: we're going to leave town. Well, yesterday on the way back from the reservoir I was thinking about what to do, never to see each other again. Not that I'm ashamed of what happened. It was so nice! But we've got to accept it: I'm a grown woman, you're a child, and our love is impossible. Besides, during these past few days, without saying anything about it to you, I planned to volunteer to go with the circus, work in their skits as an actress. I've read the life of Eleanora Duse. It must be a wonderfully happy feeling to sense in your body, in your face, and in your voice the ability to make people believe you're someone else! Please forgive me for not having spoken to you about this. But I knew: we'd be breaking up fairly soon. With what happened yesterday I think the time has come. So I beg you by everything holy: *Don't try to speak to me.* Let's keep the picture of yesterday intact in our memory, the final scene, both of us in the rain, suspended over the town. Like two angels.

"I'm beginning to hear Hahn's musical passage sung in a chorus and it doesn't upset me. I knew that a lot of people would go with her beyond the edge of town. How could I understand such a gesture since so many of those same people had persecuted us without pity so many times with the same song they're singing light-heartedly at this moment? Can it be because they haven't got any tenderness in their lives? Yes, maybe it was our love that bothered them and they were trying to annoy us (unfortunately we were vulnerable) with their teasing. And if they're all following the elephant *it's because they love her,* for lack of anything better. Isn't it possible that I myself, when I didn't see you, loved her too? But that love, my dear, that love of theirs, is just as foolish as mine for you and yours for me. Let's break up, then, and for good. Goodbye. Things that have no future are quick to fall apart. They have to end quickly.

"I remember when, under the afternoon sky, Hahn looked blue to me, lighted by your eyes. Now she's going away, I'll never see her again. I'm saying goodbye also to our misunderstood love, which had such a short life and made me so happy. In spite of everything it was the most beautiful thing I've known in my life. I'll always love you. Your . . . Hahn."

Θ On the bus—the last one to Recife—I can barely recognize the town bathed in the moonlight. I'm bothered by inquiries I must resolve. The present is not entirely healthy tissue; dead areas continue to exist and affect the living parts. How can they be removed? How many things in myself can I rescue from disintegration? I hear the sound of steps. I imagine that some cattle must be blocking the road. I see the crowd. They're all going along silently, following the elephant. The retinue is like a funeral procession. A small band is following alongside, their instruments lowered. "She's a corpse," I say with rage. "She's going to the cemetery on her own feet. She dies in every town she visits." I can see myself just like everyone else in that crowd, trailing along behind dead things. As if in answer, one of the musicians, in a frock coat and a derby, lifts an oliphant horn to his lips and gives off a prolonged note aimed at the stars. A confused roar—there are hundreds, maybe over a thousand people going along—comes from the crowd. The band begins to play, in a slightly adulterated version, the first phrases of the Triumphal March from *Aida*. The music is repeated as in a contagion. The bus driver tries to accompany it with his horn and the man with the oliphant continues on, indifferent to the melody and the rhythm, blowing like a man possessed. Hahn, with mats on her forehead and her back, seems to be getting excited, taking on inexhaustible meanings in my eyes. I can't take my attention away from that huge, fantastic, moonlit beast until the man with the oliphant comes closer. I remember him as if he—and not I—shouted these commands to me: "Bury the dead. Write, it doesn't matter how or what. About the past, a master that absorbs you today and hinders your life force, a possession won by the blood of your days, making you a servant, no longer a sovereign entity, making you a parasite. Let memories, not evil, be the field over which you will exercise your choice, which will fall back upon your own deaths, on elephants you'll never see again, so as to give everything to the living and in that way give life to what has been devoured by Time. Pass through the world and its joys, look for love, wisely sharpen up the urge to create." Verdi's music, mangled and harsh, grew in volume. Will I be capable of obeying the roars of the oliphant? Hahn is going along more rapidly, flapping her ears. She looks like some winged creature to me, a transparent animal, almost immaterial, taller than all the houses, no longer a corpse, the emblem now of the great and the impossible, of everything that's greater than us and which, even if we go along for a while, we rarely follow forever.

TRANSLATED BY GREGORY RABASSA

Juan José Arreola

Mexico
(b. 1918)

Like Horacio Quiroga, Jorge Luis Borges, and others, Juan José Arreola devoted himself almost exclusively to the short story. He preferred the brief subgenres of the fable, the epigram, the sketch, or an entry in a bestiary, spurning longer texts such as novels (though he did publish one, *La feria,* in 1963). His collection of stories, *Confabulario* (1952), was reissued in several expanded editions and is known in English as *Confabulario and Other Inventions* (1964). Among several other professions, Arreola studied theater and worked as an extra in the Comédie Française from 1945 to 1946. He was a lifelong friend of that other Mexican master of the short story, Juan Rulfo. Arreola's signature is his humor, which ranges from the witty to the cosmic. He is chiefly interested in the absurd and likes to poke fun at the failed promises of modern technology and its monstrous by-products. In this he is a sort of light, humorous, and irreverent Kafka. Like Borges, Arreola cultivates the hybrid subgenre of the essay-story, a blend that pretends to lend authority to quite outlandish propositions. "The Switchman," the selection here, is Arreola's most anthologized story. It is certainly the most representative. Some have seen it as a criticism of the Mexican railroad system, others as an allegory of the whole of Mexican society. It is both, and in addition an allegory of modern technological society, and of the universe in general, whose proper functioning is left in the hands of this very minor employee, a low-ranking god.

The Switchman

The stranger arrived at the deserted station out of breath. His large suitcase, which nobody carried for him, had really tired him out. He mopped his face with a handkerchief, and with his hand shading his eyes, gazed at the tracks that melted away in the distance. Dejected and thoughtful, he consulted his watch: it was the exact time when the train was supposed to leave.

Somebody, come from heaven knows where, gently tapped him. When he turned around, the stranger found himself before a little old man who looked vaguely like a railroader. In his hand he was carrying a red lantern, but so small it seemed a toy. Smiling, he looked at the stranger, who anxiously asked him: "Excuse me, but has the train already left?"

"Haven't you been in this country very long?"

"I have to leave right away. I must be in T—— tomorrow at the latest."

"It's plain you don't know what's going on at all. What you should do right now is go look for lodging at the inn," and he pointed to a strange, ash-colored building that looked more like a jail.

"But I don't want lodging; I want to leave on the train."

"Rent a room immediately if there are any left. In case you can get one, take it by the month. It will be cheaper for you and you will get better attention."

"Are you crazy? I must get to T—— by tomorrow."

"Frankly, I ought to leave you to your fate. But just the same, I'll give you some information."

"Please—"

"This country is famous for its railroads, as you know. Up to now it's been impossible to organize them properly, but great progress has been made in publishing timetables and issuing tickets. Railroad guides include and link all the towns in the country; they sell tickets for even the smallest and most remote villages. Now all that is needed is for the trains to follow what the guides indicate and really pass by the stations. The inhabitants of this country hope this will happen; meanwhile, they accept the service's irregularities and their patriotism keeps them from showing any displeasure."

"But is there a train that goes through this city?"

"To say yes would not be accurate. As you can see, the rails exist, though they are in rather bad shape. In some towns they are simply marked on the ground by two chalk lines. Under the present conditions, no train is obliged to pass through here, but nothing keeps that from happening. I've seen lots of trains go by in my life and I've known some travelers who managed to board them. If you wait until the right moment, perhaps I myself will have the honor of helping you get on a nice comfortable coach."

"Will that train take me to T——?"

"Why do you insist that it has to be T——? You should be satisfied if you get on it. Once on the train, your life will indeed take on some direction. What difference does it make, whether it's T—— or not?"

"But my ticket is all in order to go to T——. Logically, I should be taken there, don't you agree?"

"Most people would say you are right. Over at the inn you can talk to people who have taken precautions, acquiring huge quantities of tickets. As a general rule, people with foresight buy passage to all points of the country. There are some who have spent a real fortune on tickets—"

"I thought that to go to T—— one ticket was enough. Look here—"

"The next stretch of the national railways is going to be built with the money of a single person who has just spent his immense capital on round-trip passages for a railroad track that includes extensive tunnels and bridges that the engineers haven't even approved the plans for."

"But is the train that goes through T—— still in service?"

"Not just that one. Actually, there are a great many trains in the nation, and travelers can use them relatively often, if they take into account that it's not a formal and definitive service. In other words, nobody expects when he gets aboard a train to be taken where he wants to go."

"Why is that?"

"In its eagerness to serve the citizens, the railway management is forced to take desperate measures. They make trains go through impassable places. These expeditionary trains sometimes take several years on a trip and the passengers' lives suffer important transformations. Deaths are not unusual in such cases, but the management, foreseeing everything, hitches on to those trains a car with a funeral chapel and a cemetery coach. The conductors take pride in depositing the traveler's body, luxuriously embalmed, on the station platform prescribed by his ticket. Occasionally these trains are compelled to run on roadbeds where one of the rails is missing. All one side of the coaches shudders lamentably as the wheels hit the railroad ties. The first-class passengers—another instance of the management's foresight—are seated on the side where there is a rail. But there are other stretches where both rails are missing; there all the passengers suffer equally, until the train is completely wrecked."

"Good Lord!"

"Listen, the village of F—— came into being because of one of those accidents. The train found itself in impassable terrain. Smoothed and polished by the sand, the wheels were worn away to their axles. The passengers had spent such a long time together that from the obligatory trivial conversations intimate friendships sprang up. Some of those friendships soon became idylls, and the result is F——, a progressive town filled with mischievous children playing with the rusty vestiges of the train."

"For Heaven's sake, I'm not one for such adventures!"

"You need to pluck up your courage; perhaps you may even become a hero. You must not think there aren't occasions for the passengers to show their courage and capacity for sacrifice. On one occasion two hundred anonymous passengers wrote one of the most glorious pages in our railroad annals. It happened that on a trial journey the engineer noticed in time that the builders of the line had made a grave omission. A bridge that should have spanned an abyss just wasn't there. Well now, the engineer, instead of backing up, gave the passengers a pep talk and got the necessary cooperation from them to continue forward. Under his forceful direction the train was taken apart piece by piece and carried on the passengers' backs to the other side of the abyss, which held a further surprise: a turbulent river at its bottom. The management was so pleased with the results of this action that it definitely renounced the construction of the bridge, only going so far as to make an attractive discount in the fares of those passengers who dared to take on that additional nuisance."

"But I've got to get to T—— tomorrow!"

"All right! I'm glad to see you aren't giving up your project. It's plain that you are a man of conviction. Stay at the inn for the time being and take the first train that comes. At least try to; a thousand people will be there to get in your way. When a train comes in, the travelers, exasperated by an overly long wait, stream tumultuously out of the inn and noisily invade the station. Frequently they cause accidents with their incredible lack of courtesy and prudence. Instead of getting on the train in an orderly fashion, they devote themselves to crushing one another; at least, they keep each other from boarding, and the train goes off leaving them piled up on the station platforms. Exhausted and furious, the travelers curse each other's lack of good breeding and spend a lot of time hitting and insulting each other."

"Don't the police intervene?"

"They tried to organize a police force for each station, but the trains' unpredictable arrivals made such a service useless and very expensive. Besides, the members of the force soon showed their corrupt character, only letting wealthy passengers who gave them everything they had board the trains. Then a special kind of school was established where future travelers receive lessons in etiquette and adequate training so they can spend their lives on the trains. They are taught the correct way to board a train, even though it is moving at great speed. They are also given a kind of armor so the other passengers won't crack their ribs."

"But once on the train, aren't your troubles over?"

"Relatively speaking, yes. But I recommend that you watch the stations very carefully. You might think you had arrived at T——, and it would only be an illusion. In order to regulate life on board the overcrowded coaches, the management has been obliged to take certain expedient measures. There are stations that are for appearance only: they have been built right in the jungle and they bear the name of some important city. But you just need to pay a little attention to see through the deceit. They are like stage sets, and the people on them are stuffed with sawdust. These dummies easily betray the ravages of bad weather, but sometimes they are a perfect image of reality: their faces bear the signs of an infinite weariness."

"Fortunately, T—— isn't very far from here."

"But at the moment we don't have any through trains. Nevertheless, it could well happen that you might arrive at T—— tomorrow, just as you wish. The management of the railroads, although not very efficient, doesn't exclude the possibility of a nonstop journey. You know, there are people who haven't even realized what is going on. They buy a ticket for T——. A train comes, they get on it, and the next day they hear the conductor announce: 'We're at T——.' Without making sure, the passengers get off and find themselves indeed in T——.''

"Could I do something to bring about that result?''

"Of course you could. But it's hard to tell if it will do any good. Try it anyway. Get on the train with the firm idea that you are going to reach T——. Don't talk with any of the passengers. They might disillusion you with their travel tales and they might even denounce you.''

"What are you saying?''

"Because of the present state of things the trains are full of spies. These spies, mostly volunteers, dedicate their lives to encouraging the company's constructive spirit. Sometimes one doesn't know what one is saying and talks just to be talking. But they immediately see all the meanings in a phrase, however simple it may be. They can twist the most innocent comment around to make it look guilty. If you were to commit the slightest imprudence you would be apprehended without further ado; you would spend the rest of your life in a prison car, if they didn't make you get off at a false station, lost out in the jungle. While you travel, have faith, consume the smallest possible amount of food, and don't step off onto the platform until you see some familiar face at T——.''

"But I don't know anybody in T——.''

"In that case, take double precautions. There will be many temptations on the way, I assure you. If you look out the windows, you may fall into the trap of a mirage. The train windows are provided with ingenious devices that create all kinds of illusions in the passengers' minds. You don't have to be weak to fall for them. Certain apparatuses, operated from the engine, make you believe that the train is moving because of the noise and the movements. Nevertheless, the train stands still for whole weeks at a time while the passengers looking through the window panes see captivating landscapes pass by.''

"What object is there in that?''

"The management does all this with the wholesome purpose of reducing the passengers' anxiety and, as far as possible, the sensations of moving. The hope is that one day the passengers will capitulate to fate, give themselves into the hands of an omnipotent management, and no longer care to know where they are going or where they have come from.''

"And you, have you traveled a lot on trains?''

"Sir, I'm just a switchman. To tell the truth, I'm a retired switchman, and I just come here now and then to remember the good old days. I've never traveled and I have no desire to. But the travelers tell me stories. I know that the trains have created many towns bedsides F——, whose origin I told you about. Sometimes the crew on a train receives mysterious orders. They invite the passengers to get off, usually on the pretext that they should admire the beauties of a certain place. They are told about grottos, falls, or famous ruins: 'Fifteen minutes to admire such and such a grotto,' the conductor amiably calls out. Once the passengers are a certain distance away, the train chugs away at full speed."

"What about the passengers?"

"They wander about disconcertedly from one spot to another for a while, but they end up by getting together and establishing a colony. These untimely stops occur in places far from civilization but with adequate resources and sufficient natural riches. Selected lots of young people, and especially an abundant number of women, are abandoned there. Wouldn't you like to end your days in a picturesque unknown spot in the company of a young girl?"

The little old fellow winked, and smiling kindly, continued to gaze roguishly at the traveler. At that moment a faint whistle was heard. The switchman jumped, all upset, and began to make ridiculous, wild signals with his lantern.

"Is it the train?" asked the stranger.

The old man recklessly broke into a run along the track. When he had gone a certain distance he turned around to shout, "You are lucky! Tomorrow you will arrive at your famous station. What did you say its name was?"

"X——!" answered the traveler.

At that moment the little old man dissolved in the clear morning. But the red speck of his lantern kept on running and leaping imprudently between the rails to meet the train.

In the distant landscape the train was noisily approaching.

TRANSLATED BY GEORGE D. SCHADE

Julio Ramón Ribeyro

Peru
(1929–1995)

Best known in his native Peru, where he was considered one of that country's major writers, Julio Ramón Ribeyro was the author of some eight volumes of short stories. In fact, although he did publish novels, Ribeyro considered himself essentially a short story writer. Ribeyro began his writing career in the early fifties, just at the time that he moved to Europe, where he remained for most of his life, with brief visits to Peru. His tales are an unusual combination of social commentary and fantasy, with a bleak outlook on Peruvian life. His landscapes are mostly urban. His is a Lima crowded by poor masses moving down to the coast from the Andes. The squalor he depicts sometimes has an anachronistic quality reminiscent of naturalism—Ribeyro purposely eschewed literary fashions and experiments. His view of the middle class is bitingly satirical. Dick Gerdes has written that "Collectively, Ribeyro's stories create a distinctive tone of melancholic pessimism that captures in ironic fashion the banality, the absurdity, and anguish of a middle-to-lower-class bourgeoisie that has no place in Peruvian society; it is a class without any history, traditions, future, or identity." And Alfredo Bryce Echenique, another distinguished Peruvian short story writer, says about one of Ribeyro's marginalized characters that, "faced with the alternative of integration, Ribeyro proposes here another, disintegration." Ribeyro seems to be the heir of César Vallejo, the great Peruvian poet of social and existential deterioration and despair. The separation of exile, however, gave Ribeyro a distance that he turned into a strange kind of aesthetic detachment, because it did not exclude compassion. "The Featherless Buzzards," written in Paris in 1954, is Ribeyro's best-known story, a flawless fable in which misery acquires a bizarre poetic aura.

The Featherless Buzzards

At six in the morning the city gets up on tiptoe and slowly begins to stir. A fine mist dissolves the contour of objects and creates an atmosphere of enchantment. People walking about the city at this hour seem to be made of another substance, to belong to a ghostly order of life. Devout women humbly shuffle along, finally disappearing in the doorways of churches. The night-wanderers, drubbed by the darkness, return home wrapped up in mufflers and melancholy. Garbage collectors begin their sinister stroll down Pardo Avenue, armed with brooms and carts. There are workers heading for the streetcars, policemen yawning next to trees, newspaper boys turning purple from the cold, and maids putting out trash cans. Finally, at this hour, as if responding to some mysterious password, the featherless buzzards appear.

At this hour old Don Santos fastens on his wooden leg, sits down on the mattress, and starts to bellow, "Efraín, Enrique! Get up! Now!"

The two boys run to the ditch inside the corral,* rubbing their bleary eyes. The calm night has settled the water, making it transparent to reveal growing weeds and agile infusories sliding about. After washing their faces, each boy grabs his can and scurries toward the street. Meanwhile, Don Santos goes to the pigpen and whacks the pig on the back with his long stick as the animal wallows in filth.

"You still have a way to go, you dirty rascal! Just you wait; your time's coming."

Efraín and Enrique are lingering in the street, climbing trees to snatch berries or picking up stones, the tapered kind that cut through the air and sting the back. Still enjoying the celestial hour, they reach their domain, a long street lined with elegant houses leading to the levee.

They aren't alone. In other corrals and in other suburbs someone has given a sound of alarm and many have gotten up. Some carry tin cans, others cardboard boxes, and sometimes just an old newspaper is enough. Unaware of each other, together they form a kind of clandestine organization that works the city. There are those who maraud through public buildings, others choose the parks or the dunghills. Even the dogs have acquired certain habits and schedules, wisely coached by poverty.

After Efraín and Enrique take a short rest, they begin their work. Each one chooses a side of the street. Garbage cans are lined up in front of the doors. They have to be completely emptied before the exploration begins. A garbage can is always like a box full of surprises. There are sardine cans, old shoes, pieces of bread, dead parakeets, and soiled cotton balls. The boys, however, are only interested in scraps of food. Although Pascual will eat anything thrown to him in his pen, his favorite food is partially decomposed vegetables. Each goes along filling up his small can with rotten tomatos, pieces of fat, exotic salsas that never show up in cookbooks. It's not unusual, however, to make a real find. One day Efraín found some suspenders that he made into a slingshot. Another time he discovered an almost eatable pear that he devoured on the spot. Enrique, on the other hand, has a knack for finding small medicine boxes, brightly colored bottles, used toothbrushes, and similar things that he eagerly collects.

Corral here refers to an enclosed, dirt yard surrounding the one-room shack in the urban slums of Peru, where Efraín, Enrique, and their grandfather live.

When they have rigorously sorted through everything, they dump the garbage back in the can and head for the next one. It doesn't pay to take too long because the enemy is always lying in wait. Sometimes the maids catch them off guard and they have to flee, scattering their spoils behind them. But more often than not the sanitation department cart sneaks up on them and then the whole workday is lost.

When the sun peeks over the hills, the celestial hour comes to an end. The mist lifts, the devout women are immersed in ecstasy, the night nomads are asleep, the paper boys have delivered their papers, and the workers have mounted the platforms. Sunlight fades the magical world of dawn. The featherless buzzards have returned to their nest.

Don Santos had made coffee and was waiting for them.

"Let's have it. What did you bring me today?"

He would sniff among the cans and if the grub was good he always made the same remark: "Pascual's going to have a feast today."

But most of the time he blurted out, "You idiots! What did you do today? You must have just played around! Pascual's going to starve to death!"

The boys would run for the grape arbor, their ears still burning from the slaps, while the old man dragged himself over to the pigpen. From the far end of his fort the pig would start to grunt while Don Santos tossed him scraps of food.

"My poor Pascual! You'll stay hungry today because of those loafers. They don't spoil you like I do. I'll have to give them a good beating and teach them a lesson."

At the beginning of winter the pig had turned into an insatiable monster. He couldn't get enough to eat and Don Santos took out the animal's hunger on his grandsons. He made them get up earlier to search unfamiliar areas for more scraps. Finally he forced them to go as far as the garbage dump along the ocean's edge.

"You'll find more stuff there. It'll be easier, too, because everything will be together."

One Sunday Efraín and Enrique reached the edge. The sanitation department carts were following tracks on a dirt road, unloading trash on a rocky slope. Viewed from the levee, the dump formed a dark, smoky bluff of sorts where buzzards and dogs gathered like ants. From a distance the boys threw stones to scare off their competition. A dog backed off yelping. When the boys reached the dump, they were overcome by a nauseating smell that seeped into their lungs. Their feet sank into a pile of feathers, excrement, and decayed or charred matter. Burying their hands in it, they began their search. Sometimes they would discover a half-eaten carrion under a yellowed newspaper. On the nearby bluffs the buzzards impatiently spied on them; some approached, jumping from one rock to another as though they were trying to corner the boys. Efraín tried to intimidate them by shouting; and his cries echoed in the gorge, shaking loose some large pebbles that rolled toward the sea. After working for an hour they returned to the corral with their cans filled.

"Bravo!" Don Santos exclaimed. "We'll have to do this two or three times a week."

From then on, Efraín and Enrique made their trek to the sea on Wednesdays and Sundays. Soon they became part of the strange fauna of those places and the buzzards, accustomed to their presence, worked at their side, cawing, flapping their wings, scraping with their yellow beaks as if helping them to uncover the layer of precious filth.

One day when Efraín came back from one of his excursions, he felt a sore on the bottom of his foot. A piece of glass had made a small wound. The next day his foot was swollen, but he continued his work. By the time they returned he could hardly walk, but Don Santos was with a visitor and didn't notice him. He was observing the pigpen, accompanied by a fat man with blood-stained hands.

"In twenty or thirty days I'll come back," the man said. "By then I think he'll be just about ready."

When he left, sparks shot from Don Santos' eyes.

"Get to work! Get to work! From now on we've got to see that Pascual gets more to eat! We're going to pull this deal off."

The next morning, however, when Don Santos woke his grandsons, Efraín couldn't get up.

"His foot's sore," Enrique explained. "He cut himself on a piece of glass yesterday."

Don Santos examined his grandson's foot. Infection had set in.

"Nonsense! Have him wash his foot in the ditch and wrap a rag around it."

"But it's really hurting him!" Enrique added. "He can't walk right."

Don Santos thought a moment. Pascual could be heard still grunting in his pen.

"And what about me?" he asked, slapping his wooden leg. "You think my leg doesn't hurt? I'm seventy years old and I work . . . so just stop your whining!"

Efraín left for the street with his can, leaning on his brother's shoulder. Half an hour later they returned with their cans almost empty.

"He couldn't go on!" Enrique told his grandpa. "Efraín's half-crippled."

Don Santos looked at his grandsons as if he were passing sentence on them.

"Okay, okay," he said, scratching his thin beard, and grabbing Efraín by the scruff of the neck, he pushed him toward the one-room shack. "The sick go to bed! Lay there and rot! Enrique, you'll do your brother's work. Get out of here! Go to the dump!"

Around noon Enrique came back with both cans filled. A strange visitor was following him: a squalid, mangy dog. "I found him at the dump," Enrique explained, "and he kept following me."

Don Santos picked up the stick. "One more mouth to feed!"

Enrique grabbed the dog and, clutching him close to his chest, ran toward the door. "Don't you hurt him, Grandpa! I'll give him some of my food."

Don Santos walked toward him, his wooden leg sinking into the mud. "No dogs here! I already have enough trouble with you boys!"

Enrique opened the door leading to the street. "If he goes, I go, too."

The grandfather paused. Enrique took advantage of the moment and persisted: "He hardly eats anything; look how skinny he is. Besides, since Efraín's sick, he'll be a help to me. He knows the dump real well and he's got a good nose for scraps."

Don Santos looked up at the dreary sky, gray with drizzle, and thought a moment. Without a word he threw down the stick, picked up the cans, and limped off toward the pigsty.

Enrique smiled with delight and clasping his friend to his heart, he ran to see his brother.

"Pascual, Pascual . . . Pascualito!" the grandfather was chanting.

"We'll name you Pedro," Enrique said, petting the dog's head as he went in the room where Efraín was lying.

His joy suddenly vanished when he saw Efraín writhing in pain on the mattress and drenched in sweat. His swollen foot looked as though it was made of rubber and pumped with air. His toes had almost lost their shape.

"I brought you this present, look," he said, showing him the dog. "His name's Pedro; he's yours, to keep you company. When I go to the dump I'll leave him with you and you can play all day long. You can probably teach him to fetch rocks for you."

"What about Grandpa?" Efraín asked, stretching his hand toward the dog.

"Grandpa has nothing to say about it," Enrique sighed.

They both looked toward the door. The drizzle had begun to fall and they could hear their grandfather's voice calling, "Pascual, Pascual . . . Pascualito!"

That same night there was a full moon. The boys felt uneasy because that was when their grandfather became unbearable. Since late afternoon they had seen him roaming about the corral, talking to himself, swinging away at the grape arbor with his stick. Now and then he would come near the room, scan the interior, and seeing that his grandsons were silent, he would spit on the floor with rage. Pedro was scared of him and every time he saw him he would huddle up and not move a muscle.

"Trash, nothing but trash!" the old man kept repeating all night long as he looked at the moon.

The next morning Enrique woke up with chills. Although the old man had heard him sneeze earlier that morning, he said nothing. Deep down, however, he could sense disaster. If Enrique was sick, what would become of Pascual? The pig's appetite grew more voracious as he got fatter. In the afternoons he would bury his snout in mud and grunt. Nemesio had even come over form his corral a block away to complain.

On the second day the inevitable happened: Enrique couldn't get up. He had coughed throughout the night and by morning he was shivering, burning with fever.

"You, too?" the grandfather asked.

Enrique pointed to his congested, croupy chest. The grandfather stormed out of the room. Five minutes later he returned.

"It's mean to trick me this way!" he whined. "You abuse me because I can't walk. You know damn well that I'm old and crippled. If I could I'd send you both to hell and I'd see to Pascual myself!"

Efraín woke up whimpering and Enrique began to cough.

"The hell with it! I'll take care of him myself. You're trash, nothing but trash! A couple of pitiful buzzards without feathers! You'll see how I get along. Your grandpa's still tough. But one thing's for sure, no food for you today. You won't get any till you can get up and do your work!"

Through the doorway they saw him unsteadily lift the cans in the air and stumble out to the street. Half an hour later he came back licked. He wasn't as quick as his grandsons and the sanitation department cart had gotten there first. Not only that, the dogs had tried to bite him.

"Filthy trash! I warn you, no food till you work!"

The following day he tried to repeat the whole process, but finally had to give up. His leg with the wooden peg was no longer used to the asphalt pavement and the hard sidewalks; a sharp pain stabbed him in the groin every time he took a step. At the celestial hour on the third day, he collapsed on the mattress with only enough energy to cuss.

"If he starves to death," he shouted, "it'll be your fault!"

That was the beginning of several agonizing, interminable days. The three spent the day cooped up in the room together, silently suffering a kind of forced seclusion. Efraín constantly tossed and turned, Enrique coughed, Pedro got up and after taking a run out in the corral, returned with a rock in his mouth which he deposited in his master's hand. Don Santos, propped up on the mattress, was playing with his wooden leg and hurling ferocious looks at the boys. At noon he dragged himself to the corner of the lot where some vegetables were growing and prepared himself some lunch that he devoured in secret. Occasionally he would toss a piece of lettuce or a raw carrot at his grandsons' bed with the intention of whetting their appetite, and thereby giving his punishment a touch of refinement.

Efraín didn't even have the strength to complain. Enrique was the one who felt invaded by a strange sense of fear because when he looked into his grandfather's eyes, they didn't look familiar. It was as though they had lost their human expression. Every night when the moon came up, he would hold Pedro in his arms and squeeze him so affectionately that he made him whimper. That's when the pig would begin to grunt and the old man wailed as if he were being hanged. Sometimes he would fasten on his wooden leg and go out to the corral. In the moonlight Enrique saw him make ten trips back and forth from the pigpen to the garden, raising his fists and knocking over anything that got in his way. Finally he would come back to the room and glare at them, as if he wanted to blame them for Pascual's hunger.

The last night of the full moon no one could sleep. Pascual's grunts were intolerable. Enrique had heard when pigs are hungry they go crazy like people. The grandfather remained vigilant and didn't even put out the lantern. This time he didn't go out to the corral, nor did he cuss under his breath. Sunk down in his mattress, he stared at the door. A deep-seated anger seemed to be welling up in him and he appeared to be toying with it, making ready to unleash it all at once. When the sky began to lighten over the hills, he opened his mouth, and keeping that dark hole turned toward his grandsons he suddenly bellowed, "Up, up, up!" as he pelted them with blows. "Get up you lazy bums! How long is this going to go on? No more. On your feet!"

Efraín broke into tears. Enrique got up, flattening himself against the wall. He was so mesmerized by the old man's eyes that he felt numb to the pain. He saw the stick come down on his head and for a moment it seemed as though it were made of cardboard instead of wood. Finally he was able to speak. "Not Efraín! It's not his fault! Let me go, I'll go, I'll go to the dump!"

The grandfather stepped back, panting. It took him awhile to catch his breath.

"Right now . . . to the dump . . . take two cans, four cans . . ."

Enrique stepped back, picked up the cans and took off running.

The fatigue from hunger and convalescence made him stumble. When he opened the corral door, Pedro tried to go with him.

"You can't come. Stay here and take care of Efraín."

He took off toward the street, deeply breathing the morning air. On the way he ate some grass and was on the verge of chewing dirt. He was seeing everything through a magical mist. His weakened condition made him light-headed and giddy: he was almost like a bird in flight. At the dump he felt like one more buzzard among many. As soon as the cans were overflowing he started back. The devout, the night-wanderers, the barefoot paper boys, and all the other secretions of early dawn began to scatter over the city. Enrique, once again in his world, contentedly walked among them in his world of dogs and ghosts, bewitched by the celestial hour.

As he came into the corral he felt an overpowering, oppressive air that made him stop in his tracks. It was as if there in the doorway his world ended and another made of mud, grunts, and absurd penitence began. It was surprising, therefore, that this time a calm filled with a sense of doom pervaded the corral, as if all the pent-up violence lay in wait, poised and ready to strike. The grandfather was standing alongside the pigpen, gazing at the far end. He looked like a tree growing out of his wooden leg. Enrique made a noise but the old man didn't move.

"Here are the cans!"

Don Santos turned his back on him and stood still. Enrique, full of curiosity, let go of the cans and ran toward the room. As soon as Efraín saw him, he began to whimper, "Pedro . . . Pedro."

"What's the matter?"

"Pedro bit Grandpa . . . and he grabbed the stick . . . then I heard him yelp."

Enrique left the room. "Pedro, here boy! Pedro, where are you?"

There was no response. The grandfather still didn't move and kept looking at the mud wall. Enrique had a sick feeling. He leaped toward the old man. "Where's Pedro?"

His gaze fell on the pigpen. Pascual was devouring something in the mud. Only the dog's legs and tail were left.

"No!" Enrique shouted, covering his eyes. "No, no!" Through his teary eyes he searched his grandfather's face. The old man avoided him, clumsily turning on his wooden leg. Enrique began to dance around him, pulling at his shirt, screaming, kicking, searching his face for an answer. "Why did you do it? Why?"

The grandfather didn't answer. Finally, his patience snapped and he slapped the boy so hard that he knocked him off his feet. From the ground Enrique observed the old man standing erect like a giant, his eyes fixed on Pascual's feast. Enrique reached for the blood-stained stick, quietly got up and closed in on the old man. "Turn around!" he shouted. "Turn around!"

When Don Santos turned, he saw the stick cutting the air above him, then felt the blow to his cheek.

"Take that!" Enrique screamed in a shrill voice, again raising his hand. Suddenly he stopped, horrified by what he was doing, threw down the stick, and gave the grandfather an almost apologetic look. The old man, holding his face, stepped back on his wooden leg, slipped, and with a loud cry he fell backward into the pigpen.

Enrique took a few steps back. At first he listened closely, but didn't hear a sound. Little by little he again drew near. His grandfather was lying on his back in the muck with his wooden peg broken. His mouth was gaping open and his eyes were searching for Pascual, who had taken refuge in a corner of the pen and was suspiciously sniffing the mud.

Enrique started backing away as stealthily as he had come. His grand-father barely saw him because as Enrique ran toward the room he thought he heard him calling his name with a tone of tenderness in his voice that he had never heard before. "Come back, Enrique, come back! . . ."

"Hurry!" Enrique cried, running up to his brother. "Come on, Efraín! The old man has fallen into the pigpen. Let's get out of here!"

"Where?" Efraín asked.

"Wherever, to the dump, anywhere we can get something to eat, where the buzzards go!"

"I can't stand up!"

Enrique picked up his brother with both hands and pressed him against his chest. They clung to each other so tightly, it almost seemed as if one person was slowly making his way across the corral. When they opened the gate to the street, they realized that the celestial hour had ended and that the city, awake and vigilant, was opening before them its gigantic jaws.

Sounds of a struggle were coming from the pigpen.

TRANSLATED BY DIANNE DOUGLAS

Virgilio Piñera

Cuba

(1912–1979)

———— // ————

Virgilio Piñera, an almost clandestine classic, was admired by a coterie of friends who protected him as best they could from his own self-destructiveness and the envy of both lesser writers and bureaucrats. His life, about which anecdotes abound, as a bohemian homosexual in Cuba's macho society was one of his most outrageous creations, and he was conscious of it. He was better known for his avant-garde theater, such as his play *Electra Garrigó*, than for his poetry or even his short stories, although he was a recognized master of the latter. His two best-known collections are *Cuentos fríos* (1956) and *Pequeñas maniobras* (1963). Piñera was associated with the journal *Orígenes*, headed by José Lezama Lima, but he was too irreverent to fit in with the group that surrounded the great poet. In the 1950s he spent time in Buenos Aires, where he came to know Borges, and his work was published in *Sur*. This sojourn in the River Plate area and his contacts with Borges and others there, including the exiled Polish writer Witold Gombrowicz, left an imprint on his work. Returning to Cuba after the Revolution, Piñera was arrested in 1961 for "political and moral crimes." After his release he continued to live as a marginal figure with few defenders among those in power, although he did win the Casa de las Américas Award in 1969 for his play *Dos viejos pánicos*. Piñera's stories combine the fantastic with the grotesque, and there are touches of a Kafkaesque paranoia. The world seems to cave in on his protagonists, who resort to drastic measures, such as the protagonist of "Meat," who proceeds literally to eat himself. Piñera was bored by the commonplace and he reveled in the perverse obsessions of his characters. In "Meat" the protagonist's actions assume a metaphysical dimension.

Meat

It happened simply, without pretense. For reasons that need not be explained, the town was suffering from a meat shortage. Everyone was alarmed, and rather bitter comments were heard; revenge was even spoken of. But, as always, the protests did not develop beyond threats, and soon the afflicted townspeople were devouring the most diverse vegetables.

Only Mr. Ansaldo didn't follow the order of the day. With great tran-

327

quility, he began to sharpen an enormous kitchen knife and then, dropping his pants to his knees, he cut a beautiful fillet from his left buttock. Having cleaned and dressed the fillet with salt and vinegar, he passed it through the broiler and finally fried it in the big pan he used on Sundays for making tortillas. He sat at the table and began to savor his beautiful fillet. Just then, there was a knock at the door: it was Ansaldo's neighbor coming to vent his frustrations. . . . Ansaldo, with an elegant gesture, showed his neighbor the beautiful fillet. When his neighbor asked about it, Ansaldo simply displayed his left buttock. The facts were laid bare. The neighbor, overwhelmed and moved, left without saying a word to return shortly with the mayor of the town. The latter expressed to Ansaldo his intense desire that his beloved townspeople be nourished—as was Ansaldo—by drawing on their private reserves, that is to say, each from his own meat. The issue was soon resolved, and after outbursts from the well educated, Ansaldo went to the main square of the town to offer—as he characteristically phrased it—"a practical demonstration for the masses."

Once there, he explained that each person could cut two fillets, from his left buttock, just like the flesh-colored plaster model he had hanging from a shining meathook. He showed how to cut two fillets not one, for if he had cut one beautiful fillet from his own left buttock, it was only right that no one should consume one fillet fewer. Once these points were cleared up, each person began to slice two fillets from his left buttock. It was a glorious spectacle, but it is requested that descriptions not be given out. Calculations were made concerning how long the town would enjoy the benefits of this meat. One distinguished physician predicted that a person weighing one hundred pounds (discounting viscera and the rest of the inedible organs) could eat meat for one hundred and forty days at the rate of half a pound a day. This calculation was, of course, deceptive. And what mattered was that each person could eat his beautiful fillet. Soon women were heard speaking of the advantages of Mr. Ansaldo's idea. For example, those who had devoured their breasts didn't need to cover their torsos with cloth, and their dresses reached just above the navel. Some women—though not all of them—no longer spoke at all, for they had gobbled up their tongues (which, by the way, is the delicacy of monarchs). In the streets, the most amusing scenes occurred: two women who had not seen each other for a long time were unable to kiss each other: they had both used their lips to cook up some very successful fritters. The prison warden could not sign a convict's death sentence because he had eaten the fleshy tips of his fingers, which, according to the best "gourmets" (of which the warden was one), gave rise to the well-worn phrase "finger-licking good."

There was some minor resistance. The ladies garment workers union registered their most formal protest with the appropriate authority, who responded by saying that it wasn't possible to create a slogan that might encourage women to patronize their tailors again. But the resistance was never significant, and did not in any way interrupt the townspeople's consumption of their own meat.

One of the most colorful events of that pleasant episode was the dissection of the town ballet dancer's last morsel of flesh. Out of respect for his art, he had left his beautiful toes for last. His neighbors observed that he had been extremely restless for days. There now remained only the fleshy tip of one big toe. At that point he invited his friends to attend the operation. In the middle of a bloody silence, he cut off the last portion, and, without even warming it up, dropped it into the hole that had once been his beautiful mouth. Everyone present suddenly became very serious.

But life went on, and that was the important thing. And if, by chance . . . ? Was it because of this that the dancer's shoes could now be found in one of the rooms of the Museum of Illustrious Memorabilia? It's only certain that one of the most obese men in town (weighing over four hundred pounds) used up his whole reserve of disposable meat in the brief space of fifteen days (he was extremely fond of snacks and sweetmeats, and besides, his metabolism required large quantities). After a while, no one could ever find him. Evidently, he was hiding. . . . But he was not the only one to hide; in fact, many others began to adopt identical behavior. And so, one morning Mrs. Orfila got no answer when she asked her son (who was in the process of devouring his left earlobe) where he had put something. Neither pleas nor threats did any good. The expert in missing persons was called in, but he couldn't produce anything more than a small pile of excrement on the spot where Mrs. Orfila swore her beloved son had just been sitting at the moment she was questioning him. But these little disturbances did not undermine the happiness of the inhabitants in the least. For how could a town that was assured of its subsistence complain? Hadn't the crisis of public order caused by the meat shortage been definitively resolved? That the population was increasingly dropping out of sight was but a postscript to the fundamental issue and did not affect the people's determination to obtain their vital sustenance. Was that postscript the price that the flesh exacted from each? But it would be petty to ask any more such inopportune questions, now that this thoughtful community was perfectly well fed.

TRANSLATED BY MARK SCHAFER AND REVISED BY THOMAS CHRISTENSEN

Augusto Roa Bastos

Paraguay
(b. 1917)

Augusto Roa Bastos is a poet, essayist, short story writer, novelist, and author of children's books. Like several writers of the Southern Cone (Argentina, Uruguay, Paraguay), Roa Bastos spent many years in Buenos Aires, beginning in 1947. Later he moved to France to flee the military dictatorship of Alfredo Stroessner. Like Miguel Angel Asturias in Guatemala and José María Arguedas in Peru, Roa Bastos is passionately invested in the plight of his country's native peoples, the Guaraní, many of whom do not even speak Spanish. As with most of the major writers of Latin America, this concern makes Roa Bastos view the historical break of the Spanish Conquest as a continuing event, still pitting a relentless Western modernity against people innocent of its foundational and everyday beliefs, practices, and habits. It gives Roa Bastos's work an apocalyptic quality in matters of language and storytelling that endows it with astonishing freshness and power. Roa Bastos, who was awarded the Miguel de Cervantes Prize in 1990, is a modern master in his own right. He is the author of many collections of stories and novels, most famously *Son of Man* (1960) and *I the Supreme* (1974). The last is about José Gaspar Rodríguez de Francia's dictatorship (1814–40) following Paraguayan independence. It is, among other things, an exploration of the origins of Stroessner's rule, but also a very modern consideration of the interrelatedness of language, writing, and power. Roa Bastos has returned to the topic in *El Fiscal* (1993), and to the Discovery and Conquest in *Vigilias del Almirante* (1992), whose protagonist is Christopher Columbus. "Unborn" (from *Moriencia*, 1969), the story presented here, braids the voices of the mother and the child she carries to plumb memories that span the whole of life and death, as if they were uttered before the beginning of time, or after its end.

Unborn

When you tell me that I can't remember that far back, nobody in his right mind can, and that I'm old enough now not to go around wasting my time in childish prating, I shut up. Only on the outside. Without anyone to talk to about such things, since you don't want to listen to me either, I go on talking to myself, on the inside. I may waste my words; why should I waste my silence? I hug the wall, press my mouth against the plaster, and feel the words moving on my breath with a taste of whitewash, of little blond cockroaches. I chew them a little and let them come limping up. They climb out and get caught in the spider webs on the ceiling.

And you say: Don't go on mumbling like that, don't keep harping on the same subject. You're going to ruin your life with that empty head of yours. Just the way your father did with his guitar. But he at least was a man in every sense of the word. And the only thing you know how to do is whisper claptrap, or pound all day long on that damned drum so as to drive a person out of her mind. Once and for all: start making something useful of yourself, because you weren't born to be a drummer, much less a singer; heaven only knows what you were born to be.

I hold my tongue, just so as not to annoy you. So as not to see your eyes take on more of the wolfish color of sadness. A color like that of those weary plants along the roadsides, with dank little leaves, covered with dust, with pellagra. And the whole of you like those plants, underneath your faded mourning dress.

I hold my tongue so as not to bother you, looking at the litany that beats against your lips and that makes me sad too because I know very well that it comes from a suffering that's a little bit dried up by now and as drained of color as your clothes, as your voice. Above all when you remember Papa. Then you don't say a word, overcome by the silence that's stored up inside you, and I take advantage of it to talk to you again, emboldened by the way you're looking at me; my confidence bolstered by those looks in which I feel myself suddenly growing and maturing till I'm the same size and have the same look about me as Papa, whom I see reflected, as clearly as can be, in your eyes. With my thought I try to make my throat swell out as far as it will go, so that even my voice comes out sounding like an imitation of his. I hasten to speak of those memories from before I was born; there aren't many of them, but I strain to make them last, so that you won't get mad again right away as you did before; so that I'll go on being praiseworthy in your eyes. I strain to bring those memories closer to you so that you too can see them the way I see them, like big, broody birds sitting on the other, smaller memories of what came later to hatch them. When I'm left alone with them, seeing them stirring in the darkness, a profound feeling of helplessness comes over me; not fear, you understand; just great loneliness, too much. I take the bottle full of little fireflies out from underneath the cot. That's worse, because then I also see the darkness opening up with greenish edges around the glass. The memories crawl about as though they were hungry and begin to eat the little bugs till the bottle is empty; and now I can't get to sleep as I wait for them to peck at me and devour me too.

When you go to town with the donkey to sell your little jars of milk and your cheeses, I lie down in the yard, face up, looking at the sun till

I'm struck totally blind; but I also see the soldiers come; I see them argue with you under the acacia tree, and I'm huddled up there inside you, not knowing where to go.

But if you listen to me, it's different; I curl up in the happy feeling it gives me, however sad those memories may be, and there's no denying they're sad ones. Seeing as how I don't have anybody to talk to about those things, that is; the kids my age have soon learned to make fun of me, to gang up on me and put me in a daze with their shrieking at me in their wild parrot voices. It's Unborn here, Unborn there; the biggest ones evil because of an evil nature I don't understand since it seems unnatural, borrowed. The thick brush rains stones and rotten oranges down on me when I head for the hills to hunt pigeons, without being able to get there. And you yourself have given me beatings because I've come back bare naked with hen feathers stuck in the burn marks from the rubbery milk of the curupicay tree. Nowadays I don't dare go past the boundary line of the sewer, ever since the time I came back with the feathers of my backside all bloodied. The farthest I ever go is to the bridge to hear the train roar past, with my head under the water, breathing through a little reed, holding on tight to the piling, so as to hear the shuddering sound in my teeth. Or else I hide myself away in the cave in the ravine with my drum. The only one who listens to me is Usebio, as he scrapes mold off the stones with his fingernails and eats it. But he's a deaf mute and I don't know if he understands me when he listens to me with his gummy eyes, his trembling head saying no all the time, even to a falling leaf.

But to me these things don't matter. What does matter are those memories from before being born, so downright stubborn they never escape my memory, even at times when I'm not paying attention. Now that what are memories to you aren't memories to me; what to you has happened once, to me happens over and over again, the same way each time, continually.

Every morning soldiers enter the house looking for Papa, who is hiding out in the hills. They shout at the top of their lungs as they turn the house upside down with their rifle butts, smashing the standing wardrobes and even the tiniest drawers where only a mouse could be hiding. But at that moment an insult rings out from the yard, and immediately thereafter the sound of a pugnacious polka being sung; Papa's own voice, but falsetto, as though anger and rage had thrust a rubber tube down his gullet. The voice comes from overhead, as if Papa were straddling a fork in a tree. The soldiers aim their rifles and are about to shoot at the voice that is now roaring with laughter amid the branches. You go and say to them fearfully, abashedly, as though you were revealing a secret: It's only Panchito. For the love of heaven don't do anything to the poor man.

They get him down, hitting him with the flat of their swords; they kick and drag him to the middle of the yard, and there the volley of rifle fire from the platoon raises a cloud of green feathers, spattered with red: the bits of the parrot's death that you and I see falling very slowly, as though held aloft by the dense gunsmoke and the gently cradled fire of the sun's glare.

But now the soldiers move closer to you, dragging their heavy boots with fierce slowness; they grab you by the arms; they are about to knock you to the ground; they lift up your clothes and rip them off you. You scream, writhe and scream; you bite, kick, and scream; you won't stop screaming even after you're dead. Each time you retch, it squeezes me tightly all over, it shrinks me to my very smallest, to the last limit of my nothingness, that I never should have come out of. The galloping of a horse is heard; it may be Papa's horse; more people keep coming; a sound of horseshoes, of firearms, of hoarse voices; nothing can be seen in the darkness of the sun. Papa is hiding out in the hills; he'll never come back.

You don't like to hear these things mentioned and you order me to shut up, telling me to stop talking nonsense. You keep endlessly repeating that my empty head is going to ruin my life with foolish babblings of an idiot, of a little one weaned too soon out of necessity. From the height of your smallness, of your thinness, you shout to me: Make a man of yourself once and for all, because I too may not be around anymore and then I don't know how you're going to get along, for as the saying goes an orphaned calf won't find another mother to give him her first milk. Go get the cows out of the pen instead of hanging around here playing the fool.

But I don't go off. In silence I watch you busying yourself at your tasks in the corners, bending down between the various pieces of furniture, disappearing at times behind a little cloud that rises from the swipe of the broom; and a little later on in the yard, in the kitchen garden, getting smaller and smaller with your every move until you're no more than a breath of air amid the scorched leaves of the banana trees. Only then do I grab the drum and take off for the cave, to shut myself up in the double rumble of the drum and the strong current. Through a little hole in the cave a ray of sunlight enters, beaming into the darkness a coconut tree feet up, the little ripples of the river gleaming face down, instead of the sky, without being turned over. Just like when I was stored up inside you and looking through your eyes; a larva all by itself in the honeycomb hearing the honey drip on the other side.

When there's a storm coming there's nothing I can do but begin to lick the windowpane till I feel all through my body the taste of the rain, the flavor of burned sulfur of the lightning flashes. And when the great storm clouds burst from the cudgel blows of the claps of thunder, I stop licking and start pounding on the leather drum head without being able to catch those rhythms outside, which intertwine in a frenzy and give me cramps in my fingers, my hands, my stomach, until I begin to vomit up my fault, my most grievous fault, the dark sugar-cane liquor of the "I a Sinner" that you make me pray every night and that goes to my head, making me rave like a madman and spit out the holy name of God in vain against the wall.

If you would only listen to me, everything would be better. Because what makes me melt with pleasure and heals me is talking of those things from before being born; not so as to make you suffer, believe me; just so we'll be closer to each other; they make me feel that I am going back inside you again till I'm drenched to the bone with your darkness, snugly wrapped in the warmth of your anxiety, feeling in my head the gentle swaying of your footsteps that calm me with your own concern, in the course of that endless journey through the hills in search of Papa. Let's see if I remember.

The point where we begin to separate from each other is always his death; such a stupid one, you maintain; a death that turns out to be the negation of what he was all his life: a life full of vivacity, of anger, of strokes of luck, with him always knowing more than the others; more carefree and joyful, more courageous, more everything. A giant. It's hard to believe that he could have met his death when he fell off the chestnut horse, bringing him back home after one of his all-night sessions singing and playing his guitar, and hit his head on paradise, just at the door of the house. The fall also broke his guitar, which woke us up as it alerted us to the fatal accident. We found nothing but the lifeless body of a man brought low, unnerved, thrown into the trash.

Without another father to talk these matters over with, I hear what you are willing to tell me about the dead man, about that dead man who is never going to stop dying inside you. And as is only natural: If I must see him with your eyes, I find he has that look about him that makes your soul grow. But I see him differently, and this is what annoys you most. When we reach this point, the blow on the head immediately shoots out of your hands and echoes in my head, my head against the wall, with that rumble that makes me tremble from head to foot. Oh, the sadness of not being able to want what you want, of not being able to make you understand what I want. I scratch at the ants that the blow has left me with, hungry ones, underneath my scalp, and I stay there where I am looking at you; I think that, because of the great love you bore your husband, it may be that you want to give me a death just like his, so as not to be unfair to the two of us. That is what I think, and perhaps this is best for the three of us. Who knows. I bow my head waiting for that blow that will make everything come out even; if you don't thrash me again, I myself will ram my head against the adobe wall, against the trees, like a kid goat, till I knock myself senseless and fall to the ground, just to show you that we're of one mind.

I know that you're right to beat me because of those memories that hurt you; but you're not right to beat me because I can remember so far back. My guilt and my remorse may be very forgetful. I don't know. What I do know is that I have to keep kicking my feet in the same place all the time, hemmed in on all sides, trampling on this heavy, waterlogged sky, that's pushing on my feet; struggling so as not to fall to the earth like a flat shapeless lump, an orphan before being born, disliking life before ever coming to know it.

So my weariness is growing more than yours is. Before being born, I am already older than you are, older than my dead father, much older than the oldest people in town. Why don't you believe me when I tell you that I remember these memories very well?

And you say: Stop going on and on about what you know nothing of. You've heard me talk about those things, and that was how you got the idea that you yourself saw them happen. No one can remember anything except what has happened to one's very own self. And that only after a person has the faculty of reason.

With all due respect, I tell you that to me that is not remembering but forgetting. I don't remember those things with my power of reason: You yourself say I'm half out of my mind. I feel those things in my belly button; even if I close my eyes I see them: *They're there.*

And it's when I start in talking about Papa that you fly into a rage and shut me up. Don't be stubborn. You can't think badly of him. It's plain to see that you never got to know him. And how could you have known him if when he died I had been carrying you in my womb for barely six months. He was a real man and with his instrument almost two men. When he sang he grew to the size of paradise, and people sat in his shadow thinking that life isn't all that bad. He knew how to put his finger on those things that to poor people are always beyond their reach and how to bring them to the surface. An everlasting pity that he didn't leave his seed in you. He surely knew that his destiny came to a dead end in himself. Just a little while before he died he made me swear that I'd make it my duty to bury his guitar with him. And I fulfilled his last wish.

I remember that very well too, and tell you so not so much to raise your spirits as because it is the absolute truth. I see you on the night of the wake, determined to put the guitar in the coffin of the deceased; nice and slowly at first, very gently, trying to fit it into an empty space; you bathe the two of them with your tears, with your widow's laments; you finger them again and again with your caresses as if to soften them, trying to make them understand, tugging so as to make the two of them one. But the dead man is big, he seems to get fatter by the moment, and refuses to make room; perhaps it's the guitar, as sweaty and stubborn as the dead man, that cleverly manages not to fit into the box. You call out to your husband, coaxing him affectionately as only you can do, reminding him of all his virtues, of the great pleasure the two of you shared, how much he loved his guitar; you beg him, you lift up an arm, a leg, his head. It doesn't help one bit. The dead man coils up inside in anger, disavowing his last wish; he doesn't want any more music now, only silence and peace; the guitar creaks and protests outside, its wooden body broken, its strings lying in a tangle on the pegbox, feeling resentment against that man who is slighting it, who wants his death to be his alone. After all that useless struggling, you too grow angry; and what you haven't managed to do by fair means you achieve by foul ones; you finish the job of totally destroying the guitar by pounding it on the floor; you pick up the pieces and dump them into the coffin by the handful. Neither your laments nor your pounding can be heard; people are laughing for all they're worth, as though they had burst into sidesplitting tears. There is a point at which laughter and weeping are in no way different; that point at which they deliriously bring out their desperation from inside their bodies, emptying them of their bad noises.

You kept your promise. And I alone know that a dead man, whom people call my father, has come here inside to share with me a place that doesn't have room enough for the two of us. And I know that sooner or later he is going to end up shoving me out of here. That's why I put up with your beatings, very humbly, without protesting; the insults that you constantly heap on me. I know that your greatest duty now is toward him; that since he is the weakest one now, the one most in need, you're obliged to devote more care to him than to me. I must place a counterweight in the balance that makes you suffer, with the double pointer fixed with such disparity on your side; like don Lucas's balance, when you send me to buy groceries; in one pan is the bit of black lead; in the other, the tiny handful of *maté* or biscuits that makes it immediately sink to the bottom. I want to relieve you of an overload that tears you in two to no purpose, that has turned your life into suffering. Tomorrow I will go to the bridge to hear the train rumble past, having put my head a good way under water; as always I am going to glue it to the piling, but I am not going to put the little reed in my mouth; I will stay under water listening with my teeth clenched till the noise that has set them on edge gradually dies down inside my bones along with the other sounds that keep drumming away inside me without a moment's respite.

TRANSLATED BY HELEN LANE

Julio Cortázar

Argentina
(1914–1984)

Julio Cortázar lived in Paris from 1952 until his death, earning a living as a translator for UNESCO. Although fifteen years younger than Borges, he attained worldwide fame at nearly the same time as his master. Cortázar's novel *Hopscotch* (1963) opened the period known as "the Boom of the Latin American novel," which brought to the fore the work of Borges, along with that of younger writers such as Mario Vargas Llosa, Carlos Fuentes, and Gabriel García Márquez. Cortázar's trademarks were his humor and witty irreverence, traits that were uncommon in Latin American fiction before the 1960s. He was cosmopolitan and part of the counterculture, and espoused left-wing causes with more enthusiasm and empathy than reflection. A gentle, playful giant six and a half feet tall, Cortázar had a very vivid imagination and became one of the outstanding craftsmen of the modern short story, his best genre. By 1963 he had published three collections of short stories: *Bestiary* (1951), *End of the Game* (1956), and *Secret Weapons* (1959). He went on to publish several others, the best known of which is *All Fires the Fire* (1966), as well as novels, including *62, A Model Kit* (1968) and *Manuel's Manual* (1973). Cortázar was fascinated by instances of the fantastic and the uncanny, a trait he derived from Borges, but also from the surrealists. A recurring motif is the repetition of places or events, the feeling of déjà vu that blurs the distinction between cities, civilizations, or eras. In "The Night Face Up" the protagonist dreams he is an ancient Aztec warrior, but the story tells of what happens to him following a motorcycle crash in the present day (or is the Moteca warrior dreaming that he is the one in the crash?).

The Night Face Up

> *And at certain periods they went out to hunt enemies; they called it the*
> *war of the blossom.**

Halfway down the long hotel vestibule, he thought that probably he was going to be late, and hurried on into the street to get out his

*The war of the blossom was the name the Aztecs gave a ritual war in which they took prisoners for sacrifice.

motorcycle from the corner where the next-door superintendent let him keep it. On the jewelry store at the corner he read that it was ten to nine; he had time to spare. The sun filtered through the tall downtown buildings, and he—because for himself, for just going along thinking, he did not have a name—he swung onto the machine, savoring the idea of the ride. The motor whirred between his legs, and a cool wind whipped his pantslegs.

He let the ministries zip past (the pink, the white), and a series of stores on the main street, their windows flashing. Now he was beginning the most pleasant part of the run, the real ride: a long street bordered with trees, very little traffic, with spacious villas whose gardens rambled all the way down to the sidewalks, which were barely indicated by low hedges. A bit inattentive perhaps, but tooling along on the right side of the street, he allowed himself to be carried away by the freshness, by the weightless contraction of this hardly begun day. This involuntary relaxation, possibly, kept him from preventing the accident. When he saw that the woman standing on the corner had rushed into the crosswalk while he still had the green light, it was already somewhat too late for a simple solution. He braked hard with foot and hand, wrenching himself to the left; he heard the woman scream, and at the collision his vision went. It was like falling asleep all at once.

He came to abruptly. Four or five young men were getting him out from under the cycle. He felt the taste of salt and blood, one knee hurt, and when they hoisted him up he yelped, he couldn't bear the pressure on his right arm. Voices which did not seem to belong to the faces hanging above him encouraged him cheerfully with jokes and assurances. His single solace was to hear someone else confirm that the lights indeed had been in his favor. He asked about the woman, trying to keep down the nausea which was edging up into his throat. While they carried him face up to a nearby pharmacy, he learned that the cause of the accident had gotten only a few scrapes on the legs. "Nah, you barely got her at all, but when ya hit, the impact made the machine jump and flop on its side . . ." Opinions, recollections of other smashups, take it easy, work him in shoulders first, there, that's fine, and someone in a dustcoat giving him a swallow of something soothing in the shadowy interior of the small local pharmacy.

Within five minutes the police ambulance arrived, and they lifted him onto a cushioned stretcher. It was a relief for him to be able to lie out flat. Completely lucid, but realizing that he was suffering the effects of a terrible shock, he gave his information to the officer riding in the ambulance with him. The arm almost didn't hurt; blood dripped down from a cut over the eyebrow all over his face. He licked his lips once or twice to drink it. He felt pretty good, it had been an accident, tough luck; stay quiet a few weeks, nothing worse. The guard said that the motorcycle didn't seem badly racked up. "Why should it," he replied. "It all landed on top of me." They both laughed, and when they got to the hospital, the guard shook his hand and wished him luck. Now the nausea was coming back little by little; meanwhile they were pushing him on a wheeled stretcher toward a pavilion further back, rolling along under trees full of birds, he shut his eyes and wished he were asleep or chloroformed. But they kept him for a good while in a room with that hospital smell, filling out a form, getting his clothes off, and dressing him in a stiff, greyish smock. They moved his arm carefully, it didn't hurt him. The nurses were constantly making wisecracks, and if it hadn't been for the stomach contractions he would have felt fine, almost happy.

They got him over to X-ray, and twenty minutes later, with the still-damp negative lying on his chest like a black tombstone, they pushed him into surgery. Someone tall and thin in white came over and began to look at the X-rays. A woman's hands were arranging his head, he felt that they were moving him from one stretcher to another. The man in white came over to him again, smiling, something gleamed in his right hand. He patted his cheek and made a sign to someone stationed behind.

It was unusual as a dream because it was full of smells, and he never dreamt smells. First a marshy smell, there to the left of the trail the swamps began already, the quaking bogs from which no one ever returned. But the reek lifted, and instead there came a dark, fresh composite fragrance, like the night under which he moved, in flight from the Aztecs. And it was all so natural, he had to run from the Aztecs who had set out on their manhunt, and his sole chance was to find a place to hide in the deepest part of the forest, taking care not to lose the narrow trail which only they, the Motecas, knew.

What tormented him the most was the odor, as though, notwithstanding the absolute acceptance of the dream, there was something which resisted that which was not habitual, which until that point had not participated in the game. "It smells of war," he thought, his hand going instinctively to the stone knife which was tucked at an angle into his girdle of woven wool. An unexpected sound made him crouch suddenly stock-still and shaking. To be afraid was nothing strange, there was plenty of fear in his dreams. He waited, covered by the branches of a shrub and the starless night. Far off, probably on the other side of the big lake, they'd be lighting the bivouac fires; that part of the sky had a reddish glare. The sound was not repeated. It had been like a broken limb. Maybe an animal that, like himself, was escaping from the smell of war. He stood erect slowly, sniffing the air. Not a sound could be heard, but the fear was still following, as was the smell, that cloying incense of the war of the blossom. He had to press forward, to stay out of the bogs and get to the heart of the forest. Groping uncertainly through the dark, stooping every other moment to touch the packed earth of the trail, he took a few steps. He would have liked to have broken into a run, but the gurgling fens lapped on either side of him. On the path and in darkness, he took his bearings. Then he caught a horrible blast of that foul smell he was most afraid of, and leaped forward desperately.

"You're going to fall off the bed," said the patient next to him. "Stop bouncing around, old buddy."

He opened his eyes and it was afternoon, the sun already low in the oversized windows of the long ward. While trying to smile at his neighbor, he detached himself almost physically from the final scene of the nightmare. His arm, in a plaster cast, hung suspended from an apparatus with weights and pulleys. He felt thirsty, as though he'd been running for miles, but they didn't want to give him much water, barely enough to moisten his lips and make a mouthful. The fever was winning slowly and he would have been able to sleep again, but he was enjoying the pleasure of keeping awake, eyes half-closed, listening to the other patients' conversation, answering a question from time to time. He saw a little white pushcart come up beside the bed, a blond nurse rubbed the front of his thigh with alcohol and stuck him with a fat needle connected to a tube which ran up to a bottle filled with a milky, opalescent liquid. A young intern arrived with some metal and leather apparatus which he adjusted to fit onto the good arm to check something or other. Night fell, and the fever went along dragging him down softly to a state in which things seemed embossed as through opera glasses, they were real and soft and, at the same time, vaguely distasteful; like sitting in a boring movie and thinking that, well, still, it'd be worse out in the street, and staying.

A cup of a marvelous golden broth came, smelling of leeks, celery and parsley. A small hunk of bread, more precious than a whole banquet, found itself crumbling little by little. His arm hardly hurt him at all, and only in the eyebrow where they'd taken stitches a quick, hot pain sizzled occasionally. When the big windows across the way turned to smudges of dark blue, he thought it would not be difficult for him to sleep. Still on his back so a little uncomfortable, running his tongue out over his hot, too-dry lips, he tasted the broth still, and with a sigh of bliss, he let himself drift off.

First there was a confusion, as of one drawing all his sensations, for that moment blunted or muddled, into himself. He realized that he was running in pitch darkness, although, above, the sky criss-crossed with treetops was less black than the rest. "The trail," he thought. "I've gotten off the trail." His feet sank into a bed of leaves and mud, and then he couldn't take a step that the branches of shrubs did not whiplash against his ribs and legs. Out of breath, knowing despite the darkness and silence that he was surrounded, he crouched down to listen. Maybe the trail was very near, with the first daylight he would be able to see it again. Nothing now could help him to find it. The hand that had unconsciously gripped the haft of the dagger climbed like a fen scorpion up to his neck where the protecting amulet hung. Barely moving his lips, he mumbled the supplication of the corn which brings about the beneficent moons, and the prayer to Her Very Highness, to the distributor of all Motecan possessions. At the same time he felt his ankles sinking deeper into the mud, and the waiting in the darkness of the obscure grove of live oak grew intolerable to him. The war of the blossom had started at the beginning of the moon and had been going on for three days and three nights now. If he managed to hide in the depths of the forest, getting off the trail further up past the marsh country, perhaps the warriors wouldn't follow his track. He thought of the many prisoners they'd already taken. But the number didn't count, only the consecrated period. The hunt would continue until the priests gave the sign to return. Everything had its number and its limit, and it was within the sacred period, and he on the other side from the hunters.

He heard the cries and leaped up, knife in hand. As if the sky were aflame on the horizon, he saw torches moving among the branches, very near him. The smell of war was unbearable, and when the first enemy jumped him, leaped at his throat, he felt an almost-pleasure in sinking the stone blade flat to the haft into his chest. The lights were already around him, the happy cries. He managed to cut the air once or twice, then a rope snared him from behind.

"It's the fever," the man in the next bed said. "The same thing happened to me when they operated on my duodenum. Take some water, you'll see, you'll sleep all right."

Laid next to the night from which he came back, the tepid shadow of the ward seemed delicious to him. A violet lamp kept watch high on the far wall like a guardian eye. You could hear coughing, deep breathing, once in a while a conversation in whispers. Everything was pleasant and secure, without the chase, no . . . But he didn't want to go on thinking about the nightmare. There were lots of things to amuse himself with. He began to look at the cast on his arm, and the pulleys that held it so comfortably in the air. They'd left a bottle of mineral water on the night table beside him. He put the neck of the bottle to his mouth and drank it like a precious liqueur. He could now make out the different shapes in the ward, the thirty beds, the closets with glass doors. He guessed that his fever was down, his face felt cool. The cut over the eyebrow barely hurt at all, like a recollection. He saw himself leaving the hotel again, wheeling out the cycle. Who'd have thought that it would end like this? He tried to fix the moment of the accident exactly, and it got him very angry to notice that there was a void there, an emptiness he could not manage to fill. Between the impact and the moment that they picked him up off the pavement, the passing out or what went on, there was nothing he could see. And at the same time he had the feeling that this void, this nothingness, had lasted an eternity. No, not even time, more as if, in this void, he had passed across something, or had run back immense distances. The shock, the brutal dashing against the pavement. Anyway, he had felt an immense relief in coming out of the black pit while the people were lifting him off the ground. With pain in the broken arm, blood from the split eyebrow, contusion on the knee; with all that, a relief in returning to daylight, to the day, and to feel sustained and attended. That was weird. Someday he'd ask the doctor at the office about that. Now sleep began to take over again, to pull him slowly down. The pillow was so soft, and the coolness of the mineral water in his fevered throat. The violet light of the lamp up there was beginning to get dimmer and dimmer.

As he was sleeping on his back, the position in which he came to did not surprise him, but on the other hand the damp smell, the smell of oozing rock, blocked his throat and forced him to understand. Open the eyes and look in all directions, hopeless. He was surrounded by an absolute darkness. Tried to get up and felt ropes pinning his wrists and ankles. He was staked to the ground on a floor of dank, icy stone slabs. The cold bit into his naked back, his legs. Dully, he tried to touch the amulet with his chin and found they had stripped him of it. Now he was lost, no prayer could save him from the final . . . From far off, as though filtering through the rock of the dungeon, he heard the great kettledrums of the feast. They had carried him to the temple, he was in the underground cells of Teocalli itself, awaiting his turn.

He heard a yell, a hoarse yell that rocked off the walls. Another yell, ending in a moan. It was he who was screaming in the darkness, he was screaming because he was alive, his whole body with that cry fended off what was coming, the inevitable end. He thought of his friends filling up the other dungeons, and of those already walking up the stairs of the sacrifice. He uttered another choked cry, he could barely open his mouth, his jaws were twisted back as if with a rope and a stick, and once in a while they would open slowly with an endless exertion, as if they were made of rubber. The creaking of the wooden latches jolted him like a whip. Rent, writhing, he fought to rid himself of the cords sinking into his flesh. His right arm, the stronger, strained until the pain became unbearable and he had to give up. He watched the double door open, and the smell of the torches reached him before the light did. Barely girdled by the ceremonial loincloths, the priests' acolytes moved in his direction, looking at him with contempt. Lights reflected off the sweaty torsos and off the black hair dressed with feathers. The cords went slack, and in their place the grappling of hot hands, hard as bronze; he felt himself lifted, still face up, and jerked along by the four acolytes who carried him down the passageway. The torchbearers went ahead, indistinctly lighting up the corridor with its dripping walls and a ceiling so low that the acolytes had to duck their heads. Now they were taking him out, taking him out, it was the end. Face up, under a mile of living rock which, for a succession of moments, was lit up by a glimmer of torchlight. When the stars came out up there instead of the roof and the great terraced steps rose before him, on fire with cries and dances, it would be the end. The passage was never going to end, but now it was beginning to end, he would see suddenly the open sky full of stars, but not yet, they trundled him along endlessly in the reddish shadow, hauling him roughly along and he did not want that, but how to stop it if they had torn off the amulet, his real heart, the life-center.

In a single jump he came out into the hospital night, to the high, gentle, bare ceiling, to the soft shadow wrapping him round. He thought he must have cried out, but his neighbors were peacefully snoring. The water in the bottle on the night table was somewhat bubbly, a translucent shape against the dark azure shadow of the windows. He panted, looking for some relief for his lungs, oblivion for those images still glued to his eyelids. Each time he shut his eyes he saw them take shape instantly, and he sat up, completely wrung out, but savoring at the same time the surety that now he was awake, that the night nurse would answer if he rang, that soon it would be daybreak, with the good, deep sleep he usually had at that hour, no images, no nothing . . . It was difficult to keep his eyes open; the drowsiness was more powerful than he. He made one last effort; he sketched a gesture toward the bottle of water with his good hand and did not manage to reach it, his fingers closed again on a black emptiness, and the passageway went on endlessly, rock after rock, with momentary ruddy flares, and face up he choked out a dull moan because the roof was about to end, it rose, was opening like a mouth of shadow, and the acolytes straightened up, and from on high a waning moon fell on a face whose eyes wanted not to see it, were closing and opening desperately, trying to pass to the other side, to find again the bare, protecting ceiling of the ward. And every time they opened, it was night and the moon, while they climbed the great terraced steps, his head hanging down backward now, and up at the top were the bonfires, red columns of perfumed smoke, and suddenly he saw the red stone, shiny with the blood dripping off it, and the spinning arcs cut by the feet of the victim whom they pulled off to throw him rolling down the north steps. With a last hope he shut his lids tightly, moaning to wake up. For a second he thought he had gotten there, because once more he was immobile in the bed, except that his head was hanging down off it, swinging. But he smelled death, and when he opened his eyes he saw the blood-soaked figure of the executioner-priest coming toward him with the stone knife in his hand. He managed to close his eyelids again, although he knew now he was not going to wake up, that he was awake, that the marvelous dream had been the other, absurd as all dreams are—a dream in which he was going through the strange avenues of an astonishing city, with green and red lights that burned without fire or smoke, on an enormous metal insect that whirred away between his legs. In the infinite lie of the dream, they had also picked him up off the ground, someone had approached him also with a knife in his hand, approached him who was lying face up, face up with his eyes closed between the bonfires on the steps.

TRANSLATED BY PAUL BLACKBURN

Rosario Castellanos

Mexico
(1925–1974)

At the time when she was killed in an accident while ambassador to Israel, Rosario Castellanos was among the most respected Mexican intellectuals. She was also Mexico's leading woman writer. The daughter of landowners from Chiapas, Castellanos had a superior education, which culminated with studies in Europe. From the first, she was interested in the role of women in Mexican society, and she is considered a pioneer by today's feminists. Castellanos was a devoted student of Saint Theresa and Sor Juana Inés de la Cruz, the great seventeenth-century Mexican poet. Her 1950 master's thesis, *Sobre cultura femenina*, was to many a turning point in the self-awareness of contemporary Mexican women authors. Her essays, novels, and short stories often focus on the concerns of women and related social and political issues. Her best-known novel is *Oficio de tinieblas* (1962). She collected her poetry under the contentious title *Poesía no eres tú* (1972), which is a variation on a well-known line by Spanish romantic poet Gustavo Adolfo Bécquer in which he tells his beloved that it is she who is the poetry, not his verse. Yet her poetry, reminiscent of Saint John of the Cross, reveals a deep religious sense, an ecstatic wonder before the bounties of the world much like that expressed by Jorge Guillén, a prominent contemporary Spanish poet. Castellanos, who donated the land she inherited to the impoverished Indians of Chiapas who worked it, expressed with equal eloquence indignation for the inequities of the world and jubilation for its radiance and beauty. She had found both joy and the deepest of sorrows in her life. Married in 1958, in 1960 she dedicated *Mi libro de lectura* to the memory of a lost daughter. In 1961, on the same night that she won the Xavier Villaurrutia prize, her son Gabriel was born. "Cooking Lesson" is one of Castellanos's best-known stories, a sardonic picture of woman's plight.

Cooking Lesson

The kitchen is shining white. It's a shame to have to get it dirty. One ought to sit down and contemplate it, describe it, close one's eyes, evoke it. Looking closely, this spotlessness, this pulchritude lacks the glaring excess that causes chills in hospitals. Or is it the halo of disinfectants, the rubber-cushioned steps of the aides, the hidden presence of sickness and

345

death? What do I care? My place is here. I've been here from the beginning of time. In the German proverb woman is synonymous with *Küche, Kinder, Kirche*. I wandered astray through classrooms, streets, offices, cafés, wasting my time on skills that now I must forget in order to acquire others. For example, choosing the menu. How could one carry out such an arduous task without the cooperation of society—of all history? On a special shelf, just right for my height, my guardian spirits are lined up, those acclaimed jugglers that reconcile the most irreducible contradictions among the pages of their recipe books: slimness and gluttony, pleasing appearance and economy, speed and succulence. With their infinite combinations: slimness and economy, speed and pleasing appearance, succulence and . . . What can you suggest to me for today's meal, O experienced housewife, inspiration of mothers here and gone, voice of tradition, clamoring secret of the supermarkets? I open a book at random and read: "Don Quijote's Dinner." Very literary but not very satisfying, because Don Quijote was not famous as a gourmet but as a bumbler. Although a more profound analysis of the text reveals etc., etc., etc. Ugh! More ink has flowed about that character than water under bridges. "Fowl Center-Face." Esoteric. Whose face? Does the face of someone or something have a center? If it does, it must not be very appetizing. "Bigos Roumanian." Well, just who do you think you're talking to? If I knew what tarragon or *ananas* were I wouldn't be consulting this book, because I'd know a lot of other things, too. If you had the slightest sense of reality, you yourself or any of your colleagues would take the trouble to write a dictionary of technical terms, edit a few prolegomena, invent a propaedeutic to make the difficult culinary art accessible to the lay person. But you all start from the assumption that we're all in on the secret and you limit yourselves to stating it. I, at least, solemnly declare that I am not, and never have been, in on either this or any other secret you share. I never understood anything about anything. You observe the symptoms: I stand here like an imbecile, in an impeccable and neutral kitchen, wearing the apron that I usurp in order to give a pretense of efficiency and of which I will be shamefully but justly stripped.

I open the refrigerator drawer that proclaims "Meat" and extract a package that I cannot recognize under its icy coating. I thaw it in hot water, revealing the title without which I never would have identified the contents: Fancy Beef Broil. Wonderful. A plain and wholesome dish. But since it doesn't mean resolving an antinomy or proposing an axiom, it doesn't appeal to me.

Moreover, it's not simply an excess of logic that inhibits my hunger. It's also the appearance of it, frozen stiff; it's the color that shows now that I've ripped open the package. Red, as if it were just about to start bleeding.

Our backs were that same color, my husband and I, after our orgiastic sunbathing on the beaches of Acapulco. He could afford the luxury of

COOKING LESSON \ 347

"behaving like the man he is" and stretch out face down to avoid rubbing his painful skin . . . But I, self-sacrificing little Mexican wife, born like a dove to the nest, smiled like Cuauhtémoc under torture on the rack when he said, "My bed is not made of roses," and fell silent. Face up, I bore not only my own weight but also his on top of me. The classic position for making love. And I moaned, from the tearing and the pleasure. The classic moan. Myths, myths.

The best part (for my sunburn at least) was when he fell asleep. Under my fingertips—not very sensitive due to prolonged contact with typewriter keys—the nylon of my bridal nightgown slipped away in a fraudulent attempt to look like lace. I played with the tips of the buttons and those other ornaments that make whoever wears them seem so feminine in the late night darkness. The whiteness of my clothes, deliberate, repetitive, immodestly symbolic, was temporarily abolished. Perhaps at some moment it managed to accomplish its purpose beneath the light and the glance of those eyes that are now overcome by fatigue.

Eyelids close and behold, once again, exile. An enormous sandy expanse with no juncture other than the sea, whose movement suggests paralysis, with no invitation except that of the cliff to suicide.

But that's a lie. I'm not the dream that dreams in a dream that dreams; I'm not the reflection of an image in a glass; I'm not annihilated by the closing off of a consciousness or of all possible consciousness. I go on living a dense, viscous, turbid life even though the man at my side and the one far away ignore me, forget me, postpone me, abandon me, fall out of love with me.

I, too, am a consciousness that can close itself off, abandon someone, and expose him to annihilation. I . . . The meat, under the sprinkling of salt, has toned down some of its offensive redness and now it seems more tolerable, more familiar to me. It's that piece I saw a thousand times without realizing it, when I used to pop in to tell the cook that . . .

We weren't born together. Our meeting was due to accident. A happy one? It's still too soon to say. We met by chance at an exhibition, a lecture, a film. We ran into each other in the elevator; he gave me his seat on the tram; a guard interrupted our perplexed and parallel contemplation of the giraffe because it was time to close the zoo. Someone, he or I, it's all the same, asked the stupid but indispensable question: Do you work or study? A harmony of interests and of good intentions, a show of "serious" intentions. A year ago I hadn't the slightest idea of his existence and now I'm lying close to him with our thighs entwined, damp with sweat and semen. I could get up without waking him, walk barefoot to the shower. To purify myself? I feel no revulsion. I prefer to believe that what links him to me is something as easy to wipe away as a secretion and not as terrible as a sacrament.

So I remain still, breathing rhythmically to imitate drowsiness, my insomnia the only spinster's jewel I've kept and I'm inclined to keep until death.

Beneath the brief deluge of pepper the meat seems to have gone gray. I banish this sign of aging by rubbing it as though I were trying to penetrate the surface and impregnate its thickness with flavors, because I lost my old name and I still can't get used to the new one, which is not mine either. When some employee pages me in the lobby of the hotel I remain deaf with that vague uneasiness that is the prelude to recognition. Who could that person be who doesn't answer? It could be something urgent, serious, a matter of life or death. The caller goes away without leaving a clue, a message, or even the possibility of another meeting. Is it anxiety that presses against my heart? No, it's his hand pressing on my shoulder and his lips smiling at me in benevolent mockery, more like a sorcerer than a master.

So then, I accept, as we head toward the bar (my peeling shoulder feels like it's on fire) that it's true that in my contact or collision with him I've undergone a profound metamorphosis. I didn't know and now I know; I didn't feel and now I do feel; I wasn't and now I am.

It should be left to sit for a while. Until it reaches room temperature, until it's steeped in the flavors that I've rubbed into it. I have the feeling I didn't know how to calculate very well and that I've bought a piece that's too big for the two of us—for me, because I'm lazy, not a carnivore; for him, for aesthetic reasons because he's watching his waistline. Almost all of it will be left over! Yes, I already know that I shouldn't worry: one of the good fairies that hovers over me is going to come to my rescue and explain how one uses leftovers. It's a mistake, anyhow. You don't start married life in such a sordid way. I'm afraid that you also don't start it with a dish as dull as broiled beef.

Thanks, I murmur, while I wipe my lips with a corner of the napkin. Thanks for the transparent cocktail glass, and for the submerged olive. Thanks for letting me out of the cage of one sterile routine only to lock me into the cage of another, a routine which according to all purposes and possibilities must be fruitful. Thanks for giving me the chance to show off a long gown with a train, for helping me walk up the aisle of the church, carried away by the organ music. Thanks for . . .

How long will it take to be done? Well, that shouldn't worry me too much because it has to be put on the grill at the last minute. It takes very little time, according to the cookbook. How long is little? Fifteen minutes? Ten? Five? Naturally the text doesn't specify. It presupposes an intuition which, according to my sex, I'm supposed to possess but I don't, a sense I was born without that would allow me to gauge the precise minute the meat is done.

And what about you? Don't you have anything to thank me for? You've

COOKING LESSON \ 349

specified it with a slightly pedantic solemnity and a precision that perhaps were meant to flatter but instead offended: my virginity. When you discovered it I felt like the last dinosaur on a planet where the species was extinct. I longed to justify myself, to explain that if I was intact when I met you it was not out of virtue or pride or ugliness but simply out of adherence to a style. I'm not baroque. The tiny imperfection in the pearl is unbearable to me. The only alternative I have is the neoclassic one, and its rigidity is incompatible with the spontaneity needed for making love. I lack that ease of the person who rows or plays tennis or dances. I don't play any sports. I comply with the ritual but my move to surrender petrifies into a statue.

Are you monitoring my transit to fluidity? Do you expect it, do you need it? Or is this hieraticism that sanctifies you, and that you interpret as the passivity natural to my nature, enough for you? So if you are voluble it will ease your mind to think that I won't hinder your adventures. It won't be necessary—thanks to my temperament—for you to fatten me up, tie me down hand and foot with children, gag me on the thick honey of resignation. I'll stay the same as I am. Calm. When you throw your body on top of mine I feel as though a gravestone were covering me, full of inscriptions, strange names, memorable dates. You moan unintelligibly and I'd like to whisper my name in your ear to remind you who it is you are possessing.

I'm myself. But who am I? Your wife, of course. And that title suffices to distinguish me from past memories or future projects. I bear an owner's brand, a property tag, and yet you watch me suspiciously. I'm not weaving a web to trap you. I'm not a praying mantis. I appreciate your believing such a hypothesis, but it's false.

This meat has a toughness and consistency that is not like beef. It must be mammoth. One of those that have been preserved since prehistoric times in the Siberian ice, that the peasants thaw out and fix for food. In that terribly boring documentary they showed at the Embassy, so full of superfluous details, there wasn't the slightest mention of how long it took to make them edible. Years, months? And I only have so much time . . .

Is that a lark? Or is it a nightingale? No, our schedule won't be ruled by such winged creatures as those that announced the coming of dawn to Romeo and Juliet but by a noisy and unerring alarm clock. And you will not descend to day by the stairway of my tresses but rather on the steps of detailed complaints: you've lost a button off your jacket; the toast is burned; the coffee is cold.

I'll ruminate my resentment in silence. All the responsibilities and duties of a servant are assigned to me for everything. I'm supposed to keep the house impeccable, the clothes ready, mealtimes exact. But I'm not paid any salary; I don't get one day a week off; I can't change masters. On the other hand, I'm supposed to contribute to the support of the household and I'm expected to efficiently carry out a job where the boss is demanding, my colleagues conspire, and my subordinates hate me. In my free time I transform myself into a society matron who gives luncheons and dinners for her husband's friends, attends meetings, subscribes to the opera season, watches her weight, renews her wardrobe, cares for her skin, keeps herself attractive, keeps up on all the gossip, stays up late and gets up early, runs the monthly risk of maternity, believes the evening executive meetings, the business trips and the arrival of unexpected clients; who suffers from olfactory hallucinations when she catches a whiff of French perfume (different from the one she uses) on her husband's shirts and handkerchiefs and on lonely nights refuses to think why or what so much fuss is all about and fixes herself a stiff drink and reads a detective story with the fragile mood of a convalescent.

Shouldn't it be time to turn on the stove? Low flame so the broiler will start warming up gradually, "which should be greased first so the meat will not stick." That did occur to me; there was no need to waste pages on those recommendations.

I'm very awkward. Now it's called awkwardness, but it used to be called innocence and you loved it. But I've never loved it. When I was single I used to read things on the sly, perspiring from the arousal and shame. I never found out anything. My breasts ached, my eyes got misty, my muscles contracted in a spasm of nausea.

The oil is starting to get hot. I let it get too hot, heavy handed that I am, and now it's spitting and spattering and burning me. That's how I'm going to fry in those narrow hells, through my fault, through my fault, through my most grievous fault. But child, you're not the only one. All your classmates do the same thing or worse. They confess in the confessional, do their penance, are forgiven and fall into it again. All of them. If I had continued going around with them they'd be questioning me now, the married ones to find things out for themselves, the single ones to find out how far they can go. Impossible to let them down. I would invent acrobatics, sublime fainting spells, transports as they're called in the Thousand and One nights—records! If you only heard me then, you'd never recognize me, Casanova!

I drop the meat onto the grill and instinctively step back against the wall. What a noise! Now it's stopped. The meat lies there silently, faithful to its deceased state. I still think it's too big.

It's not that you've let me down. It's true that I didn't expect anything special. Gradually we'll reveal ourselves to one another, discover our secrets, our little tricks, learn to please each other. And one day you and I will become a pair of perfect lovers and then, right in the middle of an embrace, we'll disappear and the words "The End" will appear on the screen.

What's the matter? The meat is shrinking. No, I'm not seeing things; I'm not wrong. You can see the mark of its original size by the outline that it left on the grill. It was only a little bit bigger. Good! Maybe it will be just the right size for our appetites.

In my next movie I'd like them to give me a different part. The white sorceress in a savage village? No, today I don't feel much inclined to either heroism or danger. Better a famous woman (a fashion designer or something like that), rich and independent, who lives by herself in an apartment in New York, Paris, or London. Her occasional *affaires* entertain her but do not change her. She's not sentimental. After a breakup scene she lights a cigarette and surveys the urban scenery through the picture window of her studio.

Ah, the color of the meat looks much better now, only raw in a few obstinate places. But the rest is browned and gives off a delicious aroma. Will it be enough for the two of us? It looks very small to me.

If I got dressed up now I'd try on one of those dresses from my trousseau and go out. What would happen, hmmmm? Maybe an older man with a car would pick me up. Mature. Retired. The only kind who can afford to be on the make at this time of day.

What the devil's going on? This damned meat is starting to give off horrible black smoke! I should have turned it over! Burned on one side. Well, thank goodness it has another one.

Miss, if you will allow me . . . Mrs.! And I'm warning you, my husband is very jealous. . . . Then he shouldn't let you go out alone. You're a temptation to any passerby. Nobody in this world says passerby. Pedestrian? Only the newspapers when they report accidents. You're a temptation for anyone. Mean-ing-ful silence. The glances of a sphinx. The older man is following me at a safe distance. Better for him. Better for me, because on the corner—uh, oh—my husband, who's spying on me and who never leaves me alone morning, noon, or night, who suspects everything and everybody, Your Honor. It's impossible to live this way, I want a divorce.

Now what? This piece of meat's mother never told it that it was meat and ought to act like it. It's curling up like a corkscrew pastry. Anyhow, I don't know where all that smoke can be coming from if I turned the stove off ages ago. Of course, Dear Abby, what one must do now is open the window, plug in the ventilator so it won't be smelly when my husband gets here. And I'll so cutely run right out to greet him at the door with my best dress on, my best smile, and my warmest invitation to eat out.

It's a thought. We'll look at the restaurant menu while that miserable piece of charred meat lies hidden at the bottom of the garbage pail. I'll be careful not to mention the incident because I'd be considered a somewhat irresponsible wife, with frivolous tendencies but not mentally retarded. This is the initial public image that I project and I've got to maintain it even though it isn't accurate.

There's another possibility. Don't open the window, don't turn on the ventilator, don't throw the meat in the garbage. When my husband gets here let him smell it like the ogres in all the stories and tell him that no, it doesn't smell of human flesh here, but of useless woman. I'll exaggerate my compunction so he can be magnanimous. After all, what's happened is so normal! What newlywed doesn't do the same thing that I've done? When we visit my mother-in-law, who is still at the stage of not attacking me because she doesn't know my weak points yet, she'll tell me her own experiences. The time, for example, when her husband asked her to fix coddled eggs and she took him literally . . . ha, ha. Did that stop her from becoming a fabulous widow, I mean a fabulous cook? Because she was widowed much later and for other reasons. After that she gave free rein to her maternal instincts and spoiled everything with all her pampering . . .

No, he's not going to find it the least bit amusing. He's going to say that I got distracted, that it's the height of carelessness and, yes, condescendingly, I'm going to accept his accusations.

But it isn't true, it isn't. I was watching the meat all the time, watching how a series of very odd things happened to it. Saint Theresa was right when she said that God is in the stewpots. Or matter is energy or whatever it's called now.

Let's backtrack. First there's the piece of meat, one color, one shape, one size. Then it changes, looks even nicer and you feel very happy. Then it starts changing again and now it doesn't look so nice. It keeps changing and changing and changing and you just can't tell when you should stop it. Because if I leave this piece of meat on the grill indefinitely, it will burn to a crisp till nothing is left of it. So that piece of meat that gave the impression of being so solid and real no longer exists.

So? My husband also gives the impression of being solid and real when we're together, when I touch him, when I see him. He certainly changes and I change too, although so slowly that neither of us realizes it. Then he goes off and suddenly becomes a memory and . . . Oh, no, I'm not going to fall into that trap; the one about the invented character and the invented narrator and the invented anecdote. Besides, it's not the consequence that licitly follows from the meat episode.

The meat hasn't stopped existing. It has undergone a series of metamorphoses. And the fact that it ceases to be perceptible for the senses does not mean that the cycle is concluded but that it has taken the quantum leap. It will go on operating on other levels. On the level of my consciousness, my memory, my will, changing me, defining me, establishing the course of my future.

From today on, I'll be whatever I choose to be at the moment. Seductively unbalanced, deeply withdrawn, hypocritical. From the very beginning I will impose, just a bit insolently, the rules of the game. My husband will resent the appearance of my dominance, which will widen like the ripples on the surface of the water when someone has skipped a pebble across it. I'll struggle to prevail and, if he gives in, I'll retaliate with my scorn, and, if he doesn't give in, I'll simply be unable to forgive him.

If I assume another attitude, if I'm the typical case, femininity that begs indulgence for her errors, the balance will tip in favor of my antagonist and I will be running the race with a handicap, which, apparently, seals my defeat, and which, essentially, guarantees my triumph by the winding path that my grandmothers took, the humble ones, the ones who didn't open their mouths except to say yes and achieved an obedience foreign to even their most irrational whims. The recipe of course is ancient and its efficiency is proven. If I still doubt, all I have to do is ask my neighbor. She'll confirm my certainty.

It's just that it revolts me to behave that way. This definition is not applicable to me, the former one either; neither corresponds to my inner truth, or safeguards my authenticity. Must I grasp some one of them and bind myself to its terms only because it is a cliché accepted by the majority and intelligible to everyone? And it's not because I'm a *rara avis*. You can say about me what Pfandl said about Sor Juana, that I belong to the class of hesitant neurotics. The diagnosis is very easy, but what consequences does the assumption hold?

If I insist on affirming my version of the facts my husband is going to look at me suspiciously; he's going to live in continual expectation that I'll be declared insane.

Our life together could not be more problematic! He doesn't want conflicts of any kind, much less such abstract, absurd, metaphysical conflicts as the one I would present him with. His home is a haven of peace where he takes refuge from all the storms of life. Agreed. I accepted that when I got married and I was even ready to accept sacrifice for the sake of marital harmony. But I counted on the fact that the sacrifice, the complete renunciation of what I am, would only be demanded of me on The Sublime Occasion, at The Time of Heroic Solutions, at The Moment of the Definitive Decision. Not in exchange for what I stumbled on today, which is something very insignificant and very ridiculous. And yet . . .

TRANSLATED BY MAUREEN AHERN

Carlos Fuentes

Mexico
(b. 1928)

Son of a diplomat, Carlos Fuentes grew up in Washington, D.C., and Santiago, Chile. He studied law at the University of Mexico and in Geneva, and he is fluent in English and French. Fuentes is one of the most cosmopolitan writers in the world today, at home in several cultures and the heir of various literary traditions. With Vargas Llosa, Cortázar, and García Márquez, Fuentes was one of the writers responsible for the so-called Boom of the Latin American novel in the 1960s. Politically engaged, Fuentes has also served Mexico as a diplomat (he was ambassador to France) and has been a persistent and polemical commentator on current events. The main concern of his fiction, made up of novels such as *The Death of Artemio Cruz* (1962), *Aura* (1962), and *Terra Nostra* (1975), is the issue of Mexico's identity. In recent works, such as *The Campaign* (1991), Fuentes has turned to the historical novel, and in *The Old Gringo* (1985), to one of his hobbyhorses, the relationship between Mexico and the United States. In his early works he was particularly influenced by Octavio Paz's *The Labyrinth of Solitude,* the classic essay on the topic of Mexico's culture and its debt to the past. Fuentes's obsession is the currency of the past in Mexican history, the enduring presence of warring forces (Aztec, Spanish) that make up the nation and determine its inclination to violence. In "The Doll Queen" Fuentes links past and present by means of the narrator's childhood memories and how they are suddenly revived. In the same way that the violence of the Conquest is resuscitated in the Mexican Revolution, in Fuentes's fiction an individual's past never dies.

The Doll Queen

To María Pilar and José Donoso

I

I went because that card—such a strange card—reminded me of her existence. I found it in a forgotten book whose pages had revived the specter of a childish calligraphy. For the first time in a long while I was rearranging my books. I met surprise after surprise, since some, placed on the highest shelves, had not been read for a long time. So long a time that the edges of the leaves were grainy, and a mixture of gold dust and grayish scale fell on my open palm, reminiscent of the lacquer covering certain bodies glimpsed first in dreams and later in the deceptive reality of the first ballet performance to which we're taken. It was a book from my child-hood—perhaps from the childhood of many children—that related a series of more or less truculent exemplary tales which had the virtue of precipi-tating us onto our elders' knees to ask them, over and over again: Why? Children who are ungrateful to their parents; maidens kidnapped by splen-did horsemen and returned home in shame—as well as those who happily abandon hearth and home; old men who in exchange for an overdue mortgage demand the hand of the sweetest, most long-suffering daughter of the threatened family . . . Why? I do not recall their answers. I only know that from among the stained pages came fluttering a white card in Amilamia's atrocious hand: *Amilamia wil not forget thus her good friend—com see me here wher I draw it.*

And on the other side was that sketch of a path starting from an X that indicated, doubtlessly, the park bench where I, an adolescent rebelling against prescribed and tedious education, forgot my classroom schedule to spend some hours reading books which, if not in fact written by me, seemed to be: who could doubt that only from my imagination could spring all those corsairs, those couriers of the tsar, those boys slightly younger than I who floated all day down a great American river on a raft. Clutching the side of the park bench as if it were the bow of a magic saddle, at first I didn't hear the sound of the light steps that stopped behind me after running down the graveled garden path. It was Amilamia, and I don't know how long the child would have kept me company in silence had not her mischievous spirit one afternoon chosen to tickle my ear with down from a dandelion she blew toward me, her lips puffed out and her brow furrowed in a frown.

She asked my name, and after considering it very seriously, she told me hers with a smile which, if not candid, was not too rehearsed. Quickly I realized that Amilamia had discovered, if discovered is the word, a form of expression midway between the ingenuousness of her years and the forms of adult mimicry that well-brought-up children have to know, par-ticularly for the solemn moments of introduction and of leave-taking. Ami-lamia's seriousness was, rather, a gift of nature, whereas her moments of spontaneity, by contrast, seemed artificial. I like to remember her, after-noon after afternoon, in a succession of images that in their totality sum up the complete Amilamia. And it never ceases to surprise me that I cannot think of her as she really was, or remember how she actually moved—light, questioning, constantly looking around her. I must remember her fixed forever in time, as in a photograph album. Amilamia in the distance, a point at the spot where the hill began its descent from a lake of clover toward the flat meadow where I, sitting on the bench, used to read: a point of fluctuating shadow and sunshine and a hand that waved to me from high on the hill. Amilamia frozen in her flight down the hill, her white skirt ballooning, the flowered panties gathered on her legs with elastic, her mouth open and eyes half closed against the streaming air, the child crying with pleasure. Amilamia sitting beneath the eucalyptus trees, pretending to cry so that I would go over to her. Amilamia lying on her stomach with a flower in her hand: the petals of a flower which I discovered later didn't grow in this garden but somewhere else, perhaps in the garden of Amilamia's house, since the pocket of her blue-checked apron was often filled with those white blossoms. Amilamia watching me read, holding with both hands to the slats of the green bench, asking questions with her gray eyes: I recall that she never asked me what I was reading, as if she could divine in my eyes the images born of the pages. Amilamia laughing with pleasure when I lifted her by the waist and whirled her around my head; she seemed to discover a new perspective on the world in that slow flight. Amilamia turning her back to me and waving goodbye, her arm held high, the fingers moving excitedly. And Amilamia in the thousand postures she affected around my bench, hanging upside down, her bloomers billowing; sitting on the gravel with her legs crossed and her chin resting on her fist; lying on the grass, baring her belly button to the sun; weaving tree branches, drawing animals in the mud with a twig, licking the slats of the bench, hiding under the seat, breaking off the loose bark from the ancient tree trunks, staring at the horizon beyond the hill, humming with her eyes closed, imitating the voices of birds, dogs, cats, hens, horses. All for me, and yet nothing. It was her way of being with me, all these things I remember, but also her way of being alone in the park. Yes, perhaps my memory of her is fragmentary because reading alternated with my contemplation of the chubby-cheeked child with smooth hair that changed in the reflection of the light: now wheat-colored, now burnt chestnut. And it is only today that I think how Amilamia in that moment established the other point of support for my life, the one that created the tension between my own irresolute childhood and the wide world, the promised land that was beginning to be mine through my reading.

Not then. Then I dreamed about the women in my books, about the quintessential female—the word disturbed me—who assumed the disguise of Queen to buy the necklace in secret, about the imagined beings of mythology—half recognizable, half white-breasted, damp-bellied salamanders—who awaited monarchs in their beds. And thus, imperceptibly, I moved from indifference toward my childish companion to an acceptance of the child's grace and seriousness and from there to an unexpected rejection of a presence that became useless to me. She irritated me, finally.

I who was fourteen was irritated by that child of seven who was not yet memory or nostalgia, but rather the past and its reality. I had let myself be dragged along by weakness. We had run together, holding hands, across the meadow. Together we had shaken the pines and picked up the cones that Amilamia guarded jealously in her apron pocket. Together we had constructed paper boats and followed them, happy and gay, to the edge of the drain. And that afternoon, amid shouts of glee, when we tumbled together down the hill and rolled to a stop at its foot, Amilamia was on my chest, her hair between my lips; but when I felt her panting breath in my ear and her little arms sticky from sweets around my neck, I angrily pushed away her arms and let her fall. Amilamia cried, rubbing her wounded elbow and knee, and I returned to my bench. Then Amilamia went away and the following day she returned, handed me the card without a word, and disappeared, humming, into the woods. I hesitated whether to tear up the card or keep it in the pages of the book: *Afternoons on the Farm*. Even my reading had become infantile because of Amilamia. She did not return to the park. After a few days I left on my vacation, and when I returned it was to the duties of the first year of prep school. I never saw her again.

II

And now, almost rejecting the image that is unfamiliar without being fantastic, but is all the more painful for being so real, I return to that forgotten park and stopping before the grove of pines and eucalyptus I recognize the smallness of the bosky enclosure that my memory has insisted on drawing with an amplitude that allows sufficient space for the vast swell of my imagination. After all, Michel Strogoff and Huckleberry Finn, Milady de Winter and Geneviève de Brabant were born, lived, and died here: in a little garden surrounded by mossy iron railings, sparsely planted with old, neglected trees, scarcely adorned by a concrete bench painted to look like wood which forces me to think that my beautiful wrought-iron green bench never existed, or was part of my ordered, retrospective delirium. And the hill . . . How to believe the promontory Amilamia ascended and descended in her daily coming and going, that steep slope we rolled down together, was *this*. A barely elevated patch of dark stubble with no more height and depth than what my memory had created.

Com see me here where I draw it. So I would have to cross the garden, leave the woods behind, descend the hill in three loping steps, cut through that narrow grove of chestnuts—it was here, surely, where the child gathered the white petals—open the squeaking park gate and instantly recall . . . know . . . find oneself in the street, realize that every afternoon of one's adolescence, as if, by a miracle, one had succeeded in suspending the beat of the surrounding city, annulling that flood tide of whistles, bells, voices, sobs, engines, radios, imprecations. Which was the true magnet, the silent garden or the feverish city?

I wait for the light to change, and cross to the other side, my eyes never leaving the red iris detaining the traffic. I consult Amilamia's card. After all, that rudimentary map is the true magnet of the moment I am living, and just thinking about it disturbs me. I was obliged, after the lost afternoons of my fourteenth year, to follow the channels of discipline; now I find myself, at twenty-nine, duly certified with a diploma, owner of an office, assured of a moderate income, a bachelor still, with no family to support, slightly bored with sleeping with secretaries, scarcely excited by an occasional outing to the country or to the beach, feeling the lack of a central attraction such as my books, my park, and Amilamia once afforded me. I walk down the street of this gray suburb. The one-story houses, doorways peeling paint, succeed each other monotonously. Faint neighborhood sounds barely interrupt the general uniformity: the squeal of a knife sharpener here, the hammering of a shoe repairman there. The neighborhood children are playing in the dead-end streets. The music of an organ grinder reaches my ears, mingled with the voices of children's rounds. I stop a moment to watch them, with the sensation, as fleeting, that Amilamia must be among these groups of children, immodestly exhibiting her flowered panties, hanging by her knees from some balcony, still fond of acrobatic excesses, her apron pocket filled with white petals. I smile, and for the first time I am able to imagine the young lady of twenty-two who, even if she still lives at this address, will laugh at my memories, or who perhaps will have forgotten the afternoons spent in the garden.

The house is identical to all the rest. The heavy entry door, two grilled windows with closed shutters. A one-story house, topped by a false neo-classic balustrade that probably conceals the practicalities of the roof terrace: clothes hanging on a line, tubs of water, servants' quarters, a chicken coop. Before I ring the bell, I want to rid myself of any illusion. Amilamia no longer lives here. Why would she stay fifteen years in the same house? Besides, in spite of her precocious independence and aloneness, she seemed to be a well-brought-up, well-behaved child, and this neighborhood is no longer elegant; Amilamia's parents, without doubt, have moved. But perhaps the new tenants will know where.

I press the bell and wait. I ring again. Here is another contingency: no one is home. And will I feel the need to look again for my childhood friend? No. Because it will not happen a second time that I open a book from my adolescence and find Amilamia's card. I'll return to my routine, I'll forget the moment whose importance lay in its fleeting surprise.

I ring once more. I press my ear to the door and am startled: I can hear harsh, irregular breathing on the other side; the sound of labored breathing, accompanied by the disagreeable odor of stale tobacco, filters through the cracks in the door.

"Good afternoon. Could you tell me . . . ?"

When he hears my voice, the person moves away with heavy and unsure steps. I press the bell again, shouting this time: "Hey! Open up! What's the matter? Don't you hear me?"

No response. I continue to ring, with no result. I move back from the door, still staring at the tiny cracks, as if distance might give me perspective, or even penetration. With my attention fixed on that damned door, I cross the street, walking backward. A piercing scream, followed by a prolonged and ferocious blast of a whistle, saves me in time. Dazed, I seek the person whose voice has just saved me. I see only the automobile moving down the street and I hang on to a lamppost, a hold that more than security offers me support as icy blood rushes through my burning, sweaty skin. I look toward the house that had been, that was, that must be, Amilamia's. There, behind the balustrade, as I had known there would be, are fluttering clothes hung out to dry. I don't know what else is hanging there—skirts, pajamas, blouses—I don't know. All I see is that starched little blue-checked apron, clamped by clothespins to the long cord swinging between an iron bar and a nail in the white wall of the terrace.

III

In the Bureau of Records I have been told that the property is in the name of a Señor R. Valdivia, who rents the house. To whom? That they don't know. Who is Valdivia? He is down as a businessman. Where does he live? Who are *you?* the young woman asked me with haughty curiosity. I haven't been able to show myself calm and assured. Sleep has not relieved my nervous fatigue. Valdivia. As I leave the Bureau, the sun offends me. I associate the aversion provoked by the hazy sun sifting through the clouds—thus all the more intense—with a desire to return to the humid, shaded park. No. It is only a desire to know if Amilamia lives in that house and why they won't let me enter. But what I must reject is the absurd idea that kept me awake all night. Having seen the apron drying on the flat roof, the apron in which she kept the flowers, I had begun to believe that in that house lived a seven-year-old girl I had known fourteen or fifteen years before . . . She must have a little girl! Yes. Amilamia, at twenty-two, is the mother of a girl who perhaps dresses the same, looks the same, repeats the same games, and—who knows—maybe even goes to the same park. And deep in thought, I arrive once more at the door of the house. I ring the bell and wait for the labored breathing on the other side of the door. I am mistaken. The door is opened by a woman who can't be more than fifty. But wrapped in a shawl, dressed in black and in flat black shoes, with no makeup and her salt-and-pepper hair pulled into a knot, she seems to have abandoned all illusion or pretense of youth. She observes me with eyes so indifferent they seem almost cruel.

"You want something?"

"Señor Valdivia sent me." I cough and run my hand over my hair. I should have picked up my briefcase at the office. I realize that without it I cannot play my role very well.

"Valdivia?" the woman asks without alarm, without interest.

"Yes. The owner of this house."

One thing is clear. The woman will reveal nothing by her face. She looks at me, impassive.

"Oh, yes. The owner of the house."

"May I come in?"

In bad comedies, I think, the traveling salesman sticks a foot in the door so they can't close the door in his face. I do the same, but the woman steps back and with a gesture of her hand invites me to come into what must have been a garage. On one side there is a glass-paneled door, its paint faded. I walk toward the door over the yellow tiles of the entryway and ask again, turning toward the woman, who follows me with tiny steps: "This way?"

I notice for the first time that in her pale hands she carries a chaplet, which she toys with ceaselessly. I haven't seen one of those old-fashioned rosaries since my childhood and I want to say something about it, but the brusque, decisive manner with which the woman opens the door precludes any gratuitous conversation. We enter a long, narrow room. The woman quickly opens the shutters. But because of four large perennials growing in glass-encrusted porcelain pots the room remains in shadow. The only other objects in the room are an old high-backed cane sofa and a rocking chair. But it is neither the plants nor the sparseness of the furniture that holds my attention.

The woman asks me to sit on the sofa before she sits down in the rocking chair. Beside me, on the cane arm of the sofa, there is an open magazine.

"Señor Valdivia sends his apologies for not having come himself."

The woman rocks, unblinking. I peer at the comic book out of the corner of my eye.

"He sends greetings and . . ."

I stop, waiting for a reaction from the woman. She continues to rock. The magazine is covered with red scribbles.

". . . and asks me to inform you that he must disturb you for a few days . . ."

My eyes search the room rapidly.

". . . A reassessment of the house must be made for tax purposes. It seems it hasn't been done for . . . You have been living here since . . . ?"

Yes. That is a stubby lipstick lying under the chair. If the woman smiles, it is while the slow-moving hands caress the chaplet. I sense, for an instant, a swift flash of ridicule that does not quite disturb her features. She still does not answer.

". . . for at least fifteen years, isn't that so?"

She does not agree. She does not disagree. And on the pale thin lips there is not the least trace of lipstick . . .

". . . you, your husband, and . . . ?"

She stares at me, never changing expression, almost daring me to continue. We sit a moment in silence, she playing with the rosary, I leaning forward, my hands on my knees. I rise.

"Well then, I'll be back this afternoon with the papers . . ."

The woman nods and in silence picks up the lipstick and the comic book and hides them in the folds of her shawl.

IV

The scene has not changed. This afternoon, as I write sham figures in my notebook and feign interest in determining the value of the dull floorboards and the length of the living room, the woman rocks, the three decades of the chaplet whispering through her fingers. I sigh as I finish the supposed inventory of the living room and ask for permission to see the rest of the house. The woman rises, bracing her long black-clad arms on the seat of the rocking chair and adjusting the shawl on her narrow, bony shoulders.

She opens the frosted-glass door and we enter a dining room with very little additional furniture. But the aluminum-legged table and the four aluminum-and-plastic chairs lack even the hint of distinction of the living-room furniture. The other window, with wrought-iron grill and closed shutters, must sometime illuminate this bare-walled dining room, devoid of either shelves or sideboards. The only object on the table is a plastic fruit dish with a cluster of black grapes, two peaches, and a buzzing corona of flies. The woman, her arms crossed, her face expressionless, stops behind me. I take the risk of breaking the order of things: clearly, these rooms will not tell me anything I really want to know.

"Couldn't we go up to the roof?" I ask. "That might be the best way to measure the total area."

The woman's eyes light up as she looks at me, or perhaps it is only the contrast with the shadows of the dining room.

"What for?" she says at last. "Señor . . . Valdivia . . . knows the dimensions very well."

And those pauses, before and after the owner's name, are the first indication that something has at last begun to trouble the woman, forcing her, in self-defense, to resort to a kind of irony.

"I don't know." I make an effort to smile. "Perhaps I prefer to go from top to bottom and not"—my false smile drains away—"from bottom to top."

"You will go the way I show you," the woman says, her arms crossed over her chest, a silver crucifix dangling over her dark belly.

Before smiling weakly, I force myself to realize that in these shadows my gestures are of no use, aren't even symbolic. I open the notebook with a creak of the cardboard cover and continue making notes with the greatest possible speed, never glancing up, taking down numbers and estimates for a job whose fiction—the light flush in my cheeks and the perceptible dryness of my tongue tell me—is deceiving no one. And as I cover the graph paper with absurd signs, with square roots and algebraic formulas, I ask myself what is keeping me from getting to the point, from asking about Amilamia and getting out of here with a satisfactory answer. Nothing. And yet I am certain, even if I obtained a response, I would not have the truth. My slim, silent companion is a person I wouldn't look at twice in the street, but in this almost uninhabited house with the coarse furniture, she ceases to be an anonymous face in the crowd and is converted into a stock character of mystery. Such is the paradox, and if memories of Amilamia have once again aroused my appetite for the imaginary, I shall follow the rules of the game, I shall exhaust appearances, and not rest until I have the answer—perhaps simple and clear-cut, immediate and obvious—that lies beyond the veils the señora of the rosary unexpectedly places in my path. Do I bestow a gratuitous strangeness on my reluctant hostess? If so, I'll only take greater pleasure in the labyrinths of my own invention. And the flies are still buzzing around the fruit dish, occasionally pausing on the damaged end of the peach, a nibbled bite—I lean closer, using the pretext of my notes—where little teeth have left their mark in the velvety skin and ocher flesh of the fruit. I do not look toward the señora. I pretend I am taking notes. The fruit seems to be bitten but not touched. I crouch down to see better, rest my hands on the table, move my lips closer as if wishing to repeat the act of biting without touching. I look down and see another sign near my feet: the track of two tires that seem to be bicycle tires, the print of two rubber tires that come as far as the edge of the table and then lead away, growing fainter, the length of the room, toward the señora . . .

I close my notebook.

"Let us go on, señora."

When I turn toward her, I find her standing with her hands resting on the back of a chair. Seated before her, coughing from the smoke of his black cigarette, is a man with heavy shoulders and hidden eyes: those eyes, scarcely visible behind swollen, wrinkled lids as thick and drooped as the neck of an ancient turtle, seem nevertheless to follow my every movement.

The half-shaven cheeks, criss-crossed by a thousand gray furrows, sag from protruding cheekbones, and his greenish hands are folded under his arms. He is wearing a coarse blue shirt, and his rumpled hair is so curly it looks like the bottom of a barnacle-covered ship. He does not move, and the only sign of his existence is that difficult whistling breathing (as if every breath must breach a floodgate of phlegm, irritation, and abuse) I had already heard through the chinks of the door.

Ridiculously, he murmurs: "Good afternoon . . ." and I am disposed to forget everything: the mystery, Amilamia, the assessment, the bicycle tracks. The apparition of this asthmatic old bear justifies a prompt retreat. I repeat "Good afternoon," this time with an inflection of farewell. The turtle's mask dissolves into an atrocious smile: every pore of that flesh seems fabricated of brittle rubber, of painted, peeling oilcloth. The arm reaches out and detains me.

"Valdivia died four years ago," says the man in a distant, choking voice that issues from his belly instead of his larynx: a weak, high-pitched voice.

In the grip of that strong, almost painful, claw, I tell myself it is useless to pretend. But the waxen, rubber faces observing me say nothing, and so I am able, in spite of everything, to pretend one more time, to pretend I am speaking to myself when I say: "Amilamia . . ."

Yes; no one will have to pretend any longer. The fist that clutches my arm affirms its strength for only an instant, immediately its grip loosens, then it falls, weak and trembling, before lifting to take the waxen hand touching his shoulder: the señora, perplexed for the first time, looks at me with the eyes of a violated bird and sobs with a dry moan that does not disturb the rigid astonishment of her features. Suddenly the ogres of my imagination are two solitary, abandoned, wounded old people, scarcely able to console themselves in this shuddering clasp of hands that fills me with shame. My fantasy has brought me to this stark dining room to violate the intimacy and the secret of two human beings exiled from life by something I no longer have the right to share. I have never despised myself more. Never have words failed me so clumsily. Any gesture of mine would be in vain: shall I come closer, shall I touch them, shall I caress the woman's head, shall I ask them to excuse my intrusion? I return the notebook to my jacket pocket. I toss into oblivion all the clues in my detective story: the comic book, the lipstick, the nibbled fruit, the bicycle track, the blue-checked apron . . . I decide to leave the house without saying anything more. The old man, from behind his thick eyelids must have noticed.

The high breathy voice says: "Did you know her?"

The past, so natural, used by them every day, finally shatters my illusions. There is the answer. Did you know her? How long? How long must the world have lived without Amilamia, assassinated first by my forgetfulness, and then revived, scarcely yesterday, by a sad impotent memory? When did those serious gray eyes cease to be astonished by the delight of an always solitary garden? When did those lips cease to pout or press together thinly in that ceremonious seriousness with which, I now realize, Amilamia must have discovered and consecrated the objects and events of a life that, she perhaps knew intuitively, was fleeting?

"Yes, we played together in the park. A long time ago."

"How old was she?" says the old man, his voice even more muffled.

"She must have been about seven. No, older than that."

The woman's voice rises, as she lifts her arms, seemingly to implore: "What was she like, señor? Tell us what she was like, please."

I close my eyes. "Amilamia is a memory for me, too. I can only picture her through the things she touched, the things she brought, what she discovered in the park. Yes. Now I see her, coming down the hill. No. It isn't true that it was a scarcely elevated patch of stubble. It was a hill, with grass, and Amilamia's comings and goings had traced a path, and she waved to me from the top before she started down, accompanied by the music, yes, the music I saw, the painting I smelled, the tastes I heard, the odors I touched . . . my hallucination . . ." Do they hear me? "She came waving, dressed in white, in a blue-checked apron . . . the one you have hanging on the roof terrace . . ."

They take my arm and still I do not open my eyes.

"What was she like, señor?"

"Her eyes were gray and the color of her hair changed in the reflection of the sun and the shadow of the trees . . ."

They lead me gently, the two of them. I hear the man's labored breathing, the crucifix on the rosary hitting against the woman's body.

"Tell us, please . . ."

"The air brought tears to her eyes when she ran; when she reached my bench her cheeks were silvered with happy tears . . ."

I do not open my eyes. Now we are going upstairs. Two, five, eight, nine, twelve steps. Four hands guide my body.

"What was she like, what was she like?"

"She sat beneath the eucalyptus and wove garlands from the branches and pretended to cry so I would stop reading and go over to her . . ."

Hinges creak. The odor overpowers everything else: it routs the other senses, it takes its seat like a yellow Mongol upon the throne of my hallucination; heavy as a coffin, insinuating as the slither of draped silk, ornamented as a Turkish scepter, opaque as a deep, lost vein of ore, brilliant as a dead star. The hands no longer hold me. More than the sobbing, it is the trembling of the old people that envelops me. Slowly, I open my eyes: first through the dizzying liquid of my corneas, then through the web of my eyelashes, the room suffocated in that gigantic battle of perfumes is disclosed, effluvia and frosty, almost flesh-like petals;

the presence of the flowers is so strong here they seem to take on the quality of living flesh—the sweetness of the jasmine, the nausea of the lilies, the tomb of the tuberose, the temple of the gardenia. Illuminated through the incandescent wax lips of heavy, sputtering candles, the small windowless bedroom with its *aura* of wax and humid flowers assaults the very center of my plexus, and from there, only there at the solar center of life, am I able to come to, and perceive beyond the candles, amid the scattered flowers, the plethora of used toys: the colored hoops and wrinkled balloons, cherries dried to transparency, wooden horses with scraggly manes, the scooter, blind hairless dolls, bears spilling their sawdust, punctured oilcloth ducks, moth-eaten dogs, frayed jumping ropes, glass jars of dried candy, worn-out shoes, the tricycle (three wheels? no, two, and not a bicycle's—two parallel wheels below), little wool and leather shoes; and, facing me, within reach of my hand, the small coffin supported on blue crates decorated with paper flowers, flowers of life this time, carnations and sunflowers, poppies and tulips, but like the others, the ones of death, all part of a compilation created by the atmosphere of this funeral hothouse in which reposes, inside the silvered coffin, between the black silk sheets, on the pillow of white satin, that motionless and serene face framed in lace, highlighted with rose-colored tints, eyebrows traced by the lightest pencil, closed lids, real eyelashes, thick, that cast a tenuous shadow on cheeks as healthy as in the park days. Serious red lips, set almost in the angry pout that Amilamia feigned so I would come to play. Hands joined over her breast. A chaplet, identical to the mother's strangling that waxen neck. Small white shroud on the clean, prepubescent, docile body.

The old people, sobbing, are kneeling.

I reach out my hand and run my fingers over the porcelain face of my little friend. I feel the coldness of those painted features, of the doll queen who presides over the pomp of this royal chamber of death. Porcelain, wax, cotton. *Amilamia wil not forget her good friend—com see me here wher I draw it.*

I withdraw my fingers from the sham cadaver. Traces of my fingerprints remain where I touched the skin of the doll.

And nausea crawls in my stomach where the candle smoke and the sweet stench of the lilies in the enclosed room have settled. I turn my back on Amilamia's sepulcher. The woman's hand touches my arm. Her wildly staring eyes bear no relation to the quiet, steady voice.

"Don't come back, señor. If you truly loved her, don't come back again."

I touch the hand of Amilamia's mother. I see through nauseous eyes the old man's head buried between his knees, and I go out of the room and to the stairway, to the living room, to the patio, to the street.

V

If not a year, nine or ten months have passed. The memory of that idolatry no longer frightens me. I have forgotten the odor of the flowers and the image of the petrified doll. The real Amilamia has returned to my memory and I have felt, if not content, sane again: the park, the living child, my hours of adolescent reading, have triumphed over the specters of a sick cult. The image of life is the more powerful. I tell myself that I shall live forever with my real Amilamia, the conqueror of the caricature of death. And one day I dare look again at that notebook with graph paper in which I wrote down the data of the spurious assessment. And from its pages, once again, Amilamia's card falls out, with its terrible childish scrawl and its map for getting from the park to her house. I smile as I pick it up. I bite one of the edges, thinking in spite of everything, the poor old people might accept this gift.

Whistling, I put on my jacket and straighten my tie. Why not go see them and offer them this card with the child's own writing?

I am almost running as I approach the one-story house. Rain is beginning to fall in large isolated drops, bringing out of the earth with magical immediacy the odor of dewy benediction that stirs the humus and quickens all that lives with its roots in the dust.

I ring the bell. The rain gets heavier and I become insistent. A shrill voice shouts: "I'm coming!" and I wait for the mother with her eternal rosary to open the door for me. I turn up the collar of my jacket. My clothes, my body, too, smell different in the rain. The door opens.

"What do you want? How wonderful you've come!"

The misshapen girl sitting in the wheelchair places one hand on the doorknob and smiles at me with an indecipherable, wry grin. The hump on her chest makes the dress into a curtain over her body, a piece of white cloth that nonetheless lends an air of coquetry to the blue-checked apron. The little woman extracts a pack of cigarettes from her apron pocket and quickly lights a cigarette, staining the end with orange-painted lips. The smoke causes the beautiful gray eyes to squint. She fixes her coppery, wheat-colored, permanent-waved hair, all the time staring at me with a desolate, inquisitive, hopeful—but at the same time fearful—expression.

"No, Carlos. Go away. Don't come back."

And from the house, at the same moment, I hear the high labored breathing of the old man, coming closer.

"Where are you? Don't you know you're not supposed to answer the door? Get back! Devil's spawn! Do I have to beat you again?"

And the rain trickles down my forehead, over my cheeks, and into my mouth, and the little frightened hands drop the comic book onto the wet paving stones.

TRANSLATED BY MARGARET SAYERS PEDEN

José Donoso

Chile
(1924–1996)

———————\\———————

José Donoso completed his degree in English at the Instituto Pedagógico in Santiago de Chile in 1949, the same year he received a scholarship to Princeton, where he received a B.A. in 1951. Donoso, whose first published stories were in English, could have become a Latin American Joseph Conrad had he adopted English as his literary language. Instead, he returned home and began to compose his intricate, minute, and brilliant fictions about the Chilean bourgeoisie. Donoso became a sort of Latin American Henry James—a keen observer of social mores and a deft artificer of narrative technique, particularly point of view. But he adds to this formula a passion for levels of consciousness and for the multiple convolutions of madness, often reflected in the musings of his wildly unreliable narrators. Donoso's first major novel was *Coronation* (1957), and a later work, *Hell Has No Limits* (1966), is a minor masterpiece. His short stories and novellas are among the best from Latin America and have been collected in *Charleston and Other Stories* and *Sacred Families: Three Novellas* (both published in 1977). In the 1960s, Donoso was part of the so-called Boom of the Latin American novel, the group of jet-setting writers that included Fuentes, García Márquez, Vargas Llosa, and Cortázar. *The Boom in Spanish American Literature: A Personal History* (1972) is a witty memoir of that period. His best work, *The Obscene Bird of Night* (1970), is a compendium of Donoso's obsessions and a masterful if labyrinthine creation. Perhaps the best description of Donoso's fictional world is the Indian myth of the *imbunche*, which informs that novel, in which the victim is monstrously transmuted by closing off all of the orifices of his body. Donoso's fiction is equally shut off, sealed and self-contained, creating a hallucinatory, autistic kind of microcosm. But Donoso's gift is to be able to create such an airless environment without its existing in a vacuum. Various sectors of Chilean society, particularly the middle and upper classes, are sharply depicted and satirized in his works. "The Walk," Donoso's best-known story, is a kind of microcosm of his larger fictions.

The Walk

I

It happened when I was very small, when my Aunt Matilde and Uncle Gustavo and Uncle Armando, my father's unmarried sister and brothers, and my father himself, were still alive. Now they are all dead. That is, I'd rather think they are all dead, because it's easier, and it's too late now to be tortured with questions that were certainly not asked at the opportune moment. They weren't asked because the events seemed to paralyze the three brothers, leaving them shaken and horrified. Afterwards, they erected a wall of forgetfulness or indifference in front of it all so they could keep their silence and avoid tormenting themselves with futile conjectures. Maybe it wasn't that way; it could be that my imagination and my memory play me false. After all, I was only a boy at the time, and they weren't required to include me in their anguished speculations, if there ever were any, or keep me informed of the outcome of their conversations.

What was I to think? Sometimes I heard the brothers talking in the library in low voices, lingeringly, as was their custom; but the thick door screened the meaning of the words, allowing me to hear only the deep, deliberate counterpoint of their voices. What were they saying? I wanted them to be talking in there about what was really important; to abandon the respectful coldness with which they addressed one another, to open up their doubts and anxieties and let them bleed. But I had so little faith that would happen; while I loitered in the high-walled vestibule near the library door, the certainty was engraved on my mind that they had chosen to forget, and had come together only to discuss, as always, the cases that fell within their bailiwick, maritime law. Now I think perhaps they were right to want to erase it all, for why should they live with the useless terror of having to accept that the streets of a city can swallow a human being, annul it, leave it without life or death, suspended in a dimension more threatening than any dimension with a name?

And yet . . .

One day, months after the incident, I surprised my father looking down at the street from the second-floor sitting room. The sky was narrow, dense, and the humid air weighted on the big limp leaves of the ailanthus trees. I went over to my father, anxious for some minimal explanation.

"What are you doing here, father?" I whispered.

When he answered, something closed suddenly over the desperation on his face, like a shutter slamming on an unmentionable scene.

"Can't you see? I'm smoking," he answered.

And he lit a cigarette.

It wasn't true. I knew why he was looking up and down the street, with his eyes saddened, once in a while bringing his hand up to his soft brown goatee: it was in hopes of seeing her reappear, come back just like that, under the trees along the sidewalk, with the white dog trotting at her heels. Was he waiting there to gain some certainty?

Little by little I realized that not only my father but both his brothers, as if hiding from one another and without admitting even to themselves what they were doing, hovered around the windows of the house, and if a passerby chanced to look up from the sidewalk across the street, he might spot the shadow of one of them posted beside a curtain, or a face aged by suffering in wait behind the window panes.

II

Yesterday I passed the house we lived in then. It's been years since I was last there. In those days the street under the leafy ailanthus trees was paved with quebracho wood, and from time to time a noisy streetcar would go by. Now there aren't any wooden pavements, or streetcars, or trees along the sidewalk. But our house is still standing, narrow and vertical as a book slipped in between the thick shapes of the new buildings; it has stores on the ground floor and a loud sign advertising knit undershirts stretched across the two second-floor balconies.

When we lived there, most of the houses were tall and slender like ours. The block was always cheerful, with children playing games in the splashes of sunlight on the sidewalks, and servants from the prosperous homes gossiping as they came back from shopping. But our house wasn't happy. I say "wasn't happy" as opposed to "was sad," because that's exactly what I mean. The word "sad" wouldn't be correct because it has connotations that are too clearly defined; it has a weight and dimensions of its own. And what went on in our house was exactly the opposite: an absence, a lack, which, because it was unknown, was irremediable, something that had no weight, yet weighed because it didn't exist.

When my mother died, before I turned four, they thought I needed to have a woman around to care for me. Because Aunt Matilde was the only woman in the family and lived with my uncles Gustavo and Armando, the three of them came to our house, which was big and empty.

Aunt Matilde carried out her duties toward me with the punctiliousness characteristic of everything she did. I didn't doubt that she cared for me, but I never experienced that affection as something palpable that united us. There was something rigid about her feelings, as there was about those of the men in the family, and love was retained within each separate being, never leaping over the boundaries to express itself and unite us. Their idea of expressing affection consisted of carrying out their duties toward one another perfectly, and above all, of never upsetting one another. Perhaps to express affection otherwise was no longer necessary to them, since they shared so many anecdotes and events in which, possibly, affection had already been expressed to the saturation point, and all this conjectural past of tenderness was now stylized in the form of precise actions, useful symbols that did not require further explanation. Respect alone remained, as a point of contact among four silent, isolated relatives who moved through the halls of that deep house which, like a book, revealed only its narrow spine to the street.

I, of course, had no anecdotes in common with Aunt Matilde. How could I, since I was a boy and only half understood the austere motives of grown-ups? I desperately wanted this contained affection to overflow, to express itself differently, in enthusiasm, for example, or a joke. But she could not guess this desire of mine because her attention wasn't focused on me. I was only a peripheral person in her life, never central. And I wasn't central because the center of her whole being was filled with my father and my uncles Gustavo and Armando. Aunt Matilde was the only girl—an ugly girl at that—in a family of handsome men, and realizing she was unlikely to find a husband, she dedicated herself to the comfort of those men: keeping house for them, taking care of their clothes, preparing their favorite dishes. She carried out these functions without the slightest servility, proud of her role because she had never once doubted her brothers' excellence and dignity. In addition, like all women, she possessed in great measure that mysterious faith in physical well-being, thinking that if it is not the main thing, it is certainly the first, and that not to be hungry or cold or uncomfortable is the prerequisite of any good of another order. It wasn't that she suffered if defects of that nature arose, but rather that they made her impatient, and seeing poverty or weakness around her, she took immediate steps to remedy what she did not doubt were mere errors in a world that ought to be—no, *had* to be—perfect. On another plane, this was intolerance of shirts that weren't ironed exquisitely, of meat that wasn't a prime cut, of dampness leaking into the humidor through someone's carelessness. Therein lay Aunt Matilde's undisputed strength, and through it she nourished the roots of her brothers' grandness and accepted their protection because they were men, stronger and wiser than she.

Every night after dinner, following what must have been an ancient family ritual, Aunt Matilde went upstairs to the bedrooms and turned down the covers on each one of her brothers' beds, folding up the bedspreads with her bony hands. For him who was sensitive to the cold, she would lay a blanket at the foot of the bed; for him who read before going to sleep, she would prop a feather pillow against the headboard. Then, leaving the lamps lit on the night tables beside their vast beds, she went downstairs to the billiard room to join the men, to have coffee with them and play a few caroms before they retired, as if by her command, to fill the empty effigies of the pajamas laid out on the neatly turned-down white sheets.

But Aunt Matilde never opened my bed. Whenever I went up to my room I held my breath, hoping to find my bed turned down with the recognizable expertise of her hands, but I always had to settle for the style, so much less pure, of the servant who did it. She never conceded me this sign of importance because I was not one of her brothers. And not to be "one of my brothers" was a shortcoming shared by so many people . . .

Sometimes Aunt Matilde would call me in to her room, and sewing near the high window she would talk to me without ever asking me to reply, taking it for granted that all my feelings, tastes, and thoughts were the result of what she was saying, certain that nothing stood in the way of my receiving her words intact. I listened to her carefully. She impressed on me what a privilege it was to have been born the son of one of her brothers, which made it possible to have contact with all of them. She spoke of their absolute integrity and genius as lawyers in the most intricate of maritime cases, informing me of her enthusiasm regarding their prosperity and distinction, which I would undoubtedly continue. She explained the case of an embargo on a copper shipment, another about damages resulting from a collision with an insignificant tugboat, and another having to do with the disastrous effects of the overlong stay of a foreign ship. But in speaking to me of ships, her words did not evoke the magic of those hoarse foghorns I heard on summer nights when, kept awake by the heat, I would climb up to the attic and watch from a roundel the distant lights floating, and those darkened blocks of the recumbent city to which I had no access because my life was, and always would be, perfectly organized. Aunt Matilde did not evoke that magic for me because she was ignorant of it; it had no place in her life, since it could not have a place in the life of people destined to die with dignity and then establish themselves in complete comfort in heaven, a heaven that would be identical to our house. Mute, I listened to her words, my eyes fixed on the length of light-colored thread which, rising against the black of her blouse, seemed to catch all the light from the window. I had a melancholy feeling of frustration, hearing those foghorns in the night and seeing that dark and starry city so much like the heaven in which Aunt Matilde saw no mystery at all. But I rejoiced at the world of security her words sketched out for me, that magnificent rectilinear road which ended in a death not feared, exactly like this life, lacking the fortuitous and unexpected. For death was not terrible. It was the final cutoff, clean and definite, nothing more. Hell existed, of course, though not for us, but rather to punish the rest of the city's inhabitants, or those nameless sailors who caused the damages that, after the struggle in the courts was over, always filled the family bank accounts.

Any notion of the unexpected, of any kind of fear, was so alien to Aunt

Matilde that, because I believe fear and love to be closely related, I am overcome by the temptation to think that she didn't love anybody, not at that time. But perhaps I am wrong. In her own rigid, isolated way, it is possible that she was tied to her brothers by some kind of love. At night, after dinner, when they gathered in the billiard room for coffee and a few rounds, I went with them. There, faced with this circle of confined loves which did not include me, I suffered, perceiving that they were no longer tied together by their affection. It's strange that my imagination, remembering that house, doesn't allow more than grays, shadows, shades; but when I evoke that hour, the strident green of the felt, the red and white of the billiard balls, and the tiny cube of blue chalk begin to swell in my memory, illuminated by the hanging lamp that condemned the rest of the room to darkness. Following one of the many family rituals, Aunt Matilde's refined voice would rescue each of her brothers from the darkness as his turn came up: "Your shot, Gustavo . . ."

And cue in hand, Uncle Gustavo would lean over the green of the table, his face lit up, fragile as paper, the nobility of it strangely contradicted by his small, close-set eyes. When his turn was over, he retreated into the shadows, where he puffed on a cigar whose smoke floated lackadaisically off, dissolved by the darkness of the ceiling. Then their sister would say: "Your shot, Armando . . ."

And Uncle Armando's soft, timid face, his great blue eyes shielded by gold-framed glasses, would descend into the light. His game was generally bad, because he was the "baby," as Aunt Matilde sometimes called him. After the comments elicited by his game, he would take refuge behind the newspaper and Aunt Matilde would say: "Pedro, your shot . . ."

I held my breath watching my father lean over to shoot; I held it seeing him succumb to his sister's command, and, my heart in a knot, I prayed he would rebel against the established order. Of course, I couldn't know that that rigid order was in itself a kind of rebellion invented by them against the chaotic, so that the terrible hand of what cannot be explained or solved would never touch them. Then my father would lean over the green felt, his soft glance measuring the distances and positions of the balls. He would make his play and afterwards heave a sigh, his moustache and goatee fluttering a little around his half-open mouth. Then he would hand me his cue to chalk with the little blue cube. By assigning me this small role, he let me touch at least the periphery of the circle that tied him to his brothers and sister, without letting me become more than tangential to it.

Afterwards Aunt Matilde played. She was the best shot. Seeing her ugly face, built up it seemed out of the defects of her brothers' faces, descend into the light, I knew she would win; she had to win. And yet . . . didn't I see a spark of joy in those tiny eyes in the middle of that face, as irregular as a suddenly clenched fist, when by accident one of the men managed to defeat her? That drop of joy was because, although she might want to, she could never have *let* them win. That would have been to introduce the mysterious element of love into a game which should not include it, because affection had to remain in its place, without overflowing to warp the precise reality of a carom.

III

I never liked dogs. Perhaps I had been frightened by one as a baby, I don't remember, but they have always annoyed me. In any case, at that time my dislike of animals was irrelevant since we didn't have any dogs in the house; I didn't go out very often, so there were few opportunities for them to molest me. For my uncles and father, dogs, as well as the rest of the animal kingdom, did not exist. Cows, of course, supplied the cream that enriched our Sunday dessert brought in on a silver tray; and birds chirped pleasantly at dusk in the elm tree, the only inhabitant of the garden behind our house. The animal kingdom existed only to the extent that it contributed to the comfort of their persons. It is needless to say, then, that the existence of dogs, especially our ragged city strays, never even grazed their imaginations.

It's true that occasionally, coming home from Mass on Sunday, a dog might cross our path, but it was easy to ignore it. Aunt Matilde, who always walked ahead with me, simply chose not to see it, and some steps behind us, my father and uncles strolled discussing problems too important to allow their attention to be drawn by anything so banal as a stray dog.

Sometimes Aunt Matilde and I went early to Mass to take communion. I was almost never able to concentrate on receiving the sacrament, because generally the idea that she was watching me without actually looking at me occupied the first plane of my mind. Although her eyes were directed toward the altar or her head bowed before the Almighty, any movement I made attracted her attention, so that coming out of church, she would tell me with hidden reproach that doubtless some flea trapped in the pews had prevented my concentrating on the thought that we shall all meet death in the end and on praying for it not to be too painful, for that was the purpose of Mass, prayer, and communion.

It was one of those mornings.

A fine mist was threatening to transform itself into a storm, and the quebracho paving extended its neat glistening fan shapes from sidewalk to sidewalk, bisected by the streetcar rails. I was cold and wanted to get home, so I hurried the pace under Aunt Matilde's black umbrella. Few people were out because it was early. A colored gentleman greeted us without tipping his hat. My aunt then proceeded to explain her dislike of persons of mixed race, but suddenly, near where we were walking, a streetcar I didn't hear coming braked loudly, bringing her monologue to an end. The conductor put his head out the window: "Stupid dog!" he shouted.

We stopped to look. A small white bitch escaped from under the wheels, and, limping painfully with its tail between its legs, took refuge in a doorway. The streetcar rolled off.

"These dogs, it's the limit the way they let them run loose . . ." protested Aunt Matilde.

Continuing on our way, we passed the dog cowering in the doorway. It was small and white, with legs too short for its body and an ugly pointed nose that revealed a whole genealogy of alleyway misalliances, the product of different races running around the city for generations looking for food in garbage cans and harbor refuse. It was soaking wet, weak, shivering with the cold or a fever. Passing in front of it, I witnessed a strange sight: my aunt's and the dog's eyes met. I couldn't see the expression on my aunt's face. I only saw the dog look at her, taking possession of her glance, whatever it contained, merely because she was looking at it.

We headed home. A few paces further on, when I had almost forgotten the dog, my aunt startled me by turning abruptly around and exclaiming: "Shoo, now! Get along with you!"

She had turned around completely certain of finding it following us and I trembled with the unspoken question prompted by my surprise: "How did she know?" She couldn't have heard it because the dog was following us at some distance. But she didn't doubt it. Did the glance that passed between them, of which I had only seen the mechanical part—the dog's head slightly raised toward Aunt Matilde, Aunt Matilde's head slightly turned toward it—did it contain some secret agreement, some promise of loyalty I hadn't perceived? I don't know. In any case, when she turned to shoo the dog, her voice seemed to contain an impotent desire to put off a destiny that had already been accomplished. Probably I say all this in hindsight, my imagination imbuing something trivial with special meaning. Nevertheless, I certainly felt surprise, almost fear, at the sight of my aunt suddenly losing her composure and condescending to turn around, thereby conceding rank to a sick, dirty dog following us for reasons that could not have any importance.

We arrived home. We climbed the steps and the animal stayed down below, watching us through the torrential rain that had just begun. We went inside, and the delectable smell of a post-communion breakfast erased the dog from my mind. I had never felt the protectiveness of our house so deeply as I did that morning; the security of those walls delimiting my world had never been so delightful to me.

What did I do the rest of the day? I don't remember, but I suppose I did the usual thing: read magazines, did homework, wandered up and down the stairs, went to the kitchen to ask what was for dinner.

On one of my tours through the empty rooms—my uncles got up late on rainy Sundays, excusing themselves from church—I pulled a curtain back to see if the rain was letting up. The storm went on. Standing at the foot of the steps, still shivering and watching the house, I saw the white dog again. I let go of the curtain to avoid seeing it there, soaking wet and apparently mesmerized. Suddenly, behind me, from the dark part of the sitting room, Aunt Matilde's quiet voice reached me, as she leaned over to touch a match to the wood piled in the fireplace: "Is she still there?"

"Who?"

I knew perfectly well who.

"The white dog."

I answered that it was. But my voice was uncertain in forming the syllables, as if somehow my aunt's question was pulling down the walls around us, letting the rain and the inclement wind enter and take over the house.

IV

That must have been the last of the winter storms, because I remember quite vividly that in the following days the weather cleared and the nights got warmer.

The white dog remained posted at our door, ever trembling, watching the window as though looking for somebody. In the morning, as I left for school, I would try to scare it away, but as soon as I got on the bus, I saw it peep timidly around the corner or from behind a lamppost. The servants tried to drive it away too, but their attempts were just as futile as my own, because the dog always came back, as if to stay near our house was a temptation it had to obey, no matter how dangerous.

One night we were all saying good night to one another at the foot of the stairs. Uncle Gustavo, who always took charge of turning off the lights, had taken care of all of them except that of the staircase, leaving the great dark space of the vestibule populated with darker clots of furniture. Aunt Matilde, who was telling Uncle Armando to open his window to let some air in, suddenly fell silent, leaving her good nights unfinished. The rest of us, who had begun to climb the stairs, stopped cold.

"What's the matter?" asked my father, coming down a step.

"Go upstairs," murmured Aunt Matilde, turning to gaze into the shadows of the vestibule.

But we didn't go upstairs.

The silence of the sitting room, generally so spacious, filled up with the secret voice of each object—a grain of dirt slipping down between the old wallpaper and the wall, wood creaking, a loose window pane rattling—and those brief seconds were flooded with sounds. Someone else was in the room with us. A small white shape stood out in the shadows near the service door. It was the dog, who limped slowly across the vestibule in the direction of Aunt Matilde, and without even looking at her lay down at her feet.

It was as if the dog's stillness made movement possible for us as we watched the scene. My father came down two steps, Uncle Gustavo turned on the lights, Uncle Armando heavily climbed the stairs and shut himself into his room.

"What is this?" my father asked.

Aunt Matilde remained motionless.

"How could she have got in?" she asked herself suddenly.

Her question seemed to imply a feat: in this lamentable condition, the dog had leaped over walls, or climbed through a broken window in the basement, or evaded the servants' vigilance by slipping through a door left open by accident.

"Matilde, call for somebody to get it out of here," my father said, and went upstairs followed by Uncle Gustavo.

The two of us stood looking at the dog.

"She's filthy," she said in a low voice. "And she has a fever. Look, she's hurt . . ."

She called one of the servants to take her away, ordering her to give the dog food and call the veterinarian the next day.

"Is it going to stay in the house?" I asked.

"How can she go outside like that?" Aunt Matilde murmured. "She has to get better before we can put her out. And she'll have to get better quickly, because I don't want any animals in the house." Then she added: "Get upstairs to bed."

She followed the servant who was taking the dog away.

I recognized Aunt Matilde's usual need to make sure everything around her went well, the strength and deftness that made her the undoubted queen of things immediate, so secure inside her limitations that for her the only necessary thing was to correct flaws, mistakes not of intention or motive, but of state of being. The white dog, therefore, was going to get well. She herself would take charge of that, because the dog had come within her sphere of power. The veterinarian would bandage the dog's foot under her watchful eyes, and, protected by gloves and a towel, she herself would undertake to clean its sores with disinfectants that would make it whimper. Aunt Matilde remained deaf to those whimpers, certain, absolutely certain, that what she was doing was for the dog's good.

And so it was.

The dog stayed in the house. It wasn't that I could see it, but I knew the balance between the people who lived there, and the presence of any stranger, even if in the basement, would establish a difference in the order of things. Something, something informed me of its presence under the same roof as myself. Perhaps that something was not so very imponderable. Sometimes I saw Aunt Matilde with rubber gloves in her hand, carrying a vial full of red liquid. I found scraps of meat on a dish in a basement passageway when I went down to look at a bicycle I had recently been given. Sometimes, the suspicion of a bark would reach my ears faintly, absorbed by floors and walls.

One afternoon I went down to the kitchen and the white dog came in, painted like a clown with the red disinfectant. The servants threw it out unceremoniously. But I could see it wasn't limping anymore, and its once droopy tail now curled up like a plume, leaving its hindquarters shamelessly exposed.

That afternoon I said to Aunt Matilde: "When are you going to get rid of it?"

"What?" she asked.

She knew perfectly well what I meant.

"The white dog."

"She's not well yet," she answered.

Later on, I was about to bring up the subject again, to tell her that even if the dog wasn't completely well yet, there was nothing to prevent it from standing on its hind legs and rooting around in the garbage pails for food. But I never did, because I think that was the night Aunt Matilde, after losing the first round of billiards, decided she didn't feel like playing anymore. Her brothers went on playing and she, sunk in the big leather sofa, reminded them of their turns. After a while she made a mistake in the shooting order. Everybody was disconcerted for a moment, but the correct order was soon restored by the men, who rejected chance if it was not favorable. But I had seen.

It was as if Aunt Matilde was not there. She breathed at my side as always. The deep, muffling rug sank as usual under her feet. Her hands, crossed calmly on her lap—perhaps more calmly than on other evenings—weighed on her skirt. How it is that one feels a person's absence so clearly when that person's heart is in another place? Only her heart was absent, but the voice she used to call her brothers contained new meanings because it came from that other place.

The next nights were also marred by this almost invisible smudge of her absence. She stopped playing billiards and calling out turns altogether. The men seemed not to notice. But perhaps they did, because the matches became shorter, and I noted that the deference with which they treated her grew infinitesimally.

One night, as we came out of the dining room, the dog made its appearance in the vestibule and joined the family. The men, as usual, waited at the library door for their sister to lead the way into the billiard room, this time gracefully followed by the dog. They made no comment, as if they hadn't seen it, and began their match as on other nights.

The dog sat at Aunt Matilde's feet, very quiet, its lively eyes examining the room and watching the players' maneuvers, as if it was greatly amused. It was plump now, and its coat, its whole body glowed, from its quivering nose to its tail, always ready to wag. How long had the dog been in the house? A month? Longer, perhaps. But in that month Aunt Matilde had made it get well, caring for it without displays of emotion, but with the great wisdom of her bony hands dedicated to repairing what was damaged. Implacable in the face of its pain and whimpers, she had cured its wounds. Its foot was healed. She had disinfected it, fed it, bathed it, and now the white dog was whole again.

And yet none of this seemed to unite her to the dog. Perhaps she accepted it in the same way that my uncles that night had accepted its presence: to reject it would have given it more importance than it could have for them. I saw Aunt Matilde tranquil, collected, full of a new feeling that did not quite overflow to touch its object, and now we were six beings separated by a distance vaster than stretches of rug and air.

It happened during one of Uncle Armando's shots, when he dropped the little cube of blue chalk. Instantly, obeying a reflex that linked it to its picaresque past in the streets, the dog scampered to the chalk, yanked it away from Uncle Armando who had leaned over to pick it up, and held it in its mouth. Then a surprising thing happened. Aunt Matilde, suddenly coming apart, burst out in uncontrollable guffaws that shook her whole body for a few seconds. We were paralyzed. Hearing her, the dog dropped the chalk and ran to her, its tail wagging and held high, and jumped on her skirt. Aunt Matilde's laughter subsided, but Uncle Armando, vexed, left the room to avoid witnessing this collapse of order through the intrusion of the absurd. Uncle Gustavo and my father kept on playing billiards; now more than ever it was essential not to see, not to see anything, not to make remarks, not even to allude to the episode, and perhaps in this way to keep something from moving forward.

I did not find Aunt Matilde's guffaws amusing. It was only too clear that something dark had happened. The dog lay still on her lap. The crack of the billiard balls as they collided, precise and discrete, seemed to lead Aunt Matilde's hand first from its place on the sofa to her skirt, and then to the back of the sleeping dog. Seeing that expressionless hand resting there, I also observed that the tension I had never before recognized on my aunt's face—I never suspected it was anything other than dignity— had dissolved, and a great peace was softening her features. I could not resist what I did. Obeying something stronger than my own will, I slid closer to her on the sofa. I waited for her to beckon to me with a look or include me with a smile, but she didn't, because their new relationship was too exclusive; there was no place for me. There were only those two united beings. I didn't like it, but I was left out. And the men remained isolated, because they had not paid attention to the dangerous invitation to which Aunt Matilde had dared to listen.

V

Coming home from school in the afternoon, I would go straight downstairs and, mounting my new bicycle, would circle round and round in the narrow garden behind the house, around the elm tree and the pair of iron benches. On the other side of the wall, the neighbors' walnut trees were beginning to show signs of spring, but I didn't keep track of the seasons and their gifts because I had more serious things to think about. And as I knew nobody came down to the garden until the suffocations of midsummer made it essential, it was the best place to think about what was happening in our house.

Superficially it might be said nothing was happening. But how could one remain calm in the face of the curious relationship that had arisen between my aunt and the white dog? It was as if Aunt Matilde, after punctiliously serving and conforming to her unequal life, had at last found her equal, someone who spoke her innermost language, and as among women, they carried on an intimacy full of pleasantries and agreeable refinements. They ate bonbons that came in boxes tied with frivolous bows. My aunt arranged oranges, pineapples, grapes on the tall fruit stands, and the dog watched as if to criticize her taste or deliver an opinion. She seemed to have discovered a more benign region of life in this sharing of pleasantries, so much so that now everything had lost its importance in the shadow of this new world of affection.

Frequently, when passing her bedroom door, I would hear a guffaw like the one that had dashed the old order of her life to the ground that night, or I would hear her conversing—not soliloquizing as when talking to me—with someone whose voice I could not hear. It was the new life. The culprit, the dog, slept in her room in a basket—elegant, feminine, and absurd to my way of thinking—and followed her everywhere, except into the dining room. It was forbidden to go in there, but waited for its friend to emerge, followed her to the library or the billiard room, wherever we were going, and sat beside her or on her lap, and from time to time, sly looks of understanding would pass between them.

How was this possible? I asked myself. Why had she waited until now to overflow and begin a dialogue for the first time in her life? At times she seemed insecure about the dog, as if afraid the day might come when it would go away, leaving her alone with all this new abundance on her hands. Or was she still concerned about the dog's health? It was too strange.

These ideas floated like blurs in my imagination while I listened to the gravel crunching under the wheels of my bicycle. What was not blurry, on the other hand, was my vehement desire to fall seriously ill, to see if that way I too could gain a similar relationship. The dog's illness had been the cause of it all. Without that, my aunt would never have become linked to it. But I had an iron constitution, and furthermore it was clear that inside Aunt Matilde's heart there was room for only one love at a time, especially if it were so intense.

My father and uncles didn't seem to notice any change at all. The dog was quiet, and abandoning its street manners it seemed to acquire Aunt Matilde's somewhat dignified mien; but it preserved all the impudence of a female whom the vicissitudes of life have not been able to shock, as well as its good temper and its liking for adventure. It was easier for the men to accept than reject it since the latter would at least have meant speaking, and perhaps even an uncomfortable revision of their standards of security.

One night, when the pitcher of lemonade had already made its appearance on the library credenza, cooling that corner of the shadows, and the windows had been opened to the air, my father stopped abruptly at the entrance to the billiard room.

"What is this?" he exclaimed, pointing at the floor.

The three men gathered in consternation to look at a tiny round puddle on the waxed floor.

"Matilde!" Uncle Gustavo cried.

She came over to look and blushed with shame. The dog had taken refuge under the billiard table in the next room. Turning toward the table, my father saw it there, and suddenly changing course he left the room, followed by his brothers, heading toward the bedrooms, where each of them locked himself in, silent and alone.

Aunt Matilde said nothing. She went up to her room·followed by the dog. I stayed in the library with a glass of lemonade in my hand, looking out at the summer sky and listening, anxiously listening to distant foghorns and the noise of the unknown city, terrible and at the same time desirable, stretched out under the stars.

Then I heard Aunt Matilde descend. She appeared with her hat on and her keys jingling in her hand.

"Go to bed," she said. "I'm taking her for a walk on the street so she can take care of her business there."

Then she added something that made me nervous: "The night's so pretty . . ."

And she went out.

From that night on, instead of going upstairs after dinner to turn down her brothers' beds, she went to her room, put on her hat, and came down again, her keys jingling. She went out with the dog, not saying a word to anybody. My uncles and my father and I stayed in the billiard room, or, as the season wore on, sat on the benches in the garden, with the rustling elm and the clear sky pressing down on us. These nightly walks of Aunt Matilde's were never mentioned; there was never any indication that anybody knew anything important had changed in the house; but an element had been introduced there that contradicted all order.

At first Aunt Matilde would stay out at most fifteen or twenty minutes, returning promptly to take coffee with us and exchange a few commonplaces. Later, her outings inexplicably took more time. She was no longer a woman who walked her dog for reasons of hygiene; out there in the streets, in the city, there was something powerful attracting her. Waiting for her, my father glanced furtively at his pocket watch, and if she was very late, Uncle Gustavo went up to the second floor, as if he had forgotten something there, to watch from the balcony. But they never said anything. Once when Aunt Matilde's walk had taken too long, my father paced back and forth along the path between the hydrangeas, their flowers like blue eyes watching the night. Uncle Gustavo threw away a cigar he couldn't light satisfactorily, and then another, stamping it out under his heel. Uncle Armando overturned a cup of coffee. I watched, waiting for an eventual explosion, for them to say something, for them to express their anxiety and fill those endless minutes stretching on and on without the presence of Aunt Matilde. It was half past twelve when she came home.

"Why did you wait up for me?" she said smiling.

She carried her hat in her hand and her hair, ordinarily so neat, was disheveled. I noted that daubs of mud stained her perfect shoes.

"What happened to you?"

"Nothing," was her answer, and with that she closed forever any possible right her brothers might have had to interfere with those unknown hours, happy or tragic or insignificant, which were now her life.

I say they were her life, because in those instants she remained with us before going to her room, with the dog, muddy too, next to her, I perceived an animation in her eyes, a cheerful restlessness like the animal's, as if her eyes had recently bathed in scenes never before witnessed, to which we had no access. These two were companions. The night protected them. They belonged to the noises, to the foghorns that wafted over docks, dark or lamplit streets, houses, factories, and parks, finally reaching my ears.

Her walks with the dog continued. Now she said good night to us right after dinner, and all of us went to our rooms, my father, Uncle Gustavo, Uncle Armando, and myself. But none of us fell asleep until we heard her come in, late, sometimes very late, when the light of dawn already brightened the top of our elm tree. Only after she was heard closing her bedroom door would the paces by which my father measured his room stop, and a window be closed by one of her brothers to shut out the night, which had ceased being dangerous for the time being.

Once after she had come in very late, I thought I heard her singing very softly and sweetly, so I cracked open my door and looked out. She passed in front of my door, the white dog cuddled in her arms. Her face looked surprisingly young and perfect, although it was a little dirty, and I saw there was a tear in her skirt. This woman was capable of anything; she had her whole life before her. I went to bed terrified that this would be the end.

And I wasn't wrong. Because one night shortly afterwards, Aunt Matilde went out for a walk with the dog and never came back.

We waited up all night long, each one of us in his room, and she didn't come home. The next day nobody said anything. But the silent waiting went on, and we all hovered silently, without seeming to, around the windows of the house, watching for her. From that first day fear made the harmonious dignity of the three brothers' faces collapse, and they aged rapidly in a very short time.

"Your aunt went on a trip," the cook told me once, when I finally dared to ask.

But I knew it wasn't true.

Life went on in our house as if Aunt Matilde were still living with us. It's true they had a habit of gathering in the library, and perhaps locked in there they talked, managing to overcome the wall of fear that isolated them, giving free rein to their fears and doubts. But I'm not sure. Several times a visitor came who didn't belong to our world, and they would lock themselves in with him. But I don't believe he had brought them news of a possible investigation; perhaps he was nothing more than the boss of a longshoremen's union who was coming to claim damages for some accident. The door of the library was too thick, too heavy, and I never knew if Aunt Matilde, dragged along by the white dog, had got lost in the city, or in death, or in a region more mysterious than either.

TRANSLATED BY ANDRÉE CONRAD

Gabriel García Márquez

Colombia
(b. 1928)

Awarded the Nobel Prize (1982) for his masterpiece *One Hundred Years of Solitude* (1967), Gabriel García Márquez is, with Borges, the best-known Latin American writer to date. Before 1967 he had published two novels, *The Leaf Storm* (1955), and *In Evil Hour* (1962); a novella, *No One Writes to the Colonel* (1961); and a few short stories. After 1967 he wrote *The Autumn of the Patriarch* (1975), *Chronicle of a Death Foretold* (1981), and *Love in the Time of Cholera* (1985), among other books. García Márquez has the capacity to create both a vast, interconnected fictional universe and a brief, tightly woven narrative in the fashion of the North American masters Faulkner and Hemingway. The ease with which the most intricate of his stories flows has been likened to that of Cervantes. García Márquez's allegiance to left-wing regimes, such as Fidel Castro's, has not affected the nature of his writings, which are devoid of crass political cant. In fact, a doctrinaire Marxist reading of the author's major works would probably yield a reactionary García Márquez. Driven by primary passions—lust, greed, thirst for power—his characters are checked by crude societal, political, or natural forces, like figures in classical myth. His fictional world is primarily that of provincial Colombia, where ancient and modern practices clash comically, tragically, or both. So-called magical realism emanates from this conflict of traditional beliefs, which harken back to the Spanish Middle Ages, with the ways of modern-day capitalism. In "Balthazar's Marvelous Afternoon" (1962), the protagonist is bewildered by the whimsical wickedness of the rich that threatens both his rural pride and his artistic integrity.

Balthazar's Marvelous Afternoon

The cage was finished. Balthazar hung it under the eave, from force of habit, and when he finished lunch everyone was already saying that it was the most beautiful cage in the world. So many people came to see it that a crowd formed in front of the house, and Balthazar had to take it down and close the shop.

"You have to shave," Ursula, his wife, told him. "You look like a Capuchin."

"It's bad to shave after lunch," said Balthazar.

383

He had two weeks' growth, short, hard, and bristly hair like the mane of a mule, and the general expression of a frightened boy. But it was a false expression. In February he was thirty; he had been living with Ursula for four years, without marrying her and without having children, and life had given him many reasons to be on guard but none to be frightened. He did not even know that for some people the cage he had just made was the most beautiful one in the world. For him, accustomed to making cages since childhood, it had been hardly any more difficult than the others.

"Then rest for a while," said the woman. "With that beard you can't show yourself anywhere."

While he was resting, he had to get out of his hammock several times to show the cage to the neighbors. Ursula had paid little attention to it until then. She was annoyed because her husband had neglected the work of his carpenter's shop to devote himself entirely to the cage, and for two weeks had slept poorly, turning over and muttering incoherencies, and he hadn't thought of shaving. But her annoyance dissolved in the face of the finished cage. When Balthazar woke up from his nap, she had ironed his pants and a shirt; she had put them on a chair near the hammock and had carried the cage to the dining table. She regarded it in silence.

"How much will you charge?" she asked.

"I don't know," Balthazar answered. "I'm going to ask for thirty pesos to see if they'll give me twenty."

"Ask for fifty," said Ursula. "You've lost a lot of sleep in these two weeks. Furthermore, it's rather large. I think it's the biggest cage I've ever seen in my life."

Balthazar began to shave.

"Do you think they'll give me fifty pesos?"

"That's nothing for Mr. Chepe Montiel, and the cage is worth it," said Ursula. "You should ask for sixty."

The house lay in the stifling shadow. It was the first week of April and the heat seemed less bearable because of the chirping of the cicadas. When he finished dressing, Balthazar opened the door to the patio to cool off the house, and a group of children entered the dining room.

The news had spread. Dr. Octavio Giraldo, an old physician, happy with life but tired of his profession, thought about Balthazar's cage while he was eating lunch with his invalid wife. On the inside terrace, where they put the table on hot days, there were many flowerpots and two cages with canaries. His wife liked birds, and she liked them so much that she hated cats because they could eat them up. Thinking about her, Dr. Giraldo went to see a patient that afternoon, and when he returned he went by Balthazar's house to inspect the cage.

There were a lot of people in the dining room. The cage was on display on the table: with its enormous dome of wire, three stories inside, with passageways and compartments especially for eating and sleeping and swings in the space set aside for the birds' recreation, it seemed like a small-scale model of a gigantic ice factory. The doctor inspected it carefully, without touching it, thinking that in effect the cage was better than its reputation, and much more beautiful than any he had ever dreamed of for his wife.

"This is a flight of the imagination," he said. He sought out Balthazar among the group of people and, fixing his maternal eyes on him, added, "You would have been an extraordinary architect."

Balthazar blushed.

"Thank you," he said.

"It's true," said the doctor. He was smoothly and delicately fat, like a woman who had been beautiful in her youth, and he had delicate hands. His voice seemed like that of a priest speaking Latin. "You wouldn't even need to put birds in it," he said, making the cage turn in front of the audience's eyes as if he were auctioning it off. "It would be enough to hang it in the trees so it could sing by itself." He put it back on the table, thought a moment, looking at the cage, and said:

"Fine, then I'll take it."

"It's sold," said Ursula.

"It belongs to the son of Mr. Chepe Montiel," said Balthazar. "He ordered it specially."

The doctor adopted a respectful attitude.

"Did he give you the design?"

"No," said Balthazar. "He said he wanted a large cage, like this one, for a pair of troupials."

The doctor looked at the cage.

"But this isn't for troupials."

"Of course it is, Doctor," said Balthazar, approaching the table. The children surrounded him. "The measurements are carefully calculated," he said, pointing to the different compartments with his forefinger. Then he struck the dome with his knuckles, and the cage filled with resonant chords.

"It's the strongest wire you can find, and each joint is soldered outside and in," he said.

"It's even big enough for a parrot," interrupted one of the children.

"That it is," said Balthazar.

The doctor turned his head.

"Fine, but he didn't give you the design," he said. "He gave you no exact specifications, aside from making it a cage big enough for troupials. Isn't that right?"

"That's right," said Balthazar.

"Then there's no problem," said the doctor. "One thing is a cage big enough for troupials, and another is this cage. There's no proof that this one is the one you were asked to make."

"It's this very one," said Balthazar, confused. "That's why I made it."

The doctor made an impatient gesture.

"You could make another one," said Ursula, looking at her husband. And then, to the doctor: "You're not in any hurry."

"I promised it to my wife for this afternoon," said the doctor.

"I'm very sorry, Doctor," said Balthazar, "but I can't sell you something that's sold already."

The doctor shrugged his shoulders. Drying the sweat from his neck with a handkerchief, he contemplated the cage silently with the fixed, unfocused gaze of one who looks at a ship which is sailing away.

"How much did they pay you for it?"

Balthazar sought out Ursula's eyes without replying.

"Sixty pesos," she said.

The doctor kept looking at the cage. "It's very pretty." He sighed. "Extremely pretty." Then, moving toward the door, he began to fan himself energetically, smiling, and the trace of that episode disappeared forever from his memory.

"Montiel is very rich," he said.

In truth, José Montiel was not as rich as he seemed, but he would have been capable of doing anything to become so. A few blocks from there, in a house crammed with equipment, where no one had ever smelled a smell that couldn't be sold, he remained indifferent to the news of the cage. His wife, tortured by an obsession with death, closed the doors and windows after lunch and lay for two hours with her eyes opened to the shadow of the room, while José Montiel took his siesta. The clamor of many voices surprised her there. Then she opened the door to the living room and found a crowd in front of the house, and Balthazar with the cage in the middle of the crowd, dressed in white, freshly shaved, with that expression of decorous candor with which the poor approach the houses of the wealthy.

"What a marvelous thing!" José Montiel's wife exclaimed, with a radiant expression, leading Balthazar inside. "I've never seen anything like it in my life," she said, and added, annoyed by the crowd which piled up at the door:

"But bring it inside before they turn the living room into a grandstand."

Balthazar was no stranger to José Montiel's house. On different occasions, because of his skill and forthright way of dealing, he had been called in to do minor carpentry jobs. But he never felt at ease among the rich. He used to think about them, about their ugly and argumentative wives, about their tremendous surgical operations, and he always experienced a feeling of pity. When he entered their houses, he couldn't move without dragging his feet.

"Is Pepe home?" he asked.

He had put the cage on the dining-room table.

"He's at school," said José Montiel's wife. "But he shouldn't be long," and she added, "Montiel is taking a bath."

In reality, José Montiel had not had time to bathe. He was giving himself an urgent alcohol rub, in order to come out and see what was going on. He was such a cautious man that he slept without an electric fan so he could watch over the noises of the house while he slept.

"Adelaide!" he shouted. "What's going on?"

"Come and see what a marvelous thing!" his wife shouted.

José Montiel, obese and hairy, his towel draped around his neck, appeared at the bedroom window.

"What is that?"

"Pepe's cage," said Balthazar.

His wife looked at him perplexedly.

"Whose?"

"Pepe's," replied Balthazar. And then, turning toward José Montiel, "Pepe ordered it."

Nothing happened at that instant, but Balthazar felt as if someone had just opened the bathroom door on him. José Montiel came out of the bedroom in his underwear.

"Pepe!" he shouted.

"He's not back," whispered his wife, motionless.

Pepe appeared in the doorway. He was about twelve, and had the same curved eyelashes and was as quietly pathetic as his mother.

"Come here," José Montiel said to him. "Did you order this?"

The child lowered his head. Grabbing him by the hair, José Montiel forced Pepe to look him in the eye.

"Answer me."

The child bit his lip without replying.

"Montiel," whispered his wife.

José Montiel let the child go and turned toward Balthazar in a fury. "I'm very sorry, Balthazar," he said. "But you should have consulted me before going on. Only to you would it occur to contract with a minor." As he spoke, his face recovered its serenity. He lifted the cage without looking at it and gave it to Balthazar.

"Take it away at once, and try to sell it to whomever you can," he said. "Above all, I beg you not to argue with me." He patted him on the back and explained, "The doctor has forbidden me to get angry."

The child had remained motionless, without blinking, until Balthazar looked at him uncertainly with the cage in his hand. Then he emitted a guttural sound, like a dog's growl, and threw himself on the floor screaming.

José Montiel looked at him, unmoved, while the mother tried to pacify him. "Don't even pick him up," he said. "Let him break his head on the floor, and then put salt and lemon on it so he can rage to his heart's content." The child was shrieking tearlessly while his mother held him by the wrists.

"Leave him alone," José Montiel insisted.

Balthazar observed the child as he would have observed the death throes of a rabid animal. It was almost four o'clock. At that hour, at his house, Ursula was singing a very old song and cutting slices of onion.

"Pepe," said Balthazar.

He approached the child, smiling, and held the cage out to him. The child jumped up, embraced the cage which was almost as big as he was, and stood looking at Balthazar through the wirework without knowing what to say. He hadn't shed one tear.

"Balthazar," said José Montiel softly. "I told you already to take it away."

"Give it back," the woman ordered the child.

"Keep it," said Balthazar. And then, to José Montiel: "After all, that's what I made it for."

José Montiel followed him into the living room.

"Don't be foolish, Balthazar," he was saying, blocking his path. "Take your piece of furniture home and don't be silly. I have no intention of paying you a cent."

"It doesn't matter," said Balthazar. "I made it expressly as a gift for Pepe. I didn't expect to charge anything for it."

As Balthazar made his way through the spectators who were blocking the door, José Montiel was shouting in the middle of the living room. He was very pale and his eyes were beginning to get red.

"Idiot!" he was shouting. "Take your trinket out of here. The last thing we need is for some nobody to give orders in my house. Son of a bitch!"

In the pool hall, Balthazar was received with an ovation. Until that moment, he thought that he had made a better cage than ever before, that he'd had to give it to the son of José Montiel so he wouldn't keep crying, and that none of these things was particularly important. But then he realized that all of this had a certain importance for many people, and he felt a little excited.

"So they gave you fifty pesos for the cage."

"Sixty," said Balthazar.

"Score one for you," someone said. "You're the only one who has managed to get such a pile of money out of Mr. Chepe Montiel. We have to celebrate."

They bought him a beer, and Balthazar responded with a round for everybody. Since it was the first time he had ever been out drinking, by dusk he was completely drunk, and he was talking about a fabulous project of a thousand cages, at sixty pesos each, and then of a million cages, till he had sixty million pesos. "We have to make a lot of things to sell to the rich before they die," he was saying, blind drunk. "All of them are sick, and they're going to die. They're so screwed up they can't even get angry any more." For two hours he was paying for the jukebox, which played without interruption. Everybody toasted Balthazar's health, good luck, and fortune, and the death of the rich, but at mealtime they left him alone in the pool hall.

Ursula had waited for him until eight, with a dish of fried meat covered with slices of onion. Someone told her that her husband was in the pool hall, delirious with happiness, buying beers for everyone, but she didn't believe it, because Balthazar had never got drunk. When she went to bed, almost at midnight, Balthazar was in a lighted room where there were little tables, each with four chairs, and an outdoor dance floor, where the plovers were walking around. His face was smeared with rouge, and since he couldn't take one more step, he thought he wanted to lie down with two women in the same bed. He had spent so much that he had had to leave his watch in pawn, with the promise to pay the next day. A moment later, spread-eagled in the street, he realized that his shoes were being taken off, but he didn't want to abandon the happiest dream of his life. The women who passed on their way to five-o'clock Mass didn't dare look at him, thinking he was dead.

TRANSLATED BY GEROME BERNSTEIN

Mario Vargas Llosa

Peru
(b. 1936)

Mario Vargas Llosa is part of the remarkable foursome of writers who brought about what has come to be known as the Boom of the Latin American novel (Fuentes, García Márquez, and Cortázar were the other three). Raised in Bolivia and provincial Peru, Vargas Llosa moved to Lima as a young man and worked as a journalist. He soon distinguished himself as a short story writer and novelist, winning several important prizes in Europe, most notably the Seix Barral in Barcelona for his novel *The Time of the Hero* (1962). This book made Vargas Llosa an international celebrity. His production has continued unabated, with novels such as *The Green House* (1966), *Aunt Julia and the Scriptwriter* (1977), and *The Storyteller* (1987), as well as several plays and books of essays. Active in politics, Vargas Llosa ran unsuccessfully for the presidency of Peru in 1992. His fiction is mainly concerned with the struggle for and exercise of power in Latin America. Violence among males vying for the upper hand in groups—be they the regular army, the guerrillas, political parties, or gangs—is central in many of his books, particularly in masterpieces such as *The War of the End of the World* (1981). Vargas Llosa is haunted by the question of guilt and personal responsibility, concern he derived from an early fascination with Sartre and Camus. He is a prolific, original, and fluent storyteller in the manner of Balzac or Pérez Galdós. "The Challenge" was published in *Los jefes* (1959), his only book of short stories. Although an early work, it contains all of the main topics of Vargas Llosa's fiction, including the brutal way in which young men come of age, even in modern times.

The Challenge

We were drinking beer, like every Saturday, when Leonidas appeared in the doorway of the River Bar. We saw at once from his face that something had happened.

"What's up?" Leon asked.

Leonidas pulled up a chair and sat down next to us.

"I'm dying of thirst."

I filled a glass up to the brim for him and the head spilled over onto the table. Leonidas blew gently and sat pensively, watching how the bubbles burst. Then he drank it down to the last drop in one gulp.

"Justo's going to be fighting tonight," he said in a strange voice.

We kept silent for a moment. Leon drank; Briceño lit a cigarette.

"He asked me to let you know," Leonidas added. "He wants you to come."

Finally, Briceño asked: "How did it go?"

"They met this afternoon at Catacaos." Leonidas wiped his forehead and lashed the air with his hand; a few drops of sweat slipped from his fingers to the floor. "You can picture the rest."

"After all," Leon said, "if they had to fight, better that way, according to the rules. No reason to get scared either. Justo knows what he's doing."

"Yeah," Leonidas agreed, absent-mindedly. "Maybe it's better like that."

The bottles stood empty. A breeze was blowing, and just a few minutes earlier, we had stopped listening to the neighborhood band from the garrison at Grau playing in the plaza. The bridge was covered with people coming back from the open-air concert, and the couples who had sought out the shade of the embankment also began leaving their hiding places. A lot of people were going by the door of the River Bar. A few came in. Soon the sidewalk café was full of men and women talking loudly and laughing.

"It's almost nine," Leon said. "We better get going."

"Okay, boys," Leonidas said. "Thanks for the beer."

We left.

"It's going to be at 'the raft,' right?" Briceño asked.

"Yeah. At eleven. Justo'll look for you at ten-thirty, right here."

The old man waved good-bye and went off down Castilla Avenue. He lived on the outskirts of town, where the dunes started, in a lonely hut that looked as if it was standing guard over the city. We walked toward the plaza. It was nearly deserted. Next to the Tourist Hotel some young guys were arguing loudly. Passing by, we noticed a girl in the middle, listening, smiling. She was pretty and seemed to be enjoying herself.

"The Gimp's going to kill him," Briceño said suddenly.

"Shut up!" Leon snapped.

We went our separate ways at the corner by the church. I walked home quickly. Nobody was there. I put on overalls and two pullovers and hid my knife, wrapped in a handkerchief, in the back pocket of my pants. As I was leaving, I met my wife, just getting home.

"Going out again?" she asked.

"Yeah. I've got some business to take care of."

The boy was asleep in her arms and I had the impression he was dead.

"You've got to get up early," she insisted. "You work Sundays, remember?"

"Don't worry," I replied. "I'll be back in a few minutes."

I walked back down to the River Bar and sat at the bar. I asked for a beer and a sandwich, which I didn't finish. I'd lost my appetite. Somebody tapped me on the shoulder. It was Moses, the owner of the place.

"The fight's on?"

"Yeah. It's going to be at 'the raft.' Better keep quiet."

"I don't need advice from you," he said. "I heard about it a little while ago. I feel sorry for Justo, but really, he's been asking for it for some time. And the Gimp's not very patient—we all know that by now."

"The Gimp's an asshole."

"He used to be your friend . . ." Moses started to say, but checked himself.

Somebody was calling him from an outside table and he went off, but in a few minutes he was back at my side.

"Want me to go?" he asked.

"No. There's enough with us, thanks."

"Okay. Let me know if I can help some way. Justo's my friend too." He took a sip of my beer without asking. "Last night the Gimp was here with his bunch. All he did was talk about Justo and swear he was going to cut him up into little pieces. I was praying you guys wouldn't decide to come by here."

"I'd like to have seen the Gimp," I said. "His face is really funny when he's mad."

Moses laughed. "Last night he looked like the devil. And he's so ugly you can't look at him without feeling sick."

I finished my beer and left to walk along the embankment, but from the doorway of the River Bar I saw Justo, all alone, sitting at an outside table. He had on rubber sneakers and a faded pullover that came up to his ears. Seen from the side and against the darkness outside, he looked like a kid, a woman: from that angle, his features were delicate, soft. Hearing my footsteps, he turned around, showing me the purple scar wounding the other side of his face, from the corner of his mouth up to his forehead. (Some people say it was from a punch he took in a fight when he was a kid, but Leonidas insisted he'd been born the day of the flood and that scar was his mother's fright when she saw the water come right up to the door of the house.)

"I just got here," he said. "What's with the others?"

"They're coming. They must be on their way."

Justo looked at me straight on. He seemed about to smile, but got very serious and turned his head.

"What happened this afternoon?"

He shrugged and made a vague gesture.

"We met at the Sunken Cart. I just went in to have a drink and I bump into the Gimp and his guys face to face. Get it? If the priest hadn't stepped in, they'd have cut my throat right there. They jumped me like dogs. Like mad dogs. The priest pulled us apart."

"*Are you a man?*" the Gimp shouted.

"*More than you,*" Justo shouted.

"*Quiet, you animals,*" the priest said.

"*At 'the raft' tonight, then?*" the Gimp shouted.

"*Okay,*" said Justo.

"That was all."

The crowd at the River Bar had dwindled. A few people were left at the bar but we were alone at an outside table.

"I brought this," I said, handing him the handkerchief.

Justo opened the knife and hefted it. The blade was exactly the size of his hand, from his wrist to his fingernails. Then he took another knife out of his pocket and compared them.

"They're the same," he said. "I'll stick with mine."

He asked for a beer and we drank it without speaking, just smoking.

"I haven't got the time," said Justo, "but it must be past ten. Let's go catch up with them."

At the top of the bridge we met Briceño and Leon. They greeted Justo, shaking his hand.

"Listen, brother," Leon said, "you're going to cut him to shreds."

"That goes without saying," said Briceño. "The Gimp couldn't touch you."

They both had on the same clothes as before and seemed to have agreed on showing confidence and even a certain amount of light-heartedness in front of Justo.

"Let's go down this way," Leon said. "It's shorter."

"No," Justo said. "Let's go around. I don't feel like breaking my leg just now."

That fear was funny because we always went down to the riverbed by lowering ourselves from the steel framework holding up the bridge. We went a block farther on the street, then turned right and walked for a good while in silence. Going down the narrow path to the riverbed, Briceño tripped and swore. The sand was lukewarm and our feet sank in as if we were walking on a sea of cotton. Leon looked attentively at the sky.

"Lots of clouds," he said. "The moon's not going to help much tonight."

"We'll light bonfires," Justo said.

"Are you crazy?" I said. "You want the police to come?"

"It can be arranged," Briceño said without conviction. "It could be put off till tomorrow. They're not going to fight in the dark."

Nobody answered and Briceño didn't persist.

"Here's 'the raft,'" Leon said.

At one time—nobody knew when—a carob tree had fallen into the riverbed and it was so huge that it stretched three quarters of the way across the dry riverbed. It was very heavy and once it went down, the water couldn't raise it, could only drag it along for a few yards, so that each year "the raft" moved a little farther from the city. Nobody knew, either, who had given it the name "the raft," but that's what everybody called it.

"They're here already," Leon said.

We stopped about five yards short of "the raft." In the dim glow of night we couldn't make out the faces of whoever was waiting for us, only their silhouettes. There were five of them. I counted, trying in vain to find the Gimp.

"You go," Justo said.

I moved toward the tree trunk slowly, trying to keep a calm expression on my face.

"Stop!" somebody shouted. "Who's there?"

"Julian," I called out. "Julian Huertas. You blind?"

A small shape came out to meet me. It was Chalupas.

"We were just leaving," he said. "We figured little Justo had gone to the police to ask them to take care of him."

"I want to come to terms with a man," I shouted without answering him. "Not with this dwarf."

"Are you real brave?" Chalupas asked, with an edge in his voice.

"Silence!" the Gimp shouted. They had all drawn near and the Gimp advanced toward me. He was tall, much taller than all the others. In the dark I couldn't see but could only imagine the face armored in pimples, the skin, deep olive and beardless, the tiny pinholes of his eyes, sunken like two dots in that lump of flesh divided by the oblong bumps of his cheekbones, and his lips, thick as fingers, hanging from his chin, triangular like an iguana's. The Gimp's left foot was lame. People said he had a scar shaped like a cross on that foot, a souvenir from a pig that bit him while he was sleeping, but nobody had ever seen that scar.

"Why'd you bring Leonidas?" the Gimp asked hoarsely.

"Leonidas? Who's brought Leonidas?"

With his finger the Gimp pointed off to one side. The old man had been a few yards behind on the sand and when he heard his name mentioned he came near.

"What about me!" he said. He looked at the Gimp fixedly. "I don't need them to bring me along. I came along, on my own two feet, just because I felt like it. If you're looking for an excuse not to fight, say so."

The Gimp hesitated before answering. I thought he was going to insult the old man and I quickly moved my hand to my back pocket.

"Don't get involved, Pop," said the Gimp amiably. "I'm not going to fight with you."

"Don't think I'm so old," Leonidas said. "I've walked over a lot better than you."

"It's okay, Pop," the Gimp said. "I believe you." He turned to me. "Are you ready?"

"Yeah. Tell your friends not to butt in. If they do, so much the worse for them."

The Gimp laughed. "Julian, you know I don't need any backup. Especially today. Don't worry."

One of the men behind the Gimp laughed too. The Gimp handed something toward me. I reached out my hand: his knife blade was out and I had taken it by the cutting edge. I felt a small scratch in my palm and a trembling. The metal felt like a piece of ice.

"Got matches, Pop?"

Leonidas lit a match and held it between his fingers until the flame licked his fingernails. In the feeble light of the flame I thoroughly examined the knife. I measured its width and length; I checked the edge of its blade and its weight. "It's okay," I said.

"Chunga," the Gimp ordered. "Go with him."

Chunga walked between Leonidas and me. When we reached the others, Briceño was smoking and every drag he took lit up, for an instant, the faces of Justo, impassive, tight-lipped; Leon, chewing on something, maybe a blade of grass; and Briceño himself, sweating.

"Who told you you could come?" Justo asked harshly.

"Nobody told me," Leonidas asserted loudly. "I came because I wanted to. You want explanations from me?"

Justo didn't answer. I signaled to him and pointed out Chunga, who had kept a little ways back. Justo took out his knife and threw it. The weapon fell somewhere near Chunga's body and he shrank back.

"Sorry," I said, groping on the sand in search of the knife. "It got away from me. Here it is."

"You're not going to be so cute in a while," Chunga said.

Then, just as I had done, he passed his fingers over the blade by match light; he returned it to us without saying anything and went back to "the raft" in long strides. For a few minutes we were silent, inhaling the perfume from the cotton plants nearby, borne by a warm breeze in the direction of the bridge. On the two sides of the riverbed in back of us the twinkling lights of the city were visible. The silence was almost total; from time to time barking or braying ruptured it abruptly.

"Ready!" shouted a voice from the other side.

"Ready!" I shouted.

There was shuffling and whispering among the group of men next to "the raft." Then a limping shadow slid toward the center of the space the two groups had marked off. I saw the Gimp test the ground out there with his feet, checking whether there were stones, holes. My eyes sought out Justo: Leon and Briceño had put their arms on his shoulders. Justo detached himself from them quickly. When he was beside me, he smiled. I put out my hand to him. He started to back away but Leonidas jumped and grabbed him by the shoulders. The old man took off a poncho he was wearing over his back. He stood at my side.

"Don't get close to him even for a second." The old man spoke slowly, his voice trembling slightly. "Always at a distance. Dance round him till he's worn out. Most of all, guard your stomach and face. Keep your arm up all the time. Crouch down, feet firm on the ground. If you slip, kick in the air until he pulls back. . . . All right, get going. Carry yourself like a man. . . ."

Justo listened to Leonidas with his head lowered. I thought he was going to hug him but he confined himself to a brusque gesture. He yanked the poncho out of the old man's hands and wrapped it around his arm. Then he withdrew, walking on the sand with firm steps, his head up. As he walked away from us, the short piece of metal in his right hand shot back glints. Justo halted two yards away from the Gimp.

For a few seconds they stood motionless, silent, surely saying with their eyes how much they hated each other, observing each other, their muscles tight under their clothing, right hands angrily crushing their knives. From a distance, half hidden by the night's warm darkness, they didn't look so much like two men getting ready to fight as shadowy statues cast in some black material or the shadows of two young, solid carob trees on the riverbank, reflected in the air, not on the sand. As if answering some urgently commanding voice, they started moving almost simultaneously. Maybe Justo was first, a second earlier. Fixed to the spot, he began to sway slowly from his knees on up to his shoulders and the Gimp imitated him, also rocking without spreading his feet. Their postures were identical: right arm in front, slightly bent, with the elbow turned out, hands pointing directly at the adversary's middle, and the left arm, disproportionate, gigantic, wrapped in a poncho and crossed over like a shield at face height. At first only their bodies moved; their heads, feet and hands remained fixed. Imperceptibly, they both had been bending forward, arching their backs, flexing their legs as if to dive into the water. The Gimp was the first to attack: he jumped forward suddenly, his arm tracing a rapid circle. Grazing Justo without wounding him, the weapon had followed an incomplete path through the air when Justo, who was fast, spun around. Without dropping his guard, he wove a circle around the other man, sliding gently over the sand, at an ever increasing rate. The Gimp spun in place. He had bent lower, and as he turned himself round and round, following the direction of his rival, he trailed him constantly with his eyes, like a man hypnotized. Unexpectedly, Justo stood upright: we saw him fall on the other with his whole body and spring back to his spot in a second, like a jack-in-the-box.

"There," whispered Briceño. "He nicked him."

"On the shoulder," said Leonidas. "But barely."

Without having given a yell, still steady in his position, the Gimp went on dancing, while Justo no longer held himself to circling around him: he moved in and away from the Gimp at the same time, shaking the poncho, dropping and keeping up his guard, offering his body and whisking it away, slippery, agile, tempting and rejecting his opponent like a woman in heat. He wanted to get him dizzy, but the Gimp had experience as well as tricks. He broke out of the circle by retreating, still bent over, forcing Justo to pause and to chase after him, pursuing in very short steps, neck out, face protected by the poncho draped over his arm. The Gimp drew back, dragging his feet, crouching so low his knees nearly touched the sand. Justo jabbed his arm out twice and both times hit only thin air. "Don't get so close," Leonidas said next to me in a voice so low only I could hear him, just when that shape—the broad, deformed shadow that had shrunk by folding into itself like a caterpillar—brutally regained its normal height and, in growing as well as charging, cut Justo out of our view. We were breathless for one, two, maybe three seconds, watching the immense figures of the clinched fighters, and we heard a brief sound, the first we'd heard during the duel, similar to a belch. An instant later, to one side of the gigantic shadow another sprang up, this one thinner and more graceful, throwing up an invisible wall between the two fighters in two leaps. This time the Gimp began to revolve: he moved his right foot and dragged his left. I strained my eyes vainly to penetrate the darkness and read on Justo's skin what had happened in those three seconds when the adversaries, as close as two lovers, formed a single body. "Get out of there!" Leonidas said very slowly. "Why the hell you fighting so close?" Mysteriously, as if the light breeze that was blowing had carried that secret message to him, Justo also began to bounce up and down, like the Gimp. Stalking, watchful, fierce, they went from defense to attack and then back to defense with the speed of lightning, but the feints fooled neither one: to the swift move of the enemy's arm poised as if to throw a stone, which was intended not to wound but to balk the adversary, to confuse him for an instant, to throw him off guard, the other man would respond automatically, raising his left arm without budging. I wasn't able to see their faces, but I closed my eyes and saw them better than if I'd been in their midst: the Gimp sweating, his mouth shut, his little pig eyes aflame and blazing behind his eyelids, his skin throbbing, the wings of his flattened nose and the slit of his mouth shaken by an inconceivable quivering; and Justo, with his usual sneering mask intensified by anger and his lips moist with rage and fatigue. I opened my eyes just in time to see Justo pounce madly, blindly on the other man, giving him every advantage, offering his face, foolishly exposing his body. Anger and impatience lifted him off the ground, held him oddly up in the air, outlined against the sky, smashed him violently into his prey. The savage outburst must have surprised the Gimp, who briefly remained indecisive, and when he bent down, lengthening his arm like an arrow, hiding from our view the shining blade we followed in our imagination, we knew that Justo's crazy action hadn't been totally wasted. At the impact, the night enveloping us became populated with deep, blood-curdling roars bursting like sparks from the fighters. We didn't know then, we will never know, how long they were clenched in that convulsive polyhedron; but even without distinguishing who was who, without knowing whose arm delivered which blows, whose throat offered up those roars that followed one another like echoes, we repeatedly saw the naked knife blades in the air, quivering toward the heavens or in the midst of the darkness, down at their sides, swift, blazing, in and out of sight, hidden or brandished in the night as in some magician's spectacular show.

We must have been gasping and eager, holding our breath, our eyes popping, maybe whispering gibberish, until the human pyramid cracked, suddenly cleaved through its center by an invisible slash: the two were flung back, as if magnetized from behind, at the same moment, with the same violent force. They stayed a yard apart, panting. "We've got to stop them," said Leon's voice. "It's enough." But before we tried to move, the Gimp had left his position like a meteor. Justo didn't side-step the lunge and they both rolled on the ground. They twisted in the sand, rolling over on top of each other, splitting the air with slashes and silent gasps. This time the fight was over quickly. Soon they were still, stretched out in the riverbed, as if sleeping. I was ready to run toward them when, perhaps guessing my intention, someone suddenly stood up and remained standing next to the fallen man, swaying worse than a drunk. It was the Gimp.

In the struggle they had lost their ponchos, which lay a little way off, looking like a many-faceted rock. "Let's go," Leon said. But this time as well something happened that left us motionless. Justo got up with difficulty, leaning his entire weight on his right arm and covering his head with his free hand as if he wanted to drive some horrible sight away from his eyes. When he was up the Gimp stepped back a few feet. Justo swayed. He hadn't taken his arm from his face. Then we heard a voice we all knew but which we wouldn't have recognized if it had taken us by surprise in the dark.

"Julian!" the Gimp shouted. "Tell him to give up!"

I turned to look at Leonidas but I found his face blocked out by Leon's: he was watching the scene with a horrified expression. I turned back to look at them: they were joined once again. Roused by the Gimp's words, Justo, no doubt about it, had taken his arm from his face the second I looked away from the fight and he must have thrown himself on his enemy, draining the last strength out of his pain, out of the bitterness of his defeat. Jumping backward, the Gimp easily escaped this emotional and useless attack.

"Leonidas!" he shouted again in a furious, imploring tone. "Tell him to give up."

"Shut up and fight!" Leonidas bellowed without hesitating.

Justo had attempted another attack, but all of us, especially Leonidas, who was old and had seen many fights in his day, knew there was nothing to be done now, that his arm didn't have enough strength even to scratch the Gimp's olive-toned skin. With an anguish born in his depths and rising to his lips, making them dry, and even to his eyes, clouding them over, he struggled in slow motion as we watched for still another moment until the shadow crumpled once more: someone collapsed onto the ground with a dry sound.

When we reached the spot where Justo was lying, the Gimp had withdrawn to his men and they started leaving all together without speaking. I put my face next to his chest, hardly noticing that a hot substance dampened my neck and shoulder as my hand, through the rips in the cloth, explored his stomach and back, sometimes plunging into the limp, damp, cold body of a beached jellyfish. Briceño and Leon took off their jackets, wrapped him carefully and picked him up by his feet and arms. I looked for Leonidas' poncho, which lay a few feet away, and not looking, just groping, I covered his face. Then, in two rows, the four of us carried him on our shoulders like a coffin and we walked, matching our steps, in the direction of the path that climbed up the riverbank and back to the city.

"Don't cry, old-timer," Leon said. "I've never known anyone brave as your son. I really mean that."

Leonidas didn't answer. He walked behind me, so I couldn't see him.

At the first huts in Castilla, I asked: "Want us to carry him to your house, Leonidas?"

"Yes," the old man said hastily, as if he hadn't been listening.

TRANSLATED BY GREGORY KOLOVAKOS AND RONALD CHRIST

Clarice Lispector

Brazil
(1920–1977)

———— \\ ————

Clarice Lispector's parents moved from their native Ukraine to Brazil a few months after she was born. She studied law and worked as an editor, translator, and journalist. Lispector was a precocious and wildly original writer who acquired an international reputation and a following of high-powered critics like Hélène Cixous. Her first novel, *Near to the Wild Heart* (1944), was published when Lispector was in her early twenties, and it had a great impact. It is an intimate, self-reflexive work that seems to mirror her own tormented inner life, a description that applies to her other novels as well. When the book was published, the so-called novel of the Northeast dominated Brazilian fiction. Like the Spanish American regionalist novel, this was a conventionally realist narrative of sociopolitical criticism. In this context, some critics saw Lispector as overly narcissistic and self-absorbed. She was also accused of taking too many liberties with the Portuguese language. Ultimately, Lispector came to be admired and imitated for precisely those characteristics, and fragments of her later novels were sung by popular singers and rock groups. Her best-known novels are *The Passion According to G.H.* (1964) and *The Hour of the Star* (1977). Lispector was also an accomplished short story writer (often using animals as characters), and she wrote children's books and essays. Her intimate, confessional style has prompted some interesting feminist criticism. "The Crime of the Mathematics Professor" appeared in her collection *Laços de família* (1960). The story sets an ironic counterpoint between the humble, personal ritual performed by the professor and the institutional one taking place in the church.

The Crime of the Mathematics Professor

When the man reached the highest hill, the bells were ringing in the city below. The uneven rooftops of the houses could barely be seen. Near him was the only tree on the plain. The man was standing with a heavy sack in his hand.

His near-sighted eyes looked down below. Catholics, crawling and minute, were going into church, and he tried to hear the scattered voices of the children playing in the square. But despite the clearness of the morning hardly a sound reached the plateau. He also saw the river which seen from above seemed motionless, and he thought: it is Sunday. In the distance he saw the highest mountain with its dry slopes. It was not cold but he pulled his overcoat tighter for greater protection. Finally he placed the sack carefully on the ground. He took off his spectacles, perhaps in order to breathe more easily, because he found that clutching his spectacles in his hand he could breathe more deeply. The light beat on the lenses, which sent out sharp signals. Without his spectacles, his eyes blinked brightly, appearing almost youthful and unfamiliar. He replaced his spectacles and became once more a middle-aged man and grabbed hold of the sack again: it was as heavy as if it were made of stone, he thought. He strained his sight in order to see the current of the river, and tilted his head trying to hear some sound: the river seemed motionless and only the harshest sound of a voice momentarily reached that height—yes, he felt fine up here. The cool air was inhospitable for one who had lived in a warm city. The only tree on the plain swayed its branches. He watched it. He was gaining time. Until he felt that there was no need to wait any longer.

And meantime he kept watch. His spectacles certainly bothered him because he removed them again, sighed deeply, and put them in his pocket.

He opened his sack and peered inside. Then he put his scrawny hand inside and slowly drew out the dead dog. His whole being was concentrated on that vital hand and he kept his eyes tightly shut as he pulled. When he opened them, the air was clearer still and the happy bells rang out again, summoning the faithful to the solace of punishment.

The unknown dog lay exposed.

He now set to work methodically. He grabbed the rigid black dog and laid it on a shallow piece of ground. But, as if he had already achieved a great deal, he put on his spectacles, sat down beside the dog's carcass, and began to contemplate the landscape.

He saw quite clearly, and with a certain sense of futility, the deserted plain. But he accurately observed that when seated he could no longer see the minute city below. He sighed again. Rummaging in his sack, he drew out a spade and started thinking about the spot he would choose. Perhaps below the tree. He surprised himself, reflecting that he would bury this dog beneath the tree. But if it were the other, the real dog, he would bury it in fact where he himself would like to be buried were he dead: in the very center of the plateau, facing the sun with empty eyes. Then, since the unknown dog was, in fact, a substitute for the "other one," he decided that the former, for the greater perfection of the act, should receive exactly the same treatment as the latter would have received. There was no confusion in the man's mind. He understood himself with cold deliberation and without any loose threads.

Soon, in an excess of scruples, he was absorbed in trying to determine accurately the center of the plateau. It was not easy because the only tree rose on one side, and by accepting it as a false center, it divided the plain asymmetrically. Confronted with this difficulty, the man admitted, "It was unnecessary to bury in the center. I should also bury the other, let us say, right here, where I am standing at this very moment." It was a question of bestowing on the event the inevitability of chance, the mark of an external and evident occurrence—on the same plane as the children in the square and the Catholics entering church—it was a question of making the fact as visible as possible on the surface of the world beneath the sky. It was a question of exposing oneself and of exposing a fact, and of not permitting that fact the intimate and unpunished form of a thought.

The idea of burying the dog where he was standing at that very moment caused the man to draw back with an agility which his small and singularly heavy body did not permit. Because it seemed to him that under his feet the outline of the dog's grave had been drawn.

Then he started to dig rhythmically with his spade at that very spot. At times he interrupted his work to take off and put back on his spectacles. He was sweating profusely. He did not dig deeply, but not because he wished to spare himself fatigue. He did not dig deeply because he clearly thought, "If the grave were for the real dog, I should only dig a shallow hole and I would bury it quite close to the surface." He felt that the dog on the surface of the earth would not lose its sensibility.

Finally he put his spade aside, gently lifted the unknown dog and placed it in the grave. What a strange face that dog had. When, with a shock, he had discovered the dead dog on a street corner, the idea of burying it had made his heart so heavy and surprised that he had not even had eyes for that hard snout and congealed saliva. It was a strange, objective dog.

The dog was a little bigger than the hole he had excavated, and after being covered with earth it would be a barely perceptible mound of earth on the plain. This was exactly as he wanted it. He covered the dog with earth and flattened the ground with his hands, feeling its form in his palms with care and pleasure, as if he were smoothing it again and again. The dog was now merely a part of the land's appearance.

Then the man got up, shook the earth from his hands and did not look back even once at the grave. He reflected with a certain satisfaction, "I think I have done everything." He gave a deep sigh, and an innocent smile of release Yes, he had done everything. His crime had been punished and he was free.

And now he could think freely about the real dog, something he had avoided so far. The real dog which at that very moment must be wandering bewildered through the streets of the other county, sniffing out that city where he no longer had a master.

He then began to think with difficulty about the real dog as if he were trying to think with difficulty about his real life. The fact that the dog was far away in another city made his task difficult, although his yearning drew him close to the memory.

"While I made you in my image, you made me in yours," he thought, then, aided by his yearning, "I called you Joe in order to give you a name that might serve you as a soul at the same time. And you? How shall I ever know the name you gave me? How much more you loved me than I loved you," he reflected with curiosity.

"We understood each other too well, you with the human name I gave you, I with the name you gave me, and which you never pronounced except with your insistent gaze," the man thought, smiling with affection, now free to remember at will.

"I recall when you were little," he thought in amusement, "so small, cute, and frail, wagging your tail, watching me, and my discovering in you a new form of possessing my soul. But from that moment, you were already becoming each day a dog whom one could abandon. In the meantime our pranks became dangerous with so much understanding," the man recalled with satisfaction, "you finished up biting me and snarling; I ended up throwing a book at you and laughing. But who knows what that reluctant smile of mine already meant. Each day you became a dog whom one could abandon.

"And how you sniffed the streets!" the man thought, laughing a little, "indeed you did not pass a single stone without sniffing . . . that was the childish side to your nature. Or was that your true destiny in being a dog? And the rest merely a joke in being mine? For you were tenacious. And, calmly wagging your tail, you seemed to refuse in silence the name I had given you. Ah yes, you were tenacious. I did not want you to eat meat so that you would not become ferocious, but one day you jumped up on the table and, among the happy shouts of the children, you grabbed the meat, and with a ferocity that does not come from eating, you watched me, silent and tenacious, with the meat in your mouth. Because, although mine, you never conceded me even a little of your past or your nature. And, troubled, I began to realize that you did not ask of me that I should yield anything of mine in order to love you, and this began to annoy me. It was on this point of the resistant reality of our two natures that you hoped we might understand each other. My ferocity and yours must not exchange themselves for sweetness; it was this which you were teaching me little by little, and it was this, too, which was becoming unbearable. In asking nothing of me, you were asking too much. Of yourself, you demanded that you should be a dog. Of me, you demanded that I should be a man. And I, I pretended as much as I could. At times, crouched on your paws before me, how you watched me! I would then look at the ceiling, I would cough, look away, examine my fingernails. But nothing moved you, and you went on watching me. Whom were you going to tell? 'Pretend,' I said to myself, 'pretend quickly that you are another, arrange a false meeting, caress him, throw him a bone,' but nothing distracted you as you watched me. What an idiot I was. I trembled with horror, when you were the innocent one: that I should turn round and suddenly show you my real face, and that I should trap you, your hairs bristling, and carry you to the door wounded forever. Oh, each day you became a dog that could be abandoned. One could choose. But you, trustfully, wagged your tail.

"Sometimes, impressed by your alertness, I succeeded in seeing in you your own anguish. Not the anguish of being a dog, which was your only possible form. But the anguish of existing in such a perfect way that it became an unbearable happiness: you would then leap and come to lick my face with a love entirely given, and a certain danger of hatred as if it were I who had revealed you to yourself through friendship. Now I am quite certain that it was not I who possessed a dog. It was you who possessed a person.

"But you possessed a person so powerful that he could choose: and then he abandoned you. With relief he abandoned you. With relief, yes, because you demanded—with the serene and simple incomprehension of a truly heroic dog—that I should be a man. He abandoned you with an excuse supported by everyone at home. How could I move house and baggage and children—and on top of that a dog—with the business of adapting to the new school and a new city, and on top of that a dog? 'There is no room for him anywhere,' said Martha, as practical as ever. 'He will disturb the other passengers,' my mother-in-law added, not knowing that I had already justified my decision, and the children cried, and I did not look either at them or you, Joe. But only you and I know that I abandoned you because you were the constant possibility of the crime I never committed. The possibility of my sinning which, in the pretense of my eyes, was already a sin. I then sinned at once in order to be blamed at once. And this crime replaces the greater crime which I should not have had the courage to commit," thought the man, becoming ever more lucid.

"There are so many forms of being guilty and of losing oneself forever, and to betray oneself and not to confront oneself. I chose that of wounding a dog," the man thought. "Because I knew that this would be a minor offense and that no one goes to hell for abandoning a dog that trusted in a human. For I knew that this crime was not punishable."

Seated on the mountain top, his mathematical head was cold and intelligent. Only now did he seem to understand, in his icy awareness, that he had done something with the dog that was truly irrevocable and beyond punishment. They still had not invented a punishment for the great concealed crimes and for the deep betrayals.

A man still succeeded in being more astute than the Last Judgment. This crime was condemned by no one. Not even the Church. They are all my accomplices, Joe. I should have to knock from door to door and beg them to accuse and punish me: they would all slam the door on me with a sudden look of hostility. No one will condemn this crime of mine. Not even you, Joe, will condemn me. Powerful as I am, I need only choose to call you. Abandoned in the streets, you would come leaping to lick my face with contentment and forgiveness. I would give you my other face to kiss.

The man took off his spectacles, sighed, and put them on again. He looked at the covered grave where he had buried an unknown dog in tribute to his abandoned dog, trying, after all, to pay the debt which, disturbingly, no one was claiming—trying to punish himself with an act of kindness and to rid himself of his crime. Like someone giving alms in order to be able to eat at last the cake which deprived the beggar of bread.

But as if Joe, the dog he had abandoned, were demanding of him much more than a lie; as if he were demanding that he, in one last effort, might prove himself a man—and as such assume the responsibility of his crime— he looked at the grave where he had buried his weakness and his condition.

And now, even more mathematical, he sought a way to eliminate that self-inflicted punishment. He must not be consoled. He coldly searched for a way of destroying the false burial of the unknown dog. He then bent down, and, solemn and calm, he unburied the dog with a few simple movements. The dark form of the dog at last appeared whole and unfamiliar with earth on its eyelashes, its eyes open and crystallized. And so the mathematics professor had renewed his crime forever. The man then looked around him and up to the skies, pleading for a witness to what he had done. And, as if that were still not enough, he began to descend the slopes, heading toward the intimacy of his home.

TRANSLATED BY WILLIAM L. GROSSMAN

Antonio Benítez Rojo

Cuba
(b. 1931)

Antonio Benítez Rojo, one of the most original short story writers to have emerged in Latin America since the 1960s, is also an essayist and novelist of note. Benítez Rojo was a latecomer to literature. Trained in economics and the social sciences, he did not participate in literary activities until his mid-thirties. Raised in Panama and Puerto Rico as well as his native Havana, he learned English early and in his youth spent a year in Washington, D.C., as a student. Benítez Rojo worked in the Ministry of Labor at the outset of the Cuban Revolution, but after winning a contest with the very first story he wrote, he switched to the cultural bureaucracy, where he rose to the directorship of the Caribbean Studies Center at Casa de las Américas. In 1980 he left Cuba and made his way to the United States, where he is now a professor at Amherst College. In Cuba he won several literary prizes, and in the United States he has been honored for his short stories and essays. Benítez Rojo is the author of a novel, *The Sea of Lentils,* and several collections of stories, such as *Tute de reyes* (1967) and *El escudo de hojas secas* (1969). "Buried Statues" is by far his best and most famous story, by now a minor classic of Latin American fiction. Benítez Rojo's tales fall into two groups: one dealing with historical subjects and concerned with Caribbean issues, and the other dealing with the Cuban bourgeoisie in the wake of the Cuban Revolution. The first group, which displays Benítez Rojo's impressive erudition in the field of Afro-Caribbean lore and history, follows Alejo Carpentier. The latter stories, ostensibly in the line that issues from Poe and goes on to Quiroga, Borges, and Cortázar, are concerned with the uncanny. The distinctiveness of "Buried Statues" lies in its ability to bring to this trend the encroachment of history, in the form of the revolution that traps the protagonists in their house, in their memories, and in their fears.

Buried Statues

That summer—I could never forget—after Don Jorge's classes had been dismissed and at Honorata's pleading, we used to hunt butterflies in the gardens of our mansion in Havana's exclusive Vedado Heights. Aurelio and I would go to great lengths to humor Honorata because she was not only the youngest of the three, having just celebrated her fifteenth birthday last March, but was also lame from birth. We usually teased her by pretending not to want to go just for the fun of watching her pout and toss her braided tresses about, although if the truth were known, both of us enjoyed as much as she did drawing lots to see who could take the hunting horn from the deserted dovecot. Our nets held ready, we would then wander among the marble statues along the flagstone path of the Japanese garden, with its unexpected turns through the wild, tall grass that grew right up to the house.

The grass was our greatest danger. For some years it had overrun the iron fence at the southeastern edge of our estate on the bank of the Almendares River, which during the rainy season threatened to flood the property and put the vegetation in a frenzy of proliferation. It had completely taken over that part of the estate under Aunt Esther's care, and in spite of all of her and Honorata's efforts, it now covered the large windows of the library and the French shutters on the wall of the music room. As this botanic siege affected house security, which was Mama's responsibility, our meals usually ended in intractable arguments. At times Mama, who became very nervous when she was not intoxicated, would bring her hand to her head in her characteristic signal of a headache, and would burst suddenly into tears, threatening between sobs to desert the house and yield her part of it to the enemy if Aunt Esther did not clean the overgrowth immediately. Mama believed that the pullulating vegetation was likely a secret weapon of the evil people who lived beyond the boundaries of our enclosed property.

"If you would pray less and work more . . . ," Mama would say as she cleaned off the table.

"And if you would lay off the bottle . . . ," Aunt Esther would retort.

Fortunately, Don Jorge never took sides in these disputes. He would fold his napkin, his face long and gray, and would retire from the table, thus avoiding embroiling himself in the family discord. Not that Don Jorge was a stranger to us. He was, after all, Aurelio's father, having married the sister who came between Mama and Aunt Esther, but whose name no one mentioned anymore. And although we did not call Don Jorge "uncle," we treated him with a familiar respect.

It was different with Aurelio. When nobody was looking, he and I would hold hands as if we were engaged. And precisely that summer he would have to choose between Honorata and me, for time was running out, and we were no longer children.

We all loved Aurelio for the way he carried himself, for his flashing black eyes, and above all for that special way he had of laughing. At the table the largest portions were for him, and on those occasions when Mama's alcoholic breath could be noticed above the smells of dinner, you could bet that when Aurelio held out the plate she would seize his hand

and serve him very slowly. Of course, Aunt Esther did not waste any time either. With the same dedication as when she said her rosary, she would kick her shoe off under the table and search for Aurelio's leg.

Thus went our meals. And, naturally, Aurelio let himself be loved. He lived with Don Jorge in the rooms of the old servants' quarters because it was so stipulated by the Code. Otherwise, both Mama and Aunt Esther would have given him rooms on any of the floors of the mansion to please him. And Honorata and I would have been delighted to have him nearer to us during those stormy nights, punctuated with flashing lights, as the house lay under siege.

We called the document that spelled out each of our duties and established our responsibilities and punishments, simply, the Code. It had been sworn and subscribed to during Grandfather's lifetime by his three daughters and their husbands. In it were gathered the patriarchal commandments, and although it had to be adapted to our newer circumstances, it became the rallying point of our resistance. Since we guided ourselves by it, I will briefly describe it.

It recognized Don Jorge as a permanent and gratuitous usufructuary and member of the Family Council. He was charged with the provision of food, with military intelligence, the administration of the family funds, with education and cultural activities (he had been an Under-Secretary of Education during the times of Laredo Brú), with electrical repairs and masonry, and with cultivating the land along the northeastern wall by the Enríquez house, which had been converted into a polytechnic school at the end of 1965.

Aunt Esther was left with the responsibility of attending to the flower gardens, including the park, to caring for the breeding animals, political agitation, repairs on the water system and the plumbing, the organization of religious acts, and washing, ironing, and mending clothes.

Mama was assigned the cleaning of the floors and the furniture, the preparation of tactics for defense, carpentry repairs, the painting of the roofs and the walls, the practice of medicine, as well as the preparation of the meals and other related tasks. However, this last commitment occupied most of her time.

As for us, the cousins, we helped with the morning chores, and listened to Don Jorge's lessons in the afternoon. Whatever time was left we dedicated to recreation. We, like the rest, were forbidden to venture beyond the limits of the estate, for that meant instant death. Moral death, that is. The death that waited on the other side of the iron fence, along that evil path onto which half the family had strayed in the nine years that the siege had lasted.

So, as matters stood, that summer we hunted butterflies. They would come across the river, flying over the tall grass, pausing on the flowers or on the marble shoulders of the garden statues. Honorata used to say that they made the air happy, that they perfumed it—poor little Honorata had such an imagination. But they upset me, for they came from the land beyond, and, like Mama, I was of the opinion that they were secret weapons that we did not yet understand. For this reason, though I liked to hunt them, I felt a hidden fear. At times they would startle me, and I would flee through the grass, anxious that they might seize me by the hair and by the skirt, as in the engraving that hung in Aurelio's room, and that they would carry me over the iron fence and beyond the river.

We caught the butterflies in nets made from old mosquito netting, and then put them in empty jelly jars which Mama gave us. Then, at dusk, we would gather in the study room for the big beauty contest, which could last for hours, for we dined late. Once we had decided which was the most colorful, we would take it from its jar, clean it, and paste it in an album that Don Jorge had given us.

Following a suggestion which I had made to prolong the sport, we would pull the wings off the others and organize butterfly foot races, betting illicit pinches and caresses. Finally, tired of our games, we would throw the mutilated insects into the toilet bowl, and Honorata, trembling, her eyes misty with tears, would pull the chain, releasing the sound of falling water, sweeping their bodies away in a whirlpool.

After we had dined, and after Aunt Esther's allegations had caused Mama to retire to the kitchen with the irrevocable decision to abandon the house as soon as she had finished washing the dishes, we would gather together in the music room, by the only candelabrum, and listen to Aunt Esther play her religious hymns on the piano. Don Jorge had taught us something of the violin, which we kept strung; but because we had no way to tune it, the piano itself being out of tune, we preferred not to take it from its box. On other occasions, when Aunt Esther was indisposed or when Mama had reproached her for being behind in her duties, we would read aloud at Don Jorge's suggestion, and; as he felt a great admiration for German culture, we could pass hours muttering stanzas by Goethe, Holderlin, Novalis, or Heine.

Very rarely, only on stormy nights when the house seemed on the point of being swept away, or on some other extraordinary occasion, would we examine the collection of butterflies in the album, feeling the mystery of their wings reach deep into us—those wings charged with the world beyond our spiked iron fence, beyond the walls topped with the sharp glass shards of bottles. Fascinated, we would sit there together in silence by the candles, under a shadow that concealed the moisture on the walls, our eyes shifting and our hands tense, knowing that we each felt the same, that we found ourselves in the depth of a dream as turbid as the river along our boundaries, while overhead the warped ceiling, cracking further, would powder our hair, our intimate gestures, with flaking calcium. And so we kept collecting them.

My greatest satisfaction during this time was to imagine that at the end of summer Aurelio would finally be mine. "A disguised priest will marry you through the fence," Don Jorge said circumspectly one day when Aunt Esther and Honorata were walking beyond earshot. From that moment on I did not stop thinking of it. It even made bearable the interminable morning session. Mama's deterioration proceeded apace. If she cooked, she hardly had time to do the dishes, and it was I who mopped the floor and shook the dust from the shabby furniture and battered chairs.

It may, perhaps, be a dangerous generalization, but in one way or another Aurelio sustained us all—his affection helped us to resist. Of course, Mama and Aunt Esther had other hopes than marriage. How else was one to explain their wild, gastronomical enthusiasms, their exceptional care for his occasional, light colds or even rarer headaches, their prodigious efforts to see him strong, stylishly dressed, content? Even Don Jorge, usually so discreet, at time acted like a brooding hen. And one wouldn't believe the way Honorata fussed over him, the poor little thing always so optimistic, so unrealistic, totally unaware of her lameness. The fact is that Aurelio was our hope, our sweet taste of illusion, and it was he who kept us calm in our rusty fetters, us, so harassed from the outside.

"What a beautiful butterfly!" exclaimed Honorata one evening at twilight, only a summer ago. Aurelio and I were walking ahead on our way home, and he was making a passageway for me through the weeds with the handle of his net. We turned around to see Honorata's freckled face flying over the jungle of weeds as if she were being pulled by her tresses. Farther above, near the top of the royal poinciana tree that grew where the path turned down toward the statues, a gilded butterfly fluttered.

Aurelio stopped. He motioned for us to take up positions in the undergrowth. Advancing slowly, he slipped through the weeds with his net held high. The butterfly descended, opening its large defiant wings, almost coming within Aurelio's reach, then suddenly glided beyond the royal poinciana down to the gallery of marble statues. Aurelio followed, and both disappeared.

When Aurelio returned night had fallen, and we had already chosen the beauty queen for the evening and were getting her ready to surprise him. But he came in serious and sweaty, declaring that the gilded butterfly had escaped just as he had been at the point, by climbing the fence, of catching it. In spite of our insistence, he refused to remain for the games.

I began to worry. I envisioned Aurelio there on top of the wrought iron fence, his net hanging over the river, just one step from leaping over. I remember warning Honorata that the butterfly had been a decoy, and that we had to intensify our guard.

The next day was unforgettable. Since dawn the outsiders had been very worked up. They shot off cannonades. White exhaust trails of their gray airplanes laced the cloudless blue of the sky, and far below, their helicopters rippled the river's waters and the vegetation along its banks. No doubt they were celebrating something, perhaps a new victory, while we remained solitary and ignorant of the cause of their jubilation. It was not because we had no radios in the house, but because for some years we had not paid the bill for electricity. And the batteries of Aunt Esther's Zenith had become sticky, and smelled of the Chinese ointment that Mama treasured in the back of her medicine cabinet. Nor did the telephone work, nor did we read newspapers, nor did we open the letters that we received from faithless friends and traitorous relatives from the world outside. It is true that Don Jorge traded through the fence. If he had not done so, we would not have been able to subsist. But he did it at night, and we were not permitted to witness the transactions, nor were we permitted to ask questions about them, although once, when he had a high fever and Honorata was taking care of him, he let it be known that our cause was not totally lost, and that well-known international organizations were preparing to assist those with the courage to resist.

In late afternoon of that memorable day, after the patriotic applause from the Polytechnic Institute had subsided, and the martial songs—which during the day had driven Mama crazy in spite of her ear plugs—ceased to be heard from over our glass-studded wall, we took down the hunting horn from the panoply, and went to hunt butterflies. We walked slowly, Aurelio with a frown. Since early morning he had been gathering cabbage near the wall, and listening at close quarters without the necessary protection from the uproar of the songs and the fervid speeches that droned on past midday. Aurelio seemed disturbed. He rejected the results of the drawing and abruptly appointed Honorata to assign the hunting areas and to carry the hunting horn. We separated silently, without the usual jokes. In the past we had always respected established procedures.

For some time I had been wandering along the trail that followed the iron fence, waiting for the twilight, my jar full of fluttering, yellow wings, when suddenly I felt something tangling my hair. At first I thought it was the mesh of my own net, but when I raised my left hand my fingers rubbed something with more body, like a piece of silk that flew away after striking my wrist. I quickly turned around, and I saw hovering in the air before my eyes the gilded butterfly, its large wings opening and closing almost at the height of my neck. Alone and with my back to the fence, I could hardly contain the panic I felt. I seized the handle of my net and swung it furiously at the hovering thing, but it avoided my blow by gliding aside to the right. Moving slowly back along the fence, I tried to calm myself and not to think of Aurelio's engraving. Little by little I raised my arms, watching it carefully, and took aim, but this time the net became entangled in an iron post, and once again I missed. At this moment I dropped the handle of the net, and it fell in the foliage along the path. My heart was racing. The butterfly flew around me in a circle and attacked my throat. I hardly had time to shout and to hurl myself on the grass. A burning sensation caused me to raise my hand to my breast, and it was covered with blood. I had thrown myself on the tip hoop of the net, and it had wounded me. I waited some minutes, and then turned on my back, panting. It had disappeared. The tall grass that grew around me hid me, like the statue of Venus that had fallen from its pedestal and that Honorata had discovered in the back of the park. I stretched out motionless like it, looking fixedly at the twilight sky, and suddenly there were Aurelio's eyes, and I watching them quietly sweep over my nearly hidden body and stop at my breast, and then his chest coming among the stalks, his whole body struggling to force me down, and finally the long and painful kiss that made the grass tremble. Afterwards, an inexplicable awakening: Aurelio on top of my body, still kissing my mouth, in spite of my biting his lips and scratching his forehead with my fingernails.

As we returned to the house, I was too disillusioned to speak.

Honorata had seen it all from her vantage point in the branches of the poinciana tree.

Before entering the house, we agreed to keep it a secret. I don't know if it was because of Mama's and Aunt Esther's glances across the steaming soup, or the nocturnal sighs from Honorata as she thrashed between her sheets, but when the new day dawned I realized that I no longer loved Aurelio as before, that I needed neither him nor that disgusting thing, and I swore not to do it again until our wedding night.

That next morning stretched on as never before, leaving me exhausted. At lunch I gave my portion of cabbage to Honorata (we were always so hungry), and I looked coldly at Aurelio when he explained to Mama that a cat from the Polytechnic Institute had bitten his hand and scratched his face before disappearing over the wall. Then we had our Logic class. I paid scant attention to Don Jorge, in spite of such words as *ferio, festino, baroco,* and many others.

"I am very tired. My shoulder hurts," I said to Honorata after the lesson, when she suggested that we hunt butterflies.

"Come on, don't be a bad sport," she insisted.

"No."

"Isn't it that you are afraid?" asked Aurelio.

"No, I am not afraid."

"Are you sure?"

"I am sure. I am not going to do it anymore."

"Hunt butterflies?"

"Hunt butterflies and the other. I am not going to do it anymore."

"Well, if you don't come along with us, I shall tell everything to Mama," screamed Honorata unexpectedly, her cheeks flushed.

"I have no objections," Aurelio said, laughing, as he seized me by the arm. And turning to Honorata without waiting for me to reply, he said: "Bring the nets and the jars. We will wait for you at the dovecot."

I felt confused and offended, but when I saw Honorata depart, limping pitifully, the truth suddenly dawned on me, and I understood everything that was happening. I let Aurelio put his arm around my waist, and we left the house.

We walked in silence, submerged in the tall grass, and I realized that I also felt pity for Aurelio, for I was strongest of the three, and perhaps of the whole household. It was curious, I was so young, not yet seventeen, and yet I was stronger than Mama with her progressive alcoholism, than Aunt Esther, who was always hanging onto her rosary. And, I realized suddenly, stronger than Aurelio. Aurelio was the weakest of all, even weaker than Don Jorge, than Honorata. And now he was smiling from the corner of his eye, rudely squeezing my waist, as if he had conquered me, without realizing, poor Aurelio, that only I could save him—him and the rest of the house.

"Shall we stop here?" he asked, pausing. "I believe it is the same place as yesterday," he said, winking at me.

I assented and lay down on the grass. I waited as he raised my skirt and began kissing my thighs—I, cold and quiet like the goddess, letting him do it to appease Honorata, so that she would not tattletale to the house and arouse those unsatisfied, envious females into open warfare.

"Move over a little to the right, I can't see very well," shouted Honorata from her vantage point astride a branch in the poinciana tree.

Aurelio paid no attention to her and unbuttoned my blouse.

It became dark and we returned, Honorata carrying the nets and the empty jars.

"Do you love me?" he asked as he removed a dry leaf that had become entangled in my hair.

"Yes, but I don't want to get married. Perhaps, next summer."

"And will you continue doing it?"

"All right," I replied a little astonished, "provided no one learns about it."

"In that case, it's all the same to me, although the grass scratches and makes me itch."

That night Aurelio announced at the dinner table that he would not marry that year, that he would postpone his decision until the following summer. Mama and Aunt Esther both sighed sighs of relief. Don Jorge scarcely lifted his eyebrows.

Two weeks went by, and Aurelio continued with the illusion that he possessed me. I would lie down in the grass with my arms under my head, like a statue, and would let him caress me without suffering the outrage. As the days went by I perfected a rigid pose, which excited his desires, and made him depend on me.

One evening we were walking along the river bank while Honorata was hunting among the statues. The rainy season had begun, and the flowers, wet during the midday downpour, stuck to our clothing. We spoke of trivial matters—Aurelio was telling me that Aunt Esther had visited him at night in her nightgown. At that moment we saw the butterfly. It flew at the front of a swarm of ordinary butterflies. When it recognized us, it flew a few zig-zags and lit on a pike of the iron fence. It moved its wings up and down without flying, pretending to be tired. Aurelio, becoming tense, released my waist to climb up the fence. But this time victory was mine. Without saying a word, I lay down, my skirt up above my hips, and the situation was brought under control.

We were waiting for the man because Don Jorge had told us after our History lesson that he would come around 9 p.m. that night. He had supplied us with provisions over the years, and he insisted that he be called the Mohican. As he was an experienced and courageous soldier, according to Don Jorge (although this seemed difficult to believe, since they had taken his house away from him), we would accept him as a guest after feigning a debate. He could help Aunt Esther exterminate the invading grass, and after that he could cultivate the piece of property to the southeast which was bounded by the river.

"I believe he is coming," Honorata said, pressing her face against the wrought iron bars of the main gate. There was no moon, and we were using the candelabrum.

We drew closer to the chains that guarded the access while Aunt Esther prayed a hurried rosary. The foliage was pulled back, and a hand was revealed in the pale light of the candles. Then a wrinkled, expressionless face appeared.

"Password!" demanded Don Jorge.

"Gillete and Adams," replied the man in a subdued voice.

"That is correct. You may enter."

"But how?"

"Climb over the bars; the lock is rusted."

Suddenly a whisper surprised us all. There could be no doubt that on the other side of the great gate the man was talking with someone. We looked at each other in alarm, and it was Mama who broke the silence.

"With whom are you talking?" she asked, coming out of her stupor.

"The truth is . . . I am not alone."

"They have followed you!" cried Aunt Esther in an anguished tone.

"No, it is not that. . . . The truth is, I came with . . . someone."

"In the name of God, with whom?"

"A young lady . . . almost a child."

"I am his daughter," interrupted a voice of exceptional clarity.

We deliberated for some time. Mama and I were opposed to it, but there were three votes in favor, and one abstention—Don Jorge. Finally, they were allowed to cross over to our side.

She said her name was Cecilia, and she walked very proudly along the darkened path. She was the same age as Honorata, but much prettier, and without anatomical defects. Her eyes were blue, and her hair a rather unusual golden color. She wore it straight, parted in the middle, with the tips turned upward, reflecting the light of the candelabrum.

When we reached the house she said that she was very sleepy, as she was accustomed to going to bed early, and seizing a candle, she entered directly into the old room, at the end of the corridor, that had belonged to Grandfather; she locked the door from the inside as if she were familiar with it. The man, who now I know was not her father, after saying good night with a weary appearance and clutching his chest, went off with Don Jorge and Aurelio to the servants' quarters, coughing every step of the way. We never found out what his real name was. She refused to reveal his name the next day when Don Jorge, who always rose early, found him by his bed, dead and without identification.

We buried the Mohican in the afternoon near the well down by the Polytechnic Institute in the shade of a mango tree. Don Jorge pronounced the sermon, calling the deceased "our unknown soldier." And Cecilia produced from behind her back a bunch of flowers which she put between his hands. After that, Aurelio began to shovel in the earth, and I helped him erect the cross that Don Jorge had made. And all of us returned to the house except Aunt Esther, who remained to pray.

Along the way I observed that Cecilia walked in a very curious manner. She reminded me of the ballet dancers that I had seen as a child at the Pro Arte concerts. She seemed very interested in the flowers, and would stop to pick them and carry them to her face. Aurelio supported Mama, who staggered pathetically as they walked, but he never took his eyes off Cecilia, and smiled stupidly every time she looked at him.

At dinner Cecilia did not eat a bite. She pushed her plate from her in disgust, and then offered it to Honorata, who, in turn, to show her gratitude, praised her hairdo. I finally decided to speak to her.

"What pretty dye you use on your hair. Where did you get it?"

"Dye? It isn't dyed. It's natural."

"That's impossible. No one has hair that color!"

"I do," she said smiling. "I'm glad you like it."

"Will you let me have a closer look at it?" I asked. The truth is, I didn't believe her.

"Yes, but don't touch it."

I picked up a candle and went to her chair; leaning over the back of it, I looked intently at her head. The color was even. It did not appear dyed. Yet there was something artificial among those gilded strands of hair. They looked as if they were made of golden silk. It suddenly occurred to me that it might be a wig. Impulsively, I gave it a jerk with both hands. I don't know if it was her howl that caused me to fall to the floor, or the fear I felt on seeing her jump about in that curious manner. The fact is, I sat stunned at Mama's feet, watching her run bumping into the furniture in the dinning room, turn down the hall and lock herself into Grandfather's room, all the time holding her head as if it were about to fall off. And Aurelio and Aunt Esther, feigning disbelief, pressed against the door to listen to her bleating. Mama brandished a knife without knowing what was going on at all, and to top it all, Honorata stood on a chair applauding. Fortunately, Don Jorge remained calm.

After Mama's babbling and Aunt Esther's tiresome response, I retired with dignity, and, refusing the candle Aurelio handed me, groped my way up the dark stairs with my head held high.

Honorata came into my room, while I pretended to be asleep to avoid discussion. Through half-opened eyes I saw her place the plate with the candle on the dresser. I rolled over on my side to make room for her. Her shadow, dancing along the wall, reminded me of the section on games and pastimes in the *Book of Knowledge,* whose twenty volumes Don Jorge had sold some years previously. Honorata's shadow limped exaggeratedly. She went from one side to the other untying her braids, opening the drawer where she kept the sheets. Then she approached the bed, looking taller, and leaning over me, touched my hand.

I pretended to yawn and turned over on my back. "What do you want?" I asked in a bad humor.

"Have you taken a look at your hands?"

"No."

"You should."

"There is nothing wrong with my hands," I said, without looking at them.

"They are stained."

"They must be dirty," I said. "Since I pulled that creature by the hair, and shoved Mama. . . ."

"They are not dirty, but they are gilded," Honorata shouted impetuously.

I looked at my hands and it was true; a golden powder covered my palms and the underside of my fingers. I rinsed my hands in the washbowl, and blew out the candle. When Honorata grew tired of her farfetched conjectures, I was finally able to close my eyes. I got up late the next morning, feeling groggy and confused.

I did not find Cecilia at breakfast because she had gone out with Aunt Esther to see what they could do with the weeds. Mama had already gotten drunk, and Honorata stayed with me to help with the cleaning. Afterwards, we would make lunch. We had already finished downstairs and were cleaning Aunt Esther's room; I was dusting and Honorata was sweeping, when it occurred to me to look out the window. I put down the feather duster and looked out over our property: to the left and to the front, the iron fence separated us from the river, its spikes overgrown with weeds; closer, beyond the orange poincianas, I saw the heads of the statues, greenish, like the heads of drowned women, and the gray boards of the Japanese dovecot; to the right were the vegetable garden, the well, and Aurelio, squatting on the ground to gather mangoes near the small cross; farther on, the wall, the roof tiles of the Polytechnic Institute, and a waving flag. "Who will tell the Enríquezes?" I thought. And then I saw her. She flew very low in the direction of the wall. At times she would become lost among the flowers and then would reappear farther along, shining like a gilded dolphin. Then she changed direction, and went in a beeline toward Aurelio. And, suddenly, she was Cecilia, Cecilia who came out from the bed of oleander bushes, running over the red earth, her hair fluttering in the air, almost floating over her head; Cecilia, who was now talking with Aurelio, kissing him before leading him by the hand along the path that crossed the park.

I asked Honorata to make lunch, and I stretched out in Aunt Esther's bed. Everything was spinning around in my head, and I felt my heart throbbing. After a while someone tried insistently to open the door, but I was crying, and I shouted that I felt sick and for them to leave me in peace.

When I awoke, night had fallen, and I knew something had happened. I leaped from the bed and ran down the stairs barefooted. I entered the hallway alarmed and muttering to myself that even yet there was the chance it was not too late.

They were all in the living room around Honorata. Don Jorge was crying softly on the edge of the sofa. Aunt Esther, kneeling by the lamp, leaned toward Mama, who was gesticulating in her rocking chair without being able to straighten up. Unnoticed, I leaned against the frame of the door, almost in the light, listening to Honorata, watching her act out her report in the center of the rug, and feeling myself become weaker by the second. She went into great detail, explaining how she had seen them just at twilight on the river road on the other side of the iron fence. Then, suddenly, there was the explosion, and the sound of Aunt Esther's prayers as Mama became delirious.

I put my hands over my ears. I lowered my head, feeling the urge to vomit. Then, through my fingers, I heard a scream. Someone fell over the candles, and we were left in darkness.

TRANSLATED BY LEE H. WILLIAMS JR.

José Balza

Venezuela
(b. 1939)

In 1957 José Balza moved from his remote native region to Caracas, where he obtained a degree from the National University, eventually becoming a professor at the Universidad Central. Balza has published essays on literature, art, and film, in addition to collections of short stories and novels. *Iniciales* (1993) is a volume of essays about early Spanish American literary figures who were born in the New World and who began to publish after 1600. His interest in the roots of the Spanish American literary imagination has led him to Garcilaso de la Vega, el Inca; Sor Juana Inés de la Cruz; and Carlos de Sigüenza y Góngora. In *El fiero (y dulce) instinto terrestre: ejercicios y ensayos* (1988) his topics were more contemporary: Teresa de la Parra, José Antonio Ramos Sucre, Ava Gardner. His collections of short stories include *La mujer de espaldas* (1990), and his best-known novel is *Percusión* (1982). Subtle and learned in his essays, as a writer of fiction Balza is interested in what could be called psychopathology (his first university degree was in psychology). His recurrent theme is the multiplicity of the self. Balza has stated: "All my works have attempted to explore, by means of especially invented techniques and concrete experiences, one sole theme: that of the psychological multiplicity of man. We change chronologically from infancy to old age; but we also change spatially—every instant—for ourselves and for others. Personal identity is a strange and mysterious equilibrium, a sort of illusion. What truly characterizes us is multiplicity." The story selected for inclusion here, "A Woman's Back," centers on that topic, but also contains others typical of Balza: displacement, alienation in a foreign environment, the origin of the imagination in deflected sexual desires. Balza writes in a deceptively plain prose that at times reveals a refined ironic perspective.

A Woman's Back

In line with his unbridled enthusiasm for the style of Tom Wolfe, the young (actually, over thirty; two divorces) journalist wanted his reporting to contain something of the poem, the novel, the drama. Or he wanted to produce articles so vivid they read like novels. Maybe all he really wants is to write fiction, but the hidden and paradoxical fear of writing with a journalist's tics keeps him a prisoner of the large daily newspaper where he

419

works. His congeniality, his knowledge of cultural affairs, the mental winks he tossed me led me to associate him with a certain superficial idea of what a writer should be.

For one hour of my morning he had been conducting—without my being able to resist or react—our agreed-upon interview. The subject: a large dictionary edited by a team under my direction. I know that any dictionary omits precisely what the reader-in-need wants to find. Also, that a dictionary is forever unfinished. But the rest of the team was satisfied, and I finally ended up accepting the glory for five years at the task. All the while the newspaperman raved about the precision of the facts, the method employed, the innovative classifications (which did away with alphabetical order), I hadn't a clue that he had not even skimmed the volume our PR people had sent him the week before. That's how he is: he improvises questions as if he knows what he is talking about. And convinces millions of readers.

When our secretary noticed—through the glass of the wall dividing our offices—that it was a good time, she brought us both coffee. The fellow was already putting away his cassettes and the notebook he had never opened. For a second or two, I tried to imagine how he would approach the article. I was afraid that more than the dictionary itself, he would high-light—following the rules of New Journalism—my inopportune sneezing. Evidently he wasn't in any rush (when he showed up, the team that had expected a prominent spot in the next day's paper had had to wait a week and a half; and then he didn't use—then *or* later—the group shot his pho-tographer had taken before our session). He went on about how enthu-siastically his wife—his third?—was poring over the first volume of our edition. Only then did he begin to talk about what truly interested him. I believe he would have given anything to be the person being interviewed, so he could be the one making subtle comments about the project he was leading up to. He began by suggesting the broad outlines for his play (a belief currently circulating, among other vices, is that any novelist can write better theater): two taut and inexorable acts. He alluded to the effort to dilute the plot, and he sketched some characteristics of the protagonist: a foreign woman, a drunk or drug addict. If I'm not hallucinating, I feel certain he told me that the plot was entirely his concept, but with his second cigarette (Could we have a little more coffee?), and in a very straightforward manner, he gave credit for the plot to a bootblack who worked in the Plaza Central. It was from that aged and diligent man—the man once the young boy who in 1910 claimed the spot where he works today—the journalist had heard this strange adventure. Yes, it had hap-pened yesterday, when in yet another example of his versatility he had interviewed the old shoeshine man in the plaza.

It was easy to imagine him convincing his editor in chief (as eager to be voguish and successful as he) to send him on assignment to the Plaza Central with its mix of humble characters. Something new, something different from their routine features on artists and poets, they would have agreed.

That's why, he tells me before he leaves, he'd gone to the plaza yesterday. He hadn't expected to see anyone but kids, and instead found the old man. He had spent several hours with him (after having his shoes shined) and had offered to buy him a drink. The grizzled old fellow had not accepted the invitation, but had given him this fascinating story from the 1930s, one that since yesterday had been buzzing about in his brain as a detective story or a play.

The old man could still recall the headlines. It had been a major scandal, and the bootblack (who is both the kid of 1910 and the present-day decrepit old man) had not forgotten certain details about the parties involved.

I become aware that the newspaperman, dying to be interviewed, is looking for questions from me, for me to point out the contradictions in what he'd said, but I don't fall for it. I pick up my second cup of coffee, and I listen until he decides to leave. I will not take the bait about the plot being his, nor point out that he also said he'd heard it from the old shoeshine man the day before. Up to him. I can wait until he turns it into fiction or into the outline for a play. (I feel sorry for the members of my team there on the other side of the glass who think that the newspaperman is commenting on our dictionary, while in fact he's spinning his own tale.)

Even listening to him, it's confusing. The journalist does not have command of the clear and uncomplicated threads needed to weave a story about a murder; he goes into unnecessary detail—in the manner of the thirties—interpolates items of local color, gets carried away by a phrase. Finally . . . a heavy-set Frenchman, along in years, a total stranger, in the port for only a week, killed a foreign woman, stabbing her in the back, right where she had a beauty mark shaped like an iris. He had forced her into a position where he could strike again and again at the iris. She was strong and should have been able to defend herself (a double of Simone Signoret?), but he surprised her, and was armed.

The account was given by the murderer himself, who had neither the desire nor the strength to escape. It didn't matter to him whether he returned to France, stayed in prison in Guyana, or died in the midst of a climate and a language he didn't understand. He told how for forty years he had mourned over losing the woman. They weren't even a couple, and had been unable to marry. He had loved her excessively. He died at the age of twenty-seven, when she died, and from that time had lived in isolation. He had always lived in Petite Ville—before her and after burying her there—but Marseille had been the site of his happiness and his love. The life of the port replicated the woman's: changeable, transitory. Maybe once he had said that, and yet he wanted to believe in his power to make her a different person with his love: a love that was both serious and insane. How old would she have been? Eighteen? He was nearly twenty-five, and even though the woman was very young, she seemed to have experienced everything—everything except a love as faithful as that he was offering. At some moment, he must have recognized that maybe neither of them could aspire to the love he had pictured. With no parents, no family, the woman had always made her way among men. (He was sure that, in her loneliness, only a very fine line—chance—separated her from becoming a nun or a nurse.) She had no women friends and probably had never known a sustained, loving relationship with another human being. Sex, money, parties. That was how he met her. At the beginning, he saw her as a great asset in one of his business dealings. Despite being so happy-go-lucky, despite her little run-ins with sailors and police, her periods of drinking and gaiety, no one could have imagined her involved in a big-time operation. She was too talkative and too open to keep a secret. But he knew how to turn on the charm and use her for his own purposes. Sensual, greedy, Marie-Jos was not actually attractive, but she could inflame sudden desire in any man. Perhaps her very spontaneity seemed artificial to him, but it was enchanting. She not only played a central role in his scheme but fell into two habits: getting out of the port and going to Petite Ville, enjoying it as a safe haven—but also participating in more and more daring adventures. They fooled the port insiders and they fooled the authorities. They began stashing away a fortune in their retreat. But François had not counted on the emotions that would grow unbidden in him and found it difficult to let her go back to the port, to acknowledge her life with other men, her partying all night. He knew he had to allow it in order to throw people off the scent and to attract new business. But a strange prickling sent him to Marseille at times when he should not have gone. Feigning unconcern, he often watched her. She would throw him a wink, and two or three days later his happiness would return. Marie-Jos would be exclusively his again. Traces of her unruly life, long nights, and libertine sexuality disappeared. An almost adolescent freshness took their place, true desire: a tender and playful, almost sisterly, persona.

François was not unaware of the dangers: former partners, rival traffickers, detected his new prudence, his new manner of operating. No one had proof of his contact with the ships (that's what Marie-Jos was for), but he knew he was being watched. Did this state of affairs last two years? He had targeted four as the necessary time to become a millionaire and fade out of sight, but the girl's death put an end to any plan to amass a fortune. The tragedy happened at night: curiously, while he was in the port and she in their hideaway. When he came home he found the house turned upside down: not a sou, not a jewel. Blood on the floor and an appointment at the morgue. He took it to be the work of his rivals: which of them? For years he found no trail, no suspect. That should have alerted him, but it didn't; he loved her too much. His loss erased all else.

What happened was that the attendants at the tiny clinic (at that point he overlooked the fact that the body had not been taken to the central hospital but to this dreary dispensary) had offered to show him the knife-riddled body, but he refused. A hideous weakness prevented him from looking at the dead breasts and skin he had cherished so dearly. He signed the necessary documents. He paid for the burial, and for months visited the small cemetery. "Marie-Jos" were the only words on the headstone. He devoted hours of silence, of adoration, to her. As the years went by, he forgot the place, and he grew old. Since he didn't know how to do anything else, he kept on in his old line of business, but now he worked with whoever came along (including some who could have been the thief, the murderer). He wasn't interested in finding out; he had lost her, it was enough to live a little. Maybe he didn't have what it takes to be a millionaire, a rich man, as he had believed when he was with her. Over time he became more meek, and even gained respect among his associates.

He had first heard the rumor five years before. Someone, an ex-convict returning from America, had told a mutual friend in the port. The news was unembellished: a woman identical to Marie-Jos was living on the other side of the ocean, in a port like this one. He couldn't judge too clearly the elements of the report, but something sharp turned over in his gut. That evening he took the bus to visit the cemetery. He cleared away the dead leaves and uncovered the old stone. The beloved name, his own story, were there, frozen in time. He spent a blurry evening thinking of her, and got drunk.

Months later, by chance, he ran into the same friend, and they reviewed their earlier discussion with calm. The man himself had never been in that port; nevertheless, he knew certain specific facts through the ex-convict. The woman across the ocean was called María-Inés; she was no longer young, and although she spoke the local language, her foreign accent was unmistakable. The con, when still living his life of adventure, had spent a night with María-Inés. The woman had an iris-shaped beauty mark on her back.

François shuddered. That coincidence settled it. An iris! A tattoo, not a beauty spot. He recalled their first meetings, his delight in Marie-Jos, like having a new toy. He, he François, had tattooed the flower on her skin. She dreamed about sailors' tattoos; she wanted one herself. He found out how to do it. Drunk, they had practiced on him—he ran his fingers over the place now—because he wanted to please her but not take risks. Then he convinced her to put the tattoo on her back; he feared destroying some memorable portion of that beloved body, but the flower took on shape and color, triumphant. Marie-Jos was happy; it amused her, using two mirrors, to look at her "beauty spot."

Now the aging François was on the alert for travelers arriving from America. Intuition told him exactly which ones to approach: a detail of clothing, certain leathery skin, a mark on the arm: indications of life in barrios and ports. In this way he established contact with a young traveler who, interestingly enough, was not European. ("Should I," the journalist asked, "put in a dark hint about the bootblack? He told me that a Venezuelan accomplice was going to help François, but didn't assign that role to himself." "No one will recognize him as a former criminal, and besides, that was forty years ago," I replied. "The kid who was the shoeshine boy of the plaza, the one who told the story, is the old man who still remembers the headlines. Therefore, he could be the young adventurer, the unsuspected link between Marie-Jos and François.")

It was true that François never again made the big money he had in his youth, but he lived comfortably, and had some savings. Nor did it matter to him if he lost that money to indulge the obsession that was consuming him. If once he had been madly in love, now he was driven by suspicion (or revenge). He allowed the young adventurer to live off him; in his house: bringing women from the port, drinking constantly. A strange bond of affection (the young man seemed to need conversation, warmth) and blackmail grew between the two men. In fact, he bought him. In the midst of all the parties and pleasure, the young adventurer knew how to return the favor. Besides, the job he was being offered would be a breeze: return to his own country, live for a while in Puerto Cabello, and locate a somewhat older woman, maybe inclined toward drugs and heavy drinking. His mission: to find out what he could about her and spend a night with her. Long enough to observe her back.

So all that was left was for the young hoodlum to make the trip. While he was away, François put his mind to obtaining permission to open the vault. He was extremely discreet (in the end, he had asked for special favors from someone in the government), and one noon, in the quiet of the cemetery, apprehensive, he had ascertained that there was nothing in his lover's urn but some remnants of cloth and a few stones. He may have been too old to feel the appropriate emotion, but from that moment waves of passion, fury, and impotence raced though his veins. Scorn and hatred took the place of love. Even so, he remembered the tenderness he had known in his twenties, his surrender, his need for her and now his violent longing to destroy her, to put an end to his prolonged dream. Marie-Jos, he concluded, had been an unknown quantity, someone capable of deceiving him in every way (as she must have done with her clients in bed); a soul untouched by the liquor, the nights. For several weeks François isolated himself, indecisive, disconsolate. Alone, he again lived as he had during the days with Marie-Jos; sounds, details of street corners, held him in a time now dead. When he excised that double image, all that was left was pure hatred.

Now he must wait for the traveler's return, but in his mind everything was confirmed. He used those days trying to pick up (so late!) a trail. Why had Marie-Jos betrayed him? Whom had she run away with? He reviewed the hundreds of faces he had seen beside hers in bars. It could have been some sailor, someone passing through, someone he had never suspected (just no one had caught on to the close relationship between them).

He spent night after night filling in that empty face, the figure of an unidentifiable man. The ghost humiliated him with its absence. And then the adventurer returned. His report (since he didn't know the story) contrasted with François's questions in its precision, its freshness, its fatal effect.

The woman was Marie-Jos. Now, at the end of her best years, the secret she had guarded for decades seemed unimportant. She babbled on about her life to the adventurer. At first, he had felt a certain revulsion toward this faded woman, but he let himself be carried away by her skill in bed, her playfulness. And when he sensed she was asleep, he discovered on the woman's back—to his surprise—the violet petals of a small flower. She was drunk, in fact, nearly every night, and suffered a terrible illness: nostalgia for Marseille. Year after year she had considered the possibility of returning, of asking someone's forgiveness, but the sweet languor of the tropics immobilized her. She never made a move to go back, even when—after cautious inquiries—she learned that during recent years "someone" had dropped out of the busy life of the port. One drifter even swore he had attended his funeral.

And whom was she living with? What was she doing? The traveler recounted details of her house, of how she had managed a huge fortune. She lived for pleasure, but like a blind woman: no aspirations, no goals. And, less credible, without a steady lover. She took pleasure, and suffered, from brief encounters. Only on two or three occasions had she taken in a foreigner, because she was mad about the local men—energetic, with narrow, firm buttocks ("Like me, wouldn't you say?" asked the dark-skinned man—whom she kept for brief periods). All that betrayal, François reflected, that long voyage, changing identity, all to be a nothing? Just nothing? Her love affairs in her new world were still short-lived. Puerto Cabello received her with festive humor. She had problems with a few wives but gradually was accepted, and even became friends with a few decent families.

The traveler talked on, completing the mosaic of the past, unaware of the precision with which François was fitting in every detail. It was Marie-Jos. But why had she done it?

There ended the complicity with the traveler, but in its place was a new desire: not so much revenge, destroying Marie-Jos, but learning what had caused her to plan the desertion, the theft, the indifference of all those years. To find out those things his spy would not be effective, nor would a new intermediary. He alone could obtain the truth from the woman, although seeing her again would mean killing her.

Once again he organized his life around Marie-Jos, as if nothing that pertained to him could be excluded from her world; as if the past, his present life, and any future invention could turn only about her, for her. He went through his papers, organized his money and a pending deal; without saying so, he was bidding his language, his few casual friends, his home, the air he breathed, the smell of Marseille, goodbye.

At the last moment, the bootblack followed François to Puerto Cabello. For all practical purposes, they were never apart during the crossing: a drink, a joke, the adventurer's interminable chatter. François never mentioned the woman; his companion had no concrete motivation for their trip. Once in Puerto Cabello, the old man seemed dazed; the excessive brilliance of the sky, the heat, inhibited him. Maybe he didn't want to be seen so clearly. It was then the friend became very useful; he kept him practically hidden in a discreet pension, he acted as his interpreter, and above all, at night—sometimes on foot, sometimes in a taxi—he pointed out Marie-Inés's comings and goings. François convinced himself that he felt nothing the first time he saw her. She was leaving her large house in her car. A little fat, a little faded, she had little resemblance to the lively girl in Marseille. But even seeing her so different, he could recognize her in a certain rigidity of her movements, something about her mouth, in a forgotten cut of her eyes.

The Creole never detected any violence in the old man's low-key behavior. He seemed only to be remembering, to be comparing the image of a former lover with the present-day woman. Three days later, at dawn, Marie-Jos died, stabbed to death by François's knife. The body was untouched except at the point of the flower.

Is it an invention of the journalist or a true comment by the aged bootblack that François forced her to answer a question? Does a novel or a two-act play need the protagonist's confession? Their two voices, at any rate, coincided at one point: Marie-Jos had acted solely on her own. She had taken advantage of François's trust in her, and left him when it suited her. Not another man, not a true betrayal—nothing more than her willful scheme. François never knew that the day he had gone to the morgue,

Marie-Jos was hiding in Marseille. Had he opened the urn, had he discovered the masquerade, the attendants—the woman's close friends—would have called her. She would have come back, begging forgiveness, somehow explaining away her terrible joke. She would have convinced him, and maybe they would never have parted. But he believed her death from the first minute.

TRANSLATED BY MARGARET SAYERS PEDEN

Nélida Piñón

Brazil
(b. 1936)

The daughter of Galician immigrants, Nélida Piñón often portrays in her fiction Brazil's poor but industrious communities of foreigners, who are attracted by the country's always imminent yet forever postponed realization of its economic potential. She herself, only the fourth woman named to the Brazilian Academy of Letters, is an example of the success of some of these immigrants, who have become an integral part of the nation, crucial ingredients in Brazil's complex melting pot. Brazil is perhaps the only nation in the Americas to have achieved a synthesis akin to what used to be conceived of as a race. A tireless worker, since 1981 Piñón has published eight novels and three collections of stories. She is a prolific storyteller who creates vast, Balzacian social panoramas of Brazilian society, spanning all classes. But she also has a keen eye for history's broad movements, with their beguiling prophetic repetitions. In this she is closer to Spanish Americans like Carpentier and García Márquez than to other Brazilian writers, like Lispector. Perhaps her Brazilian precursor in this is Enrico Verissimo. Piñón's best-known novel in this vein is *The Republic of Dreams,* published in 1981 (English translation, 1984), a thinly veiled autobiographical story about several generations of a Galician immigrant family. Other well-known works are *Guia-mapa de Gabriel Arcanjo* (1961) and *O calor das coisas (contos)* (1980), whose title story, "The Warmth of Things," is reproduced here. The story is a perversion, perhaps a parody, of Kafka's "The Metamorphosis," a central modern literary myth. Here Oscar's transformation into his nickname takes on, ironically, a quasi-metaphysical dimension. His metamorphosis, provoked by his mother's devotion, hovers between the sacred and the very profane.

The Warmth of Things

The neighbors called him "meat turnover." And his mother tenderly repeated: "My beloved meat turnover." The nickname came from the obesity that Oscar never successfully fought off, despite rigorous diets. One time he lived on water for five days, without his body showing any effect of the sacrifice. After that he accepted his exploding appetite and forgot his real name.

From early on, he fell into the habit of calculating his age according to the number of centimeters his rapidly expanding waistline measured, taking no account of how many birthdays he had celebrated with cakes, black bean stew with sausage, and platters of macaroni. So he soon felt old among young people. Especially since he had no clothes that would disguise his bulges. If he would only wear skirts with gussets, he would at least be able to hide those regions of his body that gave him a pie shape.

He constantly rebelled against a fate that forced upon him a body that was such a violent contrast to his delicate, svelte soul. Especially when his friends offhandedly admitted that they missed having him along with an ice-cold draft beer. And their only reason for not downing Oscar right there at the table in the bar was their fear of the consequences. But they did nibble at his belly, and tried their best to pry a black olive out of his navel.

The house was gloomy on his birthdays. His mother turned out half the lights. Only the candles on the cake illuminated the presents on the sideboard. Always the same ones: long-handled bath brushes, since his pot belly kept him from reaching his feet, and immeasurable lengths of cloth from the dry goods store. After blowing the candles out, he forced the mirror to show him his face with its innumerable fine wrinkles around his eyes, its drooping cheeks, its multiple chins. He saw that his extremities looked as though they had been mashed with a kitchen fork, so as to keep odd bits of ground meat from escaping from the dough consisting of flour, lard, milk, and salt that his body was made of.

Despite his visibly upset feelings with regard to meat turnovers, he ate dozens of them every day. And not being able to find them on every street corner, he tucked in his knapsack a supply of soy oil, a frying pan, turnovers to fry, and a discreet flame to be fed by blowing hard on it. In vacant lots, before frying them, he chased off any strangers who might be out to rob him of his rations.

Each morning when he awoke, his body was different. Perhaps because certain fat deposits shifted to another center of greater interest, around his liver, for instance, or because he sometimes put on four kilos in less than sixteen hours. A physical madness that played its part in stripping him of all pride. Of his pride in being handsome. Unleashing in its stead a great resentment in his heart against the friends who hadn't yet devoured him during that week, despite his closer and closer resemblance to a meat turn-over sold on a street corner.

In his hour of greatest sadness he clung to the little medal of Our Lady of Fatima around his neck, under whose protection his mother had placed him, for lack of a patron saint who watched over fat people in particular. At home, he whistled to hide his sorrow. But the tears from some of his fits of weeping flowed so thick and fast that they wet the floor, which his mother happened to be wiping dry at just that moment. She pretended not to notice. Only when his tears formed a puddle, as though rain had leaked through the roof, did his mother go, coins in hand, to special friends of his to get them to accompany Oscar to the movies at least once a month. The ones who agreed to go with him one day were reluctant to do so the next, despite the lure of the money. And just as she was running out of friends of his to ask, Oscar himself, who no longer fit in any seat, stopped going to movies that he had to watch standing up.

On Sundays, the dinner table was full of smoking platters. Oscar saw himself in the place occupied by the roast, carved with a silver knife and fork, with the whole family in high spirits. In order to avoid such punitive visions, he retired to his room on those days.

In summer, his torment grew worse, for instead of sweat, it was oil, vinegar, and mustard, his mother's favorite seasonings, that dripped from his chest. Touched by divine gifts of such a nature, she would then stroke her son's head, pulling out at the same time a few curly hairs, which, once back in her room, she examined one by one, anxious to find out how much longer she would have her son with her at home, safe and sound.

Oscar collected this maternal consolation in the same tin he used to store the leftover fat from his itinerant frying pan. And, wishing to reward the sacrifice his mother had made by drinking the oil and vinegar from his breast, he beamed a smile at her, whereupon she exclaimed: "What a beautiful smile you have. It's the smile of well-being, my son." These words were followed by ones that wounded him to the quick and which his mother, in tears, could not help uttering: "Ah, my beloved meat turnover!"

The expression of this affection, which his misshapen body could not have inspired, made Oscar creep off to his room, hurt by these corrosive words from his mother, whose one aim was to get him inside the red-hot frying pan of her fervor, patience, and hunger.

He foresaw a tragic end for himself. His friends ready and waiting, like vultures, to peck at his flesh. The prospect of his own pain led him to read on the walls a minutely detailed balance sheet of his credits. He had his doubts about his earthly estate. The column listing his debts had grown so long that he would never free himself of them as long as he lived. He owed his flesh to his fellows, because they were hungry. And even though they owed him a body that he could be proud of, he had no way of getting it from them.

Once he was freshly bathed and smelled of scented lotion, he imagined what love between humans would be like, their bodies lying in the bed unaffected by a lack of control over a hostile obesity. At such moments, misled by the hope of a modest credit balance, he reached the point of being able to see himself doing battle with his adversaries. It took no more than a brusque gesture, however, for reality to remind him of a corpulence in which there was no place for poetry and love. And immediately, the prospect of being eaten with a knife and fork was transformed into the most obscure question.

His mother put up a fight against his wildly staring eyes, his soul continually in mourning. What evil is abroad in the world that makes you look upon us with such suspicion? Oscar gave her a platinum brooch as a present, to be plunged forever into her breast. Drops of poison and the certainty of her own cross to bear were to drip from her flesh. In the face of the enigma that Oscar was posing, his mother, who throughout her life had rejected limpid phrases, uttered the words, "Oh, such a good meat turnover of a son!"

The more she extolled virtues that, in all truth, both of them despised, the more eagerly Oscar hastened to remove from the edges of his body residues that perchance had not fit inside the turnover that he was. In the end he abandoned the vacant lots where he had fried his turnovers. He no longer tolerated being stared at with a hunger that he was unable to satisfy. He had no way to feed the poor. They would have to die without help.

As his consultations of the mirror, a clouded one, grew more intense, the glass gave him only a dim view of his body tailored every day by an efficient kitchen fork. He dressed himself in a turnover every morning. In retaliation, he installed his armchair in the kitchen, leaving it only to sleep. He attended to the basic necessities, and practiced his new habit of sprinkling wheat flour all over his body. With the hollows under his fingernails smeared with fat, he received visitors there, obliging them to smooth his flour-dusted skin.

His mother rebelled against this uncouth behavior. She did not want her friends to be exposed to such an ordeal. If he was a prisoner of his obesity, let him put up with it in a dignified manner. Her son returned the insult with his teeth moving like a power saw, nearly grinding her arms to a fine powder. And his performance was so convincing that his mother took to protecting her limbs with thick pieces of wool, despite the heat. She left her face showing. And when Oscar insisted that she stay within reach of his hands, she slunk away underneath the coats and boots.

By the age of thirty, Oscar was fed up. It was his turn now to eat anyone who suggested a turnover. He had been willing to play this role for so long a time that he demanded human flesh to sate his appetite. He would select his victim very carefully. Although he was particularly inclined toward people who belonged to the household, fraternal blood. And following through with his plans, he pretended to be blind, stumbling over things, so as to distract his enemies. His mother asked the neighbors for help, and they took turns staying with her during the first week, only to leave her by herself after that. With so many things to do, his mother took to wearing light clothing, forgetting her son's threats.

Oscar for his part was surprised to discover the charms of speech. He had never before been heard to hold forth so rapturously on objects that in point of fact he claimed he could not see. He had just discovered that he possessed the power to make his hunger coincide with a verbal voracity that had always been in his blood, but to which he had attributed no importance, occupied as he was in defending himself against those who wanted to fling him into the frying pan.

His mother soon accustomed herself to his blindness. She treated him like a passenger in an endless tunnel. She described the house to him, as though he were a guest in it. She wanted him to participate in everyday life, and her face suddenly brightened on seeing her son's gentleness. That was when Oscar opened his eyes, certain that he had won. And there she was, smiling, her arms outside, her body exposed. He rapidly went over in his memory the times that, moved by the force of love, she had called him her meat turnover, coming close to eating him. At that moment his mother, having suffered for his sake, caught in his eyes a gleam that was not that of a chandelier, or of happiness, or of the remote truth of a son she hardly knew. What the mother discovered in her son was a flame bent upon living, and the unmistakable look of an executioner.

She stood there calmly at his side. Oscar would take the necessary steps. She was aware of him as a man for the first time. He drew his armchair closer to his mother's, which she had dragged to the kitchen. He asked her to sit down. He too sat down, after first plucking out a few of the woman's hairs. And only with his mother's consent did he begin to keep a close watch on her.

TRANSLATED BY HELEN LANE

Dalton Trevisan

Brazil
(b. 1925)

The title of the collection from which "Penelope" is taken says much about Dalton Trevisan's fiction: *Novelas nada exemplares,* or "Hardly Exemplary Tales," a play on the title of Cervantes's famous collection. The nonexemplariness of Trevisan's work lies in his penchant for showing the grotesque, cruel, and deviant actions of humans, particularly of middle-class people who would hardly seem capable of such deeds. Trevisan is the disfiguring chronicler of the bourgeoisie in Curitiba, the capital of the state of Paraná in Brazil. He is adept at creating an ambience of provincial mediocrity and conventionalism out of which, uncannily, something unusual emerges. A prolific short story writer, Trevisan is also the author of collections such as *A guerra conjugal* (1970), which won a national award, and *The Vampire of Curitiba and Other Stories* (1972). Trevisan's signature is having the unusual appear in the midst of the ordinary in a manner not unlike that of a Hitchcock film. "Penelope" is a case in point. The context of the classical Greek myth seems too grandiose for this homey couple, past the blush of youth, who seem more suited to appear in a painting by Rousseau, or perhaps one by Botero (given the lady's plumpness), than in such a highly dramatic context. The uncanny erupts into their dull lives in the form of insistently regular and anonymous letters left under the door, whose repetitiveness gives the story the aura of a nightmare. Trevisan's mastery is shown in how the offending word in the letters never surfaces in the text, yet its power is capable of unleashing a minor tragedy, fraught with irony. According to K. David Jackson, Trevisan "makes a significant contribution to the short story through his approach to understatement and stylist miniaturization." This mini-Joycean recast of the Penelope myth exemplifies not only these virtues but also Trevisan's rather pessimistic view of the human condition.

Penelope

An old couple lived on that street. The wife would wait for the husband on the veranda, knitting in her rocking chair. When he got to the gate she would be standing, with the needles crossed in her sewing basket. He would cross the small garden, and by the door, before going in, he would kiss her with his eyes closed.

Always together, working in the vegetable garden: he in the kale, she in the mallow patch. Through the kitchen door the neighbors could see the husband drying the dishes for his mate. On Saturdays they would go out for a walk, she fat and blue-eyed, he thin and dressed in black. In summer the wife would wear a white dress that was out of style, but he was still in black. Their life was a mystery. It was vaguely known that there had been a disaster years back, their children dead. Leaving house, graves, and animals behind, the old couple had moved to Curitiba.

Only the two of them, no dog, no cat, no bird. Sometimes when her husband was away she would get a bone for a stray dog sniffing at the gate. If she was fattening up a hen, she would immediately grow soft-hearted, incapable of killing it. The man dismantled the henhouse and planted a fierce cactus in its place. He pulled up the only rose bush in the corner of the garden. Not even to a rose did he dare give his remnant of love.

Except for Saturdays they never left the house, the old man smoking his pipe, the old woman criss-crossing her needles. Until the day when opening the door, back from their walk, they found a letter at their feet. No one ever wrote to them, with no relative or friend in the world. The blue envelope was without an address. The wife proposed burning it, for they'd had more than their share of suffering. He replied that nobody could do them any harm.

He didn't burn the letter. He didn't open it. It lay forgotten on the table. They sat down under the lamp in the parlor, she with her knitting, he with his newspaper. The woman lowered her head, held one needle in her mouth and with the other counted the stitches and, as her look wandered, recounted the row. The man, newspaper folded over his knees, was reading every sentence twice. His pipe went out but he didn't light it, listening to the click of the needles. Finally he opened the letter. Two words, in letters cut from a newspaper. Nothing else, no date, no signature. He handed the sheet of paper to his wife, who, after reading it, looked at him. Neither spoke. She stood up, holding the letter in her fingertips.

"What are you going to do?"

"Burn it."

He said no. He placed the note back into its envelope and put it in his pocket. He picked up the mat that had fallen to the floor and continued his reading of the newspaper.

The wife put her yarn and needles in the basket.

"Forget about it, old girl. A letter tossed into every house."

Does the sirens' song reach the heart of old people? He forgot about the piece of paper in his pocket. Another week passed. On Saturday, before opening the door, he knew that the letter was there waiting. The wife stepped on it, pretending not to see it. He picked it up and put it in his pocket.

Hunched over, counting the same row, she asked: "Aren't you going to read it?"

Over the newspaper he was admiring that beloved head, not a single white hair, eyes that despite their years were as blue as on the first day.

"I already know what it says."

"Why don't you burn it?"

It was a game and he showed her the letter: no address. He opened it: two words, letters cut from a newspaper. He blew into the envelope, shook it over the rug, but nothing was there. He put it away with the other one and, as he folded the newspaper, he noticed that his companion was undoing a mistake in the mat.

He woke up in the middle of the night, leaped out of bed, and went to look out the window. He drew back the curtain. There in the shadows he saw the figure of a man. He clenched his fist until the other man went away.

The next Saturday during the walk he wondered if he was the only one receiving the letter. It could be a mistake; there wasn't any address. If only it mentioned a name at least, a date, a place. He pushed open the door and there it was: blue. Into his pocket along with the others. He opened the newspaper. Turning the pages, he caught sight of the face hunched over the needles. A difficult mat she'd been working on for months. He remembered the legend of Penelope, who undid at night by the light of a torch the rows she'd finished during the day, and waiting for her husband, she gained time from her suitors in that way. He stopped halfway through the story: Had Penelope cheated on her absent husband? For whom was she knitting the shroud? Did the needles keep on clicking after Ulysses came back?

In the bathroom, he closed the door, tore open the envelope. Two words . . . He worked out a plan: he put the letter away and put a hair in it. He hung his jacket on the hook, the piece of paper showing in the pocket. The wife left the milk bottle by the door, went to bed. In the morning he examined the envelope: it seemed intact, in the same place. He scrutinized it in search of the white hair—he didn't find it.

From the street he spied on the woman's steps inside the house. She goes to meet him at the gate—in her eye the reflection of the other's necktie. Ah, lifting the hair from the nape of her neck to see if there were any teeth marks . . . In her absence he opened the closet, stuck his head in among the clothes. From behind the curtain he spied on the men passing on the sidewalk. He recognized the milkman, the baker, young men, with false smiles.

He went over his mate's movements: dust on the furniture, whether the soil in the pots of violets was damp or dry. . . . He was measuring time by the mat. He knew how many rows his wife was knitting, and when she made a wrong stitch, she had to undo it even before counting with the tip of her needle.

With no proof against her, he never revealed Penelope's purpose. As he read he would observe the face in the shadow of the lampshade. When he heard steps, sneaking on tiptoe he peeked out the window, the curtain crumpled in his angry hand.

Finally he bought a weapon.

"What's the revolver for?" His companion was alarmed.

He mentioned the number of thieves in the city. He demanded an accounting of old presents. Might she be making mats for her lover to sell? In the evening, with the newspaper open on his knees, he would observe the woman—her face, her dress—seeking some sign of the other one. She would miss a stitch, would have to undo the row.

She would wait for him on the veranda. He would pass by the house as if he didn't know her. On his return he would sniff the odors in the air, run his finger over the furniture, touch the soil of the violets—he knew where his wife was.

In the middle of the night he woke up. The pillow was still warm from the other head. Under the door a light was showing from the parlor. She was doing her knitting, always the mat. Was it Penelope undoing another day's work at night?

Lifting her eyes the woman caught sight of the revolver. The needles were clicking without any yarn. She never knew why he spared her. As soon as they lay down he fell into a deep sleep.

There'd been a cousin in her past. . . . The woman swore in vain that the cousin had died of typhus at the age of twelve. In the evening he took the letters out of his pocket—there were a lot of them, one for every Saturday—and he read them one by one, muttering.

He wouldn't accept staying at home on Saturday in order to identify the author. He felt a need for that note. The correspondence between the cousin and him, the cuckold. A game where he'd be the winner in the end. One day the other one would reveal everything. It was imperative not to interrupt her.

At the gate he gave his arm to his companion. They didn't speak to each other during the entire walk, didn't stop by the shop windows. On their return he would pick up the envelope and, before opening it, would go into the house with it. He would immediately hide a hair in the fold and leave it on the table.

He always found the hair. His wife wasn't reading the two words anymore. Or—he wondered with a new wrinkle on his brow—had she discovered the art of reading them without disturbing the hair?

One afternoon he opened the door and took a deep breath. He ran his fingers over the furniture: dust. He touched the soil in the flower pots:

dry. He went straight to the bedroom with its closed windows and turned on the light. The old woman was there on the bed, revolver in her hand, white dress all bloody. He left her with her eyes open.

He felt no pity; it had been just. The police left him alone—he hadn't been home when his wife committed suicide. When the funeral was over the neighbors commented on his profound grief—he wasn't weeping. Holding on to a handle of the coffin, he helped lower it into the grave. He left before the gravedigger finished covering it.

He went into the parlor, saw the mat on the table—the mat she'd been knitting. Penelope had finished her work; it was her own shroud she'd been weaving—her husband was home.

He turned on the lamp with the green silk shade. On the armchair the needles lay crossed in the sewing basket. It was Saturday, he remembered. Nobody could do him any harm. His wife had paid for her crime. Or—suddenly the cry in his breast—innocent perhaps? The letter thrown under other doors. Under his by mistake.

There was no way of knowing, so he could grow old in peace. If it was meant for him it wouldn't be coming with his wife dead, never again. That was the last one—the other man had trembled on finding the door and window open. He must have seen the hearse at the gate. One of those who stood next to him as the coffin was lowered—there was a little water in the grave.

He left the house as on every Saturday. His arm bent, a habit from offering it to his companion for so many years. In front of the store windows with dresses, some white, he felt the weight of her hand. He smiled disdainfully at her vanity, even when she was dead.

The two steps to the veranda—"I was right," he repeated, "I was right,"—with a firm hand he turned the key. He opened the door, stepped on the letter, and, sitting in the armchair, he read the newspaper aloud so as not to hear the cries of the silence.

TRANSLATED BY GREGORY RABASSA

Cristina Peri Rossi

Uruguay
(b. 1941)

Cristina Peri Rossi's great-grandparents on both sides were Italian immigrants. She won several literary prizes early in her career for her poetry and short stories. But in 1972 Peri Rossi had to go into exile in Spain because of her political militancy. She lives in Barcelona, where she works as a journalist, publishing in *Diario 16, El Periódico,* and *Agencia Efe.* Peri Rossi is considered one of the leading Latin American writers today among those who have acquired recognition in the period after the Boom of the Latin American novel (when García Márquez, Vargas Llosa, Fuentes, and others came to prominence). With her work translated into many languages, she is one of a group of women writers making their mark today. Although Peri Rossi's fiction is often about women, matters of gender do not limit her work, which is broadly ironic, witty, and metaphysical. Her first book, *Viviendo,* a collection of narratives whose protagonists are all female, was published in 1963 but was written earlier. The following are a few highlights from her substantial oeuvre. The award-winning *Los museos abandonados* (1968) contains a series of short stories, considered by some to constitute a brief novel. Peri Rossi received another award for *Diáspora* (1973), a collection of poetry. *La tarde del dinosaurio* (1976) is a volume of stories with a prologue by Julio Cortázar. The witty *El museo de los esfuerzos inútiles* (1983) is yet another book of stories. Peri Rossi explores sexual desire in *Una pasión prohibida* (1986) and *Fantasías eróticas* (1991). She has occasionally written vaguely pornographic stories. In "The Threshold," the selection here, Peri Rossi has managed to give a new twist to a topic that reaches back to Plato: the relationship between dream and reality, and between waking consciousness and fantasy.

The Threshold

The woman never dreams and this makes her intensely miserable. She thinks that by not dreaming she is unaware of things about herself that dreams would surely give her. She doesn't have the door of dreams that opens every night to question the certainties of the day. Nor the door of dreams through which we enter into the past of the species, where once we were dinosaurs among the foliage, or stones in the torrent. She stays at the threshold, and the door is always closed, refusing her entrance. I tell her *that* in itself is a dream, a nightmare: to be in front of a door which will not open no matter how much we push at the latch or pound the knocker. But in truth, the door to that nightmare doesn't have a latch or knocker; it is total surface, brown, high and smooth as a wall. Our blows strike a body without an echo.

"There's no such thing as a door without a key," she tells me, with the stubborn resistance of one who does not dream.

"There are in dreams," I tell her. In dreams, doors don't open, rivers run dry, mountains turn around in circles, telephones are made of stone, and we never get to our appointments on time. In dreams we don't have underwear to cover our nakedness, elevators stop in the middle of floors or smash against the roof, and when we go to the movies all the seats have their backs to the screen. Objects lose their functionality in dreams in order to become obstacles, or they have their own laws that we don't know anything about.

She thinks that the woman who does not dream is the enemy of the waking woman because she robs her of parts of herself, takes away the wild excitement of revelation when we think we have discovered something that we didn't know before or that we had forgotten.

"A dream is a piece of writing," she says sadly, "a work that I don't know how to write and that makes me different from others, all the human beings and animals who dream."

She is like a tired traveler who stops at the threshold and stays there, stationary as a plant.

In order to console her, I tell her that perhaps she is too tired to cross through the doorway; maybe she spends so much time looking for her dreams before falling asleep that she doesn't see the images when they appear because her exhaustion has made her close those eyes that are inside of her eyes. When we sleep we have two pairs of eyes: the more superficial eyes, which are accustomed to seeing only the appearance of things and of dealing with light, and dream's eyes; when the former close, the latter open up. She is the traveler on a long trip who stops at the threshold, half dead with fatigue, and can no longer pass over to the other side or cross the river or the border because she has closed both pairs of eyes.

"I wish I could open them," she says simply.

Sometimes she asks me to tell her my dreams, and I know that later, in the privacy of her room with the light out, hiding like a little girl who is about to do something naughty, she'll try to dream my dream. But to dream someone else's dream is harder than writing someone else's story, and her failures fill her with irritation. She thinks I have a power that she doesn't have and this brings out her envy and bad humor. She'd like for my forehead to be a movie screen so that while I sleep, she could see all the images from my dreams reflected on it. If I smile or make a gesture of annoyance during the night, she wakes me up and asks me—dissatisfied— what happy or sad thing has happened. I can't always answer her accurately; dreams are made of such a fragile material that often they disappear as soon as we wake up; they flee to the eyes' web and the fingers' spiders. She thinks that the world of dreams is an extra life that some of us have, and her curiosity is only halfway satisfied when I am finished telling her the last one. (To tell dreams is one of the most difficult arts; perhaps only Kafka was able to do so without spoiling their mystery, trivializing their symbols or making them rational.)

Just as children can't stand any slight change and love repetition, she insists that I tell her the same dream two or three times, a tale full of people I don't know, strange forms, unreal happenings on the road, and she becomes annoyed if in the second version there are some elements that were not in the first.

The one she likes best is the amniotic dream, the dream of water. I am walking under a straight line that is above my head, and everything underneath is clear water that doesn't make me wet or have any weight; you don't see it or feel it, but you know it is there. I am walking on a ground of damp sand, wearing a white shirt and dark pants, and fish are swimming all around me. I eat and drink under the water but I never swim or float because the water is just like air, and I breathe it naturally. The line above my head is the limit that I never cross, nor do I have any interest in going beyond it.

"It's probably an old dream," I tell her. A dream from the past, from our origins when we were still undecided about being fish or humans.

She, in turn, would like to dream of flying, of slipping from tree to tree way above the rooftops.

Sometimes while she sleeps I put a little pressure on her forehead with my fingertips in order to bring on a dream. She doesn't wake up, but she also doesn't dream. I tell her the last dream I had, of a prisoner in a small punishment cell, isolated from light, time, space, human voices, in an infinity of silence and darkness. There's a guard next to the door and the prisoner manages to inject—through the walls of the tunnel as through the membranes of a uterus—his dreams into the guard, who then can no longer rest, hounded as he is by the prisoner's dreams. The guard promises to free him if the man can frighten away the lion who hunts him down each time he dreams.

"You're the prisoner," she says with a vengeance.

Dreams are like boxes, there are other dreams inside them. Sometimes we happen to wake up in the second rather than the first, and this makes us anxious. In the second, I try to call her but she doesn't answer, she doesn't hear me; then I wake up and call her again. I open my arms to her, not knowing that I am in the first dream and that this time she will also not answer.

I propose that before falling asleep we have the experience of inventing a complementary story, the two of us together. Surely then some remains, castoffs, residue of this story elaborated by the two of us would pass imperceptibly to the inner part of our eyes (to the eyes that open when the superficial eyes close) and in this way, she would finally manage to dream.

"We'll take each other to the threshold," I tell her, "and when we get there we will separate, giving each other a kiss on the forehead, and each of us will go through the door—her and his door—and we'll meet again the next morning after a different journey. You'll talk to me of the tree you saw and I of the ship that takes me to the city I hope never to see again."

That night we go to bed at the usual time and I am the one in charge of beginning the story that is to take us imperceptibly—but together—to the auspicious door.

"There is a man in an empty room," I begin.

"The curtain is very soft," she says, "made of red velvet, but it is tied at one end."

"The man is lying in bed," I continue, "although he is still wearing the white shirt and the dark pants."

"I think the man is afraid of something," she continues. "That's why he is still dressed."

"Next to him is a woman," I say, "with short blond hair. Her eyes are blue."

"No," she corrects, "they are green with blue flecks."

"Yes," I accept. "She is beautiful, but she has the cold skin of those who do not dream."

"The woman has on a pink dress. Isn't it somewhat outmoded to wear a dress of this color to bed?"

"No, sweetheart," I say. "It looks great on you."

"He's just about to fall asleep," she observes.

"Yes," I confess. "I'm very sleepy. I am walking slowly towards a door that takes form up ahead."

"You are walking slowly with your shirt sleeves rolled up and your eyes half closed."

"I'm really sleepy."

"She's following you but every moment gets farther behind. Her steps are shorter than yours and, moreover, she's afraid of getting lost. Why don't you turn to look behind you, to help her?"

"He is very tired and the path is guiding him, pulling him like a magnet."

"It's the magnet of dreams," she says.

"The woman is very far behind. She can't be seen any longer. On the other hand, I am at the threshold."

"She's gotten lost again. The corridor is dark and the walls narrow. She is afraid. She is terrified of solitude."

"I've seen this threshold before."

"But I can't see it at all."

"If you go back, if you turn around, you'll never find it."

"I'm afraid."

"Ah! What an auspicious threshold! You can make out a light once you cross over."

"Don't leave me alone."

"There's not much space."

"Don't leave me."

"I have to go on. I'm at the end of the pathway, my eyes are closing, I can't talk any more . . ."

"Then," she continues, "she throws herself forward, following the vague and dark aura that his footsteps have made in the shadowy corridor, and before he crosses over the threshold, she plunges a knife in his back."

I stagger on the threshold, I fall like a wounded person slowly in the dream, it's strange, I slip, I collapse, now I have one foot over the threshold but the other one has stayed behind, it doesn't move forward, surely I am in the second dream although the pain in my back is possibly from the first, I'd like to call to her but I know from experience that she won't answer, she has probably gone while I try in vain to wake up and I slip in a pool of blood.

TRANSLATED BY MARY JANE TREACY

Reinaldo Arenas

Cuba
(1943–1990)

———— ⸗ ————

Reinaldo Arenas was a poor peasant from eastern Cuba who was fifteen when
the revolution came to power in 1959. His education was haphazard and his
upbringing complicated by his homosexuality. The young Arenas was fascinated
by his grandmother's stories and the soap operas he listened to with the women
who raised him. He was also a voracious if indiscriminate reader. Arenas moved
to Havana as a young man, finding work and mentors at the National Library.
He became a prolific and wildly original author, for which other writers turned
bureaucrats never forgave him. Arenas was persecuted relentlessly by the revolutionary authorities for his sexuality and for his refusal to conform to social and
political norms. His first novel, *Singing from the Well,* earned him in 1965 a second prize in the annual contest sponsored by the Cuban Writer's Union. His next
novel, *Hallucinations,* published in 1969 in Mexico City, was a great success,
and Arenas became a celebrity abroad. In Cuba he continued to be hounded by
the secret police. His manuscripts were confiscated, and he was eventually put
in prison on a trumped-up morals charge. After his release Arenas fled to the
United States during the 1980 Mariel Boatlift. He lived in New York and Miami,
published a considerable number of books, gave lectures and readings, and also
engaged in political activities against the Castro dictatorship. Suffering from
AIDS, Arenas committed suicide in 1990. He recounted his dramatic life in *Before
Night Falls,* a truly remarkable memoir. Arenas's short stories are among the best
from Latin America. A collection was first published in Uruguay under the title
Con los ojos cerrados (1973). A more comprehensive collection appeared later
as *Termina el desfile* ("The Parade Ends"). The title story of that collection, in-
cluded here, was the first piece Arenas published after arriving in the United
States. It is based on the incident in Havana when thousands crowded into the
Peruvian embassy hoping to leave Cuba.

The Parade Ends

Now she's escaping me. She's losing me again in this sea of legs so
tightly packed that they join together, in this jumble of rags and
compressed bodies, over puddles of piss, of shit, of mud, between bare feet
that sink in that flattened paste of excrement. I'm looking for her, I keep

looking for her as if she were (as in fact she is) my only salvation. But, the bitch, she's slipping away again. There she goes, miraculously making her way, sliding between muddy shoes, between bodies that can't even fall over, though they're fainting (they're jammed so tightly against one another), through the crying, the piss, getting away from me with each wriggle, while avoiding at the same time, thanks to I don't know what incredible intuition, the fatal footfall. My life depends on you, my life depends on you, I say to her, crawling along too, like her. And I pursue her, I keep pursuing her in the shit and the mud, laboriously and mechanically pushing aside bellies, asses, feet, arms, thighs, a whole amalgam of stinking flesh and bones, a whole arsenal of vociferating lumps that move, that want, like me, to walk around, change places, turn, and that only cause contractions, wiggling, stretching, convulsions which don't manage to cut the knot, take a step, break into a run, to show some real movement, something that really gets going, advances, leaving everyone trapped in one big spiderweb which stretches out on one side, contracts here, rises over there, but doesn't manage to break loose anywhere. So they draw back and push forward, back and forth, kneeing and kicking, now raising their arms, their heads, their noses, everything to the sky in order to breathe, to see something other than the compression of their own stinking bodies. But I'm following, I haven't lost sight of her yet and I'm following, pushing these bodies aside, crawling, kicked and cursed, but without giving up, pursuing her. For there (for with her), I say to myself, goes my life . . . Life, above all, life in spite of everything, life however it is, even without anything, even without you (and in spite of you) amid the din that rises now, amid the shrieks and the songs, for they're singing, singing again, and no less than the national anthem. Life, now, while I pursue you over the excrement to the sound of the notes (or shouts) of the national anthem, holding you as justification and refuge, as an immediate solution, as sustenance, the rest (what is the rest?) we'll see about later. Now only that lizard matters to me, that damned lizard that's hiding from me again, sly and covered with excrement, between the thousands and thousands of feet which are also sinking in the shit. *Life* . . . I was, again, like so many years ago already, at that extreme where life is not so much as a useless and humiliating repetition, but only the incessant memory of that repetition, which, in the beginning, was also a repetition, I was at that point, at that final place, at that extreme, where the act of being doesn't even matter, or rather it isn't really certain that it's true. So, standing, or better yet, bent over, since the garret didn't allow him to straighten out completely, he contemplated inside that old room of ancient hotel come to ruin and hence inhabited by people like him or even worse—vociferating creatures with no other concept nor principle nor dream but to be able, at all costs, and in spite of everything, to survive, that is to say, not to die of hunger right away—he was contemplating, staring in that position, without moving, not at the past nor the future, both not only dark but illusory, he was staring, in short, at the impoverished piece of improvised stairway that led "on high," that is to say to the narrow dormer where he had to walk not bent over, but on all fours so as not to smash his head against the ceiling. That's how he was, between the front wall that faced the hallway and the other wall that faced the other wall of the other building. Now he advanced a little more and his eyes met flush with his eyes, with his figure reflected in the mirror incrusted (screwed) right in the exit door of the hall, which was always being kept temporarily closed. He wasn't that one then, now he was this one. He wasn't running through the savannahs or grasslands anymore. He was running, sometimes, through the hysterical tumult, trying to catch a crowded bus or to get in line for bread or yogurt. So, making an effort, he separated himself from his image—this one for now—recrossed the cubicle, his kingdom, in two steps, sat down on a seat, also improvised thanks to a combination of poverty and necessity, a kind of bench with a parody of a pillow or cushion covering it. Then, before even thinking about a solution, before he could even think about how to think of a solution, the roar of a wave crashed violently, the scream, the howl of a boy (it had to be called something), the inordinate noise of a television, some radios, and, besides, of someone knocking at the closed door of the elevator, and another who, from a window, was calling in endlessly repeated shouts to somebody who obviously isn't there, or who's deaf, or doesn't want to answer, or died, finally his neighbors, people just like him, made him forget that which, like a puff of air, had crossed his imagination, had attempted to conceive—what was it, what was it—. And, hearing that kind of incessant paraphernalia, an enormous sensation of calm invaded him, a unanimous sensation of renunciation, of impotence, overwhelmed him, as always, since years ago, in a sort of stupor, of inertia, of absolute abandon, of mortal (hope?) grief, a sensation of feeling beyond all resistance, all competition, all vital possibility, a security (a rest, a weariness) of absolute death, of death definitive and complete, yes, if it weren't that in spite of everything he had a friend, and, therefore, he was still breathing . . . But with difficulty, with quite a bit of difficulty, raising and spreading out his hands, only in that way was he able to take in a little of that contaminated and absolutely stinking air and to continue, that is to dive again into the furor and the sweating bodies, crawling once again through the dirt, pushing aside legs, humps, feet, in order to reach where he was, because he was certain that he was there, naturally, in that tumult, someplace in that tumult forming a part of the tumult; that's why he was pushing, raising his head, breathing, searching, and continuing to brush aside bodies, bundles, without excusing himself, who was going to say "excuse me" in such a place? and he continued, calling out to him sometimes,

trying to make himself heard in the midst of that din. And the terrible thing
was that with each moment it was becoming more difficult to go on. More
were coming, more people kept arriving, more people who were jumping
the fence (the gate had already been closed) and entering; they were entering however they could, punching, kicking. What an uproar, what an
uproar. In the middle of the clamor and the dust and the shooting they
kept advancing, climbing up the fence and jumping; old people, pregnant
women, babies, kids; especially kids, all of them wanting to reach the wire
fence, while the group of soldiers was getting thicker. And they kept arriving, police, militia, men in uniform or in disguise, disguised as civilians,
preventing the others—the crowd—from approaching the fence. It was
no longer a cordon, but a triple cordon, heavily armed. Bursts from machine guns were heard now and shouts of "Stop right there, you son of a
bitch!" and again the clamor and the howling of those who, right there
before their very eyes, were being ripped open by machine-gun fire, without having been able to jump the fence, without even having been able
to touch it, without having been able to make it. Immediately, numerous
men (military and civilian) hurriedly getting out of their Alfa-Romeos,
were dragging the corpses to their vehicles and departing hastily down Fifth
Avenue. But now, not only were they running a risk out there, the in-
flamed mob, who at all costs wanted to get past the cordon (the cordons)
and enter, but those inside too were being machine-gunned. Somebody,
one of the top brass, a *mayimbe,* a *pincho,* pulled up abruptly before the
fence, and, beside himself, began shooting at them. In the midst of an
infernal roar, the mass retreated without being able to retreat, they pressed
even more tightly together, they hid their heads behind each other, they
backed up as if trying to climb inside themselves, and whoever fell, having
been hit by a shot, or simply having slipped, couldn't catch himself anymore, his last sight would be the thousands and thousands of feet in a
circular stampede, stepping on him and returning to step on him again.
"The anthem, the anthem," someone shouted. And suddenly, only a single
unanimous and thundering voice came out of the immense, besieged multitude, a single song, loud, coughed up, out of tune, extraordinary, crossing
the fence and filling the night. Ridiculous, ridiculous, he was saying to
himself, but for a moment he interrupted his search, he stopped, ridiculous,
ridiculous, he was saying to himself, that anthem again, ridiculous, ridiculous, but he was crying . . . Horrible, horrible, because everything was
horrible, terrifying, anew, again, always; but worse now, because now he
couldn't give himself the luxury, as then, of wasting time, his time. So,
bent over in his low and narrow hole, he was reviewing, again reviewing
all the time lived, all the time lost, and he was stopping there once again,
at the improvised and urgent stairway, beneath the roof, also improvised
and urgent, by the urgent and improvised table (the cover of a tank over

a barrel), improvised, improvised, improvised, everything improvised, and, what's more, he himself, everyone always improvising and accepting. Hearing the improvised and endless speeches; living in an improvised poverty where even the terror that he was suffering today, tomorrow, provisionally, would be substituted by another, reinforced, renovated, augmented, and so on, by improvisation. Provisionally suffering improvised laws that suddenly fomented crimes instead of reducing them; suffering improvised rages which naturally assailed him and those who were living like him, on the margins, in a cloud, in another world, that is in this improvised 3' × 4' room over an improvised garret, alone . . . To leave for the street, to go down the garbage-strewn stairs (the elevator never worked), to reach the street, what for? . . . To leave was to declare (one more time) that there was no exit. To leave was to know that it was impossible to go anywhere. To leave was to risk that they would ask him for identification, information, and, in spite of carrying on him (as he always carried) all the calamities of the system: identity card, union card, worker's card, obligatory military service card, CDR card, in short, in spite of going like a noble and tame beast, well branded, with all of the marks with which his owner obligatorily stamped him, in spite of everything, to leave was to run the risk of "falling," of "shining" badly in the eyes of a cop, who could designate him (out of moral conviction) as a *suspicious character, unclear, unstable, untrustworthy,* and without further legal procedure, to end up in a cell, as had happened to him already on several occasions. Besides, he knew what that meant. On the other hand, what a spectacle he was going to see if he went out, if not the anatomy of his own sadness, the overwhelming spectacle of a city in collapse, the taciturn figures, timid or aggressive, hungry and desperate, and, of course, hunted. Figures, besides, now alien to dialogue, to intimacy, to any possibility of communication, ready, simply (vitally), to snatch his wallet, tear off his watch, tear the glasses right off his face, in the event that he committed the imprudence of going out to the street with them on, and that's all, to run off through the deteriorating panorama. Besides, he, and here was his triumph, his means of escape, his hope, was not completely certain that he would be (that he would feel) absolutely alone . . . And with that hope, with that good fortune, he remained, just as he was: one foot on the improvised stairway, his face fading already before the broken-down mirror, his head bent so as not to bump into the ceiling of the garret, serene, still, waiting, since he was sure that, from one moment to the next, like every morning, yes, it had to be so, his friend would arrive. Finally, he took a step through the improvised room and sat down in the improvised seat. But where had he gone, where was he, where can he be, but you have to go on, you have to keep advancing, you have to find him somewhere, up on the roofs, up a tree, he can't have vanished, he has to be in this immense mob which is getting thicker now, more hysterical, grabbing hold of somebody, at last, throwing him in the air and catching him again only to keep throwing him, it's a police infiltrator, they say, who was trying to take the Peruvian flag down from the flag pole. And now thousands of arms, of closed fists, of desperate people, pounce on him, swinging him around. "Lynch him, execute him, tear him to pieces," they shout, and the man disappears and appears and disappears again, swallowed by that desperate sea until he's hurled outside the fence, where the shooting continues, now at the trees, in the air, at the cars, which, from a considerable distance and at great speeds, try to break through the barriers and get in. I go up to where the furor is most intense, I scrutinize, I push, I keep looking around among the desperate faces, among those who sleep standing up . . . But nothing, but nothing, I don't see you, although I know, I know very well that you're someplace nearby, here, not far from me, looking for me, too. We are here, we are here, although we haven't been able to find each other yet, amid the danger and the shooting, amid the stench that keeps getting more intolerable, and the rioting, and the punches, and the quarreling, the fights which desperation and hunger and this overcrowding provoke, but at least able then, now, right now, to scream, to scream . . . To get out, to get out, that was the question. Before it had been to join up, to liberate, to rise up, to hide, to emancipate ourselves, to gain independence, but now none of that was possible anymore, not because it had succeeded or it wasn't necessary, but rather because now it wasn't even possible to conceive of those ideas out loud, nor even in a whisper, it was pressing, and so we two keep talking, while we walk fearfully along the Malecón, all but deserted, although it isn't even 10 o'clock at night yet. The problem isn't to say "we've got to get out," I know that as well as you, the other one, his friend, was saying to him. The problem, the question, is how to leave here. Yes, we were saying, how to leave. On one or two inner tubes from a truck, you say, with a canvas on top and a pair of oars. To launch ourselves to sea. There's no other escape. It's true, it's true, I was saying. There's no other solution. I, you say, can get the inner tubes and the canvas. You have to keep them in your room. My family mustn't find out anything. But that's not the hardest part, you were saying. There's the other. The surveillance. There's surveillance everywhere, you know, one can't even approach the beach at night. The most difficult thing is, precisely, to reach the coast with two tubes, and food and some bottles of water. Yes, I was saying. That's right. First we have to go over the terrain, to study it, to go without anything, to see which is the best spot. I've heard it's Pinar del Río, you were saying. At least the current is strongest there, it can carry us, bring us way out. Some boat will pick us up. They have to pick us up, once at sea somebody will spot us, and pick us up. But listen, I say, it's possible that a Russian ship, or Chinese or Cuban could pick us up and we'll return again, not here, to the Malecón, to the streets, but to jail . . . They're giving five years now for what they call illegal exits, you say. And where are the legal ones? I was asking. Could we go if we wanted to, could we do it in peace, like others do it anywhere else in the world, or almost anywhere? Of course not, you were saying. But them, they're the ones who make the laws here and the ones who put us in jail. That's true, I said. Not only is there the problem of making it to the sea but also to the other side of the sea. To make it, you say, to make it somehow. Without their finding out that we're planning to leave. Them, them, I was saying. But for all that they keep watch, they can't keep track of everything; they can't, even if they live only for that, to watch over us, to check us at every moment, incessantly. Maybe you're right, you said. And as we were returning (it was best not to talk about it in the room) we finished rounding out the plan, the escape, the possibility, the attempt, but now that clever one has disappeared again, she's slipped away, sliding beneath the mud and excrement. Changing color, she's escaped me again. A shriek is heard in the crowd. A woman jumps hysterically as she puts her hands on her thighs. "An animal, an animal," she says, "an animal's gotten in here." And she keeps jumping up and down. Until she jumps out of her skirt. There she goes, fleeing again, changing color and trying to hide herself, the bitch, among the muddy shoes, bare feet, climbing up a thigh, leaping to a back, now sliding between stacks of sweaty necks, over a mob which falls back, forming a single mass on the ground. I pass over them too, I step on the face of somebody (a woman, a child, an old man, I don't know) without strength left to complain, and I follow, now crouched down, on all fours, sometimes raising an immense clamor of protests, kicked and shoved in turn, but watching her, following her, without losing sight, now up close . . . But they, in effect, yes, they were controlling everything, they did keep watch over everything, they did hear everything. They had foreseen everything. That's why they arrived so early. I came down from the garret hastily, thinking it was you. It was they. In that moment everything happened, happens, as if it had already happened. I had thought about it so many times (I had expected it), had calculated what could happen, so that now, when they enter, while they say to me, "Don't move. You're under arrest," and begin to search, I don't know, really, I don't know if everything is taking place in this instant or if it already took place, or if it's always taking place. Since it's such a miniature space, they don't have to spend much time searching. Two of them turn everything over up above in the garret, one stays with me, guarding me; the others feel around under the cushions, above the false roof, in the improvised closet. There they are, of course, the tires, the canvas, and something that I didn't even know you'd been able to get hold of (and now, worst of all), a compass. Quickly and minutely the search is concluded, in my presence, but without taking me into account. Papers, letters, books, the inner tubes, the canvas, and, of course, the compass, which I didn't even know that you had hidden in the closet, everything in these moments is an object, motive, body of the crime, cause for suspicion, for guilt. A photograph, a foreign sweater, arguments, for them convincing, too, parts of the same crime. Finally, they order me to take off my shoes, they take my footprint, they command me to get dressed completely again. "Let's go," one of them says to me, while he puts a hand at the back of my neck. So we leave. The hall is completely deserted now, although I know that they're all there, behind doors opened a crack, fearful, watching . . . A woman who had her eye knocked out by a stone, a man whose arm was crippled by a bullet, another with his swollen legs bursting, another woman who is squeezing her belly, shouting that she doesn't want to have a baby, because if she does, they'll take her out of here, another man who crawls along blindly because he lost his contact lenses. "Quiet, quiet, let's see if we can get the 'Voice of America.' " Shouts and more shouts calling for silence, but nobody keeps quiet, everybody has something to say, something to suggest, some solution, some complaint, some urgent business. "Let the Ambassador speak, let the Ambassador speak." But nobody is listening, everyone wants to be heard. "We're going to die of hunger, we're going to die of hunger. These sons of bitches want to starve us to death." Shouts and more shouts, me, too, shouting, yelling for you, pushing aside people more furious every moment, punching and moving forward, through the excrement, the urine, the crippled bodies and the uproar (outside, the shooting, again the shooting), looking for you . . . Nighttime, can it be night? Who can tell if it's night or day now . . . Nighttime, nighttime, it's nighttime. Now it's always nighttime. In the middle of this medieval tunnel and with an enormous light bulb, which is never turned off, above my head, of course it must be night all the time. Everyone reduced to the same uniform, the same shaved head, the same shout for the count-off three times a day. A day? Or a night? At least, if I could reach the window with its three sets of bars, I would know what it really is now, night, day, but in order to get near there you have to belong to the "leadership," to be one of the "pretty boys." Little by little they pass the time, it passes, or we pass, I am passing. It's not that I'm getting used to it, nor getting adapted, nor accepting it, but I go on surviving. Luckily, in the last visit you managed to bring in some books. Light is not lacking here. Silence, silence, yes, that's something that I almost can't remember. But the problem, you tell me, consists of bearing it, of surviving, of waiting. Luckily they didn't grab me in the room. At least I can bring you a few things. Here are some corn meal cakes, cookies, sugar, and more books. Time passes, time passes, you say. Time, I say, it passes? . . . It passes knowing that outside there are streets, trees, people with colorful clothing, and the sea. The visit ends. We say good-bye. To enter. Here's the worst moment. When in a blue line, scalped and escorted, we enter the tunnel, a long, thin stone vault which brings us, once again, to the circular cave that endlessly oozes bugs, mold, urine, those fumes, those fumes of accumulating, overflowing excrement, and that din, that constant shouting of the prisoners, that beating on the bunks and walls, that impotence, that caged up violence which has to get out somehow, to manifest itself, to explode. If, at least, I think, barricaded in the last bunk, they would kill each other in silence. But that din, that deafening and monotonous stamping, that cackling, that jargon which you have to pick up whether you want to or not, pick it up or perish. Ah, if somebody were interested in my soul, if somebody loved it forever, maybe, in exchange for it . . . But it's absolutely impossible to continue thinking, with that uproar, with that uproar which rises now and attacks . . . As if tormented by a strange plague, the trees have suddenly lost all their leaves, one at a time, like lightning, they've been torn off and devoured. Now, with their fingernails, with pieces of wire, kicking with their heels, every- one begins to tear the bark from the trunks; the roots, the grass, too, disappear. "Whoever has a piece of bread hidden away is risking his life," I hear somebody say. That's why I follow you, that's why, and even more than that. You are my goal, my salvation, my hope, my incentive, my love, my great, my only real true love. And now, once again you provoke an immense clamor when you climb into somebody's pants who had been sleeping on his feet, propped up by the crowd. "A buggering lizard," they shout, since in spite of everything, or because of everything, they keep a sense of humor. "No, it's queer," retorted someone else, "I scared it off just when it was coming up to my fly." "Maybe it's a real man," a woman is saying now, "since it went up my dress." "Grab it, grab it, it's fresh meat." And at the shout of that password, everybody springs at you. Letting out a howl, I cross over their heads. I won't let them, I won't let them, I won't let the others get you, even if they kill me (for now I see their hungry delirious, crazy faces looking at me furiously), I keep on pushing them, making my way, pursuing you. "Food, food." The voice of alarm sounds. Screaming. Now everyone, forgetting about you, is trying to reach the fence where they, the police, so they say, are beginning to put little cardboard boxes with food rations along the fence. The chaos increases by the instant, for all that some people try to impose order. We hear that they're only passing out eight hundred little boxes for the ten thousand or so of us who are here. Punches, rioting again, shouting, for the first time they've saved me, they've saved us, you and me, so that now, with greater zeal, having an open field, I pursue you. I reach, at last I reach the place again that I hate so much, and yet long for: the improvised room. Now it all looks so dazzling. The deteriorating and unpainted walls shine; the wall of the other building seems like marble to me. I touch these improvised seats, this improvised stairway; all the rustic and scarce furnishings that surround me are, for me, something new that I look at, touch, I could say with a certain love. Five years in that cave, you say to me. Of course everything must seem to shine like new to you. And you also tell me what you suffered: investigations, persecutions, who knows what, but now we've got to forget everything and go on, you say. Now we'll be watched even more carefully, I say. That's why, you say, the best thing is to forget about escaping for a while. Pretend that you're adapting and don't say anything to anybody. Whenever you've got to get something off your chest, talk only to me. To the rest, not a word. All of this happened to us for not being cautious. Yes, I say, although I never spoke to anybody about the plan. But they're very cunning, you say, more than you can imagine. They may not have developed the production of shoes, food, or transportation, but as for persecution, they're first class. Don't forget it . . . I don't forget it, I don't forget it, how am I going to forget it . . . They're out there, some in uniform, others in civilian clothes, all armed, beating, running down, assassinating, those who, crouched in the trees, on the water tanks, on the empty houses, are trying to get closer, to make it to where we are. And now they, out there, put the boxes of food (a hard-boiled egg, a handful of rice) at their feet, on the other side of the fence. They're calm, looking at us here inside. When one of us stretches out an arm to take a box, they lift their feet and squash his hand, or they give him a smart kick in the chest. If somebody screams, then their laughter is louder, much louder than the screams. Others, more sadistic, or more refined, wait for one of us to take a box and when he's already bringing it inside, they beat him until his arm breaks. And fresh laughter is heard again. But you're neither among those who, pushing and kicking, have reached the fence, nor among those who now pull back their crushed and empty hands. Maybe you're up above, on top of the roof of the building, or inside, right in the building, with the Ambassador himself, tending the gravely wounded or the women with newborns, or the old. Yes, sure, that's where I should have gone first, that's why, because you're with the sick, or, sure, sick yourself, gravely ill, that's the reason why I haven't been able to find you. If not for that, you, sooner than I, would have found me. Back, back, to go back, to return through the shoving and kicking, to get back, to enter the building no matter how, back, back . . . I had reached it, I had reached that moment in which life not only lacks any meaning, but, moreover, we don't even ask ourselves if it ever had one, I say, referring to myself, of course. In a tone no less tragic for its grandiloquence, and in the middle of this dilapidated room. And I go on: because it's not even possible to be sad anymore. Even sadness itself is abolished by the noise, by the constant eruption of the cockroaches, the siren of the patrol cars, by the what will I eat today, what will I eat tomorrow. Yes, even sadness requires its space, at least, a little silence, a place where it can be kept, exhibited, taken out for an airing. In hell it isn't even possible to be sad. You simply live (you die) day by day, I say, I said. And you answered me: write, write all of this down, begin to write everything that you're suffering, starting right now, and you'll feel better. Really, I was thinking of doing that for a long time already, but what for? For you, for yourself, for the two of us, you say. And that's just how it is. Deliriously, angrily, constantly and in minute detail, I go on giving vent to my fear, my fury, my resentment, my hatred, my failure, our failure, our impotence, all the humiliations, swindles, tricks, and finally, simply, the punches, kicks, the constant harassment. Everything, everything. All the terror: on paper, on the white sheet, once filled, carefully hidden above the false roof of the garret, in the dictionaries, or behind the window: my revenge, my revenge. My triumph. *Jail to rot, jail to be shipwrecked and never to be able to float away, jail to give up, forgetting, not even conceiving that the sea existed, and, much less, the possibility of crossing it* . . . My triumph, my triumph, my revenge. Walks down streets that burst, since the pipes can't hold any more, between buildings you have to avoid so that they won't come down on top of you, between frowning faces that scrutinize and sentence us, between closed businesses, closed markets, closed theaters, closed parks, closed cafés, sometimes displaying signs (justifications) already dusty, CLOSED FOR RENOVATION, CLOSED FOR REPAIRS. What kind of repairs? When will the so-called repairs, the so-called renovation, be finished? When, at least, will they begin? Closed, closed, closed. Everything closed . . . I arrive, I open the innumerable padlocks, I go running up the improvised stairway. Here she is, waiting for me. I uncover her, pulling back the canvas, and I contemplate her dusty and cold dimensions. I wipe off the dust and run my hand over her again. With light strokes of the hand I clean her back, her base, her sides. I sit down, desperate, happy, at her side, before her, I move my hands over her keyboard, and, quickly, everything is set in motion. The ta ta, the ringing, the music begins, little by little, then more quickly, now at full speed. Walls, trees, streets, cathedrals, faces and beaches, cells, minicells, large cells, starry night, bare feet, pines, clouds, hundreds, thousands, a million parakeets, stools and a climbing vine, everything approaches, everything arrives, all are coming. The walls expand, the roof disappears, and, naturally, you are floating, floating, floating, torn up, dragged along, elevated, carried, transported, memorialized, saved, on altars, and, by that miniscule and constant cadence, by that music, by that incessant ta ta . . . My revenge, my revenge. My triumph . . . Bodies armored in excrement, children sinking in excrement, hands that search in shit, turning it over and over. Hands and more hands, round, thin, plump, bony, face up, face down, joined, spread out, closing into fists, scratching heads, testicles, arms, backs, clapping, rising up, crawling, falling faint, black, yellow, brown, white, transparent, tightly

clenched and pale from days and days of hunger, swollen, mangled, mutilated by the beating when they tried to get hold of a little box of rations
on the other side of the fence, where the patrol cars are now circling
constantly, carrying loudspeakers that don't stop blaring menacingly for an
instant. "Anyone who wishes to take refuge with the Cuban authorities
may do so and return to his home." And day and night, day and night,
the shooting, the thirst, the threats, the hunger, the beatings. And now,
suddenly, the rainstorm, the torrent of rain, pacifying the dust, fusing trees,
automobiles, country homes, and military units, soldiers stationed, barricaded, in a state of alert all around us . . . The typical spring shower, unexpected, torrential. Some people try to protect themselves with their
hands; others, lowering their heads, huddle up, wanting to crouch down,
to take shelter inside themselves. Many who sleep, continue sleeping, while
the water runs over their foreheads, their faces, their closed eyes, without
managing to wake them up. Others attempt to bend down, to protect
themselves underneath the rest, causing an avalanche of protest, of remon-
strances, and some kick or other shot out at random. I take advantage of
the confusion, the state of near calm, of immobile stacking which the
shower is causing in order to make my way, scrutinizing the drenched
faces, the contracted and drenched bodies, shaken by contractions and
trembling, and I go on, I go on examining them, looking at them, deci-
phering the streaming faces, searching for you. I know that you're around
here somewhere, one step away from me, perhaps, that you must be here.
"They want to break us through hunger, illness, terror, this storm is surely
their doing too, one of their tricks," says a woman, gone mad in the
downpour, as she makes signs, crosses in the air and strange gestures . . .
And I return, full of fuel, arguments, fear. I run, I go up the sordid stairway,
I open the innumerable padlocks. Burning, I climb up to the improvised
garret. My treasure, my treasure. I look for my treasure which I'm going
to enlarge right now, my revenge, my triumph which has gone on growing
thicker, and now it's not one, not ten, nor a hundred pages, but hundreds.
Hundreds of sheets stolen from sleep, from terror, from rest, from fear,
slugged out in the heat, in the noise of the streets, of the neighbors; won,
striking out against the mosquitos, against the pestilential vapor (vapors)
that rises, that falls, that arrives from every floor, from everywhere.
Thousands of sheets won from the shrieks of sinister infants who seem to
have settled a tacit accord to erupt in their demonical uproar whenever I
sit down before the keyboard. Pages and more pages conquered with furious blows of the fist, the feet, the head, struggling furiously against television, record players, portable radios, cars without mufflers, shrieks, leaps,
the scraping of pots, inopportune visits, figures, bodies, almost unavoidable,
constant black-outs . . . Tapping, tapping in the darkness, quickly, quickly,
each moment more quickly, tapping, tapping, before they return, quickly,

quickly, triumphantly, triumphantly, in the darkness . . . And new disturbances, lights, bulbs, signal flares, that break out now on all sides, illuminating Fifth Avenue, the whole area, in such a way that it's as if it were
high noon. Somebody, the driver of a rented Chevy has managed to break
through the barriers, the three cordons, and has just smashed into the Ambassador's own car, which had been standing parked at the entrance, at an
extraordinary speed. At last the man gets out of the wrecked car; he begins
to crawl, injured, toward the fence, where all of us are watching him;
slowly, grabbing onto the grass, he continues creeping. Then the official
cars move in, focusing on him, the soldiers, lanterns in hand, are also
encircling him, as they shine their lights on him, members of the three
cordons, soldiers, judo experts, police, making a circle around him, allowing him to continue crawling. The driver almost reaches the fence now,
where everyone, including me, stares at him. Finally, when his hands are
already touching the wire fence, they, tightening the circle of lights, ad-
vance slowly, aiming at him. Two of them bend down and, taking him
by the belt and the shirt, they lift him in the air and carry him away. He,
looking at us, opens and closes his mouth, but says nothing, nothing is
heard, although there is total silence in these moments . . . Nothing, nothing, there's nothing, not one sheet, not the smallest trace of a sheet, not
even the last one, the one that was still unfinished in the typewriter. I turn
over the drawers, the mattress, the drapes, the improvised seats, I tear down
the false roof, the covering of the improvised stairway; with methodical
dread the books are examined, shaken out. But nothing. Of the hundreds
and hundreds of scribbled pages, not a clue remains, not a hint as to how
they disappeared . . . Them, them, of course, them, you tell me, while I,
giving up, stop turning over the junk. Of course they're the ones, you
continue. Then they'll come to arrest me, I say. Maybe yes, maybe no,
you tell me, as worried as I am, although trying to hide it, trying, even
without arguments, to cheer me up, to console me. Maybe they won't
come, you say. Everything was in order, I say, they didn't knock anything
over. How could they have gotten in? Don't be naïve, what can't they do?
They run the country, they run all of us, they know every move you make,
what we say, and, maybe, even what we think. Don't you get it? That's
what they've done it for: so that you'll know that they know. Don't you
realize that precisely what they want is for you to realize it? for us to
understand that we're in their hands, that we've got no escape? that just
the way they took those papers, without anybody (not even you) finding
out, they can simply eliminate you? And you'll appear strangled, hanged,
a suicide or dead of natural causes—a heart attack, a stroke, who knows,
however they want—and the door and the room and everything will be
intact, perfectly neat, in order. And maybe even a letter will appear, drawn
up in your handwriting, signed by your hand, your farewell . . . He stops

talking. For a moment the two of us remain stooped over the heap of overturned books. Now he takes a blank piece of paper, a random sheet, and he slowly lifts it to his lips, chewing it as if it were a blade of grass. Then you tell me, now in a very low voice: I don't think they'll come looking for you, for us. This was only a demonstration, a subtle bluff. In short, a proof of their cunning, their power, their control . . . And now, what are we going to do? I say. To play the game, you say, even lower. Listen up: to play the game or perish. Let's turn ourselves around, you say to me now in a whisper. Later, between the two of us we'll arrange everything . . . And we leave . . . That's how it was, at that point, as it had been for years, at that place, at that extreme, his hand lying on the improvised stairway, his eyes contemplating the narrow panorama, the four improvised seats, the embedded mirror (in that moment the noise of the nearest radio became intolerable), but he stayed that way, at that extreme, at that border, at that point, in that sort of unending recollection of a repetition, cautiously stooped over, looking at the panorama which stopped abruptly only two paces away: the deteriorating wall of the building alongside and the old closed door which faced the hallway where now somebody, or a group, is clamoring noisily for the elevator that never goes up. They shout and pound. But what a way of pounding on the old artifact, the skeleton, the cage, which, of course, doesn't move. Elevator! Elevator! And the pounding follows, just the same. Again, again, elevator! And the cackling, the uproar continue, everything gives signs of noise, but nothing gives signs of life . . . So, thinking, commenting in a low voice, protesting, ironizing, sometimes, very cautiously, certifying his existence only when he was outside of the room, in an open and desolated space, the Malecón, an empty street, a field, and looking, the two of them, cautiously, in all directions. Because now as his friend, his only friend, had told him, it wasn't only a matter of suffering, but of praising out loud all that was suffered, of shouting support of all the horror, not writing against it, or on the margins, but in favor, unconditionally, and to leave the sheets, as if carelessly, on the improvised table, in an evident but discreet place, in case they came in. And the two of them, in the evenings, in a natural, normal voice, not very loud, so that they weren't going to think that they were doing it facetiously (they're very clever, very clever, the other used to say), they discussed the "advantages," the "successes," the "nobility" of the system, the constant "progress." The newspaper, *Granma,* was read out loud. But not so loud, please, that they can think that we're fooling around. The premiere of the latest Soviet film, *The Great Patriotic War!* (was it that one?), *A Man of Truth!* (could it be that?), *Moscow, You Are My Love!* (that?): how marvelous, how many positive aspects, a true gem . . . But no, not so loud, please, that they can suspect, that they can realize that we're fooling. *We Are Soviet Men!* Lower, lower. *They Fought for the Fatherland!* . . . Quiet, keep quiet.

The Ballad of the Russian Soldier! Sssh. And to applaud. At the auditorium, on the corner, in the square, while we watch how they watch us with that gaze of disdain and distrust, or with the ironic faces of braggarts, for never, never are they going to admit to being satisfied, even when from so much pretending you forget your true face, who you are, your role . . . But now, in this moment, when you had just gotten out of bed a few minutes ago and were descending half-dressed down the improvised, vertical stairway headed toward the improvised plumbing of that improvised hole, standing thus, hunched between the garret and the ground floor, now, thus, suddenly, he was struck by the certainty (once more, yes, but always renewed) that he could not make it to the bathroom anymore (that box), nor take another step (through that trash), rather he couldn't even move a hand from one step to another (since whether going down or up the improvised stairway it was necessary to support oneself with one's hands, too). So, unmoving, in that position, he was looking, not at the past, nor the future (what was that?), he was looking at the rotting planks, some stain (could it be humidity?) on the wall, and, at last, suddenly, although now without being surprised, at his own face reflected in the mirror. And an infinite inertia invaded him to the sound of that pot (could it be the people upstairs? could it be the people downstairs? could it be those from in front?) being scraped furiously. And in that noise, completely undone and impotent, he felt that he was finally dissolving, becoming paralyzed, disappearing, no longer feigning a defeat in order to pull himself together later, to gain time, to go on, but rather he was simply defeated, liquidated. It was then—in this moment—that they knocked at the door. It was he, his friend who was knocking, as he always did and who was entering then, since naturally he had the keys to all the padlocks. Shutting the door, he came closer to him until he put his lips to his ear. You haven't heard yet? he said to him. About what? People are entering the Peruvian Embassy. They withdrew the guards since yesterday. They say that the place is already full. I'm going over there. Let's go, I told him. No, you said. Wait. They've got too much on you. I'll go first to see what's going on. And if it's true that there's no surveillance, I'll come and get you. Wait for me here. And he left. But he didn't remain standing any longer on the improvised stairway. He had to do something: to get dressed, to wait. And I waited the whole day, from noon until nearly dusk. People were running through the hall, sneaking, trying not to make noise, something they had never tried to avoid, even the radios were turned off. I open the door, I go down the stairway. Nobody is talking on the street, but somehow everyone seems to communicate with each other. I hurry to catch a bus headed toward the Embassy. The bus is more crowded than ever, which is difficult to imagine. Almost all of them are young. Some of them even discuss their plans openly: to enter the Embassy quickly. Before they close it. They're sure to close it any minute, says somebody beside me. The problem is to get there, the other replies. And not to leave, because not only are they making a file on anyone who leaves, but they also start kicking him and take him away to prison. And they keep talking. Now I know why you didn't return. I've been an idiot. I should have realized before that if you didn't come it was because it was impossible. And you must have thought that if you didn't return, I wasn't going to be such a shithead that I would stay in the room. Quickly, now the problem is to enter quickly. And to find you, to meet you quickly before it occurs to you to leave to look for me and they take you prisoner, if they haven't already. And everything is my fault, idiot, idiot. Quickly, quickly, since I'm sure you're waiting for me, that it hasn't occurred to you to leave, that you've thought, logically, that when you couldn't return, I would come to see what was happening . . . In droves, through the shower of rocks, the dust, and the shooting, they're entering, we're entering. All kinds of people. Some I know or at least have seen before, but now we greet each other euphorically, in a communion of mutual sincerity, never manifested before, as if we were old and dear friends. People and more people, from Santos Suárez, from Old Havana, from El Vedado, from every neighborhood, people and more people, especially young people, hopping the fence, dodging or receiving blows, running amidst the shooting and the din of the loudspeakers and the sirens of the patrol cars, entering, jumping now in a terrified parade, between kicks in the ass, shots, bodies that roll over and fall, a woman who drags a child by the arms, an old man who tries to open a path for himself with his cane. Everyone in an incredible throng, jumping over the railings, the gate, filling the gardens, the trees, even the roof of the Embassy building. So, in the immense dust cloud, between hands that push and shove, amidst shrieks, threats, explosions, forming a single almost impenetrable mass, we manage still to get past the security, which becomes stronger every minute, and we jump, we enter, we fall into the crowd that can hardly move, here, on the other side of the fence, surrounded already by a circle of official vehicles, and patrol cars which keeps getting thicker, Alfa-Romeos, Yuguly, Volgas, the whole administrative class, the high civilian and military officials have arrived in their shiny new cars to see, to contain, to repress, to try by any means to suppress this spectacle. And, as if that weren't enough, they just blocked up the entrances of the streets that lead to the Embassy with cars and barriers, and they've dispersed, everyone knows it, thousands and thousands of soldiers in civilian clothing throughout the area to keep anyone else from reaching here. Now a motorcycle cop is braking violently in front of the military cordon surrounding the Embassy. "Sons of bitches!" he shouts at us. And he takes out his pistol. Here we all retreat as much as we can, trying to move away from the fence. The cop, pistol in hand, comes up to it. He takes a leap and falls to the other side, next to us. With great speed he takes off his uniform, wraps his pistol in it and throws the whole bundle over the fence, to the other side, where they are. Here, inside, applause is heard, shouts of *"Viva!"* The cordon that surrounds us is tripled. It begins to get dark. Here the uproar we're making reaches such dimensions that even the din and the shooting from outside can't be heard at times. "They're going to machine-gun us, they're going to machine-gun us," a woman shouts suddenly. And the mass, we, attempt to retreat anew. The trees disappear, the roof of the building disappears. Everything is no more than a moving anthill, people who clamber, people who cling, who cling even tighter to one another. Screaming. Some who fall wounded. Now there is a general panic, because somebody really is firing at us here, inside. But that's not what I continue watching or dodging. I make my way, I go back, because I have to find you; I have to locate you, to reach you, wherever you are. In the middle of this terrorized crowd, hardly able to move, and now almost completely night, I must find you, so that you'll see that I came, too, that I had the courage to make it, that I didn't stay behind, that they couldn't annihilate me—annihilate us—completely, and that here I am, here we are, trying again, anew. The two of us. *Alive,* still *alive* . . . That's why it doesn't bother me now to step on this human mass which seems to be sleeping now, here, in the very entrance of the residence, maybe, surely, you're inside. This is the last place to check, and here you must be, without a doubt, ill. The commission for maintaining order attempts to stop me, but I push them aside and go on. People stretched out on the floor, old people, women in labor, new-born babies, the sick, in short those who need to be here, under a roof. And I go on, I go on looking for you, opening rooms, cubicles, pavillions, or whatever the hell this place is called. "Hey," a half-naked woman says to me now, "get lost, the Ambassador will be furious, they've eaten up everything including his parrot" . . . But I keep on searching all the little compartments. I push that door where two bodies are rolling around incredibly. I go up to them, I separate them mechanically and look at their faces, which stare at me disconcertedly. And I leave. "It's unbelievable," says an old man with his legs bandaged provisionally in some rags, "to feel like screwing when we've spent two weeks without anything to eat" . . . I leave, again I cross the sea of people, people who are collapsing already, or who can hardly hold themselves up, staggering, propping each other up and after all that, when they finally pass out, they don't reach the ground, because the ground doesn't exist. Covering the earth, the shit, the piss, are the feet, everybody's feet, feet standing on other feet sometimes, a single foot sometimes supporting the whole body. So, through that immense jungle of feet that are trying to crawl along, I crawl along. I go on, pursuing you. You're not going to escape me. You're not going to escape me. Don't think, you bitch, that you're going to escape me. Now, less than ever.

Now that nobody even pays attention to you since they can hardly look at anything, yes, now you won't escape me, and I follow, I follow behind her, who (the clever one) is now running toward the fence, toward the outside. But I continue, day and night, scrutinizing the faces. You could be one of them. Is it you? Will you be one of them? Hunger makes faces change. Hunger can make our own brothers unrecognizable. Maybe you're looking for me and you don't recognize me. God knows how many times we may have met, looking for one another without recognizing each other. Really, will we still be able to recognize each other? Quickly, quickly, for with each passing moment, we'll be more disfigured, we'll be less able to find, to discover, to recognize each other. That's why it's best to shout. Loud. Really loud. Above those damned loudspeakers. As loud as possible. Calling you. But how, then, if I shout, am I going to hear when you call me? I shout, I keep quiet for a moment, waiting for your answer and I shout again. Even though we may not recognize one another, we have to hear each other. To hear our names, our calls. And, finally, to identify each other . . . So I keep advancing and shouting in the tumult which now convulses once again. "Food, food, they're handing out food," they shout. And again the crowd, finding energy from I don't know where, advances toward the fence. The same rite, the same kicking. "They're going to knock down the fence," somebody shouts. "If they knock it down we won't be on Peruvian territory anymore." But the tumult is really uncontainable. Who can get through in the middle of that chaos? But I make an attempt, I, too, push and hurl myself through the punches, slaps, kicks. Pushing faces and bodies which roll aside, I continue toward the far end. Now I'm sure that I'll be able to find you, yes, you must be there, alongside the fence, as an intelligent person like you would logically be, ready to grab the first thing they hand out, to hear the first thing they say, to retreat before the first danger. I should have thought of it. Of course you have to be there. So, pushing, kicking, biting, crawling through the web of bodies which are crawling too, I make it to the fence, I grab onto the wire. There's nobody who's gonna tear me away from here, shit, nobody's gonna get me off o' here, I shout, and I begin to look at the faces of all those who manage to reach there. But you're not among them either, those who, risking their lives, like me, are climbing up the wire fence. I look again and again at those desperate faces, but none of them, I know, is yours. Bleeding hands that don't want to let go of the wire, but they aren't yours. Defeated, I stop looking at the fence, and I look through it, toward the outside, where they are, fed, bathed, armed, in uniforms or plain clothes, now preparing to "serve" us the food. And I discover you, finally I discover you. There you are, with them, outside, uniformed and armed. Talking, making gestures, laughing and conversing with someone, also young, also uniformed and armed. I turn to contemplate you again while they begin, you begin, to pass out the little boxes of food. Now they (you) approach from all sides, all along the fence. The gun in one hand, the little box in the other. The distribution begins. The clamoring and the pushing of those who are next to me are worse than ever. They crush me, they want to crush me, they want to stand on me to get one of those filthy boxes that they're passing out. Idiot, idiot, I say to myself while they trample me, climbing up over my body, using me as a trampoline, as an elevation, as a promontory, to raise themselves up a little and desperately stretch their hands over the fence. Idiot, idiot, I say to myself; and while they are all walking over me, standing on top of me, jumping over me, I begin to laugh wildly, as if all those feet, all those hooves covered with shit and filth were tickling me . . . "This guy's gone crazy," somebody says. "Leave him alone, he could be dangerous," says another. And they start moving away getting down off my body. Outside, laughing also, they methodically distribute the boxes of food all along the fence. They stand next to it and wait for somebody to stick out his hand to stomp on it with their feet . . . I could, right now, stretch out my arm and get that box. Anyway, even if I get stomped on or kicked in the chest, I won't die of hunger. But don't let them think that I'm going to give them that pleasure. Don't think I'm going to make you happy, don't let them believe, don't you believe, that I'm going to eat that shit, that filth, that swill. And much less let you step on my hand in exchange for a hard-boiled egg. For that reason, just so they won't have the pleasure, I stay this way without moving, triumphant, looking at them (at you), outside there, carting that filth back and forth. I'm looking at them this way and laughing, while desperate arms are waving over my head. Then I discover you, I see you for the first time, there, also outside, fleeing from a shiny boot, running, crawling stealthily along the asphalt, and entering, what a coincidence, here, in the riot, where we are. Here she comes, here she comes, there she goes, almost drowsy now, with hardly any energy left to keep fleeing, but still moving, beneath the bodies, over the hands and faces which barely blink when she crosses over them. She's had it now. She can't go on anymore after so many hours of trying to escape me. And now, she stops as if stunned, with her mouth open on top of somebody's shoulder, who's lying face down on the ground, trying desperately to leap somewhere . . . At last I've got you, bitch, yes, now, though you're covered with filth, you've got no escape.

TRANSLATED BY ANDREW BUSH

Rosario Ferré

Puerto Rico
(b. 1942)

With Luis Rafael Sánchez, Edgardo Sanabria Santeliz, and Ana Lydia Vega, Rosario Ferré belongs to a remarkable group of contemporary Puerto Rican writers. Born to one of the most powerful and wealthy families on the island, Ferré received a first-rate education at Wellesley College, Manhattanville College, and the University of Puerto Rico. In addition to being a short story writer and novelist, she is an essayist, literary critic, and professor. Her essays on feminist topics have often made her controversial. Ferré has also published criticism on Felisberto Hernández and Sor Juana Inés de la Cruz, among others. Ferré and other Puerto Rican intellectuals, writers, and critics produced during the 1970s a lively and widely read avant-garde journal, *Zona de carga y descarga*. Her stories reveal her appreciation for River Plate writers like Horacio Quiroga and Julio Cortázar, especially the former. Ferré is fascinated by the twisted psychology of her characters, often victims of violent passions, bizarre obsessions, and unexplainable illnesses. All of these often erupt in the midst of rather humdrum Puerto Rican provincial life. Her focus tends to be on the lives of women, particularly their erotic attachments. Ferré's books of short stories and poetry include *Papeles de Pandora* (1976), *El medio pollito* (1978), *La muñeca menor* (1979), *Los cuentos de Juan Bobo* (1981), and *Fábulas de la garza desangrada* (1982). She has recently published a novel written directly in English, *House on the Lagoon* (1995). Her story "When Women Love Men," taken from *Papeles de Pandora*, is one of Ferré's most pitiless probes into feminine psychology.

When Women Love Men

> La puta que yo conozco
> no es de la China ni del Japón
> porque la puta viene de Ponce
> viene del barrio de San Antón
>   "Plena de San Antón"
>
> For we know in part
> and we prophesy in part.
> But when that which is perfect is come,
> then that which is in part shall be done away.

When I was a child, I spake as a child,
I understood as a child, I thought as a child:
But when I became a man, I put away childish things.
For now we see through a glass darkly;
but then face to face; now I know in part;
but then I shall know even as also I am known.
       St. Paul, Epistle to the Corinthians,
         also known as the epistle of love.

It happened when you died, Ambrosio, and you left each of us half your inheritance; it was then that all this confusion began, this scandal spinning all over like an iron hoop, smashing your good name against the walls of the town; this slapped and stunned confusion that you swung around for the sake of power, pushing us both downhill at the same time. Anyone would say that you did what you did on purpose, just for the pleasure of seeing us light a candle in each corner of the room, to see which one of us had won. At least that's what we thought then, before we sensed your true intentions. Now we know that what you really wanted was to meld us, to make us fade into each other like an old picture lovingly placed under its negative, so that our own true face would finally come to surface.

When all is said and done this story is not so strange, Ambrosio; it seems almost inevitable that it should have happened the way it did. We, your lover and your wife, have always known that every lady hides a prostitute under her skin. This is obvious from the way a lady slowly crosses her legs, rubbing the insides of her thighs against each other. It's obvious from the way she soon gets bored with men; she never knows what we go through, plagued by them for the rest of our lives. It's evident in the prim way she looks at the world from under the tips of her eyelashes, as she hides the green-blue lights that swarm beneath her skirt. A prostitute, on the other hand, will go to similar extremes to hide the lady under her skin. Prostitutes all drown in the nostalgia of that dovecotelike cottage they'll never own, of a house with a balcony of silver amphorae, with fruited garlands hanging over the doors; they all suffer from hallucinations, such as listening for the sounds of silver and china before dinnertime, as though invisible servants were about to set the family table. The truth is, Ambrosio, that we, Isabel Luberza and Isabel la Negra, had been leaning more and more on each other; we had purified each other of all that defiled us; and we had grown so close that we no longer knew where the lady ended and the prostitute began.

You were to blame, Ambrosio, for the fact that no one could tell us apart after a while. Was it Isabel Luberza who began the campaign to restore the plaster lions of the town square, or was it Isabel la Negra who misspent the funds in making herself beautiful for the rich boys of the town, the sons of your friends that used to visit my shack every night, their shoulders drooping and dragging themselves like pigeons gripped by consumption, staring hungrily at my body as though at a promised banquet; was it Isabel Luberza, the Red Cross Lady, or was it Elizabeth the Black, the Young Lords' President, who used to shout from her platform that she was living proof of the fact that there was no difference between Puerto Ricans and Neoricans, because they had all come together in her cunt; was it Isabel Luberza who used to collect funds for Boy's Town, for the Mute and Deaf, for Model City, dressed by Fernando Pena with long, white lambskin gloves and a silver mink stole, or was it Isabel the Slavedriver, the exploiter of innocent little Dominican girls, put ashore by smugglers on the beaches of Guayanilla; was it Isabel Luberza the Popular Party Lady, Ruth Fernández's long-lost twin in political campaigns, or was it Isabel la Negra, the soul of Puerto Rico turned into song, the temptress of Chichamba, the Jezebel of San Antón, the sharpest-shooting streetwalker of Barrio de la Cantera, the call girl of Cuatro Calles, the slut of Singapur, the vamp of Machuelo Abajo, the harlot of Coto Laurel; was it Isabel Luberza, the lady who used to breed pigeons in La Sultana cracker tins under her zinc-gabled roof, or was it Isabel la Negra, of whom it could never be said that she was neither fish nor fowl; was it Isabel Luberza, the baker of charity cupcakes, the knitter of little cloud-colored *perlé* booties and blankets for the unwanted babies abandoned by their mothers on the front steps of the Church of the Sacred Heart, or was it Isabel the Rumba, Macumba, Candombe, Bámbula, Isabel the Tembandumba de la Quimbamba, swaying her okra hips through the sun-swilled Antillean streets, her grapefruit tits sliced open on her chest; was it Isabel de Trastamara, the holy Queen of Spain, patron of the most aristocratic street in Ponce, or was it Elizabeth the Black, the only lady ever to have bestowed upon her the order of the Sainted Prepuce of Christ; was it Saint Elizabeth, mother of Saint Louis King of France, our town's patron saint, lulled to sleep for centuries under the mountainous blue tits of Doña Juana, was it Isabel Luberza the Catholic Lady, the painter of the most exquisite scapularies of the Sacred Heart, still dripping the only three divine ruby drops capable of conjuring Satan, was it Isabel Luberza the champion of the Oblates, carrying a tray with her own pink tits served in syrup before her, was it Isabel Luberza the Virgin of the thumb, piously thrusting her pinky through a little hole enbroidered in her gown; or was it Isabel la Negra, "Step and Fetch It" 's only girlfriend, the only one who ever dared to kiss his deformed feet and cleanse them with her tears, the only one to join the children as they danced around him to the rhythm of his cry, "Hersheybarskissesmilkyways," through the burning streets of Ponce, was it Isabel the Black Pearl of the South, the Chivas Regal, the Queen of Saba, the

Tongolele, the Salomé, spinning her gyroscopic belly before the amazed eyes of men, shaking for them her multitudinous cunt and her monumental buttocks; spreading, from time immemorial, this confusion between her and her, or between her and me, or between me and me, because as time went by it became more and more difficult for us to tell this story, it grew almost impossible to distinguish between the two.

So many years of anger stuck like a lump in my throat, Ambrosio, so many years of polishing my fingernails with Cherries Jubilee because it was the reddest color in fashion at the time, always with Cherries Jubilee while I thought of her, Ambrosio, of Isabel la Negra; because, to begin with, it was unusual that I, Isabel Luberza, having such refined tastes, should like the shrill and gaudy colors that Negroes usually prefer. Years of varnishing the contours of the half-moons at the base of my fingernails, of carefully brushing around the edge of the cuticle that always stung a bit as the nail polish fell on it, because when I saw the defenseless soft skin of the cuticle caught between the tips of my cuticle trimmers it always reminded me of her, and I'd usually cut too deep.

I think of all these things as I sit on the balcony of this house that now belongs to both of us, Ambrosio, to Isabel Luberza and to Isabel la Negra, this house that will now become a part of our legend, of the legend of the lady and the prostitute. I can already see it turned into a brothel, which is what Isabel la Negra plans to do. Its balcony of long silver amphorae will be painted shocking pink; its balusters aligned along the street like happy phalluses; its snow-white, garlanded facades, which now give the impression of cakes coated with heavy icing, spread stiff and sparkling like the skirt of a debutante, will then be washed in warm colors, in chartreuse green fused into chrysanthemum orange, in Pernod blue thawed into dahlia yellow; in those gaudy shades that persuade men to relax, to let their arms slide down their sides as though they didn't have a care in the world, as though they were about to sail out on the deck of a transatlantic luxury liner. The walls of the house, which are now elegantly gessoed, will be painted a bottle green, so that when you and I stand in the main hall, Ambrosio, everything will be revealed to us. We will then see ourselves unfold into twenty identical images, reflected in the walls of those rooms that we will rent out to our clients, so that they may have their indifferent orgasms in them, so that we may see them repeat, to the end of time, the ritual of love.

And so here I am, Ambrosio, sitting on the balcony in front of your house, waiting for them to come whisk her away, waiting to see Isabel Luberza's wake wind its way to a grave that was destined to be my grave. The sacred body of Isabel Luberza will file past my door today, a body which had never before been exposed, not even a sliver of her white

466 \ ROSARIO FERRÉ

buttocks, not even a shaving of her white breasts. Isabel Luberza renounces, Ambrosio, as of today, that virginity of a reputable wife which you had conferred upon her. It makes no difference that she had never before stepped into a brothel, that she had never before been slandered in public— as I have been so many times—that she had never bared any part of her body, food for the ravenous eyes of men, except her arms, her neck, or her legs from the shin down. Her body now naked and tinctured black; her sex covered only by a small triangle of amethysts, including the one the bishop once wore on his finger; her nipples trapped in nests of diamonds, fat and round like chickpeas; her feet stuffed into slippers of sparkling red rime, with twin hearts sewn on the tips; her heels still dripping a few drops of blood. Dressed, in short, like a queen, as I myself would have liked to be dressed, if it had been my funeral.

When they bring her out, swaying under a mountain of rotting flowers, I'll be waiting right here, Ambrosio. I'll walk up to her then and I'll scent my own body with Fleur de Rocaille perfume; I'll whiten my breasts with her Chant D'Aromes powder; I'll do my hair just like hers, spiraled in a cloud of smoke around my head; I'll drape myself in my lamé gown and spill my silver tunic over my shoulder, so that it sparkles vengefully in the midday sun. Then I'll bind my throat and wrists with diamond strings; I'll dress exactly as I used to when I was still Isabel Luberza and you were still alive, Ambrosio, the town spilling itself into the house to attend our parties, and I clinging to your arm like a jasmine vine to the wall, yielding my perfumed hand to be kissed by the guests, my delicate creamy hand which had already begun to be hers, Ambrosio, Isabel la Negra's; because even then I could feel the tide of blood rising, soaking my insides with Cherries Jubilee.

It wasn't until Isabel la Negra pounded vigorously on Isabel Luberza's door that the prostitute reconsidered whether she was doing a sensible thing in coming to visit her. She had come to talk to her about the business of the house they had inherited jointly. Ambrosio, the man they had both lived with when they were young, had died many years ago, and Isabel la Negra, out of consideration for her namesake, had not pressed her claim to the portion of the house that legally belonged to her. Isabel Luberza was living in the house, and it would have been inelegant to try to evict her. In any case, Isabel la Negra had wisely invested the money she had had from the mortgage on her part of the house, so that her mind was at rest as to not having made a poor business deal. She heard that Isabel Luberza was a bit mad. Since Ambrosio's death she had locked herself up in the house and never went out.

She had come to her rival's house thinking that so many years had gone by that all resentment should by now be forgotten. The widow was surely in need of rent money that would assure her a peaceful old age, and this would perhaps spur her to agree to a business deal. Isabel la Negra was very interested in becoming Isabel Luberza's partner. Her brothel had been so successful in recent years that she needed to enlarge it, and it would, moreover, be convenient to take it out of the slum, because in San Antón it lacked prestige, and even gave the impression of being an unhealthy establishment. But her yearning to live in the house, her dream of sitting out on the balcony behind the silver balustrade, beneath the baskets of fruit and garlands of flowers, answered to reasons deeper than economic expediency. She knew she suffered from a nostalgia that had become incandescent over the years, burning in her heart like a childhood vision. In this vision, which flashed back to her whenever she walked past Isabel Luberza's house, she'd see herself again as a young girl, barefoot and dressed in rags, looking up at a tall, handsome man dressed in white linen and Panama hat, who stood leaning out on the balcony next to a beautiful blond woman, elegantly dressed in a silver lamé gown.

That vision was the only gray cloud, the only elusive thorn that disturbed Isabel la Negra's contentment in her approaching old age. It was true; she was now a self-made woman and had achieved an enviable status in the town. Most society women were jealous of her, because, with the recent crash of the sugar market, the old families were now ruined and had only the empty pride of their names left to them. "They haven't even enough money to take a little trip to Europe once a year like I do; they can't even afford the copies of my designer clothes," she'd tell herself with a smile. Her importance in the economic development of the town was universally acknowledged. She had lately been the recipient of numerous prestigious appointments, such as honorary member of the Lion's Club, of the Chamber of Commerce, of the Banker's Trust, but she felt there was still something missing. She didn't want to die without having at least tried to make her secret dream come true: to imagine herself young once again, dressed in a sumptuous lamé dress and standing on that balcony, next to a man with whom she had once been in love.

When Isabel Luberza opened the door, Isabel la Negra went weak at the knees. She was still so beautiful, I had to lower my eyes; I almost didn't dare look at her. I wanted to kiss her eyelids, tender as new coconut flesh and of a beveled, almond shape. She had braided her hair at the nape of her neck, as Ambrosio told me she used to wear it. The odor of Fleur de Rocaille, her overly sweet perfume, brought me back to reality. I knew I had to convince her that I was being sincere in seeking her friendship, that I would honor my contract with her as a business partner. For a moment she stared at me so intently that I wondered whether she truly was mad, whether she truly thought of herself as a saint, as they said in town. I'd heard people say she lived obsessed with the idea of redeeming me, and that she'd subject her body to all sorts of absurd punishments for my sake.

But it didn't really matter. If the rumor was true, I was sure it would work in my favor. After staring at me for a moment, she opened the door and I went in.

When I walked into the living room I couldn't help but think of you, Ambrosio, of how you'd had me locked up for years in that shack with a zinc roof. There I had been sentenced to spend my days, milking the boys you yourself had introduced to me. "Please do my son's friends a favor Isabel," you'd say. Damn it, Isabel, don't be hard-hearted, you're the only one who knows how to do it, you're the one who does it best." You'd tell them "sure you can, son, why not, just let yourself go, that's all, as though you were skiing down a mountain of soapsuds without stopping," so their fathers could sleep peacefully because their offspring had not turned out to be gay sissies with porcelain-splintered butts, because they were manly machos, thanks to the coupling of Saint Dagger and Saint Pussy. But your friends could only prove this by sending their sons to me, Ambrosio; and they knew I'd only take care of them if it was you who brought them.

And so it was that, just to please you, Ambrosio, I began to kneel in front of the boys, like a priestess officiating at a sacred ritual. My hair would blind me as I'd lower my head to sheath their penises, like tender lilies, in my throat. Until one day I got to thinking that I wasn't really spending myself with those teenage Romeos because you had asked me to, Ambrosio, but that deep down I was doing it for my sake, to pick up an ancient, almost-forgotten taste, that leaked out in bittersweet streams down my throat: the taste of power. Because in teaching those boys how to make love, Ambrosio, I also showed them what a real woman is like. A real woman is not a sack of flour that lets a man throw her on a bed, just as a real man is not a raping macho, but one that has the courage to let himself be raped. So I devoted myself to teaching the boys how to share a pleasure without having to be ashamed of it; I taught them how to be generous with themselves. Once they left my bed they could rest easy as to their future performances; they could parade confidently before their girlfriends like strutting young roosters. After all, someone had to show young men how to take the initiative; someone had to show them in the first place, and that's why they all come to Isabel la Negra—sinful like the slough at the bottom of the gutter, wicked like the grounds at the end of the coffeepot—because in Isabel la Negra's arms everything is allowed, son, nothing is forbidden; our body is our only paradise, our only fount of delight, and Isabel makes us understand that pleasure can make us live forever, can turn us into gods, son, though only for a short while—but a short while is usually enough, because after having known pleasure no one should be afraid to die. So be quiet now, my son, be still; nestled here, in Isabel la Negra's arms, no one will see you, no one will ever know you were merely human. Here no one will know, no one will care that you're trembling with ague in my arms, because I'm just Isabel la Negra, the scum of the earth, and here, I swear by the holy name of Jesus that is looking on, no one will ever know that what you really wanted was to live forever, that what you really wanted was not to die.

When you began getting old, Ambrosio, luck turned in my favor. You thought I was taking my duties with the boys too seriously and that they were meeting me secretly, perhaps even paying me more than you did, so that I would finally prefer them to you. It was then you had your lawyer write up your new will, in which you left everything you owned in this world to your wife and to me.

Isabel la Negra stared at the sumptuously decorated walls of Isabel Luberza's living room and concluded that it was the perfect atmosphere for her new Dancing Hall. She could finally move out of her sleazy whorehouse, where it was so difficult to make business prosper. As she admired the gilded *fauteuils,* the brocaded sofas, and the crystal chandeliers, she felt convinced that if the Dancing Hall remained in the slum, no matter how much she invested in it, it would always remain a gimcrack joint. But here, in this elegant setting, and as Isabel Luberza's partner, everything could be different. She could hire half a dozen professional models and charge at least a hundred dollars a night. She made up her mind to get rid of all the old whores with musty cunts and wrinkled breasts, and decided to invest in new down pillows and Beautyrest mattresses, discarding the old Salvation Army iron cots. She was, in short, set on a first-class establishment, where one could wine, dine, and dance to one's heart's delight.

When the women finally finished their tour of the house, Isabel Luberza shook her visitor's hand courteously, and in doing so, took a few steps toward Isabel la Negra. She stretched out her hand and touched the procuress's face tenderly with the tip of her fingers, as though she were a soothsayer and were about to solve the riddle of life. Just when I was about to leave, she surprised me by kissing my cheeks, and then bursting out in tears. I felt a terrible pity for her, and thought you must have had a heart of stone, Ambrosio, to torture her the way you did. Then she took my hand in hers and looked curiously at my nails, which I had just polished that day with Cherries Jubilee.

She's varnished her nails the same color as mine but it doesn't surprise me, Ambrosio, there are so many things on this earth one doesn't understand. I couldn't figure out, for instance, why you'd not only left her half your estate, but made her co-owner of this house, where you and I had been so happy. The day after the funeral, when I realized the whole town was on to what had happened and that I was being slandered to bits, I walked through the streets hoping Isabel la Negra would die. But then, after she tore down the shack where you used to visit her and she built the

Dancing Hall with your money, I began to feel differently about her, and finally realized what she'd meant to us.

The first year of our marriage, when I learned Isabel was your paramour, I thought I was probably the unhappiest woman on earth. I always knew when you were coming from her house; I could tell by the heavy way your hand fell on my neck, or by the way you dragged your eyes over my body like burning sparks. It was then I had to be most careful of my satin slips and French lace underwear. It was as though the memory of her rode you when you weren't with her, and she'd sit on your back and hit you mercilessly with arms and legs, tormenting you so you'd go back to her. So I had no alternative but to stretch out on the bed and let myself be made. As you bent over me, I'd keep my eyes wide open and look out over your shoulder so as not to lose sight of her, so she wouldn't think I was giving in to her, not even by mistake.

Then I decided to win you over through other ways, Ambrosio, through that ancient wisdom I had inherited from my mother, and my mother from her mother before her. I began to place your napkin in a silver ring next to your plate, to sprinkle lemon juice in your water goblet, to spread your linens on sheets of zinc under the glaring sun. I'd then place the linens on your bed when they were still warm with sunlight. I'd spread them inside-out and then fold them right-side up, thereby releasing, to please you when you'd finally come to bed, a subtle essence of roses. I'd place our monograms, intertwined like amorous vines, under your bare forearms, so they'd remind you of the sacred vows of our marriage. But all my efforts were in vain. Diamonds sown in the wind. Pearls thrown on the muck heap.

Thus, Ambrosio, as the years went by Isabel la Negra became for us a necessary evil, a tumor that grew in our breast, but which we nursed tenderly so that it wouldn't be bothersome. It was at dinnertime that her presence was most clearly felt. A fragrance of peace would then waft up from our dinner plates, and as the icy beads slowly ran down the sides of our water goblets, it seemed as though happiness would remain forever poised on the fragile edge of our lives. I would then begin to think of her gratefully, reassembling her features in my mind in order to see her more clearly, in order to imagine her sitting next to us at the table. It was she that brought us together, Ambrosio: she that made our marital bliss possible.

Since I'd never seen her, I invented her to my heart's content. I thought of her as bewitchingly beautiful, her skin dark as night when mine was milk at dawn, her hair a thick rope braided around her head when mine lay stylishly draped, like a soft golden chain, around my shoulders. I could almost see her strong teeth, which she rubbed daily with baking soda to whiten them, and then I thought of mine, delicate and transparent like fish scales, barely showing under my lips in a perpetually polite smile. I thought of her eyes, soft and bulging like grapes, set, as a Negro's eyes are wont to be, in a thick, sluggish custard, and I thought of my eyes, restless and sparkling like emeralds, always coming and going through the house.

Thus the years went by, Ambrosio, and thanks to Isabel la Negra I began to feel useful again. Thinking of her made me acutely aware of the importance of my duties as a housewife. I would then measure the exact amount of flour and sugar in the jars in the pantry; I would carefully count the silverware in the dining-room coffer to make sure none was missing. Only then would I lie down peacefully next to you, Ambrosio, knowing that I'd done my duty and had looked after your assets.

I thought I'd lost the fight until a few minutes ago, when I heard her knock on the door. I knew it was her before I opened it; she had telephoned to say she was coming, and so I'd had time to prepare myself emotionally, but when I saw her I went weak all over. She looked exactly as I'd pictured her. She had lavender eyelids and thick, plum-colored eyes, which made me feel like kissing them; she wore her hair undone, and it rose over her shoulders like a smoking mane. I was surprised to discover how little she'd aged. And when I thought of how much she'd loved you, Ambrosio, I almost felt like embracing her, like telling her, "let's be friends, Isabel, for God's sake, let's forgive and forget."

But then she began to sway her hips provocatively in front of me, balancing herself back and forth on her sparkling red-rime heels, her hand on her waist and her elbow askew so as to flaunt before my eyes the stinking hole of her armpit. The terrible shadow of that armpit hit me square on the forehead, Ambrosio, and suddenly I remembered everything I had suffered because of her. Beyond her stinking armpit I glimpsed the open door of her Cadillac, a piece of her chauffeur's gilded buttoned jacket. So I flung the door open defiantly and asked her to come in.

I'd been waiting a long time for her visit. She's already successfully replaced me in all the social activities of the town, in which I used to preside holding fast to your arm like a sprig of jasmine. Now she's come to claim this house, where I've fought to keep your memory alive during all these years. She'll grab on to your mementos, the relics and memorabilia I've been saving for years, until she's taken them all, until she's sucked from them the last drops of your blood's dust. Because until now these events have all been shrouded in mystery, and I haven't been able to fathom the meaning of so much suffering except through a glass darkly, but today I've begun to see clearly for the first time. Today I'll confront the perfect beauty of her face to my absolute sorrow in order to understand. Now that I've drawn nearer to her I can see her as she really is, her hair no longer a cloud of smoke raging above her head but draped like a soft, golden chain about her neck, her soft skin no longer dark, but spilled over her shoulders like dawn's milk, a skin of the purest pedigree, without the merest suspicion of a kinky backlash, now swaying back and forth defiantly before her and feeling the blood flow out of me like a tide, my treacherous turncoat blood that has even now begun to stain my heels with that glorious, shocking shade I've always loved so, the shade of Cherries Jubilee.

TRANSLATED BY ROSARIO FERRÉ AND CINDY VENTURA

Selected Bibliography

This bibliography contains sources in English about Latin American literature and important studies of some of the authors in the anthology.

Adorno, Rolena. *Guaman Poma: Writing and Resistance in Colonial Peru.* Austin, University of Texas Press, 1986.

Aldrich, Earl M., Jr. *The Modern Short Story in Peru.* Madison, University of Wisconsin Press, 1966.

Anderson Imbert, Enrique. *Spanish American Literature: A History,* trans. John V. Falconieri, 2 vols. Detroit, Wayne State University Press, 1963; 2d ed., revised and updated by Elaine Malley, 1969.

Balderston, Daniel. *The Literary Universe of Jorge Luis Borges: An Index to References and Allusions to Persons, Titles, and Places in His Writings.* Westport, Conn., Greenwood Press, 1986.

———. *The Latin American Short Story: An Annotated Guide to Anthologies and Criticism.* Westport, Conn., Greenwood Press, 1992.

———. "The Twentieth-Century Short Story in Spanish America," in *The Cambridge History of Latin American Literature,* vol. 2, pp. 465–496. Cambridge, Cambridge University Press, 1996.

Barcarisse, Salvador (ed.). *Contemporary Latin American Fiction: Carpentier, Sábato, Onetti, Roa, Donoso, Fuentes, García Márquez.* Edinburgh, Scottish Academic Press, 1980.

Bloom, Harold (ed.). *Jorge Luis Borges.* New York, Chelsea House, 1986.

———. *Gabriel García Márquez.* New York, Chelsea House, 1989.

——— (ed.). *Modern Latin American Fiction.* New York, Chelsea House, 1990.

Caldwell, Helen. *Machado de Assis.* Berkeley, University of California Press, 1970.

Dorn, Georgette M. *Latin America, Spain and Portugal, an Annotated Bibliography of Paperback Books,* Washington, D.C., Hispanic Foundation of the Library of Congress, 1971.

Faris, Wendy B. *Labyrinths of Language: Symbolic Landscape and Narrative Design in Modern Fiction.* Baltimore, Johns Hopkins University Press, 1988.

———, and Lois Parkinson Zamora. *Magical Realism: Theory, History, Community.* Durham, N.C., Duke University Press, 1995.

Fleak, Kenneth. *The Chilean Short Story: Writers from the Generation of 1950.* New York, Peter Lang, 1989.

Freudenthal, Juan R., and Patricia M. Freudenthal (eds.). *Index to Anthologies of Latin American Literature in English Translation.* Boston, G. K. Hall, 1977.

Gledson, John. *The Deceptive Realism of Machado de Assis: A Dissenting Interpretation of Dom Casmurro*. Liverpool, Francis Cairns, 1984.

Goldberg, Isaac. *Brazilian Literature*. New York, Knopf, 1922.

González, Aníbal. *Journalism and the Development of Spanish American Narrative*. Cambridge, Cambridge University Press, 1993.

González, Eduardo. *The Monstered Self: Narratives of Death and Performance in Latin American Fiction*. Durham, N.C., Duke University Press, 1992.

González Echevarría, Roberto, and Enrique Pupo-Walker (eds.). *The Cambridge History of Latin American Literature*, 3 vols. Cambridge, Cambridge University Press, 1996. (Includes Brazilian authors.)

————. *Alejo Carpentier: The Pilgrim at Home*. Ithaca, N.Y., Cornell University Press, 1977. Paperback, University of Texas Press, 1990.

————. *Myth and Archive: A Theory of Latin American Narrative*. Cambridge, Cambridge University Press, 1990.

————. *The Voice of the Masters: Writing and Authority in Modern Latin American Literature*. Austin, University of Texas Press, 1985.

Grossman, William L. Translations and Introduction. *Modern Brazilian Short Stories*. Berkeley, University of California Press, 1967.

Harss, Luis, and Barbara Dohmann. *Into the Mainstream: Conversations with Latin-American Writers*. New York, Harper & Row, 1966.

Henríquez Ureña, Pedro. *Literary Currents in Hispanic America*. Cambridge, Mass., Harvard University Press, 1945.

Irwin, John T. *The Mystery to a Solution: Poe, Borges, and the Analytic Detective Story*. Baltimore, Johns Hopkins University Press, 1994.

Jackson, K. David. "The Brazilian Short Story," in *The Cambridge History of Latin American Literature*, vol. 3, pp. 207–232. Cambridge, Cambridge University Press, 1996.

Kadir, Djelal. *Questing Fictions. Latin America's Family Romance*. Minneapolis, University of Minnesota Press, 1986.

Kerr, Lucille. *Reclaiming the Author: Figures and Fictions from Spanish America*. Durham, N.C., Duke University Press, 1992.

Lindstrom, Naomi. *Twentieth-Century Spanish American Fiction*. Austin, University of Texas Press, 1994.

Magnarelli, Sharon. *The Lost Rib. Female Characters in the Spanish-American Novel*. Lewisburg, Pa., Bucknell University Press, 1985.

McGuirk, Bernard, and Richard Cardwell (eds.). *Gabriel García Márquez: New Readings*. Cambridge, Cambridge University Press, 1987.

Menton, Seymour (ed.). *The Spanish American Short Story*. Berkeley, University of California Press, 1980.

Onís, Harriet de (ed.). *Spanish Stories and Tales*. New York, Knopf, 1954.

Peden, Margaret Sayers. *The Latin American Short Story: A Critical History*. Boston, Twayne, 1983.

Pérez Firmat, Gustavo. *Idle Fictions: The Hispanic Vanguard Novel, 1926–1934*. Durham, N.C., Duke University Press, 1982.

————. *Literature and Liminality: Festive Readings in the Hispanic Tradition*. Durham, N.C., Duke University Press, 1986.

———— (ed.). *Do the Americas Have a Common Literature?* Durham, N.C., Duke University Press, 1990.

Picón Salas, Mariano. *A Cultural History of Spanish America: From Conquest to Independence*, trans. Irving A. Leonard. Berkeley, University of California Press, 1962.

Prieto, René. *Miguel Angel Asturias's Archeology of Return.* Cambridge, Cambridge University Press, 1993.

Pupo-Walker, Enrique. "The Brief Narrative in Spanish America: 1835–1915," in *The Cambridge History of Latin American Literature*, vol. 1, pp. 490–535. Cambridge, Cambridge University Press, 1996.

————. "The Contemporary Short Fiction of Spanish America: An Introductory Note." *Studies in Short Fiction*, 8, no. 1 (1971), 1–8.

Rodríguez Monegal, Emir (ed.). *The Borzoi Anthology of Latin American Literature: From the Time of Columbus to the Twentieth Century*, 2 vols. New York, Knopf, 1977. (Includes Brazilian literature.)

————. *Jorge Luis Borges: A Literary Biography.* New York, Dutton, 1978.

Rutherford, John. *Mexican Society During the Revolution: A Literary Approach.* Oxford, Clarendon, 1971.

Schulman, Ivan A. (ed.). *Latin American in Its Literature.* New York, Holmes & Meier, 1980.

Shaw, Bradley A. *Latin American Literature in English Translation: An Annotated Bibliography.* New York, New York University Press, 1976.

————. *Latin American Literature in English, 1975–1978.* New York, Center for Inter-American Relations, 1979.

Solé Carlos A., and María Isabel Abreu (eds.). *Latin American Writers*, 3 vols. New York, Charles Scribner's Sons, 1989. (Includes Brazilian literature.)

Sommer, Doris. *Foundational Fictions: The National Romances of Latin America.* Berkeley, University of California Press, 1991.

Tittler, Jonathan. *Narrative Irony in the Contemporary Spanish-American Novel.* Ithaca, N.Y., Cornell University Press, 1984.

Unruh, Vicky. *Latin American Vanguards: The Art of Contentious Encounters.* Berkeley, University of California Press, 1994.

Varner, John Grier. *El Inca: The Life and Times of Garcilaso de la Vega.* Austin, University of Texas Press, 1968.

Williams, Raymond Leslie (ed.). *The Novel in the Americas.* Niwot, University Press of Colorado, 1992.

Bibliographical Sources

Handbook of Latin American Studies
Hispanic American Periodical Index
The Year's Work in Modern Language Studies
Bibliography of the Modern Language Association of America

Acknowledgments

Amorim, Enrique: "The Photograph" by Enrique Amorim, translated for this anthology by Margaret Sayers Peden, was published in Spanish as "La fotografía" in *Sur*, no. 91, 1942. Permission to translate was granted by Editorial Arca SRL.

Andrade, Mário de: "The Christmas Turkey," translated for this anthology by Gregory Rabassa, was published in Portuguese as "O Peru de natal" in *Contos novos*, 1956. Reprinted by permission of Villa Rica Editoras Reunidas Ltda.

Arenas, Reinaldo: "The Parade Ends" by Reinaldo Arenas, translated by Andrew Bush, first appeared in *The Paris Review*, vol. 23, no. 80, Summer 1981. Reprinted by permission of the Estate of Reinaldo Arenas.

Arévalo Martínez, Rafael: "The Man Who Resembled a Horse" by Rafael Arévalo Martínez, translated by William George Williams and William Carlos Williams first appeared in *New Directions Annual* no. 8. Copyright © 1944 by New Directions Publishing Corp. Reprinted by permission of New Directions Publishing Corp.

Arreola, Juan José: "The Switchman" from *Confabulario and Other Inventions* by Juan José Arreola, translated by George D. Schade. Copyright © 1964. By permission of the University of Texas Press.

Asturias, Miguel Angel: "The Legend of 'El Cadejo,'" translated by Hardie St. Martin, first appeared in *Odyssey Review*, March 1963. Reprinted by permission of the translator and Agencia Literaria Carmen Balcells, S.A.

Balza, José: "A Woman's Back" by José Balza, translated for this anthology by Margaret Sayers Peden, was published in Spanish as "La mujer de espaldas" in *La mujer de espaldas* (Monté Avila Editores Latinomaericana C.A., 1986). Translated by permission of the publisher.

Benítez Rojo, Antonio: "Buried Statues" from *The Magic Dog and Other Stories* by Antonio Benítez Rojo, translated by Lee H. Williams Jr. Copyright © Antonio Benítez Rojo. All rights reserved. Copyright © 1990 Ediciones del Norte. Reprinted by permission of Ediciones del Norte and Antonio Benítez Rojo.

Bombal, María Luisa: "The Tree" from *New Islands and Other Stories* by María Luisa Bombal. Translation copyright © 1982 by Farrar, Straus & Giroux, Inc. Reprinted by permission of Farrar, Straus & Giroux, Inc.

Borges, Jorge Luis: "The Garden of Forking Paths" from *Ficciones* by Jorge Luis Borges, translated by Helen Temple and Ruthven Todd. Copyright © 1962 by Grove Press, Inc. Used by permission of the publishers Grove/Atlantic, Inc., and Weidenfeld & Nicolson.

Bosch, Juan: "Encarnación Mendoza's Christmas Eve" by Juan Bosch, translated for this anthology by Susan Herman, was published in Spanish as "La noche buena de Encarnación Mendoza." Copyright © by Juan Bosch. Translated by permission of Agencia Literaria Carmen Balcells, S.A.

Carpentier, Alejo: "Journey Back to the Source" from *The War of Time* by Alejo Carpentier, translated by Frances Partridge. Copyright © 1970 by Victor Gollancz Ltd. Reprinted by permission of the Warren Cook Literary Agency as agent for Andrea Esteban Carpentier.

Castellanos, Rosario: "Cooking Lesson" from *A Rosario Castellanos Reader* by Rosario Castellanos, edited by Maureen Ahern, translated by Maureen Ahern and others. Copyright ©1988. By permission of Maureen Ahern, Editorial Joaquín Mortiz, and the University of Texas Press.

Cortázar, Julio: "The Night Face Up" from *Blow-Up and Other Stories* by Julio Cortázar, translated by Paul Blackburn. Copyright © 1967 by Random House, Inc. Copyright ©1956 Julio Cortázar and heirs of Julio Cortázar. Reprinted by permission of Pantheon Books, a division of Random House, Inc., The Harvill Press, and Agencia Literaria Carmen Balcells, S.A.

Donoso, José: "The Walk" by José Donoso, translated by Andrée Conrad, was published in *Charleston and Other Stories* (David R. Godine, 1977). Copyright © 1971 by José Donoso. Permission to reprint granted by Agencia Literaria Carmen Balcells, S.A.

Echeverría, Esteban: "The Slaughter House" from *The Slaughter House* by Esteban Echeverría, translated by Angel Flores (Las Americas Publishing Co., 1959). Reprinted by permisssion of the Estate of Angel Flores.

Erauso, Catalina de: From *Lieutenant Nun* by Catalina de Erauso, translated by Michele Stepto and Gabriel Stepto. Copyright ©1996 by Michele Stepto and Gabriel Stepto. Reprinted by permission of Beacon Press, Boston.

Ferré, Rosario: "When Women Love Men" is reprinted from *The Youngest Doll* by Rosario Ferré. Originally published by Editorial Joaquín Mortiz, S.A. as *Papeles de Pandora*. Copyright © 1976 by Rosario Ferré. Translation copyright © 1991 by the University of Nebraska Press . Reprinted by permission of the University of Nebraska Press.

Fuentes, Carlos: "The Doll Queen" from *Burnt Water* by Carlos Fuentes, translated by Margaret Sayers Peden. Translation copyright ©1980 by Farrar, Straus & Giroux, Inc. Copyright © Carlos Fuentes. Reprinted by permission of Farrar Straus & Giroux, Inc., and A.M. Heath.

Gallegos, Rómulo: "Peace on High" by Rómulo Gallegos, translated by Hardie St. Martin, first appeared in *Odyssey Review*, September 1962. Reprinted by permission of the translator and Sonia Gallegos de Palomino.

García Márquez, Gabriel: "Balthazar's Marvelous Afternoon" from *No One Writes to the Colonel* by Gabriel García Marquez. Copyright © 1968 in the English translation by HarperCollins, Publishers, Inc. Reprinted by permission of HarperCollins Publishers, Inc.

Guaman Poma de Ayala, Felipe: "*Tocay Capac*, The First Inca" by Felipe Guaman Poma de Ayala, translated for this anthology by Rolena Adorno, was published in Spanish as "Tocai Capac, Primer Inga" in *El primer nueva corónica y buen gobierno,* edited by Rolena Adorno and John Murra. Translated by permission of Siglo Veintiuno Editores.

Guimarães Rosa, João: "The Third Bank of the River" from *The Third Bank of the River and Other Stories* by João Guimarães Rosa, translated by Barbara Shelby. Copyright © 1968 by Alfred A. Knopf, Inc. Reprinted by permission of the publisher.

Hernández, Felisberto: "The Daisy Dolls" from *Piano Stories* (1993) by Felisberto Hernández, translated by Luis Harss. Reprinted by permission of Marsilio Publishers Corp.

Levinson, Luisa Mercedes: "The Clearing" by Luisa Mercedes Levinson, translated for this anthology by Sarah Arvio, was published in Spanish as "El abra" in *El estigma del tiempo* (Seix Barral, 1977). Translated by permission of Luisa Valenzuela.

Lins, Osman: "Hahn's Pentagon," by Osman Lins, translated for this anthology by Gregory Rabassa, was published as "O pentágono de Hahn," in *Nove, Novena* (Livraria Martins Fontes Editora Ltda., 1966). Translated by permission of the estate of Osman Lins c/o Companhia das Letras. Symbols from *Nine, Novena* by Osman Lins, translated by Adria Frizzi (Sun and Moon Press, 1995), reproduced by permission.

Lispector, Clarice: "The Crime of the Mathematics Professor" is reprinted from *Family Ties* by Clarice Lispector, translated by Giovanni Pontiero. Copyright © 1972. By permission of the University of Texas Press and Carcanet Press Ltd.

Lugones, Leopoldo: "Yzur" by Leopoldo Lugones, translated by Gregory Woodruff, first appeared in *Contemporary Latin American Short Stories*, edited by Pat McNees (Fawcett, 1974). Reprinted by permission of Richard Woodruff.

Machado de Assis, Joaquim Maria: "Midnight Mass" from *The Psychiatrist and Other Stories* by Machado de Assis, translated by William L. Grossman and Helen Caldwell. Copyright © 1963 The Regents of the University of California. Reprinted by permission of the University of California Press.

Onetti, Juan Carlos: "The Image of Misfortune" from *Goodbyes and Other Stories* by Juan Carlos Onetti, translated by Daniel Balderston. Copyright © 1990. By permission of the University of Texas Press.

Palma, Ricardo: "Fray Gómez's Scorpion" and "Where and How the Devil Lost His Poncho" from *The Knights of the Cape* by Ricardo Palma, translated by Harriet de Onis. Copyright 1945 by Alfred A. Knopf, Inc. Reprinted by permission of the publisher.

Pané, Fray Ramón: "How the Men Were Parted from the Women" by Fray Ramón Pané, translated for this anthology by Sarah Arvio, was published in Spanish as "Como se separaron los hombres de las mujeres" in *Relación acerca de las antigedades de los indios,* edited by José Juan Arrom (Siglo Veintiuno, 1988). Translated by permission of José Juan Arrom.

Peri Rossi, Cristina: "The Threshold" from *A Forbidden Passion* by Cristina Peri Rossi, translated by Mary Jane Treacy. Translation copyright © 1993 by Mary Jane Treacy. Reprinted by permission of Cleis Press.

Piñera, Virgilio: "Meat" from *Cold Tales* by Virgilio Piñera, translated by Mark Schafer. Reprinted by permission of Eridanos Press Inc.

Piñón, Nélida: "The Warmth of Things" by Nélida Piñón, translated for this anthology by Helen Lane, was published in Portuguese as "O calor das coisas" in *O calor das coisas: contos* (Editora Nova Froneira, 1980). Copyright ©1980 by Nélida Piñón. Translated by permission of Agencia Literaria Carmen Balcells, S.A.

Popol Vuh: "A Maiden's Story" from *Popol Vuh* translated by Ralph Nelson. Copyright © 1974, 1976 by Ralph Nelson. Reprinted by permission of Houghton Mifflin Company. All rights reserved.

Quiroga, Horacio: "The Decapitated Chicken" from *The Decapitated Chicken and Other Stories* by Horacio Quiroga, translated by Margaret Sayers Peden. Copyright © 1976 by the University of Texas Press. By permission of the publisher.

Ribeyro, Julio Ramón: "The Featherless Buzzards" from *Marginal Voices: Selected Stories* by Julio Ramón Ribeyro, translated by Dianne Douglas. Copyright © 1993. By permission of the University of Texas Press.

Roa Bastos, Augusto: "Unborn," by Augusto Roa Bastos, translated for this anthology by Helen Lane, was published in Spanish as "Nonato" in *Moriencia* (Monte Avila, 1969). Copyright © 1969 by Augusto Roa Bastos. Translated by permission of Agencia Literaria Carmen Balcells, S.A.

Rulfo, Juan: "Tell Them Not to Kill Me!" from *The Burning Plain and Other Stories* by Juan Rulfo, translated by George D. Schade. Copyright © 1953, translation copyright ©1967, renewed 1996. By permission of the University of Texas Press.

Sarmiento, Domingo Faustino: "The Tiger of the Plains" by Domingo Faustino Sarmiento, translated by Kathleen Ross, is from *Facundo*, edited by Kathleen Ross. Copyright ©1977 The Regents of the University of California. Reprinted by permission of the University of California Press.

Trevisan, Dalton: "Penelope" by Dalton Trevisan, translated by Gregory Rabassa, appeared in different form in *The Vampire of Curitiba and Other Stories* by Dalton Trevisan. Copyright © 1972 by Alfred A. Knopf, Inc. Reprinted by permission of the publisher.

Vargas Llosa, Mario: "The Challenge" from *The Cubs and Other Stories* by Mario Vargas Llosa, translated by Gregory Kolovakos and Ronald Christ. Translation copyright © 1979 by Harper and Row Publishers, Inc. Reprinted by permission of the publishers Farrar, Straus & Giroux, Inc., and Faber & Faber Ltd.

Vega, Garcilaso de la: "The Story of Pedro Serrano" from *Royal Commentaries of the Incas and General History of Peru* by Garcilaso de la Vega, translated by Harold V. Livermore. Copyright © 1966. By permission of the University of Texas Press.